CHRISTINA STEAD (1902–1983)

was born in Sydney, Australia. She trained as a teacher, but in 1928 she left Australia for Europe, where she lived in London and Paris, working from 1930-1935 as a secretary in a Paris bank. She went to live in Spain but left on the outbreak of war and with her husband, the novelist and political economist William Blake, she settled in the USA. From 1943-4 she was an instructor at the Workshop in the Novel at New York University and in 1943 she was senior writer for MGM in Hollywood.

Her first collection of stories, *The Salzburg Tales*, was published in 1934. Since then she has published eleven novels of which seven are published by Virago: *The Beauties and Furies* (1936), *For Love Alone* (1944), *Letty Fox: Her Luck* (1946), *A Little Tea, A Little Chat* (1948), *The People With The Dogs* (1952), *Cotters' England* (1966), *Miss Herbert: (The Suburban Wife)* (1976), as well as this collection of four novellas, *The Puzzleheaded Girl* (1967). Christina Stead's other novels are: *Seven Poor Men of Sydney* (1934), *House of all Nations* (1938), the famous *The Man Who Loved Children* (1940) and *The Little Hotel* (1974); she also contributed many short stories to the *New Yorker*.

In 1947 Christina Stead left America for Europe, settling in England in 1953. She finally returned to Australia in the early 1970s, where she lived until her death at the age of eighty.

VIRAGO
MODERN
CLASSIC

NUMBER
5

FOR LOVE ALONE

CHRISTINA STEAD

Introduction by
Mary Kathleen Benet

Babieca: Metafisico estáis –
Rocinante: Es que no como.
Prologue, Don Quixote

*This is a work of fiction and no character in the story
has any living counterpart*

Published by VIRAGO PRESS Limited 1978
41 William IV Street, London WC2N 4DB

Reprinted 1981, 1986

First published in Great Britain 1945

British Library Cataloguing in Publication Data
Stead, Christine
    For Love Alone.
    I. Title
    823[F]   PR619.3.S75
    ISBN 0-86068-052-5

Printed in Great Britain at
Anchor Brendon Ltd., Tiptree, Essex

INTRODUCTION

Christina Stead has had/trouble finding an audience. This is puzzling, for acquaintance with her books breeds addiction, and devotees begin to wonder at the rest of the world's seeming indifference. Three explanations for it have been suggested. One is that she has been black-balled by the publishing and criticism mafia because of her leftism. One is that her books are ahead of their time: Randall Jarrell has suggested that future generations will wonder at our neglect of her as we wonder at the long neglect of Melville. The third hypothesis is that she is a writer's writer and will always be limited to a small audience, because she neglects the fundamental laws of readability in packing her books so densely with ideas and technical wizardry – a highly concentrated essence for other writers to water down into something dilute enough to be taken at a gulp by the lazy majority.

These suggestions are not mutually exclusive. Because of her seriousness and purity (natural bedfellows, then and now, of radical ideas) she didn't spend any time at all in currying favour with any literary clique. Nor with readers, present or future. The escapism of the literary-entertainment industry she found morally repugnant and artistically uninteresting.

And yet no group has made a cult of her, the way cults have been made of so many *avant-garde* or audacious or left-wing writers. Perhaps this is because she was never an evangelist preaching salvation. The *Daily Worker* criticised her work as harshly as did the mainstream press, and for some of the same reasons: bafflement at her absence of 'message', confusion over her own attitude to her characters. Why aren't all the radicals in her books good people, if she's a leftist? If she ridicules the 'harem woman', why does she refuse to engage in the battle between the sexes? Why doesn't she tell us how to live our lives?

She is – seemingly – careless of plot and construction unaware of how little the reader can tolerate before losing the stamina to go along with her detailed, almost obsessive interest in her characters. But the Christina Stead addict comes to feel that these books are piled with detail because it is important to tell everything possible about this character, this situation – there isn't a moment or a phrase to waste on such trivia as leading you gently by the hand through a made-up romantic story, or giving you elementary lessons in politics and economics that would unravel some of the clues. You are expected to do your own homework.

That is not to say that there is no pleasure to be found here. There is pleasure of the intensest kind – the pleasure of following an adept into mysteries and having them illuminated; of being amused to the point of hilarity by the sheer quantity of truth revealed at every moment.

In her most famous book, *The Man Who Loved Children*, the hilarity turns to horror as the story unfolds: the battle to the death between a masochistic southern belle and a northern-liberal chauvinist, observed by the eldest child, a genius plotting her own escape. This is the first volume of what amounts to an extended fictional auto-biography. Christina Stead was born in Sydney in 1902, went to Europe in 1928, and did not return until after the death of her American husband in 1968. She lived in many cities of Europe and America, and her marriage to William Blake, left-wing economist, writer, polymath, was ideally egalitarian. His intensely sociable nature complemented her introspective solitude, and the stream of friends who passed unendingly through his life became the stream of characters who so abundantly people her books. She is perhaps unique in her ability to show both kinds of relationship completely convincingly: the war to the death with the oppressive chauvinist, and the flowering of full sexual love and co-operation.

Her delineation of sexual politics has larger political ramifications. The father is the 'liberal' exemplar of the imperialist period of capitalist expansion, the proponent of the 'freedom' which means unlimited room for his wishes and desires to impose themselves on the world. The husband is socialist man, asking nothing for himself, therefore beloved. But this contrast is drawn without the slightest taint of the tract: her books seem to contain a moral only in the sense that we incorrigibly expect life to contain a moral, though we know by now that what we used to call a moral is simply the working out of the laws of history and economic and human psychology. Christina Stead moves the nineteenth-century novel on to this new territory, and establishes it triumphantly there.

For Love Alone is the sequel to *The Man Who Loved Children*, the story of transition from the hated father to the beloved husband. Teresa, the heroine, resists the almost incestuous demands for submission, escapes her emotional prison, and, in solitude, plans and works for physical escape. She is encouraged by the example of

Jonathan Crow, a poor boy who wins a university scholarship to England. But when she gets to England herself, she finds that Crow's demands are neurotic, his relations with women self-defeating. And Teresa confesses that she cannot understand him, cannot fathom what a neurotic derives from his own strategies. He becomes, to her, a diabolical figure – a Mephistopheles in a black cloak disappearing in the London gloom.

The man who drives Crow from her life is James Quick, her employer. Separated from his wife, he is as wary of dependent, manipulative women as she is of exploitative, dominant men; their mutual willingness to give without thought of receiving is what brings them together. And Teresa, the solitary who has longed for love, is troubled by this unexpected showering of gifts, amazed by the fact that she has found what she always suspected life contained. The consequence of their liaison is to make her want to 'try men', to explore fully the life from which she has for so long been excluded. Quick, in his generosity, asserts that he expects many men to love her; she, in her new-found confidence and freedom, feels her adventures must constitute a secret life that will not make Quick think she loves him the less. It is the strangest and most plausible consequence of their union.

This is one of the great love stories, but not 'romantic' in the usual debased sense. The happy marriages, the book asserts, are those made privately, in the anonymity of the great city: casual, egalitarian, and completely voluntary.

For Love Alone is much more than the story of Teresa's journey from one kind of man to another. It is an unparalleled portrait of working-class Australia – the harsh, undomesticated spaces, the provincial culture, the remote and implausible connection with distant pale cold England. Teresa's journey, though a classic instance of the colonial reaching back to the old civilisation, is accomplished in lonely independence, in a random, desperate attempt at self-education.

Though the goal of her journey is love, the word is not used in its usual limited sense: it becomes a metaphor for the entire passionate life of the mind and the senses, a life that can only reach its fullest expansion as part of a sexual relation, a life that drives out hypocrisy and moves toward a sane comprehension of the world as a whole.

Christina Stead is too humbled by her vision of what this life could be to assert that she herself has accomplished such a journey. At the end of *For Love Alone*, she feels she is just beginning. But to anyone who submits to the power of this remarkable book, it seems as if she has gone as far along the road as any of the great, among whom she must be numbered.

Mary Kathleen Benet, 1978

SEA PEOPLE

❧❧❧❧❧❧❧❧❧❧

In the part of the world Teresa came from, winter is in July, spring brides marry in September, and Christmas is consummated with roast beef, suckling pig, and brandy-laced plum pudding at 100 degrees in the shade, near the tall pine-tree loaded with gifts and tinsel as in the old country, and old carols have rung out all through the night.

This island continent lies in the water hemisphere. On the eastern coast, the neighbouring nation is Chile, though it is far, far east, Valparaiso being more than six thousand miles away in a straight line; her northern neighbours are those of the Timor Sea, the Yellow Sea; to the south is that cold, stormy sea full of earth-wide rollers, which stretches from there without land, south to the Pole.

The other world—the old world, the land hemisphere—is far above her as it is shown on maps drawn upside-down by old-world cartographers. From that world and particularly from a scarcely noticeable island up toward the North Pole the people came, all by steam; or their parents, all by sail. And there they live round the many thousand miles of seaboard, hugging the water and the coastal rim. Inside, over the Blue Mountains, are the plains heavy with wheat, then the endless dust, and after outcrops of silver, opal, and gold, Sahara, the salt-crusted bed of a prehistoric sea, and leafless mountain ranges. There is nothing in the interior; so people look toward the water, and above to the fixed stars and constellations which first guided men there.

Overhead, the other part of the Milky Way, with its great stars and nebulæ, spouts thick as cow's milk from the udder, from side to side, broader and whiter than in the north; in the centre the curdle of the Coalsack, that black hole through which they look out into space. The skies are sub-tropical, crusted with suns and spirals, as if a reflection of the crowded Pacific Ocean, with its reefs, atolls, and archipelagos.

It is a fruitful island of the sea-world, a great Ithaca, there parched and stony and here trodden by flocks and curly-headed bulls and heavy with thick-set grain. To this race can be put the famous question: "Oh, Australian, have you just come from the harbour? Is your ship in the roadstead? Men of what nation put you down—for I am sure you did not get here on foot?"

The
Island
Continent

1. Brown Seaweed and Old Fish Nets

NAKED, except for a white towel rolled into a loincloth, he stood in the door-way, laughing and shouting, a tall man with powerful chest and thick hair of pale burning gold and a skin still pale under many summers' tan. He seemed to thrust back the walls with his muscular arms; thick tufts of red hair stood out from his armpits. The air was full of the stench of brown seaweed and old fish nets. Through the window you could see the water of the bay and the sand specked with flotsam and scalloped with yellow foam, left by the last wave. The man, Andrew Hawkins, though straight and muscular, was covered with flaccid yellow-white flesh and his waist and abdomen were too broad and full. He had a broad throat and chest and from them came a clear tenor voice.

". . . she was sitting on the ground nursing her black baby, and she herself was black as a hat, with a strong, supple oily skin, finer than white women's skins: her heavy breasts were naked, she was not ashamed of that, but with natural modesty, which is in even the most primitive of women, she covered her legs with a piece of cloth lying on the ground and tittered behind her hand exactly like one of you"—he was saying to the two women sitting at the table. "Then she said something to her husband and he, a thin spindle-shanked fellow, translated for me, grinning from ear to ear: she asked how it was possible for a man to have such beautiful white feet as mine."

He looked down at his long blond feet and the two women looked from their sewing quickly at his feet, as if to confirm the story.

"I have always been admired for my beautiful white skin," said the golden-haired man, reminiscently. "Women love it in a man, it surprises them to see him so much fairer in colour than they are. Especially the darkies," and he looked frankly at Kitty Hawkins, who was a nut-brown brunette with drooping black hair. "But not only the dark ones," he went on softly. He kept on coaxing.

"I have been much loved; I didn't always know it—I was always such an idealist. When girls and, yes, even women older than myself, wanted to come and talk to me, I thought it was a thing of the brain. One poor girl, Paula Brown, wrote to me for years, discussing things. I never dreamed that it was not an interest in speculative thought. I used to tell her all my dreams and longings. I could have married a rich girl. In the Movement there was a quiet, pale girl called Annie Milson. Her father, though I didn't think about it at the time, was Commissioner for Railways and was quite the capitalist.

"They had properties all around here, dairy-farms down the south coast. I could have been a wealthy man if I had become Milson's son-in-law, and I believe he would have been delighted. He seemed to approve of me. I spent the afternoon at their Lindfield house two or three times—and spent the afternoon talking to Milson! I never suspected the girl liked me.

"I believe she loved the good-looking, sincere young idealist— but I had no interest in earthly things at the time and I never suspected it. Poor Annie! She used to send me books. Yes, I believe I was loved by many women but I was so pure that I had no temptations. 'My mind to me a kingdom was.' I suppose, now, when I look back, that I was a mystery to them, poor girls, such a handsome young man, who didn't dance, didn't take them to the theatre, and worried only about the social organism."

He laughed, his brilliant oval blue eyes, their whites slightly bloodshot, looking gaily at the two girls. He sighed, "I didn't know that I was a handsome lad. I didn't know then what a woman, a married woman, said to me much later, a fine, motherly soul she was, Mrs Kurzon, but she said it with a sigh, 'Mr Hawkins, how many women have wanted to put their hands in your wonderful hair?' She said it with a twinkle but she said it with longing too; and then she asked me if she could, laughing all the time and sweetly too, in a womanly sweet way. I let her, and she plunged them in and took them out with a sigh of gratification, 'Oh, Mr Hawkins, how wonderful it is!' And how many women have told me it was a shame to waste such hair on a man, they would give anything to have it."

One of the girls, the younger one, who was blond, looked up at the marvellous hair of the man.

Andrew Hawkins ran his hand through it, feeling it himself. A thought seemed to strike him; he brought down his hand and looked at the back, then the palm. It was a large, pale, muscular hand, an artisan's hand, hairless, diseased-looking because streaked and spotted with fresh cement. "Not a bad hand either," he said. He had something on the tip of his tongue but couldn't get it out, he went on about his legs instead. "Poor Mrs Slops said I had legs like a 'dook'. And I have seen 'dooks', at that, and not half so well-calved, I'll take my affidavit. But do you know, Kit," he said, lowering his voice, and his eyes darkening with modesty or wonder. "You see this hand, my good right hand, do you see it, Kit?"

Kitty laughed in her throat, a troubled, sunny laugh. "I've felt it, too, in my time."

He said mysteriously, lowering his voice again: "Women have kissed this hand." They both turned and looked at him, startled. "Yes, Kit, yes, you disbeliever," he said, turning to the younger girl. "Teresa won't believe me perhaps, for she doesn't want to love me, but women, several women have kissed this hand. Do you know how women kiss men's hands? They take it in both their hands, and kiss it first on the back, and then each finger separately, and they hate to let go." He burst out suddenly into a rough ringing laugh. "You would not believe that has happened —not once, but several times—to your Andrew!"

"Handy Andy," said Teresa, in her soft, unresonant voice. She did not glance up but went on sewing. Each of the girls had before her on the table the wide sleeve of a summer dress; it was a greyish lavender voile sprinkled with pink roses and they were sewing roses made of the material in rows along the sleeves.

"Ah, you think you know a lot about love," went on Andrew, coming into the room, and throwing himself full length on the old settee underneath the window that looked upon the beach. "Yes, Trees is always moaning about love, but you don't know, Trees, that love is warmth, heat. The sun is love and love also is fleshly, in this best sense that a beautiful woman gladdens the heart of man and a handsome man brightens the eyes of the ladies. One blessed circle, perpetual motion." He laughed. "Many women have loved your Andrew, but not you two frozen women." He continued teasing, waiting for an answer,

> *"Orpheus with his lute made T'rees*
> *And the mountain tops that freeze,*
> *Bow themselves when he did sing."*

"We will never be finished," said Teresa.

"And there are the beans to do, I must do them," said Kitty, throwing the long sleeve on the table. "When they're done, I'll call to you and you put away the sewing. You must have some lunch, the wedding breakfast won't be till late."

"Beauty," mused Andrew, looking at them. "What a strange thing that I didn't have lovely daughters, I who worship beauty so much! Yes, Fate plays strange tricks, especially on her favourites. My dream as a lad was to find a stunning mate, and different from most youths, I dreamed of the time when I would have beautiful little women around me. How proud I was in prospect! But of course," he said confidingly to Teresa, "I knew nothing of a thing more sacred than beauty—human love. My dear Margaret attracted me by her truth-loving face, serious, almost stern—as sea-biscuit! ha-ha—but soft, womanly dark eyes, like Kitty's. I don't know where you got your face of a little tramp, Trees, a ragamuffin. If I had had three beautiful bouncing maidens like old Harkness! I saw the three of them coming down an alley in their rose garden last Saturday and I went up and pretended I couldn't see them. I said: 'Where are the Harknesses? Here I see nothing but prize roses!' They burst out laughing and Mina, she has a silvery, rippling laugh, said: 'Oh, Mr Hawkins, how very nice!' "

"Do you mean that fat one?" asked Teresa, spitefully.

"Ah, jocund, rubious, nods and becks and wreathed smiles," said Andrew, writhing on the settee in ecstasy, a broad smile on his face. "I peered in among the roses and then I pretended to see them and I said: 'I was looking for Mina, Teen and Violet, but all I see are the Three Graces!' "

"You should be ashamed," said Teresa, morosely.

"That just shows you don't understand the world and your Andrew," he retorted comfortably, leaning back and flexing and stretching his legs. "The girls were delighted! They went off into happy peals of golden laughter, like peals of bells. Mrs Harkness came running up and said: 'What have you been saying to my girls, Mr Hawkins? I must know the joke too.' We all laughed again. Mrs Harkness—I wish you could meet her —is a wonderful woman, motherly, but full of womanly charm and grace too. In her forties, plump, round, but not ungraceful, the hearthside Grace. And she too told me how beautiful my hair is. They can't help it, the desire to run their fingers through it is almost irresistible."

"Did she kiss your hand? Mrs Harkness, I mean," enquired Teresa in a low voice.

Hawkins looked at her sharply. "Don't jest at things that are sacred to me, Teresa. I have suffered much through love and when you come to know human love, instead of self-love——"

"The beans are done," called Kitty. Teresa gathered up her sewing.

"If you ever love! For I verily believe that inward and outward beauty strike one chord."

"You do," said the girl, "do you? Well, I don't. How simple that would be."

"An ugly face is usually the dried crust of a turbid, ugly soul. I personally," he said in a low, vibrant voice, "cannot stand ugliness, Trees. I worship beauty," he said, throwing his limbs about in a frenzy of enthusiasm, "and all my life I have served her, truth and beauty."

Teresa took the worn damask cloth out of the sideboard drawer and set five places.

"I want to be loved in my own home," said Hawkins, contemplating his long legs and speaking in a fine drawn silken murmur. "Sometimes I close my eyes and imagine what this place would be like if it were a Palace of Love! All your ideas of decorating the walls with fifteenth-century designs, peepholes, twisted vines, naked-bottomed fat and indecent infants on the ceiling—that's dry, meaningless, dull work, but if this house were peopled with our love, murmurous with all the undertones, unspoken understanding of united affection—a-ah!" He opened his beautiful blue eyes and looked across at her. "And yet, in a way, you're like my dear Margaret, but without her loving nature. How tender she was! I was her whole life, I and you babies. She knew that I had something precious in my head, like the whale with ambergris——"

"A sick whale has ambergris," said Teresa. "A whale that's half rotting while it swims is the sort they go after, because they hope it has ambergris in its head. And you know how they bring in every soapy thing from the beach, everything that's greasy and pale, for ambergris."

"And she was modest," said the beautiful man, joining his hands and looking down at them. "She had a curious thing she used to say: 'Andrew, how did a mouse like me get a man like you?' What charm there is in a modest woman! If you could learn that, Teresa, you would have charm for men, for they can forgive a lot in a woman who is truly devoted to them. What do we look for in women—understanding! In the rough and tumble of man's world, the law of the jungle is often the only law observed, but in the peace and sanctity of the man's home, he feels the love that is close to angels! A pretty face, a lovely form, cannot give that—or not those alone. No, it is because he knows he is loved. . . . Don't forget, Kitty, to clean my boots," he said, sitting up. "I'm going into town this afternoon."

"On the same boat with us?"

"No, later. And ask Trees if she sewed the buttons on my white shirt. Trees! Buttons—shirt?"

"Well, you could have gone to Malfi's wedding, you're going into town," objected Teresa, bringing in a vase of flowers.

"Ha—I don't approve of that hocus-pocus. You know that, Teresa. Love alone unites adult humans."

"We're not illegitimate," Teresa grinned.

He had risen to his feet and half turned to the window; now he partly turned to her, and she could see the flush on his face and neck. "Teresa," he said gently, "your mother and I were united by a great love, by a passion higher than earthly thoughts, and I should have kept to my principles, and she too was willing to live with me, bound only by the ties of our affection, but—I had already rescued her from the tyranny of that hard old man and we were too young and weak, we could not harden ourselves to hurt her mother's feelings as well."

The young girl went on smiling unpleasantly, "And if you loved someone else?"

The man looked out over the beach and bay for a moment and

the girl flushed, thinking she had gone too far. He said, *sotto voce*: "My girl, since you bring it up, I am in love again, with a young woman, a woman of thirty, a—" His voice dropped. He came towards her, seized her arms and looked into her face without bending. "A wonderful, proud, fine-looking woman, pure in soul. My whole life is wrapping itself around her, so I'm glad you brought it up for you will understand later on——"

She angrily shook her arms free. "Don't touch me, I don't like it."

He sighed and turned his shoulder to her. "This is no way to treat men, men don't like an unbending woman."

"I am unbending."

"You will be sorry for it."

"You ordered us never to kiss or coax or put our arms around you or one another."

"A coaxing woman, a lying, wheedling woman is so abhorrent to men," he said. "I have seen a woman sitting on a man's lap, trying to coax things out of him. Isn't that shameful to you? I hope it is. I was firm on that one point and your mother agreed with me. *She* never flattered in hope of gain, she never once lied —never once in our whole married life, Trees. Think of your dear mother if temptation ever comes your way—although you will never be tempted to lie, I know, but the other little things in women, the petty, wretched things, the great flaws in female character—flightiness—" He paused and forced himself to go on with a grimace. "Flirtatiousness—though," he continued, looking round at her with a broad smile, "*that* is not likely to be your weakness, nor Kit's. If, I say, you should ever be tempted to tricks like that, thinking to please some man, remember that they detest those tricks and see through them. They know they are traps, mean little chicane to bend them to woman's purpose. I was at Random's the other day. He let his little daughter climb over him and beg him for something he had refused. He gave in. It was a humiliating sight for me, and for the man. I could see her years later, because she is pretty, a warped, dishonest little creature, only thinking of making men do things for her."

"Have you ever seen me coax or kiss?" asked Teresa, indignantly. "Have I ever begged for a single thing?"

"No," he said, "and in a way it's a pity, for you have no attraction for a man as you are now, and it might be better if you knew how to lure men." He smiled at her, "Why can't you be like me, Trees? I am known everywhere for my smile. I have melted the hearts of my enemies with my smile. You know Random Senior, the man who did me that great injury—we used to pass in the street, afterwards, every morning on the way to work. I always smiled and offered him my hand. After a month or so, he couldn't bear it. He used to go round by a back way, to avoid me, he couldn't bear the smile of the honest man. If you would smile more, men would look at you. Men have their burdens. How delightful it is to see a dear little woman, happy and smiling, eager to hear them, delighted to cheer them. No one can say why a woman's bright face and intelligent eye mean so much to a man. Of course, the sexes are made to attract each other," he said with an indulgent laugh. "Don't think I'm so innocent as I seem, Teresa, but sex has its delicious aspects. Sex —what a convenient dispensation—yes, sex," he said, changing his tone and coming close to her, ardently, intently, "I am not one to inveigh against sex! You don't know the meaning, the beauty of that word, Teresa, to a loving man. On the other side of the barrier of sex is all the splendour of internal life, a garden full of roses, if you can try to understand my meaning, sweet-scented, fountains playing, the bluebird flying there and nesting there. There are temptations there but the man sure of himself and who knows himself can resist them and direct his steps into the perfumed, sunny, lovely paths of sex. Oh!" he cried, his fine voice breaking, "who can tell these things to another, especially to you, Trees? You are too cold, you have never responded to me, and my soul, yes, I will use that word, had such great need of understanding! I saw right away that Kitty, my dear girl, was a woman's woman, a womanly little girl, pretty, humble, sweet, but in you I saw myself and I determined to lead you out of all the temptations of your sex, for there are many—many of which you are not aware—"

"There is simply nothing of which I am not aware," said the girl.

"You don't know what you are saying," he said tenderly.

Her face became convulsed with anger. "How stupid you are," she cried and rushed out, upstairs, in the breezy part of the house. All the doors were open. Her room at the back of the house, painted nile green, was an inviting cell, almost bare, neat, cool. She rushed in, flung herself on her bed, and stared upwards at the ceiling, mad with anger. In a short time, however, she cooled down, and thought once more that she would cover the walls, the ceiling, yes, the walls of the corridor, the walls of all the house, with designs. She got up and began to draw fresh designs on a large piece of white paper stretched by drawing-pins on her table. She had combined all sorts of strange things in it; patriotic things, the fantastic heads of prize merino rams, with their thick, parting, curly, silky wool and their double-curved corrugated horns, spikes of desert wheat, strange forms of xerophytic plants, pelicans, albatrosses, sea-eagles, passion-flowers, the wild things she most admired. She forgot all about her dress, which she had to wear at the wedding that afternoon, and which was not yet finished. She came downstairs reluctantly when Kitty called her.

Andrew, viewing her solemnly from the end of the table where he unfolded his worn damask serviette over his bulging naked belly, laughed and chanted as he banged his soup-spoon on the table: "Ants in her pants and bats in her belfry." Teresa turned pale, half-rose from the table, looking at Andrew, and cried: "You offend my honour! I would kill anyone who offends my honour." There was an instant of surprise, then a low, long laugh, rolling from one end of the table to the other. Andrew began it, Lance with his hollow laugh, Leo with his merry one, Kitty's cackles joined in. It was far from spiteful, healthy, they had a character there in the simmering Teresa; she never paused for reflection, she rose just the same in defence of her "honour".

"Your honour," said Lance, her elder brother, low and sneering. He was a tall, pale, blond lad, chaste and impure.

"A woman's honour means something else from what you imagine," said her father, laughing secretively.

"A woman can have honour," declared Leo, a dark, rosy boy. He turned serious in honour of his admired sister.

Lance muttered.

"You would not kill, you would not take human life," said the handsome man, the family god, sitting at the head of the table. "Don't say such things, Teresa."

"Honour is more sacred than life," said Teresa somberly. Andrew said abruptly: "What's the delay? Where's dinner?" Kitty brought in the soup.

No more was said, and they fell to in a gloomy, angry silence.

13

The unappeased young girl, relentless, ferocious, was able to stir them all. They suddenly felt discontented, saw the smallness of their lives and wondered how to strike out into new ways of living. She did not know this: she brooded, considering her enemies under her brows and made plans to escape. She reconsidered the conversation; she had not said the right thing, but exploded into speech in the usual way. Her father meanwhile had been thinking it over. She supped her soup and without looking up, declared to him: "I am informed, on the moral side. You're ignoble. You can't understand me. Henceforth, everything between us is a misunderstanding. You have accepted compromise, you revel in it. Not me. I will never compromise."

Lance and Andrew, from laughing up their sleeves, came out into the open and burst into joyous roars of laughter. Leo considered her seriously, from above his soup-spoon. Kitty looked from one to the other. Teresa sat up, with a stiff face and a stiff tongue, too, and tried to crush them with a glance. She buried her mouth in another spoonful of soup. Several of them threw themselves back against their chairs and laughed loudly; but the laugh was short.

"Eat your soup and don't be a fool," said Andrew.

Teresa flushed, hesitated, but said nothing. Andrew said: "She dares to say her own father is contemptible, her brothers and sister."

Teresa looked ashamed. Hawkins pursued the subject. "Mooning and moaning to herself and it's evident what it's about—no one is good enough for her. She hates everything. I love everything. I love everyone. My one prayer, and I pray, though to no vulgar god, is for love."

"You disgust me," said Teresa, lifting her head and looking at him.

He began to laugh. "Look at her! Pale, haggard, a regular witch. She looks like a beggar. Who would want her! What pride! Pride in rags! Plain Jane on the high horse! When she is an old maid, she'll still be proud, and noble. No one else will count!"

The nineteen-year-old said calmly: "I told you I would kill you if you insult me. I will do it with my bare hands. I am not so cowardly as to strike with anything. I know where to press though—I will kill you, father." With terror, the table had become silent, only Kitty murmured: "Terry! Don't be silly!"

The father turned pale and looked angrily at her.

"You don't believe me," said the girl, "but you should, it's for your own good. Base coward, hitting your children when they're small, insulting them when they're big and saying you're their father. Base coward—to think," she said, suddenly rising, with an exalted expression, staring at him and at them all, "I have to live in the house with such a brutal lot, teasing, torturing, making small. I know what to do—keep your yellow blood, I'll go away, you'll never see me again and you can laugh and titter to your heart's content, look over your shoulders at people, snigger and smirk. Do it, but let me live! I'll go this afternoon and after the wedding, I'll never come back."

The answer to this was a terrifying roar from the father, who knew how to crush these hysterias, and the subdued, frightened girl sank into her place. Presently, she burst into tears, threw herself on the table and shook with sobs. "When we are all suffering so much," she cried through her hair and folded arms, "you torture us."

"Meanwhile," said the beautiful man quietly, "you are letting Kitty do all the work."

She rose and went ashamedly to work.

"Dry your eyes," whispered Kitty hastily, "or you'll look terrible when you go out." "I have suffered too much," said Teresa, "I have suffered too much." But the storm was over.

Meanwhile, Hawkins sat on the stone seat in the wild front garden, whistling. They came down, their hands still red from washing dishes. He saw them running for the boat, burst into laughter, then suddenly: "How wonderful is marriage—the Song of Songs . . . makes the women leap like roes. . . ."

2. The Countless Flaming Eyes of the Flesh

THE girls looked so strangely different, tearing round the bay, that their father, who was quite proud of their talents, doubled up with laughter as he stood at the gate shouting good-bye and they could hear his ha-ha-ha pursuing them. Everyone that they had known for years turned out and stood up to see them pass, fishermen, shopkeepers, as well as school children and visitors to the bay.

Kitty, with her neat brown dress, wore brown walking shoes and a turned-up brown sailor hat. Teresa's remarkable robe flared and floated on the ground and had medieval sleeves, narrow at the shoulder and eighteen inches wide at the wrist; the roses were affixed round this opening. She had high-heeled slippers and an immense palette-shaped hat in champagne colour. Their straight cropped hair, brown and blond, tossed wildly round their sunburnt faces, unpowdered and unrouged; sweat poured down their cheeks.

The day Malfi March was married, it was hot, past one hundred degrees in the shade at two and growing hotter. It was a brassy and livid day, come after a year of drought and fierce summer, at the end of February. The air was thick with dust, the smoke of bushfires drifted along the hills and the red glare and combs of flame could be seen even at midday.

The ferry trip to Circular Quay took nearly an hour. The girls sat outside and stared at the water.

"Your dress simply shrieks at mine," Kitty said.

Teresa looked down at herself complacently and said: "Not at all."

She went on thinking about married women and old maids. Even the frowsiest, most ridiculous old maid on the boat, trying to shoulder her way into the inner circle of scandalmongers, getting in her drop of poison, just to show that she knew what was what, was yet more innocent looking than even a young married woman. They, of course, hushed their voices when such a person butted her way in. She might talk coarsely and laugh at smut but they saw to it that she missed the choicest things; and of course, when they talked about childbed and breast-feeding, she had to sit with downcast eyes, ashamed. As for the secret lore that they passed round, about their husbands, she could never know that. The unmarried were foolish, round-eyed, even in old age with a round-cheeked look (or was that just her Aunt Di?) and even when withered, with pursed lips as if about to swallow a large juicy tropical fruit. That was the way they looked when they talked about the sexes! Poor wretches! Teresa would never endure the shame of being unmarried; but she would never take what her cousins were taking either, some schoolfellow gone into long trousers. Teresa gave Kitty a dissatisfied look. She was dreaming away there, with her fine short-sighted eyes, wearing that dress that ruined her lovely nut-brown skin. If she didn't change, she would never get married.

Kitty looked at Teresa.

"We're gadding lately, aren't we? Tina's engagement and now Malfi!" She had a fresh laugh, delicious, disquieted.

"They're all getting married, it seems."

"Except us—and Anne, and Anne's been a bridesmaid three times," said Kitty. "That was unlucky."

Teresa was silent, thinking: "And they never even asked Kitty once. It's a shame, they ought to give her a chance." She stole a glance at her sister, thinking: "She ought to have someone to dress her."

"Maids of honour often marry the best man," said Kitty. "I suppose it gives them the idea."

The step between being an unattached girl and getting married is so enormous, thought Teresa, how does anyone get over it? How is it done? Not by kindness. What about Malfi? She always had chances, though she was ill-tempered and now she is marrying young Bedloe, though at the engagement party she stumbled over his high boot with an oath, "Take your bloody legs out of my way", and he answered nothing, just looked, fair and flushed and timid and loving. Incomprehensible. Her first fiancé, Alec, was there, holding her thin arm, kissing one of her sharp shoulder-blades standing out above the low-backed evening dress. "Oh, leave me alone, can't you!" Malfi cried, pulling away gracelessly, standing round-shouldered and with a sly, angry, trapped expression. She was no longer pretty, her seventeen-year-old bloom gone, but the suburban boys milled round her; she was never at home alone. Malfi wasn't satisfied, though she had led a golden youth, thought Teresa, had everything and never had to work. Teresa saw in a sketchy way in her mind's eye the faces of the boys and girls who went to work with her on the ferry. As the burning sun bored into her and the reflections from the water dazzled her, she saw insistently, with the countless flaming eyes of her flesh, the inner life of these unfortunate women and girls, her acquaintance, a miserable mass writhing with desire and shame, grovelling before men, silent about the stew in which they boiled and bubbled, discontented, browbeaten, flouted, ridiculous and getting uglier each year.

Tina Hawkins, their cousin, a husky-voiced, long-legged brunette, had her engagement party in January, a cool day for summer and they had both gone out to the cottage at Roseville, to see the man, Tom Swann, to see how Tina took it. It was a blowy, sandy day. Tina, with thick dark brows and large eyes, was sullen, or timid—which? They helped to carry out tables into the back garden and there, shifting his feet, near a privet hedge was a starved little man with stiff black hair. "What do you say his name is?" "Tom Swann." She'll be Mrs Swann then, from Hawkins to Swann; not a bad exchange. "It's a black Swann," said Aunt Bea, who had already nine times offered the joke, "Her goose is a Swann." Each girl met the groom-to-be, Tom, and to each he was very kind and modest, saying: "I'm your new cousin. How are you, cousin? Call me Tom." Later Tina sat with him and Anne at one table, while the others looked at them; Tina, who knew what they were thinking, was awkward, flushed and dropped her eyes. He was counterman at a sandwich-shop where she worked.

It might have been Tina's engagement that made Malfi March send her wedding invitations out so soon. Harry Bedloe was another of those small, underfed men. Teresa suffered for herself and for the other girls; each year now counted against them; nineteen, and has she a boy-friend? Twenty, and does she like anyone particularly? Twenty-one, now she has the key of the door; she ought to be looking round! Twenty-two already! Twenty-three and not engaged yet? Twenty-four and not even a nibble? I'll never be one of those women on the boat, thought Teresa, never fail, never fail like Kitty, never fail like Malfi, never live the life of shame.

"Will you wear white when you get married?" asked Kitty. Teresa had never thought of getting married, however. Now, with a start, she saw herself in front of a staring crowd, with pressing bosoms and shoulders and staring, glad eyes. Some faceless, memberless heavy shadow stood somewhere near, keeping her company, a man yet unborn in her life.

"Would you wear orange-blossom, a veil and all that?" continued Kitty. "I don't like brides to wear a coat and skirt, although I suppose it's more practical."

This was a burning question in their circle. If a girl wore a long satin gown, she had to have bridesmaids. Then came the questions, How many, whom to ask without heartburnings and without financial hurt, and how to have a pretty wedding without impudent display. Teresa thought over all these arguments without coming to any decision; at last, she said:

"Well, I'd have a bouquet of red rosebuds."

"Then you couldn't wear white satin, Terry," concluded Kitty.

"No," mused Teresa. After a pause she said: "Yellow satin would be marvellous, wouldn't it, and you know, stiff heavy yellow lace."

"For a wedding dress! What could you use it for, after?"

"Yes, you'd just have to keep it."

"Or for an evening dress."

"No, you know how they always giggle—she turned up in her wedding dress dyed."

"I'd have something you could make over," said Kitty virtuously. "I think it's a silly waste when you need the money for other things."

"You would look wonderful in eggshell satin, with old lace," continued Teresa, looking her up and down, "with your dark skin and eyes."

Her sister smiled and meditated.

"When you get married, I'll give you fifty things," Teresa said. "Fifty, don't forget."

"Will you really?"

The girls were silent for a while, until Kitty stirring and sighing, said: "Don't you think we ought to go in out of the heat? My dress is sticking to me."

"I'm spouting rivers," said Teresa, "but I like it."

She admitted that they could go to the covered end of the boat; there might be a faint movement of air there. They looked out at the glare, wondering if there would be any change that day. There was no wind, but the sky was an immense workshop of wind where they saw pipes, bottles and horns of vapours, spindles, inexplicable flares, tongues of steam, falls of purple and orange. It was a day without white light; at this hour the birds sang no more and even the cicadas skirled drowsily. The ferry scarcely broke the oil eddies and the soot, instead of drowning, merely scudded off over the slippery waves. Middle-aged people slept in the cabins. The voices of schoolboys going to a boat-race came down from the upper deck. A Portuguese deck hand who knew the Hawkins boys, Leo and Lance, stood in the gangway and looked at the sisters. When they glanced his way, he nodded gravely and his dull, long dark eyes gleamed. The water had a ruby light in the path of the sun, the milky waves sent out by the ferry hissed round the thickly weeded shore. The deck hand looked over the water but at last said nonchalantly, with a quick look at Kitty: "Are you Leo's sister, too?"

"Yes, Mr Manoel."

Manoel looked out at the water again, slowly turned, looked aft and went inside. He stopped, however, when half in, and lounging against the upright, said to Kitty: "See you were Leo's sister anywhere."

His severe face creased, caved in and was polluted by a black laughing mouth, revealing several decayed stumps. He nodded to them and dawdled round the outside deck aft. The girls were flattered. Even plump business men put a hand to the gangplank when it happened to slue under Manoel's hand. The schoolboys came home bragging when old Joe Manoel favoured them with a joke. He would never allow the girls or the business men to call him Joe, however; he was Mr Manoel and would only answer if so addressed. He lived in the bay and owned two small cabins in a forgotten alley under the cliff. He had a wife, an old mother, and children, and when it was rumoured that he cuddled with the bay's only wild girl, genteel married ladies who had melted at his agreeably sinister smile, doubted and hesitated. Could nice Mr Manoel do such a thing? Only the other day he had helped them with a parcel, or a valise. Kitty said: "When I went into the cabin, Gladys was sitting on the engineer's bench."

"She always sits near the men."

"Do you think he really kisses her?"

"Oh, no; that's slander. She lives in his street, that's all," said Teresa.

Gladys was fifteen. She ruffled the women and to young girls this Venus was taboo. She was a large, square-faced, ragged hoyden who knew all the boys, the fishermen and the deck hands. She tumbled about with them, not caring how she showed her legs, that was the story. Andrew Hawkins said: "We must not judge, she lost her mother when she was a little thing, just like you children." The sisters still had confused notions of what her life could be. Teresa imagined that she slept in the boat sheds at night, near the fishermen who were waiting for an early start, amongst their old clothes, bottles, tackle and wading-boots. Kitty had seen two schoolboys in a cave on the beach, rolling, riding each other, giggling and shouting: "Gladys, Gladys." She was puzzled by this obscure revelation. Teresa, seeing the wild girl rush shouting down the streets with boys and go bathing with them in lonely parts of the harbour, hearing that she had the freedom of all the sheds and boats, had a pang of jealousy. Girls wanted to take the road, but how could they, how could they? She would have liked to ask Gladys certain things.

They picked up their parcels, gloves, and bags and moved towards the sheltered back end of the double-ended ferry. Teresa held up her long skirt with casual elegance in one hand. They rounded the corner and came to a breathless stop. Gladys was sitting down, while the deck hand, bending over her, had his arm plunged down her back, up to his armpit. The girls stared. The deck hand began to withdraw his arm, they saw his hand bulging under the cloth on her loose breast. He squeezed the breast, gave the girls a look and withdrew his knotted claw. He shambled off to the other side, settling his dirty cap on his head. Gladys sprang to her feet and hurried after him, tossing her hair. The sisters looked at each other, looked about uncertainly, and sat down in the place.

"That was funny," said Teresa.

"Yes," breathed Kitty. After a few minutes, her curiosity unloosed her stiff tongue and she timidly asked: "What do you think he was feeling right down her back like that for?"

"I don't know."

After another silence, Kitty pondered.

"Why do all the men and boys like that tomboy? She's so dirty, and so awful."

"You mean her figure? Yes, I know."

"Not that, but the way she behaves. She's so rough."

"They don't all."

"Well, Mr Manoel——"

"You wouldn't want him to kiss you?"

Kitty burst out laughing, and blushed, "Oh, no." But she began to ponder again and said almost in a whisper:

"But he's married!"

"I know."

"But he has no right, then——"

"He has a right."

"A married man?"

"If he loves her."

"But he's married."

"If he loves her," said Teresa.

Kitty looked at her in astonishment. "Love?"

"It's love," said Teresa.

"What do you know about it?"

"I know."

Kitty looked at her fascinated and for a moment, suspicious, but at her sister's expression, red face, grey eyes turned black with anger, she smiled slightly, and murmured:

"Oh, of course, you know everything."

Teresa, flattered, said nothing more and cooled off.

When the ferry docked, a few boys with private school caps stood jostling near the gangplank on which Mr Manoel rested his hand and then, in a spurt, they all leaped, the boys, Gladys, some more boys, over the thinning lane of water; and after them came the rope, the gangplank, and the two sisters walked off followed by the other citizens.

At the Quay, the girls had to pass along the waterfront to reach the Neutral Bay ferry. Kitty, watching Gladys flouncing along with two of the boys, some distance in front, awoke from this obsession, to see another sort of vision—Teresa sailing out in front of her, her lavender skirts swelling gracefully over the fatly wrinkled asphalt, her head tilted, her whole attitude vigorous and excited. A dark axe-faced, starved young man, with spectacles and a black felt hat cocked, was smiling at her and stopping to chat. Kitty approached quickly and was introduced—Mr Crow.

"Nice weather for fried fish," said Mr Crow.

Kitty giggled. Mr Crow gave Kitty all his attention.

"Where are you going all so gay?"

"To a wedding."

Mr Crow gave a horse-laugh.

"Just like you girls!"

"Where are you going, Mr Crow?"

"Launch-picnic up the Lane Cove." He swung out a parcel from under his arm. "My bathers. A wedding, phew! Imagine long tails in this weather—or don't they wear that any more?"

"I don't know. I suppose so."

"Some people got married in bathing suits, in the paper," said Teresa.

"Rather frank, isn't it?" he grinned.

The girls looked puzzled. "There was a scandal, didn't you see it?" Teresa asked.

"All that fuss and feathers, put on to take off," pursued the young man.

Teresa laughed, "You don't want them to live in them?"

He grinned. "Well, better shove off. I never saw you look so much of a toff," he said to Teresa, "didn't know you went in for that."

"Sometimes." Teresa seemed confused.

"Good-bye," said Kitty.

"Keep your powder dry," Mr Crow warned them.

"Good-bye!"

"Ta ta!"

He lunged past them, carrying his parcel, and without raising his hat.

"Teresa, who was that?"

"He's the one who coaches me in Latin at night."

"He's quite young."

"Oh, he's not so young," said Teresa, "and very poor, that's why he has to teach at night. He has no one to help him, all the other graduates have, but——"

"There's the boat," said Kitty.

They ran.

3. Malfi's Wedding

MALFI's husband stooped and picked up the long veil, running behind her like a woman catching chicks. By the time they reached the festal door, he had gathered up the gauze and had it frothing on his arm. Malfi was delicate, small and thin.

In the entrance, and climbing the tall wooden stairs, it was a constant hello'ing and calling out of names, rapid introductions lost in a confusion of smiles and crackling new suits and dresses, a *phew*ing and *ouf*ing over the heat, jokes about the champagne, words and phrases, family words known to them and strange jokes in the family jargon of the Bedloes and of other strangers drifted into their harbour, floating through the air like confetti, startlingly clever, with a hundred sights of old faces refurbished and new faces varnished. The girls felt happy. They allowed themselves to drift upstairs through the carnival, surreptitiously, in the crush, picking their dresses from their wet breasts and streaming thighs. "How about a nice shower! We ought to have brought our bathers! I'm sorry for the men with their collars", rang on every side. Every word was a joke, every joke successful. They were breathless in the hall, breathless on the threshold of the hall, which was to rent for "banquets, receptions, smoke concerts, etc." The church, with its wilted flowers and tangled ribbons, had been disappointing but here there was a large if shabby splendour. From the roof hung the red and green streamers of a past fête. A few white ribands hung from the walls and a white bell with silver tinsel was suspended over the centre-piece of the long banqueting table. Trestle tables covered with white cloths ran round three sides of a large square. The room was spacious, with a dais for a small orchestra, a balustrade, a piano, music-stands. To everyone's surprise, a few musicians in black were actually there, a violinist with a cloth in his hand, a pianist, a cellist, all looking very off-hand. What expense! Trust Aunt Eliza and Uncle Don for the real thing, at the wedding of their only and beloved child. And then, why not?

There was Anne Broderick, their first cousin, Aunt Bea's only child. The two girls rushed forward, "Anne, oh, Anne!" They had lived together as children. There was Aunt Bea herself, the Venerable Bede of the great Hawkins family, as she called herself, rushing up to them, again in her old serge suit, borrowed hat, cheap high heels and wrinkled stockings, all smiles and love.

"How are you doing in this heat, my chick, my cherub?" said she to Anne, whom she had not seen since the church, seven minutes away. "Did you ever see my diddums look so plump and pretty, like a spring chicken? Kiss me, my duck. How do you think my baby of twenty-four is looking, chicks?" she enquired. "My two favourite nieces! And how's your dear father, my dear brother Andrew? We are all broken up that everyone couldn't have been included, but Croesus himself would think twice about asking our tribe in its entirety and you don't know how disappointed Eliza was that Malfi insisted upon a relatively quiet wedding. Malfi herself cut down the list of guests by half. She was always thoughtful of her parents, and of course, to them, she is the pearl of great price. How very nifty, Teresa! But look, a rose is hanging by a single thread! So here we are, my chicks, in the fullness of time, at Malfi's wedding. Everything comes to her who waits, including Mr Right. Of course," Aunt Bea bent closer, "I understand that he simply adores her, he worships the ground she walks on and the love is more on his side than hers, but we never know. Malfi is settling down at last, poor child, and all is for the best in this best of possible worlds."

"Oh, Mother," said Anne. They all laughed. Aunt Bea, excited by the wedding, said: "Of course, a good many people are surprised, between you, we, and us, that Malfi with all her chances is marrying Harry—but Harry is a dear. I've met him three or four times and he calls me his Aunt Bea, the Venerable Bede, not so Venerable, he calls me, for they, no doubt, told him about Bea and her peculiar, reprehensible no doubt, but my own qualities, peculiar to myself, I don't mean strange. And though the boy, or man, I should say! is rather a simple soul, he's a good soul and after all, handsome is as handsome does, if Malfi is happy with him, we ought to ask no more questions. And it really is time our little Malfi had a home of her own with things of her own, for we all know a time comes when a girl, however much she loves her parents, yearns for her own nest. And so it is with Malfi. And if it is love she wants, loyalty and all that, she has it, I say. I was quite won over by Harry the first time I met him and I said at once to Malfi—enigmatic as Malfi is, she has a great affection for her Nana Bea —'If you want him, he's the man, he certainly has a good heart', and after all, who knows if she'd really be happier with Clark or Errol?"

"Oh, Mother," said Anne, "don't be stupid." She laughed.

"Diddums!" exclaimed Aunt Bea. She kissed her daughter passionately twice and darted off to one of her sisters-in-law. Her navy suit was frayed, and had shrunk, a tail of her blouse hung down behind the coat. Anne rushed after her to straighten it for her and (while the women formed a circle around her) pull up her stockings. When her stockings were tightened, the swollen veins in her thin legs and feet could be seen. But Aunt Bea came back, tugging at her coat and looking over her shoulder at their great-aunt, Aunt Esmay, a pleasant fat woman who had been a general servant when she married, was now a widow, and kept winning prizes at bridge parties. She had on a black voile dotted with indescribable flowers, through which her red neck and arms glowed.

"Now, Bea, I know," she said, "I'm too wide in the hips, there isn't a dress that sits well on my hips."

"You're not so very wide there, May," said Aunt Bea. "Look—there are Andrew's two girls looking like the babes in the woods, their get-up's a bit sketchy, they'd look worlds better with a bit of rouge, but I suppose my brother is still as old-fashioned as ever—you know you should wear the princess-type, that's all, May. The tight waist you have and that frill round the sitdown make you tubby, and then there should be shoulder interest, don't you see, you lift the eye away from the avoirdupois. If you have a frill round your shoulders and——"

"I like a plain dress with a couple of frills," said the old woman placidly, "and I never heard men didn't like hips on a woman."

"Well, I'm afraid you'll find, or you would find, that the style

27

has changed, May. The slinky is more the thing now, not that I don't think a woman should be a woman."

"I am as God made me," said May, complacently smoothing down the ill-cut material over her belly. "I was a thin slip of a thing once, but I don't mind how I am now, Bea. A woman my age should have a little flesh! I don't want to look like a skinny old maid."

"Well, grandmothers look like young girls now, walk behind and you can't tell the difference. A woman I know was hit on the head by a man and knocked down on the pavement. She walked nicely and dyed her hair. When he stooped down and looked at her he saw her wrinkles and he left her lying there. She got up and didn't dare tell the policeman, he would have seen her face and laughed at her."

"No one will give me a knockdown," said Esmay. "I'm off! There's that woman!"

There was Aunt Di herself, the family's only elderly spinster, a golden woman, a school-teacher, who loved her young nieces before their weddings. Aunt Di was gallant about her misfortune. "I am Miss Hawkins," she roared at people, "my nieces are Miss Teresa Hawkins, and so forth, but I am the *only Miss Hawkins.*"

It did no good. They laughed at her in public and in private, to her face and behind her back. At the name of Di's crusades, once the misery was over, one roar of laughter rocked the family. Say what you would, she was just a battling old maid and did not know what man was like, whether Mr Wrong or Mr Right. Meanwhile, her nieces, reaping their wild oats, knew, provoked new scandals which flung Aunt Di into new tempers. Aunt Di cut off each of her favourite nieces as they reached the age of sin and fell; but no matter whether babies came untimely, or girls were mysteriously ill, or babies came "beyond the pale", no matter who was deserted and betrayed, her roaring was in a desert; the more she raved, the more the matrons, the virgins and the seduced laughed at her or hated her. She was utterly a brute or jollily ridiculous, it all meant nothing: she was an old maid.

Each girl had made up her mind to risk anything to avoid being the next "Miss Hawkins". Yet she sat in the front row at all the family weddings and gave bolts of silk, silver teapots, embroidered tray-cloths.

Teresa shrank from her rather more than the others, because

she resembled her. She had the same bright hair and keen grey eyes. What an omen! She pretended not to see Aunt Di coming near and turned away, but Aunt Di bounded up, and seized her by the arm.

"Terry, don't you want to see your Aunt Di? The lavender suits you, Terry, I used to wear shades like that when I was your age, but I can't any more. I had a complexion like you too then."

"Why can't you any more?" Terry demanded.

"It doesn't suit my weatherbeaten skin, my dear, and my age! I'm not young any more like you. I'd be ridiculous."

Terry said: "Why give up?"

Aunt Di gave a kindly snort.

Terry heard it vaguely. She was steaming. Another Aunt, Maggie, bored, had drawn close.

"If you give up, make the faintest compromise, it's all over with you," said Teresa. "I hate Bernard Shaw because he says that life is compromise. It isn't. I'll never give in."

"What's the trouble about?" asked Maggie.

Di let out a hoot. "I used to be like that, just like that!"

Maggie murmured: "Yes, you were, Di, you were a fine-looking girl, with that high colour."

Teresa turned away with bursting heart. It was intolerable because it was true. She was like "the only Miss Hawkins". Aunt Di was saying: ". . . but I waited for Mr Right——" Teresa went over to an isolated bentwood chair and stood beside it, thinking: "What do I care if I am? The little world of aunts has changed. All rights, all liberties, all loves! Let the last shreds of my impotence fall away, they will be right to laugh at me if I remain Miss Hawkins!"

The tables were set, the crowd was thirsty, the air was red and dust flew up. The important persons stood about exchanging well-worn confidences and courtesies and a new embarrassment set in for the hundred mixed relations. Aunt Bea kept running about keeping up the good-will, while Malfi's parents were continually shaking hands, kissing and greeting people. But the strangers brought together by Aunt Bea broke apart again at once, rendered indifferent by the heat of the extraordinary day which had now reached its maximum and was, as the men kept saying, one hundred and twelve, right outside now, the mercury frying. At first they created a little turbulency and gaiety by saying: "Have the bride and groom arrived yet?" "Were you at the church?" Many of the guests had not been invited to the church for the queer reason that Malfi, a party-giver and the showpiece of the family, wanted a very quiet ceremony. Presently these questions failed too, especially when it became certain that the newly married pair had already arrived but were staying in a small room, because Malfi was tired.

Sylvia Hawkins, a dark cousin of twenty-eight, came bursting in with the news, creating a small unrest for a while by saying that Malfi was crying and her husband comforting her; and Aunt Bea rushed about at once saying the poor child was over-wrought, over-excited, the happiest day of a girl's life often brought tears, even though they might be deep-down tears of joy, but happy is the bride the sun shines on, and it certainly was bursting a blood-vessel to blaze on Malfi, the sun never shone so yet on any Hawkins bride, and then a good-natured joke to cover the awkwardness: "How do you like that—a June bride in February? But if all brides were to get married only one month in the year, such procrastination might cause certain things to happen, for time, time waits for no man and sometimes the Little Stranger comes out of the nowhere into the here rather sooner than he is expected."

"Oh, Mother," said Anne, Aunt Bea's daughter, blushing to the roots of her hair.

"Don't blush, my cherub," said Aunt Bea, "though a day like today no one knows whether it's blush or sunburn, but whatever anyone may say, I don't think it's out of place at a wedding to talk of babies. Babies do come, you know, and from weddings, and under some circumstances", and here she giggled remini-scently, and lowered her voice, "you might almost say it is the baby who is being married."

"Mother!" cried Anne, mortified.

"Fear not, my little darling," said Aunt Bea, ashamed, but only of having hurt her child's feelings. "Mother will shut up. I open my mouth and put my foot in it."

"Don't be a fool, Bea," said Aunt Esmay fatly. "My! my dress is sticking to me, they'll think I came in a bathing suit if this goes on much longer. We do need an electric fan. Wouldn't you think they'd have one? At the whist drive on Saturday they had one over each table."

"A ninon bathing suit is just right for today," said Bea, giggling, "or Eve's bathing suit."

"I'm just waiting to rip these rags off my back and step into a cold bath," said Maggie.

"Look at me in my old serge suit," said Bea, with a poor smile. "Well, all I had, don't think I wouldn't prefer ninon."

"Ninon over none-on," said Aunt Esmay, laughing at the old joke as if she had just made it up.

"Ninon over none-on," said Aunt Bea disconsolately. But she brightened at once. "Never say die, for my own precious cherub's wedding I'll wear purple and fine linen if I have to scrub floors for a six-month before. Anne will have whatever she wants, ivory satin, watered silk, Chantilly lace and of course, the family diamonds." Aunt Bea lifted one foot and wrenched at her shoe with a grimace. "These were a bargain at Joe Gardiner's, but you know I am so ashamed to keep the poor young man showing me samples that I just take anything. They seemed to fit in the shop, such a bargain, I couldn't resist it, twelve-and-six, bronze kid, but now they fit me all over nowhere."

They could not fill in the time. The tables waited, the musicians waited, the Don Marches had done shaking hands and the reception was beginning to fall flat; for it was queer and depressing that Malfi had not yet come in but was sitting, nerve-shaken, prostrated by the heat, in a cloakroom at the end of the corridor.

In the moist heat which intoxicated them, and the expectancy, the groups flowed together again, friends together, and the boys and the girls in different circles began to murmur jokes. From each joke flew off a flock of relieved laughs. Their bodies relaxed wantonly, they shook their hips and pressed their shoulders together unconsciously. The gaiety started up again. They stood with their backs to the tables, trying to forget the claret cup, the home-made lemonade, the champagne, only turning back from time to time to see that they were not left out, that no one had sat down. The men, ashamed of their dirty turn of mind, looked around self-consciously and tried to keep their talk decent, and a silence fell on any unseemly guffaw; but the irritated lasciviousness of the girls, on whom the heat and the thought of the wedding-night worked as an aphrodisiac, their impatience, curiosity, and discontent, threw them into a fever. It was perhaps Aunt Bea who set them off, running round to each group with a busy gossip's smile and naïve lecherous interest in the wedding only half-accomplished. She kept saying: "The new wife, the wife in name only," and "A married woman *de jure* but not *de facto*"; and made remarks about the weather, "I hope it will get cooler for the poor things, imagine sleeping together for the first time in such weather." She pushed these remarks farther than was her custom for the pleasure of hearing her nieces "go off into a roar".

Teresa and some young cousin, awkward, flushed and astonished, stood on the outside of a group of four girl cousins listening to Madeline, the prettiest of them all, a golden-brown ringleted girl with blue eyes. She kept doing a dance-step, wriggling her hips, fox-trotting in and out of the group and singing quatrains, or reciting limericks and cracking jokes at which the girls cried: "Oh, that's too raw," or "How absolutely killing!" or "You're vile," or "Where on earth do you get these things?" They stood listening, unable to believe what they heard, with red cheeks, baited but ashamed. Madeline sang: "*In the park, after dark, without pants in the park after dark*", her curls flopping, her face jovial. Aunt Bea had thrust her brown head in amongst them, its skinny stalk growing among all the satiny, round stalks, her young eyes gleaming. When the two sisters heard the conclusion of this song, Kitty turned her hot brown eyes quickly to Teresa and at this Teresa tried to walk off unobserved. Kitty followed. No one but Bea saw them go. A shriek of laughter burst from the group but was quickly hushed. Aunt Bea came after them at once.

"What is it, girls? Are you having a good time? You mustn't mind what Mad says, she means no harm, it's all innocent fun to her, there isn't a lovelier, purer girl than Mad. I know you two are two little prudes but there's a charm in a little fun. Of course, I think Mad oversteps the fine line between broad humour and the coarse, sometimes, but she's so wholesome. But you can't have too many prunes and prisms at a wedding, for, after all, what is a wedding about"—said Aunt Bea, excitedly, going far beyond what she would have said to the two little prudes at any other time. Bored with them she looked around, said: "I do think Malfi ought to make a little effort and not make her guests wait, I'm dying of thirst and that lovely claret cup, I'm so greedy for it—

that's a lovely turtle neck, dear! Just a sec", and off she ran. The lonely girls passed by another group where a smart-looking girl of about seventeen was leaning forward, stuffing her handkerchief in her mouth, while a fat brunette declared: "Oh, it was awful but we simply shrieked and I never dared tell mother", and farther on they dropped anchor by some older people who were talking about the wedding presents. "A cheque for fifty pounds from the bride's parents." Here they listened eagerly, the shame dropping from their shoulders and their eyes getting tense; for they had given two presents, Kitty a handsome tray cloth from her own hope chest and Teresa an electric iron. These were Bedloes however; instinctively they closed rank to shut out the Hawkinses, and Teresa heard the words "another electric iron" from some of their own people, right at hand. The girls moved forward. Tina Hawkins was there, the girl who had just got engaged, thick-browed, jolly Tina, sullen no more but convulsed with laughter as in the old days, Tina with her guttural voice and beside her fat Aunt Esmay holding forth.

"Three electric irons and believe it or not, a pair of chamber-pots."

"Oh, it's impossible."

"Call me a liar? I swear, I saw them."

"But did they put them with the—with the—oh—other wedding presents?"

"Under the table," said Tina solemnly, "of course."

"Oh, I can't believe it."

"Why not?" said Aunt Esmay. "You need them even after you get married. You don't stop wee-weeing."

The girls shrieked.

A cloud of obscure references hung over the girls. Tina said:

"The girls and Madeline dared me to give po's to Trix when Vic married; I said I would and she made me go buy them. I thought I would die when the man came up to me, a nice young man with hair plastered down. But I up and said: 'Two po's.' He turned red as a beetroot and then he laughed and Mad, the dusty bow-wow, said: 'My sister wants them for a wedding.'"

They laughed heavily. The humour of the afternoon was already well launched and ploughing through a choppy sea.

"Oh, I could have died laughing, I never laughed so much," said Tina.

33

"And you gave them to Vic?" one of the girls said, unwilling to give up the story.

Aunt Bea came rushing up.

"I don't want to miss any of the fun, a family wedding doesn't come every day and especially such a grand do as Aunt Eliza gives. Oh, girls, oh, girls, Tina, your sister Madeline, you two girls, you're a menace to society. You ought to be put out. I never heard in my life such an awful," she lowered her voice, "limerick. I flatter myself I'm open-minded, I relish humour, even broad humour, but there are limits, and Mad with those big innocent baby blue eyes wide open—oh, Mother Ida! But what were you girls giggling about?"

"Tell us the limerick first."

"I couldn't bring myself to. Go and ask Mad."

Instantly, there were some deserters. Aunt Bea, seeing them disband, quickly asked again what they had been laughing at. For the first time Kitty spoke and quite seriously:

"Chamberpots. Some awful presents someone, I mean, Tina, gave Vic."

"Oh, let me die!" Aunt Bea swung on to Kitty's shoulder. "Never!"

"It's not so funny," said Aunt Esmay. "I've seen po's given twice. One pair, down at Mr Vetter's wedding, some friends of his in the club gave them to him for a gag, when they gave him the bachelor dinner. This pair had eyes in the bottom."

Some vile jokes followed, but "Eyes, what eyes?" said one.

"Yes," said Tina seriously, "they had one pair with eyes painted in when I was down with Mad. They showed them to me. We nearly blew a rib when we saw them."

They all became serious. "Why eyes?" puzzled Aunt Bea.

"A big eye, with lashes, in blue," Tina explained.

"I've seen them things," said Esmay, "quite a few times. Maybe it means something. Mr Vetter's friends said it was a masonic symbol."

The girls came rushing back with the limerick and started whispering it, with side glances at the Andrew Hawkins girls, "Oh, we simply exploded."

"Now you speak of it," said Bea thoughtfully, "I heard of it a long time ago. Now what could it mean?"

"Perhaps it is Egyptian, it is the eye of Ra rising," burst out Teresa, then blushed. "It might be an old thing."

"But why would the Egyptians have hieroglyphs on their po's?" asked Aunt Bea.

"To see with at night," Tina said, and yelled with laughter.

"Venus can see at night without eyes," said Teresa. At this strange remark, they all looked at her and fell silent; they even looked a little sulky or underhand. Teresa felt herself turn red slowly from soles to hair-roots. Aunt Bea came round to them, all bonhomie. "Teresa, dear, you oughtn't to say things like that, a young girl like you, but of course we know, dear, that is just thoughtlessness. Now, you girls break it up, mingle with the others. What ever will Aunt Eliza think if we stand around in scrums? Now you two girls," she continued, bustling Teresa and Kitty off, "come and speak to your Aunt Eliza and Uncle Don, I don't believe you've congratulated them yet, and they'll feel deeply hurt if you don't. They're so fond of you, now come along, and you look so pretty, I'm sure Aunt Eliza appreciates it——"

In the natural intermittings of the concupiscent fever which had them all, she needed some arid activity. But they did not reach the circle of froufrou and decency in which the parents of the young couple stood, for the bridesmaid came rippling in, her face bloated with heat and importance, stately, as the groups flowed back before her, and she reached the bride's parents, saying: "She's coming now."

"She's coming now, the bride's coming now, the happy pair is coming now, here they come!"

The guests crushed together and then like grains through a hopper began to stream and blend their flows, they turned, swarmed and reknotted their groups, pushed back, pressed forward; nearer the door vaguely moved back and those near the table confusedly bent towards it. Someone went to the musicians and the girls pushed forward with avid expressions. Here she was, with her bridegroom, standing a moment at the door, she a little pyramid of satin, with a small oval face, looking at them, as she paused as if they were all strangers, he in a dark suit, the veil over his arm, already disturbed by a husband's worries, looking friendly. She made her way to the table, followed by him, forcing herself to speak amiably and call them all by their names. Andrew Hawkins's girls, who hung back, presently found

35

themselves at the foot of one of the tables, opposite them Aunt Bea.

"Do you see where Annette is?" asked Aunt Bea. "Malfi insisted upon having Anne beside her, because you know they were childhood playmates and Malfi has a loving little heart, bless her, whatever her quick temper may lead her to do," and she went on, "Don't think you're left out in the cold, because you're here. I'm here too, among the poor relations, but I'm lucky to be near my two fondest nieces, aren't I? I always look on the bright side, because there always is a bright side; and when I look up there and see my girlie sitting there, so pretty in her blue—do you notice how lovely Anne's hair is to-day? It's the electricity in the air, I suppose—I can't help the tears starting when I think that one of these days she will be a blushing bride and I will be losing my little girl for ever! I asked Eliza how she felt about losing her daughter, but she said: 'I am not losing Malfi but gaining a son.' You know, the old saw is true, I never thought of that. I thought, How should I like to have a son-in-law! Well, and you two girls—your time will come. Look at the chances Malfi had and she is older than you—stand up, girls, it's the toast!"

The champagne had been passed round, a speech had been made by a bald, squat man at the head of the table, and he had said that though he was best man, he was only second best to-day, and he gave them the charming bride and happy groom. They were all standing now and Kitty whispered to Aunt Bea to ask whether she couldn't have water, for Daddy didn't allow them to drink wine and had made a point of it, in fact, just before leaving. Aunt Bea flushed and said angrily: "But you must drink Malfi's health."

"Not in wine," said Kitty unhappily, the colour in her face ebbing.

"But you must drink the bride's health, it would be awful——"

"Not in wine," said Kitty several times. "Couldn't we have water?" Aunt Bea was almost in tears, and whispered madly: "It's unkind, it's rude!" They were drinking, they half emptied the glasses. Kitty's glass stood in front of her, while Teresa held hers in her hand, out of politeness.

"Silly little idiots," hissed Aunt Bea with tears in her eyes, as they put down the glasses. The Hawkins girls stood feeling mean and stupid. When they sat down, Aunt Bea protested in an undertone, while they became red with confusion, and Kitty began to weep quietly.

"Your father's not here, you billies," said Aunt Bea.

"It's wrong to drink wine," muttered Teresa, raising her eyes.

"He made us promise," said Kitty.

"It's so rude, whatever will Eliza think, and your own cousin —do you wish her bad luck? It's heartless, drink it, drink it, before anyone notices."

Teresa frowned, Kitty raised her swimming eyes and looked about. Both were in the throes of cruel doubt; they alone had not tasted. The glasses had not been drained, but stood waiting for the toast to the bride's parents, which was now coming up. When they rose again, Teresa, with an obstinate look, seized her glass, and saying: "It's for Malfi too," sipped it cautiously, and at once drained the glass. Kitty, with a startled look, sipped hers and then put it down. Aunt Bea smiled.

"Silly billies! You didn't take the pledge after all!"

"Will we get drunk?" asked Kitty.

Teresa put out her hand tentatively, seized Kitty's glass, and drank what remained in it.

The wedding party had been delayed and it was now nearly time for the bride to dress. The sun was going down behind the buildings opposite, so that the glaze on the plates shone and blood-red spindles went through the drops of claret in the jugs. The velvet air, full of moisture and dust, clung to their faces and was palpable when they moved their hands. The seats were hot to their bodies. The bride rose and the crowd with her. A fuss began round her and as she jumped up she found the tall heel of her white satin slipper caught in two rungs of the chair. Impatiently, she wrenched it and suddenly the slipper itself flew out into the room with a devil-may-care swoop, while the heel remained in the chair. Several were bending down, pulling it out, one ran for the slipper and while the bride stood one-legged by the chair with a grimace, her father and husband worked over the heel, wedging it back into the slipper. Without a word, she took it from them, slipped it on and walked smartly round the table, with an angry shrug. Then she noticed her cousins standing, round-eyed, disorderly, half-scared and half-laughing at her mishap. She walked back and took her cousin Anne by the hand.

37

"Keep close to me, Anne," she said, "I want you to get it, I want you to be the next to go," and she took her bouquet from the bridesmaid and carried it to the door.

"Get me a chair," she said to her father, "I'm too small to throw it." He smiled down at her and then at the crowd of relatives driving towards him, mothers and aunts, elderly women, Aunt Di, pushing the young girls forward towards the bouquet. Don March bent down and lifted Malfi who put one arm round his neck and with a "Well, here it is, girls!" threw the bouquet towards Anne Broderick.

What a scene! They had nearly all discarded their hats and posies and stood breathing upwards, their eyes darkly fixed, with pain, not pleasure, on the bouquet. As it left the bride's hand, involuntary cries burst from them and they leapt at what was falling towards them, jumping sideways, knocking their neighbours out of the way, pushing, and if they fell back too soon they leapt again with open mouths and eyes and not a smile, their red, damp faces flushing deeper and taking on hungry, anguished and desperate expressions, as in the fatal superstitious moment they struggled for the omen of marriage. Anne, a plump, soft, timid butterfingers, only touched a spray of maidenhair fern with two fingers; the bouquet fell lower, was batted dextrously away from her by Madeline, a tennis-player and cousin Sylvia Hawkins, the eldest of Rodney Hawkins, the rowboat-owner, a thin, tall girl, grabbed it, pushing her way through the darting, jostling mass, when it was wrenched from her by a long thin freckled hand on a bony wrist which protruded without its owner being seen. The arm to this hand, in a poor flowered stuff, was squeezed and released the bouquet; at this moment, Kitty, who had been hovering miserably, all indecision as usual, snatched the bouquet and as she did so it fell to pieces.

"A foul," said Uncle Don, laughing slyly.

The bouquet had disappeared. The slippery thing had found its way down between tossing plump shoulders, sparring elbows and tumultuous thighs. Where was it?

In the fear of having ruined the beautiful loose spray of lilies, roses, larkspur, and fern, the girls parted, billowing away from the spot like swans. Anne, desolate, stared down at the dusty floor and cried: "You've got your foot on it!"

On the farther edge of the circle stood Teresa, her long lavender dress creased and the hem dusty; from under the skirt a long branch of budding roses strayed out. She looked down, moved her foot a little and murmured: "I have not."

She had not jumped for the bouquet, though pushed forward by Aunt Bea with her sister Kitty, because in that blink of the eye she had seen the awful eagerness of the others and the smiling, waiting circle of adults, witnesses of their naked need; and so she had drawn back a bit, with a thumping heart, disappointed but grim, at the very moment the bouquet was thrown. She picked up her skirt now and retired, not daring to pick up the branch which she so much wanted. A slight pause followed.

"Toss for it, girls," said a boy's voice. Everyone burst into a laugh. They were laughing at them, at her, because they had been struggling for a husband. But Aunt Bea came forward, picked up what remained of the flowers and saying: "Is it all right, Malfi dear?" she went among the cousins, giving a flower here, a spray of buds there. "A star-burst of weddings, it will be," she said happily, saving the situation. The girls smiled timidly at her and took the offering. Malfi, having seen this distribution, picked up her skirt without a word and ran to the stairs, clicking her little high heels, but half-way up she paused again and looked curiously at the girls, getting her flowers. When her thick dark lashes flew up, her eyes could be seen, of medium size, clear grey and keen.

"It is a shame, Mother's cherub," said Aunt Bea to Anne, as she handed her daughter a pink rosebud, "sweets to the sweet, but I know Malfi meant it for you, well, all's well that ends well. What a sly one you are," she continued to Teresa, who had now crossed over to Anne's side, "kicking it under your skirt."

"But I didn't know," protested the girl.

"How's the bunfight getting on?" said a male voice, near, teasing. "Does this mean you girls have to share the same man? How about me?"

Teresa's face became sullen and she thrust back the fern spray which Aunt Bea was handing her. "I don't want it. Here, take it," she said, pushing the spray at Anne. "Put it with that!"

"Teresa," remonstrated Aunt Bea, "can't you take a joke?"

"Not that kind of joke," shouted Teresa, in a sudden blow of voice that made the crowd, now disbanding and streaming off to coats and hats, turn and stare at her. People began to smile, laughs broke out, the men guffawed and some of the women looked hurt, severe.

"You can't take part," said Aunt Bea. "Look how you've hurt Aunt Eliza."

"You ought to be ashamed, Terry," said Kitty, rather loudly. Teresa looked at them proudly; she felt immortal. The world was like a giant egg of golden glass, she could crush it. She floated; she looked at them, gleaming. "You're cruel to us, making fun of us, this is cruel," said Teresa. She swept aside, she looked down her nose, she felt her immense strength.

"Terry!" said her sister.

"Jumping, jumping—" replied Teresa contemptuously. Bouquets! She felt she had only to command and men would kneel at her feet.

"Oh, Teresa," said the kind and always gracious Aunt Eliza, as if broken-hearted. Teresa grew pale, looked at her piteously, and looked from eye to eye of the relatives and strangers, again drawing off and giving her curious cool stares. A suspicion came over her. Why did she suddenly feel so strong and fine? Deserted by all, the girl went to get her hat. When she came back, she pushed her way to the front rank of all those waiting to farewell the bride. Malfi came down in a short time, dressed for the honeymoon journey in a short dove-grey silk suit and as she went slowly past, tapping her neat little shoes, shaking hands, kissing, "Good-bye, good-bye, thank you for coming, good-bye, thank you, good-bye", Teresa pushed up to her and said: "Malfi, good luck, I'm sorry for my rudeness, I beg pardon." Malfi stopped and looked straight up at her for a moment. The two cousins had avoided each other all their lives because they were said to be alike in temperament and brain. They were the two "clever ones". Now Malfi was small and neat and Teresa had outgrown her. Malfi reached up for a kiss, said: "Don't think too badly of me", and passed on. Teresa stared after her. What could have prompted this reply?

At the door, Malfi turned round and flung herself on her mother, weeping. "There, my poor child," said her mother, "it's all right, Malfi." The young husband came up to her, kissed her and wiped her eyes with his handkerchief. The door slammed. The long car drove off.

Those who were left in the thick twilight closing in, in the splendid intoxication of the burning air, reeking with food and body smells and cheap perfume and faded flowers and all the pleasant riot of a party's end, stood about for a while talking. Soon the girls had got together and the whispers began, while Aunt Bea again rushed from hand to hand and ear to ear and kiss to kiss, saying this time that they weren't going off on the train at all, but to a hotel for the first night. No one but Aunt Eliza knew where it was, not even the bridegroom's mother—and it was better so.

"I can't help thinking," she said, "how strange it is, the first night, the very first. I can't help thinking of those innocent young babes starting out on life's journey together hand in hand and of them there together, alone at last, you know, for the first night of a lifetime. And then, you know—when you think—they were never allowed to be together till tonight, and now, tonight, it is right and proper, but it must be——" She stopped with a high giggle. Anne was silent. One of the girls said, *sotto voce*: "There'll be a hot time in the——" She was hushed. Some of the girls laughed. "I just can't help it," said Bea, "and it's only natural, isn't it? It's natural for them to be together now!"

"Mother," said Anne, in a low voice.

"What is it, darling?"

"Let's ask Terry home."

"Why, darling, I think that Aunt Eliza and Uncle Don want me to go along with them and cheer them up. Of course, they'll be feeling rather down in the mouth at spending the first night without their darling girlie, and I have such a natural gift for making people merry, that I think my first duty is with them, you see, and they want you too. They're so fond of you."

The guests drifted out, saying good-bye again, to each other, to Bedloes they would never see again in their lives, to relations they would see perhaps in another year or two at another family wedding. There were good-byes between cousins who were intimate friends and between Teresa and Anne, who had once been together for several years in their childhood and were closer than sisters. This was the best of all, a warm, scarcely articulate conversation between friends who hoped to see each other again soon.

But Donald and Eliza March went out to dinner with the bridegroom's parents and left poor Bea stranded there among the very last departing. She turned eagerly to find Teresa left and Teresa went home with them. Teresa was bursting with marvellous news—Kitty, the mouse, the nun, had gone off by herself, at the invitation of Cousin Sylvia, to a moonlight picnic. What would Daddy say? They tried to guess and they laughed.

"I am glad you girls are beginning to come out of your shells at last," said Aunt Bea. "A little drop of wine didn't hurt you, you see." Teresa would not admit she had been wrong and so said nothing about it.

Aunt Bea lived with Anne in Rose Bay. The three of them came home by tram. There was a glorious sunset, a sudden dusk, and the bays were twinkling as they came along in the tram. It was still very hot, human beings smelled like foxes, the thick new-washed hair of women gave off the scent of little woodland beasts; the paint and dust on the tram, the heated metals, the summer trees outside, the petrol in the air made a delicious, stimulating, heavy drink, taken in by the nose. At first Aunt Bea was inclined to grumble because she had turned down a ride in a Packard, to wait for Eliza and Don, but her easy good humour soon returned and she said how nice it was of Uncle and Auntie to think of the poor Bedloes, poor things, she was like a second-hand stuffed armchair and he was got up like a sore thumb, Uncle and Auntie had only met them once before today, but what did it matter, it was Harry she was marrying. Bea accompanied this with a great many other consoling reflections and in a short time was saying that they had never, never had such a lovely wedding, and that Malfi was such a tender, youthful little bride, that she had cried at the church, and dear Harry was such a young man to be taking up the burden of a household. At this moment they were on the rise of Darlinghurst and Aunt Bea broke off suddenly to giggle with them about the "juicy details of that den of iniquity", just discovered thereabout, and now going through the newspapers. "A black man and three sailors, four to one, my dear, so they said——" and so forth; and to follow was the mystery of the hypodermic needle, which, it was said, strange men suddenly thrust into young girls passing by innocently, on their own business, even in broad daylight. "What do they do it for?" "So and so was just waiting for the traffic to stop when suddenly she felt a prick and a tingling sensation. . . ." The crowd in the tram, coming home from all the suburbs, was stretched out, relaxed but lively, women in bright-coloured short dresses and men in shirt-sleeves and sandals. Anne shook some confetti out of her upturned hat. It fell on the ribbed wooden floor of the tram and everyone looked at them and smiled.

"You look as though you've been to a wedding," said a fat red woman with a crocheted white hat.

"Yes, my niece's, a lovely girl, a tiny bride," said Aunt Bea. "When you see a little girl taking on the responsibility of a husband and home, it seems pathetic, doesn't it? Pathetic is hardly the word."

"You mean she's a small woman?" said the woman, interestedly.

"It's a little early to talk of it, I suppose," said Aunt Bea, "but small women usually have small babies, it's the fitness of things. Though I have seen fat women with mere wisps of infants."

" 'Ot for a wedding," said the woman, retreating.

"We're in the dog days," said Aunt Bea. She looked hopefully at the woman, but she said no more.

4. *She Had——*

BEATRICE BRODERICK and her daughter Anne lived in a single front room in a small brick bungalow at Rose Bay. Bea got the room at a very small rent, in consideration of doing most of the work of the bungalow for the tenants, named Percy, a mother with a grown daughter, going to work. The woman was small, pasty-faced, with pepper-and-salt hair curling naturally, and large, steady eyes, a plain, impressive and unsettling personage. The daughter resembled her father. She was blond, ruddy, oncoming, an attractive girl whose clothes were red, blue, white, yellow; she was slender and well-made, too tall, five feet nine, but overcame this defect with an interesting restiveness, a quick attention, impulsiveness, coquetry. She was boy-crazy and worried her mother, Bea explained as they neared the house, but Bea wanted Teresa to meet the girl, Rose, because she was such an interesting type, above all, kind-hearted. Whatever you might say about Rose, this she was, kind-hearted. As to the mother, she was a queer body, respectable, serious, of course. Bea believed she had been something as a girl, but she did not know quite what. She married late, poor thing, at thirty, and her husband kept leaving her, after the daughter was five years old. "In fact," said Bea, "she said she was a widow, like me, but later she forgot what she had said, and came out with it. She is worried about Rose because she is so flighty, and she is afraid—of the taint, you know," Bea continued in a lowered voice. "In the asylum he gets better, and he may come back any time. He comes back at night, they never know when, and the poor woman says she is half mad herself, with fright. As soon as he comes home, he is loving to them, sorry for what he has done.

44

Then in a few days, he asks to go back to the asylum, because he feels it coming on!"

"I wouldn't live there," said Teresa.

"Well, she's so nice and such a poor little thing! She likes to have a friend in the house, she says, and I'm so naturally gay, I cheer her up with my singing and my bright words, and then she likes to have another woman with a young daughter, a widow too, although she is not a widow, but she might as well be, although it's worse, much worse, unless you could be the widow of a gibbering ghost——"

"Mother," shrieked Anne, "oh, don't."

"My chookums," said her mother, "don't be so sensitive. Annette is a bit frightened to stay there, and so I don't often leave her alone. But after all, we do get it nearly rent free and the woman is so sweet, though a little reserved at times, a bit fretful. Poor thing, she is worried all the time. She told me she doesn't sleep at night, afraid he will come back and ring the bell, or even climb in at the window."

"My goodness," said Teresa. They were coming down a winding dirt road towards a gully, still partly bushland. It was about a mile from there to Teresa's own home. They passed suburban brick dwellings with white fences in front and well-grown gardens. The name-plates on their gates said, "Mon Repos", "Idle-a-While", "Just Home", "The Raft", "Banksia".

"She told me," said Aunt Bea, very low with a slight laugh, "poor thing, that she did not believe in you-know between married people. After she had been married two years she refused to have anything more to do with men, and I suppose that is why he went mad. It might have helped anyway. 'Telopea' is the name, there it is, three houses down. It's a blessing to me, a front room, airy, use of the kitchen and bathroom, and a quiet woman, the girl out all day. She lets me use the piano too, and says it brightens the house up to hear me warble all my old light operas."

Gay and confident, Aunt Bea, loaded with parcels, swung open the gate of "Telopea", went up the neat brick path, put her latch-key in the fresh-painted green door. The first door on the right was hers. This was standing open. It was a small room, almost filled by a large double bed, the former marital bed of the Percys, a wardrobe, a wash-stand, and a kitchen table covered with a cloth at which the mother and daughter ate. The corners and free spaces were filled with sewing-baskets, trunks, knick-knacks, doilies, boxes in cretonne, all things brought in or made by Aunt Bea, to furnish her home. The girls took off their hats and sat on the bed while Aunt Bea went to see if the kitchen was free, "For if she is there, I don't disturb her, she's a little moody at times. No wonder, poor thing." Mrs Percy was there, said Aunt Bea when she came back, and in one of her moods, a bit cranky. She had just looked at Aunt Bea over her shoulder and not even given her a how-do-you-do, but you could hardly blame her, her troubles had turned her queer. So they would just sit on their stomachs and wait.

"Take off your dress, if you like, Terry," said Aunt Bea, "or stretch out just as you are. It's a very pretty dress, the colour's just right. We'll put it in a glass of water, the lovely rosebud, Anne, that you got from Malfi's bouquet. It will bring you luck. I'm glad you weren't Malfi's bridesmaid, although I did think it a bit funny at the time, but always a bridesmaid, never a bride—it's better not. What a day! My dears, I'll never forget Malfi's wedding day. My cherub, take off Mother darling's number nines. I ache in the understandings. Wootch! Flow gently sweet Afton. Ouch! I'm like the man who wore tight boots, I am the woman who wore tight boots. Soon I'll get a pair of those elastic-sided button-ups that Aunt Philly wears. Your old mother will hobble to work like Little Tich."

"Oh, Mother," said Anne, laughing, and putting away the thin, cracked shoes under a faded curtain.

"Well, my dears," said Aunt Bea Broderick, falling backwards on the bed, "—move over, Terry—what a day! I was over at Aunt Eliza's at eight. My consul was very nice and said I could have the entire day off. Perhaps that is why Mrs Percy seems resentful this evening. However—there she blows, just what I needed to make a perfect day, as old Aunt Philly said when their one and only Ming (or was it Sung?) vase fell to the floor. Your father, Terry, was there, and never can forget the philosophy of your great-aunt. 'La-di-da!' she said, 'there she blows.' 'We should all be like that,' said your father, 'see all that we cherish go from us without emotion.' He thinks worlds of your great-aunt. I must say I'm of his way of thinking, we ought to be stoics. But who is? She certainly is a merry old soul and a merry old soul is she.

May we all live to be half as young as Aunt Philly, your grandpa always said. He never subscribed to the Undertakers' Gazette either. Your dear grandpa was quite a bird, a gay dog. Grandpa kept the ball rolling."

"Oh, Mother," said Anne automatically, as her mother paused. Anne got up from the hot bed and went to the open window where she sat looking out into the street. A lamp stood two houses away. Opposite was a vacant lot.

"I think it's getting cooler," said Anne. "The moon's rising. The moon streams in here."

"This was where they slept all their married life," Aunt Bea said. "With the moon on his face I don't wonder he went off. I told Mrs Percy that. She said she didn't believe it but you know in lunatic asylums on nights of full moon they have to have extra strait waistcoats."

"It'll be sticky all night," said Terry. "I wouldn't mind being in swimming. What a day! I loved it, though. I steamed. It was pawky, the church, wasn't it? Could you understand all those dead flowers? Did they wilt or were they half-dead in the first place? The whole thing was so queer."

"Did she fall or was she pushed?" mused Aunt Bea. "My lumpkins, sweet cherubs, my lumps of love, I'm glad it's all over, the weary round, or merry, the gift teas, the linen shower, the presents, the dresses. O Mother Ida hearken ere I die! I did expect to be invited to dinner tonight and I frankly avow, my chicks, that I was a bit glum at being left out in the cold but your Aunt Eliza was right, I suppose. I suppose Liza knew what she was doing. And of course, the gown was lovely. Very choice, Malfi darling."

"Tell her about 'very choice, Malfi darling'," said Anne.

"Oh, didn't I tell you that? I did! No? Well, I told so many people and they all simply rolled in the aisles. I hate to repeat myself, as the onion said."

"Oh, Mother," said Anne.

Teresa lay back on the bed and looked out through the window at the dark-blue sky. "It's late, isn't it? I'd better go home."

"Oh, I heard the back door slam a minute ago," said Aunt Bea. "Just wait till I tell you this and I'll run and cook our tea."

"Dad said he couldn't understand Uncle Don allowing Malfi

to have a church wedding," said Teresa. "Uncle Don never goes to church."

Bea seemed flustered. "I don't say we're great church-goers, but a girl feels happier if she can have her little pageant when she turns from girl to woman, and you can't go to a registry office in a veil. To continue, Terry, I went over to Miss Smith-Wetherby's —where she got the Wetherby from I don't know, but anything is better than to be mere Smith I presume—you know, don't you, oh, you know, Malfi's new husband's, so very new, aunt by marriage, maiden aunt, of course. Don't you think we ought to have words for all that? I don't think we have half words enough! Well, it seems poor Miss Smith-Wetherby took rather a fancy to Malfi. She saw her first at Dot Hancock's wedding, a mutual acquaintance, and being herself without chick or child, of course it would be rather queer otherwise——"

"Mother!"

Aunt Bea laughed. "She at once took Malfi under her wing and promised her half a trousseau. It does seem a pity when Malfi already has so much, but to her who hath shall be given, I suppose. Fortune has favourites, far be it from me to cultivate the green-eyed monster—it is just fate. Do you believe in fate, kismet, Teresa?"

" 'There is a tide in the affairs of men which taken at the flood leads on to fortune', I suppose."

Aunt Bea laughed, lying on her back, looking up into the dark ceiling and swinging her thin corded legs. "My darling cherub is ashamed of her Mother's irrepressible foolishness, bless its heart."

"I am not, Mother."

Aunt Bea laughed and asked them if they wanted the lamp. Anne said quickly: "No, let's stay in the dark till the moon is up."

"Let's sit in the dark till the moon comes up," sang Aunt Bea. "Do you know, cherub, you have a perfect instinct for lyrics, you ought to try your 'prentice hand. Anyway, to resume, well, Miss Smith-Wetherby—a ridiculous name, just with Wetherby tacked on, just to avoid being in the telephone book under the innumerable race of Smiths—Aunt or Miss Smith-Wetherby, a respectable maiden lady, invited yours truly to view the trousseau she had collected for Malfi. Well, poor Annette couldn't get away—*oh, I couldn't get away to marry you today, my wife won't let me—*

48

Harry Bedloe evidently didn't feel that way, or Malfi would have been in the soup——"

"Really, Mother," said Anne, in a soft, crushed voice.

"Yes, teeototums, Mother is sorry. I am shameless, kiss Mother darling, otherwise its Mother will repent. Thank you, cherub. To resume, a summary of the preceding chapters will be found on page seventeen of the current issue. What a push was there, oh, my countrymen. Canapés of every rank and degree, caviare actually, I never saw it before, cake-stands full of cake were to be seen in the drawing-room, dainty silver forks, handworked napkins, very choice, Malfi dear."

"You didn't explain that yet," said Anne.

"So I didn't! China tea, ginger beer and spirituous liquors. My dear, I've never seen it before in a lady's drawing-room, she must be a gay old dear even if she is an old maid, not a fussy old maid, as the saying is."

"Mother," said Anne, in a tone of reproach from the window niche.

"Knock, knock," said Aunt Bea.

"Who's there?" came an interested voice, Teresa's.

"Fornication."

They giggled. "Fornication who?"

"Fornication like this you need champagne. I heard that in the bus. Well, to proceed. There you would have seen the *ne plus ultra* of the trousseau for the modern bride-to-be. Of course, Malfi has her own bottom-drawer treasures, some of which, poor child, she made when she was looking forward to marrying Alec, such a lovely boy, but it is better she should know her own mind before the fatal words were said. Part of the secret annals."

"Go on, Mother," said Anne.

"Yes, the trousseau," said Aunt Bea. "Miss Smith-Wetherby kept it there till the end of last week on show, but sent it to Malfi of course in time to pack it, and Aunt Eliza had a constant stream of visitors, oh-ing and ah-ing, for there was everything contained therein that the heart of young woman could desire. She had six voile nightgowns for summer, and two ninon, well, ninon over none-on is ravishing I think and for a bride—well, it's too, too— though I was surprised at an old maid thinking of it, they are generally too shy of the facts of life. So dainty, such marvellous work, you would say fairy-fingers had been at work, for Malfi is such a little thing, a Dresden china doll in physique and I suppose that that is what first attracted him. She has fallen in a bit lately, it was time she got married. It is a pity he is so small. Six dozen hand-drawn handkerchiefs, and half a dozen hand-made panties, three *crêpe de Chine* and three lawn with Madeira work and hem-stitched borders. Of course, on the machine. The panties were blue, pink and white, the nighties were of all the hues of the rainbow, or I should say of Tintex—filmy grey, exquisite pale blue, baby-pink, coral-pink, eggshell and nile. Green for a young girl I never thought quite—but nowadays girls have no superstitions! It was nice of Miss Smith-Wetherby, though. And, my dear, she insisted upon the Smith-Wetherby. Of course, very right, I suppose when you consider the great Psmith Pfamily. Isn't it a scream. Oh, Mother Ida, hear me ere I die! To proceed, six face-cloths, I can't think what for, has she six faces——"

"Oh, Mother, don't," said Anne. Aunt Bea gave a gratified laugh and went on, "—in checks and stripes. Six slips. Let me tell you about those slips. All hand-done. Two in *crêpe de Chine*, two in lawn, two for sports in flowered silk, very sweet, white sprigged pink, and each one, mark you, embroidered separately with an appropriate motif. Miss Smith-Wetherby had done the motifs herself, though the slips were shop-bought, machine-stitched and hand-finished, I noticed. One was with sprays of maybuds, in white, in satin stitch, another with bluebirds in satin stitch, blue of course, the sports ones just niftily embroidered with pink and white initials, very smart and tailored-looking and for the rest, one with fine silk net whipped in and with a silk thread run through and the other with an old-fashioned, that is so new-fashioned, val lace insertion and lace with a dainty bébé ribbon threaded through, blue for luck, of course, very 1860—is that the period?—and in a way the smartest of all. She had six dozen handkerchiefs, you know, three of each, very useful, really, three plain white with hemstitched border and initial in corner, three hand-embroidered in grey, six linen of different modish shades, grey, tangerine, ultra, peach, coco, six mixed tartan in mousseline, six handprints from blocks made by a Russian woman who lives near Miss Smith-Wetherby, very handsome—but I wonder if the ink comes off—in choice arty combinations, so to speak, of navy and leaf, lilac and rust, eau-de-Nile and salmon, chaminade and ibex, Mediterranean and coral, black and chromium, if I remember rightly, these last six on fine soft linen, of course—otherwise they wouldn't take the designs, which were of a delicious, this-is-the-spray-the-bird-clung-to sort, sprays, birds, all that I mean, and six shadow prints, the very latest you know, they have at Farmer's. I suppose she got them there. Six wide-bordered, hemstitched cottons in colours, sport type, one dozen all champagne with variegated designs in off-white, eau-de-Nile, plaque, and scarab, to go with her travelling costume, one dozen house hankies to stuff in the pocket of a tennis wrap-on, or summer cottons—the sort young housewives wear—in checks, black and white, rust and white, green, blue, red, nothing to speak of, just the usual sort, and one dozen assorted *crêpe de Chine* and tulle, outsize, darlings, for evening and head kerchiefs. I know Miss Smith-Wetherby had personally made the collection, it was rather a scream to think of the old dear fussing over it, but sweet, going from shop to shop picking it up. A sort of hobby. Such a nice thought, though. We must admit that Malfi, dear as she is to us, has done well by herself, picking out a family where she is so much loved, though I don't doubt for a moment that the Bedloes are rather flattered to find themselves connected with the March branch of the Hawkins, for we're queer, but we are above the average, not quite the common herd and the usual family-in-law. Well——"

"But, Mother," said Anne, "you didn't explain."

"Oh, the cream of the joke was that Miss Smith-Wetherby's married sister was there, fair, fat and forty, a regular Mrs Rustle-bottom——"

Anne giggled. Aunt Bea went on with a rush, "She had not seen the trousseau and at each thing, all the exquisite little things like cobwebs in their tissue paper, she exclaimed: 'Oh, very choice, Malfi darling', and 'How nice, Malfi darling', and '*Very* choice, Malfi darling'."

"So now we always say it," said Anne. "Very choice, Malfi darling."

"Annette is too shy to have a bottom drawer, but my pet shall have them—those delicate flimsies fine as a spider could spin, in lawn, silk and lace, pintucked, with gentle easings, I can visualize it as I lie here, those veritable treasures of a young creature starting out in life, those dainty dreams of dessous, as the French would say—where was I? Oh, yes, I wish Anne would begin to put by a few things."

"What for?" said Anne in a practical voice.

The moon was just coming over the hill; its beams still shone above them but were lowering. Aunt Bea spoke lazily of making tea, but did not get up. In a few minutes the moon was on the house and was moving down the wall towards them, soon it whitened the outline of Anne's hair. "It's lovely tonight," said the young girl, "and the bay is so still, you don't hear a sound, only the crickets and the cicadas."

"Lor lumme," sighed Aunt Bea, "heigh-ho. It was a lover and his lass, with a hey and a ho and a hey nonny no. Oh, oh, what a yawn! I dreamed that I dwelt in marble halls with vassals and serfs at my side. Yo-ho! Yoo-ee! Lumpkin! Go and make the tea for Mummy."

"Yes, Mother."

The two girls went out into the small kitchen smelling of oilcloth, old plumbing and tea leaves. A few things left from Mrs Percy's meal were in the sink, unwashed. While Anne was frying eggs Teresa got down the plates and cups and in the middle of this they heard the back door clap to.

"Mrs Percy?" called Anne, in her uncertain contralto. "Mrs Percy?"

The door from the laundry opened and the dumpy, large-eyed woman stood on the threshold, looking at them. She said in a meek voice: "Yes, dear?"

Anne introduced them with the unction she had learned in the office. The middle-aged woman came into the room, begged Teresa to go into the parlour, showed her a chair and sat down to talk with her, all in a refined way which made the visitor ill at ease. Mrs Percy sat deep in her chair but leaned forward, holding to the arms, and as she spoke looked closely at Teresa with sage, luminous eyes; the girl had the feeling that an intelligence and a soul lived restlessly behind the eyes. Teresa began to talk rapidly and brilliantly, quite beside herself, in an apprehensive frolic; she talked about her Latin teacher, Mr Crow, about her ambitions, and for some reason, said that Mr Crow believed in free love and was discussing it in the suburbs. She felt that Mrs Percy was not easy. The older woman rose suddenly and begged the girl to excuse her, saying she was tired; the girl must pardon her, she had so many headaches that she had had to give up reading altogether, she who had been so fond of reading, just as fond as Teresa herself. This brought Teresa to a stop and she thought back over what she had said. She could scarcely remember it, but no doubt she must have said something which called up the "reading" remark.

When the things were ready, the girls carried them into the front room where they ate, under a little pink-shaded lamp. When they were finished, and the dishes carried out, they turned the light out again and sat silent, fanning themselves, while mosquitoes strummed in the moonlight.

"I knew there was something I wanted to say," began Aunt Bea. "I heard you talking to Mrs Percy before. How did you two get along? I've always told her about my brilliant niece, the schoolteacher."

Teresa did not like this at all, for she was ashamed of being a schoolteacher and remained silent.

"You two should get along," remarked Aunt Bea. "She was quite a modern woman in her day, a bit eccentric, I gather, she went in for Darwinism, free-thinking, women's movement. Her husband left her and she used to teach, I understand, to keep the child."

"She asked me what I did," said Teresa, "and I told her about the children I teach."

"You did put your foot in it," said Aunt Bea, in a low voice. "Didn't you remember what I told you?"

"Oh, heavens, I never thought of it!"

Teresa had a special class in the public school. In this class had been dumped the truants, the deaf, the mad, and the imbecile, who had been undisciplined in all the other classes.

The back door shut and this time they all heard it.

"There she goes," said Aunt Bea. "I do hope she isn't offended."

"She doesn't know I know."

They heard the steps down the cement passage. The side gate clicked and her footsteps passed down the street beyond the street lamp.

The heat and the moonlight were now pouring in. They moved their chairs back, not to be dazzled. Aunt Bea turned on the pink lamp at a side table where she had her sewing.

They heard the water running in the bathroom; it squeaked

and went off. Anne came back. "I just soaked in," said she. "I'll go back in a minute." A long discussion followed on the best way to wash, wring, and hang stockings, together with numerous accidents that had befallen the stockings of all their friends; dogs, faults, cars and long fingernails.

"What a lovely glow the lamp casts on your face," said Aunt Bea. "But Anne always did have a flowerlike complexion and that dear little tip-tilted nose—oh, you young things, you do not know what you have. These are the happiest days of your life. When you're my age, you'll catch up with an old woman on the street, it will be yourself."

"You're not an old woman, Mother," protested Anne, pouting.

"No, I'm younger than Anne is in some things," agreed Aunt Bea. "But not in looks. Oh dear. Such is life without a wife. What's the matter with me? What've I got? Dandruff, I expect. A depression is approaching from Iceland."

"Mother!" said Anne tenderly.

"Nothing to wear but clothes, nothing to eat but food, nowhere to sleep but bed, nothing to marry but men, nowhere to go but home," mused Aunt Bea. "Nothing to do but live. My poor feet! Now I know where the shoe pinches."

"Why don't you soak them?" asked Teresa.

"Yes, I will. Go and get Mother some hot water, Annette."

She mused: "Very choice, Malfi dear. I'm waiting for the day when you and Anne—Oh, but you, dear—and besides, you're so very reserved about your affairs, you never tell any of us. If you did have someone in the mind's eye, you would never tell us till the fatal day, not even your little Nana Bea, I know," she said in a disappointed tone. "Have you anybody, dear?" she continued, hesitating. "Not that I want to pry, if you don't want to tell me, say so."

"I have a young man travelling in Europe at present," said Teresa.

They both looked sharply at her. "Really, dear?" Aunt Bea did not dare to disbelieve it.

"Yes." Teresa laughed suddenly. "Oh, no, I'm joking."

But now she could not get the idea out of their heads; whatever she said, the deeper she saw the suspicion root. At last she gave it up. Aunt Bea sighed, "Well, dear, as you like, it's your own affair. My darling Anne, too, is reticent about her private

54

affairs and thoughts, not like her foolish Mumsy, who broadcasts her ideas to all and sundry, selfishly, I dare say, though I only do it to cheer people up." She stopped for a while, drawing her feet in and out of the water and hummed, "Me, me, me, me, me." She burst into song, "I love me, I love me, I'm mad about myself!"

"Oh, Mother," laughed Anne at this very old joke of her mother's.

"Oh, Mother Ida," said Aunt Bea, taking her feet out of the water. "The towel, dear, hearken ere I die!"

Teresa said dreamily: *"For now the noonday quiet holds the hill, the grasshopper is silent in the grass——"*

"What's that, dear?"

> *"The lizard with his shadow on the stone,*
> *Rests like a shadow, and the winds are dead."*

Aunt Bea said: "What is that, dear?"

"Oh, Mother Ida, harken ere I die!"

"Is that it? I've forgotten, long ago. Isn't it funny where we get our tags? Anne never recites now. You remember her as a little thing? You remember when she was Red Riding Hood in the school panto? I thought she would go on the stage, such a sweet little pipe. But Anne's such a modest thing. Now would you believe she is so modest—*A violet by a mossy stone, half hidden from the eye*—that she is afraid of young men? I don't believe Anne's ever been kissed. Eh, darling? Ha-ha," she said softly. "For if she had she would tell her own precious Mother, wouldn't she, my precious? Perhaps not. I doubt it, said the Carpenter as he wiped away a tear. Sweet twenty-three and never been kissed. Eh, darling? Tell Mother!"

"Stop it, Mother," said Anne, troubled.

"Have you been kissed, Teresa?"

"Yes," lied Teresa.

"Oh, do tell," cried Aunt Bea excitedly. "What was he like? Dark, fair? What's your ideal, Terry? Like your father, I suppose. My brother Andrew is such a handsome man, always was. I rather think Anne's ideal is different, she seems to have a liking for tall, dark, and handsome. Eh? Oh, but Malfi's sachets! Oh, that was a scream! I believe Malfi inherited them from Miss Smith-Wetherby's bottom drawer of long ago. She had put in sachets of pink and blue, with a marvellous old nightdress case—of course, that was the high point of the afternoon—in old rose point, imagine it if you like, lined with pink silk—pretty of course, darling, and the lace is valuable, but who uses them? They went out with whalebone and Malfi says: 'Yes, but who uses them and what for, Aunt Lena? I always wear my nightdress under my pillow, especially when it's as darn hot as this,' Malfi said. Well, you can imagine the fluttering of the dovecotes —old Lady Droopy Drawers, her sister, turned a faint laburnum—" Aunt Bea waited for Anne's response, but not hearing it, still cantered cheerfully on—"and from that went to blush-violet as she set her lips grimly and said, brisk and respectable: 'But, Malfi dear, now you'll be living with someone else.' And Malfi nearly upset the apple-cart. 'I always did,' she muttered, but I assure you the respectable Dame of the British Empire did not hear that. Anne, my duck, you seem sad?"

"No, no," said Anne. "Mother, let's put the light out, the room will be full of moonlight. It's nearly full." The light went out.

"And there within the moonlight in his room, making it rich and like a lily bloom," said Teresa. They were silent for a moment in the warm dark. Then Aunt Bea said: "Put out the light and then put out the light. I saw Oscar Asche do that. He was too fat. Like Ray's husband. Oh, at the altar, he blotted it out. We simply howled afterwards."

"Mother," said Anne.

"We did. She likes them pudgy, though. The last one was, too. Type is a sort of kismet, I often think." She hummed for a moment and continued: "Ray had dark-blue shoes made of alternate strips of suède and kid with elastic insets and stilt heels of kid, which made her look very dainty and shortened her feet. It doesn't pay to have a small last, as I have, size three, when the makers with all kinds of nifty tricks can make even girls with English feet look like thistledown. She was very dainty in every detail. It was truly pathetic the care the poor motherless girl had put into her toilette."

"Another motherless girl?"

"Yes, isn't that funny? They were well-matched, the attraction of opposites. He's blond, like a perambulating door-mat, and she's a lovely brunette. She carried a bouquet of dark red roses——"

"Really?" cried Teresa.

"Yes, original, wasn't it, and sweet for a bride, dark red for love. I thought it such a nice notion and a frank sentiment, you know. That's the advantage of a girl without a family, she can do what she likes. Of course, I want Anne to have white on her wedding day, a girl looks so dazzling in white and I expect when the happy man sees this vision at his side, at the altar, he must wonder how he got her. I don't even like rouge, for there is generally a natural flush which is most becoming, though a little lipstick against the ivory or dead white does no harm, but as little as possible, a mere touch. Ray's bridesmaids had nasturtium, powder-blue—that was Anne, I made it myself—and fuchsia robes of the same material and the skirts were cut the same, though longer, which gave her a youthful look, and she has nice legs. The sleeves were shorter and summery, which lent her dignity you see, in the centre of the tableau. I was worried that Anne's were too short, I love to show off Anne's soft rounded arms, but it passed unobserved. I should be so happy to see Anne established in her own home, with her precious Mummy near her, looking after the material wants, while the young couple billed and cooed, as is only right, for the responsibilities come later."

Aunt Bea sighed. The fierce moonlight had now retired from the bed where she lay, and spotlighted the gathered ribbon garters which Anne had left lying on the window-sill. Anne herself was sitting on the other side of the window, her dim face looking towards the street. Mosquitoes buzzed, a gate clicked down the road, and someone called "Good night".

"It must be getting late," said Teresa.

"Oh, stay, idle-a-while," Aunt Bea urged her; and looking at the ceiling, she continued her miraculous descriptions of weddings and feasts long past. She did not notice when her daughter stole from the room.

"Do you want to get married, Terry darling?" asked Aunt Bea.

"Oh, yes, who doesn't?"

Aunt Bea sighed again. "Heigh-ho! Oh, Mother! It's hard to get married nowadays. But you will, I know, Teresa, you always did know how to look out for yourself."

"I certainly will," said Teresa.

"Sugar lump, where are you? Where's Annette?" said Aunt Bea.

"She went out a minute ago. To the bathroom, I think."

"Oh, yes, the stockings. Poor child, she too dreams of her wedding day and standing up at the altar with her own true knight, I expect, just as we all do or did. And there is the pleasure, the excitement, the pride of flashing a sparkler at your girl friends at the office." She sighed, "I thought it would come before this, but there is time enough for the greatest event in a girl's life. Malfi had such lovely presents, did you see them?"

Aunt Bea then went on to a marvellously detailed description of Malfi's presents whether in silver, china, ivory or linen. Of each she knew the origin and the cost and she knew the intentions of each giver. In the middle of it, Teresa saw the small figure of Mrs Percy trundling up and turning into the side gate.

"She came back."

"I'm glad of that. Nights of moon she worries, because lunatics get lively then and she thinks he will escape. She has probably been now to look down the street."

"Does she want to see him?"

"It's hard to say, but she is afraid for her daughter, though personally, I think, she frets without cause. Rose is quite normal, just a bit flighty. I should say Rose is a clever girl. You would notice nothing and I know you're observant, as I am myself."

The back door slammed. "She always slams it so," said Bea.

Another door creaked. "That is the kitchen door, I know its song," Bea remarked. "Oh, I tore that hangnail! Why doesn't it shut? She must have wedged it, to make a draught I suppose. No wonder. Yes, there, she switched the lights on. What is she opening and shutting the drawers for? Did you girls wash up? No? What a pity! We are supposed to do it, but I forgot time was passing. Well, no use crying over spilt milk. I'll put on my slippers and run out and do them. There, she's closed the door again. Now I'll run out. You go and get things ready, Terry dear, while Nana gets her slippers on. Put a towel round your pretty dress."

Terry went out and on her way down the short hall, looked into the bathroom, where the door was ajar and the light on. She heard a scuttling sound there. For a fleet second she saw nothing, then perceived that Anne had got on to the floor and was after something, stretching after something with her hands out cramped, but her head was sideways, resting on one ear on the tessellated floor. A fat tear dripped out of her closed eyelid. The steady bright light shone on her fair tendrilly hair and flushed plump face. Teresa went in and shut the door behind her. She whispered: "Anne!"

"Go away," said Anne.

"Anne?"

"Go away, go away," said Anne, in a sob.

Teresa stood looking at her, and as she did so, the girl's body began to writhe, a powerful slow rhythm beginning with the pelvis and twisting the shoulders and the head; the body moved strongly and the head was tossed up and sideways alternately. Anne brought her head down and beat it on the floor. Teresa bent down and grasped her cousin's left arm near the shoulder. Anne slowly brought her face close to the hand and bit it. "Let me go, go away and leave me." She took her little teeth away. Teresa rose, looked at her forefinger, wiped it on her dress, and moved out of the bathroom, closing the door after her. She went into the kitchen and began scraping the plates. The door to the laundry opened and Mrs Percy entered with a disordered expression, her large eyes wide open and anxious. She came close up to Teresa and brusquely drew a small black book out of a fold of her skirt. It was the bible of a mumbo-jumbo religion widespread among women in small houses, but Teresa had never heard of it.

"If you read this," said the woman earnestly, "you will be happier, you will find life worth living, you will not be so restless."

"I am not restless," said Teresa, wiping her hands on the towel pinned round her waist and looking the woman full in the face.

"Don't leave home," said Mrs Percy in an intimate tone. "Be careful of what you do, don't leave home. I did. It is a great mistake."

"All right," the girl said, and politely opened the book and looked over a few pages.

"Read it at home," said the woman. "And now I will leave you. If I had known you were going to do it, I should not have left my plate and cup, but of course, I thought Mrs Broderick would do it. That is part of our covenant, you know." She seemed cross.

"Yes, yes, I know."

59

"Yes, otherwise——" the woman paused carelessly, and then finished: "Good-bye, I won't see you again before you go."

"Good-bye. Thank you for the book."

"Yes, yes. Good-bye. Read it, read it, that is all."

The creaking door opened and shut. Did she sit in the laundry or go into the garden? The moon flooded the garden, everything could be seen in it, but there was no sign of the woman.

When Aunt Bea came, Teresa showed her the book and then remembered her cousin. "Anne is in there, on the bathroom floor."

"On the floor? What doing?"

"Crying."

"Oh, my poor child—"

Teresa put her hand on Aunt Bea's thin arm. "Don't go in."

"You mean—" Bea's eyes flew back. She said: "Anne?"

Teresa laughed. "No, it's because she's not married. A woman who is ready to marry must marry."

"No, no, she must have a pain, poor baby, she often has," and Aunt Bea flew in. Teresa heard their voices, Anne's sobbing, Aunt Bea's consoling. She felt annoyed, because she had given the wrong advice. She put away the things, hung up the towel, and trailed gracefully up the hall to get her hat. When she was dressed, hat, gloves, bag, she looked in at the bathroom door and said: "Good night!"

"Are you going, Terry?"

She went after Bea had brought Anne into the bedroom; and when she went past, in the street, she saw their dim forms at the open window. She waved. They waved back. She walked home, along the unpaved roads, her long gown gathering dust and prickles.

5. *It Was High Tide at Nine-thirty*

IT was high tide at nine-thirty that night in February and even after ten o'clock the black tide was glassy, too full for lapping in the gullies. Up on the cliffs, Teresa could see the ocean flooding the reefs outside, choking the headlands and swimming to the landing platforms of jetties in the bays. It was long after ten when Teresa got to the highest point of the seaward cliffs and turning there, dropped down to the pine-grown bay by narrow paths and tree-grown boulders, trailing her long skirt, holding her hat by a ribbon. From every moon-red shadow came the voices of men and women; and in every bush and in the clumps of pine, upon unseen wooden seats and behind rocks, in the grass and even on open ledges, men and women groaned and gave shuddering cries as if they were being beaten. She passed slowly, timidly, but fascinated by the strange battlefield, the bodies stretched out, contorted, with sounds of the dying under the fierce high moon. She did not know what the sounds were, but she knew children would be conceived this night, and some time later women would marry hurriedly, if they could, like one of her cousins, who had slept the night with a man in one of these very grottoes; and perhaps one or two would jump into the sea. There were often bodies fished up round here, that had leapt when the heart still beat, from these high ledges into waters washed round these rocks by the moon.

Some fishermen came slowly up through the rocks to the edge of the curved lipped platform over which they began casually to drop down by the iron footholds to the lowest ledges, wet by the unusual tides, and from these they waded out smoothly to their fishing posts on the edge of the square-cleaving shale. The bay, the ocean, were full of moonstruck fish, restless, swarming, so thick in places that the water looked oily; their presence, the men thought, with other signs, meant storms at hand.

Terry, who knew them all and to whom they said: "'Lo", in their meditative voices, watched them go over, some by the front cliff, shining blue, some by a small funnel where volcanic rock had crumbled in the sandstone. She went up to watch the latter and stood against a giant boulder staring out to sea. Nothing was between her and a two-hundred-foot plunge from the pale rock but a hand's breadth. She knew the funnel too. She had climbed in it as a child, but now she was even less sure-footed than then, a powerful, full-blooded young woman whose head turned easily. If she could only go to the bottom of the dike now, with the men, and spend the night with them, thigh-deep in the sweet water, catching fish, saying nothing, looking out to sea!

In the quiet harbours of the coast, the unfrequented estuaries, full of beaches of white sand and tangled scrub, she had often seen the lucky women, fishers' women, picnic women, holiday women, the wives of workers and loafers and misanthropes, who lived on boats and beaches, in shacks by the shoaling sand, with their men moving about them, free by the campfire and burning hearth, easy-going, tattered, ugly, very likely starved, beaten, but embraced by men and endowed with men's children. She had seen, the last summer, a dark-haired woman, at the bottom of a huge cliff, near Barrenjoey, at dawn. There were two boatloads of fishermen with her, Australians of Italian and English blood. They put in to shore about six in the morning, after the night's fishing. Some of them had already got there and lighted a fire, on which was a large iron pot. The woman, in black clothes, with high cheek-bones, and thin, was helped on shore by the men, from the stern of the boat where she sat and she went calmly to the pot in which they were throwing fish which they brought from the boat. She said something, a man brought a piece of wood; she said something else, they laughed all about her.

Teresa came down to the foot of the cliff. Below the cliff was a lane unknown to most of the inhabitants of the Bay, although lovers walked through it, the lane where Mr Manoel lived. The wooden cottages in it faced the steep cutting where hardy trees grew twisted out of split rocks and rough grass had spun over the bores of the dynamite charges. The dirt lane was flooded with light. The blinds were not drawn and weak lamps shone out. In a room stood a double bed with a honeycomb quilt thrown back over its foot. A foxy yellow, bloated little woman stood on the far side in an old-fashioned camisole and bloomers. A high chest of drawers with a crocheted cover was behind her. In another part of the cottage, men were talking. A window on the veranda with a single bulb behind it showed sticks of chocolate, bunches of carrots and cans of milk. There was worn oilcloth in the hall inside the netted door, a mop and bucket stood on the wooden veranda. A woman with grey hair moved round the kitchen table at the end of the passage. The woman was Queenie, a one-time schoolmate of Teresa, who had disappeared from school and married a man twice her age, in her fifteenth year. Now she had a long married life already behind her. The dirty back yard with the Datura tree, the broken flooring, a rag on the window and even the strange old clothing the girl wore, filled Terry with languor. She regretted now that, like them all, she had despised this miserable, plain child. She went on along the row of houses with their sway-backed roof-trees. All the time, the moon, rising higher, reduced her shadow until it was at her feet; shadows began to move out of the cottages and at the sound of her foot-falls, a blind was drawn somewhere along the lane.

In this hot night, not only the rocks above her, half-naked among twisted, tooth-leaved trees and spiney bushes, but the little open park she was now approaching, the grass above the drip-ping rocks of the military reserve, and the tram-shelters, were full of semitones and broken whispers. The roots, the trees, the timbers of the houses, strained by storms, the back yards full of plasterers' rubbish, the niches in the stony undercliff were refuges of love.

She came out from the lane, crossed the road and skirted the park. Near the seesaw, on the short grass, lay a black shape, un-moving. When she passed it, she saw it was a man over a woman, the woman's white gloves and bag lay on the grass beside them. They caught pickpockets in the Bay. Near the Old Hotel two more, the woman on her back and the man on his elbow, lay looking into each other's eyeballs, reflecting the moon. There were none of them on the beach tonight, drowned under the high tide; none in the boats drawn up across the footpath. People sat in their moist warm gardens, talking and hitting out at the mosquitoes; the smell of eucalyptus oil and pipe-smoke reached out. Across the harbour, on the oyster-coloured water, a large Manly ferry full of lights moved southwards toward the city. She felt the swarm of lovers thick as locusts behind her when she turned into the beach path. Tied up to the fourth pile of the wharf was a rowing-boat covered with a tarpaulin. Under the tarpaulin was a woman's body; she had been fished out of the sea just outside of the cliffs that afternoon; it did not cause much comment. They lived there, among the gardens of the sea, and knew their fruits; fish, storms, corpses, moontides, miracles.

In between Teresa and her house, on the beach path, lay the old park which she had skirted on the far side, the wharf, and a few cottages. The young girl walked gravely, with a balanced stride, her back and neck straight, pretending she had a basin of water on her head. She was so intent on this as she came down by the park that at first she did not hear the people splashing in the Old Baths, now dismantled and which were no more than three strips of narrow boardwalk, awash in the present high water. But the shouts and splashes stopped as she came abreast of them, under the light of the lamp on the promenade, and in surprise she looked. She saw her brother, Leo, a seventeen-year-old, with three girls standing about or sitting in the water in careless attitudes. She did not know the girls, some girls from the Bay, in school after her time.

Leo grinned in his endearing, shamefaced way: "Hullo, Tess."

"Hullo," said a girl's voice, satirically.

The others said nothing. One of the girls, dragging her legs through the water, was absorbed in looking down at them; the other, standing up in a wrestling attitude, cast back her tousled dark-red hair. A second lamp shone on the beach path between the Old Baths and the Old Hotel. The Old Hotel had ceased to be a hotel, but stood in the park without fence or outbuildings, a white-painted two-storey building with trees topping it, as old as the Hawkins house, but dating from the military settlement of the Bay. Someone lived there in the Old Hotel. There were no lights there nor anywhere in the Bay, except the street lights. From the open back windows came voices. In a bush near at hand in the park a boy's voice said: "I seen your sister; black man kissed her."

The girls laughed.

"Lady Vah de Vah!" said the voice.

Leo laughed in a troubled way. Teresa had not stopped walking. Glancing quickly behind her, she saw Leo take a step towards the red-haired girl, who was standing in an arc, shaking the water out of her curls. She sprang upwards and wrestled with him in a beautiful bold way, the two of them winding in each other's arms, conscious of Teresa who had just gone by, excited by the boy hidden in the bush. Something hurled them at each other.

Coolly, Teresa walked on till she passed the wharf, glanced at the water and came to the first of the fishermen's cottages, Joe Martin's, it was. There the light falling through a few inches to the submerged sand showed three sting-rays swimming in a row. Some man was sitting on a boat near, stuffing his pipe.

"Sting-rays," she said. "And I was just going to paddle."

"I seen three caught round in the Cove," said the man. "This morning when the tide was out. I suppose it's the same three."

"They give you a nasty wound."

"We got one in the boat with us yesterday," said the man. "It was dashing round like a mad cat. Your brother Lance picked it up and threw it out. I thought it would get us all."

She went on. She thought: "Tomorrow, the night after and the next will be the three nights of full moon, the time I dream of blood, too." The tide would be higher still. A man's voice called out. She muttered: "Hullo," and went past. She wished she had stepped into the bay back there; it would have been queer to feel the long wet skirt round her, like sea-weed. But the sting-rays, the possible sharks which could come in close at such a time? She did not care if the dress were spoiled, she now had no use for it; but the hat? And of course they would think her a freak. Already, there was the Green Dress. The green dress was an old wool dress she had embroidered with all kinds of things, pagodas, butterflies, geraniums. She wore it only at home on Sundays, in the mornings, because it was thick and she need wear nothing under it; but Leo's friends, the Bay children, had seen it, touched it, asked her about it. She did not know herself why she kept this dress and wore it. She did not want to be eccentric, but on the contrary, to be noble, loved, glorious, admired; perfection as far as she could be perfect.

The tide still washed the kerb in front of the Hawkins house at the end of the beach path. She could bathe there still. She rushed breathlessly up into the garden, holding up her dress, and through the wire-netted door, up the uncarpeted staircase to her room, which was at the back of the house. In the front were her father's two rooms, his bedroom and his study in which he studied nothing, but which contained the out-of-date text-books, grammars, and botanies which he had once used, Wood's *Natural History*, the prizes of his poor youth. The south-eastern room was Kitty's, the north-eastern, Teresa's. In between was a long corridor in which a small flight of stairs led to one of the turreted attics. This corridor was also a kind of dais. One stepped down from it to reach the stairhead. All about, there were wooden passages, open windows and light and air streaming in. It was a spacious stone building, which had once been a military stables. The floors were always gritty with sand and stone-dust, as well as dirt from the hill which rose just behind them. At night, on this dust, lay the moonlight and starlight; in rains, streaks and pools of water lay about. It was rarely that Teresa put on her light to go to bed or to dress, only on dark nights of smother and storm; but Kitty was usually there, the "woman of the house", under a lamp lingering over some sewing, visible through the half-open door, bowed close, looking like an old mother, except for her short dark hair. Kitty's room tonight for the first time was dark. Teresa leaned out of one of the back openings and called to the yard: "Where's Kit?"

Her father's voice answered her from the shed: "Is that you, Terry? Isn't Kit with you?" She heard him cross the flagged yard and enter the kitchen. She came across to the stairhead and shouted: "Kit went somewhere with Sylvia."

"Sylvia who?"

"Sylvia Hawkins. You know."

"By herself?"

He reproved her for leaving Kitty, standing at the bottom of the stairs and looking up. Then seeing her long dress in the luminous shadow, he began to laugh. "You two girls were figures of fun today running for the boat."

"I'm going for a swim," she said, retiring.

"Don't swim alone," said he.

"Just in front."

She shed her clothes hastily and ran downstairs, barefooted, dragging on a black bathing-suit she had grown out of, too small to wear in the daytime, but sleek and fishy to swim in. A tall, dark form slouched through the mosquito-door, grumbling.

"Come for a swim?" she asked her brother Lance.

"Too tired," he said. "Don't swim alone, and look out, there are rays and Portuguese man-of-wars about."

"I'll stay in the light. You come and be look-out."

"Not on your tintype."

Her father, sitting on a stone bench in the garden, slapping mosquitoes, said: "Have you got a look-out?"

"You come and watch," she said.

"Nuh," said he. "Too tired. Been making Kitty's hope chest all the afternoon. More hope than chest."

Lance from behind the door said: "Hmff," disgustedly.

"Lance doesn't care for women," laughed the father in his soft voice.

"Really?" cried Teresa. "Really! Doesn't he? Oh, no!"

The father laughed. Teresa dropped her towel on the steps and splashed into the water; it was so still that the splash could be heard all over the bay.

"Not out of the light," called her father. "I saw a large basking shark up Parsley Bay yesterday." The basking shark was pale, changing colour with the bottom and all but invisible.

She was floating about under a street lamp where the beach path ended. Swimming here, she could see anyone coming either from the wharf or from the little end village of several streets arranged in a square of green called the Lawny. She floated in the water and thought she would not be afraid to go down at sea. To burn at sea—yes! But to go down! People had floated for thirty-six hours on a smooth ocean. You just let yourself go—you can even sleep floating, but the ocean she dreamed about under her lids was a wide smooth expanse under the moon, a halcyon sea. A man approached from the wharf way. She turned on her front and began to crawl about aimlessly, like a young prawn, over the sand. The water was only a foot or so deep. It was Georgie Martin going home. They exchanged hellos.

"See what Leo caught on the reef?" asked the big young man shyly.

"Kelpfish. We ate them," she said, wishing him to go. As soon as he mounted the grass slope towards the street where he lived with his fat, timid wife, she turned back and began floating. It was impossible to swim in the shallows. The sky above was blond and delicate and the water far and wide was pale; she could see the bottom sand to a certain distance and it was too shallow for a shark in there.

"I'd like to sleep out tonight," thought she. The moon gave her ghastly dreams which she enjoyed. She remembered school-yard tales: "You will go mad, if you sleep with the moon on your face." She had a cousin who took fits at full moon; she turned blood-red also at full moon. That was some story she had heard. Like-wise, this cousin had a great charm, men ran after her; she was not precisely "no good", but she was fly.

Voices came from the baths, saying good-bye. She even heard Leo's voice faintly calling: "So long, so long." Then she heard him nearer, his young baritone talking to the men, his whistling as he approached. She floated feet first to the edge of the path under the lamp and looked at him over her feet. His voice was full of delighted surprise. "I say, why didn't you come in with us?"

She did not reply, only grinned at him. Leo flung his towel on the path and sat down with his toes in the water.

"That was Marion Josephs," he said in a low voice.

"Which one?"

"The one with red hair."

There was a silence in which Leo wordlessly implored Teresa not to mention his romping with girls in the Old Baths; and in which Teresa, by suddenly turning over in the water and swim-ming a few strokes out and back again, answered that she would not.

"Come in, come in," said Teresa, pulling at his leg. He went in, but came right out again, because he had been playing football, fishing, and swimming all day.

"Moon's nearly full," said he.

"Next day too," answered Teresa.

"It's a pity you can't go swimming in trunks like I can," he said, considerately. Teresa swam a few strokes.

"You look nice in that bathing suit," Leo continued with an eager, timid smile, looking into her face. She lay on her back looking up dreamily at the Milky Way: "I'd like to swim all night."

Leo ducked his head and murmured: "Do they hurt really?"

"What?" said Teresa, looking round for jelly-fish. Then his tone recalled her. She stared at him. He flushed but said mildly:

"Your—those," he pointed at her breasts.

"Don't be silly."

"I don't know," he murmured. "I thought perhaps."

"How?" She plunged into the dark.

"I say, Tess," he pursued in a clear voice, "I say, what's your feller like?" he laughed. "Your boy?"

"I haven't got one."

"You must have."

"I haven't."

"Yes, you have," he persuaded her, laughing gaily. "What does he say to you, uh?" He was very eager. "What sort of things, huh?"

"Nothing. I haven't one."

He laughed, knowing better.

"I say, can I take you to the Maroubra Motordrome on Saturday?" he asked. It was a long trip, but she knew he had a girl down there, an Italian, black-eyed, pasty-faced, with a long English jaw and thick eyelashes; he had shown Teresa the photomaton picture, begging for her opinion; her name was Eunice. She despised Eunice, the latest of Leo's succession of black-eyed girls, and she disdained Leo, this loving, handsome seventeen-year-old who already wanted to get married.

"I'm out," she suddenly cried, bending upwards and getting to her feet. The sky behind the high attics of the old house was bubbling with radiant air. The water was receding fast. A curious flattening of the light had been coming in quick pulsations for minutes from the east and now a faint, very wide ring appeared round the moon, but the disk sailed free, without a cloud. She ran up the steps.

The bay, the headlands for miles, and all the districts of suburbs with their deep-etched gardens, the pallid streets, the couples walking, the parked cars, every buoy and rowboat, even flotsam and crabs stiffly promenading on rocks were intensely visible, and yet had dulled since half an hour ago. In the garden the trees were black against the flown moon-scarves. Leo followed her in.

"Where've you been?" inquired his father.

"Swimming," said Leo.

"Alone?"

"No, someone was watching." Leo sprinted for the house.

6. Lance with His Head in His Hand

LANCE, with his head in his hand, was at the dining-room table poring over his engineering books. She stood in the doorway and asked: "Did you get your dinner off the stove? If you stay out with the fishermen, you can't get it fresh."

He turned slowly towards her, flashed a look at her bathing-suit, and then spoke to one side of her, his eyes downcast. "Of course."

"Was it all right? It was kept from lunch."

"Of course."

With misgiving and a real touch of pity for him, she looked over his lemon-coloured face, its hollows and long lines from nose to mouth. His pale-red lips were slightly apart and showed the two gaps where his front teeth had fallen out. He was still dirty after his afternoon. His long ash-blond hair, slicked back, dark-green with water, was coming down over his forehead again. His skin was very fair, his neck and all his features long and soft; his neck and face drooped easily under trouble and fatigue. He had docile brown eyes, so that however despising or sarcastic he looked, he seemed gentle too. He had a changeable face that he could never control—just when he was trying to be harsh, superior, cold, a sheepish or reluctant look upset the expression. He was estranged from them all, a young man of twenty-two, who had already spent several years on the treadmill of working boys, college at night. He worked in the daytime as a chemist in a factory where the men were always nauseated at lunch-time with the smells. He did not eat his lunches. In the week-ends, Lance lighted out early with a friend, cycling furiously for long distances, practising for reliability trials on his motor-bike, or exercising for marathons. He was an intolerant faddist. Tess searched his dusty face until he withdrew his sidelong glance and went back to his books. She knew why he careered all over the country that way in the week-ends, wearing himself out.

"You ought to go to bed," she ventured.

"Shut up," he said softly, working at his figures.

"You'll be all in."

He turned slowly and looked at her with eyes great and unfocused.

"You'd better go and get that off, there's a split on the side, anyhow," he said with quiet dignity. She giggled.

"You get out of here," he shrieked, leaping out of his chair, starting towards her. She vanished. He fell back on his books. Going up the stairs, slowly lifting each bare foot and putting it down voluptuously on the dusty wood, she thought vaguely of Leo's shouts of wrath in the mornings, when Kitty packed his lunch and blacked his boots, Kitty, in tears, rarely answering back, the father quietly letting it pass over him, drinking his black tea off the hob. Lance also mistreated the young woman who did everything for him.

"She oughtn't to clean their boots," said Tess to herself, lifting her fingers one by one out of the dust of the balustrade. Why did Dad let the boys rave and never intervene? "Least said, soonest mended?"

Lance even hit Kitty, knocked her roughly out of his way as he plunged in to breakfast, a desperate look in his eyes. Leo, flaming with anger, red-cheeked, bright-eyed, leaped into the kitchen, his shirt half on, shouting complaints. Tess did nothing for them except some housework, but she did, of course, earn money, while poor Kitty seemed a burden to them, a mouth to fill. Thinking of this, Teresa remembered that she had not paid her money to Kitty this week. She went into her room and took it out of her drawer, all in silver. At this moment she heard Kitty come in and waited with some curiosity till Kitty had explained herself to her father and gone up to her room. Then she went in, still in her bathing-suit, which had now dried on her.

Kitty was sitting by the lamp, her hat still on, her short-sighted eyes looking off vaguely, a faint silly smile on her face. Teresa put down the money on Kitty's work-table. Kitty looked up with a smile of gratitude that had nothing to do with the regularly paid money. She had been a very pretty little girl, slightly cross-eyed with large black pupils; she had become a stocky adolescent with pleasant little cries and laughs when playing with the village children she was fond of, then a dull, clumsy, and slow housekeeper for the family. Teresa looked at her in her new mood with curiosity, thinking:

"I don't know what goes on in her head!"

Kitty said: "It was a nice wedding, wasn't it?"

"Not bad."

"I thought you'd forgotten," said Kitty, pointing. "You get paid on Thursdays."

"I know, I'm sorry, I forgot. What's that?"

Kitty showed her a crocheted cap, emerald green.

"It's for Joycie Baker. Her mother provides the wool, I only get two shillings for that. If I provide the wool, I make them for three and six. I made them for a few of the mothers. It's the style now."

"You can't make anything on them?"

"Two shillings, but of course I don't get many and it's only a fad."

"I'll give you some money," said Teresa, in shame.

Kitty laughed eagerly, but said: "No, no. I ought to earn some. You pay enough."

"We ought to pool some pocket-money for you."

The younger girl's lip curled as she looked at her sister's dress. That brown! If she had real money, she'd make her wear different things, but Kitty was obstinate; she wanted to be safe, respectable. Teresa sighed and went back to her room, and had forgotten her sister before she was half-way along the passage.

The room! She literally jumped across the threshold and stood panting with pleasure near the middle of the room. Then with a silent, shivering, childish laugh, she closed the door, quickly and softly. She stripped off the bathing-suit, which she hung out the window to get completely dry and felt her flesh, cold as marble in the warm air. She shivered again with excitement and went to kneel at the uncurtained window looking out on the back road, the road into the camp and the hill. This hill was half a hill. On the other side it fell straight into the sea, part of South Head; the open sea was not more than two or three hundred feet away from where she stood. She envisioned it tonight, a water floor out to the horizon, with a passage strewn with moonrushes and barely breaking at the base of the cliffs.

"Oh, God, how wonderful, how wonderful!" she muttered half-intelligible exclamations which were little more than cries of ecstasy as she stood in the window. If someone was crouching among the rocks on the hill, he could see her, but otherwise she was safe here. She leaned over the sill, her round arms and full breasts resting on the woodwork. Her flesh was a strange shade in that light, like the underside of water beasts. Or like—— She began to think like what. She did not care if she never went to bed; the night stretched before her. "I know every hour of the night," she said joyfully and repeated it. It seemed to her that she knew more of the night and of life than they all did down there; hunched Kitty, cheesy Lance, girl-mad Leo, slow Andrew Hawkins, entombed in their lives. She heard footfalls in the Bay, far off—people going home—voices, a pair of lovers perhaps, climbing higher up on the cliffs. The footsteps of anyone going home late to the camp, the permanent staff, going by the paved road, could be heard long before he came in sight and so too in the blind road underneath the house.

She was free till sunrise. She was there, night after night, dreaming hotly and without thinking of any human beings. Her long walks at night through the Bay, in which she had discovered all the lost alleys, vacant lots and lonely cottages, her meditation over the poor lovers from the city, her voluptuous swimming and rolling by herself in the deep grass of the garden and her long waking nights were part of the life of profound pleasure she had made for herself, unknown to them. She was able to feel active creation going on around her in the rocks and hills, where the mystery of lust took place; and in herself, where all was yet only the night of the senses and wild dreams, the work of passion was going on.

She had a vague picture of her future in her mind. Along the cliffs on a starlit night, very dark, strolled two figures enlaced, the girl's hair, curled as snail-shells, falling back over the man's shoulders, but alive of itself, as she leaned against him walking and all was alive, the revolute leaves, the binding roots. This she conceived happened in passion, a strange walking in harmony, blood in the trees. The playful taps and squeezes, wrestling and shrieking which Leo had with the girls was not what she expected and she did not think of this as love. She thought, dimly, that even Leo when he sat on the beach at Maroubra with his girl, made some such picture; a turbulent, maddening, but almost silent passion, a sensual understanding without end.

She abandoned herself and began to think, leaning on the window-sill. In a fissure in a cliff left by a crumbled dike, a spout of air blew up in new foam and spray, blue and white diamonds in the moon, and in between the surges the ashy sky filled the crack with invisible little stars. Hundreds of feet beneath, the sea bursting its skin began to gush up against the receding tide; with trumpet sounds, wild elephants rose in a herd from the surf and charged the cliffs; the ground trembled, water hissed in the cracks.

The full moon shone fiercely on the full-bellied sea. A woman who had known everything, men's love and been deserted, who had the vision of a life of endless work and who felt seedy, despairing, felt a bud growing on its stalk in her body, was thirsty; in her great thirst she drank up the ocean and was drowned. She floated on it now in a wooden shell, over her a white cloth and over all the blazing funeral of the sky, the moon turning its back, sullen, calloused.

What the moon saw. The beaches, the shrubbery on the hills, the tongues of fire, the white and dark of bodies rolling together in snaky unions. Anne—Malfi, "Don't think too badly of me!"—herself! She sighed, shivered and drew in. All the girls dimly knew that the hole-in-a-corner marriages and frantic petting parties of the suburbs were not love and therefore they had these ashamed looks; they lost their girlish laughter the day they became engaged, but those who did not get a man were worse off. There was a glass pane in the breast of each girl; there every other girl could see the rat gnawing at her, the fear of being on the shelf. Beside the solitary girl, three hooded madmen walk, desire, fear, ridicule. "I won't suffer," she said aloud, turning to the room to witness. "They won't put it upon me." She thought, a girl who's twenty-seven is lost. Who marries a woman of thirty-five to get children? She's slightly ridiculous to marry at that age. Look at Aunt Maggie, everyone laughed. Take Queenie, few marry at fifteen. Say eighteen, eighteen to thirty; twelve years, whereas men have eighteen to—any time at all, fifty at least, well, forty-eight, they can have children at forty-eight.

They can marry then; thirty years. A woman is a hunter without a forest. There is a short open season and a long closed season, then she must have a gun-licence, signed and sealed by the state. There are game laws, she is a poacher, and in the closed season she must poach to live. A poor man, a serf say, clears himself a bit of land, but it's the lord's land. As soon as it's cleared, he grows a crop on it, but it isn't his crop, only partly, or perhaps not at all, it isn't in his name; and then there must be documents, legalities, he must swear eternal fealty to someone. A woman is obliged to produce her full quota on a little frontage of time; a man goes at it leisurely and he has allotments in other counties too. Yes, we're pressed for time. We haven't time to get educated, have a career, for the crop must be produced before it's autumn. There are northern countries where the whole budding, leafing, and fruiting take place in three months. A farmer said: "What do they bother to put out leaves for, when they must go in so soon?" We put out leaves and flowers in such a brief summer and if it is a bad summer? We must do it all ourselves, too, just like wild animals in the bush. Australian savages arrange all that for their women, they don't have women going wanting, but we do. Girls are northern summers, three months long; men are tropical summers. But then there are the savage women, and the Italian, Spanish women—do they have as short a time? The women of ancient Greece, the Romans, so corrupt and so libertine, but happy no doubt—there might be other women. It isn't necessary —Malfi, Anne, Ray, Ellie, Kitty—me! But they won't even rebel, they're afraid to squander their few years. The long night of spinsterhood will come down. What's to be done? But one thing is sure, I won't do it, they won't get me.

How about the boys, too, Lance and Leo? They were different, but they were pressed too; nothing that was, suited them. If nothing that is, suits people, why do they all take it lying down? Because they have so little time, no money—but is that enough excuse?

Standing upright at the window, thinking, thinking, feeling rage at her floundering and weakness, and at seeing all the issues blocked, she thought of how cocksure she had been at school. Awkward, easily faced down, of course, but confident about the future. The things she wanted existed. At school she first had news of them, she knew they existed; what went on round her was hoaxing and smooth-faced hypocrisy. Venus and Adonis, the Rape of Lucrece, Troilus and Cressida were reprinted for three hundred years, St Anthony was tempted in the way you would expect; Dido, though a queen, was abandoned like a servant-girl and went mad with love and grief, like the girl in the boat outside. This was the truth, not the daily simpering on the boat and the putting away in hope chests; but where was one girl who thought so, besides herself? Was there one who would not be afraid if she told them the secret, the real life? Since school, she had ravaged libraries, disembowelled hundreds of books, ranged through literature since the earliest recorded frenzies of the world and had eaten into her few years with this boundless love of love, this insensate thirst for the truth above passion, alive in their home itself, in her brothers and sister, but neglected, denied, and useless; obnoxious in school, workshop, street.

Teresa knew all the disorderly loves of Ovid, the cruel luxury of Petronius, the exorbitance of Aretino, the meaning of the witches' Sabbaths, the experiments of Sade, the unimaginable horrors of the Inquisition, the bestiality in the Bible, the bitter jokes of Aristophanes and what the sex-psychologists had written. At each thing she read, she thought, yes, it's true, or no, it's false, and she persevered with satisfaction and joy, illuminated because her world existed and was recognized by men. But why not by women? She found nothing in the few works of women she could find that was what they must have felt. By comparison, history, with its lies to discourage the precocious, and even the inspired speculative stuff, meant nothing. But it was either rigmarole or raving, whereas the poets and playwrights spoke the language she knew, and the satirists and moralists wrote down with stern and marvellous precision all that she knew in herself but kept hidden from family and friends.

In her bare room, ravished, trembling with ecstasy, blooming with a profound joy in this true, this hidden life, night after night, year after year, she reasoned with herself about the sensual life for which she was fitted. She smelled, heard, saw, guessed faster, longed more than others, it seemed to her. She listened to what they brought out with a galling politeness, because what she had to say she could not tell them. It was not so that life was and they were either liars or stupid. At the same time, how queer that she understood what was going on in their minds so well!

For it seemed to her that they were all moved by the same passion, in different intensities.

The newspapers made it appear so. Even the most sedate and crusty newspapers recounted at length, in divorce suits, what happened on worn divans in broken-down old office buildings, they all laughed together over those unlucky paramours who had been followed and caught in degrading positions, the school-children gulped down the stories of bathing parties in the bushy reaches, mad cohabitations in the little bays, dives where sailors and black men went, miserable loves of all kinds, the naked dancing in the sweltering Christmas days and the nights of pale sand. Love panted in and out of their young nostrils, and the adolescents dreaming of these orgies, maddened by the tropical sun and these dissolute splendours of the insolent flesh, spent their nights in a bath of streaming sweat and burning blood.

A faint breeze had risen, rather damp. A mosquito sang windily. "What have I done yet?" said Teresa to herself. She had had a dream the night before. This dream made her realize her age and she felt the shame of being unmarried. She had given the breast to her child, she dreamed, a small dark-haired baby. Everything was as clear as life, the nuzzling, sucking, and the touch of the child's spread hand. She was a woman, she was nineteen. Funny that at fourteen she had felt quite old! Her life was dull and away from men. Where would she get a husband?

She made a fretful gesture and accidentally pushed the bathing-suit off the window-sill into the yard. She pulled on a sweater and skirt and went downstairs.

There was no light in the back as she passed between the boys' rooms to the kitchen. Leo's room looked out on the grass slope and Lance's on the small alley by the neighbour's house. The moon had passed over, the kitchen was dark, only the yard shone. She went out into the yard, picked up her suit, hung it over the saw-horse and sniffed around for a while in the toolshed, fresh with sawdust. When she came in, Lance was at the old ice-chest, near the back door, munching and pulling out bits of food.

"It stinks in here," he said cheerfully.

"You stink in there," responded Tess.

"Good job I like sour milk, there always is plenty," continued her brother, holding up a bottle towards the lighted yard.

"Sour milk is good for pigs and goats," observed Teresa,

coming into the kitchen and lounging against the table. Lance had a furtive smile in his long cheeks.

"What were you doing out there?"

"Getting my bathing-suit, it fell out the window."

He thoughtfully munched for a while, standing side on and giving her meaningless glances; then he grinned to himself. "You pushed it out."

"What for? Don't be silly."

"You're lying."

"What!" She sprang forward.

Lance turned round and smirked, "You're a liar. You threw it out." It was the signal for battle. Teresa felt the blood rush to her head. Lance was the only one who dared to give her the lie.

"You're a liar," repeated Lance lusciously, waiting. She flung herself upon him, pounding his chest, his long neck, and his head.

"Hey, hey!" said Lance, turning his head from side to side. She panted. He could see, even in the gloom, the dark flush over her face and neck.

"Don't you dare say that."

"You're a liar," he panted.

As if delighted, though puffing and writhing in her grasp, he merely fended off her clumsy blows, his face now stark and serious. Teresa punched his face on each cheek and temple and grasped his hair. Suddenly he groaned and staggered away from her. "You got my boil."

She stood back, dark with anger, furious with him, heaving and ready to rush in again and beat him. He staggered down the hall, moaning, holding his hand to his head. "Oh, my boil."

She looked after him contemptuously; he was always a coward. It did not occur to her that he had not hit her.

She saw him in the ghastly hall light. Blood trickled from his temple, two threads reached his neck. Fists clenched, astride and full of fight, the girl watched him go towards his bedroom. Kitty was half-way down the stairs, asking him questions, getting no answer. She clattered down the rest of the way, ran in after him. She came into the kitchen for water and put on the light. "What were you doing?"

Teresa frowned at her and muttered: "He called me a liar."

Kitty said nothing to that. She went in again and said to Lance, as she bathed him: "How did it happen?"

Lance said: "The fool! I called her a liar for a joke, just because it gets her goat." Teresa choked. She stood in the kitchen door and shouted: "That's no joke, it's no joke. You knew what you were saying."

Kitty said reproachfully: "You knew he was joking."

"It wasn't a joke! I'll kill anyone for that," shouted Teresa. "I'll kill him if he says it."

Lance, satisfied, said nothing, only moaned as Kitty washed him.

"Poor Lance," said Kitty, looking at her sideways.

"I'll smash him to pieces for that," said the girl. "He knows it, too."

Lance groaned. Teresa went away furious. He had said it with a grin and kept grinning right through. That was a knife in her gall. She knew that out of malice he enjoyed the fight. She moved off sulkily. When she got up to her room, she sat down on the little sewing-box and thought about it, clenching her fists and grinding her teeth. She would kill anyone for that! She would kill for honour. A scene flew up in her mind in which she killed in hot blood, for honour and was glad of it, saw the spilt blood spreading. Ha-ha, that paid him off! For twenty minutes she sat there, her breath coming quickly and then her other thoughts began to creep in. She flung herself on her bed. Downstairs she heard the noises of the house as Kitty put things away and she heard her father beginning to lock up, leaving the door unbarred for Leo. Presently he came upstairs. He saw her open door and looked in. "You hit Lance?"

"Yes." Her temper rose again.

"You hurt him, you know, Terry."

"Let him look out."

Andrew Hawkins said quietly: "Good night, Terry," and went away towards his room. Terry felt rather flat. He called out: "Early to bed, early to rise."

"Yes," she muttered, "yes."

Her father called from his room: "Terry? You get Leo up?"

"Yes," she answered impatiently.

His door shut. She heard him wind his clock. This time she left her door open.

7. *Leo Was Lost in Roaring Slumber*

LEO was lost in roaring slumber by now. The others could be heard getting into bed. Teresa put the clock face where she could see it from the bed, then undressed, and throwing herself on the bed, gradually tweaked the mosquito-nets out of the bed top and let them fall round her like a veil. A train shrieked far off in the hills across the harbour; she had never found out where the train was, for it looked as if there was nothing there but wild bush. At the same moment, she heard a faint *boom!* The ocean was stirring again. *Boom!* Yes, at the foot of the cliffs, it was beginning again. The first sounds had come several hours before, a faint boom, washing the silent bay. In the clear still weather, with the hordes of fish and the filming of the sky, this irregular humming meant a disturbance approaching.

"Change of moon, change of weather!" There was a splash in the bay. The swell had now caught the low water and the beach hissed. Teresa went on with her more serious meditations.

She ought to run away. The only reason she did not run away was that she had not the courage. How could she teach little children when she herself knew nothing about life? She thought of the day she had signed up with the Education Department. They were all there, high-school girls of seventeen, most of her classmates. There was nothing much else for them to do and they were going to teach until they got married. The grey-headed man there had asked her if she wanted her pension money subtracted as for retirement at sixty or sixty-five. She burst out laughing. Then she saw her best friend, Viola, saying "Sixty-five", because they subtracted less each week. Viola was a chubby blonde, secretly engaged. She saw Viola at sixty-five! Then she looked round timidly, with a flush, at the man who was watching her sternly.

"Don't you intend to stay in the Department? We don't want to train women who intend to marry or take up some other profession."

"Put sixty, then." It was five years less, at any rate.

"You are not thinking of getting married?" said the man.

"No." She heard Viola denying it too.

They all walked out together, fourteen or fifteen of them, "young giggling girls", as Aunt Bea called them, who had been in high school together and who now were caught, herded into teaching until, supposedly, they fell off from old age, desiccated virgins. Teresa, frightened and horrified, had made up her mind at that moment to leave teaching, but at the time the training course was her only chance to get some higher education. But at home what rejoicing! They thought of her as fixed for life—no bother about unemployment. At school they had expected her to do better, but she was a poor student and not of the stuff that takes University Bursaries. She never could sit up at night to study. If she sat up, she dreamed, her head and body nodding with carnal intoxication. At one time, encouraged by some teachers, she had dreamed of the great universities of the old world. She knew it was only a vague wish of the teachers who had liked her and who had mistaken her intense rummaging in libraries for scholarship.

But now! Now, in the schoolroom, ignorant still, unhappy, choked with dirt and dust, with the noises of the playground which she herself had only just left, having for comrades the very same fat-waisted, thin-haired women and bowed, unhappy men that as children they had always jeered at, those very wretched slaves of a headmaster and an inspector that the children in their wicked perspicacity led by the nose in a life of misery; knowing that she was one of them, and obliged to go on like them with coarsening face and voice; something, it seemed to her, from which all ordinary human beings fled, and which, in her circle, was only associated with one phrase, "an old maid of a school-ma'am"—now she was on the treadmill. The other teachers hated the work too.

As soon as she caught sight of the school buildings in the morning, their dirty yellow, and heard the bell, the shrieks, the boots rushing across the asphalt; as soon as she smelled that thick oily and dusty scent which school buildings alone give out, human grease and neglected corners, old varnish and urinals in the heat, the little oils from lunches in paper and boot polish, old stuffs ironed at home with the soap still in them, the dirty heads; that huge, fat, sickening smell that poured down the street, on every side, and seeped from outside into the purer dust of the closed schoolroom—as soon as she saw it and smelled it, that illness to which she was condemned for life, until she was sixty, when a woman is not a woman, she began to float in her misery, not to walk. She forgot her feet and yielded herself to a kind of delirium of horror. Yet she did not have to do what the other teachers did, that is, go to the headmaster's room and sign on. She did not have to line her class up with the other classes; and her class alone did not have to stand in the sun, salute the flag, and sing "God Save the King". She laughed when she thought why. It was because she had the unclassified children, called Special Class by the teachers and Dope's Class by the children. The sight of the Dope's Class or Mad Class, eleven poor creatures, two deaf and dumb, some lame, some twitching, and all with long school reputations as madmen or idiots, standing there and yet straggling while standing, was the only pleasant sight in the whole school. Some were high, some low, some goggling, and some dignified, some amused because they were marked out and some oppressed. The sight of them the first morning behind the other classes had caused great merriment, disorder, and excitement. The king and the flag got no attention; everyone turned round. The teachers themselves had had strange feelings—shame and embarrassment; they had been shocked. Now the eleven lined up in a little asphalt patch of their own, near the flower-beds. It was not the eleven poor children that Teresa disliked; they were more affectionate, interesting, and tractable than the ordinary children who conformed, and were sly, prosy, or smug. It was rather the school system and the idea of being in jail, for she kept thinking to herself: "Why, I have never been out of school, I have never learned anything and never will!" Even more than this, she was afraid of drying up there, being forgotten by the world and dying in the chalk-dust.

Running away was not such an easy thing. If she ran away, she forfeited her bond and lost her wages and her family lost her wages. For the past two months, during the long summer vacation just ended, she had been studying shorthand and typing at night, but she had yet a month to finish the shortest course available; the other consideration which ought to have stopped her did not. She owed something to the state official who ran the special classes. He had picked her out for this relatively soft job and had talked to her of the Sorbonne, Berlin, London, where he himself had gone; his fatal words, Europe, Jena, Weimar, the Black Forest, stuck in her mind with old scenes accompanying them, just as if she had already been there and seen them. She must see them; they were part of an old heritage. But how?

It was simple enough. It was for this that she was studying at night. "There is office work all over the world." She saw the significance of the maps of the British Empire showing the world strung on a chain of pink, all the pink was Britain's. In every one of those pink patches, no matter what the colour or kind of men there, nor the customs of the native women, she could get a job, she was a citizen there. There were advertisements in the Sydney papers for typists to go to Nauru, Cocos, Shanghai, British Columbia, and these could be just jumping-off places.

She had mentioned nothing of all this to anyone in the family, to frighten them. She was bringing them thirty-five shillings weekly and could have given more. They hoped she would when her pay was raised. Only once to Leo had she hinted at it, "When I go overseas——"

"When? Are you going?"

"When I get the money."

"It's a good idea."

"Why don't you go and get a job in San Francisco, Leo?"

"Yes," said Leo restlessly, looking with a vague yearning out to sea.

"Yes, do. Yes, do." She had begged and argued with him. "Home-keeping youths have ever homely wits."

Good-naturedly, Leo laughed and tried to please her by talking about it from time to time. But now Leo was at work—at present, out of work—a lock-out; and he wanted to get married.

"Get married!" said Teresa aloud, violently, and sat up, thrusting her legs down the folds of netting. At the same time she reflected that she must leave the school as soon as she had finished the next month's training at shorthand. She would go to the

Department and tell them she could not stay, she would pay them back the bond in instalments. She would pay them back, go to the university at night, and sail away, or sail away first. She looked at the clock: eleven-thirty. She was surprised to see an ugly ring round the moon already and cloud materializing as she looked.

Bad weather! The sea was noisier, increasing gradually. By morning it would be surging round the path; they would have to go to work by the back road. "Who can does, who can't teaches!" She could not make up her mind when to run away. Should she leave home now?

She had to go down to Leo at midnight. In the meantime, to forget the gnawing thoughts about school, she reviewed some of her favourite private movies. They were mostly from old legends she had read somewhere. The first one was by her entitled, "The Cruel Huntsman." Through a thicket in the wild wood, a pale girl with flying hair darted a length in front of a supernatural black horse, its lips drawn back as if snarling. On its back, dressed in black armour, without a face except for the black visor, sat a giant huntsman, and yelling, at the sides of the foam-flecked stallion, ran his hellhounds, black and black-splashed white. The hunt raged through the thicket, leaving trembling and torn boughs dashed about, was heard farther off and reappeared in the opposite direction, in the middle distance, in sunlight. (The girl was a tormented shade and in life, said the legend, was a coquette.) This was the mildest and most sentimental of her movies, an hors d'œuvre. The others followed fast. There were halls of veined marble, strewn with purple, red, and white, with golden goblets and splendid male and female slaves to bring in the food; there were scenes of taverns, taken from Breughel, and in cathedrals; a Hogmanay party in the Highlands with the bursting of a great haggis, and the guests fallen down in a flood of pease pudding, small birds, giblets, and tripes. There were insatiable Bluebeards in some gloomy northern castle, surrounded by pale bright hosts of condemned women; monsters in sea-caves, horrible bargainings, butcheries, black masses, Sabbaths haunted by flying corpses and old wives' gatherings in hidden valleys; routs of black horses, drawings and quarterings, impalements; cannibalism from Grimm, brothels from Shakespeare. All this gave her unutterable pleasure. She believed all these things existed from time to time, if they were not daily occurrences, and it was to reach some circle, some understandings in touch with these pleasures that she felt she had to break the iron circle of the home and work; for she knew these things were not thin black shapes of fantasy, but were real. It was a country from which she, a born citizen, was exiled. She struggled towards it.

She heard eight bells from two ships in the bay a few moments before she indolently got up to go downstairs. How happy she felt at this moment! Without these orgies, she would have had nothing to look forward to. In a reasonable way, her trip overseas, the halls of learning, were part of this grand life that she lived without restraint in the caves, taverns, woods, colonnades, and eel pools of antiquity and the night. Smiling to herself, she went downstairs slowly, feeling the dust and the grain of the splintered wood with her bare toes. With this liberty of head and mind went a kind of vigorous discontent which was pushing her out into the world faster and faster. She felt at this hour strong, energetic, beautiful, full of gaiety of the invincible, untried young girl who has not yet gone to work. She was a girl for any man, geared for a long night of love. She always knew at this hour of the night that if she met any man now he would fall in love with her, such was her serene power. But at that right hour, a girl was at home, in her eyeless room.

For a moment, the house seemed chill. It was a poor fate to climb the stairs and claim that single bed, those bare neat walls, that little pile of sensible clothes and those pencil marks in a note-book. She sighed and went on downstairs. When? How long? How could she bear it? Tomorrow, again she would begin to wait for the next day. What could happen to her, taking the ferry, talking in the teachers' room? Would the sky fall if she simply walked out? She had never done a single brave thing in her life, defying the rules; just obeyed, gone to school, paid in her money.

She walked into Leo's room. The lower panes of the window were stippled over so that passers-by on the overlooking street could not see in. Hawkins had made Leo's bed himself, saying it was something like a sea-hammock and would harden Leo. On a wooden frame some old sacks were arranged, thick and firm, and on this a small, hard mattress laid. If Leo did not sleep so deep and so long, Hawkins opined, he would not walk in his sleep. He told Leo, in the daytime, that he could conquer this weakness by will power. Hawkins was much ashamed of this defect in his son and felt it might be taken as a sign of a defect in his heredity. Teresa's voiced opinion was that Leo walked because he wanted to marry, the same thing that made Lance stay up senselessly at night, and Kitty weep. The house was haunted by legends of sleep-walking. Every relative who came there had something to say about it, the men to the men, the women to the women. There were sleep-walkers who had been seen on roofs, travelling on drain-pipes, dancing on chimney-pots. They returned safely to their beds unless spoken to, when they lost their balance, their wits or their lives. It seemed that a woman having a sleep-walking son placed a tub of water at the foot of the stairs and went to bed, easy in mind. She heard a howl and rushed out to find her son dead of his footbath. Leo might get into some trouble; and so one of the watchwords of the house was, "Last to bed, get up Leo." Hawkins had another, simpler theory about Leo's weakness, that it was due to a small physical irritation and the brother or sister waking him had to see that this was attended to.

Lance was not fond of his brother and detested this duty, though he was the one who usually came in late; and Kitty had to rise early, so it was Teresa who went down to him as a rule. Leo was hard to waken; he never really waked. Though he would get up, do what he was told, walk, drink, go outside, he did it all in his sleep. He got up rosy and tousled, muttering and laughing. Sometimes he would hit out. Sometimes he snapped and when scolded would answer, but however his sentences started off, they always ended incoherently.

Teresa tonight helped the big boy up and led him flaring and staring wildly to the kitchen, to the yard, and back into bed, where he rolled suddenly over on his side, with his eyes shut. He often snored while standing up, loud, sudden, peremptory snorts, and snored at the moment of rolling into bed. Sometimes he fell sideways across the bed and seemed unable to move further, so that she had to drag him in, tugging at his heavy muscular limbs, fighting with him for the bedclothes in which he was entangled. Many times he fell into her arms, leaned on her neck, her shoulder, stood like an apple-cheeked country drunk with his head against her cheek while he slept The fragrant moist heat of his brown body came to her nostrils in gusts from his open nightshirt, sliding off his smooth chest; in summer he slept naked. His nakedness was nothing to her; she did not even think of him as a man. He was only her brother, her own flesh. It was pleasant, friendly, to help the adorable boy, staggering with his eyes shut and often a silly smile on his mouth; or the brown eyes peering as if wickedly in the slits of the weighted lids, his hair ragged, a glimpse of the square white teeth as he answered with his comical mad babble. She remembered the funny things he said, to ask him afterwards:

"Last night, you said: 'Oh, gemme, gemme, down on the Lawny'—what did that mean?"

"I never did," he would grin at her sideways.

"And you said: 'The lights were down at four o'clock.' "

He grinned and shook his head. He was proud of her, he did not know why.

She was staggering about there with Leo for fully half an hour tonight. She heard the single bell ring from the ships while she was still in the lower passage. Presently she came up to bed. The house was shut and locked now, Leo could not get out, no one could get in. It was night, lingering, drowsy, real night.

She was in her room again with the door shut and suddenly she threw herself on her knees at the side of the bed, where the nets and sheets were tumbled. Into her hands she whispered: "Let me find a lover soon, let me get a lover soon, I must, I must, I beg, I beg." She was willing it, not praying. She believed firmly in the power of will to alter things and force things to an end. Cheerful, she got up and jumped into bed, as if she had heard a promise. She did not sleep yet; she was too tired for her legends but she tossed convulsively. She thought: "Oh, I'll never be able to sleep." The girls in the Botanic Gardens last Saturday had all given their remedies for sleeplessness; one said: "Breathe deeply." She tried that and it woke her up. Another said: "Take hot milk." There wasn't enough milk for everyone to be having glasses of milk. Teresa said: "Read an abstruse page, it's infallible." But the other girls, one a young doctor, one a social worker, said reading kept them awake. She tossed and turned. She listened to the sea, thought of it rolling in, and herself began to roll, like a ship at sea, moving quite ignorantly as women move with their lovers. "A storm far out at sea, coming in," she muttered. "Love, learning, bread—myself—all three, I will get."

A cry was ringing in the air when the girl started up. The moon was down, and a pallor and a cool air creeping in. She remembered she too had been calling for help: "Mother! Mother!" Now she heard faint noises downstairs. She jumped out, pushing the stifling mosquito nets aside and stole out in her nightdress. She could smell strong tea, so she knew Leo was going out with the men. She came quietly downstairs and stood in the kitchen door.

Leo turned from the stove with his smoke-blackened billy-can in his hand. "What ya doin'?"

Teresa laughed.

Slowly his face cleared. He turned his back and finished making his tea by pouring in the boiling water. "It's for the men," he said.

"Did Dad say you go out with them?"

"Yes! No! Can't I go out by myself?"

"Got out of bed the wrong side," remarked Teresa.

Leo muttered.

"What's the matter?" asked his sister.

"I know he'll make a row. He wants me to look for other work. I'm locked out, aren't I? Can I help it? She," he pointed upstairs to the room where Kitty was still sleeping, "doesn't pay any keep."

"Well, I do."

"Well, I wasn't saying——" He turned away to get the loaf of bread. After cutting a couple of thick slices and wrapping them in newspaper, he went into his room and she heard two notes of music—he had picked up his guitar.

"The fish won't come with that," said Teresa.

"I'm taking it round to Joe Martin's house. He wants to have a try, I'm teaching him," he explained.

"You're teaching Amy," she smirked.

Leo smirked too. "You think you're clever."

"It's windy," said Teresa. " 'Last night the moon had a golden ring and to-night no moon I see.' "

"We'll be back in a coupla hours," said Leo, throwing his coat over his shoulder and setting out through the front of the house, billy-can in one hand and guitar in the other.

"Storm signal isn't up at the lighthouse yet. I don't think. Look."

"Joe wouldn't go if he saw it."

"There's a Newcastle coaler in the bay. I wonder what for?"

"One of the boys jumped overboard and swam ashore," said Leo. "The bunks were bad and there were rats. I wouldn't take a berth in them. I saw the bloke. He went back home."

At the screen door he turned round, speaking in an undertone: "You see, Dad gets mad seeing me here. Perhaps I'll be back at work tomorrow. I don't know why I can't catch a few fish, and today's Sunday." He looked up at the ramshackle building. "He gave me a regular jawing last night. He said I wasn't to picket." Leo gave a dulcet laugh. He opened the screen door, shut it, and stood outside, whispering to her through the wire: "Gee, it's——" he shook his head. "I'll vamoose the ranch if he keeps after me. Nag, nag. Well, so long."

"Will you be back for lunch?"

"Unless Joe asks me."

She watched him loping down the garden, in shorts, barefoot, his curly hair uncombed. It was almost dark still. The gate clicked, a note came from the guitar.

Along the beach path in the early morning, she heard the first soft hollow sounds of oar and killick, bait-tin and dinner-pail and a soft conkling in boat-houses and slipways. On the ferry wharf someone was swinging a lantern, meaning "More this way". Men's voices came fitfully.

She went back to her room, looked at the stifling mosquito-tent, the hot bed, and slipped into her sweater and skirt. There was a big black rock always dripping, round which the path wound on the way to Pearly Cove, a demi-lune of white sand at cliff bottom. From the cliffs and grassy slopes one looked in both directions, south to the city's pale aurora, north to the distant pines of Manly. All the shipping of the harbour slid by that point, from fishing-skiff to warship. There you could hear the words said on the bridge by the skipper to the pilot taking the ship out, or the remarks of fishermen on their way out. Behind the headland the tide drummed. The girl took a drink of water, a piece of bread-and-dripping and went out the back way. The tide, though far out, was coming back in short leaps. She went up the military road and out round the black rock, avoiding the guard-house because it was too early. She went slowly, biting into her bread and trying to make up her mind about the school. On Thursday,

89

she had got paid. Thursday afternoon last, she took George Wadling, the Mad Boy, with her to buy a pot-plant, and gave it to him to look after overnight. He was to have it, keep it at school. Next morning the plant just watered was on her desk and she saw the poor boy's dirty overgrown head flash up over the window-sill for a moment and then disappear. When she looked out the window there was no one in the playground. Was he hiding directly underneath?

The sky was now getting clear, but light sinewy airs were nosing about and the air had thickened. Back in the bay behind the two points, the Martins' outboard motor started, muffled. Presently they came sweeping round the point. A man standing up, sang—

> *"A life on the ocean wave,*
> *A home on the rolling deep,*
> *Where the scattered waters rave*
> *And the winds their revels keep.*
>
> *So now good-bye to land*
> *To the dull unchanging shore—"*

and they were out of earshot. It was stoutly sung; the singer strangely glided and bobbed over the choppy water, with the three hearers at his feet, one Leo, singing seconds. The boat headed outwards.

The ground was moist and the mosquitoes singing round within the shelter of the rock. The girl turned home. She was worn out and went to sleep when she got home.

8. It Was the Hot Intolerable Hour

THE infant breeze died after sunrise, though the swell continued. Inside the house and out, the merry bay jigged. The egg-beater rang in the basin, they were sawing in the shed and Andrew Hawkins was singing—

> *"Ye mariners of England*
> *That guard our native seas . . ."*

—above the rhythmic hee-haw. They were launching a fishing-boat in the bay, a ferry could be heard coming in to the wharf. Seagulls flew overhead with their *queer-queer!* increasing in number as the surf increased and darting at the basins of scraps thrown overboard by sea-cooks before entering the harbour. Neighbours up the street were talking on their front verandas, the warm rich air was full of eleven o'clock smells, an iron tool fell in the paved yard, *clink!*

> *"As ye sweep through the deep;*
> *While the stormy winds do blo-oh-oh-oh-ow!"*

A boy laughed. The strong smell of drying fish-nets came in. When the beans were cut, the potatoes scrubbed and the roast ready, Kitty sat down in the kitchen to hem some dish-towels and Teresa skipped to the empty upstairs to "do the rooms", as she said. She made the three beds, shook the mats and then was free to prepare the lessons for the next day. She had made six dozen little cards on which she had written simple problems for the weak intellects of her class. Besides this, she was learning basket-making out of a book and had half-wound a mending basket.

But as she sat with the raffia in a bundle on her table she imagined a new dress for herself. She had on her green dress. She took it and all her clothes off. "If anyone comes, I'll say I'm going swimming," she thought. She did nothing but sat down on the sun-heated iron-bound sewing-box again, twisting a piece of raffia in her hands.

"I am beautiful, why can't I be photographed like this?" She put the piece of raffia, red, round her waist and drew it tight. "I am sure I look beautiful like this. The weather's hot——" She laughed aloud and looked hastily to the door. She had just thought that tonight, when all were asleep, she would walk out naked, in the garden. Who would be about? Some lovesick boy? And he'd think he was having hallucinations. He'd think, "I'm going mad," and would hurry past, run home. Or he might come into the garden, "What are you? Are you real?" She would say: "Is this real? Is this flesh? No dream of yours is as solid as this." She laughed again. One such daring act and she, the boy—several daring acts and they would all be free. She came back to the idea, "But how can we all suffer when none of us wants it?" She stood up beside the open window, behind the light curtain and looked out at the ragged grassy slope. A pink shadow fell from the shutter, strapped across her arm and body. "Who knows under our clothes what we are like? Why do they imprison Venus? I am Venus, too. If Venus is a goddess, I am a goddess. The poor old schoolteachers in the teachers' room worship Greek culture. They know nothing about Greek culture. But they love it. Why? They don't know. I know. The naked Venus. Now Kitty leans out of the window looking under her lashes at the boy next door. Her olive skin as a little girl; how beautiful she was! Feminine race, woman's beauty, and then the boy next door. Oh, no, it's just the result of prison life. 'Young desire—' They don't mean it though. Get married first and see! Then after all, any man wouldn't do. I want to be adored. If I showed myself at the window, what would happen? 'Breasts that bore at men's eyes.' The young men in the Bay round here, who are half-mad with desire this hot damp morning, would fall down at my feet, worship me, kiss my waist, knees, hips, clinging round like vines, snakes—what a shame it is! I want them and they want me! There's something I don't understand in the whole arrangement. No, I'm not mad, they are."

At the thought of this injustice, how they would fly to each other, she felt as if she would burst from a fierce pain. "Last night, those fallen on the grass, unable to stand up, they were ugly, coarse, but in full life. In art courses, we see women's bodies, not men's; we're shown how to admire our own beauty, but when it comes, then we must hide it. And it's wrong, too, we can't see naked men, we're robbed of our pleasures." Her head whirled with confusion and frustration. "It isn't anything to do with me. Malfi was pretty, wealthy, clever—she, too."

She walked out of her room to the head of the stairs. The light airs came from every door, window, and chink, up the staircase, down from the turrets at her, feeling thoughtfully over her body, giving her caresses that could never come otherwise. The softly haired wood was like a beast under her feet. Circe? The men-tamers? What had they? She looked down the staircase, to the shaded hallways covered with worn oilcloth, the oilcloth strewn with sand carried in. She regretted her youth, like an old woman, "At fourteen, I was——" and "At fifteen, already I——" and so forth. "I remember that cornflower blue voile, all the men stared at me—why didn't I know then? Are the old people jealous? Those fishermen now wouldn't mind at all. They'd like to see me walking down the beach, say, through the salt water, or at night, a night like tonight will be, at moonrise. They might faint at the sight! And then open his eyes, rouse himself, come through the foam like a sea animal, with his mouth full of salt water and kiss, kiss, embrace, like a vine coming up the calf, the knee, his mouth salt and stinging, but always hungry till he would either get drowned with salt water or pull me down into the waves with him—to roll for hours in the foam! And it's more misery for the men who make the laws than for me who never made a law, for women are outside the law; they make nothing, they say yes or no, to some collection of whereases. Why do men make the laws, say, about marriage, decency and the like, to shackle themselves? It's all incomprehensible."

She leaned against the head of the stair, pressing the smooth greased wood into her side. It was getting hotter.

The most curious thing is, thought Teresa, that men like undressed women better than dressed, they have places where they can enjoy them, but we can't see naked women. I should like to be one of the *hetæræ*, thought she, that's different from a harlot, it's

93

a mistress harlot; govern my own household, do as I liked, have no one say no to me. How would I get the money, that's the question. Poor men can't give you money and rich men want another sort of woman. But will I begin with men like those down at the Bay, or at work, poor beachcombers, so to speak, schoolboys, failures, that lop-eared doctor on the boat, ugly men, broken-backed child-whackers trembling before a Mr Prentiss, a headmaster? No, no. Never venture, never win. I'll have to go out and look for a man. The hands, dark, passionate, clawlike but beautiful, firm, long and muscular that move over my body, like a crab moving over the sand, a big spider and his shadow moving over a whitewashed wall, are no schoolmaster's, no fisherman's hands. She heard the oven door clang; Kitty had put in the roast. Leo's joyous shout came from the beach path, "Look at our catch!"

She came away from the stairhead and went towards the back and climbed quite naked into the little open tower. "If I show myself at the opening here, only breasts, only belly, or only thighs, what a joke! What we all want and what we don't take. What cowards. It's a naked woman, just the same, not a schoolteacher in a skirt that is the ideal of beauty; not a man, a woman, and not a married woman, a naked young virgin, like me. Oh, Aphrodite, I wish you were a goddess, I wish you were the real thing and I could pray to you and dedicate myself to you. What words would I say? You would know everything. I would say, Venus, or Aphrodite Pandemos, mother of all living, listen to my troubles. When I was fourteen, I was sick with love, when I was fifteen I was so round and red-cheeked and burning with love that everyone knew it, I was ashamed myself to walk down the street, because I knew they knew it. It wasn't only my body, it was everything, the sleek eyes, the long silk hair, the walking, the legs and arms; the boys called after me and I was ashamed then. At sixteen I was tired with putting my arms round thin air at night, at seventeen I drooped, my face got sad. Venus, what am I to do? Yes, what am I to do? No one will help me."

Discouraged, Teresa came down from the turret and went into her room. Opening her sewing-box she pulled out what she had there; some yards of lace, bits of velvet and silk, an old beaver hat, a pair of ruby gloves she had bought for the colour and never worn, a piece of chamois leather, a cord. She considered all these for a time. The sun increasing to midday beat into her brain and she moved slowly, almost stupefied. After a while she opened a box and got out a pair of scissors and some thread. She began making a pair of buskins. Feverishly, with a big needle, with ugly stitches, she sewed them up and pulled them on her naked feet. Then she put on the beaver hat and went into her father's room to admire herself. It was a striking get-up. She returned to the room walking firmly, imagining herself some goddess athwart the woods; and now invented a new dress for herself. It was her custom on Sundays when she was free and the family were out roaming the bay and the cliffs, to invent these costumes, fantastic to the last degree, colourful, all had the same intention; they bound the thighs and showed the belly, or covered the face, neck, and arms with a hood and wimple which fell short of the breasts; they were all obscene. When she was tired of invention and sick of her gee-gaws, she would throw them aside, stuff them into her bottom drawer where they became more and more crumpled, and would throw herself on the bed, half asleep, while slowly, as she became hotter (for she became chilled in her parades in the empty upper floor, in which the wind always blew) a swarm of new inventions filled her mind, patterns which she put by for the next time, for too thick they came for her ever to make them up, they required a wardrobe mistress.

First, now, she imagined a city-state with short walls of white and blue marble, with clear water running down the gutters and the people, in laced leather and metal sandals, taking these off to bathe their feet when it got too hot. There was no dust anywhere, the air sparkled. It was high up in the mountains, near the sun, so that it was both cold and hot at the same time, a wind blew but at certain hours of the day it was perfectly still. Each day at the same time, a soft rain fell and for this hour the people either went into their marble-floored houses or put on cloaks, all of the same style, but of different colours. At midday it was perfectly still and they all tanned themselves, but some of the men and women remained absolutely fair always. The children were naked except for wreaths of flowers and bunches of fruits round their arms, necks, ankles, or middles, just as they pleased. The adults were variously garbed; the men in tights of all colours, cloths, and cuts, showing their limbs, muscles, and sometimes split on the thighs or breast; sometimes a mere jerkin, or even a

95

circlet round the breasts, a coating of paint over the rippling skins and never the loincloth or sporran. The women were clothed (in her city-state) more gorgeously, in fashions beyond description. Some hid their flesh, some showed it. Through a dress of lemon velvet the pouting breasts of a young mother stood out, bursting with their thick white wine; she suckled her child as she walked. They had a thousand ways of showing their breasts. She designed madly for them, but they moved about unconscious of her as if they really existed. It staled, her eyes shut. What had happened? She would dream no more, but got up dully. She went down languidly and softly. If only Kitty had not done everything without her!

Lunch. First, the big kitchen ready, robust, steaming, with the oven, cupboards, dishes full of the food they had earned, a food grove that was their own; inside, the long table with Andrew Hawkins sitting sideways so that he could look out at the bay, Kitty at the bottom near the kitchen to serve, Teresa next to her, the boys on each side.

Today, Kitty was happy but flustered and the father kept making remarks about "her boy". Her two brothers eyed her with less than their usual disdain. Teresa saw them all only in a dream. Why couldn't she cover the bare walls of the dining-room with designs? Andrew Hawkins never disapproved of handwork itself, only of bought painting. The entire wall and ceiling could be covered with leaves and flowers on vines, for instance, and in each wall a painted window or vignette, through which a painted scene would show. On the ceiling—

It was time to change the plates. "The two girls are fast asleep," said their father indulgently. Leo grunted. "They burned the potatoes in their sleep," Lance remarked after some reflection. He had not spoken to his father for a year, for no particular reason; but to avoid scandal, he dropped remarks into the room when others were present. Leo added: "I'll bet Terry is thinking of some teacher at school." Teresa put the plates at her sister's place and went out for the lemon sauce.

"Aren't you, Terry?"

"Do you think I'd marry a schoolteacher?"

The men laughed. Kitty said, with a laugh: "Nobody asked you, sir, she said, sir, she said."

> *"If he should ask me to marry him,*
> *What shall I, what shall I say?"*

"Say yes, Tess," said the father.

"I'll ask him if I like," said Teresa.

Lance enquired: "Who'd marry you?"

"Who'd marry you?" asked Teresa.

Kitty laughed as she sat down.

"You're sickening," Lance flung at her. "Going on a moonlight excursion and"—he was unable to bring himself to say the word "kissing" so he growled instead, "Look at you, with paint and powder on you now. As soon as they see a man, they put on cold cream."

They all looked at her keenly; she had blotted the lipstick clumsily.

"Well, Kit!" said her father.

Smiling with embarrassment, but without an apology, she got up and went into the kitchen where she scrubbed her lips with a duster.

"You're all the same," said Lance. "As soon as a man comes within half a mile, it's giggling and flirting and lipstick, spending your money on clothes, fussing yourselves up, brazeers to look beautiful——"

"Lance," cried Teresa, leaping from her chair.

He paused disdainfully; the father smiled slightly.

"That's all you think about the whole morning," he said evilly.

"What do you mean by that?"

"Never mind. I know what I know. You lie on your bed reading, your eyes are all red, you don't do your schoolwork." He snickered. "When they go to a wedding, the girls go boy-crazy. There, but for the grace of God, go I."

Kitty came in with the steamed pudding and put it in her place, to cut it up.

"It's like wet flannel," said Lance. "Why can't you learn to cook? You've been at it long enough. Why don't you go to cooking school?"

Kitty cast down her eyes and began to divide the pudding.

"Your Malfi now," said Lance.

97

"What's the matter with Malfi?" enquired Leo with lazy interest. "She's all right."

"She runs around with her dress cut down to the small of her back, with her bones sticking out and salt-cellars in her neck. She thinks the boys are sick over her."

Leo laughed shortly. "She's got enough boys."

Lance nagged: "She'd better look out, she'd better not try anything on now." Kitty was looking into her plate. Teresa gulped down the sweet wet pudding. There was a pause until she finished and she then said to Lance: "What a pity you're so jealous!"

"Jealous! Of that flirt!"

"Yes. Of that flirt!"

Lance folded his napkin and got up from the table, turning away to hide the irresistible grin stealing over his face. Kitty, unnoticed, messed with her pudding and said stormily: "Do you want a second helping?"

"Not of that rubber," said Lance.

"Well, now, we can live without the critic," said Kitty.

The father remarked: "You shouldn't torment him. Pass my plate, Terry. You know poor Lance is overworking and probably has his private worries."

"Why is he so mean?" asked Kitty.

"Born mean," remarked Leo, getting up without ceremony and stretching himself. "Going down to the men."

"You're always with the fishermen," said his father. "I don't mind you being with your mates, but I'd like to see you stay at home and try to read a bit, improve your mind. Lance does that, that you've got to say for your brother."

Leo's face darkened. Teresa said: "Leo's the fastest workman in the shop, they had to tell him not to go so fast, he was speeding up. All the men like him and when they walked out the other day, it was Leo made them walk out. He got up on a stone at the gate, the stone that holds the gate back. He got up on it and made them a speech and they walked out afterwards."

Leo came back into the room. "I told them to down tools till the boss got rid of the foreman, the foreman's his son-in-law. They just started to stroll out the gate, nothing wrong, it looked like. Then they locked us out."

Kitty, incredulous, said: "You, a boy of seventeen, told men what to do?"

"A man of seventeen," said Teresa.

The father, balancing between admiration and disapproval, said: "Leo's a hothead, he ought to have looked before he leaped. Now they're all out of work."

"He talks big," said Kitty. "I can't understand grown men listening to a boy like that."

Teresa, playing with a spoon, bursting with pride, imagined Leo, with tossed dark hair, his eyes lively, on the stone. She said aloud: "Leo could get married now, he's a grown man himself." Kitty lifted her head and gave her a puzzled look; then she said: "Leo has nothing in his head but girls. He runs around with all the tomboys in the Bay, even that Gladys." She put down her table napkin and got up to clear the plates. Teresa got up to help her and their father sat at the table looking dreamily over the bay until the cloth was taken off, when he got out a huge book of orchid prints and started going through them. He called the girls in from washing the dishes, to look at various species.

"I've seen that one over behind Stoney Creek. I found that one twenty years ago in a gully up the Lane Cover River that's just a suburban development now."

When Teresa hung up the towels to dry and came out of the kitchen to go upstairs, she found Leo hanging about the stairfoot. He threw himself at her, whispering resonantly.

"Teresa, come here a minute. I heard what you said just now, that I ought to get married, I mean. Do you think so? You see," he began explaining in his low warm voice that he was earning the basic wage. "Lots of men live on the basic wage and—" He flushed hotly and he rumbled in the bass, something about a girl he wanted to marry, he wanted her to meet, not Eunice out at Maroubra at all, that was all over, a mistake—"you can't tell a book by its cover"—but a girl named Esther, a beautiful, smart girl, not one of those fly-by-nights, the kind of a girl to settle down and make a home for a man. "Do you think I could get married?" he pressed her.

"Oh, get married, get married," she begged.

His eyes shone. He threw his shoulders back, pulled his arms taut. His powerful head braced on the thick neck towered above her. He said softly: "I bet you'd like to get married too, wouldn't you, Tess?"

"Of course."

"I knew it, I knew it," he said. He padded off, velvety and ungainly, not yet fully grown.

"Donkey," said Teresa to herself, grinning.

She went upstairs. There was a real breeze; the afternoon was cooler but vaporous. The corners, the landing, and the rooms were burning with a faint rose colour. Her room, the door ajar, invited her, blazing to her with the gem-like colours of past saturnalia, the heavy air thickened with fables of lust, beckoning without beckoning, self-content, streaming with sylphs of ancient style and Priapic hosts, shaken from floor to ceiling with the presence of monsters, no heavier than smoke. The door and window open, inviting them, made her stand still on the landing for a few moments as she looked into her room, trembling with expectancy, as certain of joy as if it were a grotto of the satyr-woods, breeding the miracles of incarnated desire, waiting for a rustle, a voice, unheard by them downstairs but heard by her. She deceived herself with joy, hoping for a powerful hallucination; if she could hear or see them only once! It was the hot, intolerable hour, the hour when in hot countries the sun begins to embrace the earth and crush it with his weight; when he changes everything in it. At this time, there is no more love, conscience, remorse, or sin. In that room, in the furnace, she understood herself and knew what was wrong with the world of men. She felt like a giantess, immense, somehow growing like an incommensurable flower from a root in the earth, pouring upwards into the brazen sky, "the woman clothed with the sun". At this hour each day, the sun, reckless, mad with ardour, created her newly. This was the hour when she lived as a heart lives inside a beast, she was the blood and the convulsion; outside was a living envelope, the world.

After a long pause, savouring it, foreseeing the mad fervour of the visions to come, but hearing nothing, not a single note from another world, seeing not the hair of a haunch, she went in languidly and stretched herself out on the square of grass matting her father had bought for her, saying: "A young girl should have some luxuries." It was too hot to lie on the bed. The ceiling was of the palest nile green and to her obscured eyes, swimming in the maddening heat, it was curtained already; as she looked up, her head resting on her arms, the dark of the heat closed in round it. It was not sleep, but the swift dropping curtains of the play. The play was about to begin. There was no music, though there was a faint rustling; there were no feet though there were forms all about that she never quite caught in the tail of the eye; and she was not asleep. At this time of day, it was no longer the polite conventional romances built on Rome's bric-à-brac authors, but the stories of the shameless Greeks which first rushed onto the stage like a whirlwind and were thrust into thin air by the oncoming wind of the next. Now her mind cleared and she began to think.

Of course, we must change things. A man goes to the Judgment Seat and when God threatens him with hell, he says: "Thou canst not send me there, I came from earth just now." In Oscar Wilde it is. Everything can be changed, for this is not hell, just the same; it is only earth. Below every cathedral is a tangle of fancy-named streets where harlots live; there are follies in every large town where naked women dance and even in country towns and in suburbs there are smoke concerts where some woman writhes before them, with smoke in the air and smoky spirals of gauze, and flounces in embroidered tatters; they pass around their books of nakedness. We should have had male brothels. But who wants a bought male? One wants love. Men are corrupted by power and want submissive women, but we— the corruption of weakness fortunately is a mere surface, like house-dirt; the human being sleeps underneath and can be roused. I am certain that as I lie here now, frenzied with desire and want, all women have lain for centuries, since innocent times and never an ounce of bravado to throw off the servitude of timidity. If ever I have money, I'll build hostels where youth can go free, no watchman, no fee. Is this a life? And calmly we live it. They want to educate youth. Let them send us to school, university, good, but during that time let us be hidden in some green town, away from everyone and live together. Old age and youth cannot live together. But everyone would have to be rich for that. And who would pay for our pleasure? Could we young people with money get up some community of our own? This is just a question of the village of youth. There would be a council of themselves, a ruler, like myself, elected of course, all the people of one age and absolutely no penalties; only it would be necessary to study all the time. There would be a thousand Romeo and Juliets, Paolo and Francescas. Why did these couples so famous die unhappy? Because there was no village of youth. Then when men fell in love with women, they could go away too—another community with people coming and going at will, no questions, no fees, only work between them, and each would have to work and no lover-snatching. Anyone who left his or her own lover would have to go. Another could follow them. Would this leave the house and larder bare? In this house we work for the house and we don't love each other; but then, if Lance and Leo brought their women and we our lovers——

She trailed off, Leo and Lance, and Kitty and I, we could all go away to this palace of youth, this phalanstery of learning and suffer no more. But that's fantasy. Who is going to build it, who lead it?

There should be places, bureaux, where we could go and register when we wanted a mate, a stranger's place away from all those who know too much about us. We could get the names of boys and girls and when they needed someone, when life in the world as it is became unbearable, they could disappear, go there and find a mate.

What a waste of our time! Then we could work—study—not always be mulling over the same anxieties. I put up with it because I belong to the bloodless rout of women. If only I have the will I needn't suffer as I do.

But she was suffering now and she turned away from those painful thoughts and began to go over, word by word, with intense preoccupation, the *Lysistrata*. She had never learned it; it had burned itself into her head, the words as if printed on the blue and burning sky of Greece, or else of her own country as hot, as naïve, as open.

She must have fallen asleep. When she opened her eyes suddenly, she saw Lance standing looking in at her.

"What do you think you're doing?"

"Exercises," she said promptly.

"In counting sheep. You were fast asleep." He guffawed.

"What do you want?"

He had not come any farther than the door. "Your face is flushed."

"Yours is pale-green."

She got to her knees, feeling ashamed of teasing the poor willowy wretch. She and her sister Kitty did the housework and helped the washerwoman with the clothes; the two knew the secrets of the family in the way that servants know them.

"Lance," she said, getting to her feet, "why don't you get married? Get a girl and get married. We'll manage here. I don't see why you should use your money up in this old hulk of a house. I won't stay here long myself. I'm going to get away. You get out too."

"Get married," he muttered, lowering at her. "That's all you girls think of, to get a man stuck."

"Oh!"

He looked at the floor and then at her as he turned away. "Where could you live?"

"In a room."

"To ask boys up?"

"Why are you so nasty to everyone?"

As he lounged off, he said: "Anne's downstairs to see you. She's got something for you."

"Anne!" She rushed out calling: "Anne!" Anne, rosy and brown, handed her a letter. "I happened to mention to Mrs Percy that I was walking over and she asked me to give it to you. She wrote it last night." Flattered, Teresa tore the many close-written pages from Anne.

My Dear Miss Hawkins,

When you come to visit Mrs Broderick next I hope we shall all be less distraught and able to review life's mysteries with clearer vision.

There are one or two out of all the myriad passers-by, who compel me. I mean they, these few, get into my soul so that I cannot not care how they travel their path, even though each one's path IS all his own and for no other's pointing out.

You may wonder who and what I am to presume to teach anyone? Well, you will know, as time goes on, that the matter which I have for the work is not trivial, and this momentousness has nothing to do with this obscure person, but only with its vital bearing upon all fundamental human problems.

No truth is maintained by ANY credentials of its exponent be he never so famous or worthy; but only by its own illuminating quality, as it is tested and applied in relation to FACTS & EVENTS.

Only these hard ugly concrete external, or even "material" things can teach wisdom to any man.

Our dreams whether waking or sleeping all spring from that quagmire of emotion which gives off its evanescent vapours—mostly very unhealthy; but sometimes to certain types—wholly pleasant.

Now I'm going to tell you a little more, for you are one of the very few who do need a special wakening mood.

Almost all upright and right-minded humans come into life with an instinctive sense of good & evil. Whether in themselves, or in the world around them, they are for ever at war with some form or other of "evil" or "wrong" or "sin" or "temptation" as they call it, and they from childhood know a sense of shame when guilty, a secret will to do the right & so on & so forth.

These are the rank & file of true humans.

But here & there are "white souls"—never mind where they come from—but they have no shame, no inner strivings against temptation, no horror of evil in the world, no will to resist or strive against anything. They enjoy loveliness, they are lovely, very much as angels are. But they have all yet to learn about man, human strifes & the unutterable hatefulness of that source & essence of Evil which has made the degenerates what they are.

Will you try to live in actualities and shake yourself from your sweet dreamings?

Look into the eyes of the worst humans you meet in slum or Bourse, oh, I almost wrote "brothel". You do not know what that means. Clean men never mention it. Clean women mostly know nothing of its true horror & forget such things. But you are in the very midst of Hell's worst outrages and you are as innocent & oblivious of it all as a new-born babe.

To human life you are new-born.

These words are no fanatic's outpourings. I charge you, Miss Hawkins, weigh them well. Examine ALL that life shows you & learn to discriminate between what is good & what is bad.

Study facts, happenings, & events and get out with your excellent brains your own diagnosis of THE GOOD & the bad.

Then write to me—after some months of survey, & tell me which quality you find predominant in your world.

Now forgive me, but I must say one word more, presumptuous though it may seem—

Your sweetheart is getting you because he wanted to use for his own ends a very rare tool, namely, a woman as guileless & unsuspecting as a child who yet had very exceptional mental acumen.

Well, he got you, kept you, used you, & now YOU have what you could never have got otherwise, the rarest insight into one department of deviltry. Not so strong a word, please? All right, wait till you know all that IS going on about you, and all that it means in intrigue, malicious defeatment of the innocent, all in the name of love, and then see how much trickery & cunning deception has to go along in its train.

Ask yourself what all these things are. Look on it as from Mars —or Heaven—whence you came & tell your own soul whether or not you like & admire the things you see & lend your hand to.

I am a wise woman now—but I have had to gather wisdom only by getting into closest quarters with devils & deviltry in order to be awakened to what deviltry is, hate it, withstand it & go on to discover more & more.

Only so do any of us learn. But you, you babe in white raiment, have plunged straight from Heaven, that is the spirit realm behind all human life, right into Satan's pet stronghold, the trickeries that call themselves respectable, or cultivated or artistic & so forth.

Do get away from soft dream-fantasies & touch realities. You came into this grim battleground of human life to learn what evil is—because no soul however lovely can withstand evil or further the good till he experiences it, & stand against it in his own life.

Auntie is as far removed from you as woman could be. She is an ancient warrior—knows evil instinctively & understands shame, remorse, misgiving, will to strive & so forth. She sees you in a whirlpool of infamies, evidently enjoying life. SHE cannot explain your wondrous innocence, and I cannot ever talk to her, to enlighten her.

Do you see how it sways any undecided mind, to see an innocent and obviously pure soul actually upholding the very things all upright haters-of-evil agree to shun, if not loudly condemn?

There is no argument that can convince you. No man ever sees & hates evil because he is taught to, but only as his own innermost self (which can whisper only when thought is still) shudders at it, writhes in its presence, feels sick, nauseated and revolted in the presence of evil-minded persons. It is a SENSE not a mental attitude & you have yet to cultivate that sense.

You have been led into your world of evil for a great purpose. When you DO awake & know you know, & come out, you will be a great force for good.

Yours who would be your friend if it may be,

AMABEL PERCY.

Anne, when she read it over her cousin's shoulder, cried: "What is she talking about?"

Teresa told her about Crow's talks on free love; it must have been that! Anne laughed comically, flushed. "Free love—does he really talk about that?"

"Everyone does."

After a silence Anne asked in a subdued voice: "Do you—do they, I mean, when you're there? What can they say about it?"

"The old way of marrying and settling down is all finished," said Teresa, curtly. "Malfi and all that—do you want to do that? Well, there's no reason why you shouldn't, if you want to."

"What about the children?"

"Oh, the children—of course, it's all for a different world."

"What's the advantage, though—I wouldn't like it, I don't see the advantage," pursued Anne, confused, anxious.

"Well, for one thing, children shouldn't live with their parents and be annoyed by them."

"Annoyed by their parents!" cried Anne.

"Yes. You shouldn't live with Aunt Bea—you ought to be out on your own, you could easily get married then, in a month, in a day."

Anne stared at her, her face strained.

"It isn't Aunt Bea's fault," said Teresa hastily. "But now you ought to be alone, it's time."

"But what would Mother do?"

"You never are alone—how can you look for a mate? Aunt Bea thinks she ought to be there with you—men don't want that."

"Oh, the man I want to marry wouldn't think of having mother live alone," said Anne.

"Then you'll never marry." But Teresa looked kindly and sorrowfully at her cousin, and continued: "Anne, live by yourself, be brave. It takes a lot of courage—but you must."

"I've thought of it," said Anne, suddenly, in a low tone, her eyes dropped. "But Mother would be so cut up. She's done everything for me, since I was a baby. How can I?" she implored her cousin, raising her eyes and seeming to ask for a practical answer.

"I don't know, but you must."

"I'll try," said Anne hesitantly.

"Do it, do it, don't think it over."

"Oh, but how can I?" Anne begged again. "It's out of the question."

"Then it's all over with you. That's all."

"I want Mother to meet any young man——" Anne began, stopped. After a short silence, she began to cry in a small, troubled, baffled way. "I know it's stupid," she cried, "I know I'm so stupid, but I'm afraid I won't meet anyone."

"Leave, leave," Teresa importuned her, going too far. "Only leave——" She saw the hope already draining out of Anne's eyes, as she raised her face and wiped it.

9. The Deed Was Extreme

ON the eight-thirteen boat in the morning, which most of the office-workers took to the city, Terry Hawkins sat always with two girls from her own part of the Bay; Martha, who had been a stenographer for eleven years in a tyre salesroom, and Elsie, who worked a Moon's accounting machine. Martha was a pale, sedate, but spirited brunette, with wiry hair, long pious nose, and stiff purple mouth. She had been engaged for five years to a clerk in the Treasury Department and was always urging him to pass some examination or other, while they saved up to get married. When they had two hundred pounds she would leave work and they would marry. It was not considered respectable among these girls to work after marriage; a girl was supposed to find a man who would keep her, and if she worked after marriage, it was a reflection on man and wife alike. This was Martha's entire theory of marriage. Since she had first got her job at the age of fifteen she had been making her trousseau, which now filled a tea-chest and a trunk. This alone marked her out as a woman with strength of mind; for the law of the boat was that while every girl might start on her trousseau, that is publicly, two or three mornings after her engagement, even her secret engagement, provided her secret engagement was properly given to rumour, a girl was vapid, a dreamer, silly, even pretentious, who worked on her trousseau (in these circumstances called glory-box, bottom drawer, or hope chest) before her engagement. This was observed so strictly that any girl doing sewing on the boat was believed to have a secret engagement to marry.

A girl, before the diamond ring, belonged to Martha's category of the Great Unwanted. Martha was the wit of the party, a village gossip of the forbidding, dangerous, upright, churchly kind, with a rapid, penetrating eye, who could strip a congregation down to its underlinen and who, completely integrated, feared neither man nor God; to the latter she gave lip service. Martha was respected over the whole boat, on the female side, for her ability to first guess how love affairs were going; who was about to leave, who about to return to, the Great Unwanted. For this reason, Martha held herself apart, and had only two regulars, that is comrades: Teresa, who was neither flesh nor fowl nor good red herring, and Elsie, a natural adjutant. Teresa's other friend, this Elsie, was also an Engaged Girl. She had been in tutelage to Martha for eight years and after four years she got the ring. She was a dark, slow-voiced, simple-hearted girl who loved accountancy, and was nearing the end of her engagement. She was going to give up work, too, but she said she was going to miss the office, she knew. From time to time she put a few stitches in a piece of sewing, but she did not care much for it; she dreamed the hours away on the boat. Martha chattered without end and Elsie would sit back with drooping shoulders, her eyes shining, a soft expression round her lips. Sometimes Martha's eyes would tire of sewing, and then the two girls would sit devouring fiction, "outwardly passive, inside a seething volcano", in Aunt Bea's description. Teresa, belonging as yet to the Great Unwanted, could not, of course, do any sewing. She bent over her book. Beside her, through the churning of the screws, the *whsh-to*, *whsh-to* of the open engine and the gush of water, she would hear their intimate give-and-take, a discussion of some book.

"What do you think of Laurette, as a character?"

"I think she's true to life."

"I don't think any girl would say what she said to Mr Vansittart under the circumstances. She doesn't know him well enough yet."

Occasionally, they came out of their private life to poke their noses into Teresa's affairs. She would show her book at once, anxious to explain it. Martha always wanted a résumé of it, Elsie listened because Martha wanted her to. Martha was implacable.

"But painters just paint. They don't think out all that! Why is it called *Dawn*? How can dawn possibly look like a woman? When is Man a pentagon? Why can't Prometheus have clothes on? We have monkeys now, did a man ever come from them? How do we know the sun goes round the earth? They have globes and things, but how do they know? You can't prove it, can you? You merely accept what they say in school."

This Monday morning, going in to school, Teresa had with her Louys's *Aphrodite* and Ovid's *Art of Love*, illustrated. The two girls, while not daring to touch the books, considered them, on Teresa's lap, with a mixture of shame and curiosity. This, too, she had to explain and even to speak for. Martha, the implacable, said: "Are they really classics? Why do they have such things for classics? How do you know people did them in the olden days? Supposing they wrote down such things, why do we have to read them? What is the purpose of printing them so expensively? What are they read for? If you don't have to read them, why do you? Do you like reading that?"

Teresa said: "Everything in the world was produced by the act of love, it would be queer not to think about it," but so wrapped up were they in husbands-to-be, they seemed never to have heard of love. They knew all the scandals in the newspapers, of course, and much about whether Mrs X was found on the lap of Mr Y or not. For all the men they had names: boy friends, fiancés, husbands, and co-respondents, and there were flirts, engaged couples, married couples, and misconduct, but they recoiled at the improper words, *love* and *lover*.

"Doesn't the word—lover, I mean," said Martha, at length, faintly disturbed, "seem indecent to you? I mean, sweetheart is better, or fiancé is better."

"Lover!" cried Teresa, shocked out of her exposition. "Lover is the only word there is."

"You want a husband, don't you?"

"Of course."

"Don't you want a man to marry you and keep you?"

"I'd work my fingers to the bone to keep my lover," she said violently. "I'd live in a tent, what do I care about a house?"

"A nice thing that would be. I'm afraid the world couldn't run your way."

Teresa laughed angrily. Martha picked up her book and tried to return to the page she had wandered from, but something still attracted her to Teresa. She looked sidelong at her for a moment, and asked: "What is your ambition?"

"I can't tell you."

"Don't you want to get married?"

"Of course."

"Wouldn't you wear an engagement ring?" said Martha, attacked by a rare doubt.

"No," said Teresa timidly.

"Why not?"

"Love doesn't consist in publicity!"

Martha looked at her with disfavour.

"When you are engaged, you will understand," said Elsie kindly, meaning to save her from further attack, for Martha's face was dark. Said Elsie, with an effort: "I didn't understand either, till I was engaged. I thought the same."

"Why wouldn't you want anyone to know?" said Martha suspiciously.

"What business is it of theirs?"

"Why would you be ashamed?"

"It isn't shame."

"Love," said Martha bluntly, looking her up and down. "What do you know about love? Have you got a young man?"

"No."

"Then it's all simply theory," said Martha indignantly. "How can you talk about what you don't understand?"

"Surely I can understand about love without being engaged?"

"It's a funny thing if you can, something I wouldn't talk about if I were you!"

Teresa grew angry. "Oh, and what do you know, being engaged?"

Immediate the two girls assumed sage expressions; age-old smiling wisdom sat on their lips, Martha's hairy and Elsie's smooth.

"Being engaged—when you are beginning life with a man and everything is before you, everything seems quite different," said Martha.

"You have something to live for," said Elsie. "Otherwise you have nothing to live for. Oh, Teresa," she exclaimed in sudden simple rapture, "isn't it true?"

Starched Martha was silent, a little perturbed and hungry.

"I sent for those books," said the other, ardently. "You know, what we were talking about, *How She Became a Happy Bride* and *The Secrets of Men's Love*, and they did send them under plain cover. My mother gave them to me." She leaned forward and her sweet, puffing breath came to Teresa: "And what they say is true, but they taught me so much I did not know," and shyly, she looked at her friend. "All that they say is true."

Martha said tartly: "Yes, but you got engaged before, didn't you, so what did you want them for?"

"Look," said Teresa, "after you get engaged and after you get married, you have to know things. For example, Aphrodite, in this book, when she bathed, used herbs to scent the water."

"What for?" said Martha, needling her with a look.

"To smell nice."

"I am afraid I don't think those things count in marriage," said Martha. "Marriage is different altogether."

The two other girls were downcast.

The day was like all days. The frantic old woman with bird's-nest hair who taught Lower Third slashed the boys' legs with a ruler, although it was against the law, and no one told on her because she had gone queer. The young brunette with Upper Third said the life was rotten and if any woman could get out of it by marriage, she ought to, no matter what the man was like; she'd take anybody herself. The jolly married teacher of Fourth, ungraded, and on lowest pay because she was a married woman, an old hand, did her embroidery, slapped her brats with her open hand and chuckled at Teresa's crowd.

"You certainly have a nice lot, especially that boy, George Wadling. I don't say I envy you, though you've got a lot to learn before you're finished. Bad blood in their veins, you'll do nothing for them; all that comes from heredity, bad blood, the parents are no good."

The woman of thirty-five with faded fair hair grumbled incessantly about her feet, about not sleeping with her "arthuritis", the inspectors, new methods which they expected to see, and the notes mothers sent her by the children. Sitting blowsily in the teachers' room, standing dully in the playground, patronizing, wretched, dull, deaf to hope and with no thought of a way out, they groused helplessly, in their own minds condemned to servitude for life—till sixty-five—and they might go queer before, like the old woman in Lower Third, especially if they remained, as desired by the Department, unmarried.

"You're not alive yet, my girl," said jolly Mrs Keeling, at her embroidery. "Wait till you've been kid-whacking for twenty years, then you'll know that the children of good parents are good youngsters, smart, prompt, and the kids of that sort can never be any good. I don't see what good you think you're doing. Wouldn't you rather have a class of normal youngsters, where you could see some improvement? Besides, you can't get round those young monkeys! I had that Stephen for two years. Yes, you don't know what life is."

"I don't know," said the faded blonde, wretchedly. "Perhaps she does."

"What does it matter who she teaches, she's only in till she can get a man to take her out of it," said the brunette, a lively young-ish woman of twenty-eight who liked to wear white and red. "Aren't we all? The kids don't give twopence for us, why should we wear ourselves out over them?"

"I hate it, I hate it," said the fair woman, rocking herself. "If I can only keep the kids down, I don't care if they never learn a line. That Milly Brown came in with a note from her mother again this morning about ink on her dress. I wish some of the mothers had to take care of my class for a whole day."

"I wish that, too," said Mrs Keeling. "They'd wake up."

Teresa burst out with: "Why do you stay in it if you hate it so much? I can't go now for I would have to repay the Government my training expenses, but you have all been teaching for years, and are free." There was a pained silence, then the brunette said: "What else can we do? The pay's good, where else would you get it? They can't throw you out. I don't know how to do anything else, do you?"

Teresa said: "No, but I'm learning stenography."

"Good for you," said the white-and-red.

The blonde woman sighed: "Who would be here at kid-whack-ing if they could do anything else? Oh, gosh, I'm on playground duty, where's the list?" The bell rang, they picked up their purses and exercise-books and hurried out. Teresa had a classroom between Mrs Keeling and the woman who had gone queer, Miss Abbott. The shaded path where her children collected led straight to this room, through a corridor, so that no one saw her children at any time, except through the two glass partitions of the neigh-bouring classes.

George Wadling, the Mad Boy, was again late, dirty and noisy.

He came rushing into the room, shutting the door with a bang which startled the classes on both sides. He shambled grotesquely into his seat, a comic act, pretending not to see the pot-plant on the teacher's desk. When he was sent out, to come in again properly, he stayed out. As he was lurking in the corridor, Head-master Parrott came prowling along, in his soft, shining shoes, and saw the imp up to his tricks. Parrott was seized with irritation; he had beaten the rascal many times, in the street he had heard George caterwauling after him, shrieking his name with hate and contempt. The slender, genteel man had a blood-hatred of the boy. He talked about him freely, in his presence, to upper-class children, teachers, and inspectors, predicted the penitentiary or madhouse for him and deliberately dogged the boy, hating him.

Although glad to have the feeble-minded children taken out of his classes, he had at the same time a feeling of bafflement; and he had begun to hate the supervisor, Teresa's friend, who meddled in the affairs of his school. Every boy in the defective class, even the pretty little deaf one, had tasted his stick. He knew the use of the stick, too, and was prepared to defend it against departmental rulings and murmurings of under-teachers; no use being mild with the little roughs from slum homes; it would be better not to teach them at all, but put them to hewing wood and drawing water.

Dr Smith, Teresa's supervisor, a tall and large man, a former footballer, was too big to think of hitting such children but he had no interest in them; his object in starting a community for them was to take them out of the classes so that they would not clog the progress of the normal children. A few years would be filled in, enough to enable them to fill in their names on slips of paper and count money, and then they would be "put to hewing wood and drawing water"; this was his idea too. "There must be some who do these jobs," he said, "and these unfortunates are as if designated by nature for it."

For several weeks, Headmaster Parrott had not seen George Wadling during school hours, though he had been able to catch up with him in the playground, when he was at his tricks, and to assault him with a cuff or a kick, during recess. Before that the Mad Boy had spent most of his time during school hours in the playground dawdling between the queer old woman's class and the headmaster's, between running away from school and being fetched back, creating diversions by entering the wrong classes with a silly grin, being sent to the headmaster again with a normal pupil as gendarme, and so forth. And now, for weeks, no sign of Georgie! Parrott missed him; his cutting jokes were getting rusty. No longer he and the giants of the Sixth Class trembled and roared with laughter as he whizzed down with his cane and a sneer at the same time. Parrott the Disciplinarian he called himself, and he repeatedly told the teachers under him that there was only one method in teaching and that was to hold the class down. "The rest is frills for romantic inspectors." His career in the schools, very successful, because he was young, was built on this principle.

George had been crouching at the door, alternately scowling and grinning at his hilarious classmates within. The headmaster, coming stealthily up behind, seized his prey. Cuffing him soundly about the head and shoulders and giving him a punch in the middle of the back, the headmaster helped him forward with a kick. Georgie ground his teeth and turned his wild fighting face to the man, lashing out at him with his squared fists. The headmaster kicked him two or three times, opening the door meanwhile, and dragged him into the room. Holding him there by one fist and his collar, he turned to the young teacher with a clean gleam of satisfaction. He shone with clerkly success from head to foot. Georgie, stained, weeping, in an old Norfolk suit of no colour at all, so queered was it by rain and dirt, had given in.

"Is he giving you trouble, Miss Hawkins? Is George Wadling misbehaving?" he asked gallantly, smiling at the girl. "Because if he is, I can deal with him, just send him to me, we're old friends, we understand each other, George Wadling and I. I know George pretty well and his tricks, and I won't let him give you any trouble."

Towards the end of his little speech, he clouded over and now looked down at the sullen child sharply. "You hear! I'll cane you to within an inch of your life, my friend, if you start any of your monkey tricks here. We've got you here to try and help you a bit, but if you give this nice young lady any of your smartness, do you hear, you'll hear of it from me at the end of a stick."

He let the boy go. George did not move and had to be pushed

two or three times before he trudged to his seat, which was in front. He sat down on it sullenly and managed to knock his books on the floor while doing so. Parrott let out a warning which caused him to pick them up again. As he piled them, he dropped one of them again. He now sat staring glumly and rather hopelessly in front of him. After a few more words, the headmaster footed it out in his neat style and politely closed the door. He was seen the next minute gossiping about the incident to Mrs Keeling, this large and untidy woman acting maternal benevolence with him.

Teresa's class was crushed, all their unsteady wits shaken like butterflies in a gale.

"Open your book, George," said Teresa, faintly, to the boy. He opened it with a bang and sat staring before him, his elbows on the desk, his lips hanging.

He was ruined. Miss Hawkins was with the enemy, protected by the enemy, who sidled up and danced down and smoodged around, but was lurking somewhere to tear his flesh with kicks and beat in his skull. George, who had a very timid, fitful intelligence over his books, was not to be fooled like his classmates upon the characters of persons; he made his own living in the streets, found his own bed. He had no friends in the class; while the poor things were flattered to have a famous criminal with them, they were frightened by his outrages and hid behind the skirt of good behaviour. Only one person understood him in the least; this was Joe Calton, a newsboy of ten, starved and dirty, of course, classified as feeble-minded but bright and lively in the streets. Joe also lived in the streets and often bedded down there. He showed his sympathy by getting up and saying brightly: "George will go to the reform school, Mr Parrott says," because the reform school hung over them all with its terror; even the normal and respectable little girls in the playground talked of it with dread.

"George will not go to reform school," said Teresa. "No one will go to reform school."

The children were astonished and also scandalized.

"Bad boys have to go to reform school," said a boy.

Georgie turned round and flapped his hands at them, sneering: "Ah, you pimps, you——" He grinned widely and looked round at the teacher, but contented himself with muttering: "Reform school!"

The children began to babble excitedly about reform school, they kicked you, beat you, if you didn't behave; they were engrossed by it. After a moment, she told them about another school they would go to some day, when it was built, and drew a plan of it on the blackboard. Georgie, peering at it through his hand, when he caught her eye said: "Uh-huh!" with contempt. The other children, however, were calm and listened as if to a story.

Teresa did not even try to talk Georgie over. When the master left that wing, George began his tricks again, but now as never before, with a savage, hateful air. He saw through the coquetry of the headmaster, and to him, the woman was the man's; that was what he knew about life. Before, Teresa had been able to calm him but now—now—he was twelve years old.

Lunch-time came and they filed out in their funny irregular chop-chop walk. The sky was overcast and the weather blustery, but it was close and there were intense moments of sun. The girl ate her lunch in the classroom and thought miserably of the beating of George in the morning. There was nothing to be done with him, only a struggle, day after day, without end, against him and against Parrott secretly (for Parrott envenomed could be a nasty enemy), and against the school, and against the night of the streets which was George's life. George was not allowed into the workshop of the school because he played tricks. There was nothing to occupy him but a pen, pencil, and a bit of paper, and over these the poor child had bent as he could, with glimmers of application; but his restlessness, the origin of which she did not know, gave him little time. He would do two or three lines with his untamed fingers and throw down the pencil. "I can't do it, I can't do it, what do I have to do it for?" She stood at her desk, looking down, frowning; he was ruined. Presently she raised her eyes to the neighbouring classrooms, sat down, got up, walked round with clenched hands; at one moment, her hand on her chest, leaning against the desk, she panted. Her head was on fire, she felt as if she had been beaten, while a poison seemed to be running through her. What was to be done? This torment of desire came every day as the sun mounted. At midday a sleep strong as death approached and hovered round her, ready to snatch; she had to stand up during the lunch hour to keep awake, and with it came this paroxysm. When the children came in, she would look at them through a haze, she had to walk carefully not to stagger, and these feelings mounted, mounted.

Now she heard herself groan, as she stood by the desk, and she looked sickly round to see if anyone was near. But no one was near, and she remained standing against the partition, pressing the back of her head against the cooler glass, staring wildly through the farther partition into the other empty room. If she could only lie down now, yield to her sleep and forget her troubles. "What will I do?" She walked heavily over to the windows, and stared at the backs of the tenements in that street. These were not horrible to her even though she knew what they were like inside; they were the verminous, dangerous, soot-blackened nests from which George and his classmates came. But they were a refuge. The narrow windows and chimney-pots meant that the people there must be very poor and glad to rent a room very cheaply. In the Bay, she shuddered away from every boy who approached her, for gossip was attached to each one. She pretended not to see a hulking, aggrieved young medical student who tried to talk to her, because, though they said he was a "genius", the girls laughed at his ugly pallor and loose mouth. There, if she took him, they would think she was desperate. Here, in the streets at nightfall, she could take anyone, labourer, middle-aged man, boy, anyone who appealed to her, and no perspicacious friends, sage brothers, or anyone at all who had ever known her, would come between.

At two o'clock, when the class was back again, George, after an access of gaiety, re-established his lost fame with the little class when he ran to the window with a wild whoop and jumped out. The children had the best time of their lives, and some of the children next door, in ravished astonishment, stood in their seats, paying no attention to Mrs Keeling's commanding voice. The boy looked two or three times through the window with his peculiar whistling, his expression no longer vicious, even a tentative smile of friendship on his face, but Teresa looked at him dully and helplessly and he vanished.

The deed was extreme. The rest of the class, after their laugh, were afraid and simmered busily at their work. Stephen, the silly, soft-eyed boy, tall for his age and well-dressed, got up and said: "When Georgie comes back will I take him with a note to Mr

Parrott, please?" Hopeful and eager he looked. In his other classes, he had always been considered too silly for this mission, but here, among his equals, he might be picked.

Just as they were tumbling out of school, bubbling with the joys of the day, preceded by the newspaper boy, Joey, who had to dart off to call at the newspaper offices for the early editions, she was visited by a Sixth Class boy with a message from Mr Parrott that she was wanted in the office. She went there with wildly beating heart, although the headmaster was smooth with her and she was not in his jurisdiction. She distrusted the small, malicious man, false-debonair; he might have some curious scheme for George or one of the other boys and she was in a difficult position between the warring potentates, Parrott and Dr Smith.

"Don't be frightened," he said, however, on seeing her face. "It is nothing terrible, only the father of Sylvia", and he smiled sympathetically. "You look as if you expected to be scolded."

He took her to an empty classroom, where she talked across a table to a thin-haired, middle-aged man with a sweet, long, oval face, who was reticent, earnest, as if he had been struck. He asked in a murmur if she had "tested Sylvia's intelligence"?

"Yes."

"What did you find out?"

She hesitated. Sylvia herself sat in the headmaster's room, adjoining; she held herself quite erect, by the table, still, looking in front of her and smiling faintly. She was a well-built, early developed, graceful, soft-complexioned girl of twelve who sat all day long thus, in a stupor, for ever wrapped in the slumbers of infancy. She had a sweet, timid manner and was beautifully dressed and cared for by her father, a widower. Teresa glanced at the girl.

"She is not doing much here at school."

"There is no hope then?"

The headmaster vivaciously broke in. "No, you see, nothing can be done for her, it is quite impossible."

The father looked at them both. He got up, took his hat, and said with habitual gentleness: "Thank you very much, thank you for telling me the truth, and thank you for anything you have done for my poor girl."

She went back to get her bag and papers, but lingered in the quiet room, from which, in the cool of the afternoon, all madness had departed. The yard was still, too, the yelling and scrambling was over. She looked out the window and saw Georgie Wadling lingering round the washbasins in the long empty shed. He was looking at the windows and saw her at once. He continued to look at her, as if with regret, half-expecting to be called; but she did not call him. He stood hulking near the basins, turned on a tap, turned it off, and dawdled away up the yard. As she turned away, she saw Sylvia's father walking slowly, his stricken face slightly bent, leading by her small tapering fingers the girl Sylvia. Sylvia, her hat straight on her head, her curls arranged primly over her shoulders, her dress neat, exactly as she always sat in the playground, all the hours of recess, minced beside him with her faint smile. She was exactly like a life-sized doll. The father turned to her and said something. Sylvia, still smiling faintly, came abreast of him. He arranged the neat curls on her shoulder, took out his handkerchief, and wiped something off her cheek.

"A fiendish job," said Teresa to herself.

She walked out of the now silent school and to the Y.W.C.A. cafeteria where she had something to eat and waited until it was time for her hour of Latin at the coaching college to begin. After the Latin, she went to a business college to learn typing and shorthand.

10. Mr Jonathan Crow Who Coached in Latin

Mr Jonathan Crow was the young man who coached Teresa in Latin at the Tutorial College where she went three times a week before Business College. He had a gentle, plain manner while teaching, a thin face and dark eyes, and seemed to be about twenty-eight. He was poorly dressed, always in black, with white shirts and heavy-soled boots in which, he had told her, pointing to them with a grimace, he walked home several miles every evening, saving the fare.

The Tutorial College was a dingy, penurious private school, run by an old high-school teacher on the sixth floor of an old office building, near the Central Railway Station. A maze of wooden partitions had been run through a whole floor, cutting it into cubicles, in each one of which there were two or three seats, a table and chairs and a single electric bulb glaring overhead. Poor teachers, poor students, and graduates without jobs coached there and were of all ages, but all were men. The teachers were mostly thin, tense, fretful and with tired eyes behind spectacles.

There was no joy in them; they had long since run through the hope of good jobs and timid affairs with girl students. But Jonathan Crow's smile was very young; he was really only twenty-three, his teeth were white as a dog's. The grey hairs in his head he had paid for by his intense labours and by these he had dragged himself out of a slum home and the prospects there as errand-boy or paper-hanger. He had just graduated, was a Master of Arts, and had earned by his academic successes a travelling scholarship to a European university. But the sailing date was months off and between that and now he had to pay his own expenses and buy himself a reasonable wardrobe. In all these years he had had only one suit and one pair of good boots at a time. It still looked as if this was all he might have to take with him on the boat, if other necessities were to be bought, although he might help out his wardrobe with new slacks and a sweater and perhaps a university blazer. After his years in London were through, what then? A pedagogue's career—it would then be too late to enter the government service, too late to become a draughtsman, lawyer, or doctor. All this he foresaw now, when he had only just graduated, and he foresaw a whole lifetime of stumping wearily up and down city streets in thick-soled boots, in some clerk's or teacher's job, even as he was doing now. Only, perhaps, with an accumulation of degrees, he would get a little more money. As for luxury, the ordinary suburban life, even though he had given his whole life to the prospect of success and safety, he would not be able to indulge even in that. For him, no wife without money, and if no money, then no wife.

All this he told Teresa, from time to time, in his soft doleful tones, as he sat by her elbow correcting her exercises. Sometimes he walked down a few blocks with her, late at night, when the tuition was over, telling her how dreary was his life. He had never been able to buy football boots or a school jersey, though he was tough, strong, and active, so he had had no school sports. "I'm old before my time, I've already joined the ranks of those seedy old duffers," he said, pointing back over his shoulder with his hand as he tarried with Teresa at the narrow slot which was the doorway to the old building. "As for kids," he said despairingly, "when can I have kids? And what kind of youngsters do teachers have? They never have brilliant children, and if not, I know the grind isn't worth it, I'd make them bricklayers. I'd have been a corker bricklayer myself——" and suddenly the flash of his smile. "Revolutionists or government serfs, that's the kind of youngsters pedagogues have—that is, unless a person has influence," and he drooped again. Then abruptly he would leave her, stopping, saying "Ta-ta", making a right-about-turn and starting off at a rapid pace.

To Teresa, all that he said was marvellous, full of the mysteries of adult life and full of the wisdom of the university hill in Camperdown. The university seemed to her a gleaming meadow, in which beautiful youths and girls strolled, untangling intellectual and moral threads, but joyfully, poignantly, and weaving them together, into a moving, living tapestry, something into which love, the mind, the soul, and living beauties like living butterflies and early summer flower-knots were blended. Though he was morose he had woven part of this mysterious fabric with the others, girls and boys up there, in its halls of splendour and little rooms; he was wonderful, to her, learned. She was astonished within herself at his pity and kindness which made him, such a learned man, so humbly talk to her, an ignorant girl, of these things and of his private life. The university seemed to her a suburb of Oxford, Jena, or the Sorbonne. If she could get the fare to that suburb, she too could spend glorious days, full-blown hours teasing out the ideal and the real. She thought of how he had suffered and of the noble ideal which had kept him going, in his poverty and pain, for so long. She would do it too.

She never cared to sit down and work out how many years she would have to study to get to the hill in Camperdown, how much money she needed, how many nights would be put in falling over textbooks, or how much money was needed for them either; nor did she compare the wages of young teachers and typists with the cost of a university education. She merely put it vaguely to herself that the sessions at the business college would help her to a quiet office job, out of which she would pay her share at home, pay all expenses, learn Latin, and so be admitted to these classrooms of the ideal and the real.

At night, jaded, yellow, hungry and unable to keep her eyes wide open, she peered at the copy of *Pro Murena*, set for the next university entrance, and at the English crib alongside. Jonathan alone tried to teach the grammar a little more systematically. The teachers knew little themselves, or they were too tired from teaching in the daytime to bother about the hopeless, drab creatures who came to them at night. If a brilliant student turned up by rare chance among them, well and good—he would get himself through the examination, and as for the rest—it kept up their hopes for a few more months or years, before they faced the last failure and the death of the last hope. That was how they looked at it. Jonathan was not yet so dulled. He encouraged the poor girl and believed that she would accomplish some little thing, just as he himself had done. He thought she was older than she was; she, too, was worn with disappointment and work.

One evening he walked all the way down to the Quay with her, a distance of a mile, and now he told her his age was twenty-three and that his looks came from grind, from starvation too. In his low melancholy tones he quoted—

> *"This mournful truth is everywhere confessed,*
> *Slow rises worth by poverty depressed."*

She thought this was his own poetry.

"I never took a tram, do you know," said he. "I walked everywhere, even miles out into Leichhardt when I had to go and see my aunt there, through those rows of yellow slums——" and he made a sound of revolt.

He always ate at home, or carried his lunch, never having had money for lunch out.

Teresa told him she walked everywhere, too; and so every night to the Quay, from the Tutorial College, uphill and downhill. It resulted in an outlay on boot-leather, however, and was it worth it? Of course, they got the exercise. Mr Crow again showed his thick soles, standing on one foot in the middle of the pavement just as they were passing Hyde Park, to do so; and she showed what she wore, crepe rubber soles, which never wore out and were light as a feather. They had first walked across the park in front of the railway and then down Elizabeth Street, which runs along one side of Hyde Park, and then up King Street to Macquarie Street to the waterside. He would have to make the trip back again, but he said he did not mind, he was in no hurry to get home. He felt fresh tonight and could walk for miles. He was out of the penitentiary; he was free to starve now until the time came for him to sail to England, five or six months off. Laughing, glancing brightly up through his spectacles, he looked down at his boots again. "I got them at Stonewall Jackson's."

"Mine are from Joe Gardiner's."

After dark, the streets, especially near the parks, were filled with loungers who solicited the women walking by, calling, whispering, commenting, laughing, whistling, joking, or cursing. The men stood near the kerb or just outside the kerb on the street, or leaned against the shop-corners or against rubbish tins, or doors, just outside the light from the street lamps. They held themselves outside a certain line, defined no doubt by the fall of light, and the female pedestrians passed quickly in between those two lanes. Their lean, narrow-cheeked faces under their cheap hats looked fierce and evil in the half-light. There were prowlers, too, slouching along, without the assurance of the standing men. Sometimes, a couple or a party went down a dark street, or a tiny alley. Two dishevelled women tottered in front of them, holding a sailor between them, skirted two rubbish tins and dragged their man protesting down a brightly lighted paved entrance which led behind two shops. An angry drunk, hanging on to an iron pillar supporting an awning, confessed to them as they strode past: "I'm flamin' bloody sick, that's what I am." He looked to them for an answer. When they passed he said in an aggrieved tone: "You can't say that to a woman, it's not polite. I'm flamin' blanky sick, that's what I am."

"It's like this every night," said the girl. She told Crow what a bad street it was at night; how she scurried past, on her long way home, listening to their muffled words, pretending not to hear.

He growled. He had strange moods. He said: "You see, if women didn't try to make themselves so different—for example, if they wore short hair and pants—you wouldn't get this. It's your own fault."

His tone was brusque and cold, she thought she bored him; but as they passed under the lamp-posts, she looked and saw his starved skin, the sparse stiff hair, the rain-bitten hat, the stuff of his summer shirt, the plain spectacles set in silver over his liquidly sad brown eyes. There was something pathetic in the way he walked, dragging one foot a little, hunching one shoulder slightly, and in his tilted hat and the firm twist to his long dark mouth. He had been stamped by poverty. Strange, more curious than insulting, were his sudden grunts, mutterings, his rude sayings. In the midst of her thoughts, he blurted out: "See that little nipper there? I was a newsboy too, when I was his age—I say, he seems to know you."

She saw Joey Calton running through the traffic to her.

"Hullo, Miss Hawkins."

"Hullo, Joey."

He was holding out something to her. She took it and saw a coloured picture of the Virgin Mary in red and blue, her heart in red, bloody flesh, visible.

"I got it at the City Dumps," said Joey. "Can I put it up on the wall?"

"Yes, Joey, tomorrow."

"All right, Miss," he said pertly, and dashed off again, in front of a car, slippery as a sardine.

She told him about this boy who sold papers in this area and sometimes watched for her, when she was coming from late classes.

"Can he be an imbecile? The tests say so, but he's so smart and quick in the streets, and he scours the city from end to end, he knows every street, all the back streets. He goes out two or three times a week to the City Dumps to see what he can get. Is that stupid? Or is there something wrong with the tests?"

"Little devil," cried Jonathan Crow, appreciatively. "You're wrong about that youngster, that's the trouble with girls, they don't live the same way as boys. You see, you don't know boys. They're devils, take my word for it, and what you take for smartness is just a slick way of doing and saying things, they pick it up from the street gang. Don't get soft over them, if that's the kind of kid you have. They need a lamming sometimes." He laughed. "Gee, don't I know! I'm a slum kid myself, I've got friends still there. Snowy Mitchell, that's my pal, goes down there into Golden Grove with the University Settlement to entertain the kids. He tried to get me along. Nothing doing. Snowy's all right," he amended, "but my cousin's a social worker there." He paused. "A church organization it is, really, some sort of a church army." He looked apologetically at her. "He believes that old stuff, can you believe it?—I've jawed at him——"

He waited for the cue.

"Yes, yes."

"How did you get out of the church?"

"What church?"

"I mean religion, God."

"Oh! We're atheists."

He looked at her admiringly. "Gee, I wish I'd had that grit——" He said dolefully: "I tried to believe in God for months, after I broke away."

"Why?"

"Don't you think a person needs to believe in something? I mean, you've got to have something to believe in. I tried a personal God; no soap, it didn't work."

She looked sideways at him.

"Can't you live for yourself?"

"Myself alone?"

"Yes."

"Can you?"

"Certainly."

"That's wonderful," he said frankly. "I wish I had your grit."

After a glowing pause, she asked: "And what about the man in the church organization, what does he say about the slums?"

"He says the good stuff rises and gets out, and the bad stuff just stays there and rots, then the bad 'uns from above go down."

"That's bunk."

He said, with choler: "He ought to know, he's spent his life with them. Now, you see, that's just what I mean, with you girl school-ma'ams, you're idealist about those kids, you don't see them as they are. A real educational system would take them and knock them around, give them what they give themselves and turn them into real tough guys. This coddling weakens them. What have they got to do with fancy reading-methods? I know I just ground it out, I came before the fancy reading-methods and I sweated blood and it gave me what little grit I have."

These ideas were new to her, and she supposed they were his invention. He had a hectoring tone, commanding her what to do and think, which both aroused and intimidated her. He must have felt it himself, for he immediately changed his tune and told her about himself. The coaching lessons and clerking in an office downtown kept him in bread and beer for the present; he had not taken a summer vacation, but had been teaching ever since last November and he felt fagged out. He was living at home with his parents as he had done since childhood. His mother was a sturdy, brave woman who kept the family together and his father a weak kind of fellow, without any backbone, who would have turned into a rouseabout probably long ago if it had not been for the firm will of his mother. He had often longed to be like other boys, with new clothes and the time to play football, but he had borne the misery, the self-sacrifice, and slavery patiently since he first got the notion, at the age of ten; because as far as he could see, for a poor man the only way to get out of the rut was to follow it to the end.

Now he was at the end. How queer it was to be free. He felt like a lifer who is pardoned and is so frightened by the outdoors that he wants to go back to his cell. But he was forcing himself to idle and take notice of new things. When August came, he would sail first class "among the nobs" and lie at his ease for six weeks at sea. After that came the untrammelled life of a post-graduate student in London, with no set classes, his own thesis to work out, no responsibility save to his student adviser, no living to earn and no will to follow but a youth's will. "Perhaps I can learn to enjoy life a little."

Softly, he bent his eyes on her, with the humid brightness of a little dog.

"What do I know of life but grind, a knack of biological survival? Would you believe it? When they gave the intelligence tests in philosophy in second year, I came away down near the middle of the class and Snowy was among the first three. But I get the University Medal and Snowy just makes an average pass. That shows what the game is worth," he continued dismally.

His university talk was wonderful to her. She had never before had anything to do with a university man and it dazzled her that he was a medallist, a scholar, a coach, and yet so modest that he would explain himself fully to her. She told him, greatly moved, that she too wanted to get her degree and later go abroad.

"But I have no money and I must be my own scholarship out of my own earnings."

"That's wonderful," he cried. "I've never met a girl with such grit."

At the wharf he touched his hat, saying: "I don't take my hat off, on principle, just to get rid of those relics of chivalry."

He smiled at her winningly, wheeled round, and was off with a steady stride, on his way back.

11. *Coming Along in the Blowy Dark*

SHE sat outside on the boat and stared at the frothing water. She thought: "Could I love that man?" Continents of cloud were passing across the moon and the moonlit sky; it was dark at times, the wind on the whitecaps had a reedy sound. The boat hand, Manoel, came round near her at the port, looking at her, and after a while went in. The engines changed sound.

Coming along the beach path in the blowy dark, that night, she heard strains of music. One of the boat sheds was open: Joe Martin's; a lantern inside threw its long dim beams across the narrow footpath. When she reached the lighted patch, she stopped and craned her neck. It was Leo playing, but in a weird way; the song that Leo was playing, something unknown to her, went on and on, winding out, with patches of frenzy, patches of melancholy, an untold misery telling itself in hysteria; and an improvisation, a long breath, a returning idea, like a life, moving as the wind of this night. People were drifting nearer along the silent beach path and a few persons had already collected along each side of the ray of light; most were in the dark and one could see only a few of the figures standing there at the entrance to the little boat shed, shoulder to shoulder, mournfully enchanted, speechless, looking in. There was anxiety in their listening faces, drawn as if they heard the steps of danger coming nearer, and of something queer but true in such wild, wanton, miserable music.

Leo sat on a box, his guitar half-embraced on his knees, his dark curly head bent so low that nothing could be seen of his face behind the fallen hair. One lock hung loose from his head. His muscular hands moved fast and small. There he sat, without moving otherwise, so bowed, his head so low, minute after minute, playing on and on at that music they had not heard

129

before. He stopped, raised his head, and flung back the lock of hair. His eyes, as they spun over the people, on their way to the roof, narrowed, had an angry look. He stayed for a moment with his head lifted to the roof and his face pale, convulsed; then bent forward over the guitar again and began one of the old airs, *O dolce Napoli, O suol beato!* which the Italian fishermen sang day and night. Some of the people moved away and Teresa came closer, but he weakened, began to strum. His audience had now dissolved. Some could be seen passing like thick shadows under the single light of the sandwich shop towards the wharf; some were on their way home towards the Lawny and passed under the light which stood by the large flame-tree.

The wind started to sing, with intervals. The moon, at times, bolted out of the clouds and tottered boldly by itself in threadbare black space; round it, then, almost invisible, immense in diameter, was a vapour-ring, that looked a hundred yards across. How the sea groaned! The tide, half-way down, made running jumps at the beach as it retired. The small collier was still anchored in the bay, her riding lights shining. This was surprising, for the coastwise vessels never used the bay, and it should have been easy for her to replace one boy who had swum ashore. They tried to get one of the local boys, but the reputation of the ship and of the firm was bad; the colliers were called coffin-ships, one had gone down with all hands off Bulli in the last storm, and anyone could see now that big weather was approaching. The storm signals had gone up this afternoon at the signal station. Beyond the collier jogged the bucket-dredge, which slept in the bay month after month, when it came in from its day's work in the deep channel. She had one riding light and the small tip of the night watchman's pipe. The night watchman was a friend of Leo's and sent messages to Teresa by human telegraph, "Tell your sister to come and see me, you bring her, it's lonely here at night. I can hear you all, but I don't talk to no one."

There was still a light downstairs in the Hawkins house. When she opened the screen door, Kitty called: "Is that you, Leo?"

"No, it's me. Leo's along at Joe Martin's."

"How do you know?"

"I just saw him."

She heard her father leave the staircase and go to his room. She went out to the kitchen to get her dinner which had been kept hot on top of a saucepan since the family (Father, Kitty, and Leo) had eaten at six-thirty. There were two plates covered on top of two saucepans of boiling water. One was Lance's, one hers; they were the same, divided with absolute fairness, so many chunks of meat, so many potatoes. She sat down at once at the oilcloth-covered table and ate greedily.

There was a soft noise and there stood Kitty in a chocolate linen dress. Her dark hair, in a bob, fell straight at each side of her oval cheeks and in a straight fringe across her forehead. Her large eyes were tired tonight, with dark smudges under them; her dark soft mouth seemed to tremble. "What was he doing?"

"In the boat shed, playing the guitar. Some people were listening to him on the beach path."

"A fine time of night to be playing."

"Well—he'll be home soon."

"I don't know."

"What's the matter?"

"He said he was going to leave home. They had a squabble, Dad wants him to come home and go to bed."

"Squabble about what?"

"Dad told him that those who didn't work didn't complain of the food, Leo said he'd go and get a woman who would cook for him, Dad said what did he mean by that, and Leo said he was going to get married. Dad blew up."

Teresa became conscious that the meat was leathery, grey.

Kitty said: "They had an argument. Dad said he was too young to leave home, and Leo said he'd rather give the money to his wife than here to us." Kitty sat down at the table, put her round brown arms out in front of her and bent her head; Teresa saw the fat tears roll.

"Dad said he not only didn't work but wanted to leave home too, all the burden would come on Lance and you."

"Leo ought to leave home if he wants to."

"They had a terrible argument. Leo said he was going to take a place on the collier that wants a hand."

"He has to go back to his factory."

Kitty, looking very soft, with her habitual stoop, glancing down at the table with eyes blacker than ever, continued: "Leo gave Daddy lip and Daddy kicked him, then Leo saw red and began to shout at Daddy. He said he was striking camp, he kept saying: 'I'm going, I'll vamoose the ranch, don't worry, I'll settle down myself.'"

Kitty, shadowing into tears, stooped farther over, scraping with her fingers at a candle-grease spot on the table, her lip trembling. "He said he hated me."

"Who said?"

"Leo said. He said he hated me, he wouldn't be nagged at by all of us, he wouldn't be keeping me when I didn't work." She tried to go on with the story. She gave up and simply cried; her hair bobbed round her cheeks and the little fringe stuck to her low, well-curved forehead, while her living eyes rose at Teresa, momently, as she told her story and wept.

"What for? What did he say he hated you for?"

"Because I nagged him, he said. I was mending his shirt, and I said what you said last night, that I ought to get some money for doing it—it was just a joke on my part—and he jumped up from the table like a loony and threw a glass in the corner of the room and smashed it. I had to sweep it up—I just had to sweep it up——"

She pointed to a dustpan full of glass and dust. She looked at her sister, pushing her fringe back, her eyes blinking away the tears. The fine olive skin was faintly mottled; then her eyes brightened and a flush flew into her cheeks.

"It isn't fair. I do everything for him. For Lance too. Why doesn't Leo try to get another job?"

"He says he's not allowed."

"Do you think it's true or he's just lazy? Why can't he get a job at the same trade when they're locked out?"

"Oh, I think it's true," said Teresa.

"It's stupid to keep him from making a living. Then he gets no pay."

Teresa pushed aside her plate and looked at her sister. "Why don't you go and get a job yourself?"

Kitty sank into her usual brown study for a while and then bashfully confessed: "I answered a couple of ads for secretary."

"For secretary? You can't do that."

"Where it said beginner, or shorthand not needed. I can type. I got one answer. He said to go and see him. I telephoned him, but he said I had to have a neat appearance, to interview people——" Her lip trembled again. She got up, picked up

Teresa's plate, and took it to the sink. When her back was turned and she was scraping, Teresa heard, "Where am I to get the proper dress? I could have managed the fare! I couldn't go in this, this isn't an office dress."

"What about your dress you wore to the wedding?"

"I hate it. You think I don't know it's ugly?"

There was a silence.

"This old dress," said Kitty, "and that brown voile——"

"You'll have to get out of here before it's too late."

"But how? To get money, you must have a job, and to get a job, you must have money. Nancy Palmer got a job and I heard her talking, she had on her best dress, silk stockings, and a permanent. Her mother and father gave it to her.

Teresa cried, stamping out of the kitchen: "I'll give you the money, why don't you ask for it?"

Kitty became quiet, polishing the sink round and round.

"Will you really?"

"How much do you want?"

"I think two pounds."

"All right!"

Kitty turned round and looked at her. Unexpectedly, her face broke up into a crowd of little joys, she smiled, her irregular white teeth all showed, her hair danced, her eyes closed half-way and looked like Leo's, and a gleeful laugh struggled in her throat. What a buoyant, jolly young woman she really was, thought Teresa, better than I am—charming!

"Really? Two pounds! I could manage with that. Two pounds . . ." She stopped laughing and became serious, plotting, planning her outfit, her journeys to the city, and looking anxiously at her sister and with guilt, "I have a few shillings of my own," she added apologetically. "It isn't fair to take it from you, you work hard enough for it, but I need stockings. At work you must look decent, you mustn't look as if you needed the job, they take notice of that, they don't want to take you on if you look as if you needed it."

"It's all right," said Teresa.

"I think it's funny, don't you, that they prefer people who look as if they don't need it?" She laughed gaily.

Teresa looked at her with disgust. "What do they care whether we need it or not?" she said. "They don't care about us."

"I don't mean they care about us, but you must look decent."

Teresa leaned against the doorpost, studied the worn patterns of the oilcloth, tried to think of Jonathan Crow.

Kitty said in her husky tone: "Martha was with the same firm seven years! Imagine getting paid every week for seven years! She must have a lot of money." She looked at her sister.

"Well, get a job," said Teresa. Kitty, circulating in the kitchen, straightening things, excited, stopped near her sister and looked short-sightedly at her, very happy, wanting to hug her, wanting to tell her about the man she loved. Teresa, with a glance at her, hauled off and lounged into the passage. All the time she was thinking: "I must leave school, it will show whether I have any chance of success or not." She heard the roughening wind outside and the water lapping; she was conscious of a stirring within and without; she turned round to her sister, and said: " 'There is a tide in the affairs of men which taken at the flood leads on to fortune.' "

Kitty's face fell. She paused; she took two steps after her sister and said timidly: "When would I be able to get the money?"

"Now! I have it now," Tess said roughly. "Now, you can have it now."

She walked to the stairs, bolted up them three at a time and strode into her room. Kitty disturbed her when she wanted to think of what she must do tomorrow.

On Friday she had cashed her cheque at the bank, withdrawn five pounds although she had no plans made, and the money was all now in an open drawer, thrown carelessly in. She took two of the notes, without considering her own plans, and thrust them into Kitty's hand, as Kitty came upstairs.

Kitty looked at the money, dazzled, and burst out in a flurry of thanks. As soon as Teresa could she escaped into her room to think about her tomorrow.

She saw herself, again and again, walking from the boat, up Macquarie Street, by the bowling green, down William Street, up towards Darlinghurst; and then George Wadling toiling down the same hill towards her, tugging at his little wagon full of kindling wood. His dirty face looked up at her and then down again without recognition. She saw his head on the window-sill. Dr Smith was standing beside her, large, obscurely unhappy himself, clumsy in his relations with people in some hopeless struggle she knew nothing of. Irritated by some quarrel with the headmaster, he had walked across with her and said: "I no longer sleep with my wife, I sleep on the back veranda." He had said that, walking down the street. Walking across the gardens, he said: "I get my collars at Larbalestier's."—Such stupid, unworthy remarks that she was ashamed of him. This was the man who had told her about Glasgow, Paris, Jena; Héloïse and Abélard, a wonderful story in which Abélard taught Héloïse everything in the world; philosophy, languages, about Faust and Marguerite, an old German story in which an old man changed into a young man. The university welter-weight champion was already eaten by middle age; he was thirty-three.

Yet even thinking of Dr Smith, and Aunt Eliza, who had paid for her to continue school, she thought more of the mess of raffia wools and frames in her cupboard, of the darned holes in her stockings, of the chalk in the schoolroom air. She had been stuck in there too young, she was incapable of looking after them, she knew nothing of any kind, not even to teach madmen.

12. *A Train for Narara, Fifty Miles North*

A TRAIN for Narara, fifty miles north, left the Central Station in the morning, at nine-thirty-five. On one side of the large central hall is a dark pavilion lighted by clerestories. In it is an island of ticket-windows. Above this soared far up the sandstone canopy, with light criss-crossing as in a cathedral and pigeons flying about thirty feet above ground; and the shadows of people passing in the sunlit tram terminal. The hall is in shadow cut by the light of four entrances. Near the arch which leads to the train indicator for the northern lines, Teresa had been walking, much agitated, about twenty minutes, when she heard a voice from the ticket-windows and saw one of the clerks, a light-faced young man with reddish hair, leaning forward to look at her and beckoning to his friend. At this she picked up her little bag and walked rapidly to the Newcastle ticket-window, where she could get her ticket.

"What do they think? That I am going to commit suicide? It's queer how you give yourself away, in any case."

She walked out of the other door and to the platform gate with a busy air, and after a few minutes was admitted with the others to the waiting train. She had not been thinking about her plans, so much as seeing two scenes which ran themselves through her mind. At first, the playground, empty at this hour, quiet and fresh with the wind blowing across it from the uncut grass, the Public Gardens and the Domain; and then the teachers' room, smelling of coarse wall paint, hot face powder and sweet tea. They were scenes to which she would never return, bygone days; she thought of them both agonizedly, nevertheless.

As soon as she entered the railway carriage, the last link snapped, she forgot the school. She felt as strong and clairvoyant as one in a rage. Where were the others in this carriage going?

Was there another here, perhaps that dark-haired man nearly opposite who was markedly observing her from the corner of his eye, who had found out that chains evaporate as soon as you try to throw them off? Chains do not exist, they are illusions.

Most of the people sat congealed in a sort of sullen despair, doing what they must, going where they must. If they only knew that it was only a matter of running away. She understood her own former timidity for the first time.

Outside it was very dark and a storm-wind howled round the train. When they saw the sky between cuttings, there were black bombs of rain bursting into the hills; the lakes and watercourses had an intense ghastly shine, a glittering, streaked and daubed silver skin, rolling out there like an earth-creature married to the sky, wind, and wet.

The people in the almost-dark carriage crouched more and more. The lights came on. They rattled over bridges where the swollen water gushed a few feet below; going through the hills the new water, like the rolling of many chains, was heard running off.

What was he thinking of, the dark-haired, thin-faced, middle-aged man who had been looking at her? Now he was sunk in himself, sorry for himself. She had never felt so well in her life. She could hear laughter, from the hills shouldering off their forests, from the rivers slipping away down, the cries of the bitter trees struggling against each other, rooted in one spot, killing the small things in their shade. Looking out over the numerous crests, rising now towards the range, she felt at once a horror of the rooted forest and its secular, aimless, but stern struggle, and a joy, a veritable jubilation in the road which had been cut through the wild, that goes down to water holes and skirts bluffs and rises to prospects, to the tops of the hills, where many ridges are only horny ripples in a withered beach long jilted by the sea.

She did not know where she was going; she was outward bound. This first train journey was only the first stride on a grand perilous journey. All the other people in the train seemed to her now buried in strange debris, not really alive as she was, as her excitement increased. Alone, she found the way out, which alone does not lead to blindness, years of remorse and hungry obscurity.

For the next stage of her trip, at any rate, after sleeping at her aunt's house at Narara, a wooden cottage in an orchard, she would find the road to Harper's Ferry. Up here, a few summers ago, when she was still a high-school girl, they had gone picnicking in the range with the Carlins, a family of three young people, and Tom Carlin had told her: "Harper's Ferry is over that way", his westward pointing arm in a careless wave taking in the valley, the foothills opposite, and beyond, the faint blue ridge of the Nepean range. She had often heard of it since, a beauty spot in wild country, a lone road taken by summer walking parties of university girls and young teachers, leading to a ford, or a ferry where a settler named Harper had once ferried people across.

She remembered the sunlit day. They had mounted the dripping wooden staircase by the rocks, out of the deep gully, a mere pothole in the hills. Delicate ferns and moss grew in the shade and the young eucalypts shot fifty and sixty feet into air to reach the sun at the top of the cliff. The air was wet with spray, in the heat the aromatic oils of the hardy plants intoxicated the air. Behind Tom Carlin and her, flirting and laughing, had been Jerry Carlin, the older boy, and her cousin Ellen. Tom was a tall, thin, attractive boy, with black hair, an engaging voice.

"What will you do when someone makes love to you?"

"I'll wait and see. Perhaps I'll be the one to make love."

"Would you make love?"

"If I wanted to."

"Make love to me?"

"You're not the one."

Later, when evening came, she had repulsed Tom again; she was ashamed of the silly scene of Ellen, a tall girl, sitting on the knee of Jerry, a middle-sized man, on the piano stool, while they both sang "The Last Rose of Summer". This was Ellen, the starched cousin who had sung in the choir on Sundays and wanted to marry a modern young Minister of the Gospel. But she was even then twenty-seven and her morale smashed by an unlucky affair that lasted five years without marriage. She despised and disliked Ellen with her soul. She was her dead mother's niece and in her father's words had been "educated out of a husband". Ellen had been not only to high school but to technical college and it was this, thought the family, which had frightened off the men. Ellen had a certain talent in sculpture. "Of what use is that to a housewife?" was the family saying. The whole venture had been absurd, and Ellen's parents were regretting it, while Ellen, with bitter tongue and endless tantrums, took it out of them. The house with Ellen in it was only a shelter for a night, and she would turn from there into the mountains to see what she could see. If she had any plan at all, it was this then: to walk somehow, asking her way, to Harper's Ferry, which was about sixty miles from Sydney and then walk back. When she got back, the first flurry would have died down and she would get a room somewhere, where no one would come to bother her; no one would take any further interest in her and she could begin as a typist and save up to get her degree and go abroad. Her ideas about going abroad had developed slightly in the past few weeks. She now wanted to go to the Sorbonne, like a friend of Mr Crow's, another travelling scholar who was taking ship at the same time as Crow, a Mr Fountain. As to Harper's Ferry, she had asked no more questions about it than about fees at the university. She had never looked at a map, and if there was an obscure reason for her choosing this spot of all spots, it was perhaps that she imagined it as a lonely, dark, dread, endlessly solitary, inhuman place and had heard that a murder had been committed near there. She had a vision of a dreary wild crossing, ancient trees; beyond that nothing, but it was her way.

Yet she loved that broad, soft Narara Valley which runs north and south for many miles. Narara Creek, a clear creek, runs at the foot of the eastern slope down to Brisbane Water. On the east, where her aunt lived among the small holdings and orchards too sheltered from the rising run, the unprofitable land rises roughly into small, round, spurred hills covered with new scrub. From the flat tops of the bluffs, which are reached by following a sharp spur, the rich and broad western side which gets all the day's sun, in its entirety, is in sight, laid out in a cloth of dark orchards and light fields with the light brushmarks of pines and the black young forest of the pine nursery to the north. There are big-globed fruits fattened on the first rays and the fat midday light of the sun. The well-kept master houses to which they belong lie a little higher, all over the flanks of the western rise, which is spurred and starred and ends in a long upland, itself a spur.

So the hills conjoin, running towards the range. In this spur are steeps, gullies, and pockets, all blossom and young branch, with little houses, only their roofs visible, at the foot of a stiff green precipice hung with ferns, seedling pines, and many woods. In some of the gullies are small sawmills, logging sheds.

Coming through the bit of woodland which was her aunt's but which they had not been able to clear, in its tall timber, she saw that the two-year-old orange-trees at the top of the orchard, in the bad soil, had scarcely grown, but the bean-rows on their frames grew tall.

Coming in the open gate, she thought: "Now I am coming home", as one does in a place where one is sure of welcome. Her knock on the shut screen door and on the shut window was not heard. The door was not locked but she did not want to surprise them too much, so she went round the house to the front veranda, where she stood under the brick foundations, built very high. It was there with them she had graded the oranges and lemons, and packed them.

Passing the first window down she heard a woman's naughty sob and recognized her cousin's voice, Ellen's. She returned and now entered the kitchen quietly, while a bundled female form came towards her in the passage from the front of the house blazing with noonday sun.

"Is anyone there? Aunt Terry?" she was calling when the woman appeared and Ellen's mewing voice stopped.

"It's Tess," said Teresa softly.

Almost at once, her cousin appeared in the doorway, surprisingly tall, fair, pretty, in an old wrapper of faded pink which suited her delicate skin.

"Tess!" She rushed forward and squeezed her hands, bent and kissed her. "A surprise!"

"I'm not staying," Teresa said. "I'm walking to Harper's Ferry!"

"In this weather? Sun one moment, rain the next."

Aunt Teresa, in an old print dress, had just come in from the orchard. As soon as they began to talk, the daughter went back to her room. Aunt Teresa made some fresh tea, keeping an old brown pot on the hob "for Uncle Ned" as she said. When they had their tea in front of them, in large breakfast cups, Aunt Terry whispered: "We're doing very bad, and with 'er too. We've sacrificed everything for our girl and she's no better here than she was in the city. It's that affair that did it, she used to meet him in the Gardens every day for five years. One day I dressed her in a tussore silk suit I made myself and I went in with 'er to the Department and she asked him to let 'er have the truth, whether it was yes or no, and 'e said no. Since then, she's been another girl. Look at 'er now, and she 'as no cause to be like that, she 'as a chance, the man likes 'er."

"What is it?"

"She's invited to the Townshends' for dinner, that big house on the opposite hill. She went there first when the Minister was 'ere. The boy likes 'er, and she won't go. Sid Townshend is courting 'er and she's too proud to go unless she's sure, she's afraid to seem to be 'anging around."

"She's too sensitive."

"I know it, but she's getting worse and worse. She ought to take a step or two 'erself, she ought to show the young man some encouragement, this coldness, these 'igh-and-mighty airs, she just shoos the young men off. She's afraid she'll be thought forward and laughed at. I understand the poor girl."

There were soft sounds inside the closed door and Aunt Terry's face lightened. "Perhaps she's changed 'er mind, she may at least go to the Carlins'." Ellen banged a drawer shut. The mother frowned and got up to pour water from the big black kettle into the small brown teapot.

"Your uncle will be in soon for 'is tea," she said, "and won't 'e be pleased to see 'is Little Treasure! It was nice of you to come up for a few days, you know we love to see you. We wish our girlie knew 'er own mind as well as you do."

Something fell in Ellen's room. Aunt Teresa compressed her lips and made signs to Teresa. She rose to do some potatoes; after a while she came back to the table and, sitting down, explained about the Carlins again, asking Teresa to go and persuade Ellen to go to see Jerry.

"Jerry is perhaps the serious one, she's been in and out of there for months, every day singing like a bird and with colour in 'er cheeks, like she used to when she was at Technical College. I don't know whether we did right letting 'er go—nothing but unhappiness since—she became so ladylike there and she's afraid now people won't think 'er a lady. . . ."

"Oh, of course you were right."

"Yes, she took two medals at the College and she was always the fastest typist in the Department, she was getting six pounds a week." Aunt Terry was silent a moment, pressing her heavy, slightly-moustached lips.

"Your uncle and I have suffered a lot for 'er, but she is our own. It 'appened that last night she sat with Jerry in the old car near the barn and because they teased them when she came in, and asked 'er when the wedding would be, now she won't go, although she's promised to be there tonight."

Teresa found Ellen stupid, with her frigidity and coquetry; she said nothing about Ellen's affair, but explained that she had come, not to stay for a week, that there was no school holiday, and that she had left school for ever, and was going to walk to Harper's Ferry.

Aunt Terry said nothing and bustled to the stove to look at the stewing tea, then said:

"What did your father say? Whatever 'e says is right."

"Oh, I didn't tell him, it isn't his business."

"What do you want to walk there for?"

"Just to see the world, as they say," Teresa answered, quite at her ease.

"The weather—just look at the weather," remonstrated her aunt.

"I love rain, I never catch cold," said Teresa.

Presently in came her Uncle Edward, already faintly powdered by old age, though his long folded cheeks were tanned and sun-dried. He put his arms round Teresa and kissed her; a good old man, one of those who always have a smell of strong chaw tobacco, leather, and clean old clothes.

"My Little Treasure," he said, grinning delightedly under his tobacco-stained moustache and settling himself in his chair at the scrubbed deal table. "My tea, Mother!" and he kept smiling at his young niece. "Those fresh young roses," he said, kissing her cheeks with his whiskers. "And 'ave you got a 'oliday?"

"No," said she.

"No? Then 'ow's that?"

"I ran away."

He raised his thick greying eyebrows to his wife, and in one glance, the old pair had conversed with each other. He merely said: "Bad weather for the orchards", and shook his head seriously. "The old Narara Valley is covered with windfalls, the orchards are rotting underfoot. Men are going out everywhere getting sacks of windfalls for a shilling."

"Every morning, the tugs tow out barges of fruit past our place and dump them out at sea," said Teresa. This called up all the splendour of the spring and summer mornings when, just before she set out for school, down the harbour roads, so still and shimmering, came one or two portly little tugs, sometimes three, with lighters behind them, the dipping towline visible as they turned. Those rafts carried the unsold good fruit from just such districts as this; in the bottom of each, two doors which opened when the lighter was out at sea and let the freight of oranges, apples, and the like fall among the fishes. Joey the newsboy knew where the barges lay up and went there to get the rejected melons, bananas, oranges, of the markets, those that were thrown out when the price fell too low, fruit sacrificed because it was too cheap. Joey, at midnight, skimming from dump heap to dump heap, hazardously on the back ends of trams, buses, and cars, collected a few of these and sometimes had brought her one.

"Jones, in Gosford, sent a load in by the agent and all 'e got was 'e had to pay ninepence excess freight for the return of 'is unsold fruit. I don't know why they didn't dump it," said Uncle Edward, laughing. "I 'ad to pay twopence, two weeks ago, that was my profit."

"Working all the day there," said Aunt Teresa. "I don't like to see poor Ned, at 'is age, working down there in the 'ot sun, weeding, 'oeing."

Edward laughed. "You work a whole year, I don't know what you don't spend, sacking against the codlin moth and spraying, picking, and packing, and then you've got to pay twopence excess freight to get it sent out to sea." He laughed again goodnaturedly, slapped his spoon down and drank a whole cupful of black tea. He wiped his whiskers on his hand and looked gaily at Teresa. Then he became ashamed, calmed down and said: "It's all for 'er, after all, if it makes 'er 'appy." He turned and nodded at his daughter's room.

"I don't know if we've done any good, bringing 'er out 'ere where she meets no nice fellers," said Aunt Terry, restlessly, picking up the cup and taking it to the stove.

"Well, if she was to get settled, you know, your Aunt and I

would pack up traps tomorrow." He broke off with a glance at her door, as he took the cup of black tea. "Is she still hupset, Mother?"

Edward Paton and his wife misplaced their *h*'s; he said "hupset" and " 'ard work"; he had a gentle, caressing way of speaking and never scolded in his household more than to say firmly: "Now, Teresa", and "Now, Ellen".

Ellen, hearing her father's voice, came out of her room, dressed now in a soft blue dress.

"My darling," said Edward, " 'ow do you feel now, a little more cheerful? To 'ave Tess 'ere will cheer us hup a bit, p'raps."

"Don't say *'ave*, Father," cried Ellen nervously. "Have is easy to say."

"I'm sorry, daughter," said the man. "Come 'ere, my dear, sit on my knee."

"You should be ashamed to speak to your father that way," said Aunt Teresa. She went over with the teapot, filled the cup to the top, and kissed her husband on the head.

"It suited 'er," said Edward with a laugh, looking up at her with sea-blue eyes. "It suited your Mother 'er life long."

"It doesn't suit me," cried the daughter, kissing his cheek petulantly, "and I think you and Mother ought to learn for my sake. What do you think people think when they hear you? They think we're ignorant." Uncle Ned laughed heartily and kissed his daughter. "Your young men are ashamed of us, is that it?" He looked at her as he cradled her in his lap, then reached behind her long back to drink his tea.

"Ouch, Father, do be careful, you spilled some."

"But," said he, "Ellen, I won't 'ave you speaking that way to your mother, you see?"

She put her arms round his neck and kissed his ear, saying babyishly: "Do you love your poor girly?"

Aunt Teresa looked impatiently at them. "Don't baby 'er Father, she's old enough to know better. If we 'adn't spoiled your cousin Ellen," she explained gloomily to Teresa, "she would've been married and settled down long ago, but she thought she could always pick and choose."

Teresa gave Ellen a look and dropped her lashes; but Uncle Ned, not seeing it, beamed at her. He wiped his moustache with neatness and dexterity, pulled Ellen down (she was taller than he), kissed her forehead and said: "There, kitty, you know Mother and Father would do anything for you." Then pushing her a little, he continued with gentle severity: "Get off my knee, Ellen. Go and play Father a piece."

Frowning, she got up. "A *piece*! What *piece*?"

"'Believe Me, If All Those Endearing Young Charms.'" He looked up at her and touched her hand. Frowning, superior, she stalked into the front room; in a moment they heard her thin voice and her firm touch; she was singing "The Holy City".

Uncle Edward beamed but there was a pathetic twist in his mouth. Aunt Teresa said: "We spent a lot of money on Ellen's musical education, she has so much artistic talent, we thought she'd do something with it."

"She exhibited at the Narara show here this year and got first prize," said the father.

"She didn't do nothing with what she had," said the mother. She continued, looking at Uncle Edward: "Father, Tess isn't on 'oliday, she wants to go on a walking-trip to 'Arper's Ferry. She says she doesn't mind the weather."

"Yes?" said the elderly man, looking steadily at Teresa while he stirred his tea. Stirring his tea was with Ned Paton a prolonged, restful occupation; it was something like chewing tobacco. Presently he poured himself a saucerful of tea, blew it gently, and lifted his moustaches expertly as he slid it into his mouth.

"Good tea, Mother," said he as always. "Have you got any more?"

"Father!" exclaimed his wife. "All day long that tea is stewing there for him. You drink it too black, Father, it'll ruin your stomach." He laughed. "Been drinking it that way since I was a shaver," he said and started off on the long anecdote of how he had lived in a village in the Isle of Thanet, and walked to work at a brick-kiln, four miles there and back with his father, a brickmaker, from five years old. At twelve he had run away to sea, like nearly all the local boys and had never seen his family since. "Nor ever 'eard," said he, bending his head to blow at his saucer. He began to tell the other story about his travelling up and down the coast of South America rounding the Horn several times in one of the last of the sailing-ships, and about his settling down in Sydney, "Where I met my fate, I met Mother."

"Tess is like her mother, my dear sister Emma," said Aunt Teresa. "And I promised Emma I would look out for her, if need was."

Teresa meanwhile was lost in thought, that Ellen in her pale sterility, at twenty-nine, twitching like a filly, kissing like a girl on her father's knee, was fit for the bone-yard. Of course, she would never get a man, for she smelled and looked like an old pancake.

Ellen, white Sunday shoes, a high laugh and playing the organ at church! How could a marrying woman produce a daughter on the shelf? Teresa was sure that Jerome Carlin was not thinking of Ellen at all. She heard her name "Tess!" and looked up.

"Tess was in one of 'er brown studies," said Uncle Edward. "I said your cousin Lily Foster was out a couple of months back, she stayed 'ere a week."

"She primped herself up every time your uncle took her in town, powder all over the dressing-table and the floor, for me to clean up," continued Aunt Tess, heavily. "My sister Anne's girl, but always pretty much 'er own way." She came to the table to say in a low voice to Teresa: "When she 'ad her days, you know, she got worse than ever, very excited and red in the face, and she drenched 'erself in perfume—your uncle was quite ashamed driving 'er into town, every man in the street turned to look at 'er. A regular exhibition."

"Yes," said Uncle Ned. "She is a dandy, your cousin Lily Foster, the men were all staring after 'er——" he looked slightly ashamed.

"Because of 'er red face," said the aunt. "Of course, poor Lily can't 'elp it, she takes fits—at that time—you know."

"About every two or three months, they say," said Ned, comfortably. "She was kind and loving to your aunt but careless and lazy and your aunt got upset, your aunt got real upset."

The wife whispered: "Your cousin Ellen can't stand 'er, they didn't get on at all." They showed her a photograph of her cousin Lily, whom she had never seen, a sturdy, middle-sized girl with a long, plump face and smiling eyes.

Teresa had a vivid picture of her driving through town in white organdy (they went on to describe her), smelling of Houbigant, with a scarlet face covered with powder and all the men looking, Uncle Edward alongside.

"All the men looked?" she asked.

"Because she was so red and 'er eyes were shining," said the aunt.

"She was something to see in our town," said Uncle Ned. "She was so fussed up."

"Is it because she takes fits she is like that?" asked Teresa.

"Oh, of course, poor girl, she can't 'elp it, I'm not blaming 'er, but she went out of 'er way, just the same, to catch the eye. A big, bouncing girl like that—she should 'ave tried to tone it down a bit."

"Tone down what, do you mean?"

"Her colour and her fat, but she didn't even wear a corset."

The young girl was puzzled; the married women of the family kept speaking of girls who went without corsets, or who wore garters, or rolled their stockings, as if they were evil.

"But why should she wear corsets?"

"A decent girl doesn't walk up and down town without corsets."

Good: it was one of those moral laws she did not yet understand. She asked no more, but continued:

"Is that hereditary, those fits, I mean?"

Lily was her first cousin. She herself as a child had been noticed everywhere for the great red flags in her cheeks, surprising in such a tan-skinned country. It was for this reason that the young flop-eared medical student on the ferry had spoken to her one day. Since then he had sought her out, a peculiar creature with the figure of an angleworm, tall, slobbering too, lonely; interested in her colour. She hated him because the girls laughed at him, but now she thought she saw why he ran after her—it was perhaps the hereditary red face.

The uncle and aunt were looking at each other, thinking something out in concert.

"Is epilepsy a kind of family disease? Might I have it?" she asked pleasantly.

Her uncle and aunt looked at her; then Aunt Terry said shortly:

"Some say. But you 'aven't got it, if you mean that."

"What is it like?"

Her aunt seemed embarrassed and murmured a few words. Teresa became absorbed again, while the adults went on quickly talking. She was putting the jigsaw together again. There was nothing really serious to it, then; a red face that men looked at, gaiety, charm, people "waiting on you" as Aunt Terry had said, self-confidence, a fall—what harm was there in it? At school they taught that genius is to madness near akin, and she had already remarked that men were attracted by a little madness. Of course she had not her cousin's talents, she had never done those things that Aunt Teresa had murmured so quickly, but it might be cultivated. She stirred uneasily, wondering if she really could become a Lily, when she noticed that her uncle and aunt had left her and gone into the front room, while Ellen's drink-of-water figure was moving lengthily up and down the front veranda. Her cousin stopped and looked over the wide valley full of storm rain. The elderly couple were talking earnestly about something and soon Uncle Ned went off through the timbered lot towards the station. No doubt it was some family conspiracy about Jerry Carlin or the Townshends. There was no help for her here. There was nothing for it but to set out exactly as she had planned, and when she got back to Sydney, she would go on with her night-classes, get a job and go abroad. That was all she could see ahead of her.

13. *Air of Pride, Fire, and Water*

It was time to go to the Carlins' and Ellen was sulking in her room, dressed, her long fair hair carefully braided round her head, but marching up and down behind a closed door.

"You go in," said Aunt Teresa to Teresa, "and tell her she must go." Teresa arose, knocked at the door.

"Who's there?"

"Tess."

"Come in."

Her cousin was standing near the bed. She could be pretty, thought Teresa, seeing her oval eyes, teeth gleaming in her parted lips and the air of pride, fire, and water with which she looked at the intruder for an instant. She doubted; perhaps Jerry Carlin really liked her. She certainly did not look twenty-nine.

"It's time to go to Rhoda's," said Teresa.

"I hate Rhoda, she's common."

"Don't you want to see Jerry and Tom?" went on Teresa, indifferently.

"Get out, you little idiot, you don't know what you're meddling in," cried Ellen.

"You come along, you know you want to go," said Teresa, laying hold of her cousin's arm.

The tall girl freed herself in a kind of spasm and between tears and cries of fury and gentle slaps, drove her young cousin to the door.

"Get out of here, I don't want you. I hate you," shrieked poor Ellen.

Teresa stood looking at her.

"Get out, get out of here, get out," shrieked Ellen at the pitch of fury.

Teresa went out and went to sit with her aunt and uncle after closing the door. They heard the drawers slamming in Ellen's room. The three said nothing, but looked at each other.

At last Aunt Teresa said: "It's not your fault, Little Treasure."

Suddenly Ellen's door opened and she marched out, dressed for walking in a storm-coat and hat, with overshoes and an umbrella. Her bright hair was already escaping in tendrils from her hat, and her eyes blazed.

"Come along, then," she shouted at Teresa.

Teresa started up, after a doglike glance at the elders, and went out the door with her. When they reached the road, a matter of ten steps, Ellen was already quite calm. She seemed to be zig-zagging along the road, hopping from one rut to another.

Teresa, absorbed, followed her, kept by her side.

In her satirical voice, Ellen exclaimed: "You have no character at all, you are spineless."

"How's that?" asked Teresa, surprised.

"You follow me wherever I go," said the young woman.

Teresa said nothing.

"You ought to cultivate character," continued Ellen.

"So I do," said Teresa.

"Well, you can't have any if you dog my footsteps that way."

"I wasn't dogging you, I was walking with you."

"There's no need to *shadow* me, to walk with me!"

Teresa fell behind a few steps, much annoyed.

"What are you lagging for?" cried Ellen.

Teresa moved to the other side of the road and kept abreast there.

"You're just on the opposite side, because of what I said. That isn't showing character, to do the opposite," called her cousin in a more cheerful tone of spite.

"How can walking along a road show character?" Teresa replied at last.

"Everything shows character, the smallest thing—handwriting," said her cousin spitefully. "It plainly shows your character."

Teresa made no reply. She had for a long time thought Ellen resented her pet name, "Little Treasure", with the Patons. Ellen had a long stride, not ungraceful with her height.

"I always lead," said Ellen.

"Well, that's good," remarked Teresa. "Good for you, I mean."

"Don't tell me what you mean, you little fool," cried her cousin. "Don't you patronize me. What are you? You think you're somebody. I know you, you don't pull the wool over my eyes, I've always known you."

Teresa listened in surprise, almost with pleasure; perhaps Ellen really knew her. Ellen shouted:

"You wrote home to ask about the flying foxes that time. I read your father's letter."

The flying foxes of two summers ago! They descended from branch to branch over wide spaces, the membranes between their feet spread out like wings, wonderful creatures at nightfall, on the green sky. Teresa remembered her letter and did not reply; they had argued about whether they could really fly or only glide. She followed her cousin a few paces behind. A silence fell. She saw Ellen biting her lip; she was on the other side of the road. Suddenly Ellen said with an angry sparkle: "Sorry I lost my temper."

Teresa, thinking about that lost summer, made no reply. That summer, just after the picnic, Tom Carlin had got into trouble with a girl at the local agricultural show; he had been doing something with her behind the cages of the Rhode Island Reds. Now these were friends of Ellen's, the prude's.

"Don't sulk, now," cried the young virago.

They were coming down the hill. On one side was an old wood; in a small clearing stood a shuttered cottage. On the other side was a long close-shaved slope. At the bottom of this slope a road ran and beyond the road, under an immense wild fig-tree, ran a slate-roofed cottage with white-painted walls; five small rooms in a single row, with a number of doors to be entered from the yard. In front was a grassed strip; at one side about an acre of blackberry bushes and at the other side a wilderness of hardy pests, lantana, castor-oil plants. Beyond these were a neglected fowl-run, several pig-pens, a barn, a car without its wheels, and a few tumbledown sheds. This house had been in the hands of poor farmers, city people, and country wanderers down on their luck for about twenty-five years. It was the oldest house in the district, built of large stone blocks by convict labour, and the story was that a convict had been flogged to death, tied by rope to this particular fig-tree, in its youth. In the most deserted hours of country night, some people said, cries were still heard, there was a "ghost", but no one could describe the ghost. The Carlins, a good-natured, shiftless family, and the family before them, had been so weak in character that an air of mere folly and stupidity hung over the farm and the legend of loud cries was no longer interesting or popular.

The father Carlin was a rouseabout on some station up-country, where they had all last come from. They had a photograph of a weatherboard house on their own "station", a small holding near Collarenebri, from which they had been burned out, losing every stick and stitch. For some months they had camped near the burned house, living on a few home-grown vegetables and Tom's shooting. When a flock of parrots flew over, they had some good eating; otherwise, they ate rabbits when they trapped them. They were not popular with their neighbours, who took them for silly city people and their misfortunes for their just deserts; the country people did not like them eating the vermin either. Then Mother Carlin went back to Sydney to work in a lunchroom, where she still was and having a merry time with a proposal of marriage once a month, according to her own story; while the two boys and the girl, Jerry, Tom, and Rhoda, coming down country by car, had run out of petrol at Narara, and stopped there.

Here they led a gipsy life which suited them all, not liked by anyone in particular because they were "shiftless". Rhoda Carlin was a big brown girl, fleshy, strong but lazy, who did a little cooking for the boys. She was about to marry the catch of the district, a middle-aged bachelor, heir to one of the largest mixed orchards, only son of a jealous mother.

"Is Tom there now?" asked Teresa finally, by way of making peace.

"Tom! That good-for-nothing," murmured Ellen. "He's up-country—a boundary rider, near where his father is. He married a girl here—she works in the general store—or did. Now she's going to have a baby. Such a shiftless lot as the lot about here—she married him without either of them having a penny. They got some room in the town. Jerry's working at the sawmill up on the mountain. The crazy fool comes coasting down that mountain every sunset in that lorry of theirs that hasn't any brakes. He'll crack his neck any day."

"What harm will that do?" Teresa sighed, and shrugged.

"Don't you say that about any human being," said Ellen. "How would you like anyone to say that about you?"

"What difference would it make?"

"Every blessed evening," went on Ellen, meditating, "when I see the sun going down, I think of that shiftless boy crashing down that road."

A pig ran round the house. "Those beasts," said Ellen. "I hate this place, two people died here. Do you remember Gregg, the man they had here? He was taken away to the Cottage Hospital at show time, he died of eating in the water-melon contest. They picked him up just near the fence here. And they say they found a body in that paddock, they don't know whose."

The door stood fast shut against the wind. Through the uncurtained window, where they went to tap, they saw Rhoda and Roger, her rich friend, lying down together on the worn horsehair sofa, hugging each other. One leg of the sofa was made of a couple of wooden blocks. Ellen tapped. The pair turned up their red faces, rolled off the sofa looking proud of themselves, and came swaggering to the door, not making any attempt to smooth their hair or their collars.

"We'll soon have another pair of lovers," said the young woman. "Who's that? Why, Tess! What a shame Tom's up-country. We could all sit on laps."

"Tess wouldn't do that," simpered Ellen.

"She can have half my lap," Roger said with the nasty smirk of the timid, unpractised bachelor.

"She can't have half of Jerry's lap," said Rhoda with a roar of laughter. "I know who wants all of that."

Ellen marched into the kitchen to put her rain clothes there. Rhoda followed her out and to Teresa's surprise they did not start quarrelling, but at once began an intimate conversation in a low tone.

Teresa sat down and looked contemptuously at Roger. His hair was thinning, he had an egg-shaped head and the used look of a too-friendly house-dog. Of course, here, for this cabbage-patch, he was a catch. Rhoda was well off.

The two young women came in with tea and a tin of iced biscuits which they put on the table. The table was covered with an old red cloth and strewn with the remains of meals, with books, music, and other things.

Jerry was out in Gosford, the market town, trying to sell a pig and some produce; the market days were Monday and Thursday.

"He's changing my books, too," said Rhoda. "I'm such a lazy slug, I do nothing but read all day. What would your mother say to that?" she asked Roger.

Roger shifted and for a moment stiffened nervously.

"His mother simply loathes me," said Rhoda.

"No, she doesn't, Rhoda," began the man.

"She *does*," expostulated Rhoda, her flat contralto voice vibrating. "Oh, the time I went into her drawing-room! She received me in the drawing-room——"

They spent several hours, while the rain beat on the windows, waiting for Jerry and talking about Roger's mother, about women's health and what was the best time to conceive a boy or girl. Roger seemed delighted to understand, now at last, how things were in the world. It was Ellen who remained a little finicky, but she too had led a closed life and eagerly learned all she could from the tomboy. When it became really dark, they still sat talking there, not lighting a lamp; but Rhoda got up and sat on Roger's knee, her arms round him. From time to time the two cousins heard loud kisses and the sound of nestling.

At last, Rhoda exclaimed: "There's Jerry," and jumped up to go and help her brother put the horse in. They no longer used their car, not having the money for petrol, and having no credit in the district.

A glow approached them, and in a minute a rain-wet, golden-brown, tired boy came into the room, holding the kerosene lamp under his face, so that the cleft in his chin was lighted up.

"Guess who's here," called his sister, putting her hands over his eyes.

The lamp wobbled. "Careful, Rhoda."

"Guess who's here!"

The strong smell of hot kerosene filled the room.

"You spilt some," said Roger anxiously.

"Guess who's here!"

"Ellen," he said slowly.

"Right!"

She took her hands off, and when he put the lamp down on the table and was still dazzled by the light, she took him by the sleeve and dragged him over to the sofa where Ellen was sitting.

"The lovebirds," said she. "Come, kiss, don't be shy. Roger and I have been sitting here hugging and kissing for hours and Ellen has been sitting patiently waiting for you."

Jerry bent tenderly over the blushing Ellen who half-rose in protest, with her stiffest little air.

"My tender white lily," said he. "My sweet lily, have you been waiting for me?"

Teresa blushed to see her cousin put to shame by these hobble-dehoys.

"Will it kiss its sweetheart?" asked Jerry, still bending over her. He took her limp, shapely hand, and raising it, kissed it.

Rhoda clapped. "Oh, good work, and now a real kiss."

"No, no," said Ellen, rising in confusion. "No, no."

She half-ran into the kitchen. Jerry followed her, paying no attention to the others in the room. They heard his cajoling tone and her frightened little voice. They heard several kisses.

"Ah-ha," shouted Rhoda, "good work. Good egg!"

She turned and smacked the happy Roger several times.

"Oh, God, love is good," cried she, now turning to Teresa. "What a pity Tom isn't here, we could make it a party. Oh, can't we get someone for Tess?"

At this moment Ellen reappeared, her hand lying in Jerry's, while Rhoda hummed the wedding march.

"Down the ai-isle we must go, we must go, we must go," sang Rhoda. Ellen snatched away her hand and came to stand near her cousin. Elfish, Jerry danced forward, seized Teresa by both shoulders and kissed her on the lips.

"Ah-ha, I wouldn't do that to my lady, my lady is too stand-offish," said Jerry.

Teresa was trembling with shame. This was the first time she had ever been kissed and it was an affront, in a kind of debauch which she scarcely understood.

"You should not do that," cried Ellen, her voice trembling.

"No, I should not do that, I should not do that," mimicked Jerry. "Did that offend my pure white lily?"

"You devil!" cried Rhoda, slapping her thigh, and turning her laughing fat face to Roger, she said: "Isn't he just a devil?"

"Are you hungry, Jerry? Hunger and love don't go together they say."

Jerry looked round the room carefully. "You haven't eaten yet? Let's have something."

There was a long scramble in the two rooms, so that at the end of about twenty minutes, the brother and sister were able to produce some fried eggs, quite fresh, some rancid butter, stale bread and home-made jam, which they all ate hungrily, with newly-made tea.

At the table, Jerry said: "Tom's baby was born today. She was all alone there, someone found her. There wasn't even a basin in the house, not a rag. Do you think you could go down, Rhoda? I was there. I think someone ought to write and tell Tom, too, he never thinks of anything."

"Boy or girl?" cried Rhoda at once.

"A girl," said Jerry.

"What a shame," said Rhoda.

"I didn't see it," Jerry continued.

"You'd have to see it to know if it was a boy or a girl," said Rhoda with a nudge, looking for approval at them.

"Do you think Tom will like a girl?" asked Ellen.

"Tom always was crazy about girls," said Rhoda loudly. "That's why he got a girl. A man that's mad over the girls always gets girls, he likes his wife too much. It means he has a feminine nature, his wife wears the pants."

"I took her something to eat," said Jerry, "but she didn't feel like eating. I think there's some old woman with her tonight. I like Hattie."

"Tom must have liked her, or she wouldn't be where she is today," said Rhoda, roaring with laughter. "Well, when you get me into that state, Roger, it'd better be a boy."

They went off again into the same discussion of how to get a girl or a boy.

After this meal, they did not clear up, but Jerry said: "Let's have some music," and went into the adjoining room to get his violin.

"It's Tom's violin," he explained, bringing it back. "Tom's real clever, he has a real good ear. He learned to play it in six correspondence lessons, and he taught me."

"They've both got good ears," said Rhoda. "Both those boys are wizards, not me—I'm tone-deaf, one letter from stone-deaf."

"He plays real good," said Ellen, to Teresa's surprise. She had dropped unconsciously into her mother's old idiom, which she criticized at home.

Standing by the lamp, the fiddle and bow held roughly, his face serious, Jerry was a handsome, romantic figure, slight, flushed.

"Listen to the storm," he said, pausing with his bow lifted.

"The trees are just like violins too in this storm," said Ellen bravely, in a thin, ladylike voice.

Jerry looked at her and, turning towards her with a grand gesture, began to play to her. It was unbelievable! Teresa stared wildly round at the others, cuddling, and at Ellen with her hands folded in her lap, sitting quite straight. Should she laugh to show that she knew it was a joke? They did not laugh.

When Jerry finished, they clapped, he grinned and Ellen said: "That was real pretty, Jerry," once more quite softly, speaking as they did.

"Oh, yes, it was pretty," said Teresa hastily, supposing it was a bizarre, stupid joke.

"Play again, Jerry," cried his sister. "Play 'The Last Rose of Summer'."

"No, I'll play 'Mary, Gentle Mary'," said the boy, and once more turning to Ellen, he began to drag his bow over the shrieking, spitting, hawking strings; not a note of the tune came out of them, though Rhoda's voice could be heard humming it.

Teresa gave a hunted look round. They were brutally, devilishly spoofing Ellen and her, but mostly Ellen, who was flushed, and in a pretty admiration of the young man.

"Let's go," she said to Ellen.

"Oh, not now," replied her cousin affectionately.

"Come out into the kitchen a minute."

"What for?"

"I'm taking Ellen into the kitchen and don't you follow," laughed Jerry, pulling the willing woman to her feet and taking her out into the kitchen, with his hands still clasped in both of hers.

The two stayed out while the others kept shouting jokes, saying that it was darker still in the barn, and repeating that Ellen, that Missy, spent three hours in the old car with Jerry the night before. "Doing what, I wonder? Come on, tell us, Ellen, what went on in the old car? What is he like? Is he good?"

The couple stayed in the kitchen a long time, and then reappeared unconcernedly, as if they had just finished washing the dishes. Teresa was so upset that she started to go away several times, hoping that Ellen would put on her hat too. Ellen was not happy; she seemed to doubt, too, whether some part of this was not a mean trick, but she was too weak-willed to refuse them.

It was midnight when they left the house. The rain had stopped, but a high wind was blowing and clouds rolled fast over them.

"That old tree will come down on their heads, some night," said Ellen, looking up.

Walking down the road, she pulled on her gloves and tied on her oilskin cap. Teresa seemed to hear through the wind yells of laughter from the Carlins' sitting-room where Rhoda, Jerry, and Roger must be nearly killing themselves over the antics of the two old maids, and Ellen's peachy bloom of love, come out on her soft cheeks, and the credulous, girlish look in her eyes when she glanced up at Jerry, with his howling violin.

"Never will I marry the neighbour's son," she said to herself. "What misery, what shame!" And all because Ellen had not the courage to look farther afield.

They were mounting the long hill at the top of which stood the Patons' cottage, concealed by roadside eucalypts and a wood of turpentine. Ellen did not speak.

Just after they had passed the shuttered cottage in the wood, a human yell pealed out through the wood, marvellously loud, ringing through the air as if carried by the high airs and after two or three shouts, dying slowly, groaning away into the empty grass paddock beside them, as if tingling in the grass roots as they were treading on the neighbouring ruts. The young girl, in a paroxysm too great for fear, looked at her cousin, expecting some violent sign in her. Ellen lowered her head and trudged on against the hill. It was inconceivable! When she was opening her mouth to speak to Ellen, as if out of her own mouth, the cry pealed again, a little farther behind, but ringing tremendous, from the things on the land, from some martyred and bleeding field, or a giant old tree being murdered in the wood there. What a cry! And there again!

When it had died away again, Teresa said: "Didn't you hear that yell? What is it?"

Ellen, bending her head a little farther forward, hurried her step.

"Ellen, Ellen," she panted, "didn't you hear that awful cry?"

A terrible thought went through her head like lightning, that she was mad, or had herself uttered the cry; that was why Ellen did not answer, but pressed on. Was she asleep? Was this a nightmare? What was it, that that timid woman, hearing this thing on a country road at night, yes, at any time, in bright sunlight too, would not start and run? Was it herself?

"Ellen?"

"Come along," said the woman.

"Didn't you hear it?"

There was a breathing-space, then. "Do come along," said the woman.

"What is it? Oh, Ellen, what is it?"

"You don't know, so don't worry," muttered Ellen.

Teresa was not afraid, but the cry was too great to be that of hunting, pursuing things. Who was concealed in that shut house? Was it one of the inaudible sounds of creation, suddenly by a freak made audible to them? How did Ellen, that stupid thing, know how to take it, if so? Was Ellen also a sensitive, a living soul? Was it the howl of empty Creation, horrified at being there with itself in its singleness? Or is it the cry of the chase I am on, said the young girl? At any rate, if the cry is here, I must be off; where the cry is, that lonely, dreadful cry, I must be off. To-morrow I will go over the hills yonder.

When they came in, Aunt Teresa was sitting up for them, gentle and affectionate. She kissed her daughter warmly and when Ellen's door was shut, she kept her niece talking a few minutes.

"Are you going walking tomorrow?"

"Oh, yes."

"In the morning or the afternoon?"

"Oh, straight away. I only want to take a few days, then I must look for a job."

"What kind of a job?"

"As a typist."

"Ellen was such a good typist, the best in the Department, and much good it did 'er," said the aunt.

Teresa was silent.

"Do you know which way you're going?"

"No, I don't know the way but I'll take the road that goes straight across the creek."

"Do you think that goes to 'Arper's Ferry?" she asked. "You don't mind walking off by yourself? It seems your friends went in groups."

"What friends?"

"Your university friends."

"I have no university friends, I just heard of them through a Mr Crow, who is there."

Aunt Teresa pressed her, and she asked: "What can happen to me?"

Aunt Teresa looked at her with haunted eyes, almost angry, "They can tear you."

"What do you mean?" asked the girl, startled. She thought her aunt referred to the murderers lurking possibly round Harper's Ferry. What did her aunt murmur in reply? Horrible things, old wives' tales. Teresa took no notice of this bogy talk but said she would be off in the morning, she could not wait, she had little money.

Her aunt rose, taking the kerosene lamp so that the shadows danced about like immense moths. Teresa hesitated and then boldly said: "Down the road, there was a cry, someone yelled out."

"Yes," said her aunt, coming back to the table and looking down at her grotesquely above the yellowing lamp, her dark eyes shining like idol's eyes, "it's a madman who lives there with 'is mother. She won't even go to town in case 'e needs her. Suppose 'e got out one night and you met 'im?"

"A madman!"

"Oh, 'e's chained up, 'e can't get out."

"Why don't they take him away?"

"'Is mother says she will kill 'erself if they do."

Teresa, after a little thought, asked how old he was. He was twenty-eight.

"Did he ever have a wife?" she continued, thoughtfully.

"The madman was about to get married when 'is madness came upon 'im, lucky for the young girl, she just escaped a terrible thing. She's living down in the valley now."

"She didn't get married?"

"They said she was in love with this man and that she still 'asn't given up 'ope, but 'is case is 'opeless."

"Oh, why didn't they let them get married?" cried Teresa. "Oh, the poor things! But how can they expect mad people to get better if they have no husbands and wives? Why, I should go mad if they shut me up that way. Why, we would all go mad, if we were shut up and not allowed to get married."

Aunt Teresa explained to her how the mad must never procreate; but Teresa did not listen. She thought of the madman, down in the house in the wood, shut in with his old mother. She thought someone ought to go and let him out, but she said nothing about this to her aunt. Her aunt kissed her, saying: "You know where to go and where to put your things, Little Treasure. I promised my dear sister I'd look after you and I've always thought of you just like my own daughter. Your mother was a brave woman, a very serious woman. She never had a chance or I think she would have been quite a brainy woman. But when she wanted her own way, she got it. And so will you. You are a good girl——"

Teresa did not listen to her as she prattled on, for she felt she got no clue to her character or future in this, but when she heard that she would get her way she looked attentively at her aunt. "Do you mean that? I have will power?"

"You were always a very firm little thing."

Teresa thought: "Ah! Good! Then it is all right, in that case, I know I will find a man and get married, despite what they say at home."

She kissed her aunt good night affectionately and went off to bed, but she did not sleep for a long while, disturbed by the moon and by the thought of the lonely house of the madman.

14. There Are Many Abandoned Orchards in the Valley

THERE are many abandoned orchards in the valley. Farmlands are under wild grass, crooked apple-trees turning back to nature lean over lichened palings with festoons and knots of sour apples, yellow and streaked russet. The waters that feed Narara Creek trickle down bluffs and empty light meadows; the doors hang from their frames in slate-coloured weatherboard farmhouses, broken open by the seasons.

At four o'clock in the afternoon, Teresa, a pack on her back, was trudging along an unknown road, not five miles from her aunt's orchard. After she had heard her uncle and aunt go down the orchard at sunrise, she had got up, taken tea from the big blue breakfast pot where it was stewing for their return, and strapped together a bundle for her shoulder.

At the sound, Ellen had got up, but let her go without a protest. There was no highway north at this point, but there were roads which twisted through the valley and which must join the great northern road, which began a few miles further on. She had at first asked farmers, women she saw feeding their chickens, where was the Newcastle road? They had very vague ideas, but had pointed to the western side of the valley and there she had at first gone.

The weather cleared up about two in the afternoon, the clouds piling away to the north-west and the washed-out sky beginning to clear. It was hot by four, but coolness still came out of the drenched lands.

At this moment she was following a broad cart-track under the shoulder of a stony hill and curving back south. She had eaten a cold-meat sandwich and some chocolate, the same diet that Lance ate when away over the week-end, but now she was very tired. She hardly knew what she was doing. She no longer looked for the north road but trudged patiently along the track she had got on to, hoping vaguely that at some moment or other she would turn into something better. She was hot and her head thumped. She could not think any more; phrases and ideas from last night had begun to turn themselves round in her head and she imagined she saw things alongside the road, tails of things disappearing, shadows twitching. It was not fear, it was the delirium of fatigue.

She had taken no hat with her, and perhaps she had got too hot in the sun.

"Your dead mother had very serious qualities. . . ."

Who could worry about the qualities of a dead woman? If, for example, she had known what her mother's qualities had been, and what she had wanted, and if she had succeeded in getting it, she might know something about how to proceed now.

"What you will to have you will get. . . ."

But will what? It seemed to her that she was just willing without knowing what it was she wanted. She was out here with her will only and no plan, no intelligence. She trudged on. What was she doing here? What was it for? Why Harper's Ferry? Perhaps it was sixty miles away. Did you pay at Harper's Ferry? She set her teeth, because she knew that if she gave up, *they* would get her, she would be dragged in, she would never get away, she would go back, become their slave, until she was sixty or sixty-five, never know how things were in the world, be what they wanted, an old maid. That, never. She felt rigid as the iron in her will. They would never get her; it would stand there till the end of her day. Also, she would never marry the neighbour's son as a last expedient.

What a valley! Great, fruitful, silent as paradise. She would have liked to go into one of the old orchards and sleep, but the ground was very wet. She had not brought a ground sheet, or a blanket. She might have thought of that when everyone took one, walking.

Nearly two years ago it was that she and the Carlins had gone to that cleft in the western hills; they had their car running then. The tree-ferns, eucalypts, and other things were very frondy, slender, green and delicate; it was cool and wet there. Flying foxes dropped from tree to tree, birds sang. At the top was dry bracken country, open cleared land, and a few sheds which had looked very comfortable in the setting sun. There had been some talk about dossing down in one of them, for a lark, a rather indecent lark, as things were looked at among the respectable families. Tom had said: "Tell me what you will say when you make love to a man."

"I don't know now, I will know then."

How glorious to make a declaration to a man, say just what she felt, throw prudence away, be herself, make love generously to a beautiful man *Thou art beautiful, my beloved; thou art as*—— If she could say that to the right man, who would go to Harper's Ferry? Who would be so ridiculous as to be out on a lonely road going nowhere? Above, the tall spray of green fronds and here the sweet hot smell of bush flowers—but that was two years ago. Tom, Tom's wife. She was dizzy with fatigue, hunger, and her tattered mind. She was profoundly troubled but did not clearly remember why. She could not remember a single trouble.

She heard a shout. She had been passing a split-rail fence for some time. It was low, rich ground. Wattles and eugenias grew along the fence. Away back, near the creek, which was broad and shaded at this point, lay a rather large three-storey farmhouse, well-built, but with a wide veranda and a few yellow dogs lounging in the shade. She was just passing the slip-rail which lay on the ground. A foot-track only led to the house through deep grass. On the veranda three youngish men were sitting or standing. It was too far to see what they were like. She stood a moment in the opening, trying to catch what they said, but could not, and went on with rapid step. But the voices frightened her.

A fourth man, much older, she fancied, was standing near the line of trees that ran down to the creek, with a white rag in his hand, perhaps a "trespassers" notice. It seemed that he turned to come to the slip-rail as she moved off, no doubt to shut the gate against intruders. It gave her a hunted feeling, as if she had nowhere but the winding road. She had been feeling hunted for an hour or more; it was just tiredness. She had all kinds of floating thoughts without being able to put her finger on one of them. What dreams she had had in the night! True it was full moon and they were full-moon dreams. There was a ship running with blood on the open sea; still water, the deck slanting, a man in torn shirt with a bloody cutlass in his hand. Then she had been explaining something for a long time, she did not know what, to her brother Leo. She had been very restless, excited, perhaps she had not got enough sleep.

Suddenly she was sure that she was really pursued. She walked on in the same way, and listened. Yes, someone was following her in the dust, rather softly. She looked behind. It was the old man from the paddock. After all, she could not stop the man walking along the road. It was probably a private road, at that; and perhaps he wanted to tell her that. Perhaps it was all an estate which had never been worked. But everything can tell when it is being hunted. She walked a little faster. Did he want money? Did he have a message from the men in the house? She slowed down to let him pass her. She heard him now approaching and turned round. She had been walking south-west with the sun across her eyes and she did not see the gesture the old man made; and then he came hurrying towards her with a kind of queer white flag out beneath his belt. When he was a few yards away he stopped, stood there in front of her shamelessly, making his gestures. She turned round and walked fast. How would it end? What would stop him? She did not even know why he did it. She heard him following. For no reason she was seized with flight and began to run, but after a short sprint, she was all in and fell again into a walk. The old man had begun to run too and was now just behind her. She turned round and said in a hoarse voice that she did not recognize:

"What are you doing it for? Go away, you go on back."

The old man muttered hastily.

"Go away, go on back."

He stood there in the evening light, like a marionette, not a man. Overhead, the birds were wheeling, or making straight across the sky; the little animals croaked in the grass. Everything else was natural, except this madness on the road.

She started to walk again and he followed. She went very slowly now, being so horribly confused, troubled and tired, that she could hardly see in front of her. Only behind her, now at her side, and now in front of her, walked the wicked old appearance. For a few moments, he was in front of her with his idiotic dance, and then fell behind again, and at this moment, as she felt a new spurt of energy, she took to her heels and left him behind in the road.

When she looked back at the turn of the road as it rounded a stony hill, she saw him still standing there in the middle of the road straddling, the only human figure in a great grassy landscape. She did not understand the whole thing. It was a shame and disgrace; in the Bible they were punished who uncovered their father's nakedness. Why would an old man publish his own shame?

It was a queer, queer valley. She must get out of it. All this day she had wandered here, looking for a road which perhaps did not exist. She now recalled the little shed where sawing was done above the gully where she had gone with Tom Carlin, in a clearing. She would sleep there tonight and tomorrow she would go into the market town and find out exactly how she could get to Harper's Ferry.

It was miles and miles south-west, this shed, and on top of a hill, and only to be reached by climbing and following a ridge on the other side of the creek.

She asked herself once: "Why am I doing all this?" but she knew that there was a reason.

Tonight the moon would not rise until late; she could travel all the way in the dark. All at once she thought of a reason why she should never be on the road at this time, on this night. She began to perspire profusely, and flushed. How stupid she was! How could she have been so? She sat down on the side of the road in the dusk to think what she should now do. In spite of the shame of going back to the Patons after leaving them this morning and of not having covered more than five miles as the crow flies, and of not having discovered the north road, it seemed that it was all she could do. And now, no more anxious or hunted, knowing where she would sleep at night, a deep melancholy came over her at the sight and smell of the great valley with all its slopes far and untrodden by her. She loved it. What a hidden life it had. She got up and calmly began to retrace her steps.

She reached her aunt's at eight-thirty; the trees of the uncleared woodland tossed their heads against a clear starry sky.

They were still sitting round the tea-table and then, as she approached, she saw two new faces there, Jerry Carlin's and her brother Lance's.

"It was right to come back", and her uncle held up his cheek to be kissed. Ellen, in a fit of kindness, made room for her and went to get her a cup of tea. Lance looked over her queerly, his mobile face startled, shadowy, as if he saw her for the first time in his life.

"Where did you go?"

"Not very far."

"The school rang up," said Lance, "and then we looked in your room and found your note, and I rang up the Department to let them know you were taken suddenly ill and would be away for a few days. You could be dismissed for that, going away without leave." She was silent, feeling their criticism.

"Dr Smith came down to see Dad."

"To the house?"

"Yes, and Dad told him, and he said he would get you out of it."

"Dr Smith said?"

"Yes. After all, what would they do if you went mad?"

"What?"

"It's the same, they'd have to let you off."

"Lance came to take you home," said Aunt Teresa.

"I'm not going back to the school."

"What are you going to work at?" inquired the aunt, curiously. She told them that she had nearly finished her business course, at night, and would get that kind of job. They mourned over the good safe position she had thrown up but believed that she was going to Europe, and to some European university.

Lance said: "You'll never do it, you can't stick at anything."

They talked about the storm, the coffin-ships, an old collier that had gone down in the last storm and another that had taken three days to beat up to Newcastle. Young men had been saved, swum ashore, from other small rotten ships that were used in the coastal trade. There were no newspapers handy. If the ship was overdue they might send a plane out to search for her, she might even now be in port and all hands safe.

"Is there a train back tonight?" she asked Lance.

"You'll go in the morning," said Uncle Ned. "We'll put you both up tonight, Mother'll fix up something."

"I'll lose two half-days at work," said Lance. "Everyone suddenly going mad and running away. I lose two days' work."

"Two half-days."

Jerry got up now and took Ellen out on the road. Immediately, the old folks began to whisper.

"He's getting very attentive." "He seems really to be sweet on our little girl. It would be the end of our troubles if she'd settle down." Then, with infinite kindness, Aunt Teresa turned to her niece and said: "A girl's a great worry unless she settles down early. We shouldn't have given in to her whims; it's our fault. Don't you give your poor father trouble, Tess. A girl don't understand what a worry she is to her family."

"She don't know where she's going," said the uncle kindly. "You settle down, Tess. But she'll settle down," he continued cheerfully. "The weather's been very unsettling, some people take it that way, I've known grown men to run away in this kind of weather, change of seasons, too. We feel the weather just like animals. So it isn't Tess's fault. She won't do so any more." And he got up to get another cup of black tea, chuckling to make it all a joke and he patted her on the head as he went past. "Tess always had such lovely hair."

The couple were still walking up and down when Lance and Teresa went to their beds; the mother went to bed, while Uncle Ned sat up with an old almanac to read, to wait for them.

Before they left in the morning the brother and sister heard that Ellen had had a proposal, and was going to marry the "neighbour's son". She was in a curious mood, half-regretful but determined; all her previous life had disappeared. A small cool sun, the first sun of autumn, shone.

15. *At No Cost to Himself*

IT was March, getting cold and the evenings drawing in, but
Jonathan Crow still walked home and back in his summer suit.
At the end of March, he put on a vest, with a sweater on a very
cold day, and in April or May risked a muffler. He never wore
a winter coat and had come to believe that everyone could go
without a winter coat if he wanted to. Everything was a matter
of discipline.

He did not even shiver in the blasty wind as he came up the
Parramatta Road this night in mid-March, nor hurried his step
in the least, but footed it imperturbably in his stiff and solitary
style, along by the sandstone walls of the university, up the steps
and to the lighted side door of the Men's Union in the falling
dark. He could see the western sky, still a sombre lake of green
and slaty clouds; he thought: "Just my luck, I'll have two winters
this year", for he was sailing for England in August, the very
end of winter here, and would have only a month of their light
summer when he arrived.

He went to the pigeon-holes and got out a couple of letters and
a note. The note he opened first, with a slight smile; it was a day
late, she had held it for a day, but it had come! As he opened the
other letters, he thought: "The whirligig of time brings in its
revenge!" He had loved the wild-faced, black-eyed Clara Rasche
when he was a green student in his first months at the university;
she was the first "bourgeois girl", in his language, that had paid
attention to him and then she had such a bold, independent air,
not running after men at all, but seeming to be soaring in regions
of intellect; a brilliant girl, too, and the only woman in the
brilliant Rasche family, with three brothers, older than herself,
who had all made their mark. He had sighed after her, smiled

credulously at her; and now look at them both! Clara Rasche had married his best friend, Cooper Endor, but only in desperation, because it was him, Jonathan, she loved. Jonathan half-read one of the circulars he had received, and then went back to her note—the hand-made paper, lightly scented, the small, fine handwriting, the words, *she would wait for him if he could come* —how out of character! What remained of the splendid girl of several years ago? How could she give herself away to him like this? For surely Clara knew that he suspected what she wanted —she merely hankered after what was withheld, the oldest lure in the world. "It's defeated pride, not love," thought Crow. He put the letters in his pocket and went into the common room.

There he found Stephen Rasche, Clara's brother, now a journalist who had been in China and other seats of fire and smother, holding court in a circle of six or seven. He was tall, burly, big-headed, with a shine on his large dark face. He had begun to make a name for himself in court as a barrister, with bluff eccentricity, quips, a loud voice, a long memory; to build up that kind of personality which reaches the general public and impresses jurors before ever they are jurors, when he had suddenly married a wealthy woman and given up the bar for the quill. A grand, theatrical slob, mysteriously henpecked and who liked to talk about his henpecking, he was exemplary at home, and filled his outside life with fatal though short passions for Clara's friends. He did not like Lovelaces, his own affairs all sprang from passion; he did not like mediocrities, and as he belonged to one of the reigning families of Sydney society, his people all professional people, he let his tongue loose on those he hated. He knew well the Cooper-Clara-Jonathan trio for having seen them so often on their launch-picnics and in the discussion groups when they were undergraduates; they used to come to his chambers or to a place he kept downtown to talk about Chiang Kai-shek and Soviet Russia. To his mind, only one of the three had any ability, his sister Clara; but in the weak manner of clever women, she allowed herself to fall in love with one incapable man after another. Why? To dominate, or for peace and quiet in her home life? He regarded Jonathan Crow as a kind of wraith, a mere invention of his sister's incorrigible weakness, but being a family man he had come to be fond of his weak brother-in-law, Endor.

"Hullo," said he, stopping his windmill gestures and coming down on four legs, "one black Crow."

"Hullo, Rasche," said Jonathan pleasantly. "When are you off again?"

"Mr Master-of-Arts Crow," declared Rasche, drooping his eyelids, slewing his eyes round and studying Crow's boots, "back from a trip to the nearer suburbs with lectures on free love in Croydon, contraceptives in Strathfield, and sterilizing the unfit in Balmain. All sex, my dear fellow. Copulation, stopulation, depopulation."

"What's up?" said Jonathan cautiously, looking round the circle. All were his friends but a tall, dissolute fellow, with straying hair, hollow cheeks, large sunken eyes burning with love, drink, and debauch, and a deeply wrinkled forehead, who was half hidden by the pillar against which he leaned.

"What's biting you, Rasche?" asked Jonathan more pleasantly, making as if to leave the room.

"I'm afraid of the big bad wolf," said the dissolute man.

"How's your love cult, Crow? Crow here runs a little discussion circle, with the permission of the Dean, seven foolish, and seven wise virgins."

"By Jove," said Jonathan easily, "they'll never get any lies out of me. They go through life in blinkers anyhow; they'd be happier if they faced life the way we do. Life's no different for women. Your gallantry, your chivalry is only your way of keeping them in harness. And," he smiled, "satisfied desire. What else do we want in mistress or wife? I'm talking of the average man, who's no Kant, or John Stuart Mill—they're freaks. What's the good of these girls thinking they're going to run up against a Romeo? The fellows they meet are you, me, us. For you, Rasche, I can't say. You're the great lover. But I thought you agreed with Shakespeare—virginity is like a medlar, the worse the longer kept. Thus I am doing a salutary job."

"A job of sanitation says the bawd, the go-between, the marriage broker, a necessary job, a very excellent job," shouted Rasche in his heavy, dashing, hammy style. "Why don't you hawk your wares in the market-place like the pander in 'Pericles, Prince of Tyre'; and the little proviso, *on condition*, says you, that I may have a cut myself. A Spaniard went to bed to her very description, a Portygee made water in a sink space, and an

Englishman asked if the blame thing were legal, but you, O Crow of Crows, merely throw down orange-peel from the second gallery. 'Dost not taste thy wares thyself, first?' said the governor of the place. 'Dost not debauch by thy conversation, pander?' 'Nay, there are even now some shaken from the tree,' said the pander, 'for I am only a poor man, I have my way to make.'"

Jonathan flushed. "Pretty cheap, isn't it? I'm going. I'm no match for the lion cub of Inner Mongolia, the heir of John Rasche."

Rasche sneered: "I congratulate you, sir, on the love of woman, fair woman. Nobly cutting himself off from his equals, he goes out among the women and will prove to anyone—if she wear a spirit—that she must modify herself for men. If she don't suit, too bad for her. No, she must accommodate herself to being the universal mother, and he takes a yardstick to her skirt, too, to find out if it's too short or too long. Mr Crow, after much floor-scrubbing in the university, will shortly go abroad to try his excellent new system of female education on the English, the French, and so on. Or How the Modest Man Can Ravish Women with No Cost to Himself, Lonely Woman, or the Town. Why don't you act like a decent chap, eh?—go to bed with the girls and cut out all this hanky-panky. You know darn well what you're doing. It's an old trick, every lady-killer of the church does it."

"Isn't it too bad that you're dead wrong?" said Jonathan bitterly. "You organize groups in your chambers, that's different. If it's so what you say is so, then it's just a case of the kettle calling the pot."

"Tell me," said the drunk, "what is a woman but a sewer? What is this all about?"

"Clara Rasche," muttered one of the men to another.

"As for your scholarly career," said Rasche, angrily, "a man gets out of Europe what he takes to it, as they say, Mr Nix-nought-nothing, will you take our money?"

"Share her. Why fight?" said the drunk.

"I'm going," said Jonathan disgustedly. "Good night, chaps!"

He went out proudly, with a haggard look, his foot dragging, and he had gained the moral victory of the victim, though he was really wounded. Who knew better than himself that he was but an ordinary man who had got to the top by observing and following the rules? What they knew about him, he had himself said a dozen times.

A few minutes later, Clara Endor, Rasche's sister, saw him coming down the slope between two buildings straight towards the Women's Union. There was only a small lamp half-way up but she knew him when the gloom first moved.

He came slowly across the sandy slope full of footholds and pitfalls, under the next lamp, brushing under the tree, over the drive, without looking up, his head averted as usual. They laughed at him good-naturedly in the Women's Union; he was the only man, they said, who had ever been inside the Union except on dance nights, the only man who was not afraid to call there, to take messages to them from other men, to laugh with them on the terrace while their short skirts swung by him. Crow had a sober friendship for all women; one of his friends was "little Redtop", a smart first-year girl of seventeen, and his closest friend was Miss Alice Haviland, a woman of thirty-six. He wrote them all friendly notes and lent them his essays.

Clara looked at him and trembled. He did not love her, but here he was, here when she called. He climbed the steps slowly to where she stood, not caring that he was standing in the lamplight and could be seen by everyone for half a mile around. He raised his hat and smiled with a swift sideways glance, his soft strong voice said: "Hullo, Clara!"

"Hullo," she muttered.

He held out the note, crushed it, and put it into his pocket: then held it out again, "Unless you want it?"

"What for? Are you walking up to the class?"

They moved towards the steps. She put her arm on his when they reached the bottom step and were out of the light. He did not flinch, though he did not take her arm. "There's time yet, which way?"

"Did you eat yet?"

"Never mind. I eat at home."

She pointed to the terrace outside the library, on to which no door opened. "Let's go up there a minute."

"O.K."

It was cold and the lights were only on high in the end arch of the Gothic library. The traceried windows shone dully from deck-lamps within. No one ever went to the terrace. Beyond was the Medical School and acres of grass and unflowering plantation behind the iron pikes, with asphalt paths leading to City Road, at a considerable distance. He went that way to reach home.

"It's cold, Johnny, you have no coat."

"I don't wear a coat. Besides, what does it matter? When ladye fayre commands——"

"Your voice is husky, are you sure you haven't caught a cold?"

"I saw a doctor Saturday. He said it's just clergyman's sore throat. I'm going to give up this class here at any rate——"

"Oh, good!"

"I don't get paid for it and so——" He coughed apologetically. "Laryngitis," he said. "It'll go away if I rest it."

"Is he a good doctor?"

"He's my brother's—a panel doctor, he pays in there. A quack in City Road."

She slipped her arm through his as they walked up the three or four grassy steps to the silent terrace.

"What a starry night, Demi-johnny."

"Demi-john because I'm only half-there, or demi-john I am half-john, a smell?"

"Oh, Johnny! Really!"

"Yes, I half-stink because I am half-dead, your brother would say."

"Stephen? What has he to do with it?"

"You know that old rhyme you sing in the closets when you're a youngster, *ink, pink, paper, star, stone, stink*? Funny, isn't it? Someone ought to explain where these things come from, I don't mean the meaning, I mean the obscure poet and why it took on. There's no sense in it. We take to nonsense more than anything else. I suppose we ought to hold that in mind when we're reading the philosophers; how much of this is interesting hocus-pocus, to please the following. Come on, what do you think? You with your medal in philosophy?"

She said seriously: "Why, I think philosophy is the answer to all that. It's the attempt we make to find out what things really mean."

He laughed and went on: "What dirty words meant to us as children! It wasn't mumbo-jumbo, it was a new thrill per word."

Clara said: "I never could understand why they drew roosters on the fences."

"Roo— Oh, I see. Yes, dirty little beggars we all were. I was up to my nose in it when I was eight and liking the muck, mind you. I was a slum kid and precocious from your point of view, though they're all precocious down there in the gutter, like a feeble-minded kid I saw the other night. You should have seen that kid slither through the traffic with his papers! Reminded me of myself when I was a nipper. I think anyone who comes from down there steals a march on you sheltered kids. Our eyes are unsealed, in the words of the poets."

"You mean," she said, "that what you see there, in Darlington, in Golden Grove, in Tempe, in Redfern, is the truth, the only truth?"

"But truth disturbs the golden mean, doesn't it? The bitter truth. No. We get distorted, too, and for life. That's the trouble. We don't see the truth either. But who does? What is it? 'What is truth, said jesting Pilate', washing his hands of it." He coughed.

"Oh, your voice! You're catching cold."

"Don't worry about me," he said. "I'm tough."

There was a long pause as they walked up and down the terrace, again, close together. He coughed lingeringly. She said:

"Why did I bring you here? It's so exposed."

"I like it here," said Johnny.

"Why did I get married? He tells me I only want to go on working because I don't love him, if I loved him, I'd give up work and work in the kitchen. I told him it was only because I could get out and see other people that I stayed there at all."

"What makes you behave like kids? I thought you and Cooper had more brains. You know what it's all about."

"It's cruel that because I want to see you above all, you're just the one I can't see, it's so stupid. It means I only see those I don't care to see. What a paradox."

"Under a different system, with free love, you could see me and I could see you. We could both have you."

"You don't want me, do you?" she said sadly.

"What do you mean, Clara?"

"If I left Cooper, it wouldn't mean anything to you?"

"You know what I believe, that monogamy is rusty, it's tied up with the old system of property, it's simply making woman man's property. If women didn't hold themselves as something apart, think so much of their bodies as property, we wouldn't have all this flesh-tearing and grinding of teeth, don't you see? Friend and friend would lie down together like the lion and the lamb."

"In a thousand years—and I live now."

"There it is! I can't have you."

"You can have me."

He said nothing.

"There's something about being a woman. I simply want to be a cave woman when I think of you. I want to work for you, I'd wait on you, I'd wash your feet and dry them with my hair."

"Like Jesus," said Jonathan.

"Yes," she said grudgingly, "like Jesus. As Martha, as Mary— but I wasn't thinking of Jesus."

"No, I know, slavery is a kind of instinct with women."

"We call it love."

"I call it the instincts of the millennial slave," and he ground his teeth, a startling sound.

She laughed uncertainly.

"When women are free, we'll see other emotions, no love. Love is a slave emotion, like a dog's."

"I love you, Johnny, I love you so much."

He said gutturally: "Yes, I know you do, I know you do", and taking her by the arm he pushed her towards the wall and into the arch of the unused doorway.

She said: "Why, you can't go in that way, that door's closed."

He made no reply, but roughly, silently, as if he detested her, caught hold of her and lifted her up one step, and pressed himself against her. She understood, then. She had seen rough, poor couples in dark streets, in passageways, against trees. She began to kiss him coldly, because she was frightened, but he held her in a firm grip, said nothing, gave no kisses, looking over her shoulder at the door with a set face. She felt humiliated. They stood thus against the door for several minutes, while the wind blew round their shoulders and legs, getting colder. Without a word, he released her, and went down the steps before her. When she reached his side he moved towards the end of the terrace without looking up, but when they got there and stood looking out towards the lower ground, the hollow depression where the Union stood, the buildings with lighted floors where night classes were going on, the cricket-ground, the distant denominational colleges, he grumbled softly: "I hope you haven't told Cooper anything about all this?"

She felt as if thistledown were drifting about her eyes, and laughed drunkenly. A minute before she hated him, now she loved him.

"Oh, my dear, as if he didn't know! I've said nothing, of course, but doesn't he know both of us so well?"

"A nice kettle of fish," he said accusingly. "Now he'll be angry with me, now I've lost him." Sulkily, with his hands in his pockets, he climbed down the steps and began to lurch towards the lighted ground, leaving her a few steps behind.

When she caught up with him, he said in a reasoning voice: "You know I don't want to lose Cooper, you oughtn't to have said anything."

She laughed, "I didn't", but the time was running short and she began to have her say. "Look, Jonathan, tell me the truth, I'm not going to be a model wife and I want you, but if it's not you, it'll be another because that's the way I feel. I'd leave Cooper altogether if I had to stay cooped up. I'm only twenty-three, I'm not going to stay cabined, cribbed, confined all my life."

"Now, now. Keep cool, old girl."

"Well, just make up your mind now, Johnny. I don't want to go on like this."

"Look, Clara," he said sweetly, "perhaps we shouldn't meet any more. Don't do anything hasty. I'll be gone soon. You'll soon get over it." He went on persuasively, looking down at her: "You don't know much about love yet, neither do I. But I wouldn't lose Cooper." She said nothing; they had skirted the wide pool of light and were going towards the steps that led to the cloisters. He went on, tenderly: "So you see, dear, we ought to cut this out."

She answered nothing. He ruminated, and inquired, still with the same husky reasonableness: "Where is Cooper now? Is he at home?"

"Yes."

"Well, there you are, you see. You get hot in the collar, you're not reasonable, that's just womanish. Don't you think you ought to go home?"

She laughed, puzzled by his change of mind. As they climbed into the cloisters, she said: "But, Jonathan, explain something to me, you told me this last year that you were going to find out something about this business of love, as you said, and you made up that questionnaire, then you said you'd be scientific and experimental, and you said that you—you know what you said to me. So I was willing to let you experiment with me. . . ."

He said nothing, but guided her towards the steps.

"Johnny," she rushed on, "marriage is dull and narrow for me, don't you see? It's not love for you but passion. I don't want you in particular, if it isn't you, it'll be someone else and I picked you because——"

"Because," he said, with a tender sound of laughter.

"Because I love you. I will never love the others, don't you see? Choose now, Jonathan, it's now or never. I won't hang around you."

"You see, you're a complete woman, Clara, and I can't get you involved. You can't take it, you get too involved, so the best thing is for us to part now."

Clara said: "One minute——" She waved her arm, helpless.

"Yes," he said, staring her straight in the face, not unkindly, "we'd better part friends, just as it is, we'd better not meet again." Seeing how pale she was, he added quickly: "At least not for a year and I'll be away by then, not for the next two or three years. Then I won't be bothering you."

"Good-bye."

"Don't take it like that, Clara," he whispered.

"Good luck."

"You're very pale," he said.

"I'm hot inside, so that compensates," Clara said, tearing her hand away from his strong grasp and walking hurriedly round the other side of the cloisters.

He saw her shrug her shoulders. "Good-bye," called Jonathan mildly, after her.

He turned and walked along the corridor to the small lecture-room under the stairs which he was allowed to use, in this off-hour, for his group.

16. A Girl without a Coat and with Smooth Bare Head

CROW did not know that he himself had founded the love cult, but he knew the sensation he produced when he entered a room of these people of his own age, with his casual bright smiles and his stiff walk. "Every entrance is a sexual experience," he remarked to his friend Cooper, and Cooper not only knew that it was so, but noticed with what coaxing humility, broadcast fragments of flattery, and ingratiating twinkles the remarkable Jonathan exercised his charm. Cooper admired him. He had been too poor and also too bored to try to finish at the university and had left at the beginning of his second year. He still had the unsatisfied hunger for learning and argument of broken students. He admired Jonathan for his success, his amusing peculiarities, and his naïve cynicism, which Cooper put down to inexperience, just as the girls did. Cooper usually came to all of Johnny's discussion groups and brought with him his young wife, Clara.

"What matters to me," said Crow, to them both, "is not whether I stir their bowels, but whether I can reach through the bowel to their brains, I want to start a fermentation. I want to see the wheels go round, that is my function, to start trouble, to disturb the sleep of the world." Thus whatever produced excitement in the young people pleased him; he started discussions on sex purely to start up that want and restlessness. He was the gadfly of desire.

"Without unsatisfied desire," he said to Cooper, "there is no progress. Man is easy-going, he has nothing but the vapid curiosity of his simian ancestors, he has to be hungry, crossed in love, wounded in his self-esteem, and need patches on his boots before he will make a discovery or go to work. Don't I know? I work best when someone injures my pride. The insulted and injured? The future inventors—— Let 'em lick them. Down with social improvement. In short, necessity is the mother of invention and hunger invented that which destroys it, bread."

This windy March evening he expected an outsider at his class, Teresa Hawkins, the girl he coached in Latin.

There were still long cold gleams in the cloudy sky and a gritty biting wind blew over the quadrangle and round the pinnacles of the clock tower. The windows of the classroom, looking towards the Medical School, showed only a black sky of stars and clouds, no light was left. The lights of the classroom burned dimly. Near the window stood his platform and desk. All this he saw coming along the corridor. He looked round at them and smiled waggishly. The eight women were seated in the two front rows and behind were three men, two of Crow's unfailing guests and a visitor, Everett Keane, a raw little blond man from one of Jonathan's downtown classes, a poor young man from a dairy farm who was studying and saving to get to the university; Jonathan rubbed his hands. If Miss Hawkins came, he would pit these two rank outsiders against the paddock-fed, high-paced college product and we should see what we should see. If it were not that degrees were asked for, in good jobs, he himself would have backed the University of Life every time.

He hailed the men, said respectably: "Good evening, Keane!" and went to the girls, handing an essay back to one, taking his own essay from another and handing this to a third, chatting pleasantly with them, chuckling, talking about some past or coming Saturday outing. There were Miss Alice Haviland, a large-faced poor and dowdy woman; Elaine, a gentle blonde, in a blue dress; Joyce, a swarthy, impatient friend of Miss Haviland's, who criticized him bitterly; "little Redtop", the seventeen-year-old who was already engaged, but a playmate of Johnny's, and several others.

As he turned to go to the little platform, there were steps in the corridor. He looked and saw Clara Endor there, her hair windblown. She must have gone quite a distance before she turned back. He nodded brightly to her and plunged into his notes, while she settled herself at the far end of the second seat. They were glancing at her and she spoke to them, all old classmates, in a constrained manner. They knew her trouble. At a new sound, he saw a form standing near the outer door, a girl without a coat and with smooth bare head. It was his protégée, Teresa Hawkins. He smiled.

"Come along in!"

She advanced, and hesitated in the door while she looked at the class, then came towards his desk. He kept smiling at her. There was something strange about her, though it was perhaps only her wind-blown hair. Her eyes were reddened, her cheeks rough and pale; her short straight blond hair had just been combed back, leaving the forehead naked, her pale mouth was parted in a timid smile; grey eyes shifted uneasily over high cheek-bones. She was too plain, dressed too poorly, and looked older than he had thought. But her timidity pleased him. He came to stand beside her as he introduced her, and Miss Haviland, smiling, beckoned with a finger, pointed with a finger to the bench beside her and said audibly: "There!" with a quick coy flirt of her head. Crow said: "Thank you, Miss Haviland," and returned to his desk.

"We want to get at the truth," he said self-deprecatingly, "and in a subject like this, so wrapped up in fear and sham, and social tradition and perhaps even race-memory, we have to begin at the roots and then dig, dig in." He put on his glasses and at once became sharp.

"All our habits are the vestiges of outmoded social customs which remain with us as prejudice. Prejudice is as strong as law, it causes people to commit suicide and to imprison others. In the beginning, we had marriage by capture, and today the woman still believes that she must be coy and retreat in order herself to capture the attentions of the male. The male, on the other hand, retaining much older animal habits"—this was a signal for a general smile—"is curiously moved to show off and brag in front of the female, with sundry grunts and his best suit of clothes, even if he does not want her!"

The women stirred. A faint complacency came into his face. He went on and on in this strain. It was a disordered, impertinent paper; but no one seemed to notice that and to himself it seemed the pure fluid of thought; it was reason arraigning hypocrisy. He had a collection of ideas like the above, injected with eccentric legal, eugenic, and medical fancies with a few facts about the sexual act (still unknown to at least some members of his audience) and which was constructed on the plan of those wild religious books of visionaries and secretaries which have a crumb of everything and appeal to one great need. For sixteen pages, written out in his clerkly hand, now beginning to loosen a bit, he discussed love. Miss Haviland clicked her tongue now and then with a *tchk*, *tchk*, looking at him with a faint motherly smile and biting her lips, and Clara started when he said that perhaps the brothel was not a bad idea; while one of the men gave an ironical cheer. He went on coolly.

"What, in fact, is wrong with masturbation? What is wrong with homosexuality? Nothing, perhaps. We won't know until we calmly inquire." He looked at them with a laugh. "Let us mop up all the debris of our accepted beliefs!"

He then read the results of the famous questionnaire which he had sent out secretly to graduates, asking them about their sexual lives, at what age they first felt desire, how many children they had and the like; for, he explained, "Higher education, the prolongation of the childhood of the race, is destroying or distorting that impulse which reproduces the race. Youths who are able to procreate at fourteen or fifteen, and who must wait to establish themselves in a society which rejects bastard children, do not have offspring till they are twenty-seven or -eight, or even later. Women who could be mothers at seventeen are forced to compete with men in the professions and usually deprived of motherhood altogether, since the conservative male's objection to a blue-stocking in the home is well known." He smiled again at the miserable women whose sufferings he had tabulated. "The worst is," he continued, "that college graduates have less children than workers; that is, the elect of the race, elect through long struggle for survival, the strongest and best, with good bodies and minds, are going towards the vanishing point, while the voting majority is becoming increasingly that of the second-rate and the misfits."

Forestalling objections, he said that he came from the slums, though none of them did and he knew what was there, he had never there seen real honesty, real idealism, real ability. He gritted his teeth and said grudgingly: "Because of them I am what *I* am, just a shock-worker of grind. The slums starved me and gave me base ideas. Your idealism, your fine emotions, your æsthetics are not for me, because there are basic ideas I must accept to get on in your society. I was poor. I might want to deviate. They are not buying me. Aesthetics are for well-known families of talent." He looked ironically at Clara. She was unable to endure it, and dropped her head. He went on stubbornly.

"Especially is this sexual selection, by some need of nature, away from brains though not physical perfection, in the case of women. We, every man jack of us, prefer the beautiful woman to the drudge in books. What can a student of mathematics do for us and our children? It is for our firesides we want our women and so the sexual selection amongst the mothers of the race has had only one tendency, to divide brains from beauty, a scission which is not inevitable, but which hangs heavily over the fate of learned women and tends to force them into spinsterhood. The marriage rate among the graduates of Girton, Barnard——" and he went on to show these dreary figures, deducing that such women "failed in their biological purpose". He attacked the university too.

"The university system is wrong itself, stealing from us our youth and strength to get their degrees, to learn their subjects, to follow their professions."

"What do you want to do, Savonarola?" shouted Miss Haviland's wire-haired friend.

He grinned, delighted at the stir. Only a moment of silence and he went on: "Science must now take a hand; women must not imitate men's civilization which had only a bread-winning purpose, but must be selected for motherhood and impregnated by the state, from phials containing the seed of elect males, brilliant in body and mind. Women would not then have to capture young men, to marry them, and man could study in peace; arts, sciences, letters, all the work of men, would go ahead by leaps and bounds. As to women, if any of them showed exceptional ability, they would not suffer their present handicaps, but if suitable, would become the mothers of brilliant men." He gave them the motto "Two races with different needs".

He warned them against miscegenation, against marrying Japanese, Chinese, Bantus, or Malays, not only because they weaken the breed, "mongrels are always weaker than true strains", but because white women could never know what was going on in the brains of those men of other ancient races. There was a physical difference in the constitution of the brain. *Homo pekinensis*, their ancestors, differed materially from the Cro-Magnon race. He knew an Australian woman who had married a Japanese gentleman and had never been happy; in the end, she left him. To us, they were unreliable; they considered deeds proper which were repugnant to us and perhaps we did not act to coincide with their views of honour. For instance, we laughed at ancestor-worship, Mikado-worship, yet that was almost an instinct with the Asiatic races.

"But the Mikado has just been reimposed by main force," shouted the wire-haired girl, angrily. A discussion arose to which Jonathan listened patiently. He managed to finish his paper, but their attention was scattered and all kinds of issues arose. The wire-haired girl said: "There's so much to say against your paper, Mr Crow, that it's a waste of time to criticize it at all." Miss Haviland said: "For shame, Joyce!" Clara got up and defended him. One of the men started to discuss schools in the workshop, factory, and field. His statistics and inquiries, experiments on monkeys, and reports of Galton went by the board. Crow began to feel that he had started again that magnificent fret.

It was not a class, as Crow thought, but a group of admirers of himself, sedulously collected, carefully selected; sentimental admirers who heard of the hard row he had to hoe in life and some loving women who would not attack him before the rest. He still fancied that he had got all those girls together as part of his study of Love; first the questionnaire to graduates, then an exploration of the female mind. He thought he was original in this; he had come out with it, what bothered them all. He might some day publish a book that would be quoted, on "Female Psychology"; it might rank with other standard works. He knew that in academic woods, he who pursues a single spoor, however faint and old, will in time run down a post and title and why not the sexual problem? It was a very popular one and adorned with the greatest names. He had lost some of his original modesty, he had begun to rely on his "biological knack" and thought himself something of a sly, clever man. By pursuing his way alone he meant, shouldering away every contentious student, and forgetting the existence of those who despised him (and who would mostly fall by the wayside, anyhow), to beat the men who got on by flights of talent and certainly to get ahead of the few of dazzling brilliance, quite clearly cut off from careers. He thought only, of course, of men without much influence, like himself. The family men, the Rasches, were out of his book. He was not so much jealous of them; they were merely another breed. But amongst the mongrels, the orphaned, he knew how to get on.

The sexual problem was wide. It allowed him to range from genius in by-blows, through sexual differences and the recidivist criminal child, by racial purity, to trial marriage and easy divorce; practically the whole of life.

When the class was over, they stood round for a few moments, rattling over the irritating things he had said. Clara, shaking back her ink-black hair, in her slow, vibrant voice with its rumble of suppressed passion said: "But Jonathan seems to think that men only feel a certain sort of desire, and only wish for momentary pleasure." Elaine, the fair and reticent, said that men of the most gifted sort, Balzac, John Stuart Mill, Comte, were famous for their loyalty. "What about Shakespeare?" said Miss Haviland. Clara said he only put his brothel scenes in and his bawdy lines because he was forced to by the low taste of his audience; one of the men declared he put them in to drum up business for the entr'acte. The girls thought of Shakespeare as a pleasant, unfortunate English teacher, unfortunate because of Anne Hathaway, invalided because of genius.

"Everyone likes the obscene; that is real life," said Teresa, the bare-boned girl, unexpectedly, opening her lips for the first time.

"Not a great artist," stormed Clara.

"Those more than the others, because their violence is more," said Teresa.

Clara frowned. "I don't know, I can't see it that way."

"He wrote *Venus and Adonis* against his will?" asked Teresa triumphantly.

"It doesn't seem possible, I admit," declared Miss Haviland.

Mr Everett Keane, like a stray cat, suddenly stood up stiffly near them, scolding on the outer edge of the group of three men, little and thin but bristling, his sun-reddened face aflame with anger, his rough yellow hair seeming to shoot sparks. In a rasping farm voice with the most miserable accent in the world, he asked them if that was what interested them, whether Shakespeare liked smut; if they were interested in the family, if they had read Engels. He was somewhat put out when the wire-haired girl, that other stray cat, flung "Yes" back at him in her strong voice. But apart from the wire-haired girl, not one had even heard of Engels and he began to talk about him, wanted to send his copy up to the group for them to read. This astonished and offended them; it amused them also. But distasteful to them, used to the jolly bear-pit of their discussions, was his angry, accusing style and the phrases he threw out at them, in raw, torn pieces, scratched out of the polemics of a poor man's paper. Miss Haviland smiled in a motherly way; the other girls, after listening with a show of manners, began to turn their backs. They were really impatient with any speaker but Jonathan Crow. Mr Keane ranted. "Whether Shakespeare liked bawds or whether the mind of the Orient is a mystery," he cried to them in poignant tones, "I wanted to go to the university, and I still do, if you don't put me off. It isn't that I'll get out of the university."

His violence and power of sudden eloquence moved them for a moment, like a wild wind that had blown in the glass of the windows; dark thoughts, restless desires whirled round them, but when the yellow-haired man walked off by himself, indignant, on his short legs, they all began to laugh, a healthy, happy murmur that trembled through the whole group; this laugh was led by Jonathan Crow who started off with a few words of appreciation of the young man; he had great ambition.

They moved out in a body. The boys legged it across the quad, loose and tall in their successful youth, the girls, still fat-calved and fat-hipped, strong creatures, flocked more like fowls through the cloisters. There were left apart Miss Haviland, her wire-haired friend, a gangling, bitter person with brilliant eyes, and Teresa, who came out last, expecting Mr Crow to speak to her, but not sure, since she had seen his many friends. She joined the two older women who were also waiting for him.

Jonathan said, coming up, that what they needed, most of them, was a leader.

"Why not you?" he said to Teresa. "You have the power."

This jolted her. "I sometimes feel I have, but I don't know enough, they know so much more than me."

"They don't know anything," said Joyce, the wire-haired, in her rude, strident voice. "It's like a Sunday School picnic."

"I know," agreed Crow. "That's why I brought Keane and Miss Hawkins up. It's curious how the brains of the university graduates close after graduation."

"Do you think the brain really closes?" Miss Haviland asked. "I know, myself, I feel as if there's nothing more to work for.

All my life I've had one ambition, I've had my eyes fixed on that little bit of sheepskin. Now I've got it, and it doesn't seem to mean anything."

"Mr Keane doesn't seem to feel you are worth leading," remarked Teresa, coming back to the tremendous compliment Mr Crow had paid her.

"Young Mr Keane has a lot to learn, especially in manners," Miss Haviland said, laughing primly.

"He has the manners of a promising labour politician," Joyce said.

The four of them, the three women and Crow, walked along the cloisters in a body, closely united, and Teresa, who suddenly felt hot with ideas, was disappointed; Crow would go off with them and not give her a chance to explain her ideas to him. Joyce and Crow disputing, Miss Haviland and Teresa got to the front as they reached the archway and stood there talking, with the others twenty yards away, and very strident. Miss Haviland, with a mysterious smile, tapped her companion on the arm and murmured: "He likes you. I've often wondered what type of girl would really suit him and now I see. He talked about you before you came up." She went on with a roguish smile: "Oh, Mr Crow and I have been friendly enemies for three or four years, we divided all the prizes between us, and I have been like his sister, his oldest sister," she said briskly. "He has told me so many little things about himself, he was rather attracted to Clara in his first year, but that was soon over, now she is happily married to his best friend, it's strange, isn't it—but we were waiting to see you because he spoke of your particular personal power and said you had some exceptional quality which he couldn't quite put his finger on, and he wanted us to judge. Let me tell you, you made the right impression."

Teresa looked at Miss Haviland with a hangdog look. She said finally: "I don't know enough myself."

The other two had stopped, were looking at them and came up to them. Miss Haviland briskly invited Joyce to have tea with her at the Union, and Crow, at the signal, swung off with Teresa, whose heart was ready to burst with pride at being picked out by him like this. Miss Haviland, on leaving, had a coy but affectionate smile, wrung Teresa's hand and invited her to have tea with her next Thursday evening, "as ever is," at the Blue Dog tea-room downtown near Martin Place, "at six, now, don't forget."

The lights were on in the quadrangle and down the long drear descent of the university avenue. On the terrace a cold air fluttered their garments and hair. The early evening was around them, the lights of City Road, George Street West, and the blaze of the city below them. They stood there a moment on the brink, breathing the cold air. They knew a little about each other. This poor young man and woman prided themselves that they were hardy enough to do without an overcoat through the winter, that they need not use trams and buses but their legs could carry them anywhere; they were proud that they ate little, that they had few advantages and that they were going very far in life and in the world before they would be satisfied. When Teresa said that the Miller of Dee's song—

> *I care for nobody, no, not I,*
> *And nobody cares for me—*

—was her watchword, Mr Crow said it was a healthy sentiment, regular armour plate, and it was his too, but when he said it, his voice came out of his boots and she felt very sorry for the lonely man.

Said Mr Crow: "The Glasgow strikers and the Welsh protest marchers walk in midwinter, without coats, to carry their demands for bread and work, through the snow, through the wind, between walls of grey granite or through the black coal forests", and he gritted his teeth. "Bread and work and love, the poor man's trinity, and by all three needs they chain him down. In the need for one and three."

"In the need for one and three he struggles," said Teresa, thinking of herself.

"If he has bread and work, will he struggle for the other, or just wait and take what comes, do you think?" asked Mr Crow, jutting his blue chin towards her.

"Don't we?" Teresa said, looking by him.

"I expect women are different," said Jonathan, sighing. "I read about the mountaineers who only wear their shirts in winter in the high mountains, looking after their flocks, baring their chests to the *tramontana*. That's my ambition, when I get there, to stand where they stand and do as they do. Won't it be strange to see fields of snow?"

They laughed. Neither of them had ever seen snow. It was to them something heroic, primeval, belonging to the possible antique history of their race; and the icy seas, the fog-bound coasts, the groaning walls of ice, the night-, crime-, and misery-beleaguered island of Great Britain, something that occurred in the legends of Norsemen, something that froze Little Time and that existed also in the black latitudes of dead planets. It was not the dainty snow of Christmas cards that they believed in, broken by tinsel, robins, and ivy, but the icy death of the whale-gate, Ultima Thule. They shrank from the land they were going to, a land of tyranny denounced by English patriots and abandoned by their own grandfathers, a land of unrest, the land of Dickens, poor seamstresses in Poultry and mud-spattered Watling Street, a London, cloud-sunk, an adamantine island chained to the shifting bank of the Channel, the city of Limehouse and Jack the Ripper; and the Alps they saw in imagination were sky-piercing, snow-blazing pinnacles, sharp as wolf-teeth, in a pass of which, over-looking a pine forest, a blue-shirted shepherd opened his hairy chest to the *tramontana* and dangled at his belt an unsheathed knife with which he attacked the wolves. At the same instant Hannibal crossed with elephants panting out of wells of snow and a brave little drummer boy drummed from a crevasse; upon the glacier, the ice-maiden beckoned; in an evergreen flow of ice issuing from the side of a precipice a corpse lay for ever fresh. In the forest, long-haired timber-cutters worked, the wolves howled; in short, the land of ice-Cockaigne, without time or race. Their land of the sun seemed to them a sparkling land, set in blue seas, and much preferable, but they had to go, called out by the sea, driven forth on its ships, they could not stay in the busy port of Sydney and not take all the chances it offered of distant seas.

After these dreams of the cold, cold snow, Jonathan murmured: "What are you going over there for, exactly?"

"I want to go to the Sorbonne."

"And your young man, who is travelling abroad, is he there?"

She was silent, for she had forgotten she had told him this story as a joke. He went on: "That's some undertaking! When are you going?"

"I have to be my own scholarship, don't you see? I have no

money now and I haven't even landed a job yet, though I expect I will soon——"

"Gee——" said Jonathan, and stopped short, remorsefully.

"You are going in the spring?"

"End of winter, in the spring if you like. It will be winter here and winter there, so I'll have two winters. I'll have to get a coat for over there." After a moment he reflected aloud: "In the spring——" and laughed. "In the spring——" she said, laughing. It was complete night, and taking his hand she went down the few steps to the avenue. He let himself be led, then withdrew his hand gently and took her arm.

"In the spring," he said at last, looking closely at her with his short-sighted eyes, "even I, you know, begin to wonder whether there isn't such a thing as love. Effect of temperature on experience. That's a hard row to hoe, yours," he continued quickly. She did not reply. He cleared his throat and asked: "Do you believe that climate changes men's characters? There is some evidence to show that it changes their head form. A girl I know, Clara, you saw her, thinks people's characters change with every wind, every storm."

"My character would never change. I was always the same, single-minded and selfish. If it weren't how could I do what I'm going to do?"

"Perhaps we will see each other over there?"

She continued, arguing with herself: "You see, perhaps you are right, this climate hardens us. If you can sleep out in the park like those men do in the Domain, and like those poor children do, you do not dread unemployment so much, hence you do not dread the employer so much, hence we are hardier about the future."

"That's true," he struck his leg. "I believe that's true. Well, that's an argument on Clara's side."

"Over there, in Europe, you are likely to freeze to death, you are more afraid of being out of work."

"Braver if you resist?" he queried.

"Yes, our first settlers were brave then."

"Then why are you going?" he insisted. "I know some of the girls are going for one reason and another and some of the men. Some of them are getting up a cruise on a thirty-foot boat and expect to end up in Portsmouth. If you stayed here, you'd have a home and a job. Isn't it running a risk?"

"What do you mean by a risk?"

"There's so much unemployment everywhere and Europe's in a mess. They'll never assimilate Soviet Russia. There'll be another European war, they'll have men to fight in two years," he said grumpily. "I don't blame them, I'd go myself. Book-worming isn't my idea of life."

"I couldn't be happy if I didn't make a venture."

"Bravo," said Jonathan indifferently.

They had kept stopping during their talk, slightly shivering, in the cold breeze. They came to the bridge over the pond. The large fig-trees overhang it and a light shines beyond the leaves and the lodge-gate.

Here they stopped again. He said abruptly: "You have genius, I don't know, something that's for you. If any one of us is to win out, it will be you. What have we? Suburban brains, acquiescence. You are a free spirit."

"I know." He lifted his head at her candour and admired her. "Not so free, I am tied to all kinds of things." He didn't want to hear that. "No, no, only one of us is free." For some reason, she thought to ask: "Miss Haviland?"

"What is the use?" his voice came dolefully. "She is too old, it took her too long to fight her way upstream. She says herself her brain was closed."

She wanted to defend Miss Haviland but the cowardice peculiar to private conversations fell on her. He looked at her, sticking out his face and peering in the dark. She came forward into the light and he saw the thin face, hair combed flat and the pale long hands grasping her lunch box. Her absolute confidence shining through her drained face struck him like a blow, shook him up; he ought to have this confidence too.

"What is it you want to do?" he urged her. Suddenly intrigued, mystified, and in a mystic state of mind, he wanted to hear some revelation. Meanwhile, she felt a recession of all sensation, but a lamp seemed to have been lighted in her brain; outside all was dark but for this one believer who questioned her. She wanted to tell him everything and forget her silent plotting and planning, to simply yield her babble of projects to this man, make him a companion and have an end of gnawing secrets. The secret life seemed dry as dust; this humble, sweet man might understand her, comfort her, and even receive her love, which was for no one.

"I can't tell *you*," she said. Another moment and she would have said: "I want to love."

They went on their way, their casual relation of admiration and encouragement continuing as if no anguish had at the same moment entered them both. It was novel to him. He had from her neither Clara's tirades and gallant recklessness, nor Elaine's firm gentleness, prudent, watchful love, nor Tamar's good-fellow boisterousness. These were the three girls between whom he had hesitated last summer when he had made up his mind to go on a voyage of discovery to women. Nothing much had come of it yet. "We might meet in London. An affair might come of it." But he did not prevent it either, anxious to see how far she would go, touched by her. What did it mean, this self-control? She would grow out of him? He could await the issue, as with the other girls, Clara and so forth. The impatient girls came back to the rein and whip; he did not care, he was going elsewhere; the restive tumultuous breed of women always did the work of passion for him. He liked to remain passive.

Teresa heard his weary dragging footsteps and her own. Neither had said anything for a few minutes. A tram rattled past the gate, there rushed past the night traffic of City Road.

"I am only directing the group because no one else has stepped forward, but I believe when I go, the group will cease to be," said Crow softly. "It's a pity, there's this anxiety to learn something outside, to discuss our problems, nothing is given to us, the hungry sheep look up and are not fed. We are turned out of here completely unready. Ignorant too. You and Keane won't believe that. You are out in the swim, you two, you have to swim for it, it is sink or swim. You are in touch with real things. I'm going to be coddled for another two or three years, *prolonging the adolescence of the race*." He laughed sadly.

"If you think my life is real to me—it's only a passage," she cried rudely.

"To?" They stood on the footpath waiting to cross to the safety island where she could catch the downtown tram.

"To our secret desires," she said huskily. "To Cytherea, perhaps," and "night passage, isn't it? To Cytherea, or whatever island—but I always think of coral atolls, submarine volcanoes, the pearl gulfs of the north, a kind of Darwin's voyage of discovery, as the voyage to Cytherea. I do not think of their old islands", and she waved a careless hand towards the citadel of culture which the trees hid.

"Their old islands." He smiled at her.

"Did you know that there was a real Cytherea? The painting of Watteau is not all imagination? The men and women of the French court joined secret orders, where they only had names of minerals and plants; one sex, minerals, one sex, plants. Those islands were in the Seine. They had mysteries, what are called mysteries, but what anyone can imagine. Those were the orders of Cytherea. It was not the first time in history, either."

"Really?" He was enchanted. Then he changed his tune. "In the lives of the rich there is nothing that has not taken place. All our morality, all our history is just the history of the disinherited, the oxen, like me." He flung his words at her. "When you have learned that you have learned everything. They have wasted your youth for you. You come to the end. Your friend feels it."

"She's not my friend," began Teresa, ashamed of the old maid.

He went on: "It's for that I respect her, Miss Haviland, I'm talking about. For them, every luxury, every vice, every freedom, every dishonour, and all with honour. What is honour? Intangible honour is just another appurtenance of the poor. That is why Pilate said: 'What is truth?' He was a gentleman. What honour they want they take out of their wardrobes and jewel-cases. Diamonds, sapphires, purple and fine linen, *gude, braid claith. J'accuse.* The poor can't divorce their wives for adultery—they have to lump it." He flung his hand out towards her, and she saw it coming towards her with a shock, a muscular firm hand coming out of the dark, seeking, ready to grasp and imposing. She thought suddenly, with a thrill of fright: "Do I love this strange man?"

He hung his head with such a sorrowful gesture that she began to observe him. She saw the shining enamel of his extraordinary eyes. After all these years of reading, bluish-white they remained, the eyes of the short-sighted, that can shine liquidly with sorrow; in them the visionary look of self-pity. She was throttled with emotion. She did not believe that the university was a sham and that he had been desiccated by it as he said. Living so passionately as she saw him, suffering every moment he spent with her, from remorse, soul-hunger, diffidence, it was himself who merely strained upward, not the university that was bad.

"There's a tram coming now!" He trod on the pavement a moment, showing his teeth, said pleasantly: "You take the high road and I take the low road."

"And you'll be in Scotland afore me."

"Probably," he agreed, shaking his head. "Well," he concluded, brightly, "I don't despair, perhaps there is something to be learned. Is it teachable? I am willing to learn."

"Learn what?"

"The joy of living, is that it? I'm willing to learn that. If it can be taught. Teach me that, and I'll teach you Latin free." He laughed joyously.

"Oh, I can't."

"I like you," he said suddenly, as he handed her into the tram. He took off his hat for the first time. It was an old-fashioned car with two long benches facing. She sat down in the shattering light and looked out vaguely, saw him standing there. He waved his hat and replaced it, his face still looking in, his pedantic glasses shining. She did not even smile. She sat in a blaze, remembering the moment he had begged to be taught, his hand on her arm, his vibrant voice as he spoke his last, "Good-bye, Teresa." Through the end of the tram-car, she then looked back along the darkish road where he would walk homewards, and she imagined it all from his description.

City Road runs back into the poorest tenement areas of the northern city. Jonathan Crow had footed it along here for many years, starved, thin, dull-complexioned from being shut in with books, and in broken boots; this was his Calvary road. A tram rattled past going in the opposite direction. Why couldn't he climb into the tram and rest his body? Why this martyrdom of penury? It was that that had made him what he was, nervous and uncertain. She saw him walking along by lamps and trees, by pubs and small dirty shop fronts, as he described it, the girls at their gates waiting for their boy friends, above them the lighted room with squalling children; he had been one of those squalling, squabbling children. Beyond this, it ended. All that he had said about the other end was that he owed everything to his mother and himself. What street, what suburb? What house or dark flat? And was it a wretched, abandoned woman who waited for him?

17. *This Embarkation for Life*

As for Jonathan, deeply excited, he strode along City Road under the trees of the university park. He had said: "You are a free woman", and the reply had been, "Yes, I am." To his mind, it meant only one thing. What the Hawkins girl said was unmistakable. Her emotion, her liking for him, made it seem that he had found the free woman who would suit him, in this brief interval, before he set sail. He was timid. He liked women. He had heard shouts and the footsteps of couples in the evenings beneath his window as he worked. He willed himself to work. He willed himself to sleep so that he could work the next day. Now the long sentence was really over and he was a free man; but he was a book-worm with scarcely any knowledge of women but unfortunates, and he lived at home and all the girls he knew lived at home. During one summer he had gone to work on a farm and had an affair, but had not had the courage to bring it to anything. He had regretted it ever since; he was at that time only in his second year, though, and dreaded more than anything a tangle with a woman, the threat of paternity. Some men at the university in his year were already entangled and one had left to support a coming child. He was still ignorant of how to get rid of women and feared an early marriage. Women liked him too much and he yielded to them. He yearned for their advances that gave him so much pleasure; he had not yet the hardihood to lie outright, he was afraid of hearing his own words flung up in his face. If only Miss Hawkins would get a job—he knew how it was at home, one of her brothers away, lost, working somewhere up and down the coast, one sister studying at business college, the father not working for years, the whole house at present falling on one brother, Lance. Why didn't they sell the house? Why not rent rooms? Apparently, they had enough. Could he, for example, take a room there for a while? But he dismissed this idea at once. She must get a room in town.

Could he wangle a job for her? What do they pay such girls weekly? Could she afford a room? Jonathan abandoned this idea for the moment to imagine himself with a mistress. He had loved Clara madly at one time, believed in her, looking upon her as another Olive Schreiner or George Sand, but she was just a coltish child of talent, who spent her week-ends fishing, yachting, playing tennis, and now, quarrelling with Cooper. She wanted too much from a man, a man couldn't keep up with her and study as well. As for Elaine, after several summer nights, in her subtle innocence, she had invited him down to her place one Saturday afternoon, and there he had met the father, mother, and brother with a question in their eyes, and in fact, the father had taken him aside and shown him his patent razor, the brother had shown him his motor-bike and the mother had said: "Elaine tells me that you see a lot of each other?" He remembered now the furious beating of his heart and how long it had taken him to get out with courtesy. He was not cold and suffered the torments of the southern sun, but church lectures had scared him away from street girls, and for the rest, he was dependent on his parents for pocket-money. He neither smoked nor drank; he had one suit of clothes. Thus he cast up his accounts. "The end of the family," he thought, "would mean freedom for us all, she away from hers, I away from mine, the Elaines away from theirs. Work of course, and there I am—work, bread, and most certainly love. Yes, she is right about that."

Only one thing made him balk. He had turned away from it with incredulity and forgotten about it, but he came back to it cautiously. He had seen the girl's pale face blazing with ecstasy as she sat in the moving tram. He settled his hat with a smart tap on the crown, took two or three dull lunges, spat in the gutter and then swung off on his way. But now he tried to fix the disagreeable picture in his mind. Could he manage her? He faced it. It irritated him to give this great naked slobbering joy to one who could not make payment in kind; the wretched woman could get pleasure out of him when she wished, merely by looking at him; he did not own himself, it made him feel helpless. He did not want to see that look on the face of any woman in the world.

This he put in the terms of a naïve prudery, "She should have more reserve, a man doesn't care for a woman who gives herself away." So many women loved, so few men. It was an illusion necessary to them, but why? He detested unholy mysteries. He had soon got over the infatuation with Clara and seen it for what it was; and Clara was a high-class girl, her high-nosed handsome face was mobile with the inner flame.

"Darn it," he said, "darn it!" The last thing he wanted to give her was the gift of love, from him, the unloving! He ought to have been more cautious. All he had said was "I like you." He suddenly flamed. He wanted to run after the tram and tell her firmly that he could never love her, he could give her nothing, and all women gave him a feeling of absolute cold. Only to wipe that expression off her face and make it droop, as he liked to see it, thoughtful and wretched, wearied, with the spurt of resistance breaking through. He thought of Cooper and Clara. All went down on their bellies and chins into the fleshpots. His poor flesh shivered and crawled. He did up the last button of his jacket, unthinking. Rather a clean-minded brothel, after all, a bargain struck at once and at once carried out, with no riders, no poetry, than these tentacles of self-indulgence trailing all through life, suffocating the years ahead—they called it hope. Something to live for—he wished he knew if it was.

He sighed and looked sideways with reproving lips at a woman in her thirties, a faded fat blonde with an arm in a sling, who was in her usual post, in a cold slot between two buildings, a disputed two feet of land, in litigation for twenty years, which she squatted on and made hers. It ran back ninety feet, held garbage tins, thin grass and a thin wind. On one side was the window of a poor mercery, the light of a single bulb coming through from above the counter. The woman nodded to him. He gave a faint curt nod and hurried on. To the next girl, a young dark one who looked like a factory worker, he lifted a finger to his hat. Why not? What was his reward for going against his principles and taking his hat off? This frightful grin of the fleshpots. With this courtesy to the dark young girl, he felt that the bad mark, the fraud of courtesy to "ladies" was wiped out. His sullen soul was white again.

Jonathan, for the first time in his life, was almost alone. His life until now, and he was twenty-three, had been spent in class. His class comrades now were working or were looking for work every day. A few were married and joining small suburban circles of the respectably ambitious. This embarkation for life of his friends made him feel old for the first time. It was true he was on his own, not a prize student, not someone to be watched for in the next examination results, not someone who might pick off one of the plums of next year. He had to render his accounts. He was just a poor man who had made up his packet and was trudging off to sell himself, reduced once more to his original situation and talents, with a poor and jealous family and that drawback to success which is a thin, hungry face, with brown avid eyes, the stealth of the evil eye. He was not insensible to his own looks; when he faced himself in the bathroom glass in the morning, shaving, he studied and meditated upon this starvation face, that single leaf of flesh which had been given to him to write his own history upon.

Meeting Teresa Hawkins in her proper role, as a sad and hungry-looking girl, without family or prospects, he felt at ease; they might give each other a few hours of shelter from the raw climate of life; but if she was going to expect anything else? "Well," he thought, "she will soon find out, I'll teach her too, the bleak truth. The hungry cannot feed the hungry, they merely march near them in the struggle for survival, they shudder together merely in some night-refuge, but out of the night-refuge, next morning, they are wolves. Man the wolf of man and woman. What the devil, I've got to start somewhere. Who am I to be picking and choosing? Who am I?" Very depressed, in that state of indifference to life which borders on horror, he went through the dark streets, looking dully at the customary sights; fruiterers' and pastrycooks' windows that he had pasted his nose against, stationers' windows full of exercise books, very tempting to him at high school, the open doors of men's outfitters and haberdashers, that he had never entered, and the bootshop of thrown-out specials where some "Blucher boots", the class mark of the very poor child and man, were marked at seven and sixpence.

He had trained himself from earliest childhood to stoicism and had no daydreams; nor did he dream at night of what he could not have. What he could not buy, it was unmanly to desire. In the course of years he had reduced himself to a miserliness of mental life out of this sense of honour and revolt. If he desired or dreamed, he struck himself a mental blow; it was not *thus*, wanting like the weaklings, that the ambitious reached the moral and material heights; he had wanted to wear a hair shirt at one time, but where to get a hair shirt? That too, he saw, was a luxury for him and so was a weak fantasy which he quickly suppressed.

But tonight, in the paroxysm of horror that the sight of Teresa's joy had given him, estranged from humanity by his meeting with Clara, he saw his bareness. He not only wanted nothing but he had nothing. By God! They had taken him at his word. He had forgotten how to want. What sterility! What meanness! Loving is giving; they gave me nothing and I have nothing to give, so I cannot love. Is that it? O Lord, they have taught me not to want, only to work with my bare hands and in the sweat of my brow. *J'accuse!* A fire was lighted in him. All right, he said to himself, all right, from this out, from today, I am alone and all the others are scrambling for the largesse, I will teach myself to want and to take. Let's see what I *want*.

I want a woman. I want a new suit with chalk stripes, cuffs, and a high waist, the shoulders padded, breast pockets, shoes, socks, blue, red. I want dinner, and for dinner what? And after dinner, the movies—I'm a rotten wanter yet. I want to be with those who can want and who are crass enough to know no self-denial, who all their lives have wanted and are satisfying themselves now. Rasche, that bull-thrower, Cooper—no! But even Cooper has Clara.

I want, I want, he said to himself, let that be me from now on. I went for it, the holiness story, denial and self-sacrifice, and I had to have it to get through, but no more, that's all over.

He felt miserable. He had a mental misery which came back at intervals. He would feel grit, see glare, all sounds would be raucous, the world hopeless and full of oppressors and haters; and everything, with thick outlines, in crude black and white, stood out like figures in a stereopticon.

This vision to him was reality; when it came, he felt horror, but when it passed he knew he had been *reality*; but he did not expose it to anyone, it was a mystery known to him. Come down to brass-tacks, the world was like that but mercifully we had to have illusion to go on living; it was a race-wide, world-wide, perhaps, *knack of biological survival*.

He lost this despair occasionally, but only with a crowd and this he called a *phenomenon of crowd psychology*, it was the humour of the crowd invading him; he gave up his personality blissfully and became an atom of the crowd. In the Eight-Hour Day processions, though he hurrahed for strikers or martyrs of labour, shouting himself hoarse, feeling a glow of heroism, hot youth, sympathy running like melted gold through his veins, making his limbs leap, the crowd receded, leaving him with the orange-peel and papers on the pavement. He felt himself over curiously; he had been drunk with crowd psychology, he was nothing by himself, and the terror of that, knowing what he knew, reality, and seeing those illusions go past, struck deeper into him, as if at each transport the cancer ate at once into the opening soul. It was now deep in him, this suspicion of every-thing, which was at base a fear of not eating; and whatever unhurried but persistent calculation he had made of how he was to eat for the rest of his life, was to govern him from now on.

Clearly, anyone depending on him was an octopus dragging him under; worse, a heavy stone pulling under. If he could get a woman who felt the same way, all suffering would be avoided. Looked at rationally, it was hard to understand why they took the stony way. *Gather ye rosebuds while ye may*; they could have him if they would give him back again, but it was not him they wanted. The look of the girl in the tram, was it for him at all? Exaltation perhaps? He did not care either way but he would have liked to have picked up a little happiness. He turned into St Michael's Street, home, repeating: *"Mortals deserve some happiness, mortals deserve some happiness."*

When he got home, he rushed up the slippery oilclothed stairs three at a time and threw himself on his bed, his heart mad. As he lay there, words came into his head. He had written so many ardent, innocent letters to the women in his years; to Miss Havi-land, Clara, Elaine, others, free with his pen and boyish affections. Presently, he swung his legs off the bed, went to his pine table and began to write fluently with pen and ink. The first line began, "Dear Miss Hawkins," and he went on to the end of the fourth side before he signed himself, "Yours sincerely. Johnny Crow." So easily did he write now after all those essays and letters, in engaging, acceptable confidences, with a soft, modest indiscretion; it flowed like peaceful maundering, he scarcely knew what he had written. Yet afterwards, he could remember the phrases and chewed them over, smiling to himself. When he had finished, he said to himself, with a smile: "Sublimation! Sublimation is the secret spring of style! That's a bull's-eye, I'll put that in my next lecture."

18. Innuendoes of Love

THIS was the first letter Teresa ever received from a man. He began to write about once a week. She had noticed the tender, yielding way in which Jonathan spoke to her and was surprised at the simple good nature in his letter. She exclaimed: "The callow youth!" The simple and mediocre man. The letter was full of the innuendoes of love, while skimming over all sorts of subjects. A short, plain path led from it to a love affair, but this ordinary fellow, anxious to be loved, was not the sort of man she could love; he was too ready and he said to her: "Teach me", with an empty delighted soul, blazing with eagerness; at other times, he was mean and had no faith in anything. But she was flattered and she began to think about the "teach me" and his hand out-flung in the dusk. She saw gradually, for the first time, the torn-off, separate beauties of the body. Sensuality began to steal over her.

She took his letters with her to Miss Haviland at the Blue Dog. It was a place in a cellar with small tables and bric-à-brac. Often, Joyce was there, censorious and restless as ever. Miss Haviland read the letters with a smile, but once, at a very tender letter, became restless and declared: "I have a headache" suddenly, when asked. Teresa became nervous, guessing the resigned love of the older woman for the young man, and said: "I have a headache too, Alice!" and the wild girl flung a coarse laugh over the table, crying: "There's a plague of headaches—I just left Clara Endor and she had a headache!" and she gave them a contemptuous, irritated look. "It's that young man," said she. "Nonsense," said Miss Haviland, recovering herself. "And why should it be? That young man could never give me a headache."

Presently they were left alone and they smiled at each other comfortably. Teresa disputed points in philosophy with Miss

Haviland, with the rash loftiness of the autodidact. Before this passion, Miss Haviland retreated. She gave her a list of mid-European dramatists to read; Teresa argued about their theses, even without reading them. During the last few months of association with these university folk, she had discovered to herself and to them, a prodigious memory, she confuted them out of their own books and rapped them over the knuckles with what they had told her. She had once, in the university grounds, offered to make a citation "from English literature", on any subject whatever mentioned to her. Jonathan was there grinning, observing this feat. At another time, she gave them one of Edmund Burke's speeches, she gave them whole splendid parts of *Zarathustra*, of the Biblical prophets, or Jeremy Taylor, and Donne. Her memory had not been ground down by drudgery or examinations. She had few ideas, and argued in an unacademic way, but the magnificence they had thrust on her and that she had read, came whirling at them out of her mouth. Certain people began to say there was something strange there: a consummately elegant schismatic leader of a religious order offered her a position in the order; a young politically minded youth tried to educate her in politics; Jonathan, looking for something to believe in, and believing spasmodically in every person of talent he came across, believed in her and came walking round her with a shining light in his eyes. It happened that this was the moment when she was in flower. Fruit might come, but this would never come again. For a few months only this lasted. Crow, Miss Haviland, a few women became strongly attached to her. Her own views changed, she began to despise their provincial university culture. She would go to Europe and perfect herself; she no longer saved to go to the university, but intended instead to enter London, Cambridge, Paris, as a student. All this was mad dreaming. She had not saved a penny.

She and Miss Haviland met every day and talked over all these things. Crow was a man who ploughed in a furrow, Miss Haviland admitted her limitations, but the girl with no experience admitted no limitations and was like Mr Keane, the angry dairy farmer, rude, ribald, and harsh towards the little world of textbooks they had come from. They enjoyed this rough treatment. They spoiled her and tried to educate her. She saw how little they knew and thought it would be easy for her to get up among the heads of the living world; eagle's feathers sprouted.

Crow continued to write to her. He had three or four other female correspondents; the months wheeled past, his departure drew near and there was a lingering, regretful affection in what they wrote to each other. Only Teresa did not write like this, first because she had not known him in the old days, and then because she was going abroad "to enter a foreign university". This impossibility several of her friends already believed.

One day Jonathan took her to the "forum" set up by a free-thinking professor who felt the university curriculum was narrow and that students should not be shut off from workers and citizens. The professor invited such outsiders to his forum and invited them to read papers there, an innovation. He was said to be a Marxist. Jonathan took Teresa to this class, and introduced her to the professor. This one afternoon alone, she realized her dream of the classrooms stormy with debate. Dusk fell, the jewels of the city were laid out, the trees waved below the high tower room in which they sat, benches dropping down to the platform and the great blackboard, and the hot tongues wagged, while the genial and humane professor encouraged them to go far out of bounds of university classroom decorum. Johnny walked down the avenue with her in the dark. They were still gushing, warm with the intensities of the classroom. Teresa said passionately: "How cut off I am! I know nothing!"

He sighed: "Yes, what do we know?"

"It's maddening."

After a silence, he said: "Are you still at home? I thought you were going to try to get away."

"I've thought of taking a room but I don't know where to look. I get only thirty-five shillings a week now because I'm a beginner; I used to give them that at home."

He looked downcast. After a pause, he continued, gloomily: "Perhaps if you looked in the right places you could get a small room for ten shillings, we'd have to look, it would have to be in a slum, I suppose. If you could get a room with a family with a separate entrance——"

"I wouldn't like it with a family," she said. "I have a separate entrance, if you like, at home, where I am."

"You could always go home," he muttered.

"Yes, I could." She looked at him, hesitating. She understood nothing of this bad temper and sudden dislike of her, for that's how it seemed to her.

He scolded: "But I suppose you wouldn't do it. You'll just stay at home like all the others."

"I'll do what I like." He followed a pace behind. Why did he follow her, badgering her, and humble, cowardly in the same moment? Was he afraid for his reputation, afraid she wouldn't do properly the paper she was doing for his class?

She went on: "I can tell whether the tide is running in or out with my eyes shut. I can tell where the boat is in the harbour with my eyes shut. It's the sound coming back from the hills and shores." He doubted. Hotly, she affirmed it. He laughed idly. "If you like. I don't say that you can't do it, I'm sure I couldn't."

"You could if you tried, why do you say you can't do things?"

He grumbled: "I'm not sensitive, I'm afraid. When they gave me the scholarship, they told me it wasn't because I deserved it, but because the other two fellows ran amok, one married a woman twice his age and one wrote obscene lyrics on the profs. Miss Haviland was next in line but she's a woman and women marry. So that's exactly why I got it."

"They all believe in you, Miss Haviland believes in you. Never mind what the profs say."

He said, mysteriously: "Miss Haviland's a woman."

"Well, I believe."

"You? You might do much. But you're on the outside. It's easy for you."

"Then leave the inside. For heaven's sake!"

He smiled shyly. "Oh-ho! That's too much to ask. Otherwise, it's clerking in the public service, or teaching, is that worth it? If I'd somewhere to go, some friend's room."

She said dolefully: "You mean get a room?"

He said with embarrassment: "No, no, I meant in general. But if you want to get a room?"

She said, childishly: "But where would I look? I looked on Saturday. I went out to a place that advertised rooms cheap and it was terribly funny. Jolly queer, I mean. There was a large old house with two floors. In the centre of the second floor was a kind of ballroom, you would have said, with rooms all round. Each room was a cubicle, not bad, clean, but just as I was going out I noticed that there was no lock and no bolt. The woman was a nice-looking woman, and very friendly, young-old, about forty with quite black hair, but when I asked for a bolt, she said it was so safe and friendly that there was no need for a bolt, all were friends. I suppose she is right, but it seemed strange. Perhaps she runs a kind of phalanstery. But I certainly felt queer."

"Perhaps," said Jonathan, "if I went round with you, you would get on better. I know these back suburbs better."

"And the tram rides," said Teresa, dubiously.

"Why shouldn't you get a room somewhere near the university? Then you could drop in to any free discussion groups and—I could see you."

He said the last so quickly that she asked in confusion what he had said.

"I could drop in on you sometimes, help you a bit." Then she said: "But you're going away soon."

"Yes," he said miserably. "It isn't much to induce you to leave, is it? Me, my company, for a month or two."

"Oh, it's worth it, I dare say."

"I don't know either—if it is."

"Oh, I know, good heavens, I'm going myself. I wouldn't stay for anything."

"And that's another thing that makes me feel like a squib," he continued. "This trip's handed to me on a platter and you have to get it in the sweat of your brow."

"That's all right, I take the high road and you take the low road. I'll see you in London just the same."

"In London, then!" he cried, turning to her quickly. "And God bless us all."

She said: "But if I want to look for a room, would you come round with me? I don't know where to go." His reply lagged; he sounded as if his enthusiasm was all gone: "If you want me to, but it might make it hard for you."

"Why? How could it?"

"A man with you."

"A man with me? Why—don't they like men boarders?"

He laughed, troubled, but only said: "People don't always take to me at first sight, you see. I look what I am."

"How can you say that?"

He impulsively took her hand. She continued: "I think I'll look first in the suburbs near me, so that you can get the fresh air on Sundays, you see."

"Doesn't that seem silly, to live right near home?"

"I suppose it does."

They were half-way down George Street West, approaching the station. He made her laugh at some girls clustered in front of a jeweller's. He said: "Would you like a ring?"

"I never thought of a ring."

"Bravo! I'll bet you don't like to wear these conventional clothes, either."

She glanced down at herself. "Oh, yes, I do! I can't really wear what I want, can I?"

"A lot of fuss and feathers! If women didn't go in for that, they wouldn't have half their disabilities. They ought to wear pants."

"Why?"

"Then they wouldn't have to have men to keep them company. Their conventional clothes mean sexual frailty. Frailty means a protector. That's all wrong. If you wore pants, you could go any-where."

"Here's the station!"

"That's right. Well, ta-ta! I'd go farther, but I'm starving. Nineteen-twenty, my belly's empty."

"Let's go over there and have a cup of tea." She pointed to a small, badly lit shop across the tram tracks.

"No, thanks," he said stiffly, lifting a finger to his hat and bearing off. She was used to his changes of mood, but humiliated all the same. She did not know that he had not a penny in his pocket and that, though he believed in the equality of the sexes, he could not tolerate the idea of a woman paying for her food when with him; it wounded his poor man's vanity. Cold, sad, and hungry, she went on clippity-clip in her broken shoes to cover the next mile. The sole of her shoe had come loose, she had fixed it with a hairpin in the office, but it still flopped on the asphalt.

When she got home to the Bay, she took her dinner off the stove, said nothing to anyone, went upstairs to her room. The old varnish-crusted top of the desk she had covered with thick brown paper and on the paper had written the words of Isaiah, "Of whom hast thou been afraid or feared, that thou hast lied?" Beneath this was written in gold and blue, on the brown paper, also from Isaiah, "And that thou hide not thyself from thine

own flesh? Then shall thy light break forth as the morning."
She put her papers and ink on top of these words of the prophet
and wrote a letter to Jonathan. Why did he suffer? Things were
not as sordid and hopeless as he imagined. This was a miserable
state he'd got into because he had been too long shut up at school;
he had no hope because he was a poor man who thought what
was needed was money. He was a man now; he should forget his
teachers. She could show him the world of Orpheus and David—
his young lawyers and foal-lipped doctors crying because they
had not enough influence to get on! Orpheus and his lute made
the trees and the mountain tops that freeze dance to him when
he did sing, the mountains skipped like lambs for David. Was
this mere imagination or was there something greater in the
world than the law courts and the doctor's office? Why should he
be miserable when the world was his? He had only to look at it
as she did. The world was hers and she had no doubt for the
future. In the threatening eloquence of the prophetic virgin, she
wrote to him, and she knew that Jonathan, who had been made
to eat dirt for his success would tremble at this. She had no doubt.

A day later, the next evening, she had an answer to it, written
post-haste:

I burn to be saved from my vices of all kinds, intellectual, moral
sloth, envy. You lead and I follow. You show me that what you
say is and I will try to hear it and see it. I have never paid any
attention to these things but I am sure I could see, hear, feel
as you do. I know my pal Bertram does. I know they exist, but
not for me, so far. I will follow you anywhere, any time. If you
knew how tired I am of the life I lead—but I cannot force myself
to believe in anything, I have to be shown. I suppose the trouble
with me is I am a grind who has passed by all that matters, the
old mess of pottage. I'll meet you at the tram stop at eight, as you
say. I put myself into your hands; it's your affair entirely. We
shall see what we shall see. I have no will of my own, I only
want to be saved and I don't care who does it. Let it be you. I
prefer that.

When the letter was posted off, he felt happy. During the few
days that intervened, he was very happy at times. Other men had
found women, been happy because of women, and it was possible

that he could become like other men he knew and was not condemned by nature to a mean, parasitic, carping, second-rate life; or, if so, then still he could make a go of it. His father, a quiet sort of man, could not have been entirely unhappy with his mother's harshness and firmness. "We're the meek sort of man," he said to himself. "I'm no genius, why fight? I am like this, this is my nature, why shouldn't I yield to it? I'd be a fool to hold out for some quixotic ideal. If she proposes some sort of life in common, whatever it is, at least I'll perpend. I couldn't have been plainer the other evening." He imagined how she would lead up to it, in the evening, in the dark, tree-shaded, meandering streets of the waterside suburbs where they were going to walk. He felt gentle towards her; she was at work, she had the money for this room and he was a dependant. He borrowed half a crown from his father and set out, after a light meal at home, bread, butter, jam and tea.

In the tram, on the way out, he tried to remain sober, to think about his friend Jackson's schemes for a Youth Party, to be a disappointed man of the world, but he could not. He had with him an old magazine she had lent him, written and illustrated by the young artistic set in Sydney, run by the Brimley family, dominated by the Brimley family, in which, with imitations of Marlowe and Shakespeare, Donne, and free verse, it was chiefly a question of free love and naked women; on each page were drawings of voluptuous, fat-faced, naked women, running away from a crowd of satyrs, carried off by centaurs or tempted by evil-eyed fauns. In between were prose pieces, either condemning the masters of English literature who had written with reticence, or recounting the adventures of the young men of the circle, with "good, easy girls" or "lusty wenches". The *Quarterly* was elegantly printed; being of small circulation it would become a "collector's item". It was too expensive for Jonathan, but Teresa had managed to get a few copies. It was the only magazine she bought; she read no newspapers. Jonathan had tumbled the book well at home, but here, in the tram full of home-going suburban people, he did not dare to look at it. It was enough that a naked, buxom "wench" flew along the cover. To tell the truth, the full-blooded Bohemian joys written up by these gifted and for the most part moneyed young men mostly took place in the near suburbs with an occasional trip to a holiday place and there were few Don Juans among them; they were mostly ambitious young artists trying to make their way in advertising, architecture, and commercial illustration. To poor Jonathan and others of their followers, it was the full use of all powers and all senses dreamed about by hot-eyed youth. He thought: "Will I buy her something? But what?" and thoughtfully clicked in his pocket the few shillings he had borrowed from his father.

The moon was a bonfire just below the horizon when he got to the tram stop. A narrow strip of dunes stood between the tram stop and the ocean; beyond some meadows was the harbour. They could roam the dunes, cross to the ocean beach or walk the long walk to Teresa's home. Above, from where he came, rose the dark lights and the brightly lighted night tennis courts; above, in front, were bluffs crowned with the stout walls and the old trees of a convent.

She was there, her thick fair hair bound in a loop, in a sweater and skirt. They had the whole night before them. They set off to walk at once, almost without a word, and he did not ask where they were going. In these suburbs lived some of his wealthy classmates; he had never been asked to their homes by "the toffs". They climbed the long hill, passed down the road by the convent, off the high-road, down among the deep gardens in the sunken states of three following bays. He said nothing, obedient, gentle. She talked of the water, the moon, and the gardens and he listened, full of his own thoughts, and worried by doubt and fear, tingling with anticipation when she made some sudden movement, and eagerly agreeing to all she said.

As for the girl, she had written her letter under the inspiration of the moment and she had only a feeble idea of what she would say if he really asked for guidance as she promised. She read only one sentence in his return letter, and at these words, "I will go with you, any time, anywhere", she had thought of nothing more but the wonderful night walk, their first outing together. When she came home would she be a changed woman, would she have been kissed by her lover? Certainly it would not be nothing that came out of a walk with the man. . . .

But a silence had fallen between them and Jonathan, shaking himself, croaked some old stand-by of theirs, that he was going abroad living on velvet while she was going to have to work for years to do the same thing; and he went on heavily, about "the man abroad". Was he waiting for her?

"Yes, he will be," she said, smiling.

Jonathan drew closer to her. When they reached the natural park on the shore, she pushed aside the branches to show the way into a bower of shrubs and trees from which they could scale down to the waters. He walked a few steps into the bushes and then the girl's attitude, casually unprovocative, innocent, her homely scrambling down among the stones to the still water, put him off. There was a seat in the centre of the clearing and there he sat watching her for a moment, waiting for her to look back. What was she doing, dabbling in the water? Fishing something out? He waited. She laughed inquiringly and started back. At that moment, they both heard two loud smacking kisses from the bushes on the right. She came up and sat beside him, close to him. A murmur came from the bushes. She looked closely at him and laughed. In his embarrassment and fright, he was repelled. He saw all the cheap couples before and after who had used this glade, the clumsy sitting side by side, the girl waiting for a kiss, the fumbling, it was not for that that he had come out. He jumped up with a guttural cry, turned his back on the girl and broke out of the ring of shrubs with a fierce, forward thrust of the shoulder and stood, full of spleen and shame, in the smudged dark of the hillside, visible in the shade, silent and crouched as a night bird haunting the dust of a lonely road.

She came out, putting the branches aside and as he moved forward, followed him a pace or two behind, humbly. He was thinking that the pair in the bushes had seen the whole thing, laughed at him. He waited for her, putting out his hand, but not touching her when she came out. In a minute or two they would see the full water, the headland, the pines on the last cliffs where the continent plunged into the Pacific.

He now turned against himself. If she had made a kind of promise to him, she must still expect some kind of initiative in him, women were bred to it, taught to be recessive. He thought miserably about all he knew of women; it danced in his head, the textbook maxims and the gay knowledge of his wealthier friends. He was sorry for the opportunity missed. What for? For two rough kisses in the dark! He was half in despair, and tempted to run up a side road he saw branching back into the quiet roads they had left. He could run round the corner, disappear, and keep running, far out of sight and call, never see her again, reach the tram, get home, without any more thought about the wretched business. "What does she think I am doing?"

When they came round the headland and saw before them the wide double bay with its thick wooded slopes to the tide, she said: "Isn't it cold, Johnny?"

He said, in muffled tones: "Yes, feel how cold my hand is," and suddenly grasped her hand, so that he felt her start and draw in her breath. His hands were capacious, smooth and fleshy, hers were thin and restless. In his firm pressure, her left hand fluttered and ducked, as a small animal, and after forcing it to lie still for a moment, she dragged it back and drew a step away from him. He smacked his hand against his trousers seam and scarcely repressed a "damn" of embarrassment. He thought angrily she was after all a gawky, inexperienced girl who had just meant to go spooning with him on a moonlight night, and he was angry with himself at being taken in by a few glowing words. He ought to have known that there was no such thing as he expected. She was a lonely girl, love-hungry; dynamite, not for the likes of him. He got back his wits, and was inclined to laugh. Coming along in the tram he had been worrying about the little bit of money he had on him, not to be in her debt too much when she made love to him and everything fair and square. Now he saw he needed nothing, nothing was expected from him, except the love-making and "that's not in my line", he said to himself, "that's not my lay".

Now the girl regretted her mistake and timidly took his hand, but he moodily pushed her away and said:

"Know what place this is? It's a regular palace."

"That's an Indian princess's." She was offended and drew ahead.

"Go on, you have princesses here!" His tone distinctly said: "Then you don't need me, do you?"

"But we live a couple of miles farther on," she said hastily, ashamed of the princess.

"Oh, not with the nobs, then?" He stuck his hands carelessly in his pockets, turned to the bay and looked around him. He sighed, "Well, you were right. Q.E.D. It's not half bad. Glad I came. Is it much farther?"

"There are two wharves nearer, you can catch a boat at either. You must be tired."

"And the last wharf, yours?"

"To reach the end you go by that bay and that bridge, it's just scrub, you miss the cliffs but it's quicker, while at this time of moon——" she stopped, struck by her own vision of the heaving, brilliant sea, a winter moonlit sea—"but you're tired, we'll stop at the next."

"Let's go through with it," he said. "I'll try anything once, that's my motto, and I stick to it. Lead on, Macduff."

"It's late. It isn't so fine. The lights are going out, there are just the buoy-lights and the lighthouse, the moon's rather grey tonight."

"Yes," he said, stopping, looking at her askance. "Then you see it for what it is, naked, in the rough, beastly——" he threw out a hand with a fascinating gesture. The ferries were infrequent in the harbour now. They had consumed hours in their futile walk. Under the ghastly high light, the land was limp and slaty as a dead fish; the unliving light which had blasted the centuries, the light of the great dead eye, was sucking out the marrow of this night. The tide was rising still. What she said was true, thought Jonathan, become keener in the access of distress; he heard the strange sounds on the rocks, like little pickaxes, like endless elfin boats, grounding, the walnut-shell of the Willow Pattern, grounding on shingle. He heard the faint rustle in the trees, a soot-winged night bird flying, a dog yawning. He heard a deck hand speaking a long way off, on a ferry. He heard insects, harsh grass brushing its way upwards against a bit of newspaper.

"Yeah," he said, turning his head to her, "I am a brute, I've lived on a tram line, near the railways with the engines whistling in my ears since I was a youngster. I had to stop my ears by will power or I'd never have got where I am——" he ground his teeth at this—"never have passed their beastly exams. Nothing but noise and dust in my face—and then apart from that, what do you think was my ambition, when I was a kid?"

"To study?"

He burst out into a rough laugh.

"Not on your tintype. I did that because it was a way to eat. That's what I am. I wanted to play footer, that's what I wanted to do. I never had a sweater, the colours of my school, and you couldn't play without. That jersey used to hover about in front of my eyes."

She said: "Leo—my brother—was in your school. I made him one, primrose and violet." He said: "Primrose and violet, dainty colour-combination, eh? I liked it. One of the greatest days of my life was when my uncle gave me twopence and I could buy two sheets of transfers, because all the kids had them. I stuck them all over everywhere and then I couldn't see anything to it. That's what I'm like anyway. That was my kind of art, transfers on fences."

They were passing behind the princess's house, an immense white, slate-roofed house with a small garden going down to the water. He looked at her doleful back and said more kindly: "I don't say you're wrong and I'm right. Let's say I'm wrong and you're right. There are more things in heaven and earth, Horatio. Live and learn. You can hear those sounds. I would have sworn you couldn't. But I don't see life like you do, it has no promise for me."

She said softly: "If you think I believe in fairy godmothers, you're wrong."

He hung his head. "No, you're darn right. This is just trick lighting and the whole thing's a sideshow to get us in. Cheap melodrama, you're right there."

She tried to explain that he would see more, tell more, if he tried to get out of himself. He listened under the influence of the grisly moonlight. She was like a nerveless spectre that had entered his soul, and was vapidly uttering some girlish story that interested him not at all.

"Ulalume, Ulalume," he moaned, "by the light of the silvery moon." She was silent, thinking this a stroke of devilish wit; she had never heard of Ulalume.

He came close, putting his arm round her waist, his bold cleft chin above her shoulder, spitefully. They walked on for a few steps, embraced and then broke apart. The walk went on like a nightmare, mile after mile.

Each was glad when the ferry came round the point. It was nearly one in the morning. The lights were out all over the Bay. They ran down the wharf and stood at the top of the steps. When the gangplank was put out, there came off two silent huddled men who had been sleeping through the cold journey, and he waved his hand gaily and ran down the steps. She turned and began her walk home before the boat cast off.

Jonathan sat in a mournful stupor, unwilling to review the lost evening. Teresa, going home, was the prey of the voices. One said: "If you had made a move, you would have done better"; the other said: "Men despise women who make the moves." By the time he reached the Quay, Jonathan thought: "I should have done better, but she was coy to bring me on and I won't be the first victim of my own atavism, led by the nose in that degrading mimicry of the chase simulated by woman to enhance her own value in men's eyes." Teresa, by the time she had got to bed, had altered her ideas to, "It's my fault. If I'd been bolder, both would have been happy by this time." She thought: "None but the brave deserve the fair."

19. *Property Is Everything*

THEY needed each other. Two weeks later, on a Saturday morning, after two letters, they went out again. Again, Teresa had made the proposal and Jonathan accepted it. He thought to himself that by now she must have made up her mind to go farther with him. He still had nothing of his own, she was still his only affair. He visited elsewhere, was admitted to the homes of girl friends, but one after another they were beginning to walk out with boys who thought of marrying. He was like a sailor; his ship was waiting in the harbour.

Teresa, meanwhile, taking upon herself all the blame of the previous failure, had prepared for this morning for nearly two weeks, and in a strange way. It was early morning, long before six o'clock, when Teresa and Jonathan, setting out from their suburbs, took the workmen's trams in to the centre of town, where they met at the gate of the Public Gardens, which open at six. They had got up long before breakfast and had brought nothing to eat, but it was a fairly fine morning heavy with dew, the scent of the plants and flowers so strong that neither of them felt hungry. They waited outside the tall gates, both without coats, in their mended shoes, and they talked in low voices, almost fearfully, on the coming day. They had come here to see the sunrise. She said: "An open hearth, flaring out at intervals, today is the very kind of day, a burning fury which rouses up life as lust rouses up love."

"Is it really?" he said. "A burning fury? You have to make good on that."

"And on the rest too, I can. On all. Haven't you seen it, a cauldron tipping over and pouring rust on the new-built steel-grey world on its stocks?"

"On the world in the morning! Can I see such a thing in my back yard?"

It was a warm day, a threatening, oppressive day, sea-fog hung about the coast and had not rolled in upon them but lay upon the still ocean. As soon as the guardian came, clinking his keys, and undid the high bronze-piked gates, they walked in, along the paths so well known to them, past the familiar lawns, down the steps and towards the far end of the garden. The sun was rising but hidden. It rose furiously, with purple and sulphur colours. The grass was bowed down with dew and was hoary. A gunboat came in, saluted the harbour as it rounded the point and the slight echo came to them. They went through the gates at the other end of the gardens and out on to the Public Domain, where they might have gone an hour ago or all night, since it was open all night, and sat down to face the east. They were on a grassy slope facing the harbour. Men were still sleeping huddled close to tree trunks. Some were burning damp papers with much smoke. The dew weighed down their clothes and the smoke was in their eyes.

Jonathan, in black and white, lay on his side in the dew, plucking out grass.

"After I had been in Law School a few weeks I understood that I hadn't a chance, no influence, no family—what's that but no property? Property is everything. They don't want talent, or hard work, or even belief in the system, they want property or the evidence thereof. Where's your visible means of support? Here— my two fists. No, that only shows you can fight, we don't want fight. Where's your property? See! What are our lords and masters? Those with property. What are the despised? Those who have no property. Don't you see? You're full of fight. I don't say it's no good because you might win, you might get property— through some man, probably. But I can't marry some man. I beat them all at studies, where am I? On the footpath, looking for a job. Ergo, being despised, ergo, being an outlaw, it is my first duty to myself and society—since man cannot live with himself despised—to acquire property. But I shall never acquire much, not having enough—ability", he bit the word and flung it out. "And so it is my duty to myself to acquire titles to esteem, that is, titles which enable me to look after other people's *property*, to wit, estates, libraries, and the learning of the ages which, because the poor can't learn very much, is property too. You see! My father was a socialist and believed in Darwin, the survival of the fittest. He thought it meant his kind. Logical error. I know it means the fittest to survive in any given conditions. There might be conditions where hunchbacks are fittest to survive. So I shall survive. I know what is fit in this society. I shall acquire titles to respectability which can sometimes be exchanged at a discount for property. The more degrees I have, the more they will feel themselves obliged to give me jobs. They know that a rut-man like me never takes up arms against them. For this subservience, a tip. And I'll marry for property, a little bit, I'll see to that. If I have to have their marriage to slake my appetites——" he looked fiercely into the grass, plucked some roots out, "—they'll pay for it."

She paid no attention, she thought it was a mania of all young graduates, because the lop-eared young doctor on the boat also kept saying that he could go nowhere without influence. She chewed a grass-stalk, swallowing the sweet sap. She looked sideways down at him and saw the clothes he had on. Underneath his thin white shirt, which lacked a button, she saw his hairy chest, strong and slender. He said violently, after waiting for her answer: "But marriage is only an excuse for the state to delude poor parents like mine. Slave to bring up new citizens. Give 'em the chance you never had. Yes? My parents didn't do that duty to the propertied and so I had to myself. I was," he paused, biting a bit of grass, "a sap! Playing their game, bringing up a citizen for them, by the sweat of my brow. Now I know the ropes. Now they can keep me my life long while I take more human clay and force it to my own image, their image."

He turned over on his stomach, calmly chewing the grass. He cast an eye at her to see how she had taken the remark about marriage and upbringing. She had noticed nothing; she was looking east, the sun was just visible through the thinning locks of sea-fog, which had a snaky look. The fog was beginning to churn and roll away. The water began to ruffle beyond, and cold air reached them.

"You're soaked, Johnny," said Teresa, plucking his wet sleeve. "If a woman does something for a man, is that self-interest? Isn't there anything but property?"

"Unenlightened self-interest," he grunted.

"You mean, no sympathy, no parental feelings, no love?"

"The protean branches of self-interest."

He rolled on to his back and lay looking complacently at the fair blue sky and the edges of branches nearly overhanging him; he continued meditatively: "You see, if women were enabled to reproduce without men, we would have a much clearer idea of the emotion called love. Would it exist at all? For decency's sake, there has to be an architecture, some Through-the-Looking-Glass, an anithetical balance—perhaps it's nature's art at that, I don't say no," he raised his head and looked at her with bonhomie. "But the whole object is to obfuscate the real purpose."

She didn't understand. What real purpose?

"Yes, alas for civilization. If I'd been a black boy and not a white boy, I would have been initiated and become a man and married long ago, at fourteen, now I'm nearly twenty-four and I still haven't had a woman! What have I gained? Would I have spent ten years crouching over their books? It's a mistake."

"What?"

"Civilization. I'd rather sleep all day in the sun and do a bit of hunting and fishing." He laughed pleasantly. "Oh, boy, oh, joy, where do we go from here? There, I do believe in it. You've converted me."

"You see," she said, "we should have youthful marriages, from the time we're fourteen, like the blacks, but we don't have to go back to living their way to do it, surely. We should be taken away from our parents. We should have community houses while we're learning. We should find out everything for ourselves, learn from scientists, the best artists and writers and no theory, no theory—we'd invent the theories ourselves. The world wouldn't hold together for two minutes." She laughed. "All that is for older people, it's so old it doesn't fit us."

"That would be all right," said Jonathan, yearning into the sky.

"And love should be taught, so we'd make no mistakes. We don't know what we're doing. Now love, the most important thing, is neglected. We hear about Romeo and Juliet and we hear about the danger of illegitimate children, and nothing in between. We don't know anything, that's why we're so miserable. We prey on each other, but we don't want to."

He sat up and looked over the water at the gunboat just coming to anchor, and then fixedly at her. "Instead of which—yes, the world is upside down. But where are you going to get those youth colonies? No, pardner, I'm afraid we have to face the world as it is. There are no green colonies," he said bitingly. "But dust and back rooms, tram-lines, influence, property, brothels, and nice girls wanting to rope a Mr, and that's the only kind of love there is. That's why I don't believe in it—not that I ever had it," he said in a miserable tone, drooping. He went on, more spirited: "Perhaps there's some solution. I'm sailing, in the spring, to find out."

She waited, looking sadly at him. He went on: "The answer? Free love! But women are not free. They want to be and acquire property. Do they want to? I don't know. Does property want to be property? There isn't a girl will live with you freely." He raised his long lashes and studied her. She was looking away, downcast and embarrassed, pulling out a stalk of grass. He continued:

"The disinherited may not marry, John Lackland has no offspring." There was a sad silence.

"And yet," said Jonathan, "I want to love, I am lonely. Even I? Do I have to be deprived of the full use of myself as a man just because I have no property? Must women be a luxury?"

"Used to be! But you wouldn't marry a poor woman?"

"Nope. Not knowing what I know, and the charming women are a luxury. And we want charming women! Man's delight, man's rest from his struggle, it's his right."

The girl looked blue. She said, very low, angry: "And men are a luxury to poor women. Both are a luxury."

He sat up and whistled. She had nothing more to say. He stirred her with his appeals. Before them was a coppery sky and rolling harbour; a tugboat breasting up the harbour pushed the heavy water aside in waves like conch shells, the waves slowly decreased, broke beneath them. For a moment, both of them wanted to be out of this misery, and gone to some far island of the Pacific where broken men and women lived, unseen and unlawed, to have their lives in peace and wantonness. Out of a cave underneath their feet, a hobo crawled, with his bundle of sleeping-paper in his hand. He did not look up at the murmur of voices, but went on down to the water and around out of sight.

"Why wasn't it decided ages ago?" asked Jonathan savagely. "Do you think there is an answer?"

"Yes. We must try, we must have courage," she said roughly. Jonathan shook his head.

"No, no innovation is possible, not until property is abolished. No, we must conform or die out. That's Darwinian. It is not for me, it is not for you, it is not for others—perhaps someone will break through."

"I can break through."

He shook his head. "You are brave, you see, but it is easy for a woman. No one expects her to make a career. That's right, isn't it? Don't your parents just tell you to get married?"

"I have no parents, exactly, in that sense. I mean——"

"I mean, just marry. Do you want to get married?"

She hesitated.

"Do you? We were talking about it up at the class, some said you were too free for that. I said you were not a bluestocking, you'd get married."

She stared at him: "I'm a bluestocking?"

"Wouldn't you?"

The reticence taught to her since birth made it difficult for her to answer this question, but she said at last: "Of course."

"Any man, eh?"

She flushed and shook her head, her eyes sparkled with anger. He smiled and continued: "I mean a man without much of a chance—a poor beggar. But you believe in love, don't you?"

"Yes."

"Would you marry a chap in my position, I mean without anything, and who didn't believe in love, without anything, like my brother Eddie? I'm taking him because he's like me, absolutely without talents or future, and I've stopped him getting married twice because I've just felt that the girls were getting a meal ticket. But perhaps they *love* him."

She did not answer but looked at him suspiciously. He laughed idly, dug a hole in the ground and went on: "Well, we all have our means of escape, delirium tremens and God and love, I suppose." He looked at her darkly, raising his lids.

"You stopped his marriage?"

"You bet."

"Why?"

"Mum wanted it, and he was getting himself into a trap. I went and told the girl. I called for her at her father's house, she was pleased. Thought I'd come to bring greetings. I told her she was robbing my mother. I told her what my mother had done for us. I told her we all opposed it and none of us would see her if she did it. He doesn't want it. He's only doing it because he's afraid. He's given his word. She tried to get her hooks into me. Ah! I sent her to the right-about. The next day, she broke the engagement." He rolled over and looked up at her, laughing in an abandoned, charming way.

"Does your mother know?"

"Yes, but it wasn't for her, though I said it was. It was for Eddie. I can't see a poor man stick his head in the noose. I've seen enough of it in my particular back street, the bottomless pit of horror and filth and the vile, what they call marriage in the slums, vice on eight feet, two rowing parents and two squalling children. Do I want me and mine in that? Never while I can stop it! Don't you see what's the trouble with us? The rich take their time, the rich marry late so that property will be divided little and late, while the poor rush to marry and to divide the little pay that one gets. Do they fool you like they fool other women? I can't believe it." He looked into her face sarcastically. "Sink-or-swim wives, that's my name for them. He can marry after I sail, if he's donkey enough, not while I'm here to stop him."

"He puts up with you doing that?"

He was firm. "He knows darn well that if he marries that girl Flora, I'll never speak to him again."

There was a long silence. Both were stirred. At last he rolled himself round, sat up, and grinned friendly at her.

"How I gab! But you were going to tell me something about the sun."

"Only what is written in the Book of the Dead. 'Oh—Oh, Thou who wanderest across the watery abyss,' that is Ra rising! I was going to tell you about Ra rising. I was going to wonder if we wouldn't be different from all other races but the Egyptians perhaps, because of the sun, the desert, the sea—but our sea is different—each Australian is a Ulysses—'Where did you come from, O stranger, from what ship in the harbour, for I am sure you did not get here on foot?' " But these particles were not what she had prepared.

"Well—" he tugged at her hand and pulled her up. "Well, it's getting late, you ought to get some breakfast before you go to work and I'm going out on a jaunt all day on a picnic. You work, I shirk, eh? It'll be a grand day if it doesn't blow, no swimming now, but a bush walk, I suppose, then a picnic in this girl's house, Elaine's, you know her, and I don't know what—movies, necking, I suppose." He finished with an off-hand air: "There's a lot of that, you know, they can't get enough of it. Not for me!"

They walked along the flower beds, passing some fine flowers. "Yes, it is beautiful," he said, pointing enthusiastically at the flower beds. "Wonderful colours, striped too, you're quite right. It's worth doing. If I could appreciate beauty I would be happy but all I can do is read up on aesthetic theory!" He laughed affectionately, taking her hand. "Well, thanks for the outing! So long!" At the outer gate he lifted his hat with a jolly smile and put on his glasses. He turned down towards the Quay and Teresa uptown towards her hat factory, which was beyond the Central Station.

20. *The Infernal Compact with Herself*

TERESA had been obliged to join the Teachers' Union, and for her money had received a little badge in red and silver which she had refused to wear, supposing that she would be ridiculous in the streets, that people would know at once she belonged to the legion of condemned bachelor women and would shy off from her. In the office now, she refused to join the office workers' union, feeling that if she entered their lonely ranks, she was equally condemning herself to servitude. She said to them, believing that women who joined trade unions were hopeless, desperate women who had no husbands, and if she joined them she would be marked off, beyond chance: "I'll be here such a short time that it doesn't matter." She gave them the impression of being friendly, unassuming, and intelligent, so this caused great surprise. This was all based on another superstition, that if she bound herself to them, she would never get abroad.

At the same time, she supported all strikes, detested blacklegs, in general accepted prevalent socialist ideas and gladly walked to work when the ferries struck; if the factory or office had gone on strike, she too would have gone on strike; but she did not think logically, all other things were secondary to the need to leave the lonely state that galled and humiliated her as woman and freeman. It was an accident, perhaps some early song, some tale of Britain, that made her think she could escape by sea. It was perhaps the first visions printed on her mind as a child of the sailors who, from de Quiros to Cook, had sailed all the seas and discovered Australia, and England's sea history, and the voice of the sea behind the language. She loved the sea with a first and last love, had no fear of it, would have liked to sail it for two years without seeing land; she had the heart of a sailor. How could she be satisfied on the dull shore? It seemed the haunt of street nuisances. She wanted to get married but had never formed any idea of the marriage ceremony or the suburban home she might occupy, for she only wanted to marry in order to have love, and if she had any vague idea of a home at all, it was in some coast town overseas, in some mysterious unseen spot where perhaps they spoke a foreign language.

She was ashamed of her timidity and aimlessness, she knew she was not a brave woman. Her twentieth birthday was approaching, she felt old, dull, abandoned, a failure because she had no man. Lance and Jonathan said in effect: "Women are cowardly, women only want to tie a man down, women won't make a move themselves, women only want a man to involve himself, women won't take a chance." She felt that this was true and she asked herself: "What would men do in my situation? Men are brave. A man would tell a woman he loved her and take the consequences. He would take the plunge."

She cast about for a man to love; the nearest man was Jonathan, but she ran over the others. Dr Smith, a man resembling Crow in the office, the medical student on the boat. She went to and fro to work for two days, thinking over what she must do. She must put herself to the test, could she write to poor Jonathan telling him she loved him? Am I afraid, she asked herself. Yes? Then I must. This is the proof. If I haven't the courage for this, I'll fail everywhere. I'll never get anything done.

At about eleven o'clock at night, she wrote the fateful letter. She got up at six o'clock and walked round the Bay, meeting the milkmen and their yellow-and-red-varnished carts. The letter was in her bag. She posted the letter in the red box just outside the ferry, on a cold, dusty morning. She had to put down her paper satchel to unfasten her bag and get out the letter. She slipped the letter in the red pillar-box. Bending to pick up her lunch-case, she stuck her left leg out. Why not?

An engaged youth and girl from the ferry passed her and laughed aloud, at her antics, she thought. She was pale with fright at what she had done. She heard the voices of others, very loud, and saw the fluttering of their clothes, their shoes brightly shining—hers were dusty. The winter sun struck her dry flesh, she was dry as an old maid. She walked to work with a vacant mind, and she arrived at work late. Life, that is to say, indecision, had stopped. She believed that no woman had ever done this bitter, shameful, brave thing before. If people knew of it they would think she was pushed to it by fear, as she was. If it were known, her family would insult her, people on the boat would vomit jokes as she passed. They were safe, closed up with their fiancés, and their marriages to come. She was in the howling wilderness. It was like a crime, she felt, in her terror, and she was a lost woman. It was at the hour she committed this crime and for some time after, till Jonathan sailed and so relieved her of the dread, that she went about with all the feelings of a young anarchist preparing to overthrow authority in secret, for strangely enough she now hated the accepted world, and triumphed over it too. She had undone it all. The deeds of the moral inventor are always criminal and their most evil effect is that when done secretly they cut the doer off from society; put around, they attract adherents. But she was too much ashamed ever to tell it.

This day, walking to the office, a terrible thought came upon her, the only thought during the whole walk; it was, "Once I was interested in everything, in Latin, in going to the university, in the childhood of Goethe, in the apprenticeship of Dürer, even in going to Harper's Ferry. I wanted to know everything, go everywhere by myself, alone. Now I am forcing myself to think only of Jonathan. In the morning, as I raise my head off the pillow, I force myself to think of Jonathan. Everything has changed since I knew him, is he good or bad? Good, good! But if there were waters of Nepenthe I would drink them and forget him and my whole life up till now."

She was like a madwoman, sulky, monosyllabic, torn to pieces by the fear of her solitary deed. At times she trembled and did not dare to look at the black mantelpiece where his letters always stood beside the clock. Sitting alone on the boat, avoiding Martha and Elsie, shivering in the cold winds, she thought: "It's like being in jail, why can't I forget? I don't want this. It isn't that half-starved, half-grown man I want. It's passion, but there's no such thing, that I see. Shall I die hungry?"

Then she superstitiously came to think that if she gave up this boy, she would lose him and all other men, it was a symbol; this or a life without men, a body without children. If she won him, she would succeed, and in some mysterious way conquer her life and time. He did not answer for two days. Each evening, she wanted to beat herself nearly to death so that she would fall into bed and sleep a brutal sleep, remembering neither the infernal compact with herself, nor the disgrace of having failed. There was no way open ahead.

In three days, she received an answer to her letter. The young man wrote:

I have carried your letter about for three or four days trying to understand the real meaning of it. It is too much for me. I feel humble when you say that you love me, because I know I have not those qualities you see in me and I have nothing equal to give in exchange. You are better than me and this shows it. Believe me I will always be your friend.

Sincerely,
Jonathan S. Crow.

She did not like this letter much and she understood suddenly that she wanted him to write something else; *I love you.* But he let her down lightly; she admired the simple honesty with which he wrote. Then she thought she must try to understand him. She studied each sentence, and then each word. What did he really mean? At some times during those days she had been afraid that he would write an angry or cold answer. But she felt there was something behind this mild and sweet answer too. She cudgelled the meaning for a warm answer. In order to compare the two notes, two styles, and two sentiments, she copied out from memory the words of her own letter and then put the two pieces of paper side by side.

First, she forced herself to read her own, which she still could scarce read from shame:

DEAR JOHNNY,

I have loved you for a long time and now I am writing it to you because we are going to be separated by our fates and distance, perhaps for ever. In writing to you I do formally renounce real love and it is not of that I am thinking. But I hope you will think of me and remain a friend of mine. I will be able to keep on struggling if I know that you are watching me from a distance.

Yours,
TERESA HAWKINS.

The first phrase held her up. She had not loved him for a long time. It was a lie. She had played with his emotions merely to help herself out. Then it was a cowardly letter; she prostrated herself before him and at the same time declared it all meant nothing, it was a ritual act. She blushed as she read on. She read hurriedly, thus tearing to pieces every word. Not one seemed true; it had a bad odour, it was hypocritical. What had made her write it? She detested Jonathan Crow, a stupid, carping youth. He could do nothing for her. She became angry. She had given him an immense power over her. She would never see him or write to him again. And then suddenly she thought, but what was she to do? Where could she turn? A surge of hope and confidence rose again and the meekness of his note charmed her. She began instead to worry over each phrase of his letter. "Three or four days" he had carried it about—then had he shown it to his friends? Undoubtedly. Of course it was all over the university. She would never go there, then. She would forget the whole episode, that or death from shame.

At the end she thought he must realize that she was very far from trying to trap him into marriage. In this she was close to his idea, and from there she began to hope again that he might come to love her. She would improve herself so much that she would be lovable. She made up her mind to work harder and she thought of some way to show herself so that her talents would be recognized. Her prospects were worse than ever before, but she had more hope, soon she would be no longer miserable, neglected, and poor. She sat apart always now from Martha and Elsie and all other acquaintances, and avoided the strange young doctor, with his slobber-snouted, mobile face. She did not notice how her bones were showing, nor was ashamed of her threadbare clothes; she appeared to others an ill-kempt sallow woman five years older than she was. She burned with internal flame, her hope and desperate energy, the hope that she would be loved, and at times she thought that her affair with Jonathan was only a step to the unknown man; she would use him for that. She laughed contemptuously at her father, who, seeing how she faded, declared that she would never marry and that someone would stay at home with him in his old age; and at her brother Lance, who drew back at the sight of her and told her she was ugly, hideous, dirty. She said nothing to either of them; both she and Lance spoke to no one at the table.

Jonathan had passed a week in considerable excitement and some happiness. From time to time, he had heard of men who had received declarations and looked upon these men as Launce-lots. He showed the girl's letter to his best friends and received their advice, without taking it. He could see himself go up in their estimation. He had begun to be bored and disappointed with her, now he saw her charm, she was brave and disinterested. When, by accident, on one of their Saturday outings, one of the women said something cutting about her, he defended her. What they laughed at in her, he said, was poverty and the lack of property or status. He was pleased when he saw how this remark quietened the women; he began to use her discreetly as a weapon with them. After a few days, he needed to meet her, look at her, think what kind of human being it was who had written this letter to him. He wrote her a note asking her to meet him when he came to town one night. They would look for a room, if she still wished to leave home; he recalled, he said, the other day, that they had never done that.

After work, he met her outside the teashop in George Street West where she had a bite to eat and they set out along the streets of Ultimo, inhabited by so many college and university students, the best for her he thought. Miss Haviland had once lived there and many other of their friends. Teresa said she had given up a free lecture at the university to do this. She looked him over in the dark of the winter evening, careful not to meet his eye in the lamplight. He looked at her in the light. She was poor and shabby and he would have felt ashamed not to help her. What a miserable thing life is! She had written to him because she was desperate. Fated to a solitary and hopeless life, she clung to him. He was sorry for her. While he was still on this continent, he could be friendly to her. What could a woman do in this world who was not beautiful enough to cadge jewels and lunches?—for women had to be cadgers, he saw that. He felt a responsibility towards her; but now that he saw her again, even worse dressed than before, and much plainer, with her straight hair, colourless lips and cheeks, he felt the hopelessness of the young life of them both. He wished he were sailing right away; the room, which was just a pretext for their walk—he knew what it would be like. His mother let such rooms. They took their way down the main street leading into the Glebe, a dark old street with some trees and old houses mostly divided up among families and with rooms let out. A street lamp stood between two old-fashioned houses with iron railings and stone steps. He said: "I was thinking about you last night."

"I was thinking about you—last night."

He put his arm through hers and looked down kindly at her. "I wish you were free and we could see each other in the evenings."

"Yes, but we can now. I get home late, no one notices."

"They don't keep a watch on you?"

"Oh, no." She hesitated and looked at him. "I don't seem to belong there any more."

"I was thinking of you all last night," he said.

"That's silly," she said. "Just thinking of each other. What's the use?"

"All people like us, homeless, are silly."

They walked on looking at houses. He would point at one, saying: "You ought to live there, perhaps." But it became too late, they could no longer go and ask for rooms and she suddenly saw that at this hour she could not go with a man and ask for a room. All this time, they had said nothing about her letter, though her timidity and low feelings and his tenderness referred to it. Now he said: "I liked your letter."

"I liked yours, too."

They walked farther and turned back. At the turning of City Road, where he must take his way home, he left her. She took a tram to the Quay. He went home thoughtfully and quietly, thinking about her. Could she do anything for him? She was so awkward and weak. She put herself out for him. He believed it was "against the law of the herd" for women to make declarations, but she had done it for him. It was refined pleasure such as he had not yet had, and the letter had marked a stage for him, too. He could never go back to the intimate, confiding belief he had had in women before; now he could dominate them. He saw that his understanding, that he had thought dried up, could develop through his experience with women. He now knew he would never feel love, that time was over. People loved in adolescence, as they wrote poetry; it was soon over, it was over at twenty. But in some belated adolescents, such as virgins, it persisted.

It amused him to go out with Teresa sometimes in the next few weeks and talk in the gentle, off-hand way he had acquired. She asked nothing about his life, merely speaking of what had happened on the last walk, and waiting for him to suggest another. He met Teresa in various moods, sometimes casual, almost rude, overbearing, sometimes kind and affectionate; she could not understand him and began to dread meeting him, even though these meetings had become the whole reason for living through days and nights.

Jonathan lived in a dream. He was beginning to part from his friends, pack his trunk of papers; friendships that had pressed too heavily on him were lifted, criticism blew over him; he was not afraid of Clara and Teresa, they became slight acquaintances whom he would never see again. Many years might have flown past before he set eyes on any of them again. He intended never to return. He thought he had solved his "sexual problem", too. He now for the first time understood what sophisticated love-writers were talking about. He saw a new life for him. But sublimation, too, was a way of cheating the poor. Did rich men sublimate? He was so absorbed in this and in pottering round an office downtown where he did work with a friend to get experience —for no pay, of course—that he did not notice a certain strange, subdued and soundless fuss at home. One Saturday afternoon, in midwinter, in July that is, as he lounged into the passage of his home, he met his father and mother dressed in their best; his mother, he saw with astonishment, actually had a pair of white kid gloves on, perhaps the first she had ever worn since her marriage.

"*Where to?*" He turned her round with affected admiration, looked at the white kid gloves. "Who's getting married? Oh, you great big beautiful doll!"

Smiling stiffly with embarrassment, she withdrew her hands sharply and dusted her gloves. "White kid soils so easy, stupid."

"Where are you going?" He smiled quizzically.

"Never mind, we'll tell you when we come back," said the mother. Mr Crow was saying: "Come on, Attie, we'll be late, you spent an hour fidgeting and—your mother curled up her hair!"

"You'll be attending funerals next."

Jonathan heard the silence of the house; it was swept, clean, silent.

"Come on, Holland's waiting," said the father, referring to one of the two lodgers they had upstairs.

"Oh, it's Holland?" He let out a roar of laughter. "And is he going to bring the blushing bride here? It's the first time Mum ever weakened."

"Let me go, Johnny," she said, tugging away the skirt he had been holding playfully. "You'll tear it."

"Is Eddie going too?"

"Your brother Eddie's going," said the father jovially, and the mother stiffly assented.

Jonathan looked at them both, his eyes opening, and he cried: "You're going to Eddie's wedding?"

"Yes, son, that's what it is. Now you've guessed. Now let us go. We weren't going to tell you till it was all over, knowing you would take it funny, perhaps. But he wheedled us into it, and there we are!"

Jonathan threw himself in front of his mother and put his arms firmly round her. "You're not going."

"Come along now, Johnny, come along now," said the father warmly. "What business is it of yours, I don't see. Mum and I made up our minds to go through with it, since he was so set on it, and here we are."

"You can go," said Jonathan. "I won't let Mum go. You know how she got him. You go, but Mum has no right there. It's blackmail. Take your hat off, Mum, and sit down."

"Let up," said the father. "What good can it do now? It's all over—or will be if we don't hurry. And Mr Holland's waiting. He's best man. It isn't fair to keep them waiting."

"Mum's not going," said Jonathan firmly, pushing his mother into the best room and making her sit down on one of the crochet-covered chairs. "Listen, Mum, that woman's two years older than Eddie, she's been his mistress for years, waiting for him to marry her. I went and told her he'd never marry her and that must have got her dander up, now she's done it to spite us. If you go, you're just playing her game."

The mother looked angrily at the father, who twisted his black moustache, and said: "What's done can't be undone. What do you want to bring tears to your mother's eyes for? You shouldn't have said that. Now bear up, Mum. Give us a smile, go on. Dry those tears."

Jonathan said coldly: "You go with Holland, it's all settled. But I won't let my mother meet that woman, and I'll never speak to Eddie again. I told him what she was. She's getting herself off on him now that she's shopworn and getting too old. She's shopworn on the shelf. Do you think I didn't follow her up? Let him have his rag and bone and hank of hair, but I'll never acknowledge the marriage and I'll never set foot here while he's here."

The mother sat rigid, sullen in the chair. Jonathan turned to her and said: "I'm warning you now, Mum, if you go to the wedding, I'm leaving the house today. It's that daisy or me."

She unbuttoned one of her gloves and rebuttoned it.

"Eddie wouldn't marry a woman like that, Jonathan!"

"I know all about that, what Eddie wouldn't do," he said sharply. He went and opened the front door. "Go on, Dad, there's Holland in front of the gate. I see Mum's washed the veranda and done the steps for the bride. I won't let you go, Mum," he said fiercely as she advanced, sorry to miss a wedding.

"Eddie's my son too," she said firmly. "And was before you, Jonathan."

Jonathan smiled nastily, unpinned her hat, pushed down her hands when she put them on his chest, took the pins out of her hair and let her grey hair fall down her worn old face and neck.

"You do look a sight," he said, laughing grimly. "Fit for that kind of a wedding, I'd like to see you turn up like that."

"You'd better go, Dad," the mother said. "Johnny's set on making a row, and perhaps he's right—I 'arf thought myself. And if she's that kind of woman——" but Mr Crow ran down the white steps and joined Holland, who was beckoning and showing his wrist-watch. Jonathan closed the door.

"Sorry to be a spoil-sport," said Jonathan angrily, "but I meant it. If that drab comes here, I'm off, and for good. You won't see me again."

"What do you want to be so mean for, and just before you're going away for years from us, too."

He shut the door of the best room, picked up her hat and gloves and, going down the passage, aimed them at the kitchen table.

"I hope you'll never speak to that woman," said Jonathan. "She

233

copped a sucker. You're just as weak as he is. Have you seen her?"

"Yes."

"Isn't she an old woman?" he said savagely. "Ugly, worn, thin old hat-rack. You could see she's on the shelf and he was her last hope."

The mother sat down and began twisting up her hair.

"She doesn't look so old!" she said nervously. "I'm an old woman. I wouldn't say she is."

Mrs Crow, with her mouth full of pins, raised her eyes secretively to him; a faint gleam of satisfaction crept into her face. When she had finished, she said: "Well, you are a tartar, aren't you? You've certainly got a will of your own."

"I'm through," he said suddenly, seizing his hat. "Now you've done this, you can take the consequences. I'm going down to the pub. You'll see me when you see me."

"Johnny!" she cried sternly. "You come back 'ere, where do you think you're going like that, in a temper, and leaving your mother with that kind of language. You come right back 'ere."

"You sit and wait for the happy pair," he said. "I'm going to get drunk."

" 'Ave you got the money?" she said cruelly; then she looked at the clock. "Well, it's all over now. No good cryin' over spilt milk, they're man and wife."

"Congratulations," said Jonathan. "Mum, give me a bob, darn it, I've not got a penny to get away on my own for half a day."

"It seems to me you go out pretty often on your picnics," she sneered, putting her hand in her purse.

"As a beggar," he said. "I'm always accepting hospitality. Ugh! How glad I will be to leave this damned town behind me and all my friends and the whole mess! I hate it here. I've been a mendicant here. Give me the money and let me go, I'm begging from you too, but from you I'm not ashamed. I cannot dig, to beg I'm not ashamed. Ta-ta. Expect me when you see me."

He went out, clacking the back door, and hurried down the passage.

" 'E always 'ad such a will," said the mother to herself. " 'E'll make 'is way, of that I'm sure." She looked at the clock, got up, and smoothed out the white gloves given to her by Eddie. "What Eddie'll say I'm sure I don't know, I don't know what Dad'll say!

That poor boy is a fair terror. You must do this, I won't let you do that! 'E's got a backbone, at any rate." She looked round the tidy kitchen. "I'll tidy up a bit. I've no doubt they'll stop by to persuade me to come to 'ave a bite, Dad and Eddie—and 'er." She arranged the folds of the curtain. "The place certainly looks like a new pin, it does me credit. I don't believe what the boy said, what does 'e know about such things? 'E's just took a dislike to 'er and 'e says anything, as 'e always will. She's no great shakes, but what's done, is done."

21. Love Is Feared: It Dissolves Society

THIS affair Jonathan wrote, boiling hot, to his confidante, Teresa. What a shame, what a swindle, and what cowardice on Eddie's part, to allow himself to marry a woman without love! And Jonathan's parents who lent themselves to the farce, the official union in holy matrimony of two persons who were now indifferent and would soon hate each other.

Is that a way to get beyond the reach of penury? Is it a way to improve the lot and character of women, to allow them to put over the old fraud of marriage and a hearth, a man to keep them, a legal meal ticket? But I am sure that if she had loved him passionately, my mother and father, Holland and the others would not have been anxious for the marriage at all; it is because marriage binds up their game and any kind of love dissolves it. Love is feared: it dissolves society, it's unpopular, and it's very rare. That is why they put over this ritual, because it keeps society together. And what society? The erotic fraud ought to fall to pieces. As for me, I stick my hands in my pockets now and look on. It took me a while to reach this state of beatitude—for indifference and contempt is the only beatitude I know. I was going to quit the house, but now I have laid down a rule, if he comes, I go, so I suppose they will keep him and the woman he's taken out a licence for. Perhaps you don't see eye to eye with me. I was in a lather, as you see. I forgot, you are a woman, perhaps that makes a difference? But could you want to imprison yourself in marriage? Well, forget it, anyway. It was just a flare-up. But it goes from bad to worse, I am more and more unhappy—odd word, that, can one be unhappy who never was happy?—and the shaking my dust from my feet can't come too soon for me.

I don't mind taking their money. I have no illusions, I'm the ideal merchant in dull impartiality, I'm a down-at-heel déclassé, risen from the ranks, with no axe to grind, no canoe to paddle, and no song to sing, a piece of wood that they can hew and carve. They don't know whether they detest me or laugh at me, my perversity is theirs. I'm their dream, the average man, that statistical fiction, a conveyor-belt intellect—but no danger from me. And this is my only use, I'd say, since I'm indifferent to everything and can't be fooled, I'm a good sieve to strain facts through to others. The world's a mart of chicane, cheat and compromise; "idealists" go surrounded by their own brass band and don't know it. I don't cling to the old, either. The old for the most part is a mess of conventions and private interests held together by the cement of L.C.D. needs. My ideal? To live without illusion; in brief, that means without love, doesn't it? That's my reason for existence, not to be duped like the great nor like the petty. This came to me in my third year after several years of aimlessness and personal despair, I might say, I felt at first that since I had always been supported by the state, I ought to do something for it.

It seems I'm getting a reputation as a wit, at least Cooper told me so, but I don't know how, it's just my undeviating common sense, for nothing can distract me, neither Atlanta nor her golden ball. As for men of genius, I suspect they start trouble to satisfy their instinct of pugnacity, like big-fisted young drunks running down George Street West on Saturday night and challenging every mick and dago to a fight. This makes them unreliable, their instincts are big within them, they might run amok any time to satisfy them, they have a limitless adolescence. I grew up before my time—where was my youth? I am not enceinte with any instincts. I am austere. The state likes that kind of man—and why not? He's a worker. He doesn't cry for superfluity. Or am I just a brain sensualist and want to be a theory-taster all my life? Maybe it's sublimation of the love instinct after all. But let it be. I like it this way!

Teresa cried over this letter. She thought feverishly how to console him. She created a design as long as the dining-room table, a panel in seven sections, in colours, the design of his life. She called it the Legend of Jonathan. All the pictures were in draughtsmen's colours. The panels were about nine inches by eleven and in each the central figure was Jonathan: first as a child selling newspapers; second as a child looking in a window of toys; third as a boy of thirteen wearing a striped sweater, a second and ghostly boy looking at him from a high Gothic tower; fourth as a youth, hesitating before the philosophers in a colonnade, that is, pictured as hesitating before a green forest into which many paths entered; fifth as an academic youth, loaded with prizes and laurel crowns, and bowed down, looking at a bird soaring up in a cloud; sixth as a man, alone, before the giant figure of a naked woman, while loves and women, naked, young, peered at him from the innumerable members of the statue; and seventh as Ulysses, afloat on an ocean on which the innumerable curled and dark-blue waves were the locks of a woman's hair, the woman far off, half Pegasus, leaping into the sky; and all these were pictures of incidents Jonathan had talked about, his sorrows and longings, while the last two were a picture of what Jonathan said was his present loneliness. She had a little skill in drawing, a wooden, naïve, but energetic skill, like a vigorous man talking in a foreign language, strangely, upside down and yet so full of ideas that even aesthetes listen to him. Like this was the strange drawing and underneath were titles, invented by the girl, "Jonathan as a child must work for his bread"; "Jonathan, though he works, cannot have the toys children long for"; "Jonathan, looking from the school window, wishes he could play football"; "Jonathan is afraid of the colonnade"; "Jonathan is crushed by honours"; "Jonathan desires womankind"; "Jonathan sets out for the unknown".

It was quaint, laborious. She delivered it to the house one evening at nightfall and said to the man who opened the door that the university had sent it, but did not hear from him whether he received it or not.

She kept seeing Miss Haviland and heard from her when he went to dinner with his old classmates and when he saw Clara, Elaine, Tamar, on last outings. He wrote to Teresa at last, a few lines, about a fortnight before he sailed, arranging to meet her at lunch time, near her factory; a postscript said: "By the way, did I ever mention that I got that drawing? Too bad, you shouldn't take so much trouble over me."

She went out and spent a lot of money on a green felt hat with a cockade. She saw them smile when she wore it to the office, and an odd, sallow young man who was fond of chatting with her, came in suddenly and hissed: "Violetta, for God's sake, throw away that awful hat." Mad with shame, she really did throw it out the window of the factory, into the vacant lot, and he laughed. During the lunch hour, she waited near the factory, not knowing where to meet Jonathan, and when she came back at two, with hanging cheeks and lids, she found a telephone message on her desk: "Mr Crow rang up to say he took the boat to Mosman and clean forgot his appointment with you." This, with the green hat, told everyone the story. She looked at herself in the glass and saw how pale and ugly she was.

Though everyone who knew him went down to the boat to see him off, he did not invite her. The morning of his sailing she received a coloured postcard with the words, "Cheerio! See you in England. Yours, Johnny". She had asked for the morning off. She did not dare to go to the wharf for the sailing and she knew by now that Jonathan would be ashamed of her bare bones and bad clothes, before all those girls and university men. He would walk with her in the dark streets, but not in the daylight. She had chosen a post in the Domain, where they had once sat at sunrise, and where they had seen the gunboat come in. She could see the boat sailing from there.

It was raining. Teresa wore a light grey stockinet suit with a grey woollen pillbox cap of the same material; she had no coat or umbrella and was soon wet and bedraggled. She had washed the suit herself several times. They had confusedly heard of sending things to the cleaners at home, but they had heard of the high prices charged and would not have thought of paying them. They cleaned the men's clothes with ammonia and soap, or else washed them and did the same with their own. This stockinet suit, so cleaned, was an extraordinary sight, something you don't see in the streets every day. It had shrunk, and the colour had come out unevenly and run in streaks. With her high nose and forehead, Lance's drooping cheeks, her small mouth and salty eyes, cropped hair and this brindled costume, she looked exactly like a loutish page in some medieval canvas. People stared at her and either smiled openly or looked away, ashamed. She knew what a figure she cut and yet she pushed on through the rain, her shoes going flippity-flop, the water streaming from her nose and her fingers as from a guttering. She would see the boat sail because this day was the end of her life, was the beginning of life

239

too; in a few years she would sail, and in her heart she was aboard down there.

At ten, in the steady downpour, she reached a tree-grown, lawny ridge in the gardens overlooking Woolloomooloo, where the great ship lay at Wharf No. 5. She could see only part of the buff upper-works as she lay, but precisely at ten-thirty the giant bulk moved slightly, amidst hooting and distant shouts, and the girl heard three-times-three from student's throats. This ship was carrying not only Jonathan Crow but several other scholars, going to medical and art schools abroad, to Paris, London, and even to Germany, for few thought then that Hitler's regime would last more than a month or so longer. It was a madness of the year. There came the nose of the boat, like Leviathan, and streamers already hanging limp, trailing in the water. They were off, land ties had already been broken. This made her happy, for she had a part in this going, the very first move of all the moves, that would take her abroad. She knew he was no longer shaking hands with them all, responding cheerfully to good wishes; he was already on the water, the life of the ship had claimed him. She saw the long rails black with people, and the ship was now half visible.

At this moment, with tears and raindrops mingling on her face, she saw that the young man in a raincoat who had been standing under a near-by fig-tree for some time was coming nearer. She looked quickly at him. He raised his hat and said: "Why are you standing here looking at the boat?"

"I'm watching it go out," she said, looking steadfastly at the ship.

"Do you know someone on her?"

"Yes."

"A man?" hazarded the stranger.

"Yes. A student who is going to London."

He looked at her for a moment before he said: "Is he your boy?"

"No, just a friend."

"And why are you standing here? Does he know you are here?"

"Yes," lied Teresa.

"But he can't see you from there."

"Yes, he has glasses."

"Why didn't you go down to the wharf?" he persisted, looking at her.

"No, I told him I wouldn't."

"Why not?"

"Better not," she said stiffly.

"He doesn't want people to know?"

"No," she said, jumping at his suggestion.

"Did you say good-bye before, then?" asked the young man.

"Yes."

"He kissed you?"

"Yes."

"And you won't see him for a long time," said the young man, sadly.

"I'm going, too. I have to save up, though."

"It costs a lot," said the young man.

She told him: "Forty-four pounds for the boat-fare, third class, and of course I must have ten pounds to land with."

"You'll get a job there?"

"Oh, of course."

After some thought, the young man began to speak again and saw that Teresa was waving, for she had thought that if her young man had glasses to look at her, he would expect to see her waving.

"Can he really see you?" the stranger said, incredulously.

"It isn't so far, with glasses!"

"No, I s'pose not. It will be a long time, though. Won't you be lonely?"

"No."

"Will you write to him?"

"Yes."

"Did he ask you to write to him?"

"Yes," she said, gladly.

"Is he going to write to you?"

"Yes. Every week," she added.

"The first letter will take a long time to get here," said the stranger. "Three months." He continued sorrowfully: "You will be lonely, it's a long time." Teresa suddenly said: "Yes, I will be lonely."

The boat had turned tail and was going up the harbour; she could see nothing but its name and port of registry. She turned to look at her companion. He was a fawn-coloured, middle-sized, fleshy man, young, with a soft brown hat, fawn raincoat, and black shoes. His eyes were large, long-lashed, dark-blue. He had a dawdling baritone, mournful, flat. He was dripping with rain. He stood there, half-turned towards the ship, watching its wake in a lumpish, sympathetic way. When he saw her studying him, he turned back, turned polite, and said: "I was standing here to get out of the rain. I walked all over town and all over the Domain. It's no fun. I'm on my holiday," and his voice was more depressed than ever. "I have a fortnight, fifteen days really they give me, and I've only spent seven days and I want to go back already. It's dull, isn't it? You wouldn't think it would be so dull. I don't know anyone here. Isn't that bad? I was looking forward all the year to my holiday, thinking I'd have a good time in Sydney. I'm from Mortdale on the Illawarra line, do you know where it is?"

"Yes," Teresa began to move, because the boat had turned the point.

"Don't go yet, you'll get wet," said the stranger.

"It's been raining all morning, it won't stop now."

"You don't like to speak to me. I'm all right. Perhaps I shouldn't have spoken to you. I know girls, ladies, don't like it."

"That's all right," she said. "I don't mind a bit."

"I was just standing here, can you beat it, thinking I'd go home. I've got eight more days of my holiday but I'm going back. I can't make any friends here. No one seems friendly. Don't go yet. Or perhaps I shouldn't have spoken to you?"

"I've got to go now," said Teresa.

"Where are you going?"

"To the Art Gallery," she said, pointing to the building not far away.

"Could I come with you?"

"No, don't do that."

"What are you doing after that?"

"I'm going back to work."

"How did you get time off?"

"I told them he was sailing."

"And they didn't tell you to come back right away?"

"I got the morning off."

He said: "They don't expect you back right away then, wouldn't you pass just a few hours with me? Don't you want a

cup of tea?—it's nearly lunch time." He was following her slowly,
his long face convulsed. He was begging, begging, coming slowly
to the edge of the tree where they both halted because the shower
was heavier at that moment. He put a hand inside his coat and
pulled out a little notecase.

"Look," he said, "I'm all right. Here's my licence, and that's my
photograph, George E. Smethers."

She carefully read the card, looked at the photograph, and then
at his face. He watched her.

"Look, wouldn't you go to a movie with me? I don't want anything, only your company. I just want to go to the movies with
someone. I never spoke to no one," he said, lapsing suddenly.
"I've been here seven days and the girls don't want to talk to you.
I'm all right. I'm a counter man in a little ham-and-beef up there,
on the other side of the station, in Mortdale. I saved up the whole
year to come to Sydney for me holidays. They always say Sydney
is lively. I never met nobody here. Yesterday, I took the train up
to Arncliffe. I just took any ticket. The day before I went to the
Zoo, I spoke to a couple of girls but they wouldn't speak to me. I
came back. I've got a room in Darlinghurst."

Teresa started out across the lawn, she was wet through and
beginning to shiver.

"Are you going?" said the man, following her, with an excess
of despondency. "You don't trust me."

"It isn't that, but I've got to get back to work this afternoon."

"You don't trust me," said the man.

She hesitated. He looked so uncouth. She knew she wouldn't
lose her job, but she didn't like the flabby man. She thought, two
miserable human beings. As she wavered, she saw, in a flash, herself, picking up men in the city, on the boat, anything for company, like this man, beginning to slide into cheap ways, looking
for men for an hour's conversation, anything to fight off the fear
of being alone and unmated, loveless love-affairs with no conclusion, or an evil one, and the great desire to go abroad wither-
ing, her will ruined, while she was eating with strange poor
boobies, dressing for hopeless men, going to the movies with
failures. Impossible. This too was a symbol. And then she was
afraid of him. Why was he so lonely? That was queer. He had
been watching her eagerly, hoping that she was going to stay
with him.

Briskly, she said: "No, I can't. Good-bye." And she walked off quickly through the rain. She went into the Gallery and looked back. There he was sloping down the landscape at a distance, diagonally, in front of her, his hands in his pockets, his shoulders bent, and the rim of his hat turned down. What was he? She thought, at this hour the city is full of miserable souls wanting each other, or someone else, but we can't take anyone at all, it's dishonourable to take anyone but the one we want. It's lax.

When she got back to the office she looked like a tramp, the suit had turned all shades of grey and the lining of the hat had turned to jelly; her stockings were splashed and the toe-cap of one shoe had come unsewn. She threw away the ruined hat, dried herself as best she could and, in her shorthand book, began to calculate how many weeks, at how much a week, she must work to pay the forty-four pounds and other expenses, clothing, food, rent, in the meantime. She saw at once that she must ask for a rise in pay. She went in to Remark, the boss, and asked him for ten shillings extra. Perhaps she was worth it, or perhaps she looked so uncommonly wretched and strange that the healthy, ruddy, hot-tempered, self-made man was touched. He granted her the extra money. She went back to her office and did her calculations again.

The next night there was a great clear sky. The girl, going up the headland, stood between the light-tender's cottage and the Hornby light and looked at the heaving sea, thinking of the ships it carried, and at the rhinoceros-horned headlands swimming out to sea. The sky was pallid, the stars scarcely visible; in the high north-west, one after the other, two meteors burned themselves out. She felt her youth and strength, her thick hair loose on her shoulders, being quite alone, and facing the Pacific. Long ago, if she had been born a black Australian girl, she would have gone off now, paddling by herself up the coasts and daring the passage to the islands. All that was needed was a boat, and then, her lover could not have gone so far. "All the same, I'm as young, strong, and brave even if my skin is white. It's the same sun, the same air. They didn't marry me at fourteen, as they would have if I'd been black, I must do it myself. But do it I will."

Her dark heart moved over the sea with the throbbing of a ship. The ship had already passed beyond all this coast and was in new waters. "What would a man do?" thought the girl. "Would he let this accident stand between himself and his love? Would he if he loved me? No. And I am worthy of him. Nothing will stand between me and him. I will make him love me."

She stood there, the wind teasing her hair on her shoulders, till the last light went out in the cottage and only the steadfast Hornby light and the great ray of the South Head Lighthouse went sweeping overhead. Then she went home, planning a life of extreme hardship, to save the more. She was tormented by what she had heard this day from Miss Haviland. "Elaine, Clara, Little Redtop as he calls her, Dorothy, you don't know her, Tamar, they were all there; it was quite a send-off. He introduced them all to his mother and he seemed a little moved when he said good-bye to Elaine and I thought he introduced her to his mother in a particular way. I met her too. Only you were not there."

"I didn't want to be," said Teresa.

"I only realized then," said Miss Haviland, with a pitiful smile, "how many friends he had, how much he is loved, and how we are going to miss him."

He had treated Teresa as an outsider, but had been proud to introduce the pretty blue-dressed graduate, Elaine, to his mother. So much the worse; she would overcome all rivals too. She buckled down to the immense task.

22. *Still Three Years to Go*

THEY knew in the family that she had been taking walks with a man and that he had now gone away, but as she said nothing about her affairs, friendly estrangement began between her and her relatives. At home, things were bad, they never spoke to each other. Only Kitty spoke to them all. Teresa had found out that Kitty was still in love with a married man, Bayliss, whom she had only met once, on a picnic. He had never written to her but Kitty wrote often now to her cousin Sylvia, who knew the man. Teresa found this out from Lance. Cruel insinuations flew about when Lance was angry. Lance was more comic with her, Teresa, because he knew that her man was a university graduate and Lance, still struggling in his night classes, respected the degree.

The year had nearly gone and it was summer again, December, before she had the first letter from Jonathan Crow, who had sailed on a day in August of that year. He had written to her soon after his arrival, combining a few pages written on board ship, and a few pages written after he was housed in London.

I went with Eugene Burt, a pal I met on the boat, to a theatre in Kingsway. We waited a long time in the rain in Sardinia Street for the show to come out and the crowd waited patiently, with monotonous, habitual patience, reading papers, eating oranges, for about an hour. Meanwhile, in the mud, thick to the ankles, in the middle of Sardinia Street, was a man dancing with his little daughter and two sons, acrobats doing tricks in the filth to amuse the crowd. They slipped and fell in the mud and took advantage of it to raise a laugh. No one saw anything wrong in it that I could see. They are poor; the poorer still, without a coat, are entitled to amuse them. The bobby didn't interfere. Some few threw pennies, the others were indifferent. Burt and I were so sickened we nearly went away, but we, wet like the rest, waited for dry entertainment within at one-and-twopence. We threw them a couple of sixpences, the man stopped and came up to us to say: "Thank you, gentlemen, God bless you", not "God bless me!" You have no idea of the poverty here. Wait till you come and you'll see. Imagine, there are regular beggars who show their sores in public, and the waiters and the servants are beggars too, they all expect tips, because they are underpaid. You hear "Thank you, sir!" Sir is used everywhere by everyone to everyone. He sirs me but I'm damned if I'll sir the next, I'll teach them a little Australian. Yesterday, in a street off the Strand, a beggar with his ulcerated legs on view, crippled and begging everywhere, the cap in hand, the pestering and the disgust allowed by the boys in blue. I don't know how I'll stick out my two years in this misery of hunger. The English have been revolting since Wat Tyler but the People of Property are still in the saddle. I am in no mood to take it, that's the rub. I had nowhere to go, and no money, having used up all my allowance. The first night, I went to a doss house of some sort that Burt knew of, the next day to L.S.E. to register (he's in his second year, by the way, and showed me the ropes) and then tucker in a teashop, worse than anything we have in the way of food, and out to look for rooms. All cold, dingy. None found; so another sleepless night in the doss house, and the following day we ran to earth an old landlady of Burt's, a yellow-faced old hag called Bagshawe, and with her a pothouse servant, they run the house. Burt and I now share one room on the first floor—back—only two floors. It's in Marchmont Street, No. 92. Write to me there. Keep me cheered up. One taste of life here and I know I'm going to be lonesome. Some of the others said they would write, Clara, Cooper, Elaine, but I don't know if they will. Gone and forgotten is my epitaph. Why not?

She showed this letter only to Miss Haviland, and put it away in a box of scented wood she had bought. She answered the letter at once but had no reply to hers till another three months were out; that was in late March 1934, but after that she began to receive one letter from Jonathan by every mail, and sometimes, when he felt melancholy, two. She sometimes showed them to Miss Haviland, but generally did not and no one else ever saw them, though the family stood each one against the clock, saying slyly:

"There's your letter, Terry", but preserved a silence about the affair otherwise. They expected her to wait for him to come back. They did not know he might not come back and only to the stranger in the Domain had she told her plans for sailing. His next letter said:

I will be pretty strapped the whole year. Burt and I sit here and shiver and live on bread and cheese; my work goes slowly, but I have another year and a half and it looks as if I might extend it to another year. I haven't used any of my introductions yet. One is to Buxton, one to Marcus; I might get a political job. It might be the solution. So it looks as if there'll be plenty of time for you to come over here.

She tried to study at night. She got her friends to give her their free library tickets and had books piled on the floor in her room. She spent her free time in the office composing letters to Jonathan. She worked over them, studying early and late, to beat Jonathan's university education with her own subtlety, though he was so many years in advance of her in learning. She had come to think of her wild dreams as impure and kept them apart from Jonathan, who was to her holy, pure, admirable, and whom she had begun to love with a mystic love into which no fleshly thought entered. Once or twice when the moonlight lay across the earth she wondered if they might marry and she imagined some wedding night in which she and Jonathan, standing in a splendid garden of heavy-limbed southern flowers, white and odorous, would kiss each other, and he would pull her backwards by her long hair into his arms. But in this embrace in the moon, apparently, they stood for ever. She told herself that if she ever allowed one impure thought to creep into her mind now, she would never have Jonathan; it would be her punishment, and a just one. "Love has nothing to do with all that." Her former fancies fell away, withered, things hideous and unspeakable began to take their place, since the room could not be left empty, but Jonathan was far apart from all of it, a knight of poverty battling on a frozen island of the north.

Each letter of theirs was a monologue, because of the three months' interval, and this gave their sentiments a false beauty and elevation.

248

Here, *he said*, it is as if I was in a kind of hospital or prison. Outside in the world is the richness of human life and experience, here I am tunnelling through libraries; I get out of it, a prison holiday, from time to time, to dig ditches in the country, my country lectures, where there are some nice fellows but the girls particularly are more interested in modern problems than the men, and who try to talk things over. But often enough my life is so meaningless and vapid that I don't even want consolation. To prove it—it is often Gene who reads your letters, not I, and I even give them to Bentham, the artist, to read. They take an interest in them and speak of your ambition—did you know it? —but say you have no courage. You must have the courage of your convictions! That is the impression you make. You know for yourself that I am no judge either of originality, power, or style. However, I appreciate them, at least by proxy, and with this you must be satisfied, for I can do no better. But then you know me and I assume, therefore, that you are satisfied with me as I am.

A week later after such a hard letter, he would make haste to please her again:

I am longing for you to come over, *he would write now*, it will be company for me. I can never adapt myself to their infinite social strata, all signalized by different accents. A man with my accent is an outsider, I could not possibly get a job at the L.S.E. —all I can pick up are country lectures. That's all that goes here, pukka sahib or rank outsider—gentleman or bounder—and it's accent, accent, all the way. I have begun to see the web of their social system. It is built up on precedent and the "by accident" or "muddling through", which is true enough, is only the outside. Inside, they're tough; the muddle is not so muddled that an outsider can stumble inside. Stumbling down from accident to accident! How they love to believe that—I wonder why? You wouldn't think a whole nation would be proud of its confusion. Mysteriouser and mysteriouser, curiouser and curiouser, but I haven't got them by the tail yet. One of these days, I'll write the great solution! I suppose I could go in for parvenu-ship like another, by electioneering to secretary and mayhap to Parliament —in one of those shires where Magdalen and Balliol are despised.

But is it worth it? I don't give a darn for their whole game! So you see what I am feeling. Dull stuff. My landlady, who looks like an old horse, is pretty good to me and gives us both a kind of rough mothering. She brought us up a coverlet and a hot-water-bag during the last cold spell. I envy you your hot weather, open air, good wages and independence. I compare myself with you and ask, What am I doing at my books at this age? Yours is the better part. Write me to keep my pecker up.

Your affectionate,

JOHNNY.

At the end of two years, Jonathan had made up his mind not to return to his native land nor to stay in England but to go to America, where greater academic chances were, perhaps he could get a job in Columbia. This damped Teresa's spirits, for she could only go where she could get a job without troublesome formalities, that is, within the British Empire; and she knew that following her schedule she might only reach England just before Jonathan left, or indeed, after he left. This was a chance she must take.

Jonathan had now begun to talk about her coming, and somehow the question had cropped up of what their relations would be. Jonathan said:

I can make no decision about it, it depends upon you entirely; I have no will. If you want to come over to me, make the decision yourself. I am willing to take the chance. As you know, I don't know what love is, but I don't say that it is utterly impossible and if you are willing to try me out, so be it. In any case, I shall be glad to see you.

Teresa thus was not deluded, but admired Jonathan for his plainness, and felt that she was behaving as behaves a gallant and a brave man who passes through the ordeals of hope deferred, patience, and painful longing, to win a wife. She might win him, it was up to her. She accepted his conditions without any surprise, was grateful for them, and would have been indignant if anyone had commented upon her willing sacrifices. This was her affair and Jonathan's; it might be the prelude to a marriage.

In the beginning of the third year, came a letter from Jonathan which greatly startled her. A paragraph wedged in half-way down the third page of his letter said:

Now that it is settled that you are coming over, I have been thinking things over seriously. This is mere speculation, but I want to ask you a question: Will you, rather, would you, live with me when you arrive? Would you be able to do this? What is your feeling about me in this respect?

This surprised and disabled Teresa so much that she was unable to reply for some time, thinking all the time that it made no difference, it would be a year yet before she could go; and then she wrote, shamefaced: "You must think of yourself and your position. If it got out what would they think at the university? This is for you to say." She was punished for this when, three months later, she received the answer:

About my question to you: it was out of order and I am sorry I made it, if it upset you at all. Let's put it down to scientific curiosity, a reaction test, and forget all about it, except on the dusty records of Time's laboratory, to be poetical. I don't want to spoil our friendship. But if I'm too Boeotian you'd better give me up. I'm always putting my foot in it and hurting somebody when I only pose a problem. We aren't really willing to see where we stand, we don't want our naked desires dragged out in the callow light of day, do we? So, as I said, let's forget about this whole episode.

In his usual style, a week later, he wrote a pleasant letter:

Let's forget the living together, or rather, let's put it another way. I want you to go walking with me during the summer next year, I think Wales; it would have been Germany, but Germany is now *ausgeschlossen!* Do you care for that? Will you trust me that far? Or we can go down into Cornwall. I think we ought to make some sort of trial, so let's make it Wales and the future comes after Wales, if we have a future.

She became more and more understanding. These letters read from end to end were very like Jonathan, the moody and inexplicable, with his changes of voice and tone, his hopes of love and hatred of love. There was nothing to explain, this was Jonathan himself. She had swallowed everything, disappointment, rivals, girls in the country, casual "pals", an American girl he had a crush on for a time, coldness, unadvised letters, but she felt she had won; and a little later she received a letter in which he said he must love her.

I feel I love you and you feel you love me, but time will prove, in any case I am anxious to see you. What does that mean? I won't swear to what I mean. I like to get your letters, I am looking forward to the day you come and if that is love, take it for what it is worth, take me, if you can persuade me. You see how I put myself into your hands. Perhaps you will find me changed, but in one thing I have not changed, I have not been happy and if you can alter that, you are welcome. London is drizzling again, the cold is aching in my bones, this is the life I lead. Man is a sun-machine. I have spent three years of misery, I ought to say three lives of misery. All kinds of promises were pie-crust. I'm an unhappy man but you don't mind that. Well, my dear Teresa, it's in the hands of the gods, if you love me, if I can love you, I will and I feel that I do. This is all I can offer! Life has nothing for me, so as well this as that, you understand. You see the kind of man I turned out to be. But come to London, come to me, and let us see how things turn out. With love,

> your Jonathan, if you wish.

In one, he put a bashful postscript:

By the by, have you kept any of the letters I sent you? Bring them along with you if you have room. But I suppose they didn't interest you enough to keep, I'm not much of a fist at it. No, better not! I might be sorry to see what I had written! Blessed is she who preserveth not from rust and moth!

In her second or third letter, in February of the first year of her saving up, Teresa wrote to Jonathan:

To solve the question of why students suffer when they come out into the world: for one thing, learning is too general, there are

252

not enough particular sciences. If there are fifteen or sixteen shades, and more, in the sky we call sky-blue, and so in everything we have a simple name for, how can this one word, "sky-blue", satisfy every perception? This sky-blue can be depicted in a hundred ways. Again, sensation is vague, the five senses boiling in the brain, a stew of insight, confuse us farther, that is, given nothing definite, and so fifteen or sixteen blues can produce a hundred or more sensations; also feelings of joy, melancholy, despair and sensations without form or which have not yet borrowed a form, such a simple poignancy which exists by itself without any human relation attached to it, until we run into sorrow, pain. Does pleasure exist by itself? Joy? Joy is more definite because we begin early to experience joy, our parents try to give it to us; but it is the most primitive ecstasy. All the ecstasies are things within for which there is no name and which have never been described. The greatest sensations become the most general and the least concerned with that particular adjusted interlocking which is any kind of relation to the outside world. If the greatest sensations become hooked on to any outside thing or person, our heads are turned: our heads are turned by confusion. Language is simply not large enough and though English is said to have the most synonyms and the most words altogether, it still lacks hundreds of thousands of words. The words, joy, love, excitement, are bald and general. That is why love stories I suppose sound so dull, for the heroine or hero cannot feel just love, it must be one of a hundred kinds of love he feels.

Poets, mystics, addicts of drink and drugs, young turbulent children, seem to have a different world from ours, something like we remember vaguely from our childhood and what Wordsworth stupidly called "apparelled with celestial light" the vague notion of light before our eyes grow stronger. If we could see light, in all ways, that would be "terrestrial light". I attribute much of the inexplicable longing for childhood joys, which of course never existed, as they are imagined, to a longing for this general, easy, undifferentiated inward sensation which gives the greatest pleasure, that sensation of crawling, living within, of having a fire within, which poets and mystics have. A professor once asked me (Dr Smith) how I told the difference between vivid dreams and reality. I did not know how to answer. I suppose it is in the greater activity of the senses and the power to differentiate in so many more ways. Professional dreamers, hoping for a great synthesis, shed these differences. They are the ones who develop what we abandon, the sensation called coenaesthesia. It is wrong for us to lose this; those who have lost it complain of feeling cold and unfeeling, of being unable to experience joy and even anguish. Some people must be born who lose this general inward sensation early and if this leads to a sharpening of the five senses (which I doubt, though it may lead to a firmer warp of logic) it also leads to a peculiar misery, an absence of emotional life. Others develop too much towards this joyous feeling of general expansion and confusion within. Perhaps the so-called crowd instinct is nothing more than a desire for this general confused and relaxed feeling which is obtained by the multpile vague sensations of contact, sight, sound, smell, fear, expectation, hate, blood-lust, all at once, in the crowd. For it is true that the lunatic, the lover, the poet and the nervous child have no use for the crowd.

At night, lying on her bed, she reasoned, arguing beautifully with him, it seemed to her. Out of the money she was saving she took a little for a few life-classes, a few voice-lessons, things he would never take, so that she would have arts outside his, to amuse and surprise him. She was as late home every night as Lance himself, but she spent the hours after work reading in the library. She picked up all kinds of strange learning, wrote to him about Maimonides, Spinoza, tapestry, the real nature of love. She said:

Where we have passions that are uncontrollable as in sex, a difficult social web is consciously spun out of them, with the help of oppressor and oppressed, so that practically no joy may be obtained from them, and I believe that it is intended in society that we should have little joy. Religion, morality, consist of the word No! Intended, because the happy man is not willing to become unhappy, nor to slave for a crust of bread and go dirty, aching. Let a man come along full of the joy of life, bounding, hilarious, hurrahing, and after carefully inspecting him who will not get slapped, they fawn upon him, and take him in, kick him upstairs, give him a few slaves to look after. Then he thinks: "Why don't they laugh like me?" The laughter of Triumph runs through all the stages of life. He begins to despise, he is irritated, he has become infected with unhappiness; then he is got down. For the poor, those who learn to cry young, they are careful to teach impure, unhappy, harsh laughter, amusements that bring only sorrow—like the lovers in the bay. By "they", I don't know who I mean. But I am trying to get by them—whoever they are.

Her twentieth birthday had come just after Jonathan sailed, in August. When the same day in the next August approached, her twenty-first birthday, she noticed the fret of excitement in Kitty and in her Aunt Bea who visited her and ran whispering through the kitchen, and made signals in corners, and she knew they were preparing a surprise party for her. She was disgusted by it—what could they give her—money? She wanted money most of all. The rest of the things, love, an engagement, jollity, girlishness, she had nothing of, she had nothing to give them. The day of the party she was at home although it was a weekday. She coughed and sniffled and pretended not to see the preparations and hear the oven door banging. She sat up in her room, as of old, and saw there the tedium and sickness of life, but as the smells from the kitchen floated up, she stirred herself. At least, they would bring something good to eat, and the extra good would be almost as good as money towards her trip.

They were shocked to see her. Many of them had not seen her since Malfi's wedding; she looked many years older, terribly thin, and distracted, almost as if she did not know they were there. She was pleasant, greeting each one and thanking them but with the distant air of a very sick person; since her secret attachment had been whispered to everyone, they could only think that she had had some bad news and had been disappointed.

Everyone brought some packet of food and some brought presents for her also, although not all were rich enough to bring them both. At about six-thirty they sat down, with cakes, cold roast beef, and tongue sandwiches, tea and soft drinks, and toasted her in lemonade, and when the meal was almost finished, they threw a large door-key on the table, and sang—

> "Now she has the key of the door,
> Never been twenty-one before."

—and after that—

"For she's a jolly good fellow,
And so say all of us."

Stupefied, unable to be moved by the touching affection of her relatives, when they cried "Speech", she dully got up and dully said a few words, at which she saw their faces fall. Then she understood at once that they hoped not only for her gratitude but also for an announcement about a "certain person", for several of them already, indiscreetly, irrepressibly, had asked about that certain person.

She sat down, they clapped feebly, and they finished up the meal. Soon, they were singing their family songs round the piano, and early, they set out for home. Once more, she thanked each one for the surprise party, but each one left with regret, like poor relatives leaving the house without anything, after the reading of a will. She should have given confidences that they could tell each other on the path, in the street, at any rate, but what confidences? That she was loyal to a man who had never made a declaration of love? They would have thought she was desperate; and then she had her sense of honour too, he had said nothing, what could she say?

She hated to let them go so, empty-handed, empty-hearted, but all familiar joys were forbidden to her. She supposed it was because she was ugly, because, like all poor, timid people, she blamed herself. When she looked in the mirror and saw this pasty face, the face of a devout monk who has felt love-pangs and denied them, she believed that she had no right to pity or indulgence or love. If she won Jonathan Crow, it would be by superior will and intelligence; but this will and intelligence she had to devote to diverting her passions, because she had evolved the curious idea that she would only win Jonathan Crow by bridling passions as far as she was able, because of Jonathan's own self-denial.

During the afternoon Anne had told her that Malfi, some six months after her marriage, had brought to light a little daughter, now three years old, born of a one-night lover whom Malfi had never called back, out of pride. She disliked both the father, the adoptive father and the child, but now she had taken the poor little girl to live with her. This scandal raised the roof, they had only heard of it eight days ago. Even Aunt Bea was running around talking about "the poor little thing beyond the pale". Anne told this to her cousin Teresa and drew back a few paces, waiting for her verdict. Teresa said: "She had more courage than we have!"

The glance Anne gave her was a horrible avowal. Why were they all such cowards, every woman that came there to the party, suffering, knowing neither joy, triumph, nor the pleasures of debauch, living the life of poor women?

Teresa said to her cousin: "Our fault if we suffer, she was right; if we all did the same, we'd have children and they couldn't ostracize us *all*!"

Anne shrank from her, backing against the pale green wall of Teresa's room.

"Don't wait to marry," hissed Teresa, looking fiercely at her cousin, her eyes gone black. "Don't wait to marry or you'll never marry." Then as she saw how ashamed her cousin was, almost bent double, she muttered: "Why conceal it, Anne? It's too horrible. Get married, marry anyone, but marry soon. Not only women—men suffer too." She threw herself stormily on the bed. Her cousin, petrified, stared at her, raising her pale lids; at last she murmured with trembling lips: "I suppose we'd better go down." She pointed downstairs with her eyes still fixed on her cousin's.

"I suppose," said Teresa angrily. "What does it mean to be twenty-one? They're kind but you know it doesn't mean anything."

Her dearest cousin raised her china-blue eyes to her and looked straight at her, for a moment, a clean glance. Anne said: "If I don't marry, I don't know what I'll do. Life isn't worth living."

Teresa hustled her out of the room. "Let's get down there, I suppose I ought to."

What she could, of their few presents, poor things, she laid away in her trunk, to serve her for a trousseau. None knew at present that she was going away.

She had, at twenty-one, still three years to go in her saving, and already she felt the resistance of the body. She walked to and from work, a distance of nearly two miles each way, the factory being beyond the Central Railway in an old settled, slum district, not far from Jonathan's home. Her only amusement was to go out of her way to St Michael's Street, to walk up that street slowly on the far side, smell the smell of the seasons there and see Jonathan's house as she went by. She had to hurry by it, for opposite it was a vacant lot and she could easily be noticed, in her same dress, month in and month out.

It already seemed to her like a misfortune that she had to pass an extra day in 1936, for the leap year fell before her sailing date. She walked to work from the Quay, walked back, and at lunch ate some sandwiches from home and drank water. She gave them now the same money at home, thirty-five shillings, so that they could not complain of her, but to any hints about her way of life, or their own poverty, she was deaf.

During the next one thousand and ninety-six days, she spent no money on herself, either to go to a movie or to buy a stick of chocolate or to buy a newspaper. She would not visit Malfi's father, dying in a suburban hospital, because, in her calculations, she could not afford the fare. At Christmas time they had a tree, and she spent weeks at home making presents for them all, including Aunt Bea and Anne. She had learned to embroider, carpenter, and paint so that she spent almost nothing on these gifts. In the first two years, she made her trips to and from the office quite easily, observing, as a discipline, everything that went on around her, types, languages—Yiddish and Italian—the weather, the architecture and what interested people in the street, dutifully attending Eight-Hour Day processions and the like.

After that, with semi-starvation and weakness, she lost interest in these outside things. She no longer heard the men calling to her, or whistling at night. She divided the walking into stages, which became more and more numerous. To reach the Law School, up Phillip Street, where Jonathan had spent a year, was one stage; then the Law Courts, where he could never plead because he had no property, was the second, and the old Girls' High School was a third; then came the long stretch by Hyde Park; then the moment when she smelled Tooth's brewery, Mark Foy's on the right hand, a bazaar on its own piazza, and the long easy trip downhill during which she almost slept, the picture-framer's with "The Stag at Eve" and barber's sunsets, blood and lather; another park, the station, a short street in Surry Hills, full of slum houses whose domestic tragedies boiled over on the pavement before eight in the morning and at any time of the night; a park again with obscene pictures on the stone gates, a war museum, and across country in the park, past foreigners out of work reading their strange papers, fat sparrows, and the thoughts of Napoleon and Goethe and others of great voluntary output, and another street with houses, the Old Lutheran Chapel, the railway bridge. On she went, counting off her stages, relieved to pass each one. The factory, when she came to it, seemed heaven. She was happy to reach it and sorry to leave it for, leaving it, the same immense journey stretched before her, unvarying, for this was the shortest way, as she had calculated it, to the Quay. She scarcely varied from her carefully designed route in three years. She was careful to say nothing of her régime to Jonathan, being ashamed to complain when it was all for him. She knew too that nothing could change his heart; he had suffered too much as a child and youth.

23. A Photograph from the Tyrol

WHEN she had less than a year to go, she became very weak. Kitty now gave her meat for breakfast in the morning; but she would have to sit down before she walked out the gate, and if there was no seat free, she sat down on the top step at the wharf, not caring what they thought. She became indifferent to everyone. She began to break away from the route of shortest way laid down for the past two years, and carefully counted the route of fewest steps taking her from boat to factory. At several stages in the journey, there were alternative routes, possible cuts around hills and across parks, interesting quiet alleys through which she had been to count the steps, for comparison, in the past year. She was beginning to notice the noise in the streets, which increased her fatigue; the smell of brewing was getting stronger and sickened her. She avoided food shops and lemonade stands. She had found the kind of step that cost her the least fatigue, a firm lope, though it might not have looked as easy as a drag and slouch. She walked straight, but not stiffly, with a bounding step and even when she was half-fainting, she never forgot to walk with this peculiar, life-saving step which cost the least energy. Looking for one stage after another, she dreamed; she saw fewer people on the crowded streets, but she bumped into no one, since the bumping and apologizing, the stepping aside and subsequent emotion, for she now felt intense emotion on every occasion, cost her energy which she could not afford. She recognized no faces and never in all these years, though she had been bred and brought up in this city, saw a person she knew on the street. She recognized noises and smells, however, things which guided her when her eyes became milky or dark as they did occasionally, and which did not distract her. She developed the acuity of a savage, in sound and in smell. A loud sound made her secretly tremble and start.

She steeled herself against all tremor but the starting at a noise and the suppression cost too much energy and if they were drilling in the streets, or if there was a brass band, it cost less energy to go round by another way. Therefore, she took the next best way, some quiet alley, in which perhaps there were ten steps more, but there was silence.

But in this year, she had to develop this science of life-saving further, for she had become so tired she could not get through the journey without sitting down. She lost a few steps each day on each of the two journeys, there and back, particularly on the home-going trip, in order to rest on certain seats. Fortunately, she passed two parks and through another. Without any outward faltering, therefore, she was able to sit down three or four times between her goals. She sometimes lost labour so much as to climb the ramp into the Central Railway station and sit there for a while on the seats intended for travellers. Each time, she took the nearest seat and at the same time she knew how to sit down with a casual air as if she were waiting for some passenger. This seat was right near the ticket-window where she had bought the ticket to Narara. She would look at the window dimly, begin to fix it and sometimes think of it. Then she would rejoice austerely, thinking, I did the right thing—that led me to this, and her present condition seemed to her a triumph in life, because she had really a man who wrote to her every week. She had only one dress at the time, which she washed and ironed every two days and darned in places, especially under the arms above the waist where her arms, swinging as she walked, rubbed holes. In sitting, she had to arrange the dress so that the mending did not show, and when the darns doubled, she took an old newspaper from home, always the same newspaper, which she carried under her arm.

A very young salesman in the factory, named Erskine, the delicate, yellow-skinned, sickly man with blue eyes who had induced her to throw away her green hat, came into her office in the mornings, calling her "La Traviata". On Fridays, he brought her large bouquets of flowers from a garden on the North Shore. He grasped her arms, in the early morning hours when the factory was just starting up and said: "What soft, soft flesh!" She now had the soft white flesh of children bred in the dark. Her pale gold hair was twisted in a knob on her neck and two winter's back she had begun to cough, a mere irritation as she insisted, due to nervousness; who could cough in that country of the sun? Erskine, who had once had a fine alto, had a voice, curiously floating from floor to floor which could, in its softest tones, be heard everywhere. He made a very good salesman; he was brisk, cajoling, friendly and disillusioned. Best of all, old Remark had taken to him, as he had taken to young men before, and had tried to set them on the road to success. Remark was a self-made man with a liking for struggling youth. One lunch time, there was a knock on the door of the girl's office and she found Erskine outside, with a glass of grape juice for her. It happened that she had spread out on the desk in front of her a photograph of Jonathan Crow sent from the Tyrol where he had gone with Bentham, the artist, for a holiday. He wore a hard black felt hat, a black scarf and a black jacket and looked diabolically handsome. This photograph surprised Teresa with its dashing, mature, operatic beauty.

Erskine snatched the photograph off the desk. "Who is that?"

"My friend—in Europe."

"I don't like him!"

She laughed. "You don't know him."

But Erskine persisted; he was worthless, treacherous, unreliable, no good, the face was no good.

Teresa smiled; *he* was no good, Jonathan? She thought, how little men know each other! They are wild animals towards each other. She said: "But I know him, he is very good—Cyprian!"

The pale, sparkling man looked at her with lowered lids, with a half-smile. She had discovered that his third name—he had three baptismal names—was Cyprian, given by a romantic mother, and that was what she called him.

He murmured, smiling: "Cyprian! If my father heard you call me that! He has always despised me."

"But I don't despise you! And I love Cyprian!"

He turned to the mirror hanging on the wooden pillar of the factory. "God, what a face I have," he said. "Don't I look as if I had jaundice? What a complexion."

"No, no, you always look sweet—to me, I mean." He turned away quickly and went out with his native dancing step. He was born, probably, for the ballet, but he came from a respectable circle and would have thought a male dancer ridiculous or wicked.

When he left, she drew out the photograph of Jonathan and looked at it with a smile; he was actually very handsome, he aroused the jealousy of every other man. She did not see the assiduous Erskine for three days; but on the fourth day he came suddenly into her room at a quarter past eight in the morning, before old Remark had arrived, sat on an upturned waste-paper basket and suddenly observed: "I love you madly, Terry."

"You must be mad."

"I do, I say I do."

She looked at him angrily. What a thing to joke about! She got up to open the file-drawers. He jumped up, came over to her, and grasping both arms, began to shake her. "Oh, what wonderful flesh you have!"

"Cyprian! Good heavens! Don't be ridiculous."

"I'm not ridiculous," he continued, holding her tighter than before, and beginning to slide his arm up to her shoulders. "I dream about you."

"Fine dreams," she said. "I don't dream about you."

"Who do you dream about, that fellow in the black hat?"

"Do you think I'd dream about a man?"

"Terry, Terry," he said, shaking her fiercely.

"Good heavens, there's Remark," she cried desperately, believing that he was holding her up to shame, making her a laughing-stock.

"I don't care," said Erskine.

Two girls were going past, late, and saw them; they turned into the passage, grinning and talking.

"You're making me ridiculous."

The terrible voice of Remark burst forth: "Erskine!"

"You see, he heard you."

"Everyone hears me," said Erskine, imperturbably. He went off, turning back at the door to wave his hand. "I want them to."

He began to plague her, always visiting her in the morning, and remarking on her appearance and figure, and putting his hands on her whenever they met, though naturally, in the factory no place was safe from observation. The girls and floor-managers began to grin when they saw her, though in a good-natured way, for Erskine was well liked. She thought he was putting her to shame. She had so whole-heartedly accepted Jonathan's cool treatment, and thought it just, that she did not believe any man could love her. Erskine held long conversations with her on the office telephone and Remark, who liked them both, increased her pay at the next Christmas lay-off (he laid off the factory employees for a week). Erskine often came late into her office now, when Remark was next door, and after a long time Remark would call Erskine, with a gentle, patronizing inflection. She saw nothing in all this, absorbed by the letters she had to write to charm Jonathan, and as before, walking down to the Quay, she would stop at the library, to read some book Jonathan had mentioned, and would then proceed home to get her dinner off the saucepan where, by Kitty's care, it had been steaming since six-thirty.

But it became hard for her to cross wide open areas like the parks. One day, walking home, she thought illogically, angrily: "If Cyprian really loved me as he says, he would walk down with me, as Jonathan did, he wouldn't let me go here alone." One day, walking home, she saw that the streets were quite empty, although it was only five-thirty, and were of a gem-like blue. There was a silence with only a distant murmur, at times, and as she reached a hoarding then at the end of Elizabeth Street, though it was the rush hour, the time for home-going, it seemed as if only a few vehicles spun past her noiselessly into the street. She felt an access of energy. She bounded along, her legs moved with their long practice, their exquisite ease. It was a pleasure to walk, it was almost like flying. Things had a strange, friendly aspect, they were outlined with light, they had no human look and yet one would say they nodded. Evening closed in suddenly around the lamp-posts and the posts supporting awnings. She could not see! In fright, her legs trembled, her face seemed to float away, and she began to sleep. She felt a blow on the forehead. She opened her eyes and saw that she had walked into a telegraph pole that had not been there before. She dropped down without meaning to. Around her, at a distance, she now saw a few people. Fortunately, people are too modest to get mixed up with someone very thin and threadbare who drops down in the street, and she was left alone. Two typists coming home from work laughed. A very tall, big man in blue worker's shirt lunged past. A respectable man with a brief-case looked severely at her and walked on rapidly, his head lowered. At this moment, a young man came and helped her to her feet, saying: "You ought to look out. Are you hurt?"

Since she had lost the power of speech, she looked vaguely at him and shook her head. After a minute, she managed to say, gutturally: "No, I'm all right."

The young man, who looked ashamed of himself, and had a white shirt, open at the neck, took her to the shop wall and left her leaning there; he walked backwards for a few steps, and said:

"Now look out, look out, next time."

Teresa said: "Yes, yes."

"I was thinking too much about Jonathan," she said to herself. "It's stupid, I really must stop it, there are other things in the world," and she wondered once more whether there was not in existence some drug, perhaps fabulously expensive, which a person could take to forget his past and some too harassing resolution. But out of habit she went on, and went on in the succeeding days, because she was not strong enough to form any new great purpose and she felt too downtrodden, and ridiculous in ordinary eyes, to have any small aim now.

She had no real shame, having a distant goal, and she did not even look in the faces of the people on the ferry, the quay, the platform or the streets. If they looked at her and laughed, as she sometimes thought, it heartened her, it seemed a proof that she was very strange indeed—and to strange persons, strange visions, strange destinies. In a few months, she would leave them for ever, this herd trampling shoulder to shoulder in its home march. They married, settled down in the Bay or in the suburbs along bus routes to the city, in order to reach their work in the shortest time, and that was the end, then came the marriage-sleep that lasted to the grave. She would sail the seas, leave her invisible track on countries, learn in great universities, know what was said by foreign tongues, starve in cities, tramp, perhaps shoeless, along side roads, perhaps suffer every misery, but she would know life. She did not once try to imagine what Jonathan's greeting would be, nor what would happen between them. She knew by now that she was wretched-looking but said to herself: "Just the same I need Jonathan as an aim so as not to fail, even if he rejects me." Any thought of affection from Jonathan she repressed, not really hoping for any, merely hoping that he would see her; she did not want a reward for what she was doing, God forbid, or even thinking of it, to force Jonathan in some mental way. Any show of affection from him would be too great a payment; her sufferings would wither away, be nothing, just as life withers away when death is reached and there is no connection between things so different. "Say not the struggle naught availeth," she said to herself as she marched along and the curtain of strange blue light began to drop round her, as before. "The struggle is the joy, that is the only sure joy." About six months before she sailed, in September 1935, she booked her passage, made a down payment, then felt puny, and it was as if this part-accomplishment weakened her.

A new idea occurred to her. If she could get a room opposite the factory, she would save shoe-leather, boat-fares, and energy. She would have to pay rent and get her own food, however, and she certainly did better eating out of the family pot than she would by herself. The factory was in a short street, a mere by-pass behind the meeting of two thoroughfares. Two factories occupied one side, and a row of slum houses ran along the other, houses built stupidly, out of the greed of early landlords, with twenty-five-foot frontages and no garden space. The doors opened on the street. Brawling and drunkenness went on in them; aged, debauched women, filthy, full of liquor, staggered in and out and roomers there would occasionally be thrown out in the street, first their goods, with small vases and basins crashing and cheap silverware clinking and clattering in a delightful smash, then bits of tawdry, or a spare pair of pants, some cracked satin slippers, a hat, and last the personage itself, shouting, quarrelling, but finally bundled out. And there on the pavement the poor thing would stand, swearing and crying, almost sexless, merely degraded, picking up its poor possessions, while the other miserable creature, like a wild animal, fierce, black-eyed, would peer and shout at it through the corner of some lifted dirty curtain.

Teresa had long ago, but slowly, formed the idea that rooms must be very cheap indeed in this district and if she could get a room, perhaps not right opposite the factory, but in the very next street, where she could not be seen entering and leaving, it might be a saving to her. One Saturday, she had a sandwich in a small shop near and then returned surreptitiously about two hours after the factory closed and everyone was gone away, to the same street; and she walked up the street and down the next, cautiously surveying the windows, looking for a window with clean curtains and the notice, "Rooms to let". She knew she might be taken for a street-walker, and was afraid of going up to the doors and asking, and yet she said to herself that honest girls lived here also, the poor living side by side with crime, and she reproached herself for this false shame. Spurred by this thought, she went up and knocked at a door in the middle of the row. A blonde woman opened to her, when Teresa said, thoughtlessly, gazing at her: "Will you give me some bread and meat?"

At the flash in the woman's face, she realized what she had said and slowly turned red. She stuttered that she was stupid, that she was thinking of something else, and asked the woman how much was the rent of the room she had to let. The woman closing the door slightly, said: "I can't let it to you."

Flushing deeper, Teresa stumbled away and walked quickly up the street, feeling the woman's eyes on her, the slight breeze cooling her skin. What a strange thing! It was true that sometimes, when walking down the streets and feeling very tired after work, she had dreamed about going up the steps of some house and asking for "some bread and meat" which was what tramps always asked for and she had thought about the thick slices of fresh bread and cold roast meat which were usually given to them. She began to laugh to herself. Who would believe that she had gone up to someone's door and begged? It was comic. Everything she did was so strange and comic that no one would believe it. She had managed to get out of the goal, she had found out how original real life is.

She walked on doggedly till she turned into another street and began asking at one house after another, assailing their front doors, asking after rooms, like a stray cat running from one entry to another. The fifth room was a front room with a double bed in brass and iron, a clean cotton coverlet, and three autumn scenes on the walls. It was dark, bare, small, unlike anything she had ever seen before and she was afraid of it, but she said she would take it, and paid the woman five shillings deposit. She would move in on the next Monday, she said, with her clothes. This was only one street away from the factory, one of those long, cheerless, asphalted streets of semi-detached houses all exactly alike, with closed-in, railed balconies on the second floor and dust in the small front "garden". She came away with relief, already hating the yellow walls, and when she heard the door shut behind her, she was afraid, but she was obliged to follow out her plan.

Sitting on the boat in the cool afternoon she thought about the Bay; it seemed delightfully remote, silent, she bitterly regretted the way she would be forced to live from now on, but the saving in time and money would be enormous. She wondered if her family would allow her to come and see them in the week-ends, or if they would be too angry with her? She came rolling in to the house with her usual proud, silent, and bounding air, which it cost her much energy to keep up, especially at the end of the week. She went up to her room and sank on her bed, her mind darting round the room she had just left, the dark rented room which was now hers. She thought of things at the factory, of what clothes she would need for her travelling trousseau and she got up to write down on a piece of paper the number of days she still had to save money before she sailed. She calculated that on the ship she would have six weeks to rest in, and that a sea-cure is recommended to all frail people; and she thought that by the time she reached London she would be quite fit and able to look for a job the first day. Presently she felt well enough to go downstairs to eat her lunch, which was steaming on top of a saucepan as usual.

The house was silent, the doors and windows all stood open, but everyone was out. She thought: "Next week, I shall not have this", but then: "I'm leaving it soon for ever, what does this matter?" She did nothing the whole afternoon, but lay on the grass in front, thinking that sooner or later she would rise some-how, get on her feet; once she was on her feet, she felt all right and could get about the house and street without anyone noticing that she could hardly walk. No one had guessed, no one dared to ask her questions and if asked, she would not have answered. As she lay she began composing her next letter to Jonathan, phrases fitted themselves together vividly, soon she had whole paragraphs, and before half an hour was out, she got up and went upstairs to begin to write it down; she passed an hour in a delicious dream of communication. The others, Lance, Kitty, her father, behaved silently and oddly as they had begun to lately, they were more like people passing at a distance. To avoid them, she took her meals out by herself under a tree, hidden from the road, and though her father sent messages to her to come in, as always, she did not answer, except to ask to be left alone. The two men had little sympathy for her because of all the money she had in the bank; she sometimes thought, vaguely, that Kitty had been crying on her account.

This evening, after the meal, at six-thirty, Lance went off to go to the movies, and the father went off also by himself, to the movies. Teresa asked her sister sulkily if she was not going as well, for she hoped to be left alone, to wander idly over the house, touching things, looking out of windows; and tonight, especially, she had to pick out a few things to take to the room with her. But Kitty was not going out, and had a disagreeable air as if about to reproach her. When the dishes were washed, Kitty went up to her room and closed the door. Teresa sat on the back step and began to smile as she recalled Erskine's words of that day. Erskine was her solace. She had formed the habit of going to Kitty's room when anything amusing had happened, and babbling about Erskine's tricks and charm.

She went upstairs to knock at Kitty's door and heard her rustling papers inside. "Who is it?"

"Terry."

"Come in."

She was astonished to see Kitty with an open valise on her bed and some clothes already packed in it.

"Where are you going?"

"I've got a job."

Teresa was delighted, she clasped her hands and her face shone with happiness. "Where is it?"

"In Petersham."

"In Petersham? What sort of a job?"

"Housekeeper, it's a widower with a child."

"Oh!" Teresa looked at her quickly and saw Kitty's face colour. Kitty said quickly: "It's all right, it's someone we know, Mr Bayliss, in Sylvia's factory."

"He isn't a widower."

"Yes, yes, his wife died."

"Ah! Well, good luck then."

Kitty became tremulous, "Yes, I think I'll have good luck," and suddenly her shadowed little girl's face became that of a woman.

She smiled, she said huskily and guiltily but with a smile: "I'm in love."

269

"I know. Do you think he'll marry you?"

"I don't know. But I don't care."

Teresa opened her eyes and looked at her sister. "What sort of a child?"

"A little boy aged eight."

"That's not bad."

"Oh, I can manage any children," said Kitty. She rolled up a pair of stockings. "I explained to him that I couldn't buy a uniform yet, but I would as soon as I got paid and he understands all that. He said he knew you were getting good wages from old Remark and Dad could afford to pay someone to cook. Or Aunt Bea might."

"Ah!"

"Don't you like that?"

"Of course, go and take your job. You should have done it years ago."

"I know, but anyhow I'm doing it now."

Teresa turned on her heel and went into her room. Kitty looked after her piteously, she was angry. But, thought Kitty, why is she so selfish? She has money and has a boy, why shouldn't I? A few tears wet Kitty's sensitive eyes, but she went on packing.

Teresa, sitting in her room, looked across the landing at the little domestic picture of Kitty in her bedroom. Was there a crack from ceiling to floor, zig-zag across the whole building? The house was falling. "Well, too bad," she muttered to herself. "I can't take the room and I've lost the five shillings." She called out: "When are you going?"

"Shh!"

"Why?"

"I'm just going to leave a note; Dad wouldn't let me go. He says I must look after the house till I have a home of my own. But I can't meet men here. I'll never have a home of my own at this rate."

"Are you going to try to marry Bayliss?"

Kitty stopped rolling some clumsy garment and sat down, looking at her sister across the landing. Her attitude said yes, eloquently, but she did not dare to say it.

"He's quite old."

"I don't know any young men," said Kitty. She bent her face

to her work. "I had no dresses, I had nothing." She began to cry.

"Don't cry now, it's too late to cry now," said Teresa, irritably, and the tears stopped.

"So I won't see you," said Teresa, after some thought.

Kitty laughed. "You see Cyprian every day."

"I don't see him." After a moment she called: "Kitty, come here a minute."

Kitty came over with a lace collar in her hand. Teresa stopped and opened the bottom drawer of her chest of drawers. She pulled out a petticoat, saying, with a flushed look, to her sister: "Here, this is for you, you need things."

Kitty smiled. "It's from your glory-box."

"You know? But it's not a glory-box."

"Yes, I looked. I shouldn't have."

"Well, take it."

"No, you want it. If it's not a glory-box, what is it? You're secretly engaged, aren't you?"

"No," said Teresa, "but I'm going to England."

Kitty was surprised but not staggered. "When?" she whispered.

"In six months or less, one hundred and eighty-one days, to be exact."

"To him?"

Teresa nodded.

"Does he know?"

She nodded.

For the first time in their lives, Kitty bent and kissed Teresa, whispering: "Oh, good, I'm glad! I thought so."

Teresa recoiled proudly. Kitty, however, was used to Teresa's cold ways and asked: "But what about Mr Erskine?"

"What about him?"

"Everyone says he's after you. He rang up here. Dad said not to tell you."

"He's nothing to me."

"It's a pity." Kitty considered her.

"I don't want him," said her sister fiercely. "If I stay here, I'll never get anywhere."

"Well, you know best."

She took away the little lace-edged petticoat, saying her thanks and apologies for taking it and came back with something of her own, a fichu she would never wear, because it made her look like a grandmother. Then she went off again, bubbling, youthful.

"When?" called Teresa.

"On Monday morning. I'll just stay to make the Sunday dinner and clean up the house."

"I hope I don't have to do it all after you go."

Kitty came back with round eyes: "You won't do it?"

"I can't do it all. I'm not strong enough now."

"We'll have to club together to get someone, when I get paid."

"No, I won't, together with you or anyone else. I pay enough," she scolded. She turned red.

Kitty looked helpless, but murmured: "I won't give up this chance."

"I don't want you to."

"But about the house?"

"I don't know. I'll do what I can, but not too much."

"Let the men do it." Kitty uttered this revolutionary idea sharply.

"They wouldn't."

"Then let them live in the dirt," said Kitty. These two remarks made in quite a different voice, must have been the result of months of thinking things out and made Kitty sound quite sharp and hard. Teresa looked at the new woman with new eyes.

24. "So Haggard and So Woebegone"

On the Monday morning, a sharp, rainy morning, Kitty was up early, set the breakfast table, made the breakfast and then, snatching a cup of tea, ran upstairs, changed and was down with her valise while they were at the table. They heard her run downstairs and the front screen door bang.

"What's Kitty doing?" asked the father.

No one answered.

The front gate banged.

"She went to the shop," growled Lance. "She's never got anything in the house, we live from hand to mouth."

"I've got to run," said Teresa.

"You look a wreck," said Lance kindly. "You're ready to fall apart. You look like a skeleton."

"I have a skeleton underneath," Teresa told him.

"Your bones are sticking out," said Lance.

"Well, Terry never was Joan Crawford," the father said with a spiteful laugh. He was always angry with his daughter now, partly because she would not dress and look better when she had so much money. He would have liked to have had two pretty daughters and to point them out to his mates in the Bay.

"Terry's going mad," said the brother, rising and staring at her. "The way she's going on, she must be going mad."

"Women go mad if they don't get married," said the father. "It isn't their fault. If Terry would get herself up a bit, make herself more attractive, she'd probably get a nibble, but she can't expect men to go after a bag of bones. Now Terry was quite beefy when she was sixteen, she was quite an eyeful."

Teresa looked at them coldly as she got up, wiping her mouth. "What you don't know about me would fill a library," she told her father. He laughed.

"I've got to run," said Teresa. "Look, here's a letter for you", and she put in her father's place the letter that Kitty had given her to hand to him. She ran for the boat, though she heard a long frantic whistle behind her. She looked over her shoulder as she ran. Lance was not coming, he would miss the boat. That was one blessing. She joined her sister. Kitty, with her valise, sat on the engineer's seat, looking round. Flushes of happiness came over her, anyone could see it. She was like a runaway bride.

"I'll see you in town sometimes," said Teresa, "when you can get away. Let me know your days off. I'll take you to tea, I get more than you."

"Oh, I'll be able to take you to tea." Kitty laughed, and looked slyly at her. She gleamed, shivered alternately, as she thought of Bayliss or of her father.

"Bayliss will be at work when you get there."

"I know, but I have the key. I'll just straighten up and he's coming home for dinner tonight. He wants Irish stew, he's very fond of it, so I'm making it for the first night," said Kitty, looking eagerly in front of her.

Teresa had a sharp pang of jealousy. By tomorrow, she would be washing, sweeping, ironing, cooking for the man she loved, and he had given her a home. For a burning moment, she wondered if she, too, ought not to become a housekeeper. There were plenty of advertisements in the papers, where middle-aged men, doctors, lawyers, all kinds of respectable, gentlemanly men, widowers, bachelors, asked for housekeepers. It seemed such a quiet, decent job; at the same time a woman was doing for a man, she was not alone in her life. A man came home, she had something to live for. If she starched things properly, polished the tables and oilcloths, brasses, silver, blued the sheets nicely, looked after his clothes, he praised her, talked about her to his friends. "I have a wonderful housekeeper, Miss Teresa Hawkins." It was a kind, decent life, and one had a man at once, without the struggle, just by going to an agency. In the end he might marry her and they would go together into the dark, high, over-polished, starch-smelling bedroom, cold man and wife; not love but honourable marriage. Clever Kitty, to have thought out all this, thought Teresa, looking at her; and I am so clever—I never saw this solution! Clever Teresa! Yes, I am very clever. I am killing myself for a man who might possibly, if it suits him, if he is still there, if he is not too much put off by me, kiss me.

But her destiny was cast in bronze. By the time she reached the Quay, she knew she could not go and wash dishes hopelessly for some man, waiting for the day when he asked her to marry him. Better the rough and rolling sea than this convent with one nun. She no longer understood how she could have been tempted. On the way to work she went and told the woman that she could not take the room.

"I'll have to keep the five shillings deposit."

"I know," said Teresa. "That's all right. I'm sorry I let you down." The woman smiled involuntarily. "I'll give you back two shillings," she said. "You probably need it as much as I do," and she fetched her shabby black purse from a lace-covered table in the hall and handed Teresa two worn shillings. The small round coins felt grateful in Teresa's hand; she would bank two shillings more at the end of the week. She smiled at the woman, thanked her profusely.

To be hungry was her life and a necessary condition of getting to Jonathan; therefore she did not mind it at all, and it made life more interesting than it had been for years. She began to love the streets through which she passed and which were her life, she began to notice avidly shops, stands, and men and women lifting things up to their mouths. This evening, coming home, she thought only satirically of the scene that awaited her; perhaps they had already fetched Kitty home, in any case. But had Kitty been fool enough to tell where she was going? She felt a hot flash as it occurred to her that Kitty, wildly, might have told that she, too, was going—to England, the irrevocable journey. Surely not? Surely not? It worried her through the trip and spoiled her game.

She did not really care about her beggared dress, since everyone at work was kind to her. Erskine protected her and even "the Old Man", Remark, put up with her peculiarities and had a sympathy for her, remembering his poverty. She took two or three days off every few weeks, when she was not really ill but pretended to be, in order to rest. These days of sick leave she spent at home in the back yard, lying on two chairs with her hair covered against the sun and wind, her body exposed to the warm light. For economy's sake, they never lighted fires in the old house, and lately they had substituted beans and spaghetti for meat meals, margarine for butter and the like. For four winters, whatever the cold, she had worn summer dresses and no coat, and she often arrived home wet through, but pretended that she felt nothing and could never take cold. She had a deep cough which shook her whole frame and did not leave her even in summer. If she had not taken off one or two days of sick leave occasionally, she would not have got through. This trick of hers was allowed at the factory and she was grateful to them for allowing such a patent fraud. For a long time, she had not noticed the cold weather nor her cough, which, she said, was not really a cough, but a perpetual hunger which had slipped out of consciousness for several years, lately coming back, so that cheap sweets, dirty jars of pineapple and coconut juice, fruits in windows, crawling with cockroaches, and even sticky, bright cakes attracted her fearfully. Several times, on her way to the boat, she came to herself, to find that she had ceased to walk and was lounging dreamily against some window looking vacantly at one of these objects. While she looked and dreamed, she ceased to feel the hunger; it was as if she was masticating. Then she would smile at herself, hitch herself away from the window-pane, start walking with a rush, and a few blocks lower down the permanent hunger would begin blowing through her like a draught. Once or twice, lately, she had stopped and bought a sweet drink, unable to resist a wave of pleasure and gluttony which overwhelmed her as she drank; afterwards too, she experienced no shame, but would rub her hands secretly, and would walk close to other such places, to enjoy the warm rich smell. She never went to shops where people sat down, she felt more inconspicuous standing at a street bar. Later, the sight of her purse a few pence poorer shamed her as if she had embezzled. But two or three days later, she would fall again, and with the same low pleasure would buy another sweet drink. Recently, she had begun to reason with herself, saying: "If I fall again and again like this, I must need the food, it would be more sensible to live near the factory and buy myself a lemonade every two or three days." Her father would say she could not now take a room near the factory, when Kitty was away. What else could she do? If she could find one of the factory girls to live with, somewhere near. But she knew none of the factory girls. She knew only the office staff, and as most of the factory girls were very young, lively girls, she was afraid of them. Sometimes, in a white glare of anger, she would wish for Erskine. He pretended to like her, men succoured women, but he would not even give her twopence to go down to the Quay in a tram. (He did not know she walked to the Quay.) He would not even give her a lunch. He would not even share a room with her.

This same evening, as she crossed the park in the heat of the setting sun which she was facing, she looked round to see if there was not somewhere to sit in the middle, some hummock, a stone, but there was nothing. The heat, confusion, irritation poured into her. She thought: "Much he cares for me, to let me stagger home like this, to others he pretends he likes me, but I don't know about it, I don't feel it, he's a mere doll." At the same time, she was absurdly carrying a bouquet of fresh garden flowers, immense, colourful, an old English garden, in her arm, which Erskine had brought her that day. She put the bouquet down on the grass and sat beside it. How heavy it was! She only got the bouquet to make it harder for her, to make her more grotesque, staggering home with it. It was only her illness that made her wish for him. She was nearing the end, but there were moments now when she was afraid that illness would get to her before the end. She was not now walking only to save money. She was outstripping illness and failure. Wherever she walked, something of bluish-white with long stride came after her a pace away, bowed forward, not malignant, only natural, but that bluish-white thing of her own height was Exhaustion itself. Why did not Erskine, if he loved her, give her a glass of milk before she left work, so that she could walk down to the Quay? These mad complaints battering round her temples, the staggering landscape, her fear of falling, accompanied her with her lunch box, her purse, and her bouquet, while she walked in her rubber-soled shoes, crossed over the parks. Once this week, she had been forced to take the tram from the station. It was like the lemonade. What a mad excessive delirious luxury to sit in the tram and let it carry her along the roads! She had not a movement to make. She merely sat there, smiling to herself, looking with rapture at the people who rode in the tram. If they looked well and happy, she understood how they felt! If they looked sad and peaked, she wanted to nudge them and say: "Rejoice, you are riding! Ride, ride, people can't ride every day! I myself know someone for example—but never mind that, just enjoy yourselves!" In no time at all she was at the Quay.

The tram ride only cost twopence, so that it might seem folly to wear oneself out in this way, but she was afraid to give in on any count and in some way the endless walking, walking, meant England. She was walking her way to England. In three years to the day, less Sunday and Christmas Day and one or two other holidays, she would have walked 2,772 miles and by the time she sailed she would have walked just 3,000 miles. But on the other hand these three thousand miles represented seventeen pounds, three shillings, and fourpence and perhaps a bit more, saved to take abroad. Now as she would not have more than a few weeks' money, about twenty pounds, when she landed in England, and the Australian pound was going down in relation to the English pound—and she considered twenty pounds a very generous margin—she considered the wear and tear of the body and beauty as nothing. With beauty and health she could not get one wave nearer England, but even though her bones poked through and she was carried aboard, she was welcome, if she paid her fare; she could sail the seas like any free soul, from Ulysses to the latest skipper of a sixteen-footer rounding the world. She thought of death, indeed, but only as an obstacle that might prevent her sailing and must be circumvented.

She looked at the ground as she walked and considered things, cast-off shoes that might have served her, a crust of bread; often a piece of green paper fluttered like a banknote. She was astonished at the Salvation Army singing in the street with so many people starving—how could they expect converts? She was surprised that people were so honest—Mark Foy's had their bazaar open day and evening, people could steal some of these gewgaws; for people were beginning to seem to her strange things, creatures like parrots, that liked sweetmeats and baubles. For herself she kept away from all these, they were the barbarian tastes of head-less, heartless monkeys. She never looked at the pretty things that go into trousseaux, though the time had now come for her to buy her travelling wardrobe. She bought yards of rough Chinese silk, cotton, lace and cut out underwear for a cold climate, nothing for a marriage, but solid, plain things that would last for years if she was unlucky and he rejected her. All this she began to make up on a sewing-machine. In turn, this sewing-machine became for her the dream of her life. At the office, she would see it, standing towards the back street, the sunlight falling across it through the old lace curtains, its cracked veneer, and the virgin cloth with straight selvedge lying across it. When she got home, carrying her hat and bag in her hand, she would go and stand by it, smoothing down whatever had been left upon it. Now she always had work on it. This picture began to draw her homewards, she dreamed about the skilful gathering and running of the stuff as she marched along. How beautiful if she had piles of exquisite things in silk and lace, fine things, not strong and sensible as she had now! How would she cut the silk, put in the lace? She devised as she walked along. If she had linen and linen thread sufficient, she would make such and such a tablecloth or bedspread; couldn't one learn to imitate Brussels, Irish rose lace, merely by looking? She felt sure she could. She would take with her a blanket that really belonged to her, a lace mantelpiece runner. She would make six lawn handkerchiefs with drawn thread work and Johnny's initial, on the boat. She would embroider something for him—what?—in which their history would be pathetically referred to—she would show him on a cloth, as a priest of learning in a chasuble, green, gold, and white. He could use the cloth later on for his household when he had one and she might be dead. What matter if she got nothing out of it? To love is to give for ever, without stint, and not to ask for the slightest thing. Such is woman's love. There are women who do not do that, but when they become mothers, it is the same thing, they give lovingly and in suffering and without requital.

All the time, she looked about. There were plenty of places where she could curl up unseen at night, once dusk had fallen. She could be stirring early in the morning. Not the Domain, because the walk was too long from the Domain to her factory.

Her breed could stand any hardship. Her own grandmother, Eileen, had come out on a sailing-ship with only one pair of boots to her name, and had picked up a husband in a hut with an earthen floor on the goldfields, the whole thing done on her savings as a servant, in the old days. No teachers' salaries and highly paid stenographers then!

Between buildings in this hot weather were places cool and protected where no one went, surely, where a person could sleep all night. A coat, blanket or something else would be necessary.

What about washing? She could get to the factory early **and** wash, or go to the Central Railway Station. How did vagrant women wash? In pools and streams. But here? In the factory then. At the station, money was needed to wash. The factory was her home. It failed her in nothing. Money, washrooms, even affection, she was liked there and everyone knew there what no one knew at home, that she was sailing soon. Such was the good-nature and solidarity of the factory.

The factory backed on a paper factory which had been burned out not long ago. Beside the burned-out factory was a junk and lumber yard, and between the two a small grassy area shut in by a loose arrangement of palings. No one ever went in there. It was no man's land. She had often seen it from upstairs in the hat factory. There was also a vacant grassy space in between the two factories, but this was open to men and dogs. Her green hat had been there for several days, then one day a man had come poking at it and taken it away. Supposing one night, when she was very tired, after nightfall, she went in through that plank gate and slept there? No one at all could see her till morning. Light came early—about four-thirty or five. The night watchman would not look down—in any case, she could sleep right up against the fence nearest the factory and he could not see her. On the other hand, perhaps she could secrete herself in the factory itself, sleep on the roof or the like? But how would she get out to get her food? It was all a question of not walking the two miles back and forth, but if she was to pay extra for her food! Then, could she undress in the grass patch? She could not sleep in her only dress needed for work the next day. Besides, it might rain and she could not arrive drenched in the same dress, a thin silk. She observed all kinds of things, thought about the silk lying on the machine at home, and sharply kept a look-out for a hiding-place where she might sleep at night. How about the cathedral? The Art Gallery? The latter had a bare open hall where she would be seen. The cathedral was an excellent place, but surely they swept and looked round for tramps who wanted a roof over their heads? There was an infectious disease hospital in the Domain and a little morgue with a very pretty blind corner, covered with vines and half-filled with old gardening implements. But surely it was at night they came to remove the corpses? A funeral with plumes and lights—? Then again it was so far from the factory. She went on. She came to the boat. She sat and dreamed on the boat as it choughed over the waves and she was almost home round the beach path when she remembered that Kitty had run away this morning.

She found the two men stricken, like two old men who had lost their sister, but to their questions: "Did you know?" "Why didn't you tell us?" she returned languid replies. "She ought to get out and make a place for herself, she ought to get a chance." Lance, with hollow eyes and a suffering air on his cheeks, she saw was near to tears. She said: "It will be cheaper with only three of us instead of four." Lance asked: "Am I going to stay here all my life?" She went upstairs and found Kitty's room turned upside down—why? She stared for a moment at the familiar mess, forgotten things which Kitty had stored "to come in useful some time." Now she had left them all behind. All no use now. She was very far from picking and prying into Kitty's things; with a great disillusion about the young girl's life she surveyed everything from the door, when suddenly she saw a very long dark green shawl in wool, which Kitty had knitted at one time, ugly but heavy and nearly a yard wide. It had served Kitty instead of a coat for a long time. This would do! Teresa stepped forward, shook out the shawl and contemplated it with a beating heart. Wrapped in such a shawl against the dew she might do very well one night, if she could find a place in the factory or elsewhere to sleep.

The next day, she packed it in a small valise. The two men questioned her so much about her little valise and looked so frightened that she opened it up smiling and said the shawl was for a poor woman she had met in the street near the factory, who sold matches. Erskine, too, noticed the little bag and wanted to know if she were going away. She said: "Yes, for the night." Later, she went up to see Erskine in his room, a thing she had never done, and leaning on the window-sill while he chatted and while he approached and put his arm round her shoulders, she studied the empty spaces underneath the two factories. The one she coveted was well closed. Inside were three or four notice-boards, "No Trespassers", and "Trespassers Will Be Prosecuted", which had perhaps been thrown over from the junk yard. Or was there an entrance from the junk yard? This frightened her. She realized she would be trespassing and could be fined or sent to jail if she set foot on the little enclosed patch. Was there an entrance through the burned factory, without forcing an entrance? She slowly revolved phrases in her mind, "breaking and entering", "*vol avec effraction*"—but she would not be stealing. Meanwhile she was answering Erskine, pulling away from him. His hand had wandered up to the gathers on the shoulder of her dress, and now wandered down, he played along the gathers and his eyes shone. She looked at him mildly, unable to understand why he was so restless and bright, his eyes glittering, whispering madly at her. A girl sent by a workroom head for some samples of braids came in the open door and laughed aloud as she said: "Mr Erskine, Miss Allbright wants the Italian braids." Erskine fretfully, but with a smile, dropped his hands and said: "On my desk, on my desk." The girl picked up the cards and went out, looking back and laughing.

"You see," said Teresa thoughtfully, still puzzling about the entrance to the vacant lot, "you are making a scandal!"

"I don't care," Erskine replied. "I want to make a scandal. You take no notice of me, so I must make a scandal!"

She laughed, and looking out the window, asked: "Do you think anyone could get into that empty lot down there?"

He looked. "I don't know."

"Would it be hard to pry open those boards there?"

"No, I could do it easily," he said. "What for?"

"I thought I saw someone in there."

He turned back to her and came back to running his finger over her dress. "That's the first time I've seen you in a pretty dress."

"Yes, I made it for my trip abroad."

"Why don't you wear pretty dresses like that all the time?"

"Why?"

"For me," he said fiercely. "For me."

She laughed. "For you? No. I've got to keep them to wear to my jobs in England."

He dropped his hands and went behind his desk, coolly. "Oh, do you still insist you're going to England?"

"In just about four months." She smiled. "In three months, I'll give you notice," and she stared at him, smiling blissfully.

He looked her full in the face, angry but puzzled. "You're a strange girl."

282

She said: "You know it's funny I've never been all over the factory, I'd like to some time."

"I'll show you over."

"Won't they think it's funny?"

"You're my secretary," he cried in a rage. "Who's to say no?"

"All right. When? At lunch time today?"

"At lunch—all right, but why?"

"I just want to see it."

"All right," he said softly. "Anything you like."

She went back to her office on the ground floor.

At lunch time he took her over the whole factory; the heavy machines on the top floor, the workrooms, the trimmers' rooms, the showrooms, everywhere. Nowhere but in one department was there anywhere that she could spend the night; that was in the men's felts, a small cramped place full of corners. She asked if there was a night watchman. "Not inside," said Erskine.

"Can you get out once the place is locked?" she asked.

"I don't think so. Why?"

"So no one might be locked in by mistake."

"Oh, no, they're too anxious to get home." He laughed whimsically.

Looking at the factory opposite a horrible thought struck her. "If there was a fire in the night no one could get out!"

"Oh, I suppose they'd break a window and jump out, it's better to jump than to burn."

Her spirits fell, she lost interest in the factory. He went back with her to her office and stood with his back against the shut door watching her. Then he came round and looked in the mirror hanging on the wooden pillar. Gazing in the mirror, stroking his pale cheek, he asked:

> "Oh, what can ail thee knight-at-arms,
> So haggard and so woebegone?"

She ran the sheets into her typewriter for her letter to Jonathan. "What's the matter with you now?"

"Don't I look pale, ill and yellow?" he asked, turning round and exhibiting his face.

"You don't look very well, no."

"It's your fault."

"Don't be so stupid, you know it isn't."

"You don't care for anyone but that sly-looking man," he said spitefully, coming and tearing the paper out of her typewriter.

"Jonathan is not sly-looking."

"He's the most deceitful, malicious, dishonest-looking man I ever saw."

She laughed tenderly. "You don't know him, he is wonderful, tender, and so truthful and modest."

"I don't like his face."

She looked at Erskine distantly. He went to the window and turned to say: "And such a time to go to Europe! There'll be war."

"What do I care?"

"Yes, what do you care?" He came beside her, saying: "You're so pale and beautifully distracted, you're like a woman out of Shakespeare." She smiled at him.

"Yes, out of Schubert too, Death and the Maiden in one person, you look like death and yet you've got that silly maidenish face too." She laughed outright. "Go on, get out of here, I've got to write my letter." He went sideways, looking at her regretfully and angrily and pursing his lips. At the other side of the factory, where the corridor turned, he stopped to look back at her. She smiled. He blew a kiss and at the same time bumped into two young girls coming back from lunch. They all laughed, Erskine airily went on his way. Teresa went on typing to Jonathan. This day, Erskine seemed forced to tease her. He came back towards the end of the afternoon when the long red rays of sun were falling on the dusty floor in the men's felts, which was opposite Teresa's office. Teresa sometimes looked up to see the shadows of the manager or one of his assistants falling with a milk-and-ruby outline hotly on the floor.

Erskine's form, small against the light, fitted into the men's felts and then she saw it pale coming towards her. Her heart began to beat. A resentment stole into her against Erskine, who lately had begun to have the power, with his repeated caresses and embraces in public which were a kind of attack, to excite her. She was afraid she might lose her head and begin to like him, such liking might turn into love and she did not want to love anyone here just when she was going. If she loved him, she might stay here—for ever, anchored in the little harbour where she was born, like a rowboat whose owner had died and which had never been taken off the slips. With concealed trembling she saw him saunter into her room, nonchalant, airy. No sooner was he inside that he started his tricks. He leaned on her desk and remarked: "I just came to tell you you're mad."

"Go away."

"You're mad."

"I want to be mad."

"I'm better than that fellow over there."

"How modest!"

He suddenly fell into one of his little rages: "You don't understand anything about men; he's a rascal."

"It isn't only him. I have a great destiny."

Erskine straightened up with surprise: "What do you mean?"

"I have some kind of a great destiny, I know. All this can't be for nothing. Glory and catastrophe are not the fate of the common man."

"God!" he said, feeling his pale chin, his pale eyes on her. "All that you're doing, you mean? You mean, all or nothing?"

"Yes. I know. I have to go, it isn't my fault. I am forced to. If I stay here, I will be nobody. I'd just be taking the line of least resistance." She said very earnestly: "My father wants me to stay at home and keep the house together, he doesn't know I'm going. Some people years ago asked me to join a certain Eastern order because I had psychic power, at least they said that to attract me. If I stayed here, I'd fall in love with someone—you might make me, for instance—then I'd get married and stay here. I can't do it."

He looked at her in wonder, his mouth slightly open, his eyes wide open. He turned round and marched out. He went into Mr Remark's office, said something about some orders and came marching past again but wheeled, and coming straight up to her desk, said severely: "I love you. You say all that to annoy me."

They wrangled as usual and he went marching out again round the room and up to his room. In a minute he was on the telephone.

When five-thirty came and the office staff went home, she picked up her bag and took a new turning that led past the two vacant lots and the burned factory. She strolled past, glancing around, but actually sizing up the open spaces and the nailed-up gateway. It was too bright for her now to pause and there were

285

other people in the street, soon the six o'clock stream of workers would be coming past. She went to the railway station and sat in the waiting room for a long while. She went out to get a glass of milk and came back. She hoped that as she was saving the walk home, and yet had the extra expenditure of supper out, she might be able to eat only a sandwich and some milk. If it was going to cost her extra for supper, it might be better to spend the energy in her usual walk instead.

About eight it was dark and she was dead tired. She went out of the station again carrying her little bag and once more strolled in the street with the burned factory. There were still people about for it was quite near one of the big station entrances; likewise, she saw a policeman passing thoughtfully, on the other side of the street, under a light. She went back to the waiting-room and waited till about ten o'clock. How slowly the time passed. Women who had been waiting for hours gradually left for their late trains, the attendant began to look at her with wonder, so she went out and bought a sandwich, which seemed to disappear in her without leaving a trace. A few minutes later, however, she felt stronger and went out to walk the streets until it was time to try the vacant lot. Unfortunately, this closed gateway could be seen for a long way, from the station ramp, some of the platforms, the long road that went by the station and even a forking side road near the factory. The only thing in its favour was that it was not under a street lamp. She slipped first into the open door-way of the burned factory but the floor of the space was a death trap, piled with stones, charred beams, and tangled wire, with deep hollows between going into some basement. She never had a chance to try opening the gateway itself when she came out and passed and repassed it, for she always heard some footfalls or heard someone. At last she was afraid to be seen flitting there back and forth and she had already used up as much energy as she would have done on her well-accustomed route to the Quay, so she went round the corner of the wedge-shaped lot on which the junk yard stood and round into the lot which stood between the factories. Pressed against the paling fence, she looked up at the windows where she had stood today.

She began to think about Erskine. Did he love her? No, no, she thought, he's just a trap that is being set for me, to try to stop me from going abroad. If he loved her, again, why was she wandering like this at dead of night without being able to get into the vacant lot? Wouldn't he have followed her after work, seen where she had gone, wouldn't he be here now? He was selfish and light-hearted. It was nothing for him to bring her flowers, his father had a magnificent rose garden in the suburbs. She sank down on the ground against the fence, with her bag clutched in her right hand and all kinds of visions raced through her head; perhaps they went slowly through her head, she had no idea of the hour. She started and opened her eyes cautiously. A man was in the lot, at the far end near the entrance. She felt her heart beating so that she was afraid he would hear it. He went up close to the fence, stood there a while facing it, then buttoned his clothes and went away without looking towards her. There were, in her end of the lot, heaps of stone and bits of wood fallen from the factory and these had hidden her. In her ignorance of men's ways, she supposed this man was like the man on the road long ago at Narara, and she became very much afraid. She rose, trembling—what excuse could she give if she was seen coming out of the lot at this time of night? She came out boldly; so much the worse, she would explain that she had had to fix her stockings. She walked out and saw the clock on the station—ten minutes to midnight. She would have to hurry to catch the last boat. She began to walk down her old route, heel and toe, heel and toe, in the old strong rhythm, carrying her valise. When she got on the boat, she remembered the lie she had told about the scarf, that it was for a poor woman, so she took it out of the valise and threw it into the water. In a few ripples from the boat, the scarf had gone. Lucky scarf, dropping slowly down, without personality and without cares, to rest in the tide-bottom.

Both men were waiting up when she got home, anxious and angry. She told them she had been in the library.

"Doing what?"

"What do people do in libraries?" she asked and laughed in their faces.

"You might have known we'd be worried."

"I might, but I didn't. I don't think of this place when I'm away from it."

"We heard nothing from Kitty and we thought you had gone off too."

"Well, I soon will."

She had to explain herself, and to get out of the confusion sooner, she told them that she was going to England in a little while, in about four months."

"It's not impossible," she said when they cried out. "Everything's arranged."

"You're leaving the home empty," cried her father.

"Fill it with other people then."

"You're selfish and hard."

"She's mad," said Lance furiously.

"Chateaubriand says you have to be mad to get out of certain situations."

"Who's he?" said Lance.

She did not answer, but sat gulping down the food her father had kept for her over a saucepan, just as Kitty had done.

"Are you really going to England?" said the father, slumped in a chair.

"Yes, and glad to leave you and get away from everything here that ruined my youth, robbed me of my youth, I never had any youth. I don't know if anybody has any, the whole lie is foisted on us. Young love? Did I ever have any? Or Lance either?" And she looked with challenge at her brother, who did not dare to say he had. "You kill us and then you tell us we had a lovely youth. The whole thing is made up. I hate you all. I'm going away and hope I never see any of you again. Leo had to run away, Kitty had to run away, I'm going too, and if Lance doesn't he's an ass."

Heavy-eyed, the father sat looking at her, humped in his chair. "All this out of nowhere," he said. "What have I done?"

"Nothing," she admitted. "You've done nothing."

"She's mad," said Lance. "She always was mad, she's got softening of the brain. She's gone mad because she hasn't got a boy."

"Yes, that's it," cried Teresa. "So it is. Is it my fault?"

"Yes, it's your fault, because you're so ugly, mangy, thin as a skeleton." Lance kept crying at her, himself stirred and enraged at the bottom of his heart. "It's your fault. Look at your hair and the hollows in your cheeks, you can almost see your teeth through your cheeks. I've seen you in bathing, you can count every rib you've got, your arms are like sticks, your legs are like broomsticks, it's your own fault if no man will have you."

She laughed cunningly. "No man will have me? Eh? A man told me today he loved me."

"You lie," said Lance, looking at her angrily but with a gleam of his old slyness.

"Yes? I lie? This time I'm lying, too?" She merely laughed.

"Who said he loved you?" said Lance, forcing out the words.

"I wouldn't tell you."

"Who was it?" asked her father.

"Someone!"

"That Erskine," said Lance. "Poor fool!"

The father, after studying the table for a while, said, quite mildly: "Why don't you bring him down here?"

"Erskine? What for? He doesn't want to see us."

Lance, surprised, watched them.

"Bring him down, perhaps he'd like to come down."

"What for?"

"You ought to introduce to your family any young man you're friendly with."

"He doesn't want to know you." Lance was now convinced and sloped out of the room sulkily. Teresa finished her supper and now went quite openly to the sewing-machine to finish some garment begun the night before.

"Is this other fellow going to marry you?" Andrew Hawkins asked.

She did not answer.

"No?" said Hawkins.

No answer. He got up, put his hands in his pockets, and went outside where he ran into Lance and began to talk with him in low, sulky tones. Since the departure of Kitty the two men had had to find conversation in each other. Lance more and more became the head of the house.

When she went upstairs, the two men being still outside, she undressed and went in a dressing-gown to the tall mirror in the wardrobe in her father's room. It was months since she had looked at herself. What Lance said was not quite true, but it was very curious and touching, even to her, to see certain delicate and rounded forms, like the limbs of a pretty, sick child. As a child she had been large, robust, brown, and firm, now she was like a child with tuberculosis. What she thought was: "I still have time, still have some faint beauty where Lance can't see it." She had time till all her bones became apparent. When she lay in bed she, for the first time, compared the two men, Jonathan and Erskine. Jonathan's last letter came back to her:

Who can revolt from the bottom up, and if he does revolt, where does he get? In the end he is thrown to the dogs and the opportunists of revolution come in. So what use is it to revolt? It's really more stupid than the other. Better the devil you know. To know yourself—that is the ultimate wisdom. I know myself. My real baccalaureate. I'm only saying this so that you won't expect too much from me! I don't give a hang about the high places in the feast of learning, it's the same meat, but you get too much of it, you get indigestion in the end. I have still a hungry patch left in my stomach, I can look around and laugh at the others. I know that behind my tail is a tag of sulky beggars whining and crying —I'm not deaf and blind also. You see? You see the kind of man I am? You have to see that if you want to understand me. But there's something in the "thousand generations of mothers" theory—women understand a man better, perhaps it is intuition as they say, I don't know. I only know that academic psychology doesn't get you far. It isn't analysis that gets you anywhere in these human beings, but touch.

She remembered this writing word for word and lay on her back, her eyes blazing with pity. She recognized the blame on herself in the last few sentences and was ashamed. It was true that she was purely a reader of books and had little experience to help a man. But this tenderness and philosophy compared well with Erskine's lightness. She thought: "Johnny first and the rest nowhere."

Port
of
Registry:
London

25. *After Two Days of Yachting Weather*

It was May, in southern England. After two days of yachting weather, a wet stormy wind began and when the liner docked, it was raining. Just before six there were already clots of people in the long shed staring up, and about six some passengers came up ready to land, while by eight the wharf and the decks were crowded. People waved and shouted, the rails were stacked with elbows and handbags.

Jonathan reached the dock at seven and pressed forward to the picket fence. He wondered if he would recognize Teresa, and thoughts of his friends in the hot southern country he was born in filled his imagination. He saw healthy, round, jolly-voiced, sporty girls, full of opinions, and lanky, lively, pugnacious boys. How depressed he had been on coming to London to find everyone so far behind the times, girls drab, dowdy and frightened, shops dingy and Dickensian, opinions backward and smug. He had looked down upon the English at that time as a provincial race, provincial of their own imperialism. Now he had got used to living in the seat of empire and had smoothed down his prejudices, the raincoated crowd he stood with was his crowd, he too had a heavy raincoat, galoshes, and an umbrella and in the London crowd were others of his thin-faced, sallow, dark-eyed breed, men and women of Scottish or Irish descent. They all stood together lowering in the gloom of the shed; while those up on deck, not yet acclimatized, in overcoats of different shades, with flowers in their hats, some with tropic umbrellas under their arms, all in their best, were another sort of people.

About eight the rain ceased for a while. The people in the shed pressed Jonathan against the railing. By tipping the policeman he got to the front and waved a rolled-up newspaper from time to time to draw attention to himself. The first-class passengers had been coming off for some time and he watched them too, as he was not quite sure what class she was travelling in. It was funny to see some stewards who thought themselves ill-treated standing sulkily near the gangplank hoping the first-class passengers would relent. One, a middle-aged, bullet-headed, swarthy little man of Mediterranean type, was actually pestering a male passenger for a tip. Johnny could not hear the words but could see the steward's insolence, a go-to-the-devil fellow evidently, with no fear of being fired, and the man's bluster. The man put his hand in his pocket angrily and spun a coin into the steward's hand. One could see the different attitudes of the other passengers.

Jonathan scanned the third-class passengers, a full deck. Now they began to come off too, the crowd on the wharf surged forward, there were yells and blown kisses. On the upper decks was a light-haired young woman, bare-headed, in a light dress, talking to no one. She scanned the faces of the people on the dock earnestly. She was very slender with straight features, the high cheek-bones well marked. His eyes rested vaguely on this figure for some time; everyone else was in an overcoat. She stood up and began to wave at someone. He looked around him, straightened his glasses, peered. She picked up her bag and coat, and came down the gangplank and only when she was nearly down was he sure it was Teresa.

She had changed a great deal. Her hair was curled and brought up off her forehead so that the disproportion of certain features, the forehead, eye-sockets, nostrils, appeared. Around her thin neck she had a string of beads, but no scarf or fur piece. The drizzle had begun again, but she did not stop in the stream of passengers to put on her coat. She came on, in thin silk stockings, new shoes, summer dress, in the rain, looking about. Before she had seen him, he examined her intently. He would have hardly recognized her in the street; her expression was quite different. He took off his spectacles, put them in their case, pushed open his well-cut coat to show the black-and-white scarf and brought out a large silk handkerchief. She had just seen him, and seriously, her eyes fixed on him, with little steps, under the weight of the bag, she turned towards the gate. But he beckoned her with a smile, and smiling at the friendly policeman, pointed to an opening in the fence. The policeman, heavy hand on picket, smiled at her too and helped her through the slit. Teresa flushed, put down her bag and stared with a shy smile up at Jonathan. He raised his hat, said: "Hullo, Tess." "How you've changed," she said. "For better or worse?" She blushed. "I don't know, I like you any way." He bent down and kissed her on the cheek. "So you got here at last," he said, picking up the bag. "There's your letter, H, over there, let's get through."

He hurried along, got someone to pick out her luggage, was agreeable to customs examiner, got her luggage off the wharf before most of the other people had even got their bags together, and took her to the train for which he had two tickets. No one had ever done anything for her before, of this kind. She had not really been sure that Jonathan would come to meet her until she got a telegram from him on arrival. Since then she had grateful love for him and she had at last opened her mouth and told some passenger that she was going to meet a young man upon landing in England. The whole trip she had said nothing of her plans, though her silence and the several large trunks she had, which she kept locked, and a magnificent Chinese gown she had suddenly shown one night, had made everyone think she was going to be married.

She looked at nothing. It was nothing to her that she was in England. She had never wanted to see England. It was Johnny she was seeing. He talked to her about Baldwin, MacDonald and a number of other people, pointing out the strange flat country, almost Dutch, re-emergence, in fact, of the Dutch sands, the ribbon-built houses about which he had a cutting in his pocket, and he gave her the latest news about Sir Oswald Mosley. She listened, looked, and after about half an hour her eyes opened and she saw England for the first time. But all that he denounced did not seem so bad to her, pretty and new, if small and flat; she did not like it, but it was new.

He went on talking fluently about politics, Hitler, Brüning, British investments, von Papen, Hindenburg, the Westwall, a thousand references which flashed in and out of his wonderful knowledge. She listened timidly, with shame and fear. She had heard of Hitler in the past three or four years, and knew that he was some kind of dictator in Germany, head of the Nazi party, a few other things that she had picked up from chance headlines or words in the streets and on the boats. She had never bought a newspaper or magazine, or been to a cinema in all the time she had been saving up; and since everyone sulked at home round the table, after Leo left, nothing was said at home. Sometimes, at night, dull explanations were given in Lance's room, over his little radio, but to such eternal jawing she had been too listless to pay attention. Now, as the train ran towards the terminus, her heart sank under a fearful load of guilt. She would have to conceal from him that she was ignorant of all those things, until she had a few days to herself, to study it in the newspapers and a couple of books. She had studied everything, to please him, but not that, the thing he was most interested in! As he went on talking, comfortably, authoritatively, she stole a glance at him.

To tell the truth, got up like that, she might have passed him in the street—but no, not with those deep-set, narrow-set, moving eyes and that long mobile mouth; there were no others in the world like that. He had turned handsome and plump, otherwise. His voice was firmer, more melodious, but his rasping, assertive, complaining tones were there, as before. Only now he smiled more, and as if to himself, wisely, like a man quite at home in the world. Each time she looked at him, she became more frightened; he had become so good-looking and easy and he was so much the man in his fine clothes, that he could have any woman for the asking. She realized what she had been ignorant of before, how good and condescending he was to write to her as he had done, every week for so many years, how friendly to come to the wharf to meet a friendless girl.

The dull green country rattled past. He spoke of his work, his essay, his classes, his hopes of going to America. She egged him on politely, though she had a sense of bafflement which she could not explain. Why, when he was so kind and good? It was perhaps because she had not enough courage. Just the same, she had had six weeks at sea; she ought to be ready to face the world again, look for work and begin to learn all these political facts which were on the tip of his tongue. When she knew a bit more, so as not to appear an idiot, she would ask him to help her.

Jonathan, meanwhile, glibly retailing what he had said a dozen times, felt dissatisfied. Of course women, to sell themselves to men, will send these retouched photographs; and she had aged two years since the last photograph, which had showed her a pale, plain, but sweet and still plump girl. He felt a slight embarrassment. He flashed a look at her, she was staring out at the landscape. She certainly was wasted and strange, her face had taken on that curious illumined but ravaged look, often seen in disease. Tuberculosis? Unconsciously, he drew away from her a little, leaning on the window which was on his side, and looking out, pointing out some species of housing.

She felt the withdrawal of the rough, hairy coat, and trembled. Had he already found out that she knew nothing about Hitler? Good, she thought, good, if I have lost him, I have lost him. I put all my eggs in one basket, I played the grand play, it's win or lose that way, and I'm not one to complain if I lose. *He* said so. "It's up to you, Teresa." How fair he was! Lovely! Where is there a better man? And he sits by my side, but so far from me, lost in his own austere and unselfish world, thinking about mankind, other nations, while I have only been thinking about myself, my own desires! This is wickedness. How beastly I have been. It seems people have been burned alive, crucified, martyred, starved to death, driven out of their homes and all I have been thinking about all these years is my love, while *he*, poor man, with all his sorrows and his ideas of failure, has been thinking about *them* and their sorrows. I really deserve to fail.

Teresa was afraid also of the dull rainy light falling on her face. She knew how worn she looked. Every time he glanced at her she shrank. They were both glad when they got out at Fenchurch Street, for the first strain was over and in a sort, some explanation had been held between them, though he had talked about Hitler and she had murmured: "Yes," and "Really?" He was kind as ever, carried a bag for her, bought a ticket, and in her ignorance she thought that this meant he liked her, in spite of all her failings, and wanted to protect her.

They were in a two-decker bus. It was Jonathan who made her look at this. She had seen it, but did not care about it. He said: "Look, a two-decker bus, aren't they funny?" and she had looked and laughed, warmed by his grin, the old grin of the old, old days. She was here, in London, with him by her side, it was all over, the long sickness, it was all done. She laughed, she said: "I came a long way to see a two-decker bus!"

He laughed. "I didn't know if you were coming third or first and I kept looking at the first."

"Oh, I came in the middle, downstairs was E deck, a kind of

steerage, but they don't call it that any more. And underneath E deck, the glory-hole."

He laughed: "What's that?"

"That's where the sailors and stewards sleep. I knew quite a few of them."

He laughed. "Ah, you did? You had a good time, eh?"

"Oh, yes, I rested. A funny thing happened. You know my brother Leo ran away, disappeared, about four years ago?"

"Yes?"

"They told me there was an Australian sailor called Leo, they told me all about him. One day, he came up to see me—one night rather—but it wasn't my brother at all."

He looked closely at her. "One night?"

"Oh," she flushed with amusement, "just before he went to bed, on his way, so to speak. You know—no, you don't—I travelled by night. I slept in the daytime. I saw nothing. I got up one day to look at Suez, I left my work, well, it wasn't work exactly, to see Stromboli. It was about a quarter to midnight when we passed. I was so surprised when it could not get dark in the Bay of Biscay. I don't like the pale nights when it doesn't get dark."

He seemed to be picking his words when he said: "I don't understand, why did you sleep in the daytime?"

"There was a drunk woman aboard in first class. Two women volunteered to nurse her, since there weren't enough stewardesses and she wouldn't be put ashore. They were afraid for her because she's an heiress, so they asked for volunteers out of third class. Two volunteered, a woman called Mrs Brown and myself. Mrs Brown was with her husband, so of course I had to take the night shift, twelve hours, but in the Mediterranean they took me off at two in the morning."

He stared at her in an unfriendly way. She hastened to say: "Oh, I should never have got to know the sailors and night watchmen any other way! Do you realize I had a first-class breakfast, all the way across? They gave me that. When down in third class, for which I had paid, they had stewed apricots and tea for breakfast, up in first class I had marmalade, toast, cream, bacon and eggs. And that was only the nursery, out in the restaurant they had dozens of things, haddock, all kinds of fish, meat, fruit cup, all kinds of things. I did not do so badly. But the nurses only got a restricted menu and they called me a nurse."

"How long did you do it?"

"Oh, five weeks. It was about a week out of Sydney when they found out she couldn't move. Well, she could. She dragged herself to the cannon port and tried to throw herself overboard, they say. She had D.Ts." He was stupefied and his dark eyes stared at her inimically. She regretted telling it to him. She had made up her mind not to, because she knew he disliked anything peculiar; it had slipped out. It was her whole trip. She had led a very peaceful life with a couple of night watchmen and a steward for friends. She had known no one on board otherwise but the drunken woman, a good-natured though cranky girl with unfortunate affairs. In some queer way this seemed to Jonathan Crow an unexpected calamity. It bored and irritated him. Why had she done it? Did she know, he asked her.

"They asked us to!" she said. "The ship, I mean, the ship's doctor and the captain."

"They asked you to," he said sarcastically. "So you were helping out the Orient Line."

"That's silly, they actually did not have enough help, the stewardesses were overworked, the ship was full."

"It's silly?" He looked at her furiously. She hastened to repair her mistake. "Not silly, I don't mean that, I just say that all the time."

He said in a husky, hollow tone: "And to think I travelled like a lord! Twelve courses for breakfast, maybe fifteen, I don't remember." He cast a sweet smile upon her. "I know though. Pah! I didn't see the nursery, I saw what the real other half was like. Middle-aged women and old hags, flaunting their paint and powder and the youngsters smeared over with lipstick showing their breasts in their sun-suits—starting their cocktail parties in the corridors at eleven in the morning. I saw them. I guess you didn't see that if you were asleep." He smiled at her with pathetic sweetness.

"No, but she went up to one or two dances at the end of the trip and she told me a few things when she got back. She wore her dress only. She said they all do."

He looked out and spread his hand, in its grey glove.

"Fleet Street—you're not interested? I noticed you passed St Paul's without looking."

"Oh, I saw it. But I couldn't see much, that is."

299

"Oh, I know, girls can pass Vesuvius in eruption and talk about frills and flounces," he said good-humouredly.

She laughed. "Is this really Fleet Street? Where are we going?"

"To Bloomsbury." He peered at her. "I think you'll probably try to get a room in Bloomsbury, so we may as well go straight there."

"Bloomsbury? It's a boarding-house area, isn't it?"

"Why do you say that?" he asked with great amusement.

"There's some song, *My little back room in Blooms-bu-ry!*"

"Is that all you know about it?"

"Yes. What is it then?"

He smiled good-naturedly and whistled a moment between his teeth. Then he said: "I'll show it to you, then you'll know. It's no good in the telling."

She was so touched that she slipped her hand under the hairy arm of his overcoat. He said: "Temple Bar. Now we leave the City of London and enter the City of Westminster." He changed from his first mood. At first he had thought that she would be writing home to their friends in common and saying: "Thus was Johnny when I first saw him," and he had wanted to show himself at his best; mature, intelligent, sophisticated, a political man, but now he began to think that she too had some peculiar life behind her of her own. She had come for him only and this intrigued him. It was not the "Teresa Hawkins" of the letters but a sick young woman quite different. Poor thing! How she had aged! He noticed the first signs of crow's-feet round her eyes. She was peaked, a young hag, yet what age was she exactly? Was it possible that she was younger than himself? He said, reminiscently: "Yes, the boat! So you saw the other half, anyhow? You beat them to it? You saw the women they have? She must have been a nice handful, your young drunk. How old was she?"

"About twenty-seven."

"Did she look bad?"

"No, she looked about eighteen, she was a beauty, she looked wonderful, a soft pale skin. Besides, I saw the whole of her, she wore chiffon nightdresses. She was in love with one of the stewards, and he was forbidden to come to the cabin. You would have said that drinking was good for the skin."

He laughed shrewdly and glanced at her askance. "She was a high stepper, I suppose? All these women in first class have no morals. You mean there was something between her and the steward?"

"The steward, André, was not supposed to see her. But one night he came along and I let him go in because I knew she wanted him. She was so lonely, really. He was nice to everyone."

Jonathan frowned. "A lady's man. Well, these stewards must see the women half undressed, or quite, you can't blame them."

"Oh, André told me it made no difference to him whether they had all or nothing on. He was too damned tired." She blushed. "Excuse me, that's what he told me. They used to call me 'Nurse'," she explained.

"Nurse." He grinned. "I'll bet you saw a lot of queer goings-on, at dead of night, Nurse!"

"Yes, I did," she laughed. "Yes, I did. A captain from India who was always tiptoeing somewhere with a lady, and a bottle under his arm. It was terribly funny, and only old Pillicock, the night watchman, got angry with them."

"Ah, you knew him? Pillicock? Rum name. Old English? Pillicock's Hill? Isn't there something? What was he like?"

"White-headed, an old man, this was his last trip. Now he's retiring to Brighton, where his wife lives. He has a garden." She smiled. "He invited me there if I couldn't get a job; he told me you had to work six months here to get on the dole."

"We get out here," said Jonathan, inserting his hand under her arm and picking up her bag. "Now we'll get you a room. I looked the last two days but thought you'd better look by yourself. You'll get it cheaper."

"Oh, Jonathan, did you? How kind! But I expected to look myself."

He grinned. "At one place the woman said she wasn't used to having black people. At another the old fraud said she didn't like young women who had men to visit them."

"Oh, you didn't tell her——"

"No, that's why I say you'd better go yourself."

"Yes, yes."

"At the same time, you'd better make sure to begin with, ask her if men friends can visit you. I don't want to get thrown out."

"Oh, no."

"Let's have some breakfast? I didn't have any."

"Oh, Johnny! Why did you do that?"

"I wanted to meet you, you know." He gave her an impudent smile which tickled her. "There's a teashop near here, Lyons', that's the name of the big chain, I've been going there for years, I know the girls there. Let's go there."

"All right, but," she said timidly, looking up at him, "Johnny, I'll pay for myself."

"This time I'll pay, the other times, you'll pay."

They went into a small shop with gold lettering and cakes on glass shelves in the single window. She did not know where she was and was never again able to find it, but Johnny was well-known there. The woman at the cash-desk greeted him askance, and Jonathan said: "My friend from Australia." At once the woman gave Teresa a kind smile, and when they sat down at a marble-topped table between a window and a water-pipe, and a dark-haired waitress in an ugly frilly cap came up, Jonathan again said: "Hullo! This is my friend, Miss Hawkins, she got off the boat from Australia this morning."

"Pleased to meet you," said the waitress. Teresa became absorbed in Jonathan; in her excitement she had little appetite, but since her father had always said: "A man hates a woman who does not eat what is put before her," she tried to finish what was put before her to the last crumb. Teresa told Jonathan about the dipsomaniac on the boat, in whom he was interested. "She said that her mother corrupted her, she put her to bed when she was only thirteen with a bottle of gin on the night-table."

"All these society girls are depraved by their mothers," Jonathan said with distaste.

"Another time, she told me her mother was a sweet, good woman, and I saw her photograph, she was very nice-looking."

"She was keen on the steward, André, do you think?"

"I suppose so, I felt sorry for her. She was nice to me, in her way."

"She patronized a girl with no money and you're grateful," he said with a slight sneer.

Teresa laughed at him. "She told me where to get an expensive perfume, the only one that makes men flock round, she said, *La Petite Fleur Bleue*, on the Champs Elysées, she said it was a secret, and she told it to me." Teresa laughed, daring him.

"*La petite fleur bleue*," he mused. "What does that mean?"

"Little blue flower."

"A secret, eh?" He laughed. "What is the French word for ravishing, something just like it?"

"*Ravissant?*"

"And there is another word they use all the time, something like sympathetic?"

"*Sympathique?*"

"No."

"It must be."

"Well, I don't know, *vous êtes très sympathique*, is that right?"

"Yes, it means——"

He continued, greedily eating, and raising dark strange eyes at her occasionally. "I forgot you knew French. Everything is *très sympathique* with them, is that right? And the way they say it—*très sympathique. Sympathique*," he said, listening to himself. "Yes, that's it. It's a pretty word, isn't it?"

"Yes." She was puzzled.

"I was told I was *sympathique*," he said, laughing. He smiled at her and drew a packet out of an inner pocket. Fumbling in it, he at last produced several photomaton pictures and showed them to her. "Do you recognize the man?"

"Of course, it's you, the one you sent me."

"Oh, did I send it to you? That was the one the girl said was *sympathique*." He found some others of the same size and pushed them across the table at her. "That's a little girl I picked up at Carcassonne, she was only thirteen, she looks sixteen, doesn't she? Those southern girls mature early." Teresa looked at a picture of an exuberant, black-eyed, laughing beauty of a Spanish type; this was with a little photograph of Jonathan and another young man, with two girls, the black-eyed one and one rather fair, both young; all four stood arms round waists, laughing, against a crumbling stone wall.

"We were only three nights there," said Jonathan indifferently, taking the photographs out of her hands and putting them back with solicitude in his pocket. "But those little southern girls are fully developed at twelve or thirteen, they don't wait to twenty-four or -five like the English type."

"Did you have a nice holiday?"

"Oh, I couldn't have much of a holiday with my money; it was just a flit, kind of Cook's tour, but Bentham conducted it and we all clubbed together; he knows France and he said he didn't care if I was poor, every young man ought to see France before he dies." He laughed. "Don't you think so?"

"Of course."

After a silence Crow ruminated: "You can buy, mind you, every kind of corruption in Paris, men prostitute themselves in Paris." He leaned towards her mysteriously looking into her face. "Not only gigolos who go with rich women and make their living off them—why not, say I? I knew a fellow who went to the Beaux Arts and lived off a woman when he had no more money. But rich women", and his expression deepened, "buy butcher-boys and carters from Les Halles—that's the markets; those kids know to what addresses to go when they want some money."

Teresa laughed frankly. "I know! There's a story called La Corvée, or something—" then she stopped and blushed, but she laughed again. "I know, but it's so funny, isn't it? Men—oh!"

Jonathan said stiffly, and with melancholy: "They have every kind of corruption there, just feeding vice. Women come on the stage completely naked; you can go there any day, it's dark, the lights gradually come on, and you see the naked women standing there, then the lights go out." Drawing designs on the table in the spilled tea, he raised his strange dark eyes upon her.

"You went there?"

"Oh, I didn't know where I was going. We just paid in our money to Bentham, it was his conducted tour, and we promised to go blind wherever he said. They all think you want that. I got sick of it. You don't enjoy it. It's a show for men only. So I suppose—anything, once in a lifetime."

"Don't you think it's funny they don't allow women to see women?"

"Why not let women see everything?" said Jonathan roughly. "Abolish the conspiracy of silence. They're afraid of losing their husbands to the scarlet woman and all that. I think women ought to be taught the whole game anyhow so men would like them better."

"I think so, too."

"Let's go," said Jonathan, looking round. "Bill, Miss!"

"Let me pay half, Jonathan."

"All the other times, not this."

At first they went straight to his room in Marchmont Street, still the top room he had occupied when he first came to London, with his friend Gene Burt. Gene, he explained gloomily, was lost to grace. Some toffee-haired Margery, from the yellow-belly country, a beanpole in a meal-bag, had got him to marry her just because he lived with her and the ass was now in married bliss. But it suited him, he could stretch his legs, and the old dame Bagshawe was rather fond of him and let him have the same room for two-thirds of the original rent.

They had brought along the small bag that she had had on leaving the boat. She looked everywhere as they walked towards his diggings, noticing with relief all kinds of placards in pasteboard and wood, advertising bed and breakfast. She asked him what she should do about getting a job and he at once bought a morning paper. Passing along Kingsway, he showed her a large agency where she might apply.

She felt a great emotion at passing through Cartwright Gardens, a demi-lune of boarding-houses, and into Marchmont Street, the name of which she had typed on all her letters to him, far away on the other side of several seas. She looked at the houses, fixing them in her memory, at the pavement, the road— it was down this street that his footsteps had echoed all these years, he had passed by these houses, in his queer hat, heavy coat and flying scarf. Eyes in these windows had seen Jonathan go past and had wondered about him. "What a lonely man he is, how pale he is!" She was almost suffocated with joy, seeing him open the rusty iron gate, go up to the doorway. She looked up at the half-moon fanlight, she saw the curtain stir in a window at the side, she saw a servant shaking a mop in the basement and looking up at her, and felt an unspeakable gratitude. Here she was, she was allowed to see them, to enter his home. Nothing was in vain. Jonathan appreciated, in a measure, her emotion. Her joy at seeing his room and her inspection of its poverty-stricken detail, the iron bed, ink-stained table, gas-ring and wooden cupboard, were touching. He sat on the unmade bed and watched her pause by the table and look down at some ink-written sheets when he suddenly said: "Don't read, verboten!" She smiled.

"Sit down," he said. "Take off your bonnet and shawl. Make yourself at home."

Two trunks lay open near the windows. He told her she had just arrived to see him move. He was going through his papers. Old Mrs Bagshawe had taken a larger and better house on Malet

Street, near Bedford Square, where she could get higher rents. Nevertheless, for him, her old boarder, she would rent a ground-floor room, in the court, airy and quiet, for only a pound a week, and he had jumped at the offer. He had even been able to make a condition because the old woman preferred to have old tenants she could trust on the ground floor, rather than new ones. Ceasing to talk for a while, Jonathan became thoughtful. A gentle smile presently played across his face and he asked Teresa if she knew the opera, *Lucia di Lammermoor*.

"No."

"Listen, there's a song—" he sang it. "Don't you know it?" He sang the phrase twice in which the name "Lucia" occurred.

"No, I don't know it, Johnny."

After humming for a minute, he stopped, smiling. "Well, I'll have to take you to see that opera if it's ever played. Do you like opera?"

"I've never seen any, I don't know."

"I used to be prejudiced against it," Jonathan confided, "but since I found out there's a kind of general sense for art, I realize I was wrong, not the opera. Why, I've found out that washer-women, girls in teashops, even my landlady, know some music. It makes you feel pretty small, doesn't it? When I came across here and found out I knew nothing, I felt like twopence."

"Yes, I know."

Jonathan smiled confidentially. "I sing that bit to Lucy, the maid, it annoys her. When I found out it annoyed her, I took her to the Old Vic to see it. She had no idea that music was in it. She told me she nearly boxed my ears when she heard it." He threw himself on his bed and burst out laughing. Leaning on his elbow, he looked at Teresa.

"You were nice to take her."

"Why?" he asked. "She leads a dog's life, under the orders of the old girl. You should see where she sleeps—a box room full of rags and old rubbish and freezing in winter."

"Poor thing."

"I've seen it," he continued argumentatively. "It's just across the landing, I've got good cause to see it. I know when she gets up and when she goes to bed. Gets up at six and goes to bed at all hours of the night. You can see yourself. Go and look——"

"Oh, no."

"All right, look, look—she hasn't any privacy. The old cow sees to that. The old woman has the right to spy into her room, open the drawers, inspect her boxes, and Lucy's a married woman with husband and child. I hate injustice," continued the man in a sombre tone. "I told the old woman flatly that if she threw out Lucy, she threw me out too. I would never stand cruelty to a helpless woman."

"You're awfully good, Jonathan."

He smiled his absolute candour. Teresa continued after a moment's thought: "But of course, she has a husband to help her."

Jonathan said gloomily: "That's what you think. They're separated, he lives up-country doing odd jobs round some country inn for tourists, and you know what the average cheap tourist gives in tips. He's an old codger, sixty-three, and she's only thirty or so, it's a terrible difference, isn't it? It was a forced marriage, so to speak, one of those forced marriages of poverty. She had a love affair with some student who went back home and left her with his child."

"Illegitimate, do you mean?"

Jonathan nodded. "The old man married her and she was glad of his name; society demands a legal father. He adopted the child but he was out of work and she had always to work for him. I gave her ten shillings to send him several times." After a pause he said mildly: "I couldn't think of the old man starving, blacking boots for some blockheads, when he'd done that for her. He must be a decent kind of man."

"You're wonderfully good, simply wonderful," murmured Teresa. Jonathan smiled, threw himself off his bed and lunged to his trunks. "Well," he said, "may as well be getting on with this. We really are the paper animal, aren't we? Are there any other animals that collect papers? Do you mind? Or do you want to do something else?"

"Just what you like. I'll have to get a room soon."

"What say you leave your bag here and go and get a room, and then come back and we'll go out to lunch, eh?"

"All right," she said joyfully.

She put on her coat and gloves, borrowed an umbrella from

Jonathan, who said he would be in all the morning, and set out. Jonathan, squatting behind his trunk, cried "Ta-ta" and waved a merry good-bye at her across the room. Teresa went downstairs and in the hall passed a dark-haired, hopeless-looking woman in an apron; the woman scarcely glanced at her but started slowly upstairs. "Lucy, no doubt," thought Teresa. "I am glad she has one friend in the whole house."

26. *I Sit Around in Teashops*

SHE wandered about the squares, keeping her eye on Southampton Row and Woburn Place, so that she would know the way back, knocked at large green doors, tramped up and down stairs, and in the end, took a room for a week in a narrow four-storey house, stuffy, overdressed, with plush curtains, but clean, in Torrington Square. She paid her deposit and sped back to Jonathan's to tell him how lucky she had been. She had to ring his bell. A window went up, he put his head out the window, and called: "I'll be down." Soon she heard steps on the stairs and the door was opened by the flat-faced woman she had seen before.

"I heard you ring," said the woman.

"Mr Crow," said Teresa.

"He's upstairs, in his room, top floor," said the woman. "Go up, he's expecting you."

"Yes, thank you." She smiled at the woman, who looked passively at her. She burst upstairs, saying breathlessly as soon as she reached his open door: "I got a room, in Torrington Square."

"Good-o." He was still behind his trunks, fishing among the papers. He had not done very much. "Torrington Square—not much of an address, but we'll get you something better later on. Sit down till I empty this trunk and we'll go and have a bite." He was depressed and pointed to the trunk. "Look."

She came and stood by it. At the bottom of the trunk, nearly empty, were dozens of creased and opened letters, among which she recognized some of her own typing; and among these papers, some fat envelopes which, she soon saw, had not been opened. Jonathan fished in these papers and drew from underneath something which she thought was the lining of the box but which she in a minute recognized with a queer thrill. He handed it to her, a long piece of thick hand-made water-colour paper.

"I came on this only yesterday, I had forgotten all about it, it seemed to fit down there last time I cleaned my drawers out." He waved his hand.

It was her illuminated seven-panelled Legend of Jonathan. He forced it into her hand with a hardy smile; she took it unwillingly. But when she saw the work, the fingers, which leaped up at her which had cost her such pains and which seemed to her now, when it was strange, so beautiful and in such fine colours, she looked keenly and closely. "Yes," she said, handing it back, "it took some time."

"You keep it," said Jonathan. "I don't want it because you don't mean it any more."

"What would I do with it?"

"It was a waste of time," said Jonathan softly.

"No, it was a pleasure to me."

"The artist gets more than the onlooker, doesn't he?"

"I know it was badly done."

"No, I showed it to Bentham and he said you had some ability, you ought to do commercial designing. Take it, you could show it to some studios, I suppose. I can't really do anything with it."

She flinched. "Oh, no, I couldn't take it."

He smiled wryly and shrank into himself. "Well, too bad, neither of us wants it. Much water has flowed, et cetera. Perhaps I can give it to the girl to put up in her room. She would appreciate it, she has quite an eye for colour and likes design too. There's nothing on her wall at all but a calendar. There's nothing more depressing than that greyish plaster covered with finger-marks and scratches. I told Bentham you'd gone to night school for a while to study design but you'd given it up. He said it's no good if you haven't confidence in yourself and application. Well, that's your concern, isn't it—no one can ordain the life of another. We are all independent, free beings—free as air, eh?" He grinned sourly. He put the paper back in the box, however, remarking: "If you insist, I'll find some use for it. Let's go out to lunch, shall we?"

She tried to overlook the rebuff, because she believed that Jonathan was reproving her in his clumsy way for her advances to him. In fact after this he tried to amuse her, took her to lunch in a place in Oxford Street where he showed her a waitress to whom he at times had given a few shillings "to help out" when she had been out of work. Separated from her husband, who was unemployed, she was obliged herself to keep her boy of eight or nine. He knew them all, Annie, Florrie, Dorothy, he told Teresa what hard times they saw and how many of them had to make up for it by semi-prostitution. This very woman, the one with the child, had received men several times at her home, customers from the teashop. When the men came, she had to send the boy out to play in the street and was always afraid, while she was in commerce with the men, that the boy would get run over or get into mischief. "All she worries about," said Jonathan, "is her boy—What future has he? She does not worry about herself at all." She was overwhelmed by Jonathan's goodness, his ceaseless preoccupation with the miseries of poor people, her heart sank lower and lower when she compared her wretched selfish single-minded life with his elastic interests, large soul, boundless sympathy. This was how a human being should be! And how modest he was, too, never praising himself, always seeing himself as a worthless, unfortunate creature. Perhaps, thought Teresa to herself, he does it with unconscious purpose, so as to keep the common touch.

Jonathan was now describing the room the woman lived in. Once he had missed her, the other girls said the boy was sick and Jonathan had gone there with some delicacy for him. In brief phrases, in a low tone, he recounted his trip. It was on one of London's dismal Saturday afternoons, when a sea wind is blowing grey patches in the cloud overhead and grit and sharp breezes are in the streets. He had taken the bus out there to World's End and looked about for the street, a side street with two rows of the dreariest little houses, that seemed one storey high but were really two, with the meanest little rooms and staircases, fire traps, death traps for the spirit. How glad the poor woman had been to see him. He had sat there on the bed talking to the boy for a long time and the woman had brooded over her troubles, told him everything. "They like to tell me their lives," said Jonathan, in the same low tones. "Very few men have any sympathy for them."

Teresa involuntarily thought in secret of the times she had walked over to Golden Grove after work, to St Michael's Street on Saturday afternoons, and pacing slowly past the ruined flourmill, the vine-covered cottages of weatherboard and the old grave-yard, the Mont-de-Piété with the three golden balls of Lombardy, the sick man always sitting in his wheel chair, the occasional grey-haired drunk, the children running, screaming after the ice-cream man, the rapid horse and yellow trap in which the ice-cream rattled over the streets, spreading confusion and joy and sprawl-ing children, some local milk-cart, red and yellow, in front of Jonathan's house. In all the windows were cheap curtains, some yellow, some clotted with dirt and torn, none as clean as those of Jonathan's house, stiff, white, starched. The fronts of the houses were much the same, a small square of dirt overgrown with grass, or littered with children's rubbish and sparrows' feathers, a stone urn in the middle; sometimes some thin heartsease in the border. Number Fourteen's black-leaded doorstep and three white front steps, the swept brick path, and gate on its hinge, gave it an air of overpowering respectability. She had seen, one Saturday after-noon, a young man there. At first she had taken him for Johnny; but his eyes, not burning with self-contemplation and mystic pain, as Jonathan's were, were merely small, petty, and sad. He appeared starved, just like Jonathan in the old days, but without the inner fibre. Teresa thought: "I don't dare tell him I walked down his own street so much more recently than he did and saw his brother and his mother standing in the closing front door!" She felt a great pang. "Why is there so much I may not tell him? Love is hard; if we were condemned to it we would complain."

St Michael's Street debouched into a proletarian thoroughfare, between a mercery and a bakery, high old shops with painted ceilings and black woodwork in the large windows. Trams rattled, buses and cars rushed along the way which was always filled with people in poor but bright clothes. While thinking of this, Teresa began to hum—

> *Still is the night, the streets are deserted,*
> *Within yonder threshold, dwelt my love, of old.*

She noticed that Johnny was eating his food with a non-com-mittal expression exactly as if alone, and realized she had not answered him. She blushed for this solitary habit she had fallen into, this thinking and singing to herself. She said: "What you said, about going to World's End to see the waitress's son, reminded me of something else, and I wandered." She laughed in embarrassment. "But I heard what you said."

"Well," he grumbled, "you have no idea, you see, of the degradation of morals here in London. I am a lonely man and I sit around in teashops; there are no public places to sit because the local gardens are under lock and key, the property of some landlord and his tenants, all privilege and property. I talk to any-one I see because I'm interested in the other fellow—" he showed his teeth pleasantly and his spectacles gleamed "—and the poor girls are delighted to have some fellow to talk to and sympathize —you know I am *très sympathique*." He looked for approval, and when she laughed, told her a few stories he had heard from girls in parks and elsewhere, girls out of work. He always bought them a cup of tea and gave them a sixpence so that they would not have to walk home. "Some of them walk to and from work to save the penny or twopence of the fare, just like I did at home." He sank his chin and looked gloomily into his cup remembering his old privations. "Somehow that gets me down. Did you know my mother was a waitress when she met my Dad? Well, she was." He finished in a more sprightly tone, "Let's take a toddle."

This was the cream of humour to her; she laughed delightedly. There was a steel-engraved sky after lunch, spacious, dry, wind-less. They walked round this part of London. He showed her again the employment agency and told her to go next morning and register, or at once if she wished to, but with a holiday air she said next morning would do.

"Let's take a bus and do London, see the sights."

They climbed up to the top and saw London; Piccadilly, Bond Street, and so forth, got out and walked in some of the little streets behind Piccadilly, saw some of the taverns, Jonathan show-ing where the rich and idle bachelors lived, displaying his know-ledge of noble families when they passed old houses, looking down his nose at famous squares into which the loot of an empire had been poured, telling absorbing tales. They looked com-placently at each other. She knew his theories, that "a man only cavorts in female company for ancient biological reasons," and that "when a man and a woman spend time in one another's company, it is only for one reason, not for logic or belles-lettres."

Jonathan had friends among Oxford and Cambridge aesthetes; one undergrad had a room painted in black with a row of silver skulls, one dabbled in all the vices and wanted to do "murder to understand everything", one had purchased a tavern and others frequented taverns near the East India Docks; all went to low dives, which was considered the romantic thing to do. He asked her, passing one pub, whether she would take a gin and lime juice, for they could go in and take on in the company of men with painted cheeks and hair dyed yellow. At an elegant scent shop, he said: "Your little friend could perhaps get her *Petite Fleur Bleue*—what was it? What did she say?—Oh, yes, that no man could resist it, I should like to smell it," he said with a grin, looking over his shoulder. "What was she like, your dipso?" He continued to make light remarks, to joke and give her information about the habits of the great, gay, vicious world, at the same time interspersing these remarks with sentences on corruption, depravity, thoughtlessness, waste and so forth. He was then "young Johnny" the snarling, prejudiced, morbid youth of the home study circles, but he did not look like that Johnny. In that Johnny's place was a handsome, sardonic, and well-dressed man, who was at once closer and much more indifferent. Teresa, from his rather naïve and loquacious letters, had not foreseen this change. She had read of the secret life of man, rather that life taboo in polite letters, which is the greater part of man's life; his true sorrows, sufferings, his hidden loves and his loves' crimes; the excuses of the wicked, their vanity, the poor things they struggle for; and that complete ideal life which everyone dreams of alike in his vices and virtues, and which she tried to get in Jonathan; love, learning, fervour, and the flush of success. Jonathan now not only knew of all this, but had experienced it or seen it in his friends.

She had never met vice or crime in her life, or achievement either; he had. Jonathan spoke little of the stuff in books, that was all gone; now he was always illustrating his remarks with: "I saw in Paris—" "I know a chap who—" "Phil Noble told me that when he was in Heidelberg—" He was years ahead of her. Towards evening they sat down on the grass in the park near Marble Arch, side by side, while they interchanged remarks from time to time.

They were tired and discouraged, for nothing had come up during the whole day about their personal relations, either in the past or to come. Jonathan, with a patient air, kept looking across the park, which is like an open uncropped field, towards the dream-like architecture of Knightsbridge, full of turrets over trees and top corners like escutcheons in stone. His capacious white hand played idly on the grass between them. Teresa put her hand on his, and at that moment an unfortunate memory came to her of a walk round the bay, long ago, when he had repulsed her. As if remembering it too, with the same air, as if she were dirty or vulgar, he coolly withdrew his hand, placed it on his knee and then began brushing a small speck off his clothes. They continued the conversation as before, except that each felt indifferent to the other, and they were glad when it was time to suggest eating again.

Hurrying through the falling night towards a restaurant, through the miry streets, through the turmoil on the pavements caused by working people rushing in all directions on foot, to get home, they pressed close to each other and felt humble and more friendly. Jonathan began to think of her little front room, that he had not seen, in Torrington Square, and of another little front room he had seen somewhere, probably like it, with half-drawn curtains, a lamp, the gas-fire going, a kettle on the gas-ring on the hearth, the shilling gas-meter and the rest of Bloomsbury one-room comforts, the cupboard, the bed with an Indian spread over it in the background, a pale-headed girl attentive to his confidences; and she could see, in the distance, at the end of the long broad street, as if in tomorrow, a splendid sunlit forest, birds trilling in black wooded hills, early afternoon and the two of them, with packs on their backs, coming down some glade. Still visible in the distance was the town in the hollow, where they would rest in the evening—some imaginary part of Wales.

He felt, too, that he must give her time. She had just come off the boat. Every word she said and thing she did, the responses she missed, showed that she had had very little to do with men, and little to do with free love, and he thought that perhaps after all, it was because she had been thinking of him. He knew she loved him, but it amazed him that it was such a dumb love and inexpressive. In her letters it was not dumb and he had imagined he would be frankly wooed by her, a pleasant thing to think about in his quiet bachelor evenings, as he sat with a book and pipe in his arm-chair by his warm gas-fire. "You may think me a quiet fellow, not much of a Lothario, but *one* woman——" But her timid, stupid behaviour made him think of two letters he had received about her, from two friends. One, over a year back, was from an old high school friend who had never gone to the university, but who had always admired Crow in his successes. He had married some suburban girl, who knew one of Teresa's married cousins. He wrote:

Congratulations, Benedict, the married man. I hear that some cousin of Belle's friend, Madeline, is going over to join you, so I suppose that means wedding bells. Why not? In the old days we used to worry about being tied down, but we didn't know what it all meant. I'm happy enough.

The second was from his old friend and admirer, Miss Haviland, who had broken a silence of two years with a casual note in which occurred, with her old-time whimsy, the remark that her friend Teresa, *their* friend Teresa, had yet another year to work before she would be able to sail and it reminded her of one of those princesses in Grimm or Andersen (which was it—perhaps both) who had to make twelve shirts out of nettles before she could be liberated, or else stayed thirty years in an oven and came out at the end to meet a prince, both still young and superlatively fair. With malice, she continued:

There is quite a trend towards emigration here, but why? Tamar, Clara and her friends are going. Elaine was said to be going to London, too, but seems to have given up the plan. But here I stay like the penny-plain I am, and see dull sights— adventures to the adventurous. Well, young man, look to your laurels! Are you still accumulating them in your bottom drawer, or are they rusty? I expect, a year or two hence, returning migrants—at least some will return—to bring me news.

He could answer, said Miss Haviland, but she would write no more, he had correspondents enough, this was just a flash in the pan; she was an old and tired woman and had nothing to say to a young fellow full of ginger like her old friend, comrade, and competitor, Johnny, who would soon be Dr Jonathan Crow. "Splendid old girl," thought Jonathan tenderly, "but my withers are unwrung. I have not harmed man, beast, plant, government or woman."

"There's a nice place called the Arcade where I've been once or twice, let's try it."

They continued east along Oxford Street till they came near to Southampton Row, when he stopped outside a restaurant with a revolving glass door, and palms, bottles of wine, and napkins in the window. Teresa clutched his arm, saying anxiously: "Oh, not in there, Johnny, look at the wine—it must be very dear." He laughed, pushed her through the revolving door.

"I haven't the money with me," she said anxiously. "Or rather, I have, but it's where I can't get it."

He steered her to a table not far from the door and sat her down with her back to a long mirror. It was a long narrow restaurant with two rows of white-clothed tables. A waiter appeared with a cloth over his arm and a menu in his hand.

"Oh," cried Teresa, "Johnny, I have never been in a place like this. With you, I am really seeing the world."

Unsmiling, he raised his eyes to her, then looked up at the waiter and took the menu. "Hors d'œuvres," he said, "we'll choose the rest later."

"What are hors d'œuvres, really?" she asked.

"You'll find out," said Johnny.

"But what are they?"

"Ask no questions and I'll tell you no lies," in his crustily humorous mood.

She smiled timidly.

People were coming into the restaurant. The waiter came back with two plates with a bit of fish, a bit of eschalot, a bit of sausage on them, and asked what they would drink. Teresa drank water and Jonathan ordered a beer for himself.

A couple entered and sat down near them but nearer the door, the girl facing Teresa. The beer came, Jonathan lifted the glass, took a long drink and put the glass down. Then his face changed, broke up, and he leaned forward and said hurriedly: "Did you see the girl who came in, with the dark hair, and the beret?"

"Yes. I can see her now, she's facing me."

"Look, do you mind if we go now? We can eat at my digs or pick up a sandwich. I can't stay. I'll explain to you."

"Of course," said Teresa, with a frightened face.

He called the waiter, said that his lady friend did not feel well and pushed her rather gracelessly down the carpet strip to the door. Once through the door, he took her elbow, guiding her along the kerb, across the street, towards Bloomsbury. When they had crossed the street, out of the breathless silence, he said: "That girl with the dark hair—she's so exactly like a girl I was in love with last year, I thought it was Gloria at first. I felt too upset, I couldn't stay. You didn't mind, did you? I wanted her badly, madly, I felt as if I couldn't do without her. I hadn't seen anything like that before, I suppose that was it. She was a real good sort, a good pal too, and stunning, nifty, chic, what do you call it, *chic*, eh? She had it." He sighed. "She was beautiful and modern, she smoked, took liquor, knew her way about, all without turning a hair. I was in love with her. I ought to say, I wanted her more than I've ever wanted anything. I wasn't her speed, she had pots of money, or her old man did. She went back to the U.S.A., and she's there now. She said she'd write to me but just one or two letters, you know. She had other fish to fry. I suppose I didn't appeal, a poor student with no future, too much of a humdrum fellow. Well," he sighed easily, and dropped the sorrowful tone. "I soon stopped fooling myself with that gilded dream. She'll take someone with a yacht from Princeton or Harvard, or one of those six-foot fellows."

After a few steps, he added gently: "That girl was so like her, my heart flew into my boots. I just couldn't swallow."

"It's all right," said Teresa.

"She went back when she heard some fellow she was keen on was engaged, to wrest him from the other woman, I suppose." He laughed. "You women!" He became gloomy. "I wasn't good enough for her."

"Don't say that, Jonathan."

"Why not?"

"Because you're good enough for any woman."

Jonathan spat. "You think she cared about qualities? Qualities are for the poor, what she cared about was money—if I'd had money—well, I haven't. God, for a moment, I thought she must have come back."

"If she had, what then?"

"Well," he laughed boyishly, "I suppose it would have been

the same as before, I would have run after her like a hungry cur. But it wasn't. I'll never get over it, I believe. Two letters, answering mine, then my third letter unanswered, my fourth unanswered, so I stopped." He spat into the gutter thoughtfully, straightened his shoulders which had become bowed and laughed. "Have you ever seen three cats? One runs away, the other runs away after him, and the third thinks she is running away and runs after her! Not that Gloria ran after men, she didn't have to. She had it."

Teresa thought: "Men—or women—are egotists by nature and lovers must bear with them, for lovers are made differently, we are made patient, it would be cruel to quarrel over such a naïve confession." So she said: "Well, I'm sorry you have been so miserable, I had no idea."

"No, I couldn't write about it, but Gene and Bentham knew and of course gave me the good advice you don't take. They told me I'd get over it, perhaps I will some day," and as he said it, a note of sincerity deepened, as if he no longer felt it so badly.

She was puzzled by him. He was neither thick-skinned nor cruel, but he must be very ignorant of women to harp on this subject with her. She thought: "He is immersed in his own sufferings." Now, in the dark, passing through side streets straight towards his home, "Golly, I was so tired last night," he began, and went on to sweeter confidences, about himself in all the past years, when he had been here and lonely; these won her back so that she began to believe in him utterly. His adolescence had been prolonged, he said, others had grown up, finished their theses and gone away, most had positions, some had names already, many had wives and children. He was left there, abandoned in the cloisters, a derelict of the stackrooms, biting his nails, ruining his eyesight, and wretched; a youth, a boy in some things. He suffered so much through this woman and through other women. She was thinking, "Only chastity, for that is the name they give the abomination, brings such suffering, a man or woman who has loved physically cannot suffer as much, because even if he or she is deserted, she has loved." He had never been able to take that fatal step which would make him like other men. Purity, hard work, fear of disease, timidity with women, all the racial, Freudian fears had him, he was their thrall. And what woman had ever truly loved him? Girls giving chase to man had been after him, but had not loved him. Perhaps if a woman really loved him, he would make the step. He was dreadfully lonely in London and to this loneliness was added sexual desire and fear of perversion, attractive as a side-stepping of the whole issue. He did not wish to become a pervert or a neurotic and to go about cut off from the normal man. These confessions aroused in the young woman feelings of tender and passionate love. She suffered for him and for herself. The idea that he had had no luck at all, and his teeth had been chattering, his body starving and his pathetic love rejected all these years gave her an almost mortal pain. She could love and did love him, but to him she loved, she could not give the gifts of love. She felt bitter towards herself. She believed that he confessed this to her to apologize for his coldness, and she conceived that what he was setting out was a plan for the conquest of his neurosis, even though it might take him long dreary months to achieve it. She must wait for him.

Although she had no such fears as he, she believed every word he said about himself and vowed to devote her patience and understanding to helping him. He spoke about the summer and Wales and, "Wales will solve many problems," said he.

Just after this they reached his house. He would not let her go up, but went up himself to get her bag, brought it down and carried it to her place in Torrington Square. He put down the little bag and, putting his arm round her waist, kissed her on the lips. His lips were warm. She had always heard, on the ferry going to work, that the proof of real love was the kiss, that a man who received a kiss with cold lips from his wife began to think of divorce. A little smattering of ferry-lore, garbled like this, was all she knew of love in practice. Therefore, her first thought was, on receiving this extraordinary kiss, "He loves me after all." Half fainting with the shock and this conviction, she broke away from him with a low cry. Meanwhile, the young man picked up her bag, handed it to her and said in a low, intense voice: "And tomorrow you will come to my place and we will spend the day together."

"But what about going to the agency?"

"Go there in the morning and come to me about lunch time. About one."

"All right."

"Good luck," he said nonchalantly. "Oh, and take this," and he thrust an evening paper into her hand. "I don't think there are any good jobs advertised in the evening, but you can look."

"Well, I'll look."

"That's a good girl. Adios!"

He turned about and went off rapidly. She trotted upstairs. She was afraid to think of what had happened to her, that she was loved; and she looked carefully through the paper, at the advertisements first and the news next. She remembered that she had to find out about recent political affairs and she began at once, but nearly all the names were foreign to her; the journalists threw names, cities, occupations, diplomatic tangles around like feed to chickens. She cut out the political columns and put them to one side, thinking that after a week she would collate them and find out what it was really about. She picked out one set of names to begin with.

She arranged her things for the next day, got out her letters of recommendation, and did not dare to think of Jonathan until she turned out the light and got into bed. Then she buried her head under the pillow and nearly suffocated with laughter. She seemed to be swimming in a bounding wave. She felt young, beautiful, healthy, just as if she had been lying in the sun all day. She thought, he loves me, it's true, after all. Tomorrow they would be happy all day. They would say they loved each other, they would talk, prattle of the future, the days would go on reasonably, one after the other, till summer came, when she would leave her job and they would go to Wales. In Wales, he would overcome his fear, or prejudice, perhaps later they would marry, but in any case they would be lovers and it would be a love without troubles, because they had both been through so much and sacrificed so much beforehand. Sliding towards sleep, she thought, I have never known sleep until tonight.

And Jonathan, plodding homewards, felt his blood run cold when he thought of the girl who had come into the Arcade Restaurant. It had been rash of him to go there with Teresa when he had been there once a week for a long time with that woman. He thought pessimistically of the sombre-faced, dark-haired, oval-jawed English girl he had seen in the mirror when he raised his beer to drink. She was not at all like Gloria, he felt ashamed of that lie. But she was a queer and dangerous woman to a weak man like himself. She had a contemptuous and yet venomous and

321

lurking glance. She was pasty-faced, really ugly, had a whining voice and no taste in clothes, and her face was as if smudged with soot in the distance, with long folds of flesh and black marks under the eyes. Had she some liver disease? Yet she got one man after another. She could whimper and cry and she could laugh boldly in a hoarse voice that made him shudder and attracted him loathsomely. There was something horribly seductive about her, a compound of hate for men and obscenity. At the first sight of her a man was put off, the second time he was attracted and the third time he began to flirt with her dowdily, while secretly trembling.

Jonathan got to his room and sat on his thin, sagging mattress. He pressed his hands together and thought vaguely about the dull, vicious life a lost man like himself led in London. Return to Australia and join the old circle of friends that he knew too well? Become well, sunburned, easy-going, turn into a well-known minor personage and forget this visit to limbo? Go to America? To outsiders, he talked a lot about going to the U.S.A., but he had no plans and had written to no one except Gloria. He hoped, when he got through his essay and got his degree, that things would turn out well of themselves, as before. He tumbled into bed after these unpleasant thoughts, and the morning was well advanced and his packing almost finished before he remembered that he had an appointment with Teresa at one o'clock.

27. Five or Six Unopened Letters

MRS BAGSHAWE's student lodger had not meant to carry so many of his papers with him to their new address. He had left all his notes, old essays, half-done "impressions" and letters to the last, hoping to weed them out and reduce them to half the bulk. There was a wad of his letters that Elaine had returned to him without being asked. They had given him the idea for a book, about himself and his affairs, "Letters of an Obscure Man". He was amazingly fluent when he wrote letters, could pour himself out, especially to women, and surely it would be a fascinating little study, both literary and psychological, the complexity, yearning, misfiring, of a dull but tender affair that was not quite love? It was something he kept turning over in his mind; perhaps he was a literary man with a slight gift for satire. Taken all in all, his essays in sociology and the rest were more literary than scientific, but with that twist of the mind and scalpel humour that a knowledge of science gives. There lay Elaine's letters to him and his to her, and a pile of others. He had done nothing more on this project, but he was preserving the material. "I kiss and tell," he said, rollicking with himself, as he squatted over these last papers. "Or do I—all unconscious, kiss *to* tell?" If he became a literary man with a casual, delicate, effete, worldly-wise tone, all questions would be answered and he need work no more, especially if he combined it with an inoffensive teaching job of some sort. For that, any place would be handy.

The letters which he had been reading lazily, smiling, frowning, touched by his naïveties, were scattered round him when he heard his bell at one o'clock.

"Welcome to Château Bagshawe," he said, waving his hand impressively over the manuscripts. "I stayed up late reading and got up late, nothing is done and we move tomorrow." He had not risen from his haunches, but handed her up a large photograph, saying: "Do you recognize it?"

"Yes, Elaine."

"And this," said Jonathan, smiling, yawning, diving into the box and bringing out another of the same size and sort.

It was her own. "The same photographer," cried Teresa. When Jonathan had asked for her photograph for his second Christmas abroad, Teresa had found out the photographer considered elegant in town and gone there. It was not a coincidence that Elaine had gone to the same man. Jonathan handed her a third photograph of a girl, this one a postcard size. Tamar's round face and large bosom bulging from the brown background, and then there were two others, a black-haired girl in two poses in two photomaton pictures.

"Good heavens!" said Teresa, bundling them and handing them back.

"Oh, they come in from time to time. Elaine has a sweet face," he said quietly, looking down at this photograph. "I was very fond of her in those days." He shook his head, tore the photograph across and dropped it into the waste-paper basket. "I hate to do that, but it's no use cuddling old memories, is it? I've done too much of that. Look, letters I've never read—some of them must be a couple of years old." He rummaged in the letters spread out in front of him. "Look, one from Cooper, what's the date?" He peered, slit the envelope, looking up at her, pulled out the paper, glanced at the date, flung it aside. "Eleven months ago!" He showed her an envelope without an address, except for the name, Jonathan Crow, Esquire. The envelope was covered by designs making a rebus, and had been delivered by the London Post Office. "Look," Jonathan said again, waving five or six unopened letters in his hand. To her horror she recognized two of her own. "One from Tamar, isn't it?" he said. "Yes. One from Cooper? I don't know—no, from Clara on Cooper's typewriter—I say, I did fall by the wayside, that must have been during the Gloria epoch —yes, so it was!" He slit another envelope carelessly. "And three of yours. A bit of a waste of time, it all was, wasn't it?"

"I suppose so," said Teresa.

Jonathan scanned Cooper's letter for a moment. "Some bit of scandal," he said, frowning, and threw it into the basket.

324

"And three of mine, I suppose, from the Gloria epoch," said Teresa with a slight laugh.

"I used to put them in the drawer and tell Gene to open them if he wanted to," said Jonathan carelessly, "for he used to take a kind of brotherly interest in you, but it seems he didn't read very many," and as if in surprise, he looked at the envelopes again. "Three of them—by Jove—perhaps there are more!" He looked but found no more. He selected one of the letters, smiling gleefully, and slit it with his finger, his eyes fixed merrily on her all the time. He began to read, gave her a glance, grinned slyly, read the letter through, while he squatted still and she stood in front of him, silent.

"Hey! What's this?" he cried, leaping up, and standing in front of her, with the trunk between them, he read—

> "What artisan this night,
> Blew in dark glass and fine
> To imitate that bright
> And sullen glance of thine?
> Along the foaming beach
> The tide pours dark as wine,
> Dead flesh, black blood, and each
> Is white and black of thine.
> In the fierce southern night
> The whirling meteors shine,
> Like eyes; I am blind to sight
> But what seems thee or thine."

Sore with shame, the girl stood with bent head hearing those words which she had got out with such labour spilling over her head in the very voice of the man who had forced her to write them. She said in a low voice: "Don't, Johnny." As she went on to read some phrase from the letter, she tried to snatch the letter from him. He whirled away, laughing, dashed out of the door and across the landing to a window beside the maid's room out of which he leaned, shouting the poem out over the garden and casting back at her bright glances. She rushed to him, excited, laughing, the paper tore in her hand, he grabbed it back and it tore again. He finished the job by tearing the letter into small pieces and letting them float over the garden.

325

"Look," he said calmly over his shoulder, "Lucy's little boy." She looked over his shoulder to see a child of about fifteen months, sitting on a shawl in a paved yard. A few bushes grew near the paling fence. A clothes-line was strung at the end of the yard and the maid, Lucy, herself, in a grey cotton dress, was hanging some clothes on it. The pieces of paper were still floating in the pale sunny air and settling near the doorstep. The baby put out his hand to catch them and began to whimper. Jonathan whistled to the baby, who looked up at once and laughed. Johnny turned round, jollily. "Look at him, he's a bonza little nipper, I'm very fond of him. That's my doll, that rattle thing, I bought it for him. Hey, Bobby! Bobby!" he fluted. The baby looked up again.

Teresa went back into the room, picked up the two letters still unopened, opened them to see what other things might have gone into this blind alley. There was a time, during two or three months, when she had written him a few verses, not always sentimental, some limericks which she considered rather gay, some couplets. Jonathan at once returned, took the letters from her. "They're mine! Fancy opening someone else's letters!"

"Give them to me, Johnny."

"No, I want them." He held them up high.

She reached for them, and he at once dropped them and embraced her with such force that she could not breathe and stumbled on the trunk. It was clumsy. She planted her hands on his shoulders and tore away from him. He returned at once, with a downward glance, to his paper mixing. She felt ridiculous and sat down silently to watch him.

Jonathan seemed to be reflecting as he put the papers in the box. He said, at last, gently: "My mother was a servant, too, I suppose that's why I feel for Lucy so much, it's just a kind of transference, as they say. The poor little kid's fond of me, I suppose I have a streak of the paternal in me—perhaps there is a paternal instinct after all," and he chuckled up at her, affectionately. He went on earnestly: "You see, she never loved her husband, he helped her out in a tight spot, though."

"I see." The girl felt ashamed of her flurry and of the letters. Johnny went on talking gently of all kinds of sorrowful subjects; poor people, unemployment, seduced women, London's bad climate, tuberculosis, rickets, the black slums that lay back to back with respectable middle-class houses, "tenanted by vice and sordid interests in antimacassars", the horrible creatures that could be seen any night of summer sitting on the doorsteps of these high-rent warrens of noble landlords, those creatures more like large rats than men, the result of years of starvation and joblessness. "I can never forget where I came from," said Jonathan sternly. She flushed to the roots of her hair and answered nothing. "I am shamed," she was thinking, "shamed. Hunger, brutality, human beings dying and I—" She was silent until he finished, silent when he helped her with hat and coat, and it was with the humblest respect that she listened to everything he had to say. When they passed a girl hanging on to the arm of a Grenadier Guard, he said: laughing through his teeth: "Why do women admire those lazy devils? Is everything dress with women? The uniform, eh, it works! I remember Gloria was mad over some tennis champ, it was his uniform, I suppose, of flannels and racket. It's a general rule, isn't it, that those in uniform do the least work in our society?"

She said: "You see, work is dishonourable, no one would want to wear the uniform of work in our society."

"That's true. Honorific leisure in gold galloon."

"Or rather," she said, "work creates its own uniform, everyone can tell who goes to work just by looking."

He laughed. "And can you tell what I am just by looking?"

She looked at him carefully. "Do you know, I would say you were a very unusual kind of teacher, but a teacher—perhaps it's because I saw you first that way."

"The soul-twisting pedagogue," he said with a sneer. "Is that me?"

"You helped me so much," said Teresa.

"Who can does and who can't teaches," sneered Jonathan. "Well, not a very savoury subject for a schoolmaster and I suppose," he said in a biting tone, "that is what I look like. Let's drop the subject. I have a programme. We'll carry it out, right to the bitter end, for tomorrow I suppose you'll have to look for work in dead earnest."

In the evening, at Sadler's Wells, an operatic repertory company was giving *Lucia di Lammermoor*. Teresa had never been to the theatre, let alone the opera, and was terrified at first, thinking that she needed evening clothes and a cloak; but he reassured her, and gave her confidence by saying that no one in particular went to this opera, it was for students, stenographers, young artistic people without money just like themselves.

What pleasure he gave her! They were going to sit side by side for hours, then the walk home, the good nights—she looked forward to the pure happiness of the evening. She found this evening in the confetti dusk of the theatre that she had never loved Jonathan. She had never thought of his person, nor his being near, not even of touching his hand, nor of life in common. If she had not been austere in thought, she would not have been able to support his absence. Now she reproached herself with it. "Here he is, handsome, brilliant, tender, lonely, and I have never given him a real thought. Here too, all the time, it has been my own passion, me and nothing else. I never really tried to understand his wants or his world. No wonder then that he is dissatisfied with me." She now thought she had wronged him by not cultivating her physical passion for him, for this was what he wanted from her. He had waited too virtuously until she came to him, all this she had passed over like a prude. She had amused herself with writing verses about his soulful eyes and the rest of it, and worried about her own fading looks, but of his life, body, all that he had tried to put to her in his laconic way in the last thirty-six hours, not a thought. She had always been convinced that if she allowed one carnal hope to steal into her ideas about Jonathan she would never have him and would be punished with eternal celibacy by outraged Fate. Now she saw this was hanky-panky. Yet how could she have lived, if she had desired him?

This evening, for the first time, she stole glances at his shoulders and feet. He was squarely-built and looked powerful. His loins and shoulders were heavy, his hands dangled like those of a clumsy but strong man, he moved his feet awkwardly. His clothes were of heavy cloth. His hair was half grey, his coarse skin contained many London smuts.

Every time the name "Lucia" was sung, he looked quickly at her, smiled and nodded, and when they went to the bar, which opened during the interval, he explained that he was going to buy the records of this opera and learn those bits to tease the maid Lucy with. She had been "furious" with him when she found out he was going to *Lucia di Lammermoor* this evening, just to learn the music to tease her, and "even more furious" when he had told her the story of the Bride of Lammermoor, especially the bit about the half-naked child gibbering in a corner. Leaning on the bar, he went off into a peal of laughter, thinking of Lucy's wrath.

"Why was she furious?" Teresa puzzled.

"Oh, she thinks I tease her too much, she says I'm too much of a tease, she says she wouldn't go to any house where I was. I've played a few tricks on her in my time, you see!" Teresa laughed with him. Exhilarated by the good humour, the goblet of beer, her best dress, she began to put on airs, to imitate the haughty accent of some people she had heard passing, a succession of groans, sighs, yawns and lispings, according to her; meanwhile Jonathan looked at her attentively, opened his eyes and remarked: "That is the first time I've heard you speak really well." She stared. Going back to her seat she realized what he would have liked in herself—something like Gloria?—a well-born girl educated in a private school with an insolent accent, a high voice, superior to himself? Could he possibly want that? To her, then, she saw with a dawning cunning, Jonathan would offer his traditional coarseness, the sorrows and colour of his low origin, the strong, much-commented story of his origin, which he put about with such a jealous love. Now she understood why he had been angry when she said she had been a nurse on the boat, why he had been impatient with her stories about the stewards, the glory-hole, the night watchman and even the disappearance of her brother Leo, who never had been found and whom she often seemed to see in the streets, in a poor man's get-up. This strange love of the gutter in himself was his sign of potency. To him, rich women were potent. Very much astonished, she sat down beside him and looked at him cautiously through the dark. Her pulses leaped, how strange he was; complex, perverse, ignorant of himself! She drew in her breath sharply. He fascinated her.

At the same time, she revolted at the idea of making herself "a lady" for Jonathan. Besides, it was as if he had set her yet another task before she could win him. He was good, alluring, pathetic, suffering, but why so much struggle, why did he put such a value on his apathy? Despair, even anger, flashed in and out of her; did he intend it to be her fate to dangle after him? Why should she attempt so much when he was resigned to mediocrity, clung to it, in fact, with a fierce grasp? But she repeated one of her favourite phrases to herself—"hug a bad bargain closer"—and she could not give up the fight, not after such a beginning. Who knew if it was not coyness, awkwardness, mere flirtatiousness, in a man who knew nothing of women? If he was a virgin with women, he was bound to be recalcitrant. He himself had said he had a long row to hoe before he could get over his neurosis.

At the same time, sitting next to him, smelling his clothes and his skin and hair, she involuntarily formed a new resolution. As soon as she got a job there, she would go at her languages again, get a French certificate, learn French stenography and cross the Channel, so as to not to be dependent on his favours. When she made enough money there she would go to the Sorbonne as she had planned, and Johnny must make up his mind about her and women. This was a freak of her nature. Disappointed by Johnny, she instantly sought yet another country. She turned her back on failure.

During the second act, she dropped her gloves to the floor. They both bent for them and her newly-washed hair fell over his face. She heard his gasp and felt him hold his face there, in the hair. When he straightened, he put out his hand and grasped hers. When he released it, she put out her hand and put it on his knee, where he held it. For so the affair went on; after all the coolness and despair, it went on in the expected way.

When they came out, they walked the mile or so towards their part of Bloomsbury. The theatre had been packed. They left behind them the soft rustle, the hush and the stirring, the scent, the joy of being packed in with thousands of other young creatures like themselves. It was heaven to walk along the roads with that rich and delicate memory in their heads. The young man liked the opera, had a good musical memory and kept singing fragments of the music. What plays had she seen, operas gone to? None. What books had she read? None but what she had written to him about, the classics, the old guard of library shelves. Had she seen the ballet? No. What had she been doing with herself for years? She laughed. "Nothing, just slept through them, I suppose."

He shook his head, looking gaily at her. "Women are a sleepy crew, I believe they could spend their whole lives in an arm-chair."

"You won't catch me doing that."

"No? Then what *will* you do? In a typist's chair, eh? Is that it?"

"Heaven knows," she muttered.

"Did you go to that Discussion Circle downtown?" he pursued.

"No, only once, I thought they were just trifling. It seemed to me they were there just to meet each other, the men and the women I mean."

"Ah," he said, yawning, taking off his hat and scratching his poll. "Perhaps you're right there, there's a lot of he-ing and she-ing in those study circles." He grinned. "Well, why not? Male and female created he them and there's been the devil to pay ever since, as they say." He began to chatter, as they bowled along, in a gay, interesting tone. He had gone last year or the year before, perhaps, to a play about summer camps and discussion groups. It had been a hit. Why? Because every audience was either tickled in the funny bone or jobbed in the hypocrisy. They raised the roof. He had been to see it three times, so had the boys. It got them in a soft spot, since most of them, men or women, were going to teach. Some irritated young teacher in the play said that men and women could never understand each other in argument, there was only one place they could meet satisfactorily—in bed. At these words, said Crow, a shudder, a groan, a cry ran through the audience, laughs downstairs and cries of "Shame!" from the middle rows, while the young people upstairs mostly sat silent and quivered. "Shame!" cried Jonathan lustily, in the Pentonville Road, imitating them. "Shame, shame, shame." She heard him laugh shortly. "The hypocrites, shame, shame, listen to 'em. Shame on them who won't allow what all of us have in our minds most of the time, and they, the ones who cried shame, are the ones who do it."

She did not argue with him.

"Someone," continued Jonathan, "says the relation between the sexes is based on food. Savages only have their women once or twice a year. Their food is poor. All that about the love-life of the savages is balderdash for mammy-pappy consumption in the suburbs. Love is an illusion, love is food. Savages don't love. It's due to an overplus of calories, we eat more than we need, and what we admire in women is a seductive window-dressing of stored fat. Some of the superfluity goes to the brains, the nerves, and we get love, sighs, groans. Primitive love—raw fish, Cockney love—fish and chips, middle-class love—cottage pudding, the grand passion—roast duckling and port wine." He flung away

331

from her with his loud laugh and came back, slyly laughing, saying: "And how does that theory strike you?"

There was a clear sky overhead. The fresh wind had pushed away all the rain, the streets were cool but not sharp. It was pleasant again. There was a new warmth and a slight scent in the air.

"Spring," said Teresa, nosing the air.

"Spring," grumbled he, softly. "In the spring a young man's fancy lightly turns to thoughts of—well, for me, it's beer and bread."

"I got here in the spring," she said, turning to him. "Do you know, I can hardly believe it, I meant to get here in the spring and I did!"

He kicked a stone, kicked it again, said: "And in the spring, what is your idea of fish and chips?"

"Love? For me, love is quite different."

He approached and asked softly: "How is it, to you?"

"To me—" She found it hard to speak. She felt as if she were being blown out into the dark sky. She became grave. "You see, to me, it's quite different. It's like that sky, with the stars in it, dark, but longer than our lives and serene, distant, something that is there, even when we don't see it. But I do see it. I know it's there at all times. I am in love when I am not in love. I have been in love my whole life."

He gave her a side glance, made a dissatisfied sound. "That's romance, but when you found out what it was really like—the dirt, the lust and carnality, the fish and chips?"

"What was different? I don't mean I really thought it was the sky, I always knew it was flesh and blood."

"What is it," he looked sideways at her, peering closer with teeth and eyes that flashed, "then what is it, but flesh—and blood. What is it? What else? What does Shaw say in *Candida*—'we could not dwell on the mountain-tops for ever'."

"Well, of course, it is flesh."

"It is more than flesh, it is all they say it is, the bestiality, and yet we're tormented by the need for it. Spiritual beings!" He gritted his teeth with an odd ha-ha.

She was at a loss. He said: "As a girl of course you thought that, stars and all that, but later—when you found out—what was your feeling?"

She cried irritably: "When I found out? I know the flesh is life. We don't pray out the flesh like nuns."

"No, but you don't admit we like it." He went on hurriedly. "Women like self-delusion. But when—you read Krafft-Ebing, Freud, Havelock Ellis." He came nearer and spoke in a confidential tone, but shamefacedly: "I remember you wrote in some letter—" He hurried on. "When you found out what it was really like?"

"When I—" but she fell silent, puzzled by his insistence. He kept murmuring like a boy asking for something and yet she had answered him.

"It was different then?"

"A letter?" she repeated.

He laughed shortly. "I expect because I was brought up on the streets and only saw the seamy side. We were a bunch of ragged kids, filthy, hard, we were lively enough, though," he said cheerfully.

One of his strangest aspects to her was his changeable humour. In one speech he would be sardonic and naïve, cruel and gay, tender and cold. His voice, a fine one, altered all the time and was full of natural devices, slurring, drawling or sharp, keen notes, an irresistible burring of affection, soft laughs and pauses of self-blame. She loved his voice. She paused, listening to the last notes trailing away. She smiled to herself at the sound. "It doesn't prove your idea is right because you were a bunch of ragged kids." She laughed outright.

"Or yours—" After a pause he looked at her amiably, and said: "Well, I stick to my guns, that the only way you can settle an argument between man and woman is in bed."

She remained cool, but recoiled as if she had seen blood lying on the pavement.

He became cocksure, told her about his friend, a fat, jolly bumpkin named Bodkin, a Canadian student, now a journalist, last year at the university, who found his landlady with her hair down, in her nightdress, standing on the staircase with a candle in her hand, and watching the door of his room. " 'I thought I heard a noise and I was afraid of burglars,' said she, when Bodkin came, and she stepped down with a sly smile. Bodkin gave her a slap on the bottom and sent her up to her room, telling her not to walk in her sleep."

333

Crow declared that was the way they lived. They had little obscene books, went to low music-halls, and he had been along, as company, but when they went to other places, he deserted them. They had a good, rapacious, libertine, lusty, cordial yet low life and it did not please him. He was a good fellow but there were things that were not for him, not that he was a prude. Waitresses were a danger, though they could not help it, poor girls, and unlike coarse Bohemia, he could not cohabit with maidservant and landlady. Besides, he always paid his rent! And so he must suffer. To the poor student, society said: "Be vicious or suffer!"

Some time passed before another word was said. When they were near his room, he said: "I am very interested in migration problems. Bodkin was saying we are in one of the great migration ages. Now, perhaps, with the new intensities of nationalism, migration will cease for a time, but after the wars are over, mass migrations ordered by governments will doubtless take place. When we have a congress of nations, the era of migrations will begin for good, gone the little home and rent-paying. How will this affect landlords? Workmen pay rent. If they are moved from areas of unemployment to labour-scarcity areas, it will disturb the rental values."

"Yes?"

"I'm studying it at present, for I haven't a decent subject for my thesis and I thought I might take up migration. It's a bit speculative, that's the drawback. It's interesting." He was speaking hurriedly and without his usual tones. "One of the most interesting points is the free production of artificial restriction of population."

"How?"

"Well," he laughed nervously, "the prohibition or permission of birth-control for example. When migration is no longer possible out of England, they permit birth-control. See the point? For instance, does a higher wage produce more children? Or do the really poor people have more children, so that paying lower wages increases the population? See? Figures tend to show that with ease, parents become lazy and wish for their personal comfort as well as extending the childhood of their children. Poverty is perhaps better for the birth-rate. Pretty anomalous, isn't it?"

"Yes."

"Do you know anything about it?"

"No, I really don't."

He startled her by asking with solicitude whether she had read any of the literature of birth-control. She said she had seen some pamphlets but that she couldn't bring herself to ask the man for them.

"Why not? That's silly."

"I know." She blushed.

He was silent and withdrew his arm. "You ought to know."

After a time she said: "Can you get me one?"

"No," he said sulkily, "no, I can't."

In silence they passed King's Cross Station, crossed the road and stood in a paved drive-way between two small shops, a chemist's, which exhibited some of the very pamphlets in question, and a tobacconist's which had put out two racks of coarse penny postcards. The girl was afraid he was going to make her go into this chemist's, and in misery, wanted to run away. She began to tremble. A house was set back, behind the chemist's and was entered by a door under an arch some way down and a lamp shone there. It looked pleasant and quiet. After hesitating, Jonathan put his arm through her arm again and asked her if she was going to be busy the next day looking for a job. He offered her his typewriter to type her applications. There was unemployment and many people were on the dole. She might have a hard time. If she needed help in getting to know people, she must call on him.

"Oh, I can hold out for a few weeks—don't stand here," she said, pulling him out on to the road, for she was strangely upset by his standing there in the alley and had begun to tremble without knowing why.

"Tess, come over to my room now and I'll give you the type-writer." She said at once: "All right, but won't your landlady mind my coming so late?"

"She——" said Johnny ironically and bit it off there.

As they approached the crescent, the light mist was gathering. A policeman stood under one of the two lights. All round it was very gloomy, there were few lights on; it was late. A few lights shone in top rooms where the maids were going to bed.

Jonathan laughed, enveloping her once more in affection. "It was that bobby," he said, "and round that light—oh, yes, I never told you that—or did I? Burton? Burton's a kind of wild, snob-bish chap writes wild vile verse, mostly unprintable of course—thinks he's Byronic, too." He laughed obliquely but apologetically. "Flings up the mud wherever he goes, refers to himself as a stallion, a bull." His voice had changed to a grinding tone. "And then he's a hedonist, he says, wine, women and song."

"Like the Student of Prague, do nothing and go to the devil? The devil never paid for such bad bargains, I bet."

He did not hear her but hurried on heartily. "He throws away his little bit of money, he's got an allowance, gets into drunken brawls, got into the clink several times a month when I knew him and we all used to go down and get him out. He pretends to have a violent antipathy for the lads in blue, so he insults every bobby he sees. He's had ever so many run-ins with them."

"Bobbies and bushrangers," said Teresa crossly.

"No, he's really wild, a bit cracked perhaps. Once old Gene Burt, my chum, took the blame for him when Burton was on the point of getting expelled for getting up in class and singing some obscene music-hall song with gestures—" He laughed thickly.

"Here we are," said Teresa. "It's terribly late, perhaps you could bring it down."

Crow, looking away, said roughly: "No, come up, we'll make some tea, the place is in a bit of a mess, but you'll forgive that." He continued about Burton on the way upstairs, softly but with bravado, for he felt Teresa did not like Burton. "He has some-thing—braggadocio, do you call it?—but an almighty blackguard. One time we were coming from his rooms where the fellows had been on a binge. He went up to that policeman and danced ring-around-a-rosy. Burton chirped in a flossy voice and called him Oberon, King of the Fairies. The bobby smole a sickly smile at first, then he got pink round the gills. When Burton kissed him and changed hats with him, he got furious and said he'd run him in." Johnny shouted with laughter and closed the door of his room suddenly, putting his hand over his mouth. "A big burly chap, you can see him, a fairy——"

She laughed without understanding the joke. He made her sit down while he made some tea and told more tales about the almighty blackguard. As he put the tea in the green teapot, Jonathan turned round, tittering. "It's the type, you're born with it, others couldn't get away with it. You know that line of Ibsen's, what is it—you know what youngsters say—'What would you rather be?' Ibsen's hero says, 'It is better to have that kind of luck called *virtus*, the only real virtue.' Well, Burton hasn't precisely *virtus*, the word's not for his kind, but he has something, he has made a religion out of being uncontrollable, a real wild young bounder. What worse can happen to me than devilling for civilization, says he. Not bad, eh? Devil or go to the devil. Every authority in the world, says he, rests on force, violence, and crime. Even your humanitarian wants a revolution, which implies force over some portion of mankind. Civilization rests on the police, authority equals crime. He isn't a mere scapegrace," he put in, seeing her expression; "and he has the courage to carry it through. Of course, he's good with his fists." He laughed gently. "He swears he'll end up a lord, with his theory, by blackmail alone, says he. And if not, look at the fun I'll have had, he says. Oh, Lord!"

"Unworkable, though," said Teresa with melancholy. "Well, not for a man." Jonathan was getting cups from the old wooden cupboard.

"Let me do it," said Teresa. "Have you got a cloth? It's inky here."

"You see," cried Jonathan, planking down the cups, "you see! It's this habit of prettiness, the clothes you wear, the hair, the whole thing, a tablecloth—isn't a bare table good enough? My mother had a bare table and she ate in the kitchen—manners, frills and feathers—that's why you aren't as free as Burton! A cloth! No," he said with a dash of good humour, "no, we won't have a cloth. I'll always eat without a cloth." He moralized a bit more about the habits of women, but sat down pleasantly enough, pouring out the tea and telling anecdotes of his room-mate, Gene Burt, who had ruined himself by getting tied up with the cornstalk, the bony country girl. "Gene was full of self-deception, he wrote a poem about a prostitute he saw one wintry night and said if he'd sold it he'd give the money to her because she had produced it. He sold it—one guinea. Gene needed it for debts. That's your sentimentalist, isn't it?" He laughed, his spectacles shone. "Typical, isn't it?"

He came back to Burton after a moment. "That Burton, though —I could tell you tales about him all night, someone ought to write him up."

When they had finished the tea and he had forbidden the washing of the cups, he asked her to stay a few more minutes to chat before she made for home, and he reverted to Burton with the doggedness which was characteristic of him. He called it worrying a subject.

"One afternoon, we were over at his room, it's just a den like this, not much better and much untidier, the girl they have there is a slut. We were drinking tea—we were all at low water, no smokes, no drinks and Burton was fretting—no excitement. Jesus —the frowsy place he lived in! The beds weren't made and it was three in the afternoon. He almost never paid his rent, it went in booze, but he had got all the women in the place tangled up with him. That was common talk, he didn't hide it. It was a rule he had to tumble every woman, he said, it always paid some dividend." His voice had taken on the strange harsh note again.

Teresa sat stiffly on the edge of the bed. Crow was droning on. "He was fidgety and presently yelled out the window for the servant to come and make the beds. She came in, a blond, biggish girl of twenty-three or so, with big legs bare above the knee and rolled cotton stockings." He said these words in a lascivious voice, as if there was an erotic meaning in rolled stockings.

"He told her not to leave a gentleman't room in that state, he had no intention of letting his friends sit in that muck and if she was a sow and liked her wallow, he was a gentleman and he was damned if he wouldn't see that he got some cleaning up done around him. The accent, the tone, he put on! Squire Jones, oh, Lord! We simply roared with laughter. It tickled you to see Burton, unshaved, dirty, bearish, who had obviously slept in his clothes, and only half-sober after a spree, being so toney! What a character! He painted up the year for us, last year. The servant-girl grumbled that she had the whole house to do and that he had lain in bed till midday, so that she couldn't get in. He shouts: 'Gentlemen lie in bed till midday but you couldn't be expected to know that.' *'Gentlemen!'* she says, getting mad and giving us all a dirty look. 'Well, do it now,' says old Burton, in a finicky cold tone, the very image of a noble lordling, and when the girl flushed, you could see he was pleased he had got a rise out of her, for she was an old hand. She began to pull the clothes off the bed and growled, a fine gentleman and a fine thing to see a girl set on like this, she knew what sort of gentleman, we'd never so much as seen a gentleman, unless he was the judge in court, and we'd soon see more of the same sort. It was a regular comedy." Jonathan tried to control his laughter. Then he became serious. "Gee, what a *type*, as the French say, coarse but apparently *sympathique*."

He continued confidentially: "Anyhow, the girl turned back to make the bed and Burton, furious at being answered with his friends there—for I suppose he half-believes that rot of his—brutally pushed her on to the bed and invited one of the chaps to attack her. They were scared of course, so he tried to, but she twisted out of his grasp, although he's a hefty fellow—but shaky just then—and she rushed out of the room, bellowing. What a shindy! Wow! She ran downstairs, crying for the landlady. Do you know what the fellow did? A regular gallow's-bird. You've got to admire his almighty nerve in a way, none of us would have had the brass—it was this gentleman pose—he leaned over the stairhead and shouted to the landlady to send the girl up to do his filthy room, if not, he'd leave that very day. That was pushing his gall pretty far, considering what he owed in rent there. What was his pull? The old lady was sweet on him, I imagine. The girl was crying downstairs and telling what was the matter, and Burton yelling upstairs. What a din! Some of the fellows were making a row too. Would you believe it? The landlady didn't believe the girl and sent her up, to satisfy him, and he raped her, and a couple of the other fellows did, but we just sat and grinned. What a scene!" he finished reminiscently, but with a sidelong glance at her. Seeing she took it ill, Jonathan swung away to the window with a bitter contemptuous look and looked out. "The bobby's still there," he said coldly. "He does his beat and then stands under the lamp. Is he afraid? We forget that bobbies are working men too!"

He shrugged gloomily and turned away from the window, his face full of trouble. "I saw one poor chap going down a side lane to a side door of a ham-and-beef shop, to get a sandwich, and looking around anxiously to see if the sergeant was about. Then he bolted it down and went back to his beat, wiping his mouth with the back of his hand." After a moment, he burst out laughing and looked candidly at her. "It was the copper out there made me think of it! How I laughed that night when he called him a fairy and said he'd crown him—I suppose I had had a drop too much, and it doesn't often take me that way."

The girl said nothing.

"You see," he begged, "it's not really as bad as it seems, they all live in pretty much of a mess here in Bloomsbury, and she probably belonged to him, you know! You don't find female virtues in Bloomsbury! And I admit Burton's a terrible scamp, but he goes on the principle of anything once. So do I," he added morosely.

Teresa had been sitting with bowed shoulders. Now she raised her head and read his face, but she saw what she had seen before, the agonies of self-engrossment, a lonely, ingrown life, eyes that kept gleaming with secret pangs. She was swept by a flush of passion for the strange face. Seeing her face soften, Jonathan went on: "The whole thing is just to express contempt for the underdog, I suppose." He became depressed. "Give them one drop of blue blood in their veins, or even an imaginary drop, like he has, and we're just talking cattle to them. As for your romance, ideals, love—" he snapped his fingers and his eyes snapped—"your Tom Joneses didn't trouble their heads about romance or even fathering their illegitimate offspring, no state, no God, no women's honour, no such animal. Who knows if it isn't best to take the world with a swagger? The advantage of being born rich is you're born without illusions. I bet you had to struggle through a lot of disillusion, the sort of hocus-pocus they ram down our necks in school, before you realized that there was no such thing as love?"

Teresa murmured: "It certainly exists for me, at any rate."

"For me," said Jonathan, "it is lust." He said "lust" as a murderer would say murder.

"You don't know."

He hung his head. "No, that's right, I don't know. Civilization pops its hard facts at me and I don't even pop back. The bitter truth!" He stole secret glances at the girl from under his long lashes as he stood drooping. He flung away a few steps. "I have never loved a woman."

"And the girl—Gloria—the American girl?"

He sat down morbidly hunched in a chair, his arms resting on the table. "You're right! You're right! I did love her, I suppose, I wanted her, I know that. But she didn't want me. The whirligig of time brings in its revenges." He withdrew his arms, raised his

face and smiled faintly. "I suppose I'll get over it some day."
Teresa looked at him with despair, looked at the floor, and seeing
her gloves there, picked them up. She got up. "Well, I must go.
I've got to get up early."

Jonathan rose deliberately, and came a step towards her, facing
her. "I've been looking for a woman," he said downright. "It can't
go on. Whatever my philosophy—philosophy comes a cropper
every time it hurdles a hard fact—I can't get on any longer with
the hard fact of lust. I need one to love me to save me from the
desperations of—a bachelor's life." He flung his hand out, gestur-
ing at the room.

"Find someone! There are so many women, Jonathan."

"Well, I suppose, some day," said Jonathan with his twisted
smile. He made a half-turn and picked her hat up off the bed.
"Well, I'd better let you go to bed."

She supposed his timidity had overcome him again, so she took
her hat without speaking and opening her bag, took out a little
mirror to fix her hair. Jonathan took the mirror out of her hands,
just touching her finger-tips, and turned it thoughtfully in his
hand. "Do you think it's an instinct, I wonder—coquetry I mean.
Do you dress for men or for yourselves?"

"Köhler's apes in the Canaries put leaves and rags in their
hair," said Teresa. She was trying not to cry.

"Vine-leaves in their hair! Our simian grandmothers! Well,
you'd better be off."

He went downstairs with her. At the front door he let her pass
out, drew back smiling casually, holding on to the door-handle,
inside. She turned, expecting him to kiss her but he said: "Well,
ta-ta, and good luck for work tomorrow", but nothing about seeing her again and he did not offer to accompany her. As she
walked away, the long slit of grimy light round the slowly closing
door could be seen from any point in the place, and in it, half a
male figure. The policeman saw it from the other side of the
crescent, where he stood in the murk, and noticed the female
figure hurrying away. There was only the sound of her footsteps
anywhere.

Jonathan watched this figure till the curve of the crescent hid it
from sight. She did not live far away and could easily find her
way. He must not be too attentive to her, or she would think she
had him and would be unmanageable. There was a soft, cold

look on his face. It gave him a bizarre pleasure to imagine her walking alone, perhaps a little frightened, through the streets and strange squares to her room. What was she thinking? That love was like the stars? He burst out laughing uneasily, as he shut the front door. "She doesn't see the Freudian symbolism," he thought to himself as he climbed the stairs. "Jonathan's not love's fool. Well, that is that."

But he was unhappy. What way out, what end? Sordid his nights were and empty the days. He looked around him mentally, with fright. After sitting for a while in the ghastly light of the bulb, he got out writing materials from the drawer of the ink-stained table and swiftly wrote to Tamar in Australia.

How unhappy I am! I never knew that I could be so miserable. I see no end to anything and no good in anything. Do you? If you do, write to me and put me right. Have I been studying too long—do you recommend me to get out of this and go into commerce? I might try and wag my behind a bit and get a job out of doors, anything is out of doors, compared with this life of landlady's bedrooms and the U. The grey-haired student! Remember that old codger used to sit on the front benches of my class? I'm a grey-haired student now. Give me advice, Tamar, and whatever you say, I'll take it. I've never been so miserable, not to speak of the misery of the weather and the dullness of the people. Do you remember Teresa Hawkins? I heard she is here and looking for a job. I haven't seen her yet. Are you coming here, or is that just a rumour? Write to me, I'll answer.

He heard the maid coming upstairs, rose hastily, and flung his door to. He was in rebellion against her, afraid of her and her world because they had had too much of him and he was sluggish in their dusty embraces. But the maid, when she was half-undressed, came and knocked at his door, and when he saw her, standing in her untrimmed calico, her hair down, he was so excited by his misery that he went with her again, although the last week he had made up his mind to end this kind of life.

28. You Do Not Stand Anywhere

TERESA went upstairs softly, entered the long single room which she was to live in and sat down near the window. She felt that she was a woman. How remote was the foolish, romantic girl who had got on the boat six weeks ago! Although it was her second night in the Old World and things had turned out so strangely, she did not look at her room, nor think of the city, but she thought of entering offices tomorrow looking for work, or of Johnny and his new fine room, and of finding the address of a language institute she could go to as soon as she got a job, to polish up her French. If Jonathan kept her waiting too long, she would go to the Continent. She thought for a while of Jonathan's mystery. How did she offend him? Why did he blow hot and cold in one sentence? Coolly, she recalled all the unspoken misunderstandings of the last two days. What joy was there in them, except one kiss? She had not the clue to the unwinding of his sorrows. As for the kiss, now she understood why The Kiss was so much written about, she had thought till now that it was overdone in books and that in polite literature it was a euphemism for union; not now. She took the pen and ink she found in the bookcase, and wrote a letter to Crow, asking him where they stood, for she acknowledged all had not gone well between them that day or on the previous day. Either she had expected the wrong thing or she had not understood him, and she wanted to make it all clear. Was he fond of her? Did he look forward to any "association" between them? "I have put too much into this to be left in this state of bafflement," she wrote. She went down and posted it, then looked at the room and arranged her things.

In the morning she went out to the agency, which was not far from there, the one pointed out by Jonathan (which she thought would bring good luck), and was offered a job in the City in a street off Leadenhall Street. But when she heard from Miss Portfoy, the strange, rough agency woman with lacquered hair, that she must pay in to the agency the whole of her first week's salary, she suspected a trick on the innocent and refused the job, going out again and spending the whole day walking from one part of the city to another, visiting agencies in streets as far apart as Sloane Street and Holland Road. When she got back at night, she had learned much. All agencies took the first week's salary; all the people crowding the agencies for jobs thought it fair because it encouraged the agent to get a better-paid job; the wage offered her at the very beginning was, by some fluke, the best in the whole city, the very highest, a freak, a rare chance and perhaps untrustworthy, a mistake. All other salaries for women in her position, that is women with experience and a language or two, were a pound or two lower. Some of the women waiting were impressive, good-looking, well-dressed, and had worked in the great cities of the Continent for years and knew much more than herself. She was very anxious and sorry that the office was closed when she got back. She would have to go to it straight away in the morning, at eight, if it opened then. She ate something in one of the teashops Johnny had shown her, much troubled that she had not gone for the job that day, and now beginning to wonder what Jonathan had answered her; for by now there would be an answer, she supposed. She knew that mail was delivered in London at short intervals.

Under her door was his well-known envelope in his well-known writing, the very same that had appeared regularly on the mantelpiece at home for years, but now how strange it looked with her new address; tender, thoughtful, beautiful, just as if he had thought about her in her room as he wrote the address. It was as if a lamp had been lighted in London for her, and she felt that her home was here now. "Where he is, there is my country," thought Teresa, putting the envelope on the table, taking off her things and putting water on to boil. She changed her shoes, brushed her hair, looking at herself in the mirror, all the time thinking of Jonathan's affection and keeping back the pleasure of opening his first London letter. Then she sat down, smiling, slit the envelope, saw that his new address, Malet Street, was on the paper; and read:

Dear Tess,

Yes, I think it is better to be frank too. Gene Burt turned up this morning, just when I was puzzling over your note and his opinion is like mine, tell the truth even if it hurts. Here it is then. I do not love you, I never did and I feel no affection for you. I am willing to be a friend, and if this suits you, it suits me, but if not, let's cry quits! There is nothing to understand in me, I am just a "plain ordinary" academic hack with his way to make and not much chance to make it, except in the rut. Believe me when I say this—there is nothing to admire in me.

As to where you "stand"—this is a strange expression and indicates that you have hoped for much more than I had ever imagined. As far as I am concerned, you do not "stand" anywhere and am afraid you have made a great mistake. Come and visit me if you wish—though not for a few days, for I have moved with my landlady as you can see. It was only decided this morning when she agreed to take the servant Lucy with her, for the sake of the child. I stuck to my point and she gave in. She made the excuse that the reason she had not wanted to do so was the child, though what that shrimp could eat! But my rent is assured to her in any case and I have promised to get a fellow at the Union or elsewhere for any vacant rooms. She offers me a fine ground-floor room with a garden view in the back for only a guinea a week, dirt cheap, as you know, and I may as well take it. So, in a word, I am very comfortable, happy, you need not worry about me. In a few days, come and have tea with me; that is, if you can take me the way I am. If not, then not and so be it—Amen says,

JONATHAN CROW.

"Good," said Teresa, putting the letter down gently. "Good. All right, I'll take it decently." A little later, when she went out to get something to eat at the nearest teashop she was surprised to see her face so white in one of the olive-lighted mirrors. She felt as if she were walking on the points of her toes. She was suffering and yet she felt lightsome, she heard a faint little singing. The whole thing was a surprise. A face pale as death was no more a fiction than The Kiss; it was all true. For some reason, she now thought, "We should go through a bit, know what things are really like before we criticize artists." She ate, noticed people

345

looking at her and knew it was because she was so white. She went back, pulled a book from the bookcase (the room was sublet by an artist away in France) and found it was a book of alphabets. She took the pen and ink and began carefully practising the half-uncial alphabet. All the time she kept up a busy conversation with herself. "Well, I lost the gamble. That's the result of putting all your eggs in one basket. Everything is true. Cats like catnip, chickens fly the coop, dogs bark up the wrong tree, you should keep at least one egg in your hat. I made a holy show of myself. He's perfectly correct. I'm a fool. Who could love me? Do I love myself? Then why should he? It's coming it a bit thick, it's shooting with the long bow, to expect other people to love me. I tried to impose on him with my ranting and travelling and romance. Poor boy! I hunted him with love and couldn't help him out of a hole. He's looking for a woman and I disappointed him. I can't help it. So much the worse for you, says nature. So much the worse for the woman who can't get a man. I don't care, says nature, die, then. There are lots of other women, plenty for my purpose. Too bad, eh? She put sixpence into the lottery and expected the great prize, she lost—now we must have tears. Not at all. I won't cry. I'll do what I have to do, I'll work. I'll get away to France. He won't see hair nor hide of me again. Heavens! We take a chance and if we lose, it's not fair! The usual thing. Well, Fate, you and I played a long game, you won, that's all. Someone has to win, isn't that funny, I never thought of that before. I'm a fool. A fool and her folly keep open house. Naturally, I will die. 'Wilt thou not, Jule?' The pretty creature stinted and cried: 'Ay! Thou wilt fall backward.'"

Feeling the tears rush into her head, she pushed back the book and began to walk up and down the room, thinking quickly. Honourable suicide, thought Teresa, perfectly wideawake and more rational than usual during the night, is a brave death whereas impulsive bloody suicide is a coward's death. Here for years I've been thinking of myself. I'll work myself to death. In that way it will take me months and I'll be able to do something for people, I'll have the time. Her memory and reason raced at top gear, but she kept running over the much-masticated phrases of his letters of the past years, and their whole conversation of the past two days, scrutinizing every word, the ground they had covered, closer and closer, like someone who had lost a purse and goes back and back over the same ground, by morning light, at evening hours and late at night, hoping to see what was fallen and was lost. What phrase had she lost of his, what look of hers, that had changed the course of events? Something must explain this mysterious man. Melancholy, distrust, even hate in him, she could understand, because thwarted and twisted love would explain it all, or lust, as he would put it; but why did he change from jolly to cold and from kind to cruel in a moment? Why did he advance and retreat, talking about sordid sexual affairs and then pitying humanity, in one breath? She searched through their talks, looking for the clue. Some things she rejected. She threw aside without looking into it the talk about Burton's rape, this was a schoolboy's scurrility; she threw aside some anecdotes about the old woman, Mrs Bagshawe, this was a mere bad habit of gossip he had got into, living in low company in Bloomsbury; and a quick, tart question of his, like "What's wrong with homosexuality, anyhow?" and "What's wrong with self-abuse?" remarks put in to shock her, silly, pointless things that any pert boy might say. What was wrong with their natural disaccord; each wanted the other for years and now he had rejected her, and at once. She must have displeased him. She knew that she was sad-looking, frail and sick, that she looked paler still because she used no lipstick or powder, but wasn't he always inveighing against girls made up and girls dressed up, wasn't he always miserably sorry for poor sick girls who had worked in shops? Nevertheless, she knew how poor she looked and she knew she ought to be rejected for this, if only their friendship had not been on another plane, the commerce of ideas and a mutual help in their lovelessness. She passed the night in wild excitement, as if in the wild dawn of an uninhabited planet.

In the morning she got up, dressed, had a little to eat in the teashop and went at once to Miss Portfoy's. By the one chance in a hundred, the job in the City was still open, three girls had been sent there and rejected. She hastened downtown at once, blundering into wrong buses since she did not know the way, and the little streets of the City are hard to find, but she reached the building, a large modern place built of Dutch tiles and steel and hidden away in a maze of streets, not far from London

Bridge. In an hour she had reached there, was in, was out again, walking down the streets in a state of surprise. She had got the job and was free for a week to amuse herself. She would start work on the following Tuesday morning. She telephoned Miss Portfoy and had the day before her. She knew no one. She went to Chalfont St Giles, Harrow-on-the-Hill, and Richmond in Surrey, on the three succeeding days, not sleeping at all on the two nights in between. In the days, forcing herself to observe the country, strange and antique as something on a tapestry, in the fresh air, she still, without forgetting Jonathan, seemed to live; in the evenings she walked round the streets and near-by squares of Bloomsbury in the thickening air, noting the direction of streets, learning the buses she must take to work, looking in more sordid streets for rooms to let, where she could cook for herself, walking to famous places like Piccadilly and Charing Cross; and towards the end of her walk, she would come back by March-mont Street where Jonathan had lived until a few days ago, or by Malet Street, where Jonathan lived now in a new life un-known to her. She pictured him in the life he found comfort-able and happy, reading, musing, with her quite forgotten, re-signing himself for the time being to his solitude and of course with his eye and ear out for a woman who would love him. When she reached home, she read, practised her alphabets for no reason, and when she got into bed, the strange orchestra with fifes and tympani began to beat, which had been getting louder and more furious each night. Through the sounds and the open mouths of this orchestra whirled the broken and blurred images of Jonathan and herself in their eternal maddening conversa-tion, that had lost its clue; whole paragraphs of his letters stood bodily in front of her eyes, repeated so often that they had be-come incarnated, and again she heard the story of Burton, of the policeman, and the happenings at the opera, his singing about "Lucia", Lucy the maid shivering on a bench in the park some-where, Jonathan going through London pitying beggars, buying meals for hungry women—one brilliant world of Jonathan blow-ing in a storm of sunshine and bitter fog—and the rigmarole of her buffoon Odyssey torn out of privations of which Jonathan knew nothing; this last thought she hastily put away, ashamed of all she had done, because every hour of it was only a stronger proof that she was a detestable thing, an ugly, rejected woman, distorted and lost. She was lost. It was enough to know this once. No sooner had she settled this than the figures, the conversations, the tympani would whirl up again—and she would cry to herself: "But why? But why?"

The third day, she went downtown, climbed the Monument, took a bus, climbed the tower of Westminster Cathedral and at the top met a little French girl in blue who was busily identifying every landmark in London from a large map she held with difficulty against the breeze. This girl, named Francine, lived in Bloomsbury in a "ladies' club" not far from Teresa and spoke little English. She was *petite*, vivacious, sharp, a false blonde, with charm and a quick temper, a delightful person. They came part of the way home together. After leaving her, Teresa felt a twinge of conscience. Poor Johnny! He had invited her to tea and she had been so rude as to leave him without a reply. She ate again in the teashop and hurried home to write him the couple of lines that would show the poor soul that she was not resentful. She walked slower, climbed the stairs slowly, reached her room and sat down at the bare table for a long time. She got down the pen and ink, wrote: "Dear Jonathan, I am sorry," held the pen for a long time staring at the paper, got up, paced the room, and could write no more. I ought to, she thought, but I can't.

This night, the fourth night, nevertheless, she slept soundly and in the morning had more courage. The week-end passed, Monday, her last free day, and she still could not bring herself to write the letter to Johnny; it seemed an impossible task to do what she had done a thousand times. She went to the movies, roamed the galleries at the British Museum, looked round for a rental library, anything to escape the temptation which was haunting her and the fear which sickened her.

When she got back from work the next day, a lovely warm May day gilding smoke-blackened house faces and jutting cornices that were already home to her, there were two letters for her lying on the table in the hall. The middle-aged woman in a Paisley dress who ran the house hovered with bent back in the background as she took them. She had already recognized one, with a terrible emotion, the other was from Francine Bernard. But what could Jonathan be saying? She tore it open and tried to read it as she went upstairs. What he said was:

349

It occurred to me this morning that you wanted my typewriter to type applications on. Unfortunately, I'm using it just now for my work, but if you want to write a letter, come round any time, morning or evening, I'm in most times except at meal times. How goes it? Still the same spirit of adventure? Any jobs in view? Don't forget to let me know how you're getting along, you know I'm always interested. If free, anyhow, come Friday at eight-thirty, I'm free then. As ever,

JOHNNY.

She read it calmly, trying to crush down the joy she felt that he had called her back. She read it several times and sat thinking. He was sitting too, in his fine room, with his servant to wait on him, and he missed her. She thought of him with more caution and wondered what he would do if he did not get an answer. Would he care at all? Wouldn't he just let it drop for ever, out of pride? If she did not go to see him today or tomorrow, she would go on Friday she knew, because the ban had been lifted. She sat there in the dusk dreaming over him and his odd ways. He was too offhand. It was a bit too much to pretend that nothing at all had happened. But a curious smile crept into her face; was he a little shallow, flighty? The temptation to turn such a defeat into a victory was too great. She would see him, would take care; and take care, Johnny! She wrote him an enthusiastic letter about her well-paid job in the City and her new French friend, Francine, and mentioned the trips she had taken into the country and elsewhere. When she went down to post the letter, the smiling bent woman was hovering, bobbing about the hall-way again.

"A young man called for you when you were out this morning, he asked if you were in. I told him you had gone to work. He told me not to tell you, but I thought I would," the woman ended softly, estimating the girl's emotions, as she watched.

"Ah? What was he like?"

"He had a black hat, he wore spectacles, a dark young man."

"Ah, thanks," said Teresa, smiling involuntarily, and walked out. But in the street a thought struck her, why did he write the note about the typewriter, when he knew she had a job already? Just idleness—or an excuse?

29. Regular Nights

JONATHAN opened the wide green door himself and stood back for her to enter the polished hall. A fine staircase ran upwards. The second of two oak doors was Jonathan's. As they came across the hall, the swing-door opened to allow Lucy, the friendly maid, to appear for a moment. Then she shrank back.

His was a lofty, large back room painted dull soft green and full of green shadows from the garden and the neighbouring trees. A high window took in sky and tree-tops. The room was furnished in dark wood with bookcases. A cabinet in the wall enclosed the wall-bed.

He saw that her lips were darker. She had used lipstick, for the first time. He hid a smile and coldly congratulated her upon getting a job so soon, when there was so much unemployment about.

"Pure luck," she said. "Amazing, unheard-of luck. Imagine that the man himself only arrived in London last week. From New York. He really looked for a Colonial because he thinks the local English despise Americans." Soon he knew all about the office and about her trips to the country. She stirred him out of his sloth. He felt uneasy at her activity, wanted to go where she had been. He had never been to those places in his three years in London, he lacked companions, she must go with him and show him the country. She had enterprise. She flushed with joy. "With pleasure, Johnny," she cried. He had never seen her so lively, her expression had surely changed. The lipstick? Women are funny cattle. Or because he had brought her back to him? He smiled slowly and sat down facing her, leaning back comfortably in a large arm-chair, his boot on his knee. She sat with one arm on the table, in a straight chair, playing with the finger of one of her gloves, and babbled about the partners,

Quick and Axelrode, with whom she worked. Quick lied for his partner over the telephone. His partner, for instance, seemed to be mixed up with some women. Teresa had never considered honesty as anything but an absolute law, a command from which there was no appeal. Now, said she, she began to wonder if, moral questions aside, there wasn't a greater plasticity of mind required for lying. A dominant race, for example, did not lie, because it had the whip; a weak race lied, the old lied, timid children lied. Only the strong, the powerful, those in the saddle, did not lie, or rather, they need not, but they did, just whenever it suited them—for example, secret diplomatic documents.

"I have been a child and thought as a child," said the girl. "I cannot now condemn liars wholesale." She mused: "Yet, when I was a child, and of course, we used to talk about this at school, being obsessed with moral problems like all children, I used always to say I'd lie to spare people's feelings, in other words, even then I recognized a law higher than the absolute honesty."

"New man, new morals," thought Jonathan. "How woman-ish." But he smiled. "The law of perfidy?"

"Yes."

"Convenient!" said Jonathan.

"And I realized another thing this morning, in the office," she said. "Whatever I want to do, becomes a higher law with me. I am a very moral being, you see. For the first time I understand what is meant by calling puritans and the like, English people, hypocritical. Of course, they are not hypocrites, it's the singular corset of Protestantism, which forces them to invent religious law even when there is none, don't you think?"

"You're right," cried Jonathan brightly, smiling at her.

"The whole thing frightens me, how many things do I completely misunderstand then? Imagine that I had come to England to find that out!"

"That's the way we're educated," Jonathan said. "So you thought you were moral and you find you're immoral!" He laughed. "How far does that go?"

"Pretty far, I expect."

"Yes." After a silence, he forced himself again. "We don't know ourselves." A silence. "Is it worth while finding out?" A silence. "Eh?" said Johnny.

"Of course."

"Is it worth while going to the end of the night, digging in deep and finding what we really mean, our needs?"

"What is worth more?"

"And so you are getting to know yourself?" Johnny said and to Teresa he appeared to be shifting ground. She said listlessly: "Yes."

"Know thyself, a difficult injunction. We don't like what we find."

"I do," she said.

"Yes? And what do you find?"

"Don't ask me, you don't want to hear that, Johnny. I'm going to write a book about Miss Haviland."

He was full of pleased surprise. He challenged her. Why Miss Haviland, why this, why that? Wasn't she letting unnecessary sympathy run away with her? Miss Haviland had wanted an academic standing, she had it. Wasn't she a drybones? Imagine that for an ideal! When he heard she had her various sheepskins up, framed, in her study, he was through with her. Fancy bits of papers, signatures of pedagogues meaning so much to her. He had always thought she had more in her than that, but when she told him, almost with tears in her eyes, that these meant so much to her, he was finished with Miss Haviland. "Ridiculous old dowd," said Jonathan. "Isn't that a schoolteacher for you?" Teresa said she was a sheep-shearer's daughter, cooking for twelve men when she was just a child. She had studied at night, with the insects crowding the kerosene lamp. She came to the university twelve years late. Desert suns, privations, her force of character and application, also, had taken away all her feminine charm, she had no money for clothes. "I never knew," said Jonathan. He was silent for a moment. "But what is there to write about in that. It was ridiculous, wasn't it?"

"What she might have been if she had had a chance!"

"The might-have-beens—that is romance, you know. I worked with her for years, she had a second-rate brain. What had she? I'm afraid I don't subscribe to the mute inglorious Milton theory. It's easy to build on a negative, nothing contradicts you." He rolled in his chair, laughing. "I remember her, her hats—the men used to wait to see them! And you and she became great friends," he said condescendingly.

"She had to sew them herself."

"Is a person a hero to you just because he is a sort of failure?"

He laughed, got up and went to his bookcase, picked up a book, looked at her over his shoulder and came back with bright eyes. "That reminds me, she wrote me a letter about two years ago, telling me about our mutual friends."

"Yes."

He put his hand on the back of his chair and stood looking at her. He said whimsically: "She seemed to have some idea that you were coming over here for me."

Teresa looked at him proudly. Jonathan knelt down on the rug and bent over the teapot, on the gas-ring near him. "I'd like to know how she got that idea," said Jonathan.

"She was very fond of me."

"You told her you were coming over for me?"

"I dare say she knew."

He had not lighted the gas. He raised his eyes, sat up, keeping his eyes fixed on her. "Did you tell her we were going to get married?"

She flushed, got up, looked down at him. "You know I didn't. How could I?"

"Someone got the idea," he said in a hard tone.

She was silent.

"It's all right, it's all right," his tone was softer. "Only I'm not going to marry and I don't want anyone to get the idea that I am." She went to the window. She heard him laugh, he rattled something and came after her. He stuck his prominent chin over her shoulder; still flushed, she flinched and looked round angrily at him. He smiled at her. "Don't be silly," he said. "I know you always knew I wouldn't marry. I didn't mean it was you."

"All right. I didn't."

He laughed outright. "Well, what harm, if you never did?" he asked merrily. "Well, that's that, let bygones be bygones." He went briskly to the kettle and lit the gas. "Did you see that new book of Lemski's? I got it hot from the press. We had bets as to who'd get a copy first. I know a girl in a bookshop off Kingsway who promised it to me, she got it two nights before it was published from some reviewer and she slipped it to me. I hurried to the Union the next day, waving it at them. They were all furious. Chambers, that's the fellow I want you to meet, a big hulking pug, with specs, he only keeps out of the ring on account of his eyes, Chambers swore he'd been sleeping with a prof's wife, to get it first—generally does get them first. I wonder if there's anything in that tale? What do you think, eh? I told them I got it off a woman, anyway! But I wouldn't give her address. Anyhow, next day Chambers beat me to it, for he had a copy of Banquet's review, Banquet's the prof who does the reviewing, and he had an opinion all complete. I had only swallowed four chapters!" He laughed heartily. "I didn't even kiss the girl in the bookshop." He turned round to her, very merry. "But I dare say I will have to next time." He grimaced. "She has glasses, too bad, but I've got to keep up her interest. They'll trail me one of these days and my influence will be gone. For if any of those fellows offered to sleep with her, my brief day would be over. I don't think it's ever happened to her yet. In fact I'm sure. She was telling me, with bated breath, a mystery story of some man that followed her home. I bet she looks under the bed at night, fearing yet hoping." He got up, dusted his knees and flung himself in his chair. "Sit down, Tess, why don't you?"

"Shall I make the tea?"

"No," he said firmly. "I'll make the tea."

"Let me."

He frowned. "Stay where you are."

She looked at him with frightened eyes. He smiled reluctantly. "There you go, with your womanism."

She sat still while he made the tea, arranged the cups, and poured it out. He pushed the milk and sugar over to her. "Help yourself."

"You don't understand," she said in a troubled voice, "that I used to wait at table at home, on the boys and father, I mean."

"You won't wait on me."

She drank some tea. He said sentimentally: "Mum ate every meal of her life on her feet, I believe, looking after us boys and Dad. Sometimes, when we were alone, she sat down, but that was because I was her Benjamin and she felt she didn't have to put on swank with me." He laughed and poured himself some more tea. "We had oilcloth on the table," he continued, "and why not? Table-cloths mean laundry, meaning some servant or extra work for the woman."

"I wouldn't mind that extra work."

"The woman clings to conspicuous waste," said Jonathan, "because it has become unconsciously associated with servants, a fine house and all that trumpery, in other words, with ladyhood." He continued good-humouredly: "That's another of your illusions, you see, that you ought to get rid of."

She laughed. "But I won't." She got up for another cup of tea and he let her get it. He told her about Gene Burt and his wife, about the bad plumbing in his present house, not yet fixed up, and about an admirable woman on the top floor who lived there with a man without being married; both put their names on the bell on the front door. He asked her if, since she was going to write a book about a woman's life, she had read *Sister Carrie* by Theodore Dreiser. She had never heard either name. "You must," said he. "There's a woman there who lives with a man for years without being married."

"*Sister Carrie?* All right."

"Gee, I admire women who have the courage of their convictions and live freely with men," he proceeded.

She was silent, considering this state of affairs with fright. How did you go about it? What propositions were mutually made? She imagined them all as beautiful, lusty women with strong limbs and money of their own; handsome, tanned, rowdy women, full of words and arts.

"I've heard of women who proposed to men, told them they loved them or wanted them, or whatever it was," said Johnny.

"Do they here?"

He said loftily: "They're more advanced here. Could you?" he inquired, seeing her pause.

"Certainly!" Suddenly, her convictions, the force of her youth came back. "I always said I would. I'm free."

"And did you ever?" he inquired with a crafty smile.

"Not yet. But I would."

"Good on you," he said. He got up indifferently and took the things off the table, to put them on a tray at the far end of the room.

She said: "We love like men. But men don't like it. You see, they're backward too."

He carped, from the end of the room: "So you only don't do it because you're afraid to lose the men, eh, is that it?" He came back, smiling. "You see, you are yourselves responsible for the kind of lives you lead, you'd rather be an old maid than be frank about your feelings."

She was so startled that she got up. "That's quite untrue. I'm frank about mine." She looked straight at him, full of her integrity.

He smiled to himself, put his hand on the back of his chair and slid into it, one leg over the arm. He continued: "I saw Miss Hamilton, that's the girl who lives with the man, on the stairs yesterday morning. She's a fine-looking girl, clever, well-dressed, very much the girl about town, she said hullo to me. She evidently feels nothing about her position. To me, she's the modern woman, she's what women ought to be."

Teresa imagined that he was falling in love with Miss Hamilton. She lowered her gaze and sat down, defeated. Jonathan said softly: "I was thinking it all over, and I thought that perhaps you ought to come and see me on regular nights, say two nights a week, Tuesday and Friday, could you do that?"

She muttered: "I suppose so."

"It wouldn't be too much for you?"

"Oh, no, it's too little."

"It wouldn't be too much for you?"

She looked up.

"To see me on that basis?"

"No," she said mournfully.

"The other nights I have friends who drop in, classes and so forth, and I thought that instead of writing each time, it would make it easier if we had this understanding, just to meet twice a week."

"It would make it easier for me, Johnny, till I get used to not seeing you. It was a bid of a shock to me——"

"What was?" He asked it with interest but cautiously.

"You know."

"I don't know," he wagged his head innocently.

She said no more.

"What was?" he repeated.

"Well, you know, I thought you did say something about—for instance, we were to go walking in Wales. Now we're not."

"No." He frowned.

It was getting darker. She could see the white patches of his clothing and hands and face; to him, she was a dark shape against the fading window.

"That's all off?"

"That's all off."

She said softly: "Can't you get someone to go with you?"

"No." He was sullen and she was afraid of him.

She continued: "I thought we were going at one time; when I came here and found things were different, it was a surprise."

"Yes, things are different."

Their faces and forms, so new to each other, at their present age, were getting darker and softer and of grander proportions.

"This is what I meant, it would help me until I begin to look elsewhere for friends, for of course I will find other friends."

"You have already," he said harshly.

"Who? Oh, Francine." She laughed. "Yes, she is charming, pretty, friendly."

"I should like to meet her."

"If you like."

"Will you bring her over?"

"Yes, any time she can come."

"I'd like to see her," he said softly with a strange tone and motion that suggested the licking of his chops.

"You'd like her," cried Teresa. "She's pretty, dainty."

"The proof of the pudding is in the eating," said Jonathan, laughing and stirring in the dark. "Bring her over and I'll see."

She ran on, spilling all she knew about Francine. She had been brought over by a merchant, on the promise of a big salary and week-ends in his house in the country with his sister. He engaged a state-room for her on the Channel steamer. Teresa guessed that they had made love together. Francine said: "When I got here, no more mention of the week-ends, except that he said once his sister was a curious woman, changeable, and that she was in a bad temper." Teresa concluded, "I am sure it is not his sister."

Jonathan was silent for some time and then murmured: "Yes, you do that. You come every Tuesday and Friday at eight-thirty and bring your friend, if you want to—only let me know."

"I'd better go," said Teresa.

"No, no, stay. I'm lonely, no one's coming this evening. But I'd better put the light on for I believe the maid hangs round here sometimes, rubbernecking."

"Do you really think so, after you were so kind to her?"

She heard him laugh as he stood up to reach the light, then he said suddenly: "Listen, there she is!"

"The maid?"

"Miss Hamilton, I know her step already," he said eagerly. "That's the sort of woman you ought to know. Wouldn't you like to?"

She thought of the woman with fear, brilliant, young, well-dressed. "She doesn't want me," she said. "Who am I?"

He shrank into himself. "There you are," he muttered, "you're a masochist, like with the D.T. girl on the boat, sacrificing yourself, retiring. What about Nietzsche?"

"It was well for Nietzsche—he had aunts to support him, later he was a university teacher, he did not really have to work."

"Like me," he said violently. "I am supported and it's going to be for all my life, if I can."

"Why, Jonathan? Why don't you try to get out of it?"

"I have no ability. I belong in the belly of the bell-shaped curve."

"Who's the masochist?"

"I'm not a masochist, I'm a——" He clenched his fists together and looked darkly at her.

"A what?"

"A sadist, I suppose." He hunched into himself hopelessly.

She gave a long clear laugh. "Oh, Johnny, why you—you're an angel, it's only the really good people who have such remorse of conscience as you have." She laughed again. "Why, what you have done for everyone—for Gene, you told me, for Lucy, you fixed up the house for Mrs Bagshawe, you said, you got Burton out of jail, you are so good to me—it's ridiculous!"

His face had cleared, he lifted his head and looked at her pleasantly, but muttered: "You don't know me."

She said tenderly: "I don't know you? Then who does?"

"No," he said, melancholy. "You don't know me. I don't know myself. But I am a sadist and why not—" he lifted his head, challenging, "—why not try anything once? That's my motto. I was one of those kids who pick wings off flies and tie tin cans to dogs' tails."

"Boys do."

"Boys—all boys and all men—are sadists. Women offer themselves as victims, it's the sexual difference. Sex makes us suffer and men don't like to suffer, so we pick the wings off flies."

She laughed at him.

"It's a kind of sexual satisfaction," said Johnny, in a low tone, "when you can't get any other."

She looked at him. Jonathan continued: "If they deny me one, because I won't marry, won't I try all the others?"

After a silence, he continued, looking down: "The brutality of the success system! I'm bred and broken to it and I can't get out of it. No one knows how we feel. I'm haunted all the time by this need. How would you like it, never to have loved at all?"

She stared at him.

"Never to have loved once." He came up close and stared down at her. "To be tormented by thirst—lust, that is—all the time? That's something you don't understand."

After her silence, he plunged his hands in his pockets and turned away. "I suppose I have got to suffer. Who will release me? They won't acknowledge the facts." He lounged against the bookcase, hands in pockets, repeating the same thing in different words, over and over again. When she was completely broken, helpless, and silent, he said: "Well, I suppose you'd better go now."

"Yes," said Teresa. She picked up her things and went out to the door with him; he did not touch her but stood back and as he was closing the door, said: "Well, remember Tuesday, eight-thirty."

"Yes," she said obediently.

The door closed. She walked three times up and down the street, in the dark, half-inclined to go back and comfort him in some way—but what way, indeed? Then she turned home, wretched, and as desperately in love with him as ever before. She knew she was taken again, she had nothing to do but work her way out another way, slowly to die, eventually to get away from his mortal fascination. In the meantime, she needed him to keep alive, and she must keep alive to die.

30. *James Quick Lived in a Flat in Mayfair*

JAMES QUICK lived in a flat in Mayfair which he had rent free for a particular reason. He was alone in London, had made few friends, and so he walked home each night from the city, and each night by a different way, stopping at small eating-houses, if it was before closing time at seven, and going to larger and more fashionable ones if he was hungry after seven. He was abstemious by habit, neither drinking, eating, nor loving much.

This evening at the end of May, Quick was out without an overcoat and in a cast-off hat given to him by Axelrode, his partner in the business in Mark Lane, in a new English suit, and a frayed tie of feminine taste. Quick, among the clerks and juniors homeward bound, walked along fast, raising his eyes to cornices, the names of streets, sudden corners, so that he would not forget them again. He looked intently at every newspaper he passed, every newsboy and occasional pedlar, and eagerly stole from scattered bits of evening newspaper what headlines and bits of news he could, commenting upon them with slightly moving lips. When he got to a restaurant or teashop, he would read an evening paper, but he had none now, he hated carrying anything, like all fast, long walkers. All this was his usual habit, he had done it in Antwerp, in Berlin, Amsterdam, Paris, and New York.

After looking at the sky and at the lights coming on in the streets for a few minutes, and just as he reached Cornhill, in the very fast stage of his homeward trip, James Quick came to himself and thought: "Why do I feel so fresh, buoyant, why am I thinking of the days to come, when there is, money aside, Friday cheque aside, really nothing in the future, except my wife's rare post-cards, and besides that, June, July, August, and so forth?" But he went on thinking pleasurably and soon he found the glare of his pleasure was concentrated on the office, on a room in the office, and on the young woman that he and Axelrode had engaged one morning last week. The appearance of the room as she sat in it, the slaty-green light, her pale, sad, moonlit face, the large new shade hat she wore which he thought did not suit her but made her thinner, the long hands going in and out of her purse with papers and her soft, serious voice, melting away into silent embarrassment, telling him about what she had done and what her employers had said, so far away across several oceans, and the way she held out a sheaf of papers to prove it, all written far away across the several oceans. All this came back to make him smile. How could he ever know what her employers had said at the ends of the earth? But she was so sincere that such a thought had never occurred to her. He had not read her papers. He thought of her face particularly; it haunted him both in its paleness, without colour or powder, and the shining of the blue or green eyes. He kept seeing them though he did not remember the colour of the brows or hair. She wore a brownish dress in a soft material. The folds from the waist, childishly gathered, had fallen over her hips as she sat facing him. She had no gloves and in her hands a long brown leather purse out of which she took the papers; on the bench, beside her, she placed a little book by G. D. H. Cole. At this, Quick's mouth trembled and a smile appeared around it. "Another English eclectic Socialist," he thought. "Another mussed-up liberal, but it only shows what a perfect lady she is."

He went on thinking of the woman's face, her manner, nervous, anxious, hungry, her timidity in her independence. He kept remembering how she was today in the office all day, and adding comments of his own, humorous, all with reference to the English national traits. She would not tell a lie. She had reproached him for putting a false date on a letter. She had refused to type the letter and offered to throw up her job although she was plainly hungry. He had taken the letter across the street to a public typist. All kinds of funny little incidents had already occurred in which she had been timidly irreproachable, and he thought, I am, after all, a tough American, I must remember I am among people with a different style, people who never let the right hand know what the left hand is doing. As Mark Twain said: "The English are mentioned in the Bible, the meek shall inherit the earth." On the Royal Exchange they have engraved: "The earth is the Lord's and the fullness thereof." They really believe that the Lord farmed out the fullness thereof to them. The face— He was afraid she had had nothing to eat for days when she came to them, hunger had emphasized the hollowed-out face. Under the green eyes were those two pits the English have. The straw hat, worn back, showed the forehead, smooth, straight, high and soft and a nose nearly Gascon, which hunger had set in high relief. A sweet look, he thought. In spite of Shaw, Wells, Keynes, Cole and all the what-is-its that have formed it. And he seemed to see her, hurrying home, bent, in the bus or underground, over her small green serious book. She was straight, lithe, but very spare, from time to time she went into a paroxysm of coughing. He thought over things she had said to him in the strange, pleasing idioms of the English he had read in English literature. He masticated them, ran over them with the tip of his tongue. He thought of her eagerness to assure him that she could work well, and of the first day when she refused the advance money he had offered her, supposing her to be penniless. Just the same, why should she suffer, poor, silly girl? The workers are so anxious not to cheat *us*, to stand on their dignity with *us*? thought he, shrugging his shoulders as if he had taken cold. I have a butler, a maid, a fourteen-guinea suit and bespoke shoes for eight pound ten and an eleven-guinea weekly flat for which I pay nothing, because it is a whore-house for my rich partner, and *she* is anxious not to cheat *me*. He laughed aloud in the street and went on just as rapidly, not noticing that he had attracted a few circumspect glances of the hurriers home.

He presently went into a small Lyons teashop for a sandwich and coffee and as soon as he was seated there, he took out a scrap of paper on which, in the smallest visible letters, he had marked his appointments for the next week. Under the heading letters, he had several names, Lawyer, Mother, Marian, Pete, these with all the other notations occupying only the space of a twopenny stamp. Taking a stump of pencil from his pocket and a folded blank letterhead, with the name of his new company and his own and Axelrode's names, he began to write to his wife, very fast, in his large sloping hand. The writing was not at all like one's first or last impressions of the man, gave somehow the idea of an old, tall man, whereas James Quick was middle-

363

sized, white-skinned, black-eyed, with a silent, lively look and speaking lips and, in fact, a soft and truculent loquacity. He was a subtle black and white man, a prepotent, agile, clean, sweet-smelling sloven, a heady man, a sitting man, a man who loved to live by candlelight, pushed out of doors by an unspeakable greed of men, a little more—and a fisher of souls, but not this, he was, not dangerous, not ambitious, not proud, but with capacity, of old English stock, mature and steeped in the language, cured and treasured up. Distant cousins of his lingered then, as naval and army officers, in the now blasted ports of the Far East. He would have looked best, portly and ready, in a black coat with white ruffles slightly soiled, and from time to time, after being excessively aware, belligerent, angry, denunciatory, he suddenly assumed these invisibly, was courtly, lady-loving, but much as they were in the little courts of Europe before all kinds of unions of tax and race made for brusque joviality and the rough selfishness of early egalitarianism. He loved women as equals; that is, as men love friends, knowing and humbly loving all.

Yet his looks, to most people, like his writing, belied his nature. His writing took after that of a protector who had educated him as a child; his looks were those of a grand-uncle, a family lawyer, but his nature was a rebellion against the protector, a business man, and the grand-uncle.

In the tenth year of marriage he lived apart from his wife, a sweetheart of his youth. Marian lived in California with some friends in the hills, agreeably dispirited, without occupation and aimless. It gave her something to write about, her dullness, flatness, the extinction of the spirit in their childhood friends, and the failure of their marriage. Around this, which she conveyed by correspondence, Marian built a soft new life, which contented her a little and was easy to live. From time to time she wrote him a disconnected letter full of touching thoughts of their separate loneliness and the idea that two intelligent persons who understand each other too well, can efface each other in marriage. She thought this modern wisdom; "marriage is outmoded". She and James were lost, sunk, strayed, such was life with really good understanding people and neither of them, she knew, had the courage to lift a finger to stir from their webby Nirvana. Often she did not write at all. James now wrote:

I am sending you a packet by the next mail, with post-cards addressed to myself and with messages already written on them, messages to me from you—I am well, I am (not) enjoying myself, etc. All you have to do is sign your name—I know you will never write to me regularly otherwise, and I often have my tongue hanging out for some news. I am lonely.

He enclosed a cheque. James put this letter in his pocket, paid his bill, and went out to finish his walk home.

Why was he going home, to the flat in Hay's Mews? Only because people always go home. As he walked he thought about Axelrode, a young man in the office, Marian, and the pale face of the new young woman floated before him occasionally. He wondered what she was doing this evening. She was a stranger like himself. She was probably, however, spending the evening with serious and plain-looking English girl friends, other high-minded young women, or in a study circle. He would like to go along. Or with boy friends? He could not imagine her with boy friends—but after all, why not? What did he know of the English? Being so solitary he would have liked at that moment to have been admitted to that suburban semi-detached house—as he imagined it—or to that small, smoky, depressing cold-water flat in Bloomsbury; to join in the soft, incomprehensible, high-voiced circle, where people took seriously the English eclectics, and English letters. How could you despise them, after all, the race of Shakespeare, Congreve, and Bertrand Russell? The race of Newton and Haldane? Weak, tea-drinking, effeminate, ineffectual—masters of India, robbers of South Africa, bedevillers of all Europe? Yes, Americans, thought he, were still fooled by their own raw-head-and-bloody-bones Westerns. And so, thought he, what do I know, too, of the pale young woman? Where was she eating now? Did she eat spaghetti, and drink bad red wine in Soho-Bohemia, or was it tea and "shepherd's pie" at Lyons', or was she at this moment at home, spearing the gluey leather of crumpets —or was it muffins—before a leaky gas-fire? He muttered: "Except for Axelrode, yes, and his reverend-ridden wife, she is the only friend I have in London, an acquaintance of a few days. But then if she can stand it, I should be able to."

He walked on in the falling twilight. A strange, gentle, solitary race, like cats. Some called the English hypocritical. Were cats hypocritical? They blinked, calculated, purred, stole, borrowed, and hunted while others slept, and kept on considering behind their blue-green eyes. At present he called the English lithe, wiry, intense, antique, passionate, and fascinating. To know a race, you must live with it. Yes, those chap-fallen, tallowy faces, those Pool-of-London eyes, those misty polls—h'm! He walked to Trafalgar Square, down to the Embankment, over into lichened, tumbling Lambeth, through its muddy, dark and dangerous streets, back across the river to the flare of town, and all the ways up and down that he trundled, he saw hundreds of eager people, mostly drooping and lank, he saw students alone and in couples, but he did not see anyone he could make a friend of, and presently, at about twelve, he came into his furnished flat in Hay's Mews, found that the house butler, Chapman, had left out coffee with a spirit-lamp for him, took it and with it alone for a friend, went to bed. He rolled into Chapman's bed, between sheets, a tired and depressed man. He had left New York first and Amsterdam last, hoping the Old World would enliven himself and either give his wife a new spurt of love or dissolve their bloodless relationship at last, but they had continued their life as before, he at work, she living "a vegetable life", as she said, both with nothing to say and he a well of strength closed over and probably sealed for ever, as she herself said. He had no desire to leave poor Marian. What happiness could he get out of her unhappiness? Yet he was looking for a woman. For, would she ever be happier or unhappier? It was not in her nature ever to be happy. He blundered on, waiting for things to turn up. He did not like the business he was in with his partner, although it was honest and brisk.

Quick tossed, and thought over the failure of his life. What would be the end of his marriage in heaven? He was thirty-seven. They spent more and more time apart. "I must seriously look for another woman," he thought in despair. "This married bachelorhood can't go on. It ought to inspire me to work—but what?—and it doesn't! She never loved me—poor woman! She was a timid girl and took the first man she knew well, that offered. They certainly have no sort of life, to get married at the first opportunity. And then to find out the vacancy. . . ."

He tried to think of office matters. Axelrode made all his money on the produce and stock exchanges, the rest was just exercise to keep his wits in shape, a little daily dozen for idle cash.

"What a wasted life," Quick murmured. "What must I do? What can I do? Introduced to business at the age of thirteen. I'm good at it, but I don't like it. In the Middle Ages, I would have been introduced to the church and been a middle-class churchman. I have talents. No one wants my real talents. The only one who wants my real talents— This morning: 'Do I bore you with all this clatter of mine? I know most of it's foreign to you, shocks you probably, we Americans are pretty rough-and-ready, crude and obscene even', and she said: 'No, you've restored me to life'—that's odd—'I was dead to the world'—(h'm!) 'I look forward to coming to work when I get up in the morning, I see that the rest of mankind lives too'—h'm!"

"H'm," continued Quick to himself, "that's unusual, isn't it? People don't often long to come to work! Her private life can't be very exhilarating—or am I just something she's never met before—I have a kind of mental vigour of course—then the Yankee viewpoint shocks and shakes up—can she realize what is happening to her? If so—lonely, probably, rather."

He turned, lay on his back, staring up at the ceiling just visible. His bedroom was lighted from outside by a high narrow window towards the roof. It was barred with iron on the outside, and looked down into a narrow alley where no sun fell. There was usually not even sunlight above in the narrow slit of sky. Quick cast his eyes at this and thought of his friends, Axelrode, all those at home now, in bed, their children and wives around them, quiet, warm, snoring houses. He did not feel so depressed as before, however, for some reason. "A slum, a prison," he said aloud, but the warm and ruddy feeling did not depart. Through his shifting thoughts he chased the idea which had given him this glow, what was it? He couldn't put his finger on it. He went on busily therefore: "I meant to explain to her today about university professors. Talking about that acquaintance of hers, she made it plain that she—and probably he—thinks business men crafty—quite a scum. Of course, she admires profs—the bookish sort, the earnest, long-cheeked, bookish girl, as an adolescent, probably had her first crush on some college prof or man.

It's hard for girls to get over that—can't believe beggars like us are—if she only knew—yes, h'm!—but what I was saying when she said—? I must explain to her about the lawyers, though she is willing to believe that lawyers are dishonest, that's out of literature of course. I see what's wrong—yes, I must explain——"

Thinking of these things he fell asleep. He had some extraordinarily clear vision in his dreams which remained with him a long time, but he could not remember it. As he went back to work it came back to him—Burne-Jones's girl in a grape-coloured robe, and something more Pre-Raphaelite, Dante, death—he went to work absorbed by this. He had seen no one since leaving the office on the previous evening. He became excited through the day explaining things to his single disciple. Axelrode, who was going to Le Touquet to arrange some business deal, was getting ready to go and was out of the office most of the day. Presently Axelrode's chauffeur brought round his long green car and he was off. Now James was alone, the typist was in her den. He disliked the severe atmosphere of the office. He went out for coffee several times and sat at the table of the pale, bow-legged waitress that the other men shunned. He was sorry for plain, poor women. When he came back to the office he felt lonely and sick. He sent the office-boy for sodium phosphate, took it, felt worse, wished he could go home. He had to wait for a telegram from Axelrode. Nothing to do—what a miserable life it was. He spent an hour or two writing a letter to Marian, filled four pages of typing telling her things she did not care about and never had wanted to know. Then he wrote to two old friends in America to whom he had not written for six months. But the confessions did not ease him; the pale girl, opposite him, taking down notes, did not understand him and would not laugh at the jokes he told her. When she had gone away, he thought it over, and it struck him that perhaps she did not understand the jokes either—and they were rather libertine—for example the one about the Irishman and the spirit séance, "Has anyone here had intercourse with ghosts?" That Wall Street chestnut was either offensive or incomprehensible to the young lady. And the Chinese with the fluctuation of the franc—I must lead up to it. For after all she ought to go to the U.S.A. to see what women get there, no one there would work for what she works for—and if she does, she'll have to—I must work these jokes in carefully. Suddenly he laughed. He called her back and told her a very mild joke. She gave him a letter to sign, gravely, laughed, and suddenly flushed. He said: "I can see you're not used to that kind of talk."

"Not very. In fact not at all."

He was enchanted, he cried: "In fact you don't know very much about anything!"

"Since I met you, I know I don't."

He was delighted.

31. *Modern Is as Modern Does*

It was Friday, their regular meeting. Jonathan was lounging in his room, the tea-kettle on and a bright fire in the grate. It was a cold evening although early June. By a quarter to nine, Teresa was late. He smoked, and kind thoughts poured into his mind. When he knocked out his pipe, he noticed the time was five past nine and restlessly took a few steps through his room. She had forgotten the appointment! It was incomprehensible that she should not come when he had made a rendezvous with her.

He heard the bell at the front door. He was about to go when he heard Lucy's steps in the hall and he smiled to himself; Lucy too had been listening for the bell. He heard the voices of the two, he opened his door. "Hullo, Tess," he said jovially. Lucy swung past, her shoulders bent and bowed, just as usual, carrying a packet of paper. Teresa said: "Oh, you have some flowers!" He picked up his pipe and began to stuff it.

"Yes, Lucy got them out of the garbage tin or somewhere and put them there."

"Oh, don't be silly."

She laughed. He looked at her good-naturedly. He noticed that she had a certain slight, almost delicate charm when she was in a good mood. He had had nothing to do the livelong day and had thought up a more sympathetic way of approaching her. He asked her about her book, the one that was to be about Miss Haviland. She tucked her gloves away behind a vase, took off her hat, stood up against the large oak table near the door, and clasping her hands, with eyes wide open and shining, she told him about it; she had really written some pages. This astonished him. He had thought it was one of the novels of life that the girls he knew had always been thinking of writing.

"I'd like to look it over," he said. She refused. It was not ready, she had to think it out, he could not see it before it was ready to print. He smiled and said eagerly: "You mean, you'll really write a book about Miss Haviland?"

"When I first heard her story I thought, I'll write about the sorrows of women."

"The sorrows of women," he said, laughing tenderly. It was getting dark and he judged it better to leave the lights off. She was much better in the dark, something fell away from her, she became a different woman. One would have said, just to hear her softened fluent voice, her variable tones, that she had become a desirable woman. How queer to put the light on later and see her.

"Tell me about it."

"It will be called 'The Testament of Women'."

"Rather funereal?"

"Or 'The Seven Houses'."

"Ah that's more like it. 'The Angel in the House'?"

She laughed. Her voice had become contralto, it was the dark working. He had only noticed this last week. She went to the window and looked down into the yard. He had started towards her when, after a brief knock at the door, Lucy came into the room, saying "Excuse me!" Jonathan halted at the fire and bent down to turn the gas lower. He said in a dry tone to Teresa: "It is getting warmer this evening", and then to Lucy: "What is that?"

"The flowers," said Lucy. She took away the half-dead pinks and sweet williams in a small white vase, and put in their place a green vase with yellow roses. She said in her ladylike voice: "The young lady brought them and I put them in water." Then she went out, closing the door after her.

"Did you bring those?" said Jonathan angrily.

"Yes." He could not see her loving expression until she reached the gas-fire.

"Why?"

"Why not?"

"I'm afraid it's wasted on me."

"They look nice."

"Not to me, I've got no eye for that kind of thing. Take them home with you!"

"I can't take them home," she said. "Why, you had flowers here."

"Lucy—I don't know where she got them, as I said before."

"Well, don't take it hard, Jonathan."

He grumbled: "I don't take it hard, don't worry about me! I don't even notice them, just some more dead flowers for Lucy to throw out in three or four days."

She sat on the edge of the table. "A funny thing, my French friend, Francine—that sounds like a musical comedy—said she would bet I was the kind of woman that took flowers to men. How did she know? I said I did."

"And she told you not to," said Jonathan, laughing.

"No! She said it could not be helped, in real love, one must do anything, go to any extreme, the point was to love truly."

"She said that? The French know about love," Johnny conceded. "I thought you were going to bring her."

"She wouldn't come, she said some other time."

After a long silence, during which she swung a leg under the table, he resumed: "I was beginning to think that you had made up your mind it was wiser to stay away." He lounged across the room and put his pipe on the mantelpiece. "I had a letter from my mother, unopened since Christmas Day, which I only just opened while waiting for you. She reproaches me, of course, for my way of life." He laughed brazenly. "There is something uncanny and unholy in mother love, perhaps it is the absolute, unhallowed, unquestioned property of each sex in the other, the only case in which it occurs—but why argue? There it is! She is angry with me, has been for six months, and I didn't know. I was happy until now. You must own men, husbands or sons."

"We have no other property," said Teresa. She threw herself backwards across the table, her long silk-clad legs dangling. She flung her arms outwards and upwards and consulted the dark ceiling. "We don't want the souls of men," she laughed.

"I don't know," he muttered. He looked at her with surprise, put on the standard lamp to see her better. He could see round knees and thighs; her attitude was provocative but she had not sent a glance in his direction. She went on addressing the ceiling. "I almost did stay away tonight."

"Ah!" She sat up and saw his depthless dark eyes on her. She continued: "A man on the street asked me to go for a walk with him and I nearly did."

"Why didn't you?"

"It wasn't a pick-up," she said quickly.

"If it was? What's the diff?" Insolent, staring, he came close to her. "Yes, there is danger," he said, breathing small. "Just fear, it's not attractive to think that's the foundation of chastity, is it?"

"Why isn't it?" She swung her legs. "Besides, I think love makes you chaste."

He snorted a laugh. "Not likely." After a moment he said miserably: "But I don't know, don't pay any attention to me."

She looked at him standing quite close to her with resigned love, sighed: "Jonathan——"

"What was that you wrote about me?"

"What?"

"The poem—verse——"

"I don't know, 'He hath made this night', or 'Who hath made this night', or—I don't know any more."

"Funny, isn't it—it must seem funny to you now?"

"Oh, never, Jonathan," she said huskily. "I will always feel that way."

"About me—that's funny, isn't it?"

"Why——" But the word was half choked in her throat and ended on a whistling note as he flung himself upon her, grasping her tight and trying to make her bend backwards. She had no idea of his intention, only of the brutality of his clutch and his hoarse breathing. She remained quite still, her breath gone. He did not kiss her, or move, merely held her like iron. She was angry and whispered: "Stand up, Jonathan." After a moment, he coolly released her and walked away to the window. She got down from the table and sat in his arm-chair, the first time she had ever done that. After a couple of minutes she continued as before: "The man I met in the street was my boss, Mr Quick. He happened to be passing down Southampton Row when I was coming here."

"And?" He had his back turned.

"He wanted me to go for a coffee."

"Why didn't you?"

She stared. "I was coming here. Even so, I was late, just standing there talking to him. I walked to the corner with him."

"Why didn't you bring him along? I'd like to meet a City man." He added: "If he has influence in the U.S., which he probably has, he might even give me a leg up."

"Oh, he would, he's so kind."

"Let me ask him," said Jonathan. "I'm sorry you didn't bring him along."

"Next time I will."

"Any outsider might help," said Jonathan heartily. "Beggars can't be choosers." He laughed lazily. "All's fish to my fry. Could I go down to his office one day?" She hesitated, said Quick mightn't know who Jonathan was. "Wait till I ask him," she said.

He flung an angry look at her, "Never mind, let's drop it."

"Don't drop it."

He sulked.

"Let me speak to him, Johnny, he's very decent."

"All right, but just say I'd like to learn about the City, and later I'll put it to him about the universities."

"You ought to learn a bit about practical life too, it would do no harm." He was silent, raging. He flung a malevolent look. He cried: "Yes, the American spirit I suppose." Then he brightened, "You're getting it, aren't you?"

He went on about his prospects, and he placed each word so that she could see that she was no figure in his future. She presently left off thinking about Quick and the office and listened to Jonathan's monologue with bursting heart. She thought: "His life is just beginning and mine is over. What will happen to me? The work is getting harder, soon I will have to give it up and then—perhaps I will have to get work as a maid like Lucy, I will drop one day, they will put me out and next winter, for sure, that's my limit."

Jonathan perceived her gloom and became light-hearted. He did not offer her tea, which was a loss to her because she was hungry.

She had just paid in advance three pounds seventeen and six-pence to a French teacher whose advertisement she had answered. She had bought a typewriter out of her savings because Jonathan complained he had no secretary to type his notes and essays, and so she was poor again. She was trying to save money to go to France, but could not, she had lost the knack. In the stupidity of habit, she was again walking to the office in the City. When she got home, after walking back, she ate bread, cheese, and honey and drank milk. This was her supper. At lunch-time, she took a bun and a cup of tea. She had foolishly put down some money on a beautiful embroidered dress which was laid by in a shop for her. She went to no theatres or concerts, but a few extra expenses she had, which were necessary to please Jonathan; her hair, a pair of good shoes, were enough to extinguish her salary. She could not save money and her savings brought over from Australia were nearly gone. Jonathan knew nothing of all this, as he knew nothing of her previous struggles. He went on talking about the U.S.A. She borrowed a book on economics from him and returned one. When she left, he went out with her, putting on his black hat and scarf, so that he looked Italian, and he walked with her into Russell Square, where he shook hands with her, again mentioning James Quick. To his surprise, after the good-nights were said, she murmured: "Johnny, dear, let me walk back to your house with you, it's so early."

"Why not? I thought you wanted to go early."

She actually felt all of his replies on her heart, which contracted painfully and irregularly and which seemed bruised by his ignorance of her misery.

"You don't mind?"

"Why not, if it pleases you?" the young man said. He turned on his heel and they retraced their steps.

"A few minutes with you is enough to calm me," she murmured.

"Why aren't you calm?" he asked with a smile.

"I don't know—because of you, Jonathan, perhaps."

"Haven't you got over that yet?" he asked in a brotherly tone.

"Over what?"

"Over liking me too much."

"I never liked you too much."

"Oh, yes, you did, and you thought too much of me. It wasn't for want of warning, was it?"

"No, you were always fair to me, Johnny."

"That's good then," he said, squeezing her hand. "I know myself I am not to blame."

"There is no blame. You are very kind to me."

"Why not? Time's short and I'll be gone soon."

She did not answer.

"I have nothing to keep me here or anywhere," he said with melancholy.

"I know, Johnny."

"I'll lay my head on a boarding-house pillow for the rest of my life——" Abruptly he became cheerful. "But what do I care—I care for nobody, no not I, and nobody cares for me." He leaned over her, grinning.

She murmured: "That isn't true."

"It isn't true, eh? Then who does care for me, for myself, that is?"

"Others, you have friends."

He laughed bitterly. "And you, eh? The blind leading the halt. What a push, eh? We don't know what we're missing, do we? But I don't know, that's the point."

"I don't believe that, Johnny."

He ground out fiercely: "You don't believe it?" intimidating her.

"You've just been unlucky, Johnny."

"So you think I can love, too?" he said, turning and facing her. Then he swung round and went on, ignoring her, leaving her a pace behind. "Well, perhaps, but I don't care, I'm beyond good and evil." They turned into Malet Street and walked along side by side without a word. At his gate, Johnny hesitated, expecting her to say good night. She felt as if she would burst, almost threw herself into his arms, to get the momentary comfort of his arms and breast. But she saw him standing there like a stone, his arms straight at his side.

Jonathan resignedly walked to the gate, put his hand on it. "Well, Tess, here we are. Night-night."

She could not force a good night. He looked at her curiously, with a faint smile. She turned to go but after taking a step, came back just as he was pushing open the gate. She began speaking hurriedly, in a low tone: "Jonathan, let me come back for a while, inside for a while, only a few minutes."

"What to do?" said Jonathan insultingly, throwing back his head.

"Not to do anything, to be there a moment."

He turned stiffly and walked up to the door without saying a word. Afraid and ashamed, she stood at the gate watching him. He put the key in the lock, looked over his shoulder, opened the door, went inside and stood there, then he beckoned stiffly. After apparently wrestling with herself, she came up the path and stairs with uneven steps and stood outside the door. He pointed the way to his room without a word. She stood inside the door with a flushed face, then blustered: "Johnny, I'm going."

"Why?"

"You don't want me."

"I do," he said in a hard tone. "I want you very much."

She looked frightened.

"Come in," he said with rough good-humour. "After all, I didn't give you tea, that's what you need perhaps, it's been a long evening. Then I'll set you on your way."

"I didn't come back for tea," she said, slowly pulling off her gloves; but she was hungry.

He pushed her inside his door, took off his hat and muffler, pulled down the wall-bed and threw her things on it.

"I'm pretty sleepy," he said, "so I might as well air it a bit before I go to bed. The maid used to do it but old Bagshawe started to make a row about her coming here in the evening, said damned suggestive things that no doubt she chews over in her lecherous old mind, and so now I do it myself." She sat down by the fire in a low seat. He filled the kettle with fresh water, put it on, all the time casting glances at her, while she looked downwards, with shame, at the mat. He smiled wryly. "Well, feeling better?"

"I impose on you, you have troubles of your own."

"Nothing that will break or bend me. I'm not like you, sufficient unto the day is my motto, but you look before and after and pine for what is not." He knelt by her to light the gas. "Eh? Isn't that it?"

"I don't know why I'm like this," she said, still looking down with shame. "I've practised self-control ever since I was a child, never let on, never let them know what was the matter with me, that was my ideal. It just passed from me. It doesn't work any more."

"You're a masochist," he said. "Your whole history shows that, that girl on the boat, everything. You enjoy seeing yourself suffer, you see, you don't want others to share the spectacle with you, all the Christian martyrs under one hat—" he looked up, smiled, "one blond thatch. Isn't that it? Put it to yourself."

"No, it isn't."

He laughed. She went on thoughtfully: "I never meant anyone to get the better of me, get through my armour so to speak. I couldn't work it. You did."

"What do I do?" he asked gently, still kneeling by her feet.

"It isn't your doing. It's my fault. I don't know what's the matter with me."

"Don't you?"

"Beg pardon?"

"Don't you know what's the matter with you?" He looked into her face with such a strange, hard, gay expression that she felt the painful fire corkscrew through her from her knees where he knelt to her head. She looked warily at him. He veiled his eyes, got up to get the things out of the cupboard and said thickly: "What's the matter with all of us? We haven't what we need, the sweets of the world go to property and privilege."

"I don't want those things."

"If you had them would you be in the hole you're in now?"

She looked up with sudden pride. "What hole?"

"Where you are," he said vaguely. "At Quick's beck and call, working all day for a man who can sack you at the end of the week. You'll be looking for work perhaps next week. But you," he snarled, turning and looking hard at her, "now you see a lot of good in Quick. You're credulous, you believe in the boss. What's that but masochism? This masochism of yours is just a way of making spiritual capital out of your weakness. You're helpless, but you don't see it. So you go on putting yourself at the mercy of one person after another. It all comes from your inability to move freely. You're pinned down. If you don't like your job you must stick to it——"

"But I do like it——"

"If you don't like London you must live here, if you don't like me, you must stick to me——"

"I've changed jobs and countries."

"But not me," he said, smiling.

"No," she said very low.

"I'd rather you changed me too, I can give you nothing."

"I know, Johnny." Her voice broke. "Johnny, you have given me everything."

378

He laughed slyly up at her from where he crouched holding the toasting fork. "Not everything, surely, Tess."

"You gave me something to live for, a purpose; it was for you I came here, without you I might never have come. I would have failed."

"You must have had an empty life," he said with contempt.

"Empty? No, full! A burning full life, I had, while I was saving——"

"Hold on," he said easily, "hold on, there's your imagination again. You see, you're different from me, you still expect to get something from men." She recoiled and he went on steadily, with a grim smile: "But I don't expect to get anything from man or woman. I know better now. There's no rainbow for me. I want love as much as the next fellow, but it's out, and so I'm beginning to give up worrying about it. You won't face it as I do. That's why you are upset like you said just now."

"Face what?" said Teresa with horror.

"Face doing without love, face doing without a man, you won't do that."

"Of course not."

"Why not?" he asked in an impudent, boyish voice. "It's been done. Women haven't the courage to face it, they've got to fill their lives with an emotion as a house with knick-knacks. There are old maids, plenty of 'em—but it isn't from choice." He laughed bitterly. "Take a leaf out of my book, tell yourself there's no such thing as love and forget it."

"Never," said Teresa.

He grinned and turned round to her. "So, you've made up your mind not to be different. You want to be a cave woman, slave of the bedroom and kitchen, just like the rest. I'm surprised at you, I thought you were a modern woman."

"Are you a modern man?"

"Modern is as modern does. I do modern."

"What do you do that's so modern?"

"This!"

"*This?*" She pointed at the room, at the bookcase.

He pointed to the bed, laughing recklessly.

"You sleep your life away?"

He burst out laughing again. "If you like." He filled a plate with toast, and handed her some. "Drink your tea now and then trot off, so that I can get my forty winks. Besides, I'm expecting someone."

"So late?"

"Only Lucy. She's coming in to see that things are fixed for the night. She likes to when the old Bagshawe won't see her. She even said she wanted to read some of my books, to pull herself up by her boot-straps. Touching, isn't it? She might be jealous."

Teresa laughed: "But does she still live with you?"

"Eh?"

"In the house."

"Oh, I thought you meant she lived *with* me."

"Don't be ridiculous!"

He said belligerently: "Why would it be—is that snobbery?"

"Of course not."

He relaxed. "A good thing—in every way." He told anecdotes, the gossip he had heard. She yawned. "Bagshawe told someone," he said, "I don't know why, one of my friends, the old devil, that she listened at the door and heard us in bed together, the maid and me."

"Oh, Jonathan! Why don't you leave?"

"Why? It amuses me. It gave me a clue. She stays in there next door and her lecherous old imagination weaves fantasies round me. Comic, isn't it—me! But that landladies always hanker after their student lodgers, that's an old story. She's a vicious old body. She told me that women are all alike where men are concerned and she never knew what games her maids would be up to. She tried to indicate, I half imagine, that Lucy was no better than she should be."

Teresa opened her eyes wide, petrified with astonishment. Then she gave a shriek of laughter. "Oh, that's killing! Do you think she's quite sane?" she asked.

"Quite sane," said Jonathan dryly. "She just hankers after my bed, that's all."

Teresa wrung her hands. "You have to put up with dreadful things, why don't you leave?"

"Gossip can't touch me," he said coldly, "and in the meantime she pays for her fantasies—I mean, she lets me have the room cheap. I suppose there's a touch of senility in it, senile decay. I don't give a darn, I never think of it," he shrugged his shoulders. "But don't make too much of it, it doesn't touch me. But I've got one thing to say for them—they give free rein to their fantasies." He smiled askance at her, grimly.

"You must be glad to get away from here, down to the country, twice a week."

"Oh, those country girls are just clean pals." He put the cups and saucers together in a basket at the end of the room, and meditated aloud. "I'm not serious in all I say, but I suppose in a way I ought to live with one of them, it would keep me out of jams. But, you can bring a horse to the brink but cannot make him drink." He flung back his head and laughed. She saw the double whorls of hair on his head, the ducks' tails.

He came back towards her, dropping his tone. "As for that, you know, I'm getting afraid of Lucy, I think she likes me too much. That's the trouble of the near-cohabitation of a house like this. She comes in at all hours and she is free to do so, of course," he looked away, "and old Bagshawe knows my habits. If I have a girl to my room, even you," he smiled, "though they know it's not serious—I've told them so, to keep them quiet—there's a cold wave for a day afterwards. Then I have to be sweet to them, butter them up, you know. I even kissed Lucy, once, after you had been here, just to keep the house running on its tracks, you know, nothing to it!"

"Of course not," she said. "I never thought for a moment——"
He picked up one of her gloves, fingering it. "Pretty, what colour do you call that?" he asked, teasing.

"What colour? Wine. What other colour would you call it?"

He flung it down. "Wine, women, but no song. Oh, by the way, Tamar is coming this way, I've just had a letter from her, she expects to get here by September. I had a note from Elaine too, but", he smiled wryly, "I'm afraid Elaine has given me up as a bad job. A nice girl, too!"

"Are you going to marry Tamar, Johnny, is that it?" she asked.
He crumpled down on the rug, close to her, half-reclining and looking at her with half-closed eyes. All she could see were his long black lashes. He glanced at her legs. A laugh blurted out. "Marry Tamar! No fear! I stick, my dear, to the pure intellectual life. Tamar has been engaged for two years, so I suppose I don't even count in her young life. At any rate, with her, life is physical." He saw the tears in her eyes. He said gently: "Physical love, to a girl like you, is impossible, isn't it?"

She was tired of answering him. She looked at him thought-fully.

"Well," he continued, plucking at the mat, "I suppose I'm a freak! I must be, but I'll stick to it. If it be so, let it be so. Amen, says Jonathan Crow." He laughed thoughtfully. "I see voluptuous females on the street, with the requisite superfluous adipose tissue, the sort nature made to seduce men, who are always taken by profit, a bonus, you know—" He laughed and shot her a brilliant glance. "I'm a man like the rest, it would take no effort to seduce me, I'm no monster of chastity, quite the opposite. There's a girl down the country, in one of my classes, who, funny kid, said she'd teach me about life, introduce me to it, just as if she had a shake-hand acquaintance with it, initiate me—" He laughed heartily. "Would you like to see her photo?" He got up, pulled out a drawer and brought across a bundle of photographs, out of which he took three. He showed himself, lying down under a tree, his head in a girl's lap. "Not bad of me really, eh?"

"No, very good."

"She's just a youngster." He pointed to a girl in whose lap he was lying. "There's another kid, she's engaged, a bonza little blonde, she came up to London two or three times and I had her here and I thought my number was up—I'm not totally insensible, you see—but she would have none of me, she was wearing some fellow's ring, labelled for life, there's the eternal harem for you, like all the ones you really want," he said with bitter regret. He raised his eyes. "I assure you, Tess, I'm a man like the others, if you like." He ground his teeth, his curious habit. "I'm not as I try to make out. That's just self-preservation. But the two or three women I've wanted, the sweet kernel of the carnal—" he laughed, a soft, troubling tone—"those two or three darlings fashioned by insensately prolific nature, with more than usual relish, to receive man's heat and give heat and carry man's seed and make more for the next generation of men to desire—they were already some other fellows', and as for the seed—that crazy yearning you have to perpetuate yourself in some woman, purely instinctive, against all common sense, but so real, I'm mad I know, but they give it to you. There never was one of them that wasn't burning with love, I felt it myself. Your plain-faced, skinny girls, without the profit of nature, as I call it," he grinned at her, "they're stand-offish, and it's a dispensation of nature as I see it. The French say instinct is never wrong, so I was told by a French girl." He smiled a wolfish smile as he plucked at the mat. "I felt the radiant attraction, but—it wasn't to be. Our system was made for the misfits, the ugly women, who get one man and hold on to him like grim death," he said viciously. After a silence, he resumed, with a quiet laugh. "No, really, I have had hard luck, and after the dear little blonde I determined to pay nature in her own coin, bad coin. Very well, says I, Dame Nature, if I can't have what I want, I'll have none, I won't beget myself on a hangdog woman that *will* have me. That's my motto, let 'em shrivel. I won't have one of my sort. Youth at the prow and pleasure at the helm or no boat ride at all! And, provided that kind of girl does not turn up again, I'm sticking to it. I suffer like the deuce, I'm on the rack, at least sometimes." He turned over on his belly, looked up at her through his lashes and went back to scratching at the carpet. "But I'll get over it. What's wrong with that, eh? Don't you do the same? Why should I put up with a misfit, one of those?" he flashed a plaintive glance at her and lowered his eyes again. "When I've been cheated, I cheat back. Eh? What do you say?"

She was silent.

"What I suffer from unrequited and unsatisfied love," he said with a deep groan as if he had just been wounded newly, "I'll keep for my own record. Night thoughts. Pleasant, eh? The price of decency. What do you think?"

"I suppose so," said the girl. She was terribly pale and her eyes glittered. "But, Johnny, do you want to know what I think?"

"What do you think?" he looked up with a pleasant smile. "To get women to say what they think is something."

"I think that any love affair with any poor woman who loves you—even like this Lucy——"

"That's got an invidious sound—'this Lucy!'"

"Lucy, or the girl in the class who wanted to initiate you," she shuddered. "Not Bagshawe, of course, she's vicious—but anything decent is better than to suffer as you do. I hate chastity. It is torture, invented to make us suffer, and I don't know why. The people who invented it do not suffer themselves. It is for us, the young. I hate it and them, they are hypocrites. When I think of you suffering, Jonathan—" she said and then stopped. Then she said: "It was a bad idea invented late in history and not adhered to much or by many people, but by the poor and help-less. And it is a mistake wherever it is. Look at us. Think of our age! We were strong, we used to be. I used to be strong. We ought to be thinking of our futures and on the first great creative lap of our lives we are smashed, pinched in by this, I don't know why. You don't seem to be able to get out of it. I can't. But a man can, easier. I think you're holding to an old monastic ideal, you have too many ideals. Your idea that the student must be chaste or must only take the best is monastic, it's an adolescent ideal. Why should you wait for the best and die in the mean-time?"

"You mean be satisfied with carnality! Is that your solution?"

She pursued: "The student, all of us, should know about life, and what life is about. As to your feeling about Dame Nature and your possible children—I think those are the feelings of a student, who doesn't know much about life yet." She paused as she saw his darkening face, but went on bravely, "Almost the feelings of an invalid, like the ideas of a world by someone in jail so long he doesn't remember the world. When you toss about in bed, thinking of the pretty little blonde, that is a dim memory of the world, all your other ideas are jail ideas. There are lots of women in the world. Why don't you go and get one of them? There must be plenty of women who would appeal to you, the sort that makes you happy. In some way, they have managed to give you ideas of hundreds of years ago. Monks used to give up their lives for an ideal woman, the Virgin Mary. It's nearly the same with you. Don't suffer, Johnny, I don't care. Love someone. Anything is better than that."

"Why should you care?" he said slowly.

"I don't."

"Would you take anyone?"

"No, I'm different."

"You see."

"I can love."

"So you advise me to make love—that is, to go to bed with, the first girl who will have me."

"Why not?" he said mournfully.

"I will try it, he said briskly getting up, and standing above her with foggy eyes. She looked up and saw the expression, like hate, in them. She got up. "Well, I must go, it is terribly late."

"Yes, it's terribly late and you must go. Poor Lucy—I forgot her! She's still sitting in the kitchen waiting for me."

"You ought to tell her to go to bed."

"I will. Don't forget she's sweet on me," said Jonathan with a coquettish glance. "She's like you." He paused. "Well, maybe I'll take your advice one of these days." He came to the door with her, saying softly: "Well, is it all right now? Did you get what you came for?"

"Yes, thank you."

He opened the door, and she hesitated, expecting him in his soft mood to kiss her. He did not, looking her straight in the face, expecting her really to kiss him. She waved her hand and went down the steps. He started to shut the door, gave an irritated laugh under his breath, watched her curiously, just the same. He muttered to himself: "She wants me but I've got her trimmed, it's an interesting little case in psychology, by Jove! She'll come out with it some day." When he crossed the hall he saw the maid's head and long, lumpy body coming through the back door. She stopped at the muttering, looked back curiously but went on. She went into the room before him, with a composed face.

"What's the idea?" said she. "Keeping me waiting up till all hours of the night."

"You'll have to give me some advice, Lucy," he said. "I don't know how to get rid of her."

"Tell her not to come back."

"That's pretty hard, isn't it?"

"Too hard for you, I suppose."

He laughed. "Now you'd better hurry up and clear out, Bags will be back soon.

At that moment they heard the key in the front door. Jonathan quickly switched off his light, and they both stood breathing softly until the landlady's door shut. Then Jonathan pushed the maid out of his room softly; she had meanwhile taken off her shoes in the dark. She crept upstairs with tears of fatigue in her eyes. She avoided the stairs that creaked and thought angrily on the ways of young men. She was fond of Jonathan, but she knew he was weak, he went with the tide. "I know what I am," she muttered to herself, on the top landing. "Yes, I know what I am, all right."

385

32. Several Off-colour Stories

On a Friday a few months later, at the beginning of December, Quick waited till the young woman had put on her hat and gloves and gone out into the street, then he jammed on his own worn black felt and hurried after her. He knew which bus she must take to get home and he went at once to the bus stop but there was no sign of her, she must have gone into a shop. "I should have told her I was going her way," he thought, and wondered if it would have offended her. "I don't want to be thought an office Lothario." He had not heard from his wife again today; she had not even returned the addressed post-cards he had sent to her. All he knew of her was a laconic, languid letter ten days old; in it some man was mentioned who had been very nice to her in some shop, helped her, accompanied her home. "Yes, she ought to get another man," Quick said to himself. His face lengthened. She was a fascinating woman, she would soon find it out and he would be quite alone in the world. How strange it would be to be utterly alone in a world of over two milliards of people! "Yet I'm a brilliant guy," he said. "People like me."

He passes out of his route, down Old Broad Street to London Wall, and back from London Wall, down Basinghall Street and past the Guildhall, involuntarily recalling all he knows about them, that on the ninth of November the Lord Mayor and Sheriffs on their accession to office give a banquet here and that in the Great Hall took place many famous trials, those of Lady Jane Grey, the Earl of Surrey, and Lord Dudley, that Gog and Magog are here, sixteen banners of the Livery Companies hang here, from the walls of the hall and much else. Then he goes by Gresham Street and Milk Street to Cheapside, down which John Gilpin flew, and where Edward III watched the joustings in old days; and by Newgate Street to Holborn Viaduct and to High Holborn and into Lincoln's Inn Fields where he sits down to rest under the bare trees. He gets up and wanders round the square looking at the narrow, dull, styleless houses, quiet and sedate, wondering if anyone could ever get an apartment there, imagining some tall, high old tree-shadowed student's room in which he, the foot-loose, could live with a library. He loves scholarship, he spends hours each day reading, yet he has not even a shelf of books to his name, he is living in an apartment decorated with two sporting prints and two detective novels. He sighs and sits down again. For a week he has been coming to this part of London, circling it, round one building after another, darting down alleys, floating down streets, crescents, alleys, squares. Late at night he ends up in some Corner House and about midnight or a little after he crosses London, homing to Hay's Mews, sometimes, but not often, taking a taxi.

Yesterday, he came by Queen Street and Watling Street, past St Paul's and the marriage licence bureau; the day before by Upper Thames Street to the Temple and the Strand; this day was Friday.

He keeps walking with his round black head sturdily set on his square shoulders, his back straight, staring in front of him when he is absorbed, and then, when he comes to himself, his face becoming mobile, but still remarkably pale in the leaden light, he notes street names, buildings, direction and calculates the distances he is walking and will yet walk. He seems unable to stop but as if he must walk while the world turns mile after mile. This night he stopped at King's Cross Station, took a muffin and a cup of coffee and then started out again rapidly, haunted, however, by some address that he was leaving behind him, a shadowy address, a house, a street he had not seen. This time, he struck into the distressed district of Caledonian Road and reached the heart of the Islington slums, all those rows of small houses, crushed together and squares entirely soot-blackened, with shrunken front and back bedrooms and downstairs parlours where pale lodgers take breakfast before work, philosophize in thin and hoarse tones, and out of which, for a dreadful reason, human beings issue in haste to take up their miserable day— why, and with what hope, why to return, thought Quick, we know but do not repeat for fear our hearts would break. They harden.

He went on faster, now started to come back in a rough square by Richmond Road, Liverpool Road, into the Pentonville Road again and so back to King's Cross. He found a little shop where he could get some coffee, grey, lukewarm, and set out again desperately up the Euston Road, thinking he would go to Baker Street to Canuto's and get something decent to eat. Nearly there, he turned round again, plunging towards Bloomsbury, which he had been skirting for so long. It was now after eight o'clock, the air was thickening but was still pleasant. Quick thought he might wander a while in the frosty squares before getting something to eat and going home. He must eat at home tomorrow, he thought, order something from Chapman and his wife; that was only fair, they expected tenants to give them a chance at a little profit. He came down Gower Street and turned into Torrington Square to go by the British Museum. When out of the square, he retraced his steps. Now he remembered the address that haunted him—it was his secretary's. The girl had moved to the Euston Road. Since he had already looked at all the addresses in London that he knew, merely as a pastime, he would now add hers to the list. He came and stood before it. It was not yet dark. He looked down an alley between two small shops. Euston Road steamed and roared behind him. A house was set back above a chemist's shop and it was entered by a new-painted street door, which opened under an archway. He stood looking upwards. Perhaps that one he now saw, the room carried on the arch, like a howdah on an elephant? As he looked, the curtains of this room stirred and a thin face peered, someone looked out. A man? Perhaps she had a lover. He went down the alley softly to the door, looked at it and then came back, looked up once more and turned westwards along the Euston Road.

A young woman hurried in front of him—like her, he thought. He hurried after her. She walked rapidly. He called: "Miss Hawkins, Miss Hawkins!" She missed a pace, went on. He began to run, "Miss Hawkins!" She wheeled and bumped into him. He pulled off his hat. "What are you doing here?" she asked. He said breathlessly: "I've been walking round here for a week, I'm the King of Southampton Row. I was just going for a coffee, will you come along too?" No, she was in a hurry to be off. He thought of the man at the window, and asked solicitously: "Are you going home?" "Oh, no, not home, but to see a friend." "Then I won't detain you!" But he did detain her, talking. When he released her, she was off like a shot, saying: "Excuse me, I'm so dreadfully late!" "Oh, my paws and whiskers, the Duchess!" cried Quick after her. She turned round at a distance, laughed, waved her hand and bounded on.

This meeting cheered Quick up but left him with a hollow feeling too. To begin with, it was hunger. He went to a place at the corner of Oxford Street and Tottenham Court Road. As he ate, he raised great eyes over his food, looking quickly round the room and wondering if there were many like himself, so much alone. He wanted to explain the streets, the politics of London to a woman. He was busy all day explaining them to his partner, to explain them to men was not agreeable at night. If he had a woman with him, he wouldn't walk so much; then also, they could walk together, and he could point out the things of interest. Even Londoners, he had found out, did not know half so much about their city as he did. He thought, it was Old English, the face, antique, not peculiarly feminine—something that he had seen in old print shops. Perhaps it was the light in the office. He laughed. She argued with him about everything, she always thought he was wrong. He, who knew so much, and she, who knew so little—it made no difference—she seemed to think she and the rest of the English came post-graduate from God. He chuckled. "The philosophical Teresa." He had had plenty of secretaries who teased, kidded, or flattered him. She never once agreed with him. "Yes," he said, "that's it, that's what she is, a ship's captain, or less than that, a rebel lieutenant, perhaps the reincarnation of Mr Christian of the *Bounty*." He laughed aloud. This time he noticed someone looked covertly at him and he recollected where he was. He paid his bill, went out into the street and struck for home. It was not surprising: he dreamed about the girl and the dream was quite clear in his head the next morning. He had seen her, not as a ship's captain, but hanging in a frame against the wall. He was inside the frame too, and there she sat with her knees showing through a long soft blue cloth, in fact she was garbed as a Madonna, her strange-coloured eyes looked past him. "Why ever a Madonna?" he said to himself as he shaved and looked into the mirror. "I am sure she would not like that dream of mine at all." He smiled slightly. She was a funny girl.

In the office today he had explained to her, "My wife is a charming woman, fascinating. At our house, she was always surrounded by men, my friends. My only dream would be to make her happy, I have nothing else to live for." He looked at her for a moment and repeated slowly: "I have nothing else to live for."

"You!" She laughed.

He had been pleased. "Why? Do I seem aimful to you?"

"You? How could you not be, knowing what you know? I never met a man so brilliant. You light everything up when you explain it. The world has changed for me since I knew you. I felt miserable, hopeless, and now I'm anxious to come to work. I see there's a life worth living. I think of things outside myself. You tell me about other nations, other kinds of men, you explain things. You have the knowledge we haven't got and want, you could change the lives of people. How could you be without an aim?"

His jaw dropped, he turned pale and his large eyes stared at her. "I? I?" he repeated. "I seem like that to you?" He thought he heard his partner speaking outside in the hall and he said hurriedly: "Let's get on with that letter. We'll—we'll talk later." After a moment, he brightened. "If you feel like that, if I really help you, I'm only too glad to explain things to you."

"Institute a Chair of Quickery and explain them to everyone. No one knows."

"No one!" he laughed. "No one knows because she doesn't know. The U.S.A. is the place for you," he had said, "it's the place for a bright girl. The people are all dead here, polite but dead. You can't be happy here."

"Happy! Who bothers about that?"

In the afternoon, he told her that his partner was a Jew, told her about European pogroms of which she had never heard; and ended with the joke: "If I had known, Mamma could have saved the horses and carriage." He explain the status of Cuba, the Philippines, and Alaska, and told the joke of the Alaska fairy, commented upon the poll tax in the Southern States which prevents the Negroes from voting, and simmering in his own excitement and enthusiasm, capped this with several off-colour stories. Then he had kept repeating that in the days to come he would explain the United States—and the world—more and more, so that she would see how things really were, and that when he got to know her better he would tell her some really vile jokes that he did not dare to bring out now. As she looked at him calmly and smiling, he was delighted at his own mental activity and at having found a friend. He exclaimed passionately—

> *"She was a Virgin of austere regard,*
> *Not as the world esteems her, deaf and blind,*
> *But as the eagle that hath oft compared*
> *Her eyes with Heav'ns, so, and more brightly shined*
> *Her lamping sight; for she the same could wind*
> *Into the solid heart, and with her ears*
> *The silence of the thought loud-speaking hears—"*

Listening, she smiled secretively he thought, and he hastened to say: "Of course you know that quotation from Giles Fletcher?"

"I never heard of him."

"What? The English poet? 1588-1623, thirty-five at the date of his death or disappearance," said James Quick. "But alive today, if I believe the dream I had last night, of such a Madonna!"

"A Madonna," she said contemptuously.

"But don't you know Giles Fletcher?" he rushed on. "And you so English? I believe we Americans love English literature more than you do. What Englishman writes in the spirit of the Carolines as much as T. S. Eliot?"

"I never heard of T. S. Eliot," she said coldly.

He laughed slyly and pressed her to read T. S. Eliot and acquaint herself with modern American writing. The genius of the language had passed to the other side of the Atlantic, what had modern English writers done? This she did not know. She said: "I'm afraid I've been in a stupor for three or four years. I read only books on economics and politics."

"You're interested in English economics?" he asked ironically.

"Not at all, but this young friend of mine, this young man at the university here is studying it."

Quick had promised to meet the young man and guide him if he needed guidance. He had inquired his address and it was in the direction of Malet Street that he now walked.

Beside the door were four bells with four small handsome brass plates. Quick came up to the door to read these, and then went out again and looked up at the house, the corniced top of which was just visible. "Number fifteen," murmured Quick and went by Great Russell Street to Tottenham Court Road and retraced his steps to Malet Street, looking about him and exploring the side streets and alley names with the care and curiosity of a cat. He was rather short-sighted and often had to walk close up to lamp-posts and the fronts of houses. Steeples of the quarter were ringing ten when Quick came by number fifteen again. The hall-light burned steadily through the fanlight, a lamp had come on in the front room of the ground floor and a light shone in the basement and the second floor, exactly as before. Quick walked past. There was no one in the street near. He came into Gordon Square around which he walked several times, idly memorizing the names of the societies with their offices there and the numbers, and he found his imagination beginning to weave a fabric on the woman's figure that he had dimly seen leaving a house, perhaps it had been number fifteen, perhaps Miss Hawkins's friend. As he thought, he moved his lips almost imperceptibly. "For months, I've known this woman Hawkins, sat opposite to her at my table every day. I know her political and social viewpoint I might say better than she does, and who she is, as a person, that is, her mannerisms, nods, becks and wreathed smiles, the outward part that's visibly linked to the inward, in her especially—I know her in that way better than any person in London, better than Axelrode—well, not better than Axelrode, but better than—say Chapman, my butler. I know her certainly better than I now know my wife, 'the office wife' is not a false term at all, it is true. Yet, speaking very frankly, do I know this young woman so very well? There's a mystery about her, a personal mystery. I can't make it out.

"Take where she lives. Three pounds ten is good pay for London, yet she lives at 15A Euston Road, a slum, a rattletrap in a hell of noise. How much? Could I ask her? Would she resent it? Probably these English girls have a high idea of privacy and dignity. She's not English but Australian of course, but it's the English race, unadulterated by any revolution. Then her clothes, they're very poor. Of course, the women dress miserably here. Other Americans laugh at English hats, but I see in it a sign of the complete neglect and impudent disregard of women by the English male. They must be desperate. What do women do when they are neglected? Supposing I——?

"On the other hand," Quick went on to himself, beginning to twiddle his fingers in a peculiar style, holding his hand out somewhat frontwards and shaking his hand as if it were merely a bunch of fingers, "on the other hand, yes, I may be merely a provincial myself. One of your Brontës, now. The debunkers, the American wise guy tries to prove that all the Brontës wanted—they, the Brontës I mean—was a man. Is that the whole story of female genius? Speaking very frankly, America could do with a few such virgins, if that is all there is to it. However, to proceed, the mystery of this woman is that with the salary I pay her and that I purposely increased because she looked so thin and hungry, she looks like a pauper. Am I complicating it? She is the phthisic type and she coughs, it might be that. Then she has no chance. But that does not explain Euston Road and the clothes.

"But if she is going to see this man, it is a love-affair and woman's first instinct is to dress for her boy. . . .

"Is it this man she goes to see, therefore? Or what is he to her? Perhaps there is some dreadful or sordid, some tragic family story behind it, someone in trouble whom she helps out, a brother, a sister unhappily married, a brother who gambles, a wastrel—who knows? I know her, I say, as well as anyone in the world, yet I know nothing. She looks devoted and loyal, no doubt deeply affectionate, permanently attached when she loves. Perhaps there is here one of those hard-hearted family parasites for whom an elder sister sacrifices herself. Need it be this boy friend? Perhaps she was going to give lessons or take one. One of those clandestine and nasty uneasy affairs that start with the exchange of lessons in English and French.

"What does the bad clothing prove? I am perhaps merely thinking nationally. In the U.S.A. they shoot papa if he doesn't give junior a Ford to himself; here they're not so. The British vampire robs at home too—thus life is spiritual. As a result, here, youth still believes in—my mind to me a kingdom is—perhaps she and her boy friend simply don't care about clothes. They are both poor but they love—yes, why not? No, she is struggling bitterly, but against what? Here I am back to the beginning. It's certainly queer that I sit opposite a woman for several months, every day, and I see her devastated by some illness or tragedy. I could ask but one doesn't do that. It isn't done! One can't ask point-blank: 'What's the matter with you? You look as if you're dying on your feet.' How simple it would be."

Quick now turned towards Montague Street, just after the clocks had struck the quarter past eleven, and on his way passed Jonathan and Teresa, arm in arm, walking in the direction of her room. The man was muffled against the weather and wore a broad-brimmed hat. Quick could only see a man taller than himself, with a wiry walk. He was following them, on the opposite side of the street, with no set purpose, when he saw them walk backwards and forwards on the pavement for a while and then begin to retrace their steps. He had not far to go to reach the corner and from there he saw them first separate and the girl, after hesitations, enter the house with the man. Such a scene at that hour, on such a dark evening, startled Quick. He was upset and put it down to crowded memories of London stories of the two friends of the gloomy sort, Wilkie Collins and Charles Dickens and all the English writers of city wretchedness as well as the murder mystery writers—this was, after all, he told himself, the city of Jack the Ripper and of many a horrid drama which did not reach the newspapers in such a wild form but which ended badly. It was the city of unhappy, tortured men and women, it was the city of evil loves. He walked along much troubled, always in the same neighbourhood up and down the streets, returning every quarter of an hour to the proximity of Malet Street and Montague Street.

"Intelligence, energy, idealism," he said to himself, "don't help a woman at all to pick out the criminal or even betrayer of the other sex, in fact they peculiarly indispose her to suspect anything—not to mention that the sexes are made to be deceived by each other. Love is blind. Faults actually become virtues in the eyes of the other sex. Mothers know and condone, sweethearts, on the other hand, see a murderer possibly as a saint, purging the race, well not as bad as that—Nancy loves Bill Sykes. There you are! That type of sex criminal naturally picks out his victims anyhow among the unsuspecting. There is something very attractive to him, juicy, fantastically enjoyable in seeing the paroxysms of goodness, the imbecility of the victim. It's after all possible, more likely it's this brilliant, unhappy youth she mentioned. Yes, it's a love affair. My intervention isn't needed. Or this young Englishman she is walking with may be her brother, they're discussing something, she has lent him money—much money for her—she is supporting his lazy, greedy, or sick wife and children; he is out of work and she is persuading him to do something, or explaining her circumstances to him—or he is separated from his wife, yes, obviously he is living alone—or wait, have they gone out to discuss something and are now returning? But the waiting at the gate, that was strangely suspicious, why did she hesitate in that way, then the way the door shut—the house looks decent enough and there are four lodgers there, those big roomy houses, converted•private houses, are not soundproof. She's a woman of mature age, she has travelled, she knows what she is doing. But do any of us know what we are doing in sex? And as for a brilliant, travelled, mature woman—what could—what am I, a knight-errant?" he asked himself, twiddling his fingers and his face lengthening. He sighed and heard the steeples begin their long roundelay which meant the hour was now twelve. "Twelve? Is she going to stay the night there?" and he walked a little more, saying to himself that her life was her own. Nothing to him if she lived with the young man, in fact, he was glad of it, if he did not maltreat her—was she secretly married? That might explain everything. But could that be when she had been here such a little time—unless she had come with or to a husband?

He now found himself passing the house again in the opposite direction and he had scarcely gone ten steps before the door opened again and he hastily crossed the road to the other side of the street. He had convinced himself that his secretary was in trouble and that he must guess what it was in order to help her, delicately, secretly if possible.

The same man, apparently, without his hat and coat, let her out. They stood for a moment facing each other, the woman poised, the man warning, antagonistic; then, abruptly, without his having heard anything, they parted, the woman fleeing down the steps, with her head bowed and the man doing an odd thing. As he stood very slowly closing the door, Quick could see against the brightly polished oilcloth of the hall floor a squat, thick figure, with heavy hips, padded shoulders, a small craning head. This figure stood quite still, except for the right arm closing the door and appeared to be staring after Miss Hawkins. Even when the door-opening was only a slit this figure stood and peered through it. The girl glanced backwards as she closed the gate, but furtively, over her coat collar, and then rushed away. When she had gone to the end of the street, she hesitated and then turned away from her home, chose a dark street, and lengthened her step. Now she was going with the demeanour of a person deeply agitated. When she reached the end of this street, she looked quickly behind. She heard a man's step and she now struck out towards the lights of Tottenham Court Road, and came out into it opposite the Whitefield Tabernacle. Quick followed her doggedly, either she was on some urgent or odd business at this hour of the night, or she had given him the wrong address, and if this latter why? He was by this time trembling with fatigue, he had taken no proper dinner and only kept walking out of his ordinary restlessness and the feeling which can be called pity or sorrow for the world, which is the feeling of any kind man with a formed philosophical viewpoint. He walked, perhaps, because some were blind to fate and others were helpless; and he walked thinking, and on this night, the tragedy, embroilment, and heedlessness of everyone became mixed with the fate of Teresa Hawkins alone.

Just before she entered Tottenham Court Road, however, as she stood on the edge of the pavement, she turned round and looked fiercely at the man following her, and when she saw him, uttered his name softly, almost incredulous. Her startled glance flew all over his face.

"I followed you from that house you came out of," he said.

"Ah!"

"I didn't mean to spy on you; I happened to be passing, and I went out of pure curiosity down Malet Street, since you said you had a friend that you were visiting, at number fifteen, wasn't it?"

The girl was silent. Her mouth twitched and as she looked at him, her eyes widened and her traits lengthened as she looked inward. Quick stared at her. They stood facing each other again, focused intently on each other, exactly as earlier in the evening.

"Am I intruding?" Quick said softly. "Perhaps you have some errand—but if so, it's rather late, let me come with you, I won't inquire what it is."

She smiled. "I ought to be getting home, I am stupid to be walking this way at this time of night. I'll never get to work in the morning. I was just walking, for exercise."

"I'm dog-tired," he confessed. "I've been walking ever since I saw you early this evening, and when I met you, I had been walking hours and I was ready to drop then. I thought you would come and have a cup of coffee with me—tea, I know you don't like coffee. Anyhow, I went by myself and read the paper for three-quarters of an hour, but since then I've been walking about this neighbourhood. To tell the truth, I've been here three nights in succession and looked for your address, because it intrigued me, you know. It was the alley that fooled me. Of course, I was just walking in this direction. Come have a cup of coffee, I want you to like it, it's better for you."

"Isn't it too late? Is there any place open?"

"Why, the Corner House is open all night, perhaps it shuts at four or five for an hour, I'm not sure about that. There are other places too, don't you know that?"

"How could I know it?" She laughed. "I'm at home at night."

"Are you? You go to bed at night?" He laughed appreciatively. "But you walk first."

"Not usually—tonight."

"Tonight—so late?" After a pause, he added vivaciously: "As you know, Miss Hawkins—see, Tottenham Court Road, it's always like this, until two, three in the morning, and you didn't know!" She said confusedly: "Haroun-al-Wretched."

"It's not the Haroun-al-Raschid sentiment at all as you might think." He laughed. "It's simply that I lead such a lonely life. You see only my brilliant side, you see me charming people in the office, you see men writing to me from all over Europe affectionately, almost in love with me, you see British gentlemen who ride to hounds and pay four hundred pounds a year to send Wilson minimus to Eton and who worship His Majesty and ranunculi with equal emphasis, coming in to Axelrode's little den to hear what Jim Quick has to say, a Yankee, by Jove, a low fellow born and bred in a democracy where there are no lords and not even any baronets, not a single knight nor the remotest nuance of a K.C.M.G., but a beastly comical fellow, by Jove, and beastly clevah in his own way, taking it all with a pinch of salt."

Whenever he mentioned the British in his conversation, and

invented their commentaries, he most comically aped a British accent, which varied between Cockney, a British stage drawl and the cheap and chipper accent of the "Ruler of the Queen's Navee". He was not always conscious of this mannerism, but whenever he mentioned the British or even brought in the word "England" the irresistible figure of Lord Dundreary crossed his mind and he executed the part to the best of his experience.

The young woman listened with involuntary laughter, and Quick went on: "But outside all that, I am really a lonely man, a solitary, if you will. I lead a lonely life. People get the idea that I am a great mouthpiece; I am not at all. I don't care for crowds, for the glitter, the applause that follows a *bon mot* in the mouth of a man celebrated for his talk. My friends think so, but they have got me wrong. What happens to men like us? They fade out, and leave no record. If they knew how I know London, just out of my walks at night alone! For example, this evening——" but while he was talking in his inexhaustible style to which she was accustomed, he noticed that in spite of her evident trouble and her evident interest in his conversation, she glanced about brightly and observed everything in the Corner House, which was new to her.

Still talking, he wondered still about her. Was she a cataloguing type, a Dewey system in the flesh, ticketing things for the mere pleasure of arranging them? Was it that empty dry mind which notes "interesting facts", a *Whitaker's Almanac*, the foundation of one of those high-minded, strong-minded, rubber-soled old women of England who are too parochial to govern?

He said: "For example, last evening, I came from Hay's Mews, where I live, as you know, almost in a direct line. Well, I believe Conduit Street was the only street in a straight line—Hill Street, Berkeley Square, Bruton Place, New Bond Street by Argyll, Great Marlborough, Poland, across Oxford Street by Wells into Wigmore, Tottenham Court and into your bailiwick, W.C., by Francis Street, Torrington Place, Byng Place—do you know where that is? You should, you walked through it tonight——"

"Tonight?"

"But I found a cabby on Monday, I admit, who knows it as well as I do. He got me home in a quarter of an hour from Kingsway, I congratulated him, and he told me most cabbies aren't fit to be cabbies, they ought to be pavement artists or ditch-diggers because they only know one patch of the earth at a given time. They just follow the great thoroughfares, they think in straight lines, and rectangles. A cabby must think in ground plans, in networks, like an airman. Well, how do you like waffles?"

"Oh, very much, thank you."

There was a silence.

"You must think me a nut," said the man, laughing softly and appealing to her with his black eyes.

"No," she said, then, "I'd really better go, it's awfully late."

"But you live alone? No one is waiting?"

"Oh, no."

The man's face softened, took on a satisfied look. "So your friend lives in Malet Street? Near Bedford Square, the high hall of the ground landlord of Bloomsbury. The French, Belgian, and Russian consulates are in that square. Your friend likes high society. What is your friend, an architect? It is well known for its interiors, the Square."

She listened wearily. He rushed on, "You look tired, I didn't mean to detain you. Let me walk you home, or would you like a taxi?" She refused, and they began to walk home. They were both exhausted. When they reached the dark streets, the girl became silent. As they came nearer to Jonathan's house, she began to suffer horribly from disappointment and shame as she recalled the young man's peculiar hard looks, and drawling, rough tones. She knew that he had been standing at the door, nearly closed, looking at her through the crack. She knew what they suffered from. The only thing they had in common was this cancer. That there was no answer for them was now sure. Tonight had proved that no matter how far she was driven, Jonathan would never make another move, he would never touch her hand, kiss her now. He was like icy steel to the touch, hard, but the flesh stuck and burned.

She had flung herself into the street determined to walk up and down the unknown dark and fearful side streets, till a man picked her up, to force herself to do this, anything to escape from Johnny.

She was so deep in this dreadful nightmare of what was to come to her tonight, when Quick left, the next night, or the next at latest, that she heard scarcely anything of what Quick said, and she wished for him to leave her, take a taxi and go to his rich home, letting her finish the last part of her way in the darkness. She was still not resigned to going home tonight without knowing man's love; could she enter the house, loaded with the shame of refusal?

A little way off, the all-night buses thundered, they made her little arch-slung room tremble all night and day. There was only a short space between that rumbling room and this street filled with the eager chatter of her employer; she had not had much time to think, to take the last decision. She was struck by a silence beside her. She looked at the man. His strongly marked, pale face was turned inquiringly to her.

"Are you worried about something? I have asked you three questions and you haven't heard me."

"Oh, I'm sorry—what was it?"

"Weren't you very surprised to see me twice in this quarter tonight?"

"Oh, very much surprised."

He seemed pleased, and rushed on: "Won't you please tell me if you're worried about something?" He said "wurried", slurring it softly as Americans do. "Perhaps I can help. We should all help each other. You would help me."

"You don't need help, though."

"We all need help more than you think."

She did not hear him again, thinking of one evening recently when she had passed Johnny's house. It was not an evening when she was allowed to visit him. Sometimes on the other evenings she merely walked past in the gathering dark and looked at the house or did not even look at the house but walked quickly past the familiar railings and tall solid walls on which thin vines were beginning to creep. That evening she had seen Jonathan. He was sitting under the lamp with the old woman of the house, in the front room, on the other side of a cotton-spread table and a game of cards. Another evening, he had left the house just in front of her and walked rapidly away. She had followed him slowly to the corner of the street and had stood there until people began to glance at her, not looking after him, merely thinking how it was that others could see him and she not. Several times she had walked up and down the bursting street, like a person going mad, or about to take a fit, or knowing a hopeless disease on him and knowing that there was a cure, refused because of poverty to him; like a girl out of a job, tramping, knowing that in each house is a family eating and sleeping. A kind word from Jonathan was the cure cruelly withheld, not by Jonathan but by what he called "things as they are".

"You don't want to tell me," the man beside her insisted.

"It's about my friend, this young man I went to visit. He's very unhappy. He feels his life has been wasted. The universities don't prepare him for life, and he wants to go to America where he thinks he can look out a new life for himself. He doesn't know how to, and doesn't know anyone there."

"Yes, you told me. And that worries you so much?"

"Yes."

"You must think very highly of your friend?"

"I do, he deserves to succeed. He has struggled against so many —you might say—fiends, demons of adversity, he has done everything for himself without help. The roads wind uphill all the way, that is how life is to him."

"To many—but that is your only trouble?"

She was silent.

"It is not?"

"He has a trouble that no one can cure, it is diffidence—no, I am wrong in putting it down to that. It is purity, old ideals, plain living and high thinking, you know," she laughed, troubled. "He is always talking about that and believes in it."

"Do you too?"

"Certainly, who doesn't? We all can't—of course. But he has really given his life to it, and it wears him out. He regrets the lost years, 'Conrad in search of his youth.' He regrets what he feels he cannot have."

"Why? You mean money I suppose?"

"His youth—he looks in the newspaper at advertisements for men's shirts, for example, he looks through a college window and sees boys playing football, he meets women, he can't love them——"

"Why?" Quick broke in.

"I don't know, but he says so. He has become that way through years of sitting over books, he has lost all confidence and thinks he can never marry. He wants and desires love and he is afraid, he is afraid to lose his purity, too," she said, laughing softly. "I think that's it, it's a boy's fear."

"How old's the young man?"

"Twenty-seven."

"He tells you this?"

"Oh, yes. I knew him years ago. It is an ideal of learning, that the flesh must be martyred and the mind improved. It's queer how these old superstitions survive. He can't shake it off any more than a pious boy can entirely shake off religion when he turns atheist."

"And has your friend—turned atheist?"

She continued in a melancholy voice: "He says himself he is twisted for life. A St Anthony. This suffering is spoiling his work. I can see myself that he has degenerated, though he is still decent. Through purity and chastity he is becoming obscene and rotten within. Men have gone morally and mentally mad because they were saints. Why does a decent thing at a certain point turn into the thing most loathed? You would think there were demons at work. That is a possibility for explaining the co-existence of God and the devil in Christian ideas, of course," she said hurriedly. "That at a certain point God becomes—to us at least—the devil. His being is so great that it twists ours out of recognition and we become insane, murder—well, that's silly, but it's true of—my friend. Out of excessive innocence, belief and aspiration, out of application, chastity and decorum, he has grown into a lazy, hopeless man, full of lustful but important wishes. Yet he is very virile, he has no need to suffer."

"And you have talked this over together?"

"Oh, often, though how the pure becomes the impure—that is my idea. Naturally, I did not tell him that he seemed like that to me. He is desperate enough already," she said gently. "But I am just telling you this because he wants to meet you and talk things over with you—I don't mean his personal troubles, far from it, he is reserved—but about the possibilities in the U.S.A. He wants you to help him. He feels lost. He has no subject for his essay, I told him how rich you were in ideas, what a plenty, what a feast—" she laughed, looking sideways at Quick—"what a surfeit of new ideas, in fact, and of course Lazarus thought Dives would spare him a crumb."

"Well, of course," said Quick, perfectly delighted. "Did you tell him that? Is that what you think? The young man wants to meet me? With pleasure. Shall I go to his home, or will he come out to meet me?"

They had been standing for the last ten minutes inside the paved passage leading to her room. The light was on under the arch. "You will see. He is a very intelligent, sympathetic, sincere young man, brilliant really, but crushed by too much school life. When he sees you he will probably want to go into the City."

James Quick stared at her open-mouthed. "When he sees me? Why?"

"When he sees what kind of men are in the City, I mean."

After another stare Quick said good night hurriedly and turned away, hailed the first cab he saw and hurried home, gasping with fatigue. On the way he thought particularly of what she had said about the young man. It was so eloquent. He believed it but was puzzled by it, especially by some parts of the young man's account of himself. Quick did not believe that any young men were chaste and pure after about sixteen, and he had never met a young woman who thought so. Teresa's friend might be an eccentric but gifted Englishman, perhaps distorted by a public school. He had heard strange things about the English.

33. A Deserted Sawmill

IT was February. No letter from Tamar nor from others for weeks, and Jonathan was sick to death of his affair with the maid. "What to do, what to do?" Even to Teresa, hopelessly, he repeated this, whimsically too, and once more he put himself into her hands, following where she led, and grumbling gently, when the fresh moist lands of London were laid before him. "I have been put in my place by Fate; I know where I am going", though to this she now listened silently, with clouded eyes, for she knew that though he was going nowhere, their roads were separating. Already they had passed the sign-post, only a few yards more. Every moment with him, but a few rare ones at dusk, was sharp-edged and her blood flowed freely whenever he spoke. She knew now that he knew it too. They said to each other: "It's nearly spring." Even Jonathan said it wistfully and smiled at Teresa, as if he expected something from the spring. On the Sunday when he was going out with her to the country as usual, Teresa brought some fresh roses from the French south, half-opened, and pluck-ing one from the vase when they were arranged, put it into his hand and asked him to wear it. "No," he said irritably. "No, no." "Take it only to please me." He took it with him to the gutter and there dropped it, looking up reasonably into her eyes. "And now let us go—to wherever it is," he said. They went to Baker Street station, each paying for his ticket. Rain threatened, but it was a fresh and sweet day, and they stuck to their plans, going out to Rickmansworth. They tramped up hill and down dale, slipping on the sides of a canal, looked at dark trees, now hardly visible across swampy flats, through the rain which had begun to drift, and they sheltered in the mud under a culvert; proposed in a thick of rain to spend the night in a haybarn, laughing and huddling, came to a frowning plantation where they sheltered again and after passing through a wood came down a ramp of rolled earth and past a cement works to the hamlet of Troy on the borders of Buckinghamshire. A row of trees mounted the hills, trees lined the field at a distance. Watercress grew in summer in the swollen ponds at the bottom. Potatoes were heaped in barrows along the flank of the hill. Not far from there, when the wind began to blow harder, they sheltered in a deserted sawmill situated in deep meadow and standing out alone against the whole landscape of rises and open woods, in its yard and upon its mill-race. The outer wall was perfect, the casements and doors beautifully cut and fitted, but the mill, though used, had never been finished. All inside was clean. The high winds of the previous few weeks had blown corrugated iron sheets about the yard from the roof, but the centre of the floor was sheltered and none of the glazed windows broken. The stairways trembled, there was a square opening in the upper floor through which much sawdust had been shot to the lower floor. The sawdust was piled there, dry, reddish-gold, to one side, and about a man's height. They looked at the brimming mill-race and the rusty mill-wheel stuck against the fall of water by two wedges. They pulled the wedges out and waited for the old wheel slowly to begin to revolve, but it was firmly rusted onto the spindle. They opened the sluices and the water began to fall down over the blades of the wheel, faster and faster; it dropped ten feet and the pool seemed deep. At the other side of the wheel chamber, Teresa threw herself backward with a cry, for the flooring was entirely bitten away there into a great hole above the deep water and she skirted it and came to the edge of the mill-pool under the building. It was dark there, hard to see in the gathering dusk. Beyond, the water once more flowed out shallow but now more rapidly. The mill-pool was black and now agitated with a horrible swirling, as it began to lead its true life.

They looked from a window farther down the wall at the stream of water flowing down between grass, to join the brook again presently and so over the wide distant fields in a long separation of the woods, and running into the woods far off. The sun played on the rain high up for a few minutes. The rain fell broadcast and thick, moving towards them and around them; again, in a minute, they were beleaguered by roaring winds and stamping rain. For a moment, Teresa and Jonathan stood arm on arm. She prolonged the moment and he grew restless, kindly disengaged his arm and moved about the mill. "Looks as though we're in for it. Let's eat here, and then shove off."

The sun had gone and the wind was blowing louder. Teresa did not leave the picture spread out on the window. "It reminds me of a scene long ago, in the eighteenth century. I wish we could live for a while a long time ago, with everyone in the century dead. How would it be? Everything deserted, but living, like this? The mystery of human life, unsolved, like the mystery of the *Marie-Céleste*, found at sea with the log not yet blotted and the galley fires going and no one aboard." She laughed tranquilly. "Or to be on the high seas and go backwards and forwards, coming down with the spring floes to the Behring Sea, and back again, in winter."

"Why—" he raged, turning round and coming towards her, maddened by her—"why must women look backwards, not forwards? Why not the twenty-second century before everyone was born? That's a complete give-away, never the present, never reality."

"The past is quiet, it can't be broken into," said Teresa. "The future has armies of people waiting to break into it, hungry hordes, waiting to suckle."

"Yes, I suppose that's a woman's view," he said. "And never the twain shall meet. That's our fate, isn't it. I suppose Lucy would feel like that, too," he smiled. "A long stretch of quiet with everyone dead and nobody to do for. So you are sisters under the skin!"

The clouds thickened with evening and the wind blew very fiercely. The iron sheets rattled in the yard and the sound of the splashing water from the race increased. They ate out of Jonathan's rucksack and rested on their coats on the sawdust.

"We could stay here, if it got worse," said Teresa. Jonathan looked at her without making a reply and presently got up and began to walk about on the cleared floor. While he was away Teresa made up her mind to stay there. The long walk up the red wet earth, the dripping woods, the plain dull fields before the station, the cruel companionship—no more. Let him stay or go. Jonathan lit a cigarette and she saw it moving, standing by the window and his head against the window. He went into the yard in the wet and returned. The unnatural long light waned, but they could still see each other. After a while he came nearer, stood several yards off, and said: "Well, let us stay, it looks like fate, doesn't it?" and laughed in a friendly way. "But nothing about the past or the future. I like life, I'm just an ordinary man."

Satisfied, Teresa began to smile faintly and imagined him lying there all night, huddled up, unconscious of his sleep, gently breathing, and in the morning, astonished, secretly wounded because she had not gone near him. They settled into the saw-dust, one on each side of the soft but uncomfortable hill, she with a handkerchief knotted round her hair, both under their coats. It began to get cold. The storm was very loud and they wondered if any more sheets of iron would be blown off the roof or the rattling windows blown in. "We'll probably regret this," said Teresa. "Why?" he asked belligerently. No more was said and presently they thought each other asleep.

There was a great clattering in the yard as if someone were throwing things about. The floor was trembling with wind. The rain had ceased. With her ear close to the floor, she heard a regular grinding and splashing sound and remembered the sluice-doors left open; the water was pouring in, out of this weather. She sat up. Without a doubt the mill-wheel was turning and shaking the empty building. She took the matches from the rucksack and picked her way to the sluice-gate side of the wheel-chamber, lighting matches several times in the draughts. There was the master of the mill come back to life while they slept. Grinding and groaning, shrieking, it turned downwards into the boiling pool while the timbers tried to rear apart. She went back to Jonathan and said: "Help me shut the sluice, the wheel is turning."

He half-woke and said: "Let it turn."

"Feel how the floor is moving! I'm afraid something will happen."

"What can happen to us?"

She waited. Jonathan, asleep again, mumbled. She crouched beside him and looked at his dark hair with the pale lock tossed over his face; at the dark, tenacious, sorry profile.

She sat there on her haunches, with the wet draughts trickling over her cheek and down her neck, and pondered. There was a confused sound of mill, water, and storm. She looked out the window. There was nothing left of the water-colour scene of the afternoon; the doused moon and pool sheen, the smudged fields and forest, the smoking cloud and distantly drifting rain showed how unhuman life was. The wild animal, Time-without-man, sniffed its way through the damp. Jonathan snored. So—always with him, if she had her way? Sleeping there, with cold, dully. She shivered. She thought: "This is the last of the Houses of Love. Marriage?" She went and leaned over the black pool the wheel spurned. "What if I should fall in, that he would find me choking the exit in the morning? 'Teresa with drowned hair and cheeks of sod—' no, no."

Rising on his powdery bed, cramped, cold, Jonathan craned over the peak of sawdust and saw no one. Then he knew she had spoken to him a long time ago. What time was it? He looked. Only nine-fifteen, and he seemed to have been sleeping for hours. He stretched out his feet, swollen in their boots. He got up, went to the yard, saw her nowhere about, came back towards the wheel. She had moved to the other side. Making a light with his cigarette-lighter, as he moved, he went first to one side, dragged powerlessly at the wheel that closed the sluice, shrugged and came round the other side, watching carefully for the great hole in the floor. Between this hole and the lip of the well were a couple of feet of clean flooring; she had been looking in, and now stood against the wall watching him come towards her. She stood between the drop and the ragged hole in the floor. She could only come back one way, by the way where he stood. A few feet from her, he also stood now between the hole and the well. They looked at each other and the same thought flashed between them. "He (or she) could go without regret, why doesn't that thing of misery do it?" They looked at each other by the light of the flare with unveiled dislike. Teresa, looking at him, released him from her will; it happened suddenly. The harness of years dropped off, eaten through; she dropped her eyes, thought: "How stupid he is! How dull!" He looked sullenly at her, with hatred, crueller and more vicious than teased lust. He half shut his eyes and turned his head away. When his eyes returned to her, they had a natural look, but he was a stranger.

"It's cold," she said in a whistling voice. "I'm hopping it," said Jonathan. He turned round, taking away the light, and walking carefully. He looked at his watch; it was not yet ten. He got up, took his rucksack and coat and, getting to the door, looked back. She had not moved. He flung himself out into the yard and began to run. He could make the eleven o'clock train if he looked sharp.

He saw the train coming, the headlights and the window lights squirming towards him, melted in the thick rain. He almost missed it, jumped in, flung himself panting on the cushions and felt frantic, because he had left her and because he had nearly been stranded there for the night. What would he have done? Slept in the station, gone to the hotel, or wandered back disconsolately through the rain to the sawmill, his boots squelching, a cold in his throat? Whatever had happened and whatever might have happened, none of it was pleasant; his whole association with the woman was a cowardly mistake of his, dull, frightening. He coughed. Yes, in the storm he had caught a cold, and with a lecture on Monday. He must gargle, get a hot-water-bottle from Lucy if she was still up. She at any rate would be be pleased, in her grudging style, that he had returned. Lucy, too——

He had a vision of Teresa, lying in her coat in the sawdust, dreaming of what? She would not be frightened. A woman who had come some twelve thousand miles merely to see him, would not be frightened by one night alone out in the tame English countryside. Tramps, wanderers, country fellows—he became thoughtful. He got up, stuck his hands in his pockets and looked gloomily out into the rain. He thought it all over again. None could accuse him of being gallant.

He reached home, stretched his legs out and stared at the photographs opposite him on the wall. He still saw the mill. He smiled, laughed, flung his head back and let out a bellow. It was funny, all right. It would be something to smile over for years. She liked that kind of thing, it would be one more item in her total reckoning of suffering, for by this she must consider her suffering. She said nothing about it, was too canny for that; her business was to record the sweets, say: "On such a day, you were kind to me, Johnny." Quite a trick but it didn't get him, because he understood. To understand everything is to despise everything, he muttered. He rolled his head about trying to recapture the moment of fun but it had gone. He had got home relieved, but empty, resentful. What did it all come to? Why did he never have any pleasure out of things that amused other people? He hated everyone at that moment; he was deucedly alone in the world. What swarms of liars and hypocrites, cowards, they were! Yet they could get any amount of amusement or pleasure out of that kind of episode. He saw through it and the world was a bleak place for him. Passing enjoyment was all that was left; for the rich, isolated moment, there was indeed the fierce ray of pleasure. Then it left him and went turning elsewhere, a lighthouse situated on a hidden reef, in a sea no one could cross. He could not be bothered calling up the servant so he made himself some tea and got quickly into bed. He turned out the light and lay for a short time, thinking of the strange night, Teresa miles out in the country, huddled in he did not know what blackness of mood or sleep, without light, in a storm, in a half-stripped building; himself here, home in bed, thinking of her; spending the night thinking of each other, strangely united, strangely separated. He felt the faint breath of inspiration; this was an adventure of a sort. He fell asleep, heard the storm in his dreams and the leaves softly brushing the window, almost like a woman's nails. Queer night, a wonderful night. He awoke early in the morning, tossed as the night had been, with a new spring of life; something marvellous had happened to him. What would she do now? She would return by the morning train. She would come no doubt straight to his place. He thought he heard the bell ring. It was no such thing. Up, in his pyjamas, his hair tousled, he looked at himself in his shaving mirror under the high broad windows; a clear light came through from the new-washed sky. A spring rain. He saw in the mirror the curve of the smile on his sucked-in lower lip and his foggy eyes. He caught the fleeting tender and deprecating expression. Perhaps it was this expression they saw on his face? He turned away and stared out of the window, sat in his chair reading yesterday's paper. If she came and he was still drowsy, in pyjamas and dressing-gown, what a joke too! About one o'clock the telephone in the hall rang and Lucy called him to it. He took it up without thinking of Teresa and was startled to hear her voice. "Is that you, Johnny?"

"Yes," he said. "Hullo, there!"

She rang off. He waited for her to call back. She had no telephone in her room. But she did not call. "All right, fair lady," he said aloud, grinning. "O.K., I can stand it. But you can't."

She did not come on Tuesday or Friday and then he wrote:

HULLO, TESS!

I got home all right from the Rickmansworth expedition. Did you? How is Quick treating you? Expect you on Tuesday night as usual. Fortunate you didn't come this Friday, I had a study circle here, invited them three weeks ago, clean forgot it was your night. All's for the best in this best of possible worlds. Come if you want to, Tuesday, but not if you have other fish to fry.

Your friend,

JONATHAN.

P.S.—Perhaps we can try that country trick again some time soon with more satisfactory results.

She did not think for a moment of refusing him. She thought: "He needs me, I cannot refuse just because I am sick of it." When she came he gave her his last essay to convey to Quick for his opinion.

34. *Aurea Mediocritas*

It was a foggy day a week later. The lights were on in the City in all the offices and it was already quite dark. Quick felt ill on such days on the mudbanks of the Thames; many things made him uneasy, his dark flat, the silences from Marian, and lately in his office he had curious dizzy moments. The pale girl sat opposite him across the broad polished desk and his anxiety and puzzlement about her, and the way she was fading under his eyes, curdled his heart. He was not himself, he had strange feelings, he sometimes felt as if he were dying.

One afternoon, he took a taxi home about four o'clock. Teresa had to remain in the office to receive telephone calls. It was the day that Teresa had brought in Jonathan's essay. Quick took it with him but didn't unwrap it in the taxi, for his head was swimming and his eyes bad. After sitting down at home for half an hour, however, before a bright fire and after eating a little brought in by Chapman, Quick thought of the essay and brought it over to the divan on which he was lying.

He opened it casually in the middle and read:

What is called heterosexual love is a type of paranoia of greater or less incipiency, induced by obsession with one idea and exactly the same behaviour and reactions may be observed with the application of very different stimulus in other cases of obsession, as with the lunatic, the poet, the inventor and similar one-idea'd individuals. It is well known that some obsessions are, some are not, in the social "thirty-nine articles"; but it is valuable to inquire why this one (love) is not only accepted but is conscientiously induced by parents, educators, artists and even scientists who, so to speak, know better. Why the propaganda? The young man entering on the scene of life and seeing with unprejudiced eyes at once declares: "There is no such thing as love." Ten years later, we find the same person married, with children, retailing the lies and conventions which as a fresh-visioned youth he rejected. This is the great paradox of every life. I am for the moment (though I will return to him later) neglecting the youth who, for certain reasons, accepts the great socially valuable lie of love. Parenthetically, one may ask if all heterosexual love is not a shame-deviation from natural homosexual love which would seem the more logical—for what have the two sexes in common in our culture?

Quick at once turned to the front page, as he supposed for a moment that some error had occurred, but the cover and the title-page said: "Meliorism, or The Best of Possible Worlds, by Jonathan S. Crow, 1933."

Well, thought Quick, I have struck a bad passage but I am afraid Miss Hawkins's "brilliant young man" is just another typical example of the "greater or less incipiency of Ph.D.'ism". Phew! "Love is paranoia!" A fine lover he must be. A rather ordinary example, I should say, of the vacant-minded, empty-hearted young academic hedonist, for hedonist read egoist. But perhaps I am too quick on the trigger. The English are a freak people. They maunder along and suddenly a flight of genius! I must give the young man a chance. But if I am right how wrong she is! Can she be as bright as I think? Well, I had better begin at the beginning.

He sat up and started at the first page. Once he got up and clasped his head with both hands with an exclamation of horror. Another time he got up and paced about, biting his lip and twiddling his fingers with an angry expression, and the third time he stopped altogether with the pages spread out on his knee and stared into the fire, quite out of countenance. He then re-covered himself, put the essay on the table, and pacing about, began a long meditation, dark, musing, and it seemed to himself he was puzzled, he was even baffled.

The more he knew about his secretary and her friend Jonathan Crow, the obscurer became the problem. Had he misjudged her? Was it possible? Because he now realized that he had come to respect and admire her, for all her ignorance and simplicity. What were her relations with Crow? Was she a friend, a

413

mistress? How could she so misjudge him? Was it the "necessary blindness" of one sex for the other, merely? But how could an intelligent woman—he thought of all the "intelligent men" he knew who were blinded by a woman. But how could she—with himself before her eyes! Did she really understand what he said to her every day? Was she uncannily clever at pretending to understand? It became capital with him to find out whether she understood him or not. Was he the victim of a fraud, the pretended sympathy of a worker for the person who pays wages on Saturdays? For a moment he wished he were a simple student like Crow, with nothing to offer her, so that he could know if she really appreciated what he said to her. "Why am I taking it this way?" he asked himself. "It's rather a simple situation, a stenographer pretends to admire and understand her employer——" However, he got no farther in this direction. His thoughts suddenly flew off and he thought angrily: "Can I really admire a woman so stupid as to think that *this* is a work of talent?"

After much worrying of this sort, he rang for Chapman to bring in his dinner. Afterwards, he felt more genial and he took up again "Meliorism, or The Best of Possible Worlds". But now it was worse than before. Of eighty-two typed pages, the first thirty were devoted to rambling remarks about other people's ideas and the rest to sex in one form or another and this presently resolved itself into a discussion of whether academic men ought to marry, of the dying out of the superior type (the university graduate) and of women's brains and the value of women's brains to "the race". Said Crow:

> The white European male has natural superiority: for later records show conclusively, records of actual achievements in life, that neither the Jew, the Chinese, the Japanese nor the woman of talent, these four precocious groups, achieve anything proportionate to their numbers in the school or their early showing. We must conclude that intellectual precocity, like exceptional memory and emotility, by a natural compensation, is unstable, unreproductive and tends to disappear. This is the meaning in Nature of "aurea mediocritas".

Crow had other figures to show that Negroes, Italians, and

Irishmen did worse than other races of Western Europe, in English-speaking schools and this "is conclusive in the United States of America where Negroes have never spoken anything but English and therefore have an equal intellectual chance at school".

Crow now went on, rather peculiarly, to discuss a system called Basic English—but not for long. Shortly, he was back to the male-female question and did not fail to quote "Male and female created he them" although a professed atheist; and "the female of the species is more deadly than the male", although as a republican of the Empire he detested Kipling. He made remarks about a certain female spider which eats her mate and, analogically, the necessary parasitism of the mother on the father, in the human species, which destroys male intellectual efforts, although, Quick thought, he did not prove that human beings are descended from spiders. He then leapt back to a narrower discussion of why the precocious, in general, fail in later life, especially fail to attain security, respectability, "socially necessary truths", for, said he, it was so—"results show it"; and he concluded that it was better to be slow in coming to flower and fruit. He did not fail to note, however, that part of woman's ill-success "in life" as he put it, was owed to the deformation of her early training. Those who

yield to it and become members of the charmingly parasitic sorority (true women, that is) show no variation, are selected by the male to bear the next generation; while those who do not yield to it so much, gifted females with an infusion of male brains and maleness, in general (as Terman's tests show), that is, combativeness, aggressiveness, leadership and other male traits, are weeded out and their traits not passed on, because they are not selected by the conservative and possibly jealous male. Nature is a Tory, it may be unfortunate, but it is so. The race does its best, with its unconscious necessary wisdom, to the freak and the crank, the masculine female and the feminine male—we see that they are rejected so we ourselves shun them.

James Quick threw down this masterpiece of getting ahead. He walked up and down in the curious way he had when particularly incensed, while his eyes stared furiously ahead and he breathed hard. "I know all," he cried. "I see all. The stifled bestiality of the monastery, the crackpot egotism of the cracker-barrel sage—can she admire such a man? A genius! She says the footnote sage's a genius. She can bear his company. How can she? What can she be, to tolerate such a contemptible, calculating worm? Females are suspect, Chinese are suspect, talent is suspect, he alone, he alone——" He advanced staring with angry but melancholy eyes. "What's more, the all-but-perfect creature, Jonathan Crow, finds all others intrude upon his exquisite isolation, mothers are parasitic, working men breed too much——! Oddly enough, oddly enough—ugh! Men of genius can put up with their mother's children—what degeneration. What can Australia be like if it honours such men—what London, if it takes in such men? What kind of beggars in the U.S.A. that he quotes —h'm, what date? Now I'll show her—he's given himself away— now she'll see—but why blame him? The whole of organized scholarship is devoted to promoting themselves. They are busy selling themselves either to the workers, the business men or the governing class. Natural salesmen. To the poor man their line is: Here's a good easy fat job for your sons and daughters, they'll get on, they'll join the governing class; to the middle-class man, here's a bunch of people beyond reproach who will dig up so-called facts to support any of your values; and to the governing body, Christ! there they have the best job of all, of watchdogs, censors and liars—but calm down, excuse him, he's merely a nitwit, perhaps—look!—for instance, in one part of this essay he is merely selling his sex to the other sex on short-term. Part V. Computation of Population. Part VI. Male and Female Differences. Part VII. Women's Failure. Part VIII. Contraceptive Methods. That's complete. Love me and the world is mine, not yours, you bastard. Bastardess. No wonder Miss Hawkins looks like Karenina after the railway accident. Crushed by a one-horse pedant. That could be the explanation! What is he? Every man his own bride? Pederast, whoregoer at Saturday vespers? What do I know of this island anyway? Who knows what goes on in their melancholy heads, says Voltaire! It may be true, his spiel, after all. Eduard Fuchs told me, the polymath of sex—Englishmen and Dutchmen and Swedes did nothing——" He flipped a page and read:

Women are brought up to the hunt, men left the hunt long ago, women cannot be modern till they cease to hunt men, they must be taught creative trades, arts, crafts and techniques, calculation; the intense emotionalism of their lives will then cease to be an obstacle to their worldliness; their present worldliness will vanish too, and none will regret it: we can do without the St Teresas as well as the legendary libertine, coiling herself like a serpent in the poisonous dew of men's lasciviousness which without her would not exist, sterile Paphian, superfoetation of Pauline sexual fears.

A little later on, he read, however—

The Magdalen, whose love surpassed that of Martha and Mary, showed that the early Christians perceived the conditions of the freedom of women; woman is only free outside of marriage, and it is only when woman is free that man, for whom she is the "white man's burden", is free too.

Quick bounced up and down the room again, and quoted Jonathan aloud: "Christ gave no hostages to fortune." Then he rushed on: "Woman is haunted—as no man is haunted—by the fear of *biological* failure. She's desperate! They live contingently! And he knows it, the spider! We are allowed to doubt, they never."

Quick seized the essay and made a movement as if to throw it in the fire, then said: "By James, line by line, I'll talk it out of her as he's talked it into her. He's discovered women's ultimate control, desperation, the malignant spider, and he's controlling her by that, the discovering bookworm. I don't know entomology. Here he has 'spiders', that doctor of science and here 'Leibnitz'. Unread, that Ph.D."

He flung himself on his divan and looked at the clock—six o'clock. He missed her. He ought to telephone her and get her to come over now and talk to her about this man. He got up and stared at the wall in front of him, thinking of nothing, so it seemed. In two minutes, he felt a slight convulsion, as of fright, walked up and down a few strides, his ideas tossing aimlessly, a deploring look on his face, his hands clutched behind him. He shrugged his shoulders, stopped and leaned on a table with one

417

hand, turned round, faced the room and got an idea. With this simple idea, he looked over all the objects in the room, he looked out of the window into the alley which he was facing and saw a person go by the window. At once he slightly smiled, his lips moved. He stopped in front of the fire and took a few more casual steps, sucking his underlip with his face lighted up, biting his forefinger, and once more walked up and down with a Sherlock Holmes expression.

Scarcely, however, had James Quick thought, Why, I must be in love with this woman, than the improbability of it struck him and he clouded over again. He considered her simplicity, inexperience, the possibility that she was the mistress of what he bitterly called "this intellectual scarecrow", the fact that a woman who admired Crow could not by any means understand him, and the fact that he was perhaps led astray by daily intimacy. But in thinking this, an irresistible smile kept rising to his lips, a radiance brightened in his breast, as if a sun about the size of a twenty-dollar piece was rising over his heart and he could not rebuff this pleasant idea any more than a person coming out of the wintry night can resist getting warm.

He called Chapman, asked him to look after the fire, put on his coat and second-hand hat, and plunged out into the fog of the street.

Half an hour later he was at the mouth of the alley in the Euston Road. It was ten o'clock and a light was burning through the orange curtains of the little room over the arch. After walking up and down several times, in doubt, Quick went down the alley and rang the bell beside the name written in capitals in ink, "Hawkins". The door did not open but he heard footsteps running downstairs. The door opened, she caught her breath and then said his name in a voice faint with surprise. He was delighted, asked if he could go up, if it was allowed, followed her up the highly polished stairs, talking rapidly and softly. The room was pretty, with a real Dutch dresser, holding Dutch plates and tiles. It turned out that the landlady herself was Dutch.

"I knew you would live in a delightful place, tasteful," he said at once, although he had thought just the contrary. He took off his hat and put it on the table of the little dresser. "Do you use these plates and cups?"

"Oh, yes."

"Were you studying?" He pointed to the papers and type-writer on the table.

"Oh, no," she said, flushing. "Just writing something."

"May I see it?"

"Won't you take off your coat?"

His hand was outstretched towards the piece of paper. He took off his coat, however, repeating humbly: "Perhaps I disturb you? May I see what you're doing? I don't know anything about your life."

"It's just a piece of writing, you can see it if you like," and she laughed strangely, as if he could not possibly understand, shoved it towards him. She sat down opposite him, idly, flushed but stern. He was astonished to read, not something about Shaw, Wells, Keynes and so forth, but—

Introduction

The long pale evenings of the northern twilight were occupied in a strange piece of spiritual carpentry, a designed, fretted, fitted but empty box with a lock, in which would be her TESTAMENT, not now about Miss H. because this robust work was too earthy for her dying hands, but something called "The Seven Houses of Love", the ages, a sacred seven, through which abandoned, unloved women passed before life was torn out of their clenched, ringless, work-worn fists, a story of those days, perhaps of yours.

She had given up all hope of understanding the things that were talked about in the newspapers and that J. had so blithely and glibly run over when she first met him the day of her landing. The yellowish scraps of newspaper had gathered dust, unread, on the mantelpiece in her room.

Quick, involuntarily raising his eyes, saw a heap of newspaper cuttings on the marble-faked mantelpiece.

"The Seven Houses" were not for Jonathan nor for anyone then living but when she was already in the nameless dust, blown about the streets, as such women are, since the beginning, this forgotten box and this black-masked testament would lie on the table in the cold room; and these pale leaves of poor sterile women, floated off the tree of flesh, would not have been without someone to carry their words, timid, disconnected, but full of agony as those choked out of people beaten to death, these despised and starved would, dead, and dying, and to come, have an advocate in the courts of the world. The tyranny of what is written, to rack and convert.

"Who wrote this?" said Quick hastily, raising his startled eyes to her, but in a low tone of secrets.

"I wrote it, don't read any more."

"No, let me, let me, it's—it's—I can't express it to you, my girl, this minute, let me finish first."

"That's just a sketch, an introduction," she said coldly.

"Let me read, let me read."

She moved to the window, pulled aside the curtain and sat looking down in the street. The lamp striking upwards faintly lighted her. He read:

A System by which the Chaste can Know Love; Notes.

The Seven Houses, as follows, Pastorale, Bacchanale, Klingsor's Garden, Creation and La Folle du Logis (alternating houses), Heaven and Hell (identical houses), the Last Star or Extinction. (The last one is a terrible one.) The first house, or the porch. Say the word "love" and receive all floating ideas, as, say, a belly-handled jar or the belly of a jar itself, the song, "En Revenant des Noces", Maupassant's story of the pregnant woman, picked up on New Year's Eve, love of a little girl for a dark, curly-bearded man, Jesus, say, a boy in an open-necked blue shirt, Childe Roland to the dark tower came, gipsy love, Sunday afternoons, shadows under a tree on a dirt road some warm day. This may be continued for some time, say half an hour, or even more, but not to ennui, only to physical warmth, a naïve joy, an excitement which holds on to itself.

Second House, or La Jeune Fille Folle de son Corps. This excitement should be sent down by the imagination into the body, where it takes root and can be felt to grow in all members and parts of the body—this sometimes takes place very quickly, and in time, should happen automatically. All scenes of festive and dark violence. The change from one to the other, here is a sample—a fountain in secret but open sunlit woods—naked young people innocently bathing—suddenly a swarm of grotesque things, animals, men, satyrs, all a creation of beasts break out, darkening the woods, the water also darkens, turns a ruby-red and yellow, the bodies of the bathers, as they are seized or join willingly in the wild sundering of the flesh, turn dark, coppery, red, bronze.

Third House, yearning lust. The flesh, knowing, is unhappy; the age of the secret fountain is past. Night wandering, wandering by sea, the body burns to die in the desert, burned up by suns, torn by filthy creatures of the sky; satisfied mankind, waiting to drop heavily from the sky—how does the air bear them? They are leaden—to finish off the cinders of flesh and bone left by fever. Creation and La folle du logis. Suddenly, a shooting star rushes up from the earth, not downwards; out of the body thought extinct and in dust. A shrub grew beside the bones left, the bush becomes a galaxy, the bush once waving idly upwards turns into a fiery kite hitherto unseen, it is that that flashes up into the blood-rose sky. It is the leaden birds that fall down, singed, dead, they grovel and creep, what is left of them in the sand, die of hunger. The earth bursts out at their touch, thousands of sores, open wounds, scars opening and shrivelling with heat, it is desire or the suns of millions of years buried there, coming out again. Sun is born, dies each day, where is he? Buried in the earth, he bursts out, wishes to bolt upwards after the other, the phoenix, was it? All the buried suns burst out at one time, plagues on earth, the earth dies, the sky swarms.

Heaven and Hell. Relation with a single human being, knowing everything truthfully, admitting everything, beauty as horror, tyranny, skull-crushing idol, love as hatred, and humiliation. The innocent made drab; no one is admissible to heaven under this searchlight, not one is less than an angel. Devise a means of explaining all human beings in this way.

The last star. To die terribly by will, to make death a terrible demand of life, a revolt, an understanding, such as rives life, blasts it, twists it. To die by the last effort of the will and body. To will, the consuming and consummation. To force the end. It must be dark; then an extraordinary clutching of reality.

This is not understanding, not intellectual, but physical, bitter, disgusting, but an affirmation of a unique kind.

He raised his head slowly. She was looking at him. "She looks at me as if I were some object, a belly-shaped jar," thought Quick.

"I am astonished," he said. "Simply astonished——" he began to praise.

"It isn't to praise," said she. "It's to leave after me."

Presently, he knew most of the sad story. The light that streamed out of her eyes was like the fresh sky light that comes through the windows in country churches where they have no idols or images. But it was not in the conversion of Jonathan that she believed now, but in her coming martyrdom.

Quick asked her to go and drink coffee with him, and kept looking at her, overwhelmed by her strange expression. But she was too tired to go out. She told him she could not listen tonight to his "inspired extravaganzas". She said:

"With you, I feel like the devil's apprentice: I set the pot boiling and I can't stop it—it runs all over the floor, all over the village, all over the world and the tide keeps rising."

"I'm the devil?"

"You're the very devil——" Then she turned red and getting up, walked restlessly about the floor, saying: "I've never said a coarse word before, I'm getting out of hand."

Quick at once declared that she could never stand New York society where everyone was libertine, in fact, so libertine that there was no libertinism at all, the conception even had passed away. "Hell" and "bloody" made English society quiver to its foundations, at least in the middle classes, but well-bred New York girls applied outhouse adjectives to their nouns as thickly as red to their lips and gin to their livers. He did not mind it, it was the custom of the country, and it made women freer, it freed them from old slavery. As for sleeping with men, it had nothing of the European ritual to it, it had none of the taboos of the rest of the world. Women did not suffer there. Men, in fact, preferred women who were decently wanton, because they knew whether they were loved for themselves or not. A virgin woman, said Quick, knew nothing of the world, of men, of her own aims;

422

easily deceived by others and by herself. Many unhappy marriages were based on the virginity of women.

"I know you, Miss Hawkins—may I call you Teresa?"

"No, don't," she said.

"You must let me." He continued: "Teresa, I know you are a woman modern in ideas, but farther than that I don't know."

Teresa looked at him.

"In conversation with a man," said Quick earnestly, "a virgin woman is on the other side of the fence, they are not using the same language, they don't live in the same world. Do you know about that?"

"It sounds too easy a way to get an education," said Teresa. Quick laughed, rollicked. He bounced about the room, declaring: "I cannot make her confess, she *will* not tell me," and he recited—

> *"But 'twere a madness not to grant*
> *That which affords (if you consent),*
> *To you the giver, more content,*
> *Than him, the beggar . . .*

"I've altered that a bit as you'll find out when you look in Carew."

"Who's Carew?"

"You don't know Carew?" he asked with enthusiasm. "Thomas Carew, a Caroline, the most humane of libertine poets, 1595-1639. I'll lend you a copy, Teresa, I'll read it with you." She put the white enamel kettle on her gas-ring and began to measure out tea. "I'd make you some coffee if I had some."

"Don't make it, don't make it," he cried, coming close and looking at her hands. "I always look at your hands, woman's hands weaving destiny."

She laughed. He turned away. "Do you make tea for Crow?"

"No, he won't let me wait on him."

"Ah? An egalitarian?"

"No, he says women's care is a bait for marriage." She laughed quietly. "Comfort is a trap for a man who wants to devote his life to learning."

"I'd be glad to be trapped by the woman who loved me," declared Quick stoutly. He sat down at the far end of the room,

423

saying: "Don't make that damn tea. I'll take you out later and give you something drinkable, but sit down and talk to me. I know you're tired, but I'll persuade you to it. And did you want to marry him?"

She said, looking down: "I'm simply not good enough for him and he knows it; there's nothing to it."

"If a woman came after me with such devotion and sacrifice, I'd throw myself at her feet, I'd spend my life serving her."

"Ah, but he wouldn't."

"And that's why," said James Quick ruefully, moving violently in his chair. He turned sideways. "No one has done it for me. I was always the lover. There is all the difference in the world in that. I would adore the woman who confessed she loved me. But I have never really been loved by a woman. I have never been loved", and he suddenly turned his pale face, with its glowing eyes and tragic shadows, to her.

"Don't say that, don't say that, I love you."

"You love me!" cried Quick. He threw himself out of his chair and rushed to her. He stopped, seeing how tranquil she was. He became radiant. "I knew it, I knew it," he said. "I thought I knew it, but I didn't know you knew it." She looked at him quietly, concealing her astonishment and confusion. Why had she said it? Yet it seemed natural, she did not want to take it back. Quick went on declaring that he had known it for a long time, he had seen it growing and the affair with Crow must have been long dead, without her knowing it, that she never could have really loved such a man especially after all these years of trial, when she had become a woman and knew what he was. "It was just the illusion of a love-hungry girl," he declared.

"That's right," she said slowly. "I believe I never loved him at all." She was paralysed with surprise in her mind and heart. She had no feeling of any kind except a great warmth and love towards Quick, but she had not yet felt that they had any relation to each other.

"When did you find out you loved me?" he asked her pressingly.

"I don't know, I suppose I always did, from the first day," she said, puzzling to herself. "But I didn't know it."

"No, but as I talked, it gradually unfolded, as I created a world for you—eh?"

She laughed. "Oh, you think you spun the world out of yourself like a caterpillar?"

"A world for you and me," he said, coming close and beginning to kiss her hands, and then tenderly and continually, her face, hair and neck, so that she thought of the modern pictures of heads, covered with eyes or else with mouths. She was covered with mouths.

She went downstairs with him but would go no farther. There was a letter from an old acquaintance in Australia on the hallstand, and Quick at once seized it, saying: "Throw it away, don't read it, that belongs to the old life, the new is just beginning, the new is with me," but she took it from him, laughing, and put it in the pocket of her apron. They kissed in the open door-way, the quiet house behind, with the odour of floor-polish and starch, and the madly tumbling street roaring up the alley. As the first shock had not passed away, she was still cool and glad when Quick went, so that she could think about him and remember his strange words.

Quick went half-way up the alley and stood staring up at her room. The curtain moved. She looked down. He still stood staring. Presently, the face and hand disappeared. His ideas rushed about in the gale blowing inside his head and in the thunder of the street. He walked down to St Pancras, and back again, and stood again in the alley. The light went out at that moment and he saw her face at the window, but she did not see him. She was looking upwards, or over the roofs of the houses. She sat there a long time, a very long time, and at last he went away. Thus all the night, he thought, together, the whole night.

She had often wished she could have the mind of another person for a while and this evening she felt as if it had been given. Two accidents had spun her away from Jonathan and she was free of him. There he was away off in the distance, a glittering, humming, self-devoted wheel, separate in space and time forevermore. This letter was the second accident. It was from Miss Haviland. To Miss Haviland only had she written about her resolution to die and about the paper which she would leave, addressed to her, perhaps (but "do not count on it" she had said). Now Miss Haviland wrote:

Take heart and take the dreadful disappointment as well as you can. No one, not even Jonathan, is worth it; and you know how I feel about Jonathan. I loved him too, I can tell you that now. It's so far away, now, and I'm an old woman, really old. Jonathan is still a boy, but there was a time when I felt it badly. Then I gave him to you—I meant to—but of course, he wasn't mine, nor anyone's. Such a young man is no one's but his own. That's where our mistakes came in. However, whatever relics of my affection for the young man I find, among my old maid's mementoes, I owe something to you too, out of friendship. Destroy this letter and don't tell what follows to anyone. It won't be necessary. It's common knowledge now that he wrote love-letters to several girls here (it amounted to that) and even asked them to live with him. If I were you, I'd put it up to him, but if you aren't seeing him, or if you think better not, don't do it. Why and how he reconciles himself with his conscience, I don't know. He was always a peculiar young man, with notions of his own on duty and responsibility. This is a queer turn for a moral young man, and yet I somehow believe that he still means to be moral. However that may be, his freakish morals have done some damage here, at least to one of his old friends. As for me—I wasn't one of them, fortunately for me, I suppose. I wasn't even a candidate. And I won't put in a pretty sentiment and say I wish I had suffered as you did. No, I don't. And I don't understand your young man. Something has happened to him. I remember him well as a student. He was of a most unusual purity, he was an idealist, brave, almost austere. I can testify to that. Who knew him better than I did? Therefore I can't get it out of my mind that he has somehow been made vicious, has met depraved people, but that he is vicious now, of that I am sure. But how? This doesn't interest me. I am done with him, we all are. You interest me. Don't die. Live. I am thinking of you; for the time being think this, that I am living for you. Write to me. I love you.

ALICE.

Teresa, late that evening, wrote a brief note to Jonathan asking for a special rendezvous.

Jonathan, pleased by this unusual request, at once replied and invited her to the restaurant where he had first gone with her and where they had seen the dark woman. It was only after they had eaten, and when they started to walk towards his home, along a glancing street, by a row of dustbins, put out from the back of a restaurant, that she put it to him.

"Yes," said Jonathan huskily.

"Why did you do it, Jonathan?"

"For an experiment," he explained sulkily. "'Gene, my friend, said I was a fool to be so blue, any girl would have me, I said no, and the upshot was that I made the experiment. Gene turned out to be right," he ended bitterly. "Any girl would have me."

"'But you wrote only to girls that liked you?"

"You mean—where were the controls?" he asked rather brightly. "I thought of that and made Tamar the control. She wrote and told me not to be a fool, the only one who saw through me."

"What did the others say?"

"One said I was so far away, the other said she would, but—the other——" he turned and looked resentfully at her. "I was punished right enough, women don't relish an inquiring mind. Don't worry, I let them all know it was only an experiment. But the thing that came out of it, that revolted me," he cried, "was their degrading avidity."

She said nothing. He turned round, pulled at her sleeve, and pointed the way they had come. "Come back," he said. She came with him. He pointed to the row of bins standing there, some half-full, others disgorging their fragments of spoiled food. "Like that, like that."

"Like that?"

"All the women——"

She counted the tins. Five.

"Five women?" She looked at him.

He took her sleeve again, and began to talk fervidly, explaining his meaning. She combated him, but he went on eagerly, delightedly, and she felt the fragments of food, the tumbled contents of the bins, pelting at her, covering her with decay and smut, but all the time he pretended it was reality, the truth about men and women, that he was telling her.

She left him at his gate, but before she left, he asked: "And Quick? What did he say?"

"You are to meet him at the Tottenham Court Road Corner House on Friday night. Wear your black hat, carry Haldane's book, and he'll carry the *Economist* in his right hand. Be there at nine."

"O.K. Good night."

"Good night."

"Then Friday I won't see you?" he said, jeering.

"No."

"But Tuesday?"

She came back towards him humbly and said softly: "Jonathan, I am ashamed to say it, but I must cancel our engagement for the evenings."

"As you like."

"Good-bye."

He held out his hand, they shook hands, and so parted.

35. The Signs of the Misogynist

QUICK was always early. He arrived at the Tottenham Court Road Corner House (most convenient for Crow) at eight-fifteen and after looking over all the people waiting in the entrance court, among the fruit and flower stands, he returned to stand near the inner door and he took out the *Economist* which was his sign for Crow. Meanwhile, as he turned the pages, he looked up every minute or so, for the thickset, blond youth that he imagined Crow to be. Crow would have the English lantern-jaw, so often seen in American farmers of the Middle West, and a soft, brooding look, never seen in the U.S.A. at all.

He had not been watching long before he noticed a shrewd and unscrupulous-looking man in his thirties, who strolled round the stands and looked sharply at him, perhaps a private dick, he thought. The man was swarthy, oak-complexioned, with a hammered-out distorted and evil face and a syncopated rolling walk which looked like the business stroll of the second-rate spottable spy. Quick felt miserable—was Bow Street or his wife or Axelrode, for any conceivable reason, watching him? Had Axelrode, his old trusted friend, got him into some mess, or had he witlessly signed something? He tried to think. The thin and sly man, who had a tallish hat, rather high heels, a new moustache and horn-rimmed glasses, after staring at him uncertainly moved off again on his patrol. Not very secretive, thought Quick uneasily, but what dick is? They always wear an expression which says: "Watch me, I watch you." He received a shock two minutes later when he raised his head and saw the sly man in front of him, looking at him. This fellow raised his hat, came forward, and said: "Are you Mr James Quick? I am Jonathan Crow."

"Yes, I am James Quick," said Quick, coming to himself and

showing the paper in his usual good-humoured way. "And I see you have Haldane's book. You are early, so am I; good——" and he led the way into the Corner House. It was a long walk to the station he was used to, a table belonging to an old, bald waiter with a German accent and a dull face. Quick sat at his table every evening for the same reason that, in the daytime, he sat at the table of the bow-legged waitress in the teashop. Quick looked behind hospitably several times at Crow whose deepset eyes were lying in wait behind heavy glasses, and he, turning again, had observed his movements, his peculiar rolling stalk, a gait only seen on a vain man, similar in fact to Axelrode's, only awkward and slow. Quick looked intent and pleasant, rather pale; and all the time he kept wondering if some fantastic mistake had been allowed to occur—by Teresa, by Crow, or by the gods, for in Jonathan's shrewd, hard look and twisted, canny smile he saw nothing of the unhappy and inexperienced youth of talent described by the girl. Unhappy, yes, and talented, perhaps, but in quite different ways; and even the essay had described a different man, a dim-witted, dim-faced, bobbing pedant of the sort that climbs slowly but successfully on his undangerous stupidity, behind the backs of other men to be head of his department; this was all in his essay with its naked attacks on all that stood in his way. But if the man he had just caught a glimpse of—the supposed private detective—was what he seemed to be or would ever become, then he was sagely shifty. But what am I thinking of? This is Jonathan Crow, the ill-used son of the slums who is a virgin, on his own admission, and is passionately yearning for knowledge of women.

In that case, Quick, you have something to learn in psychology and you have struck a new equation in men. Oh, these English boys—but what is the answer? I will soon find out—but steady, no jumps, this is new soil. What are really the ideas of this Laski-Labour, Liberal, lover of the U.S.A., love-whiner and possible pervert? That ingrown face is the face of a devil, given the insight and the chance. But is it merely a mask? People are born with faces which do not belong to them. Milk-toasts are endowed with Hieronymus Bosch mugs. He had now steered his guest to the table of the ugly waiter and the two men sat down, with an empty white table-cloth between them. A pillar stood between them and the door, and to one side, in the middle of the back wall, was a small stage for an orchestra. The walls on either side were faced with coloured marble pieced into two immense murals, one representing Yellowstone National Park and one the horseshoe of Niagara Falls.

"Remarkable bit of work," said Jonathan, pointing at these works of art, and continued, with an easy roll from the hip. "Well, how does the blocking of currencies affect people like your partner?" Quick explained briskly and put in: "Don't mistake chemin-de-fer for politics or high finance. Some did, including Mr Léon Blum, and other eminent gentlemen. When he gets sold down the river, he shouts: 'Take me back, master, I was only having a little game of African golf, I wasn't talking about Abe Lincoln and the upside-down dipper that leads north.' The usual fate of palliators, they go where the bad 'niggers' go just as fast and a good deal faster. But they never learn. When will your labour leaders learn that you can't play the game of the rich because the game is fixed and you can't be kind to the rich because they think you're a sap?"

Jonathan grinned delightedly, and then slyly, as he was attacked.

He cried: "I had a notion you were Labour; doesn't that make you a bit out of step in the City, or are there other under-cover radicals down there?" He burst out laughing. It was the first time he had ever talked with a business man and he felt in high feather.

"My partner's pro-Soviet," said Quick curtly. "He's always been a Socialist."

"But not in his pocket," said Jonathan, "I suppose?"

"I'd rather talk to a wide-awake imperialist who knows there are Socialists than the clerks and stenographers who are related to someone who was once in Baku and who feel they have to defend their oilwells with their last shilling, thirty-second cousins on their mother's side of Sir Pompous Rubicund. Pompous and pro-Franco because they have a cousin, a drunk, who owns a cottage among the olive-fields of Andalusia or a runner of beeves in the Argentine."

"Whew!" cried Jonathan. "That's good!"

Quick, encouraged, went on improvising wildly. But when the first flush had passed, Quick, who saw in the young man what he first had guessed, an ambitious small-town man, sly, ignorant but a cudgeller of faculty cabals, a wit-picker, a notion-thief, a man bound to get on, a paste-and-scissors scholar, of the kind that often makes a name for himself by writing forewords to great works—Quick, who saw his suspicions come out in the flesh, began to attack the young man savagely, on every point, whenever he opened his mouth, and Crow, enlivened by the warm blood thus fiercely injected into him, stirred, laughed, felt again the hurly-burly of "bull sessions". When he spoke of English scientists, Quick laughed harshly. "You! You haven't a tithe of the naturalists and scientists the French have. What about Lamarck, Saint-Hilaire, the great anatomist Cuvier, Buffon, Claude Bernard—eh?—Bichat, to whom we owe the whole theory of muscular motion, Pasteur, Lariboisière, Dupuytren, the greatest chemist of the eighteenth century, Lavoisier, the greatest chemist of the nineteenth century, Berthelot, Fourier in the theory of heat, Coulomb and Ampère in the theory of electricity, and Carnot in physics, Lagrange in mechanics—Lagrange is one of the greatest names of all time—no names in France, no names? Oh, for insular vanity!"

Crow was laughing hard. He grinned ruefully, and said: "What can you do? *Que faire?* Insular vanity goes under the name of learning with us. But we do admit the Germans have something—Haeckel, Helmholtz!"

"Yes, Carlyle sold you that."

Crow snaffled pleasantly. "Well, Carlyle is a bit out of date now, he passed with Wilhelm of Doorn, didn't he? Do they still ram him down your throats over there? What kind of literature do they teach over there? All dead, of course, I know, that's required." Shifting his heavy legs on his chair, he went on at once: "What standing has a British university graduate over there? I don't mean from Oxford or Cambridge. I suppose rather high?"

"Of the rank of Ph.D.—German and French rank equally, British next, Oxford is not accepted in rank with Continental universities, Cambridge is, in sciences—in fact, Cambridge is considered about the first college of the world now in sciences."

"So the whirligig of time brings its revenges," said Crow pleasantly, tipping his beer glass and looking up at him.

"Yes," mused Quick, who kept darting puzzled glances at the young, wary, bright, and yet indifferent face. His remarks were agreeable enough, his manner indolent, yet he snarled when he spoke like a hungry animal at its food, and dark shades passed over his face. His too-soft, over-hanging lower lip was formed like a prow, jutting from the bony cleft chin and a deep crease, to meet the long grooved upper lip, the mouth, moist, red, slightly open, too soft and mobile. Above, the long nose and close-set, dark, long-lashed eyes; an olive-washed skin, dirty, thick. Looks like a cheap lawyer, thought Quick, angrily. With every glance he became more furious, he began to grimace gently to himself, he darted hot, indignant looks at the unconscious Crow. He felt sick at heart—this man, this, this one with his martyrdom?

"Yes, it's funny," said Crow, after taking out a large silk handkerchief, and blowing, much at ease. "The protocol's pretty much the same here, they retaliate, Americans have to go High Church before they're comfortable here. I haven't a chance of a good academic job with my accent, I'm a blanky Colonial."

"Contempt for everyone is the only heritage of the poor Englishman," Quick said.

Jonathan grinned sharply and picked up the long glass of beer which the waiter had just set down in front of him. "Isn't it! The cultural heritage, as they say, and by Jingo they'd rather have that than an extra shilling a day."

This all angered Quick, who now launched into a five-minute exposition of the causes of the Revolutionary War. Jonathan, stirred, smiled, his lower lip hung open damply, he sighed and murmured: "By Jove, you Yanks take it to heart still, don't you? I must make a note of that." Quick's words started to tumble over each other querulously, he stopped in mid-sentence, looked contemptuously at the young man, who was smiling into his glass, and there was a pause.

Then Jonathan softly drawled: "Did you get a chance to glance at my juvenilia? I know it's not straight textbook economics, it's more—it's almost a Meditation." He laughed. "But I thought I got out a couple of original notions there. My next will be a bit more academic, but I always like a kind of wash of original thought over the disembowelled reference books. It's not quite decorous perhaps."

"Well, to put it very frankly——"

"Yes, be frank, be frank," said Jonathan, smiling. "It didn't interest you?"

433

"To put it very frankly," Quick let fly, "it's much below standard——" and he began to rip it to pieces, page by page, quotation by quotation. When Crow raised his eyes amusedly, slyly, at the end, Quick remained silent.

"So you can expect to get into Columbia?" Quick went on, spitefully.

Jonathan became gloomy. "I've got to take what I can get, I've got no one behind me—just me and my bare hands." He smiled. "Besides, I don't think I'm going back home, nobody does. I never had any influence, so I got out. I've always had my eye on the land of—what is it?——" He gave a pleading grin. "Land of *unbegrentzete möglichkeiten,* boundless opportunity."

"It's astonishing you know all these economists," Crow continued in a flattering tone. "I had no idea business men went in for the cobwebs of theory."

"How old are you, Crow?"

"Twenty-seven. I know I look more, even after three or four years on the fat of the land. Though," he said, passing one hand over the other and looking at his hands regretfully, "the first two years, it wasn't the fat, only the rind, I had debts. You know the line—

"'This mournful truth is everywhere confessed,
    Slow rises worth by poverty depressed.'

"My mother backed me, she didn't have any money, but she believed in me. I believe she robbed my elder brother for me. I get anything I've got from her; my old man's just a vague liberal who's read a couple of books."

"Why is it every careerist tries to turn his mother into a Madonna—to prove his intellect is a virgin birth, papa had nothing to do with it?"

Jonathan, surprised at the attack, laughed clearly. "Do they? That's interesting. When observed, make a note of!"

"It's the sign of the misogynist!"

"Is it? That's all right, then, I belong to that crew, I expect, though Mum managed to keep us under her wing until pretty late in the day." He laughed. "She keeps her men! But she's a fair caution! A warning in skirts."

"So you don't marry?"

"No fear! It's easy. No concessions, that's the golden rule. One concession and you're involved, three concessions and you're

434

married!" He tossed his head like a dog, and laughed. Quick said sharply: "I've read Schopenhauer", and he denounced all canny bachelors.

"I say, you're hard on us," cried Jonathan."The women you run up against are probably cannier than the lot I know. There's another reason I'd like to get out into the world, meet the real kind of flesh-and-blood woman, the sort you can knock around with. The sort I know, they'll listen to a man until he attacks their inside defences, and then, thus far and no farther!"

"You have a lot of girl friends?" said Quick.

Jonathan said carelessly: "Oh, you know how it is, you get up in front of a class, the female naturally selects the male with some characteristic that picks him out from the herd, short horns in a long-horned herd, etc. I have what's required."

"I take it, then, that you don't live the life of an anchorite?" said Quick.

Jonathan said almost reproachfully: "Oh, when a girl gives me the come-on, I'll sometimes go to her room, if she's got one, or the little station hotel—or the hayloft. But I don't call that a love-life, it's no tribute to me, only to my function—they're a kind of industrial accident!"

"But apart from industrial accidents?" pursued Quick.

Jonathan gave him a surprised look. "Well, how does any-one—any man like you or me, I mean? It's no trick to get women, they're eager for it." He continued, his voice low and thick: "For every step backwards of yours they'll take two for-ward—the clutching hand." He laughed heavily, like a drunkard. "But it's elementary, my dear Watson. At least to men like us."

"You don't know any idealists?" asked Quick venomously.

Jonathan started and lifted his head, looking Quick in the whites of the eyes. Then he dropped his eyes and said pleasantly, looking again at his hands: "Oh, there was my friend, Gene Burt—I tried to laugh him out of it, but they're born that way, I suppose. Yes, I know there are some born with rose spectacles, I suppose there have to be some or the race wouldn't go on. Oh, girls, of course, some girls, the misfits especially, but not after they're married. It's just something to increase the intensity of feeling, something to do with heat, tension, conditions of procreation."

"What do you mean by misfits?" asked Quick, really puzzled.

"In my acquaintance," said Crow, smiling quietly, "the pretty girls are practical and those unlikely to mate are romantic. I assume that's every man's experience."

Quick said: "But you, a man of the world, don't feel anything of the sort?" Jonathan stretched out his boot, looked at it with a smile, and replied easily: "No fear. No beliefs, no illusions, not even heaven! In my second year, I tried to believe in God again. Read *The Foundations of Belief*—all the regulation stuff. No, couldn't do it. I never could fool myself, worse luck! The world seems pretty flat to a man who's found out where he stands."

Quick was taken with remorse for this man, all in black and white, with the twisted face and spectacles.

Jonathan stretched out his hand and lifted the little bubble of glass in which was Quick's liqueur. "May I smell it? Bénédictine, isn't it?"

"Yes."

"Yellow, isn't it?" said Jonathan. "Like whisky."

"I suppose so—yellow-brown. Well, what you say interests me more than you think. So none of your girls made a romantic mistake and fell in love with you?"

"No," said Jonathan confidently. "You know the golden rule, no virgins, no romantics—dangerous, it's better to wait till the next one comes along if they're not educable."

"So you have no regrets at all?"

Jonathan made a sweet grimace. "I don't know of any."

"In fact you're exemplary."

"Oh, I wouldn't say that." He laughed again. "I'm afraid my record wouldn't stand rigorous examination—but I'm just an ordinary fellow, after all—whose would? I belong in the belly of the bell-shaped curve. But what's the good of going into these things? All's for the best in this next best of possible worlds!" and he looked inquiringly and pleasantly at his interlocutor. "That is, for free spirits, critical natures, men who know their way about—in the dark that surrounds us," he ended on a miserable tone.

"You don't know where you're going, in other words," said Quick more kindly.

"To the end of the rut!"

"Maybe you'd better get out of it."

"That's why I wanted to see you."

Quick and Crow continued their conversation some time and then parted, Crow taking back his essay which Quick promised to discuss more fully at their next meeting, this one having somehow been frittered away. Quick crossed the street to buy a *Worker* from the old man who stood outside the bank door each evening at the end of Charing Cross Road, and thence, walked rapidly home, occasionally murmuring to himself, his large handsome eyes gleaming. He was trying to compose a scene with these two in it—Teresa and Jonathan—but they never fitted together.

He threw himself on his divan when he got home, quite wasted by the hidden conflict with the young man and his struggle to appear serene, for although he had been so volcanic, as Jonathan had said, he had been concealing his real feelings all the evening, "for Teresa's sake". Now he felt worn out. Nevertheless, after revolving his ideas about the young man, he got up and quickly wrote a note to him, inviting him to meet him once more on Sunday evening, at the same table, if possible, or near it, so that they could go over "many points not yet touched upon".

Jonathan was pleased with this, for he had formed a very high opinion of Quick's talents. He turned up at the meeting-place, full of good-fellowship, "with craft, like a beetle", in Quick's eyes, "scurrying in and out of the lines of his face". Quick himself was indirect.

"And now," began Quick at once, "two things. First the future of you and Miss Hawkins in the United States or elsewhere."

"Miss Hawkins!" cried Jonathan, stiffening. "She has nothing to do with my future."

"How's that? She doesn't play a part in your picture of the future?"

"If she's given you that impression, you'd better wipe it out—I'm on my own, from now on and always."

"I got the impression that you and she were friends," said Quick softly and rapidly, "and that you had at least at some time discussed the possibilities of a future together."

"That's a false impression," said Jonathan, enraged. "That fits in with some of my ideas of her. We're not even friends. I happened to run a class she came to. I don't want to go into it, it's happened too often." He shrugged. "Since then, I've been—pestered and beleaguered", he smiled slightly at the phrase-making, "harassed and haunted—you know the desperation of the sexually rejected woman, taking a kind word for love. I will confess that I studied her a bit like a case history. It's not much of a compliment to me and I don't mean it to be!" He laughed. "But what I didn't know, in the beginning, is how damn hard it is to shake the clinging sisters, they'll pity you till your head is grey. I'd rather be chased by half a dozen she-devils and carted strumpets—there'd be some fire in that at any rate", and he raised his triumphant amused eyes to Quick's for a response. Obsessed by his own thoughts, he only vaguely noted Quick's face blazing white and vaguely wondered at this violent emotion —perhaps he too was involved with some woman? Jonathan went on: "Oh, my brother too, in his street meetings, he's some kind of a soapbox radical—and the minister at home. I've seen him, coming out, down the steps in that slum street, you'd always see a couple of girls waiting, crazy Sadies, old peaked grand-mothers, specked fruit. I don't mean they even hoped for adul-tery, but just to caress, lean against, pick a speck off the coat of, breathe the breath of the outstanding, or in fact, any male." He laughed long and loud, smacked his thigh. "We're popular, by Jingo. The harem is the proper expression of the relation of the sexes. Or harlotry. Eh?"

"May I ask," said Quick instantly, in a stifled voice, "if this is a description of Miss Hawkins?"

"Oh, no," he said negligently, taking his beer and draining it, signing to the waiter. "I wasn't speaking of her, I wasn't think-ing of her at all. I may say that her intense, unfortunate and suspect—no, scarcely suspect!" he laughed shortly—"interest in me is not reciprocated, never was, never could be. I can't get that through her head. But you don't want to talk about your typist," said he, with bonhomie. "How did that come up? Oh, yes, she gave you the impression that——" he waved his right hand and asked with assumed convivial gaiety: "And how is it now, your American beer?"

"I never drank it," said Quick. "You'll forgive me, I hope, for returning to the subject of Miss Hawkins for a moment? I see her every day, which you don't, I suppose?"

"Definitely not," said Jonathan humorously.

"Quite so. I face a human being every day, after all," said Quick, "and I wonder what makes that human being the way she is. I happen to know that Miss Hawkins gets a good salary, as salaries go here, but she seems very ill. She is not ill, I suppose, tubercular?"

"I know nothing about her," said Jonathan. "Perhaps she is tubercular. In fact it might explain a lot, I never asked."

"You used to see quite a lot of her, didn't you?" persisted Quick.

"No," he shrugged. "Once in a while. She made opportunities of seeing me and you can't turn a woman out on the street. But one day was like another. I don't suppose I ever looked at her as you look at a woman—yes, now that I come to think of it, the first time I saw her after she landed, I thought she looked rather out of sorts. But then she was three years older, more than three years, and she always lacked that something that women have that attracts men, that spiritual something which is merely pretty flesh." He laughed brightly. "The great stumbling block with her is that she believes in love. I'm holding forth," he laughed. "Do we men ever love? I doubt it. I never did. Perhaps men could love each other? What is wrong with homosexuality? I never knew. I never tried it but I put it down to my prejudice." He laughed coyly. Quick gave him a sharp look, saw the waiter hovering, and for the waiter's sake, ordered the same thing again.

"Well," said Quick, "before we go on to what brought us here, your essay and your future—I seem to be marking time—I'm not like you. I can't see a human being suffering without trying to find out what is the trouble."

"Well, isn't that a bit masochist for a hard-hearted business man?" said Jonathan tolerantly. "Live and let die, say I", and he laughed vainly. It surprised Quick to see that this strange being ended every one of his sentences with a laugh. "He's a very vain man," said Quick to himself. "Or else he's a little bughouse. It remains to be seen." He bored into Jonathan's face with his burning eyes. He had become haggard, he looked ill. It was his habit of intense feeling.

"At first I thought she was starving, she looked it. It was when she first came to me, just after she arrived here. Only the other day I discovered—by accident, she didn't tell me," he lied, "that the reason was that she had actually half-starved herself for nearly four years to come here, to be near you, perhaps to live with you", and his eyes fastened themselves passionately on the man, for he did not know whether she had been Jonathan's mistress.

Jonathan lowered his eyes and looked disdainfully at the table-cloth. He shifted his boots and stretched his legs under the table. Then he remarked: "I wash my hands of that. Mild men have been chased across continents by the meekest of women—or what is that quotation?" He smiled.

"I mean, you didn't write to her and ask her to come to be your companion, wife, sweetheart, whatever you like?"

"Not on your life. She said that? She's getting the illusions of that outcast—you know, the little match girl dreaming about the roast duckling offering itself to her with knife and fork stuck in?" He laughed indulgently. Quick looked at him with undisguised horror.

"She hasn't the good taste to send in her resignation to biology. Crow suddenly laughed boyishly, and looked round with pleasure-wet eyes, not only at Quick but at two plump, blotched, sandy-faced girls he had been observing slyly from under his long lashes. His voice had become a little clearer. Then he said with a touch of professorial whimsy: "One should have the modesty of one's defects; a hunchback doesn't apply for a job as a tailor's model. I save her from herself, or rather the race from such sorry sisters. I am the instrument of Dame Nature." He shrugged and looked Quick straight in the eye, coldly. "If Nature made them parasites, she didn't make us suckers!" He laughed. Quick started.

"But you're heckling me," Jonathan declared, very jolly. "What's your theory?"

"Well," said Quick, "you'll pardon me for interpreting this one way, my way. You're a poor man and women frighten you because they're an expense. If you were a rich man, you'd have a different set of clichés about women; instead of setting traps for you, they'd be, to you, merchandise, booty."

"So they are—even to the poor man—they're poorer still," said Jonathan brightly. "By Jingo, of course that's an economic truth, I certainly get somewhere rubbing my brains against yours."

Quick said fiercely: "I have a purpose in all this, or I wouldn't be discussing the girl like this."

"Ah, I wondered." Jonathan smiled up in pleasant expectation.

"I regard you as a function of your setting, and so I am able to separate you from your detestable opinions."

"Are you serious?" cried Crow, peering at his companion. He had intended to charm and interest this influential man. He had arranged his previous conversation with this in mind and had tried to conceal his inexperience from this man of the world. He said naïvely: "But a man like you can't take women seriously? How can they compete with us? I mean, speaking frankly and seriously and without wisecracks," here he grinned, "you do not take women as your equals, I suppose?"

"Perhaps they are my superiors."

"Oh, come," said Crow, good-humouredly. "Look, have a liqueur, have a beer on me, this is my round. I'm beginning to get interested, in spite of myself, in all this. For instance, in the astounding fact that a man like you, who has seen the world, has money, lives in a man's world, thinks he takes women seriously. I wouldn't put you down as a sentimentalist." He laughed jovially. Quick started. This laugh now seemed to him to mean deep-rooted egotism. "Almost insane egotism," he said to himself intently, so that Jonathan saw his lips moving and wondered if Quick was in love with some woman who was "leading him by the nose" as Jonathan said to himself. He said tenderly, to Quick: "It's possible that one can love a woman, though I never have, but as for respecting them——" He looked down at his hands and spread them out. "I have never met a single woman who could think a thing through," said Jonathan. "They reason by fits and starts and always behind it there is some ulterior motive, of which, perhaps, they are not always, in fact not generally, aware. They are not self-knowers. They accept all the shibboleths, all the old wives' tales—don't you sometimes wonder how two nations can exist side by side in the same house, for twenty years, in the same bed? One is brought up on myths and one bringing to fruit scientific research, operational problems! Of any couple, compare the man and the woman, what do you find? Always the patent superiority of the male, even where a brilliant woman, so-called, appears to have married her inferior. Women talking about babies, frills, maids, cooking, men talking about politics and the latest inventions—or, at any rate," he smiled broadly, "football, baseball, but something outdoors, external, something to do with the real world."

"You'll let me off explaining the A.B.C. of social relations," said Quick. "I am satisfied in my own mind of very different truths. I want to get at the bottom of—if you'll bear with me a moment—what seems to be a mystery."

"Fire away," said Crow tolerantly. "What is it?" But at Quick's next words, he frowned, and buried his nose in his beer glass, sucking away at it during half Quick's question.

"Wouldn't you call Miss Hawkins an intelligent woman?"

"Intelligent? No, everything's ruined by her womanism, she's not objective, that's a case in point."

"I think the contrary. However, she seems to have had the idea that you were fond of her. Did you write that to her?"

"What? Never, that never," said Crow.

"But she thinks so. Where could such an extraordinary mistake have come from?"

"From womanism," said Crow, smiling. "I helped her in some tutorial class, told her to persevere, something of the sort. Why, you know how these things happen."

"But you never intended to marry her?"

"God forbid," said Jonathan Crow. "For me, anyway, it's out of the question, I always made that plain. No, she knew it too. She recognized a hopeless situation and threw herself into it for the romance. Masochism, it's simple. Elementary also, my dear Watson. That's the alpha and omega of the whole story."

"And then—when she came here—"

Jonathan apeared to be musing. Then he said gloomily: "I'm not a happy man, I haven't a cheerful turn of mind, I mean, and I get fed up with textbook clichés, and the only way to find out the truth is to experiment. You might put this down to the profit-and-loss of the laboratory—or even, if you like, vivisection. I was interested, finally, in her obsession. Here I was offered a true example of masochism and also a perfect example of mythomania, and I couldn't resist it. A man who's in the social sciences can't be squeamish and churchly; you've got to find out. Find out, or be found out—isn't that Nature's great dictum? So that was it. That was one of my springs of action. Secondly, I suppose, there was a kind of sexual instinct in it—I can't love, but there are certain feelings I can have, cruelty, curiosity, play and perhaps just the love of a good, old-fashioned tussle and towsle, for she has tough stuff in her, she would have got a weaker man."

"Got to love?"

"To marry!" He laughed. "That was what made the wheels go round, of course—but I'm holding forth. Your fault, Quick, you were doing a bit of psychoanalysis, weren't you, on me?"

Quick said: "So you're a scientist? That's how you look at it?"

"If I had property, I wouldn't have to use my brains," said Jonathan with false sadness. "I'd just enjoy. But I can't eat and so I think. Isn't that the urge? I've been trying to learn to enjoy for years, but I haven't got very far. In a way, yes, this was, too, an attempt at enjoyment. A poor man enjoying the struggles of a poor woman, I was a bit of a casuist with myself. And then there was the question, how far could she go? But she never had the courage of her convictions. Held back, too, by her woman-ism. A very interesting case, I suppose, but so is every defeated person, and interest in defeat is a bit morbid. I accuse myself. I know. I suppose it's fear of biological defeat myself that makes me hang trembling with laughter—and something worse—over the biological defeats of others. Perhaps now I've come down to rock-bottom, perhaps that was it. I enjoyed her misery. But this is dull stuff I'm talking. You don't want to know about my soul-stirrings," and he looked brightly at Quick. "How about you? What's the effect of the advanced sexual relations over in the States on a man's psyche?" and he pretended to be amused at the word. "That's another reason, too, I want to get over there, I really want to live free."

"And never marry," said Quick.

"There is a story somewhere—it is a regular Medusa story about a boy who at the moment of ordination sees a girl in the gallery—I forget what happens. Well, the marriage ceremony is the reverse of that. Instead of vowing yourself to chastity, you vow yourself to copulation. You are obliged to it, the marrow of your bones is hers. Isn't that an absolute horror? The bride rushes to the altar but I never heard of a man who wasn't drunk or shivering sober."

"You know a queer lot," said Quick. "But women nowadays are willing, if not anxious, to live with a man they love."

"That's merely the ante-chamber to marriage," said Crow.

"For three years, I've had a rule—never sleep with any woman who loves me."

"Then women do love you?"

"Love——" said Jonathan, laughing softly.

"Well, tell me, since we've got in so deep," pursued Quick, inquisitively, "wantonness has disadvantages; one generally has a more or less settled relation with some woman?"

"I don't trouble about that," Jonathan said easily. "Propinquity answers that."

"And who is this Propinquity?" said Quick, then he rushed on, "Well—if you don't want to tell, it's not important. Your essay astonished me, frankly, by its obsession with sex. You don't write like a cold man."

"Really? I didn't know it! That tickles me," cried the young man. "Tell me more about that. Outsiders always see most of the game! I didn't successfully sublimate, after all, then! How does that come out? Be frank. I can take it, as you Yankees say."

Quick hesitated for a moment and said: "It struck me that you must have someone that you—I don't say loved—but some-one to go to."

"Oh, yes," said Jonathan. "There's the girl in the house for instance. She's Propinquity, as you name her." He laughed. "That's good!"

"The girl?"

"The maid, not very savoury and not much to my credit, I know that, but it happens, they're used to it. That's ancient history," he said, shaking himself and trying to keep himself in countenance. "But there are others. I have a more or less per-manent relation with a girl in the country—and so forth. So I'm surprised that all this comes out in the essay, too, don't you see, for I've taken care of that kind of thing. It's a kind of caries, otherwise, eats away your bony structure, mentally."

Quick drew his entire history from him, bit by bit, and Jona-than, disappointed, became slightly nervous about his shabby life. He began to put a better face on it, to say how much he wanted to get out of it, and to ask Quick to do his best for him. He made an appointment to meet Quick downtown, to talk

444

over the subject which Quick had brought, for his essay, and to consider what he could do in the City. He thought of publishing, clerking, that was all. Quick left him in great distress and turned towards home, going over the conversation of the evening, tossing it about, improving and depraving it; then he thought now that he must tell Teresa everything, in case any affection remained for the "good and chaste scholar", so he hailed a taxi and went to her address.

36. A Fury of Only Half-spent Words

Smoking with excitement in the cab, he saw the conversation with Crow as a dreadful and gorgeous affair, his mere words blossomed into great declarations, Jonathan's admissions into the mouthings of a soul in hell. He got out of the taxi at the corner of Euston Road, unable to restrain himself any more and in a fury of only half-spent words and new emotions, he hurtled himself along the pavement, raising eddies of apologies as he bumped into people. "Sorry, sorry, sorry! I beg pardon!" and "Oh, I beg pardon," and "Sorry, sorry," he muttered.

He rushed down the alley and rang the bell. He heard steps echoing down the stairs and ideas ran helter-skelter through his mind—it might be the red-headed neighbour in a red dress who lived there, it might be the landlady, was he compromising a "nice English girl" by coming so late—but the door opened and there stood Miss Hawkins. He stared at her for a moment, scarcely able to find his voice, and then remarked quaintly: "I see you are home and still up. May I see you, my dear?"

Teresa paled in the half-light of the passage. She had given herself too much in saying she loved him, and now she feared him. She said slowly: "Yes, come up, but we've got to go and get some milk from the brass cow," referring to the automatic milk vendor on a door down the street where, during the night, milk poured out from a little cow's head when you put in six-pence.

"Getting milk," said Quick, shutting the door behind him, seizing her roughly and dragging her to him. She panted, unable to speak, yielded, released herself in a flurry of darkness, and went towards the stairs. In the hall, on the stairs, and in the upstairs hall just outside the red-headed girl's room, and as they stepped inside her room, in the open door-way, he stopped and held her again in his suffocating embrace. "My dear girl, my love, my own love." Each embrace was for her a momentary fainting. During the whole passage, she felt both completely united to the man and yet aware of the awful empire she was giving him over her, and it was always at this moment that she pushed him away brusquely. It flashed upon her, *"But this is the night of the senses!"* When he grasped her inside her own door, she pushed him away, however, and breathed hard. She sat down, without asking him to sit down, and looked comically at him, as if she were going to cry, but he was pale.

"I had to see you, after what I heard tonight", and then, "I had to come and see you also—you told me you loved me," he cried triumphantly.

She went scarlet. He waited, then said miserably: "Don't you mean it?"

She nodded.

"Let me hear you say it again," he said excitedly. "The whole evening I saw your friend, Mr Crow, I was listening to what he had to say. I was thinking of what you said to me."

She opened her eyes, panic-stricken, and flushed again as she thought of the words he was asking to hear. He studied her: "Don't you know I love you? I've been thinking about you for months!"

"About me? What about me?" she said faintly, but he did not hear, and coming towards her, drew her to him, murmuring: "I'm going to make you mine now."

"Oh, no, you're not."

"How sure you are."

"Yes, I'm sure." She laughed suddenly.

"Why not?"

"No, anyhow."

"Ah!" His face wakened. "You think men despise the girls who yield to them?"

"Of course."

"My girl, my girl," said the man, walking up and down the room. Then he burst out: "How wrong you are! On the contrary——" Looking at her eloquently, he stopped and after a moment burst out with: "We adore such women. That's what they teach you."

"No, no," she said obstinately. "I know."

He came up close to her, looked down at her, while she sat primly, but flustered and frightened, and taking her face between his hands, slowly he began to kiss it, the forehead, the two eyebrows, the eyes, the cheeks, the mouth last of all, her neck, breasts and her mouth again. In the middle of this gust of kisses, he said: "Now, do you think I would despise you?"

"I don't know," said the girl, almost crying. "Perhaps."

"Stand up to me, face me," said the man. "I see you know nothing about it."

He pulled her up and began suffocating her with embraces, fell on his knees, clasping her so that she almost fell, and as she moved a step or two, irritated, unsympathetic, he followed her, chaining her to him.

"Now you are mine," he said, rising to his feet. "All that is mine, I have kissed you all over so that you must be mine."

She laughed timidly.

There was a step in the passage under the archway.

"That's my neighbour," said Teresa.

"I want to be with you, alone," Quick murmured, "put on your hat and come on out with me—I'll take you to Lyons'—there's nobody there so late. I'll taxi you there and back."

At the end of the passage they waited between the two little shops which were closing. He hustled her into the first cab that was cruising west, threw himself upon her, and when he recovered himself, sat stolidly in one corner, panting and twinkling, and he said: "In the state I'm in it's a good thing you haven't got what the French call a *jupe-taxi*. I have one, at home." He was effervescing. "I'm sure when you were a girl at home a man who said a coarse word was abhorrent to you."

She said nothing. He became ashamed of himself. "My dear, as I said, I saw your quondam friend Crow tonight, I know all." She shrank back into the corner of the cab, stared at him. The street lamps hurtled past, lighting her up. "I never heard such a statement from a man," he continued violently. "Dostoievsky is nothing to it, layer after layer peeled off and he went on revealing himself into the lower depths, satanic depths."

"He suffered," said Teresa. "Did you talk about his essay?"

"Never mind his essay. I talked about what interested me more. I said to him, a beautiful mind and soul, a beautiful, anguished face, with a great desire and a great passion—to me,

I said, that isn't petty, that's not mean, degenerate, shameful, but something so rare and splendid in humanity, in women—you know you're capable of a great love!—that if I should find, I told him, such a gallant impassioned woman, I wouldn't let her get away from me. I didn't tell that bastard, excuse me—I know coarse words are abhorrent to you—your quondam friend Mr Crow that you loved me, it isn't for him to know. I wanted to, but I didn't. I said, if such a woman told me she loved me, I'd kiss the hem of her skirt. I asked him all kinds of questions but I couldn't make head or tail of his account. He encouraged you to come to him, didn't he?"

"Oh, yes, of course."

"You trusted him and he detested himself, he had those last elements of good-feeling. Because of the naïve, innocent showdown."

She was so puzzled that she forgot her shame.

"Don't accuse me of prejudice," he cried. "I said that to him, and your friend said: 'It might be that, God alone knows what our impulses really are.' Those were his very words, but there's much I can't tell you, I don't know you well enough. He's a devil incarnate, and he doesn't even seem to know it. He said he had never encouraged you. Of course I don't believe him. He seemed astonished that a man like me could love. He said: 'I don't suppose we speak the same language.' He was thunderstruck. He thought he was so clever, so *mondain*—when I told him you were beautiful, to me, tender, gracious, sweet, all the things we want to see in a woman, he recoiled. He didn't know what to say. I was glad to see him without a word to say. He changed the subject, and went on to his essay. I'll tell you everything that happened, but not now, not tonight. I never met such a twisted soul," said Quick.

She defended him. "He sees no good in anything."

Quick laughed. "There's a limerick about your friend Crow . . ." He was now in full feather, interspersing debate with limericks, heavenly love with obscenity. He went on—

> *"There was a young man from Cape Horn*
> *Who wished he had never been born*
> *And he would not have been*
> *If his father had seen——"*

He stopped and declared: "I don't know what you know, I don't know if I can finish that limerick." But he finished it, and it gave him a chance to explain something else. "But he couldn't wish it as much as I do," he said, reverting to Johnny Crow. "He knew you loved him and you heroically did this, and this, to him,—'to you,' I said—'and it is a coarse, mean, shameful deed, and you not only refuse her your love but want to banish her from the human race', for what else does his essay mean?"

Shrinking into the corner in shame, she came out to ask in surprise: "His essay?"

"You don't know how to read it, my girl. And why did he want to kill you—yes, that was the object, to kill you, by despair and need. Why? Because he's dead." He began laughing outrageously. "And I said to him," he explained, waving his hands, "when he tried to promote me with what he fondly hoped were American passwords, such as the vulgar populist idea that the people there get what they want, I asked him if they *wanted* the movies and got up and made a public demand for the movies when there were only peepshows at Coney Island, or if they got up a round robin when they only had stage-coaches, to invent a railway. And he tried to impress me with the names of hundreds of books he has which he hasn't read one word of, I'm quite sure. For the other, I can never forgive him. You do, because you don't know and because of women's divine compassion."

"No, I was guilty," said she. "I couldn't give up, be beaten by fate. That was it, I knew it was that. It was never Johnny. He was always kind to me, a loyal friend. Even now, he is wretched, alone, and I am getting out of it."

"You still love him," said Quick, shortly.

"Love him!" she cried in horror. "I never loved him at all. I thought I did, though. He helped me. I will always be grateful to him."

At this moment a light fell into the swerving cab and she said to Quick: "Why are you crying?"

"You are too observant," said Quick.

After a few silent moments, Quick said hurriedly: "There's something I must tell you now—about your quondam friend, Jonathan Crow. I haven't known how to tell you, but now I see I can. He has been deceiving you. Prepare yourself for a shock, I told him I would tell you, so there is nothing wrong in this."

She said: "Yes."

He had brought her to the Mayfair Hotel in Piccadilly; his home was round the corner. At a little table in the fashionable lounge, he told her something of what Jonathan had said that night, and after leading up to it, he explained that Jonathan had taken for a mistress, Lucy, the girl she knew, the woman who cleaned his rooms, "just such a miserable Bloomsbury student as you have told me he described to you, lifting the unwashed skirts of miserable servants who cannot refuse."

"I am glad," said Teresa. "I am glad he doesn't suffer. I am glad."

She looked quietly at him, thinking that he too didn't love her. She wondered if Quick knew himself.

"Thank goodness," said Quick, "no such sacrifice, no such soul-murder scars our love affair."

She looked down, very unhappy, because he had never said he loved her.

"What is the matter?" cried Quick desperately. "Why won't you look at me?" She shook her head, with a slight smile.

"Teresa," said the man, "you must have seen that I love you madly? I loved you from the very first, though I didn't know it for a couple of months, I just wondered what had happened to me. For years, I've been so helpless, aimless. A man of my age can't believe it at first, he has had other tries. He takes his time and tries to penetrate first"—he hesitated and gave her a straight look—"the character of the woman he loves. But the first day I walked down the street, feeling quite different, as if there had been a revolution and the poor were free—almost like that! I didn't know it was you. I kept seeing your face, your funny pale face and your hat and hearing your soft, timid voice, but I didn't know it was *you*."

He waited. She said nothing, looking towards the broad empty floor, and the waiter, half-way up it. "And what did you think of me?" he asked.

"I liked you—you've always been the same, since the first minute. I thought you had the face of an angel, I trusted you, you had a beautiful face," she said at last.

"A beautiful face!" he said in an astounded tone. "Did you really think it was *beautiful*? It's such a funny word to use about a man. No one says a man has a beautiful face."

451

"But men have," said Teresa.

"And you think that I have? Then you must love me," said Quick with decision. "Don't you?" he pressed.

She said: "Yes."

This was followed by a silence. Then she said: "It's nearly two o'clock. I must go home."

"Oh, I'm sorry, I'm so selfish, I forgot you were so weak. I live just around the corner, but I'll take you home, because I know you won't stay with me."

She laughed. He helped her into her coat and said: "Well, let's go to the country tomorrow, the fresh air will do us good. I'd like to take you to Canterbury, it's only about an hour and a half. Look, could you meet me at Victoria at about eleven—or I'll call for you. And we could have lunch at the old Fountain Inn, the most famous hotel in Canterbury?"

"Does it cost very much?" she demurred.

"That's my concern."

"All right, I'll meet you at Victoria."

In the taxi home, they discussed the details. She jumped out, with a goodnight and heard Quick give his address.

37. At the Altars of Antique Churches

THEY were scarcely a day at Canterbury, ambling through the streets, through a cool bright light; for just after tea at the inn, Quick wanted to go back to London. They had a first-class carriage to themselves, and for nearly half the journey he held the near-fainting Teresa in his arms while he spoke his passion for her. The countryside was white with young moonlight, the carriage dirty and even cold; neither of them had slept much the night before. Teresa, miserable and maddened by his frenzies, wandered in her mind. Through the window, she saw them speeding on through the winding sheet of the Kentish fields, the train black and smoking under a black sky, above her Quick's black eyes and blazing white face, around her his hard arms. She had never been on such a journey. When they had still a long time before them, Quick said that her hesitations, her confusion, which he could see, and even her prudery, came from his own mistake of not taking her in her room the first night when she was innocent of him. He would take her here and now. She resisted and sat up.

"It is no light thing, our meeting and our union," said he. "It must have been anywhere that we met and at any time—why didn't I know you ten years ago?"

"I was thirteen."

"Never mind, never mind," he said, disregarding her. In the dark, he became as something else, the spokesman of his passions, not the passionate. "Nothing can keep us apart. I will follow you all over the earth." She started away from him: "Like Johnny?" the idea came. He went on at this moment: "If the law says I am married, I will make you my back-street wife." Yes, even if she would not live with him as his wife but was afraid of public opinion "as so many nice girls are" he would take care of her, get her a room somewhere, furnish it, and come to see her.

She fixed her eyes on his face and listened intently. From time to time she glanced out at the long-lying fields of pale light unmarked. She had never got used to the spectral northern evening, and the light seemed created only for today, only for these indecipherable eyes and these obscure and treacherous words. But Quick, seeing her attention, eagerly rushed on; he would bring her books, music, take her to concerts, theatres, if she wished, send her to the university—make a woman of her, make a brilliant woman of her, the sort of woman who in all ages had charmed men, the Montespan of the age; for it was not rose-leaves and round-faced chits that any but the Jonathans went for, but a woman of wit and lustre such as he would make of her, who would shine anywhere. He was a stepping-stone, he told her; she would be a Staël, a Récamier, a Catherine II. He would take her to Paris, and elsewhere, no one who knew her now would know her then; he would make her over entirely.

In all this storm of words he had only mentioned marriage once and then in a dubious way. She wanted to go to the Sorbonne—but to be a back-street wife, to give with one hand and take with the other—not that!

Then he mounted the snake-faced, vulture-winged Pegasus of passion and sang the physical joys they would have—she would not have the disappointment of a drab mean bed but all the love that a man who had seen the world and many women could give her; pleasures she had never thought of and would at first be ashamed of, he would give her. Marriage was not what she thought it, the kitchen-range and the tea-table, but another thing, an academy of love, with one tutor, as Abélard and Héloïse, and all this she could have, love, joy and all in the world that women were supposed to desire, as well as those things that the women really wanted, in their hearts, dominion, learning. If she feared to be herself in marriage, he said, she could do without it. If she was not sufficiently sure, he did not mind that at all, they would be lovers.

All this she heard as a person going home through a storm and who likes wind and rain, hears the various sounds and feels the buffets with rough pleasure. He had not really proposed to marry her.

It seemed to her that this was a situation like Johnny's, as brilliant as Johnny's was mean—something splendid to look at and look through, as the Arabian Nights, but a dead blank cover when done. She did not want to go into anything that was to be over soon, either in a few weeks or in a few years. Enough of that, she thought.

When she escaped into the station, she was astonished that the storm had died down. As in the room in the alley, as the first time, now it raged suddenly out of silence, and again when he left her for a moment to buy some cakes for her, into silence it went. With him the gust returned, sweeping her up into the heart of it, and blackening her mind so that she scarcely knew where it swept her, and all the time he murmured that love had taken him into Canterbury and love brought him back with her, that he hoped for her and she must give herself up to him. He came with her to her room making love so passionately and with such fervid words, pouring out all his eloquence to her, quoting his Carew, his wonderful obscenities.

But throughout the wild scene she said: "No, no, never till *she* knows," and she stuck to this, that they must wait for a letter from the wife in California. "Nothing in the dark, *my* love is not in the dark," she said proudly, and "My God, what self-command, it's unbelievable," he exclaimed, standing up, leaving her, going to the mantelpiece, leaning on it and looking at her, flushed, her dress disordered but she laughing. She sat down on her bed, calm and feeling the surge retreat from her again.

"There you sit," he said, coming over to her. "I'll make you. Come, the time has come, and we will coin young Cupids," and he pushed her backwards.

She rolled away, got up, stood in the middle of the room and said: "Come and fix my dress, you did that!" He did so, then he went, half-swooning with emotion, but flushed, his eyes starry, and she sat alone in the silence, new fallen like snow, feeling all that youth and beauty could give, all that peace and all that triumph could ever have promised. The noises of the town fell away, struggle and misery went home, ate and slept, the world became for a short time quiet. "It's done," she said at length, got up, went to bed and slept.

They passed the cold time from December to March in these tortures, going out into the country in the week-ends, to famous churches, universities, and villages, the man with his great

455

eloquence celebrating the beauty of great places and small places, and making every glorious thing in the history of the English fold round his woman, making it all a compliment to her, finding in her all the traits of her nation, and in her face, too, its best qualities. In all such places, he wished to make his union with her, at the altars of antique churches and before a green-clothed heavy landscape, in lighted woods and raftered inns, so every part of the country became a part of their desire and consummation, a moment of their marriage, burned into their memories as the days of youth and early love. For each of them it was the first, the true love, the love of youth, and magnificent lustihood, the love without crime and sorrow. They waited all this time for the letter from overseas. The day that it came, she left him, refusing to have dinner with him, and late in the evening she came to his flat, knocked at the street-door, was admitted by Chapman and found him, grousing to himself, sick and huddled in his arm-chair by the fire. It was a cold day.

"What do you want?" he said querulously, seeing her standing there. "Why don't you go home? I thought you had to go home?"

"Didn't I promise?" she said. "The letter came today and so I came."

He got up, his mouth open with surprise and stood looking at her for a moment, not believing that she meant to stay with him. He was in low spirits because of Marian's sad and hopeless letter. He rang for Chapman, asked for tea, sherry, and cake, and when they had eaten a little, he roused himself to make love to her, but soon he said: "Go home now, my darling, I'm tired and ill and I won't be able to get up in the morning if you don't go."

"No, I'm staying all night, I came for that. I'm not going." He stared at her again, then quickly went and drew the curtains. "Where's your nightdress?"

"I don't need one."

Still startled, he rang for Chapman, got rid of the tray and said: "Well, let us go to bed at once, then, for I'm nearly dead."

She said no more, but quickly and modestly undressed, and he undressed also, before her; he turned out the light and left only the gas-fire on low, because it was still cool in the alley.

"Well," she said, "and now the great mystery."

"What," he cried, "so you really don't know?"

All through the night, he moaned in his sleep and cried, for what he foresaw, the struggle to come and that it must be fought through, because this was the woman to hold him and there was no solution but a bitter one. As for the woman, she was quiet and thoughtful too, waking in the night when he cried and soothing him, and thinking, "This is love with a man," for the rest, the "mystery" she had been able to divine it in a humble manner, it was the "Seventh House", the "last star". It was only the house of the sense, the miraculous journeys of the last few weeks that she could not foresee and that no one could build up out of lonely flesh. Now this was already over and it seemed to her, in this sad long night of the man weeping and foreseeing that he would be tormented by his women, that this was the consummation of life. In the night, waking, she found for him a terrible human passion of pity and love, such as she had never felt for any man or woman on earth. She said to herself: "This is my husband, I know it for sure", so that when they got up in the morning, although she had intended to return home and had only come this one night to keep her promise, there was no more talk of her living apart any more, but she came and lived with him and so their connubial life began.

38. Down the Flowering Lanes

THERE are bad A.B.s who make good officers and unruly innovating army subalterns who are born to be generals: Teresa was a girl who had no fitness for girlhood and its limitations but was apt as a woman as soon as she shared a roof with a man. She felt no difficulty, no need for adjustment, but at once understood her husband; all her study of love fitted her for marriage. She adapted herself so quickly to the easy connubial life that she was puzzled to know where the stumbling-block had been at first, why had she not married years before? She was conscious of two desires, to accomplish her Testament, which had now become the "Triumph of Life", and to get to understand and love men, from whom she had been wrongly, feloniously separated for so long. For Jonathan Crow, that useless husk from which the whole kernel of passionate suffering had been expelled, she had not even a thought. From the day she went with Quick, she did not give Crow another thought; and at this moment, strange as it may seem, she did not even wonder about Quick's nature nor feel surprise at his behaviour. She said only: "You never made me suffer, you never made me hunger for you, you gave me no pain, you did not set any value on yourself", and in his complete surrender, his passionate, greedy love and the recital of all he had undergone before he met her, she found rest.

She was too formed by adversity and too firm and ambitious by nature to take pleasure in her marital union alone. It was scarcely Quick who had done it, but fate, and though her only concept of fate was that she was mysteriously in tune with some inaudible, continuous single note in the universe, it was impossible to think even for a moment of how she had met Quick and of his influence on her life, without thinking involuntarily of fate. "If this is not fate, it is what is called fate." She felt towards Quick as must have felt those old-time girls educated in a convent and brought out in a fortnight to marry an unknown husband.

They had taken a flat in a renovated building at No. 10 Crane Court, Fleet Street, near Chancery Lane. There was a large window looking upon the alley, or court, but most of the light was cut away by a printers' building opposite and the rest was filtered sickly through the fogs of soot and the cloud on weekdays. On most Saturday afternoons, as soon as the chimneys stopped smoking, the sky appeared and the Sundays in Fleet Street were quiet, cool, sunny, with a marine sky and a salt wind.

Quick had led a very dull life in London, spending most evenings walking about the streets, and he was naturally a genial, loving, unsuspicious, and gay man, exuberant in company, of which he was fond to the point of vice, he now set about making friends, eager to introduce his sweetheart to them, and to expand into life again, like a robust plant. He had acquired a few habits during his bachelor life, small and insignificant, like the twiddling of his fingers and a quiet talking to himself of which he now had to break himself, and the breaking of these habits he found hardest of all.

His new life, too, was not without its hurts and scars. About two weeks after his settling in with Teresa, he had been obliged to leave her at home for about two hours one evening. He did this with great repugnance and was desolated with fear and misgivings during those two hours. When he came back, Teresa had been reading a novel by Proust which he had given her, surprised that she had never read Proust, who was then the fad of all up-to-date metropolitans of whatever profession. They threw themselves on the bed to talk and here, in the half-light, in unchecked intimacy, Teresa began to tell him about herself, what her feelings really were in this honeymoon and how she felt now that she had the whip and check-rein in her hands—he went cold, so cold, that she felt the warmth dying out of his breast; he lay like a dying man. She realized her mistake, with a pinching of the heart, and at once abandoned the thought of telling him the truth about her love. There were a thousand sides to it, it was pervasive, strong, intellectual, and physical, but he only wanted "a woman's love", the intensely passionate, ideal, romantic love of famous love affairs. She now threw herself into a frenzy of endearment, tried to charm him, went back on her own words in an engaging way with a thousand embraces, kisses and touches, such as she had never given him, but which flowered from her, from the depths of her long desire; but for the first half-hour he merely said in a weary voice: "Yes, yes, I know", or "Let me alone, Tess, it's quite all right, there's nothing wrong, only let me be", and so on; but at length the warmth returned to him and he turned over and slept. When he awakened, he was more cheerful but still serious and it was a week or ten days before she felt that he was beginning to forget the blow in the dark which she had given him.

She resigned herself now to playing a part with him, because she loved him, and in order to give him happiness. She felt the fatigue of life, believing like so many young women that she had found out the truth, which was that man and woman cannot be true companions for each other. But she did not wish to confide in a woman. What woman knew more than she did? She did not think that a child, or years of union, would alter her silence. She thought that each day would be a step farther into the labyrinth of concealment and loving mendacity. And why all this? Because she had wished to speak about the steps which had led her from Jonathan to Quick, steps which were taken quietly every day for months. "But," she thought, "I belong to the race which is not allowed to reason. *Love is blind* is the dictum, whereas, with me at least, Love sees everything. Like insanity, it sees everything; like insanity, it must not reveal its thoughts."

She was like a cornered animal before which, miraculously, an escape through rich quiet flowering country is opened; she fled away down the flowering lanes of Quick's life, and had not yet stopped to reconnoitre or to see and admire the plain. Quick could not see himself, for this, as an escape, and as for the rest —marriage was not new to him and it was part of a plan of action, while for her, involving a different kind of knowledge, a status, new embarrassments and regrets, each part of her new state merited thought and dissection. It was because it had come upon her so suddenly, without forethought or discussion, that she was restless too, wanting to find out what she had come into, like an unexpected heir of estates in distant lands. His first pleasure is to go abroad and be shown every acre, barn and hayrick of the new estate. Where a marriage takes place among relatives, the general flurry prevents the bride from thinking of her new life, except when she stops with terror on the wedding eve and asks: "What am I doing, who am I marrying, am I taking on more than I can manage?" But not so in these lonely distant unions known to wanderers. The wedding ceremony means nothing, the man is there before and there after, he and she have looked after everything themselves. The witnesses are two street cleaners and a messenger boy. They take a bus or taxi and eat their wedding breakfast alone, and then spend four hours in the cinema, being ashamed to go to a hotel in broad daylight. The whole move is made in the heart of a great city, where no one knows whether they were united yesterday or last year, or are merely brother and sister on their way to the Zoo. These are the happy marriages, but these are the ones where the social institution means nothing. No one can know and no one cares. Marriage, the institution, depends on the small town, the family house and the back-yard gossip. The big city has given it its death-blow. When nothing remains to the ceremony, the ceremony is of little importance; in the village the traditional relations of man and woman persist, and what makes them like half-effaced and nameless shrines in a pasture, is the opportunity of the modern city.

Quick, who believed Teresa to be brave, independent and passionate, expected nothing from her but affection. He had tasted and anticipated this joy, almost unknown to women, of introducing a young, pure, ardent but naïve mate to the world of social life, action and ideas. He said: "You are fitted for more than me, other men will love you and I will be prouder of their love than you, because I will understand it. Don't think I am a coward; you are free, I will share you with another man who is worthy of you." This he kept on expressing in the excess of his love. He naturally supposed that the life he offered her would not eventually satisfy her, idea-hungry, ambitious and energetic. He imagined with horror and pity the life she had led up to now, especially the heart-rending struggle for the affection of a cold, vicious man, and he thought of her as streaming with gratitude and delight, sensual pleasure and visions of the future, and knew only this with certainty, that for the time being she would be glad to rest in him. She said in answer to all this: "He giveth his beloved sleep." He loved her with the sentiment of his own generosity, he loved her because she was strange, thin, pale, hot-tempered and a dreamer, because he fancied other men had neglected her as they, with their small hearts, neglected the ugly waitresses and old waiter of the unfortunate manner. He told all this to Teresa, too, adding: "It's true we are all beefsteaks to a Bengal tiger, but why do men prefer in women the fat and tender cutlet? Cannibalism dies hard. Your inestimable friend, Mr Crow, for instance—"

"Oh, don't mention him!"

He chuckled, "—objected that you were too thin. For this stringy sultan, they must be round, fat and pink-cheeked. However, he has a theory also to cover his choice of hungry waitresses and tubercular servant-girls, he is the necessary supplement to their income. Wages are pitched so low that they must whore, says our friend. So he is there. The dear little strike-breaker."

But Teresa never mentioned Crow's name and did not want to hear of him. James mentioned him every day, insulting him and destroying his arguments, still carrying on with him, in absence, an argument that he, Quick, had long ago won. Then Teresa discovered that James was seeing Jonathan about once a week, and that Johnny was putting out feelers for a job. Jonathan had proposed himself as their dinner guest, in Crane Court, and was rather surprised to be turned down. "You could not see him, Teresa?"

"No."

"Never again, eh?"

But Teresa had no interest in these attacks on extinct Jonathan Crow. Her chief anxiety was to live from day to day. She still felt that she might only have a few months to live. Some would have said that she was unable to bear the burden of happiness. But was it happiness? Quick told her that it would take years to undo the work of that flint-hearted, evil-handed young man, who, for him, saw herself a Lucy—unloved, sinful if she put on lipstick and repugnant if she did not—nowhere able to escape the rebukes of Mr Crow; this was how he, in his perverted desire to crush all women, had moulded her. "*Evidently* a man of small sexual powers," said James, "and afraid of the empire of sexual love, to boot, he yet tried to get women in with him in every possible way, by his letters, lectures, and lamentations, but woe to those who believed him. He did call them, they did come, and what a panic he was in!"

"I shall never understand Johnny Crow," said Teresa. "I can only ask, *why*?"

"You cannot understand the weak," said her lover. "He is not conscious of having done wrong, he did all he did to survive. That is the supreme argument with the weak. They think all mankind should do them homage because they survive. Can you understand that?"

"No!"

Quick looked at her cold face and changed the subject. "I will not think the time lost if I spend many years at your feet building up what Jonathan Crow broke down!"

She was embarrassed by this devotion of the man whose idea of heaven was the rapture of married love. She respected him for his loyalty, which she understood because she too was loyal, but all her life she had expected to give passion and never thought of its being given to her. She had wished for the night of the senses but not anticipated a devotion of every day and night. Quick laughed at her, calling her his "Hard-luck Annie", but he had no idea of how his constantly proffered love, sympathy, and help troubled her; she was used to thinking for herself.

It was as if a modest young man had been made king and woke each morning to find loyal subjects singing his praises outside his window. Most young women are surprised to find themselves with a lover at all; the oblique remarks and casual slurs of relatives, the naked domestic drama and hate of parent and child, lead them to the belief that love does not exist, that it is a flare-up between the sexes, a fever, or a nugget which must be capitalized as soon as found. They are brought up with the idea that their cousins and aunts do what is next-door to blackmail, robbery, and a confidence trick to get married at all. They secretly agree with the Jonathan Crows that they are failures, freaks, if they don't. They love, but they are taught that their love is ridiculous, old-fashioned, unseemly, and inopportune, an obstacle to their life-game, an actual menace to their family society and to the lives of their children to be, for "show a man you love him and he runs in the other direction". This was her aunts' timid belief. A poor woman has only one property, her body; passion destroys all relations and liquidates property. So that open love is a serious stain on her character even if she is as pure as the Virgin. The poets killed Paolo and Francesca, Romeo and Juliet, for such lovers are dangerous. Teresa had never noticed this, but she was not surprised that Crow turned her down. What surprised her was that there was not only James Quick but another breed of men who loved women who loved. She saw at the same time that her horrible disease, her love, which she had covered up for years, was admired by this kind of man; instead of being loathed, insulted and sent to her death, she was adored.

She changed at once. She did not revel in the physical pleasures of marriage, but her secret life became more intense. She was like a scientist who has had many failures and who, once he succeeds, thinks that all his previous researches were not wasted; he regrets his dullness and the fumbling of the mind which is more like the fumbling of instinct, and yet he is proud of the blind sight that led him to this. She began to think that she could master men. She wanted to penetrate and influence men, to use them, even without aim, merely for variable and seductive power. Why the false lore of society? To prevent happiness. If human beings really expected happiness they would put up with no tyrannies and no baseness; each would fight for his right to happiness. This phrase startled her, she had heard it before. It was she who, corrupted and hopeless, had told Francine that woman had no natural right to happiness. She saw now that she was the cheated one and that Francine was right. Woman, as well as man, had the right to happiness. Only it was necessary to know how to answer the grim, enslaving philosophy of the schools.

The nauseating ideas of the slick magazines, the chit-chat of every foolish woman were, in a way, right as she was in every way wrong. Woman had a power to achieve happiness as well—but in what way? Only by having the right to love. In the old days, the girls were married without love, for property, and nowadays they were forced to marry, of themselves, without knowing love, for wages. It was easy to see how upsetting it would be if women began to love freely where love came to them. An abyss would open in the principal shopping street of every town. But Teresa did not worry about her sisters, and she was so ungrateful as not to worry even about James Quick. Her hunger had made her insatiable, and she was not content, as he thought she would be, with what he told her, she was not at all satisfied with the end of physical craving; she wanted to try men.

39. Many Men Came to See Them in Fleet Street

MANY men came to see them in the little flat in the court off Fleet Street, more men than women, many unmarried or libertine, picaresque, amiable, floating men. They came first to see James Quick who had the American's political fervour and the Marxist's political sophistication, who saw Whitehall from the American viewpoint and the White House as from the State House of some Middle-Western state. These men first loved the man and then his woman. There was Harry Girton, an Oxford graduate, a radical pamphleteer who lived in a distant seedy suburb with his swarthy-browed and sullen mistress-wife, always furious with love of him and fear; Nigel Fippenny, an ex-I.R.A. man, and his fluffy blond wife, Elsa, a one-time anarchist; a handsome, fleshy German youth, mysteriously wealthy and mysteriously travelled, who gave no name but "Alberic", but whose adoptive father was on a secret mission with Franco, so it was said; and a sturdy, sharp-nosed, salt-eyed personage who called himself "Alan Friedhofer", of vague Scottish ancestry, and his occupation, a Dantzig journalist, representing Dantzig capitalists; and many other drifting talents who called in to see them at all hours of the day and night, so that Teresa was often sitting up in bed with a shawl listening to a cluster of these people talking and coughing in their smoke, at twelve at night, or later—for indeed, they were not rich, and James Quick had much difficulty in paying for this small but expensive place which had only an uncurtained sleeping-alcove in the living-room.

With the except of the Dantziger and the German, precise, cultured but rolling in false bonhomie, their manner as uneasy in that company as a bow-legged sailor's sea-gait on land, the men had unaffected, engaging manners, with unexpected gestures, accents, delicacies, mysteries of experience, and the taking egotisms and practised anecdotes common to all adventurous men.

It was not Girton but others who told the story of his home life, a grotesque painting of the "night side of London", a terrifying legend of smoking hate-in-love. With this woman, it was said, he had rolled, crying, swearing, loving, through the forests, attics, and third-class wooden carriages of half Europe. Girton himself was a personable young man, with dark gold hair, a large English nose, a round cleft chin, and an easy-going smile. He had a north-country colour, but had now turned somewhat pale and sooty with the bad light and dirt of London; easy-going in all things, limber but lazy, slatternly, strong but underfed, he would lounge in their chairs for hours, his light baritone breaking out into notes of irritation and his accent varying from that of his home-country to the ranges of the Oxford colleges and the Cockney speech of the working men he taught at night. When discussion became hot, he usually said nothing, sitting with his somewhat bloodshot blue eyes shaded under his hands. He was alert and restless for all his slothful ways and at the back of his mind was the firm intention of getting away, wandering out, and amusing the soul of his soul by pricking his way through a very alien land, like Hudson, like Lawrence, like Burton, an Englishman of Englishmen, happy to be away from England for ever, one of those firm, ironic patriots that have been formed by England's sea-story and the brilliant pages of imperial and dangerous history, bursting with men of fibre; like a pictured Englishman in all ways he was, though in all ways dissident, a revolutionary because such a patriot.

After lounging round the flat for two hours and perhaps only making querulous remarks, he would put on his greasy and torn raincoat and go out into the dirty fog, and dirty streets, to an ill-kept suburban home; all the same, he left his casual sorcery behind him and in a short time, they both, Teresa and Quick, drew rapidly near to him, as driftwood is sucked in by waters rushing downwards round a hidden reef. His easily delighted spirit he allowed freedom in this fumy den of the world, by bursts of irresponsibility. He had loved much, and he always loved; he knew now that the beginning of every love affair had the same heat and hope, whatever the end, and that no one can tell what is in a love affair until he is well tangled in it, so he gave himself without any forethought to any woman that give him pleasure.

The second time he was at the Quicks', when Quick went to

the telephone, he leaned across the table and said in a hasty, low voice: "I never had any luck, I should have waited——" and he looked at her as if he had known her a long time, as if they were old friends. At once the young woman felt this too. Quick came back from the telephone and no more was said; there was only a pleasant and easy smile. Harry was over six feet, broad, and with shapely limbs. Now he began to glow with the soft, intermittent and still veiled fire which was the beginning of an affair to him, and when he stood in the doorway once more, in his sooty and greasy coat, smiling down at them and left them, striding away with his tired, languorous vigour, he left his presence with them, they were impregnated with him, and it seemed to both of them that he was their closest friend, one so constituted that everything was understood by all three of them without any words at all. When he spoke, his words rang true; if he lied, it was no lie, it was a convention; if he was trite, it was no triteness, but whimsy, and so forth. He bred love upon them, they came closer to the burning heart of life. They both loved him. Quick said when he left the second time: "Girton is like someone we know very well," and when she next looked in the mirror, she called out in surprise: "Like me!" and she, thinking it over, declared: "You and Girton are blood-brothers in the mind!" and he said: "No doubt of it, I always feel it."

Girton's hurried and subdued remarks, the receptive and happy mood she was in and the mysterious resemblance swept her into a whirlwind of that confused joy which any man might cause and which precedes, but is not love. She had felt in her heart for some time, emptied of the old need and ambition, an unemployment and dryness which startled her. It was her secret. "This is not right, life is love," she said to herself. She thought *this* might be marriage, and if so, marriage itself was arid, for this end of all striving and even lusting in love was wrong and not the part of any mature, joyful, human being. It was no good struggling for mere tranquillity and the death of the heart. Thus she reasoned with herself, as in a delicate, irresistible way the image and ways of Girton began to lure her, growing on her in her sleep. She dreamed of him, and presently day-dreamed of him, and, differently from any other man till then, it was of his body that she dreamed; its secret nakedness become robed in incomparable, ever-flowing, ever-born, shadowy loves and nameless pleasures,

467

as yet without form, but not without scent and touching the secret knowledge of the body.

He looked at her and a storm of the uplands blew round her ears, she reeled and felt half-mad with love, and kept thinking to herself: "It comes again, it does not die with marriage, it is not over once for all." All the time she loved Quick, and the three were closely knit all the time. Now she really felt a woman. Girton smiled long at her with his splendid oval blue eyes, lying back in his chair, and letting the fertility of his mind and flesh flow towards them. He was keen, and each knew what process was going on.

She now knew a bounding ecstatic gaiety she had not felt since her early girlhood, in the stern pride of sixteen. The golden young man called up in her mind, when she was thinking of him, an endless succession of light images, golden days, golden globes within which she lived in the murk of London. There were flashes of light, a day which was always dawning, and her feet lightly touched on the shores of a smooth sea, and such feelings of childhood, these visions which come to a child lying on its back under the sun in the grass, and blazing pictures of long half-wooded slopes down which they ran, and the running down, the slipping away of cool winds on a naked shoulder, the full glassy tide spilling over a swimmer sweetly writhing through it, all the exquisite sensations of healthy youth came to her mind when she thought of Harry; through him she began to live the sunburnt, wind-blown, nonchalant days of singing in the grass which had never yet been; she felt her flesh running into his and clinging to him, as if they had never been sundered and as if this and all life would go on in this glory for ever, as if no years would ever pass over their heads and as if, at the same time, children were springing endlessly from his and her loins. There was honey in his thighs and new-pressed unfermented wine in all of him; and, mad with love, she sucked them both into her eyes, only then understanding love of man. For the long and bitter time, the time of her imprisonment, she had steeled herself too much against misfortune; she had never dared to hope or be glad, in fear of failure; and it was only now that she was able slowly to relinquish her fierce grip on life, to relish the abandon of the senses.

It was a long time before he came to see them again. He came with Manette, who was always known as his wife, the swarthy woman who hated them all, an ugly savage woman of fire. This woman, coming in at the door, stopped, turned to wood, when she saw Teresa, and then sullenly she slouched in without a word, threw off her outdoor clothes and said nothing for an hour, and nothing during the whole afternoon except what was biting. It was she, clairvoyant, too experienced, who left them, Harry and Teresa, with the feeling that day, that a love affair between them was at hand. Neither sought it, all waited for it, tremulously, as for the buds on the earliest tree when the air begins to swim.

Manette was a volcanic, savage, cold and melancholy woman who could have been satisfied by no civilized or metropolitan man. She had dashed herself from affair to affair in a brutal Bohemia and at the age of thirty-eight had drifted into a permanent house-holding with an easy-going fellow, who never intended to marry because of the "covetousness of marriage". He had stuck to her because of her primitive force. She could always force him, in the last resort, by her deep, broken, anguished voice, her yells and the horrors of her soul which she put into words, to quell and terrify him. How many times had she threatened to commit suicide, and to murder, with such wild looks, with staring eyes, loosened hair, glabrous cheek, black shouting mouth and the stormy throwing about of her thick-set powerful body; he had never the heart to oppose her. Fiercely brooding, she walked down the streets, hideous, swart, untamed, insulting; she did her shopping, with a few gleams of unctuous friendship between her week-long glooms, she did the work asked of her in her office; and with torrents of recrimination, scandal, hatred and self-pity she won herself friends against Harry. A partner has only to be betrayed once in order to understand for ever which way his mate's fancies are turning. Thus Mrs Girton, at the first glance, saw the secret, animal understanding between them, of which they were as yet scarcely conscious. She saw, when she spent an hour with them, the flashed smiles, glances, silences between the two, heard the accord in the sentiments that they uttered separately. She had no interest in life now (she was forty-eight) but to keep her husband by this detection.

No sooner had the door closed upon Manette and Harry Girton, than Manette fearlessly threw herself upon him. In a squalling voice, she accused him of new philandering and threatened to write at once to his office, and to James Quick to lay bare their intrigue. It was so convenient, said she, so near to the centre of London, and James Quick was away all day while Teresa was at home, typing out manuscripts at so much a page and without any time-limit—it was even likely that Teresa had chosen that address in order to be near the route of Harry Girton's pursuits. He had had a mistress in the Temple and one in Covent Garden! All this was not by accident.

Harry Girton at once answered in the casual, offended tone which she knew meant innocence and threatened to leave her if she harried him. This reduced her. She wept aloud in the street and when she got to their home, she threw herself on the sofa in a fit of the sullens which lasted till midnight. At midnight, the man could stand this horror no longer and, getting on his knees beside her, told her he had never betrayed her, that she imagined all her miseries and that they could be happy if she only would. "But you need these fits of passion in order to love me, to feel you have snatched me back from the world, isn't it so?" She admitted that it was; but in the next breath asked how often he had seen Teresa Quick and how often alone. To this he replied: "Never alone, and only twice before, when not a word was exchanged." They were reconciled, but these reconciliations no longer quieted Manette nor were anything but a dull miserableness for Harry. The next day she began to pester him again. He trusted her instinct. He knew that she would not be so jealous of a woman unless she scented a real pleasure for him there. His expectancy, therefore, turned towards Quick's young woman, but in an unenterprising, debonair way, for he intended to give no sign if she gave none. She wanted him and would tell him when she was ready, he thought. As time went on (the time was short) she seemed to him more timid and less experienced. One day she gave him a book of poems to read with one page marked; it was about a love affair in the violent noonday heat. It was a tour de force which brought up the feelings of a maddening heat and dizzied the senses. He kept this book for some time.

From time to time, he came to see the husband, discussed things with him, the Spanish Civil War and the feeble efforts, or none, being made by governments of democratic countries to help the struggling Spanish government. Everyone stood aside, or covertly helped the aggressor exactly as England had done in the American Civil War. On the other hand, the true working classes in most countries sympathized with the democratic government then endangered and later unseated by force of arms.

Sympathizers of various countries were then fighting in Spain, while the only armed forces that had been sent officially were sent by the fascist governments to help the rebels. Girton and others were going round from door to door explaining the real meaning of the word "Loyalist", for this had been wantonly misinterpreted by the British Tory press. Harry Girton had intended before this to strike out along a new route into Inner Mongolia, but he now wished as soon as possible to go into Spain and fight with the International Brigade. He had duties at home, but in a week or two he would be able to get his passport and start abroad. In these anxious days, for him, he had often to be in the City and called almost every afternoon at No. 10 Crane Court, to speak to Quick, for whom he had formed a moderate but sincere affection; and there to meet, occasionally, men of his views as well as Fleet Street journalists of all kinds, to discuss the news with Quick and perhaps to write a book with him, for Quick always had ideas and Harry always needed money. He ate poorly because his wages were poor, but he liked good eating, he liked the old-fashioned fare of England which is still found in some counties, the rich pies and pasties, the great cuts of meat and smoking gravies, the roasts, baked fish and large puddings. It was convenient, when he was worn out and weak, to drop in there for a meal and rest there an hour or two in one of their deep armchairs. He would sit there, his long legs stretched across the little carpet, his eyes shaded, his pale yellowish flesh, which should have been fair and ruddy, drooping.

The first time that he found her alone, the young woman was nervous and defiant. Sitting facing her, petulant, uneasy, at the moment when he roused himself and began to speak, she received a violent impression of his virility and physical beauty. The perception of beauty is always a shock, the rest of the visible world fades for a fraction of a minute and the beautiful thing stands there alone in space, in more than lively contours; this was the way she saw Harry Girton that day. She saw then that she was falling in love with him. Adultery! Ugly word—but his beauty carried her off into love's Age of Fable: where no such words have ever been heard. His languorous movements and gentle voice, the way his voice twitched into another register, thin and irritable, the change of accents, began to float in the air round her ears; she heard, felt and saw him, smelled him. He had at all times odours coming either from his plump blond flesh or from his greasy coat and old books, or from his thick hair.

Several times after that she went out when he came. Returning too early after a third evasion, she saw him blocking the end of the passage, and his half-smile. This completed the work of weeks. However, she could not help remembering—the words clanged in her ears—the words that James Quick had often repeated since they had lived together and more often said in the rhapsodies of their first days together: "We are united by love only, you are not mine, though I am yours, and if you want another lover, you shall have him as well as me." How had she advanced in a few months from the idea that no one would love her to the assurance that she could control two men? She thought this, she moved slowly towards it, yet, at the same time, she had not even exchanged a significant word with Girton and fled from the notion of hurting Quick.

One day, about three months after what Quick called their marriage, Quick was obliged to make one of his trips to Antwerp and to leave Teresa at home. At once, a new sort of friends swarmed into the small flat, to air their opinions in a new way. In closely knit circles, the friends are jealous of each other and watch each other closely. But a pack instinct made them all turn to attack Girton whenever he was not there. Hot, filthy words flew from side to side about him. "He is unreliable! He lies! He swills all night! He lives in grease and likes to eat it! They never clean the bath! All day they lie in dirty bedclothes and fornicate and make an unholy row! How he slouches and slobbers! His pants are torn, he never has a collar clean! He has had a hundred flames and though she yells, she's justified! He goes down on his knees and cleans the floor of the house, but the house always reeks of filth and I have seen cockroaches there, where the crumbs fall on the bedroom floor!" What extraordinary tales the jealous, bitter and gay fantasies of these friends of Girton flung out. Eagerly Teresa listened, saying not a word, until before her silence they became silent; and when they were silent, she was disappointed, hungry for more words about the living, maddening, fertile man who excited them all to this wild frenzy. The wilder their insults, the happier she was; she enjoyed the hot unexpressed anger they gave her, and she enjoyed Girton in all these scenes of licence, in all this low rake's progress which was his life.

He stayed away. They went on backbiting. Once she saw him striding wearily up St James's Street. He was all about town, wearing the trench-coat that the poor Londoner wears summer and winter, a discoloured drab felt hat which he crushed under his arm, a dirty muffler and brown boots. Five days after Quick left, he turned up at the flat, and found her alone. She was dressed all in black linen. "I was just going out."

"Well, I won't come in," he murmured.

"Oh, I want you to come in."

"I'll sit down for ten minutes, I've been walking all the morning."

"Do you like port? I have some. It looks black as tar, too, look at it."

"I like port, all right," he said humorously, setting down his things neatly, and flinging himself in the same deep chair. She brought the bottle and two glasses. "I didn't have time to read the poems, just one or two," he said. "I've got five or six books promised to publishers and not one written. That's how I live, on advances." He laughed sadly. They drank two glasses of port each before he said reluctantly: "Well, I must be getting on. I'm getting off to France tomorrow."

"Ah?" she said guardedly. "You've got a lot to do then? Well, go then—but have another glass." He smiled and took it reluctantly. "I never drink in the middle of the day."

"Well, after this go and have some lunch." He said nothing, raising the glass and looking at its mantle. She explained that they got it from across the street. Since they were just inside Temple Bar, the vintners had special regulations, that is, that applied to the City, and also had cheaper and better port and sherry than elsewhere in London. They sold from the barrel, so that the wineries resembled somewhat the wineshops in Spain. In the back room, all the young lawyers and well-known Fleet Street men met at about four or five in the afternoon. Also in the street were famous taverns with a few specialities, pasties, old ale and the like, with benches arranged round the room, or in pews; and each corner, each seat in fact, was ornamented with the names of the dead. Above the pews in the "Cock" were several men in wigs and robes who resembled Harry Girton, they equally, though better developed, having his puffy drooping cheeks and the pear-shaped paunch, which he, poor man, would never be able to mature. He did his best with a little round corporation based on occasional advances from publishers and which slowly disappeared as these were expended. Harry and Manette both worked, their rent was low and neither was charitable; but the cost of living and of going on low binges with Harry's friends ate into their small cash. They had no large debts and got nothing on "easy payments", but a trip to the dentist, a doctor's bill, set them back for a six-month. They were, simply, very poor. Teresa would have liked to have gone out to eat with Harry at one of the taverns which she and Quick frequented and she knew that Harry would let her pay for him. They sat there, thinking of food. He was hungry. She thought: "If I were a man I would be as seedy and hungry as he, that's honesty."

He put down the glass, his third, and he saw with surprise that she poured herself a fourth. All the same, there was no sign of its having affected her. The telephone rang, she answered it and said: "Nigel Fippenny is coming over in five minutes to have a cup of tea. This is Fleet Street time, that means an hour and a half."

"I'm blowing," said Harry. "I have an idea he doesn't like me." He grinned slyly. Fippenny loved both Quicks and he suspected, with the penetration of jealousy, that the Quicks thought better of Girton's brains than of his own; he lost no opening for his brash Irishman's sallies and acid stories against Girton's politics.

"No, he doesn't like you."

"He looks like one of your irritable Orangemen, I.R.A. or not," said Girton pacifically.

She poured out another glass of wine for them both. Girton, who had been about to go, watched her in surprise and said nothing. He guessed she had a secret to tell him, perhaps that she was in love with him. He knew, like all charming men, that women have no hesitation in saying when they love, and he smiled tenderly to bring out the mood that was most admirable to him in the sex, the gallant and frank mood, that is a proof of love.

474

"Some more port?"

"If you like!" He watched her intently and a velvety shadow moved round his sensual mouth. She knew what he expected of her, because he had said it two or three times. "In the Soviet Union, a girl who loved a man would tell him so," but because he knew already, she would not say it. She did not care to talk about love at all, it was enough that there had been a covert declaration between them.

Nigel Fippenny came earlier than he was expected, he came twenty-five minutes after he had telephoned, and at once flung himself down in the second arm-chair, throwing his black "revolutionary" hat, old-style, on the bed in the alcove. He stretched, got out a cigar, offered one to Harry Girton, who refused it, and made a cynical comment on the aid of the International Brigade in the Spanish Civil War. This was a sore point with Nigel, since he had flourished his guerrilla campaigns against the British since 1916 and now could not give up the comforts of a Fleet Street salary, "thelegraphin' thripe to the Colonies and Dominions", to fight on the side of liberty. To excuse his sell-out, he invented a whole argument, heartily detested Harry Girton, an Englishman —therefore an "oppressor"—who nevertheless was going out to fight with the International Brigade. He opined that "Yu will never get out there and if yu dhu, yu will sit in a hotel in Madrid with all the other-r Mar-rxists and let me tell yu I can't thole the arm-chair Mar-rxist, Len'n, that I knu in Moscow in 1921 was no ar-rm-chair-r Mar-rxist", and so on. To this Harry Girton returned civil answers, or silence.

The two men made up their minds to sit each other out. However, the untrimmed Nigel, who had sold out to the British Empire, became sharp about Mar-rxists who "sell out" to various entities, including the "par-rty", and gave vent to a pious wish that Britain would fight with Hitler rather than with Stal'n, an ambitious bureaucrat, with whom Len'n would have nothing to do, so that Harry Girton got up, picked up his things and said he had to get on his way. He never argued foolishly.

Teresa left the water on the gas-stove, saying to Nigel: "Your tea is nearly ready," and accompanied Harry to the door, meanwhile laughing at Nigel's parting shot, some insult to the Marxists. Then, asking Harry what he wanted to take away to Spain with him that she could give him next day, she went with him to the street door and into Crane Court. It was only three-thirty but night had fallen. The light dropped between the half-drawn curtains from the flat above and on to the asphalt, a yard or two beyond them. There were three steps down. She stood on the second step and held out her hand.

"You're going tomorrow," she said in a muffled voice.

"Yes." He took her hand. She clasped it in both hers and looked down at him. He smiled faintly and stood still. After a moment, she said wildly: "Harry, I'll go with you."

"Where?"

"To Spain."

"Yes?" He waited, looking up at her and holding her hand still. When he withdrew his hand he still looked up, but gravely. She came down the steps, with her hand on his arm, and they turned down the court. At the mouth of the court, under the thick arch, she said: "Good-bye."

He bent down and kissed her, saying: "Good-bye."

"This isn't Spain, is it?"

He looked down silently. "I'll come back," he said at last.

She was suffocated.

"Wait for me till I come back," he said.

She came slowly up the court, scarcely able to walk. She thought: "If he comes back, I'll never see him, there was never anything like this." But when she got into the flat, she had a shining face, so that Nigel jealously noticed it.

"Yu look all excited! How's that?"

"Excited? Why should I be?"

"Maybe because James is coming back," he said sarcastically.

In the kitchen, as she made his "tay", she began to sing the "Wedding March".

"Are yu going to get married?" he shouted.

"Am I?"

"Are yu singing for joy?"

"Good Heavens!" She appeared holding the breakfast cup of tea. "For joy! No, Jimmy is not coming yet." He took the cup and smiled under his lids as he blew at the steam. "A good cup of tay. I thought yu were singing for joy, maybe", and he said no more.

40. "Today Put on Perfection"

WHEN James Quick came back from Antwerp she told him that "the boys" had been at the flat almost every day and that still she had finished the typing job. Quick inquired who they were and what they had said and seemed broken-hearted that Harry Girton had gone to Spain before he could say good-bye to him. "But you said good-bye to him?"

"No. That is, hardly. I never have presence of mind."

She wanted now to go back to the office to help Quick as his secretary, but Quick had employed a young man secretary already, not to make Teresa anxious, as he said, smiling: "And Axelrode agrees with me, since the secretary is always the office wife, as you know, and cannot help being." And he told Teresa she could employ herself at home.

"I want to know that you are there waiting for me and that when I get home you will rush to the door as you do."

She was flattered, but she thought instantly: "It's the surest way to lose me." When Quick came home the same day she told him she could never live in a back street and wait for him—— "What is every waiting wife but a back-street wife? No, I won't be that. I'll go and be someone else's secretary, and then—you know, you said before—a kept woman, *your* kept woman, yours especially, I could not be."

"Why not mine especially?" he said.

"Because I adore you."

He was radiant he but did not understand. He said: "Very well, but we must think out something for you to do. What would you like to do?" He was astonished that within three months this woman, whom he had pictured to himself as furiously passionate and to whom marriage would be heaven, should already be dull and discontented. As soon as she mentioned even the vaguest confusion in reasons for her discontent he became unhappy and said that he "had not satisfied her", and he told her hundreds of queer stories, part of the legend of the male, both obscene and innocent, in which a woman satisfied, slept, became languid, lazy and fat. She remembered in literature, too, a dozen passages where "the satyrs ran off into the wood while the nymphs slept by the banks of the fountain". For herself, she knew that the satisfaction of this great desire only made her more restless and energetic than before.

Quick loved Teresa deeply; what was clumsy and harsh in her he put down to her hard life, to Jonathan Crow's deceptions, and to her naïveté, when he felt irritated. If, sometimes, he wondered if he had not acted precipitately, in taking her to live with him at once before he had tested the strength of their union, at other times he found a great joy and glory in his absolute abandonment of which he was so capable. It was because of this great self-abandonment that he did not understand her. It was not only her own training but her age, for she was young in experience, which made her different from him. The youthful give themselves up with difficulty. When a husband or wife is a little older a sort of reticence persists. They owe these elders more reverence and at the same time they feel that it is not wrong to conceal their feelings. How can the generations meet in youth, even in the same sex?

Quick thought that her restlessness was something that would pass away when she had accustomed herself to married life, but he was not an obstinate, self-centred, or opinionated man. When he came back and saw by her silence that his wife's friendship with Harry Girton, with all its peculiarities, had developed during his absence, he asked himself: "Have I merely got her on the rebound? Is she about to love truly another man? Am I, with my possessive passion, standing in the way of happiness? I would never do that, whatever the pain—well, we must see it through. If she loves Girton and not me, if her restlessness ceases through him, I must give her up; it is better to do it now than when we are better used to each other." For restlessness in a woman, to him, by tradition, was wrong. He was very relieved to find that Girton had already gone abroad. This put off the question of their love till he returned and by then—it was far off.

But the Monday after Quick's return, about three in the afternoon, the door-bell rang and Girton appeared, to say good-bye to Quick. His departure had been delayed ten days. In the meantime he intended to go to the Midlands to see his family, from whom he had been separated many times in the past twenty-five years. He came in, sat down, and began to talk in an undertone, desultorily, to Teresa. That afternoon Quick came home early, at three-thirty, and so it was for five days, Girton each day putting off his visit to his home, and Quick each day coming home earlier. On the Friday he was at home again at eleven in the morning—there was nothing to do in the office, he said, and Axelrode off to Antwerp. During this week, when the men so mysteriously met each other, the desire for an hour alone became intense in the two lovers. They were only in love, perhaps, when Quick was there. Girton and Teresa, or so it seemed to them, only asked an hour in which to thrash out the whole matter. Nothing compared with the need to know, to hear the binding words; for the sexual act is also committed between strangers and people who hate each other, and it is the mystic words, "I love you, we love each other" which bind for life, and each waited for these words to drop. Quick, of course, plainly saw the tension between the two and could imagine only that they had a secret understanding. At last, on Friday, Girton said: "I must leave by tomorrow morning's train to see my people in Birmingham. I keep putting it off—I leave at ten-thirty from Paddington", and Teresa said: "That's funny, my people, cousins and a great-aunt, live at Leamington, that's on the same line, isn't it? At least from Paddington, that's where they told me to get the train——"

Quick said hastily: "Yes, Tess, why don't you go and see them for a day or two? It will change the scene for you before you start another job. You know, she wants to get a job, although I don't want her to——" He said miserably: "I am not enough for her."

"Why not?" said Girton. "Teresa looks like work to me, she'd make a good commissar."

"For what?" said she, beaming.

"For push-carts," laughed Quick.

"Not for care of the home," said Girton lazily. Teresa frowned. Why this? Quick said: "Tess, why don't you go up to see your Aunt Lobelia or what-is-it, for a day or two? Say I can't go along but give her an account of your luxury flat, show my picture, all the rest, so that she'll write home and say all is in order."

"No need for that."

"But still, Tess, go."

"If you insist, all right."

"And Harry here can go along with you, it'll be company for you part of the way."

She said nothing.

"Do you want to come, Tess?" asked Harry.

"Well—but what for, after all?"

"Yes, go, Tess," insisted Quick. "You'll go to Leamington, stay a day or two or three and come back to me, and see whether you like me better then."

"What?" cried Teresa, flushing. "Like you better? How could I like you better?" She frowned.

The men began to talk of Spain and local fascists. She got out some sewing and, sitting on a hassock, bent her head over it. She raised her head once to see the blond young man who was stretched out at full length in the arm-chair, as usual, staring at her. She could scarcely believe it. She lowered her head again and paid no more attention to the conversation, but at the end, Quick said: "Well, Tess, are you going with Harry on Saturday?"

She straightened up, put down her sewing. "Is it Saturday?"

"Yes, in the morning," said Harry.

She looked with confusion from one to the other. "Do you think I ought to?"

"Yes," said Quick heartily. "Why not? You'll get a chance to talk to Harry, he's going away—perhaps you have some things to talk over with him. He can chaperon you to Leamington—or why not get off at Oxford and take a look around? Harry knows Oxford pretty well, don't you?" and he laughed. He kept chattering gaily and questioning Girton who himself with warmth kept up the conversation. He told about what Oxford was like and the rest, occasionally turning to Teresa whose ears were burning. The meaning of this chatter was that the men were offering and counter-offering her love to each other, as a proof of their love for each other. She wanted to burst into tears and to go away and let them languish after her, "let them amuse each other". In the end, she rather sulkily agreed to meet Harry in the morning and to go in the train with him as far as Leamington only. Meanwhile, Quick was all good nature, saying he would get the ticket, send a telegram to "the great-aunt Minnie, *not* Lobelia", and of course, he knew she would have to traipse round the shops for half a day getting presents (for Teresa did not dare enter anywhere without propitiatory presents), and the like, and he sent Girton off with hearty handclasps, saying that he was going to get him several things before he went to Spain and that he was, or would ever be, the dearest and closest friend he ever had.

On Saturday, a bright, windy day with a fixed cloudy sky above and earth-clouds sailing near, Quick got Teresa packed in a great hurry, took her to the station early, bought her a small hamper and something to drink in the train, counted her money several times and added to it each time with a few coins out of his pocket, took all her packages, including her gloves, so that she would have nothing to carry and gave her infinite instructions. The train time drew near and Quick gaily opined that Harry, who was always one hour and twenty minutes late, by the clock, would miss the train. However, Girton turned up ten minutes before, swinging his satchel into which, this time, he had packed a few things.

His wife came with him, hanging on to his arm, and with her thick, pasty face quiet and cheerful. She seemed very surprised to see the Quicks and when she learned that the woman was was travelling alone, she turned ghastly pale and her face was convulsed.

"Did you know you were going to meet?" she asked Teresa.

Harry Girton made no sign, stood casually by; Quick coughed politely. Teresa, however, replied innocently: "Of course. I was going to see my great-aunt at Leamington and Jim thought I should go by the same train as Harry", and she pointed at Girton. "You didn't tell me," said Manette, turning wildly to her husband. "It's very funny, no doubt. Is it an escapade that you conceal it? What does her husband think of that?" and she turned furiously to Quick: "What do you think of that? Concealing it from me, I call it peculiar. I know what I call it. And do you allow that sort of thing?"

"Why not?" asked Quick bluffly. "What crime is there in going to Leamington?"

"It isn't going to Leamington they have in mind," she said

bitterly, "but a week-end somewhere—where is it?" She turned to her husband. "Where are you going with that woman?"

Harry Girton looked calmly at Teresa all this time and he now made a gesture as if to ask would she get into the train.

"Are you going?" howled Manette, in astonishment. Teresa looked curiously from her husband to Girton. Manette turned and flung herself upon Quick's left arm, which he was holding across his waist, clutching the button of his raincoat. She looked up into his face, and the two onlookers, faintly disturbed but calm, because they had their train-tickets perhaps, noticed with surprise that there was a certain resemblance between the swarthy and shallow faces now staring at each other; there was the irregularly impasted flesh around high flat cheek-bones and long-shaped shadows in the cheeks, the deep lines, flesh round the mouth, short noses, long lips, and cleft chins. Apart, they were utterly unlike, except for the colouring; Quick was prognathous and Manette had wide, semi-circular, meeting jaws; Quick's hair was smooth, short and receding, and Manette's hair tendrilly, low-growing and stiff. Quick had the sad, friendly, round but soft eyes of a fine Chinese while Manette had the iron-bound brow and sullen sunken eyes of some ancient forest race, human but stupid and brooding, shaken by forgotten pangs. But the resemblance was there. Teresa without speaking turned to Harry Girton, who was observing her. Anyone would have had the same thought. Girton thought: "By what curiosity of fate——" She thought: "Really, I am a fatal woman, I travel thirteen thousand miles to meet the same mate that Girton picked up somewhere in the marshes of the Thames." She said without thinking: "Where do you come from, Manette?"

Manette drew back and stared at her. Her pleading with Quick, which she had carried on in her usual dramatic style, had not moved either of the two fair people looking at each other and she had heard the silence behind her. As for Quick, she saw that he was obedient to this woman and would bring her no aid. Her husband, whom she loved hopelessly, now said lightly: "Well, all aboard", and saying "Bye-bye" to his wife, shaking Quick's hand and pushing Teresa up before him, he sprang on the train. Manette was in despair. Was it inexorable that these two should travel together? She turned to Quick, to gabble at him the dozen infamies which were known about Harry to everyone (by her own

482

mouth) when the train began to move. Quick paid no attention to her, except to say unconsciously: "Yes, Mrs Girton, yes, Mrs Girton", but was running along the slowly moving car looking anxiously for his woman, his face shining bluish-white in the station light, his splendid large dark eyes wide open, in a circle of white, like two wood mushrooms turned upside down. Manette could look at these eyes, the colour of her own, but melting and handsomer, and see what they were; her defeat, her denial. She wrung her hands, seeing him running now after the running train and waving. When he came back towards her, his coat flying open, his handkerchief in his hand, a smile and tears on his face, she nearly collapsed.

"Well, he'll be back on Tuesday, won't he?" he asked, smiling, in a tremulous voice and patting her on the hand, as he caught up with her.

"Why do you let them go off like that?" she asked in her hoarse voice. "Are you mad?"

"Mrs Girton," said Quick, "I read a crazy story somewhere about a wife who believed in her husband and she was right—but never mind that, that won't interest you. You are thinking of Harry because you love him. Why do you think he will deceive you? Don't you know a man can't bear to be nagged? Give the old boy a break. Perhaps he's faithful to you all along, only you don't give him a chance to prove it. Do you know what the Freudians would say? I'm not a Freudian, mark you, far from it, but in this case they might say, and with justice, that for some occult reason, you were pushing him into the arms of other women. Now, Mrs Girton, Manette," he said with bonhomie, "I've never seen a marriage break up unless at least one of the partners was working for the break day and night, and that partner is always the injured partner afterwards. Don't ask why that is so. It is so, at any rate. Now if you want to lose your boy, just make him scenes in public and nag him and he'll go to the first girlie that tells him she adores him. Why not? Manette, you've got the wrong technique. I send my wife to her relatives and I send her along in the train with a friend of mine because I know she likes him. Would I send her with someone she hated? Do you really think there is any danger in sending out together a decent man and woman? I am willing to bet—five cents—that all your troubles originate with yourself. Harry married you, didn't he? Then he must like you. You've got a clutch on him that the other girls never will have. For I know you, Manette, you love him, you won't leave him for another man, whatever the temptation."

She raised her strange black and white eyes to him and looked at him through her lashes. His eyes were wet. Her face had smoothed out and she sketched a small, scornful smile. Now she said: "Imagination isn't my strong point, that's his. I work from facts. I'll never let him get away with anything like that again—I have ways and means. And if you're thinking we're married—we're not. We never were. He was too modern to marry me. I'm years older than he is, you see, I'm almost fifty, Mr Quick. Look at me! You see a woman verging on fifty. I'm jealous because I'm an old woman and he doesn't leave me only because he's afraid of what people will say. It's his conscience. He's a nice boy and he always had a nice conscience, that's how I have him; it's to fly away from me that he's going first to fight for Spain and then to Tanganyika, if he can, and after that to the ends of the earth. The Kipling ideal, and all to avoid a woman of fifty. He wouldn't give me a baby and he said why, everybody knows. Day after day, day after day, we stuck, 'nor sound nor motion, as idle as a painted ship upon a painted ocean'. He's my prisoner, and the man that's gone off with your wife, if she is your wife, Mr Quick, is a man who's aching to escape and who will face death, if he doesn't get a fat Madrid job, rather than face an old woman. So don't give me this soft soap, because I know him."

Her raucous, deep voice went on and she clung to Quick's arm as they hastened along. But Quick had only heard fragments after the words, "he was too modern to marry me". He was overwhelmed. In spite of gossip, he had heard Manette so often called "Mrs Girton" that he had preferred to think of her as married. He knew that Teresa did not know this, she would soon find it out. His secret he would tell to none—that he and Teresa were not married. James Quick now feared that at the first question Teresa would admit to Girton that she was free. What would happen then?

Thus he imagined the train rushing out of London into the clear, spring countryside, the weighted stands of trees on old grassy hills, the trout-coloured falls, and ponds of trout rivers, the abandoned fields of half-dug turnips between turned hedges and windbreaks, the brown earth, the isolated country houses, the wide undulating fields, knotted together by copses and the whole silent countryside of England spread out beneath them, while these two, fated, marked out for each other, sped on and found out the truth about each other. He had no sign for that but his instinctive fear; but he knew that others had seen the similarity between the two and watched them, expecting some event, love or trouble, joy and anguish for them both, and all eagerly watched. Harry Girton had always been a wanderer; there was the war in Spain. Already, rumours of a scandal had flown round their small, hastily assembled circle exactly as if scandal had arisen; it was weird, shocking, frightening.

Presently Quick, no longer able to listen to Manette, put her in a bus and set off to walk home in his rapid easy trundle; but half-way there, he found he could not face the dark flat at the bottom of the Court and the silent week-end without her. He regretted his folly in sending her away. She had every reason to confide in Girton. He himself had sent her away in his care. Quick suddenly felt that he could not stand the looks of strangers and he changed his mind again, taking a bus to get home. Why had he thrown them together? He had always been like that, running on his unhappiness out of desperation, like a suicide on his knife. Once home, he took down a serious book and began to read. When he looked up, he saw before him the smiling countryside and the train, very small now, running away from him north-west.

Meanwhile, in the train the man and woman sat facing each other, saying little, but quite at ease. As they approached Oxford, Girton muttered almost incomprehensibly: "Let's get off here after all, would you? I don't want to see the old place particularly, but we could——"

"But your people? And Jim sent a telegram to Aunt Minnie."

"We can forget them," said Girton, slurring, as if he wished the recording angel not to hear those words.

Teresa looked out the window, pretending for the moment not to have heard him. She waited to hear more.

He was timid himself and glanced at her sideways, then he added casually but in a low voice: "We don't want to go there."

The "we" stirred her. She now turned and looked at this blue-eyed man with the drooping, rather shamed look. "Do you?" he inquired weakly; he seemed to shrink in size. She blushed. "I suppose not really, but—they're expecting me." She was ashamed to look at him. "I could find you a place to stay," he murmured. "I have money," she said. "He gives me too much money, always. But have you the money?"

"I don't know, yes—enough for where we would go." He looked up shyly and brightly. It was like a blow on the heart. At the same time came a feeling like a mild afternoon wind. She saw two young folk passing under some boughs, their heads bent, talking; it was herself and Girton, whose face was still youthful. She looked at Girton, he flushed and his eyes too began to shine. Without embarrassment, they said a few words in a low voice about Oxford, about sending telegrams and the like. Teresa said: "I'll just say, 'Stopping overnight at Oxford, continuing tomorrow.'"

He said: "Will that be all right?"

"Oh, yes."

So they got off there.

He did not want to see Oxford and she disliked sight-seeing; but when they got in among the colleges and saw the ugly old quadrangles, the winding walls and alleys and the strange, sexless Fellows ambling in black gowns over their sheared lawns, and especially when the evening remained so long with them, and the birds kept flying above the trees, late into the night, she liked it. He showed her the small old college at which he had been a student, but they wandered about it aimlessly like summer tourists, going to the chapels and odd corners. She was very tired and he too was miserable, worn out by his work and his domestic sorrows, of which he said nothing. It was disappointing and seedy; Teresa felt like a schoolgirl and he like a tired guide for tourists. Nevertheless, evening came, their tired faces and eyes were obscured, and they walked far and fast, talking with obscure beauty to each other; for of what they said they remembered, later, very little, something to do with their hearts, how they loved always, all their lives without knowing it, how they had thought of each other continually (although each thought that this was not all the truth) and whether one lost anything by refusing to love, and whether such things lasted, and the strange histories of men and women they had known; they talked about love.

Teresa felt all the time that there was some artifice in what she was saying and she believed he was only doing and saying what was the polite thing. The feeling they had for each other, which was without a name, a strange relation, could not flower by any other means than by this; they had no time, the world was moving, already turning from day into night and with day approaching again, when they must separate; and soon after, within two or three days, they, and not only they, but Girton from all his friends, must separate, perhaps for ever. For during this fast long walk, the course of which she could never after-wards remember, he confessed that he had no pleasure out of life, that he would only be happy again when he was among strangers, who spoke a strange language. "I want to wander, my feet ache to leave footprints on foreign soil, it is a bone-ache." She said: "I have wandered a lot too, I don't want to die in bed, or even lone wolf on lone rock. I always wanted to expire, an old hag of brown bones, on a brown-ribbed desert." He explained that if he escaped this war in Spain, and he was anxious to do so, he would go out with one of the tent tribes of Asia and wander from one part to another. "All I ask is to be unknown to all that know me." These words soothed her, for in them she heard the wind that blew for her from some remote region where she wanted to be. Relatives, home, living, and holy dying also tired her; she saw herself, too, as going alone, into other regions, even though she would probably never have the energy or strength to do so.

Presently they went to an old house in a suburb on the list of the Trust House taverns and after sitting in the bar for a while and listening to the radio play "Little Man, You've Had a Busy Day", they felt tired. The men in the bar, workers from the town, hushed their voices and smiled pleasantly, because there was a lady present; and there was an argument because a young, flushed blond man, in liquor, had mentioned the ugly word "worm" before ladies. "You're a worm!" "Shh! Ladies!" went the argument. When they asked for a room, the buxom landlady bustling, soft, was surprised: "I thought you were brother and sister, not husband and wife, you're that alike!" "I'm twice not married," murmured Teresa, laughing brashly to keep herself in countenance. "I always knew it," said the man carelessly. "I'm not either."

They went upstairs with a candle to a small back bedroom with raftered ceiling and an extraordinarily thick mattress, made of lumps of various materials and without buttons. There was a painted wooden washstand with floral china and the privy was a shanty in the yard; but the room, the halls, and the stairs, as they saw when they walked out in the moonlight across the flagged yard, were wide, bare and clean. Though they were tired, each did his best to please the other and Teresa strove to prove that she was no child at love. At first they wanted to go to sleep but the whole night passed before they slept and for hours they were as close as creatures can be. The sun rose in a clear morning and the light fell on the bare boards through the thinly curtained windows. Teresa got up quickly and dressed. The business of the night was over and she had never stayed late in bed in her life. She had a feeling of order and modesty in rising early and making everything tidy.

The young man still slept in an arc like a cat, his face tired and smaller than usual, with the closed, intense, but distant expression of a little boy thinking of his plans. On his own, at a great distance, Harry Girton was carrying on his life. She stood for a few moments by the side of the bed, looking down at him thoughtfully, and in these few moments it seemed as if all her life passed through her mind; and she saw the immediate future too, a wide, ordered, agricultural landscape, for some reason, fields ploughed and sown, with a few tall plumy trees at intervals, and a plain, fair sky in a wide sweep. She thought of the future for him too—all this without any feeling; even, she thought of her love for Quick and Harry's afflicted union with Manette, of their relatives that they would each see that day; and that they might never see each other again. She had no feeling about any of these things, because they were then satisfied with their closeness, he asleep and she standing there. She moved away and finished dressing. She was brushing out her hair when she heard him stir, and still brushing she came to the bed and looked down at him, smiling. He sprang up with a "Hullo", and took her in his arms. They felt a glow of simple happiness, without transport, almost without desire, which was like a heartfelt recognition of each other, a kind of inward smile. Teresa held him close for a moment and thought to herself: "This is life and death." They dressed quickly, went downstairs for breakfast, which they had in a quaint small room, wood-panelled, with a high ceiling, a wooden bench and seats and a few prints; outside the small window was the flagged yard.

"If I could have breakfast with you like this every morning, I would be happy," he said and she murmured, smiling: "You can, you know, if you want it," and she felt a great happiness at this untruth; there was not the least possibility of their ever living together and perhaps neither wished it. They had arranged their lives before the meeting took place; they now knew each other and what they desired was over. What more could life give to these two? They sat close to each other in a great golden calm; but since they were stormy petrels, each looking for adventure not only in physical danger but in moral and heady regions, what could they do with this simple love that depended on and gave tranquillity?

Harry wished to go out for half an hour before they set out for the station, and Teresa went upstairs to the room to see that nothing was left behind, she said, but really to think of Harry while he was away.

She stood at the window and looked into the flagged yard. The sun was higher, it no longer shone down there, the flags were shadowy. She was glad that he had gone out, now she felt something—the first feeling of all. She was in a strange state of ecstasy, she seemed to float upright, like a pillar of smoke, or flesh perhaps, some little way above the pavement. Down below flowed a great slaty river, smooth but covered with twisted threads of water, swollen with its great flow, and directly under the window was an immense dusk-white flower with drooping petals, surrounded by green and living leaves. This extraordinary flower, alive though shadowy, and living not as material things are, but with the genius of life, the interior breath of living things, after moving uncertainly like a raft began to float downstream to the left. In a few moments, it was a hundred yards away, and much smaller. She lifted her eyes and noted the houses, the back fences, the details of roofs and a large tree behind a shed, the things in a lean-to near the fence, on the other side of the yard, old and not unsightly outhouses in the yard itself, and she heard a single note of a human voice floating somewhere at the bottom of the stairs. "Time is already floating away," she thought, smiling peculiarly. She was astonished at her feeling of wanting nothing.

"Today put on perfection and a woman's name," she repeated several times, and still as if dreaming moved away from the window and put her things together. She was withdrawn into an inner room of herself and here she found the oracle of her life, this secret deity which is usually sealed from us. This oracle was now perfectly visible, in a room with a large barred window but otherwise not unlike this one, and to this oracle she said: "I only have to do what is supposed to be wrong and I have a happiness that is hardly credible. It exists. Who could believe it? Why is it that just this, this sure happiness, this perfect, absolute joy, is the thing surrounded with 'thou-shalt-not'? I seem to be in a stockade—outside, the shindy is going on, mumbo jumbo, voodoo; here am I face to face and lip to lip with a living god." She was unable to think out the reason for the taboo; she saw no malice there, but a true insanity. "We are primitive men; we taboo what we desire and need. How did the denying of love come to be associated with the idea of morality?" Lifted high, the mind was, now, by a great surge (of the pale crested black water? Or was she voyaging by air?). She continued in a fit of absence, the black river before her, the world, it seemed, silent around, and clasping her hands ecstatically together, she thought: "Chastity? But I never was chaste till now, and as for transitory passions—this *is*. Even when my mind closes for ever, this absolute love must somehow go on. . . ."

She finished packing their things in a pleasant solitude and then heard his steps on the stairs. They met again like a bridal pair; then once, before they went down, put down their bags at the door, and held each other in a passion in which their bodies evaporated.

"We are made of smoke," said Teresa, panting. "Like those genies in bottles in the Arabian Nights."

Girton had a triumphant, joyous note as he laughed. He said: "We got out."

"We will remember, at any rate," said Teresa, and as she let her arms drop she felt a new desire for him which shook her as a blow.

490

Harry, who had an eager, listening look, seemed disappointed. "I suppose we will remember."

He turned and would have gone out, when she stopped him. "Harry, this is a secret between us?"

"As if I would——" he said, stopping and turning towards her. "Do you think I do that?" he raged.

"Never," she insisted.

He frowned. "*You* will tell, you will tell Jim, I know."

"Never!" Then she came after him, kissed him, so that he relaxed and shook his head like a good dog, and she came down the stairs after him.

Her relatives, who had seen her only once before, found her even thinner than then, but "Your clothes suit you, my dear," said they. "And are you happy now?"

Teresa took a long breath before she could trust herself to answer. "As happy as I never thought a human being could be! There are all kinds of happinesses in the world and they all come together."

Her great-aunt Minnie smiled under her lashes as she bent over some charity sewing, and then she said brusquely, in the stiff family style: "And what do you mean by that?"

"Can I tell you? Can anyone put it into words?"

"How ecstatic we're getting! Dear, dear," said Aunt Minnie, severely biting a cotton thread and smiling through her frown.

"There is no man like Jim in the world—and I got him," said Teresa, throwing herself back in the chair and laughing immoderately. "Oh, how stupid, every woman says that, yes, but I know, I know."

"As long as you know, that's a blessing," severely said the great-aunt, a handsome old family trooper of eighty-two years, who wore lavender velvet ribbons, lace and scent; but she raised her large blue eyes to Teresa and frowned significantly and made the most delicate of signs. She did not wish "the girls"—her respectably married daughters, aged fifty-two and forty-eight—to be witnesses to this kind of commentary on married life. Nevertheless, she kept smiling to herself over her sewing, and when "the girls" had gone out to make supper, began to talk to Teresa about her married life.

41. I Am Thinking I Am Free

THE young woman, when alone, thought hungrily back to the flat in Crane Court and the dusks of London, and the troop of friends who invested the flat. She saw James there, amongst them, vivacious, battling, and then when they had gone, sitting alone, downcast, waiting for her. It was hard not to go out of the house at once, and go towards the great reeking city where her jewel was. She spent this time of impatience, while her relations with her aunt and cousins wore thin, while the two elderly cousins schemed against each other to have her young company, with thinking of James's passion and of the hundred devices to amuse and please him, embraces, jokes, tags out of erotic literature. She thought of her future with James—immense, rich, busy, in half the cities of the world; it was not the wide brown field of harrowed earth that Harry called up, but docks, wharves, watersides full of shipping, cities of canal-mouths, and masts, pilots and stevedores, all the Hanseatic world and the Baltic outpourings, that business that James was in, the loading and unloading in harbours, where James and Axelrode went with their lively legs and ready wits—that was her world. Yet poor Harry was off on his adventure; it was sweet Harry, a comb of honey, an ancient leafy wood, who would sleep in the olive plantation, have the salt foam, the winds of the far Cyclades, on his lips, see the tents of Arab and Kurd, be in China perhaps when the next floods came, Harry who like the foot of her wandering soul would print his foot on the world.

"So will I," she said restlessly, getting up from her bed in the middle of the night. "So will I—but not now. When then? I don't know, but not now." She thirsted after this track-making and wandering of the man in the world, not after the man. She pulled herself together at some moments of the day to think with shame: And Harry? You haven't thought of him once. But Harry in England was just a vagueness still flying towards Birmingham, although he had long ago got there and started back. In the end she cut her visit short, telegraphed to Quick and set out for London within a couple of hours; and could scarcely say good-bye to them, so absorbed was she with the thought of their first moments together, when she returned, of how glad they would be, of his smooth hair flying in excitement, his kind, loving, warm words and her intense apprehending love for him. Harry had nothing to do with this household and he was, beside the heat and activity of her domestic love for Quick, almost a wraith. Yet she possessed him absolutely, she knew he could not help thinking of her, and she resolved to give him no sign, stir him no more. She did not want to repeat the night in Oxford but she wanted him to carry it with him for ever. It was for her a foray from which she brought back milk and honey for her own affair with James. She wanted to possess Quick too, to grasp him and weave him into herself cunningly, by practising the arts of love in every form. She had learned from Harry and made up her mind, if the chance came, to learn from others. "I only know one commandment, *Thou shalt love*." No one would hold her prisoner, Harry did not, and even James would not, but she would hold them both prisoners. She thought with a kind of religious awe of his purpose in sending her off with Harry Girton. He had often said: "Can *I* fly in the face of Nature?"

She turned and looked out of the train window. Perhaps there is balm in Gilead! Perhaps this will never cease. Perhaps this *mea-culpa* story, the sadness of the world, the misery of existence is a lie, some abracadabra that for an unguessable reason, though there's certainly something sinister in it, is wished on us—but by whom?

Can I doubt my own senses? Great love exists, mad, fervent, self-sacrificing love exists, and perfect passion exists; how many other things exist, then, that merely sound like dreams and songs to us, things denied to us when children and now, when grown, foregone? All things desired, are they possible, are they already in existence? Do we only have to find them and take them, not each and each, but all—are they there for all? Because if this thing is here for me, no one, a miserable creature after all, a vain, thin thing, a wretched thing; if I, sinner and talentless, can have it, then all pleasures, all desires should be for all—weak, struggling, mean, and drab, for us all, the hungry and the dispossessed, the ugly, the dying of limitless pain, the people left behind—it must be! Yes, it must be! Yes, we will have it, all passion, all delight.

And suddenly as a strange thought it came to her, that she had reached the gates of the world of Girton and Quick and that it was towards them she was only now journeying, and in a direction unguessed by them; and it was towards them and in this undreamed direction that she had been travelling all her life, and would travel, farther, without them; and with her she felt many thousands of shadows, pressing along with her, storming forwards, but quietly and eagerly, though blindly. She even heard the rushing and jostling of their patched and washed clothes and the flapping of their street-worn shoes, their paper-stuffed soles. She began to blush deeply, deeper than ever before, into her entrails and into the brain, her heart thickened with shame, and at the same moment, life itself seemed to choke her. She suddenly understood that there was something beyond misery, and that at present she had merely fought through that bristling black and sterile plain of misery and that beyond was the real world, red, gold, green, white, in which the youth of the world would be passed; it was from the womb of time she was fighting her way and the first day lay before her. This was beyond the "Seventh House"—and when she understood this, that there was something on the citied plain for all of them, the thousands like thin famished fire that wavered and throve around her, pressing on, she knew why she continued restless and why the men, having so much in the hollow of their hands, kept on striving. At this moment sprang up in her, for them, an inarticulate emotion of excitement quite beyond anything she had ever felt. All on this fabulous railway journey seemed divine, easy and clear, as if she had a passport to paradise.

Quick met her at the station. As soon as he saw her, he came running fast, his swarthy form flying through the crowds, people making way for him, his eyes beaming, his face convulsed, as if he would cry. He seized her like a man seizing a hat that has been bowling away and carried her off, like a sand-whirl carrying off a rag. He put her down and kissed her face all over, and in the taxi held fast with both hands, bending down with his

494

head in her lap. She felt a tear drop on her hand. She was confused by this hurricane. He began to cover her with kisses. She was paralysed and without emotion.

But she did not know where she stood, any more than if a high tide had rushed in and swamped the road where she used to walk. What relation had she to Quick, to Girton, to the men who surrounded her, to all men? What was her fate? Here where she stood no old wives' tale and no mother's sad sneer, no father's admonition, reached.

Was love freebooting? But stalwart, excellent, full of glory and generous, also, were all the freebooters. She was one of them. But she suffered already from the intensity of her husband's passion, she sensed that in it was doubt, fear, and much suffering. She lay quietly in his arms while he told of his lonely days since she had gone away, she was moved by it but she could only bring herself to say: "I missed you very much, so much."

This was sufficient; he became joyful and he began to picture their home-coming a few moments off, their evenings, their home life, and their whole future life, exactly as she had done. But now overwhelmed by his storm, and out of an apposite modesty and shame, she could not bring herself to say anything of what she had thought. A silence fell. He said suddenly: "And did you like Oxford?"—for she had sent him a post-card saying she had spent a few hours in Oxford with Harry Girton.

"Oh, yes, but you know I do."

"And was Harry with you? Did he look after you? Show you round? Did he go on with you?"

She answered all the questions and a sort of anger rose against Quick that he was pushing her to the wall in this way. She wanted to keep the two men separate in her mind for ever, without intrigue; they were hers, they had nothing to do with each other. But Quick continued that he had heard from Harry, who was coming over tomorrow to say good-bye. He looked at her with genial attention as he said it, watching her impassive face in the light that came into the cab from the scarce shop-windows and street lamps. At these words she remembered her relation to Harry and she turned to Quick and embraced him with warmth and assurance, without the naïve and awkward shyness which had irritated him a little in the first days.

"I love you very much and never anyone else," she said. After

495

the episode of the first days when she felt her life would be a secret from him, she had felt lonely, unkind, and oppressed by him, who, however, said he would die for her. Now, with a secret that would perhaps kill his love, she felt able to give to him freely, unforced; she had lost nothing and would never have anything to regret. She thought: "How miserable I would have been if I had had to go on for years, wondering whether I should love another man! But now I know, this is the only love, but not the first and not the last. I will know how to make myself a life apart. If James robbed me, I would dislike him for my empty heart, but as I know how to cultivate my heart and mind in secret, now, I can only love him for giving himself to me."

She was smiling as she thought this again, and he said: "Why do you smile like that?"

"I am thinking I am free."

He stared at her apprehensively.

But when Harry came two or three days in succession, starting from the next day, she was unable to say even good-day, in an emotion without name. Thus, each time he came, and stood in the door-way looking down at her, with an inward smile, she took his hand and looked up at him without a word, or she would murmur under her breath, after a moment, "Hullo", huskily. Then she would turn away, suddenly furious with him, seeing meanings in his pauses, his slightest movement.

It was too strange. James Quick became afraid and he followed them round the room, with wide-open eyes like those of a child. He watched them intensely, without suspicion, but with his love, fear, and admiration for them both naked on his face. Then he would talk in little runs and scurries, between intense looks. They did not seem to see each other, nor touch each other. Quick, who guessed now that they had stayed overnight in Oxford, though not that they had stayed together, had to ask a dozen times and be assured a dozen times that they had not been in rooms near each other, but that Harry had stayed with a former teacher, and the like, and with each assurance, she smiled candidly and maternally. "Silly thing, silly thing!" He would look relieved, then puzzle again and ask again.

She thought: "This can't go on, I never will see Harry again." It became a terror, a mad joy to see Harry, and afterwards, a storm of jealousy and love; and she was terrified at the depths of cruel deceptions and easy lies which sprang thick in her. She thought of crimes and dishonour, ways to get rid of Manette and to prevent Harry's going to fight; she felt as if she could not give up what she had gained. "The only thing is to go myself, to Spain, fight, have the same life, but apart, by our sex; so we would be joined and I punished." But in between these terrible fits of passion, she realized a new and wonderful feeling, her duty to James Quick. It was like the hope of a child; when she fixed her eyes on it, everything else vanished and her heart became unselfish.

It was again the "last day", and seemed really the last day. Harry came a few hours before he was to leave for Spain. They knew he had told many people he would never return to England. If the fight in Spain spared him, he was for the East. He came that day, and the agile, invidious Nigel Fippenny stayed through two hours of the time they were so jealous of, that they had kept for their beloved friend, talking idly, running down not only the Spanish Government troops but any revolution or loyal national movement in which Fippenny had not participated, and in between times taunting their guest and friend, Harry Girton. Harry sat with his eyes shaded and let the talk romp over him. Presently, Nigel said grudgingly: "Och, I'm sittin' talkin' here and yu three want to hold ha-ahnds before he goes to take a soft job in Madrid, that I know. So I'll go and leave yu." And grinning bitterly he got up and left, seeing that they did not detain him.

They spoke only casually after he left, about the arrangements Harry would make to cross into Spain, about some of the fighting. Teresa drank glass after glass of wine and offered some three or four to Girton. Quick drank nothing but coffee but he took at least four cups of this. Teresa had on a dress which she liked very much at that time and which suited her, a black linen suit with black shirt and tie, all in linen and a black velvet bow on her hair, which showed up her blond pallor and soft colour; but there was no art in her get-up, it was the same she wore most days at this time, changing only for a pale grey. She had not thought of any significance in it, but she suddenly felt Harry's eyes staring at her through his fingers like an animal's through the bushes. Yes, he had spread his fingers to stare curiously at her—not only the black dress but the almost black wine which

497

looked sable in the lowering London day, must have seemed strange; the court was violet dark. Outside, near the door of the printing establishment stood the old beggarman to whom the printers threw scraps in paper bags and to whom they gave small change on pay-day. As Teresa glanced, she saw the old man's parasite, a vicious slum youth who had turned up during the last ten days, and taken his receipts, with a wicked glance at everyone and sly pinches and blows to the old man when no one was looking. The old man a month ago had had a country-man's straight thin form and apple cheeks; in one month he had become pale and bowed, frightened and huddled there, where once he had stood with a simple air. When the old man moved out, which he did at a word from the young rascal, the youth followed him, one bent back following another, and when they went it was a sign for night to come and for all the lights in the court to come on. Teresa, when she passed to and fro, gave the old man what she had, before the youth arrived. This evening she had forgotten.

She sighed. In this rough and tumble of need, egotism, and love where was the right thing to do? She fastened her eyes on Harry. He had no child. He would never have one—perhaps by some Spanish revolutionary girl or Kalmuck wife! Harry had taken his hand from his face and was looking at her darkly. She put down the glass and began to talk about the funny faces Nigel had made when he left.

"I have an idea he doesn't like me," said Harry again, smiling ruefully. "It's a fact that we're so simple that one of the hard facts of existence is that some people simply don't and won't like us."

When he rose to go, James Quick gave him the small presents he had bought for him and some money for his wife, who was being left in a bad way, for all their money had been spent on equipping him. The two lovers looked at each other but said nothing and moved into the corridor. In the corridor, Teresa walked backward, Harry following her, looking into each other's faces searchingly, but James followed up, staring at them both intensely. Harry went out the door and turned his back as if to go away, then he turned round to Teresa and said, gently: "I will try to come back—if I can fit in, I'll try at any rate. If I don't come back, remember me. Do my work for me, fill my place, be me." And he laughed quaintly.

"Well, how can I do that?"

"Just remember me," he said, smiling and taking her hand, "Good-bye," and he bent slightly, but did not kiss her, for both were conscious of the other man behind, good and loyal. As he turned he said: "I'll try to get back this afternoon, for a minute, to say good-bye, if I can—but it'll be hard." Then he turned and they both went down the stairs, Quick beginning to chat merrily at once.

She shut the door and felt very angry with them both. She flung herself on the flat to tidy it up, and then on her typewriter and began the new work which had come in, but after a few minutes she stopped and listened. She heard her husband coming up the court. She ran to open the door and stood with a great smile on her face. When he got to her, she drew him in, closed the door and embraced him with the same fervour and gladness as before and murmured: "It's impossible for me to say how I feel for you, you're so good to me, and then I love you for yourself alone."

He laughed and came into the flat, pulling off his neat little tan gloves and putting them in the pocket of his overcoat; and he told her what Harry Girton had said in the Strand. "He thanked me for my friendship and said he felt closer to me than to any other man he knew. He talked to me about love and women and how he had loved women in his life, and I listened, although you know that I'm not fond of people's confidences—but Harry is different." He gave her a side-glance. "He talked a lot about the love of women," he laughed, "and then he thanked me for the money; he said he did not want to leave Manette in utter poverty—she has her wages, but they have debts, though how they get these debts I don't know."

"Harry likes to go on beer parties," said Teresa disdainfully. "And he says he could not get on without going on the bust once in three months and he was surprised that anyone could."

"Something I don't understand, but I don't criticize others for doing it, not even Harry," said Quick. "And at the end of the Strand he stopped and said good-bye, and we kissed each other on both cheeks like a couple of Frenchmen, *Alphonse et Gaston*,

499

and he told me he felt to me like a brother, he loved me." Quick smiled teasingly at her.

She was silent, jealous of these last moments. Quick at once said hastily: "And he sent you a message too, Tess, he said he would try to come back again and say good-bye."

"Ah, good." She picked up a page and put it into the typewriter with an indifferent air. "But he won't have time to come back, I know."

"I don't think so, I told him not to try."

She said nothing, looking down at the machine, then she felt she could not bear any ambiguities in their life and she looked frankly at Quick. "Jim, it was funny, wasn't it? We really liked each other."

"You loved each other, do you think it is possible for *me* to see wrong in that? When he comes back——"

"He won't come back, I know, and if he comes back I will never see him again," said Teresa. "I know that and I promise it to you now. I don't think chastity and monogamy and all that is necessary, but somehow—I don't want you to think I love you less."

Quick was not able to get out a word.

"Let's go and have fun," said Teresa suddenly. "I'm like that loafer Harry Girton after all, once in three months I must go on the razzle-dazzle."

Quick said: "But if Harry comes back?"

"He won't come back. Let's go."

When they went out, the old man and his parasite were just going down the alley, and they followed them.

Quick went into a tobacconist's to get some cigars. Teresa, waiting outside in the dusk that fell like soot, saw a peculiar, sliding, fumbling figure go by, the typical self-pickled bachelor, well but unbecomingly dressed, dark, with a foreign-looking, broad-leafed black hat. She thought: "I'd like to write a story on that incomprehensible type, the bachelor, and here's one, the bachelor sucked into himself like a sea-anemone which suddenly sees something wrong and falls into itself, and both like a half-knit flesh wound. Where goes the bachelor? To some high, soot-green, sour room? What a shock if I heard him take a ticket to Surbiton and following him there, found him in a semi-detached villa with a black rusty-browed wife and two dirty-skinned children." She looked in, saw James Quick talking in a lively continued style over the counter as was his custom, and she took a few steps after the bent bachelor. "He really has the peculiar gait, the twisted look—if I could see his face . . ." She had only taken five steps after him, when the man, feeling himself followed and by a woman, turned quickly and viciously, darting a fierce repellent glance at the woman behind, whom he supposed to be a whore. Teresa was at the moment passing under a lamp outside a jeweller's, one of those that sell cheap watches, engagement rings, pledges and pawn tickets. In the lamp Teresa looked ghastly, blue, her cheek-bones protruded and her mouth was blue-black, the whole face unlikely. The man half-turned, stared, while the fringe of the bluish light fell on his unshaven lantern jaw and thin spectacles. Teresa felt a pang as if faced by a murderer. The vile-faced man, the bent-backed man, walking crowded with all the apparatus of melodrama was Jonathan Crow! They looked at each other, and he saw her eyes, ghastly to him, pale vapours in brilliant eye-balls, fastened upon him. She scarcely knew what he thought, perhaps that she or her spirit, in the filthy London night, was following him. At this moment, in the strangeness of it, she began to laugh and moved a step nearer to him, out of the lamp so that the shadow instead showed her bolder and warmer than he had ever seen her. Her laugh and nearness were perhaps a horrific gibberish to him; his face changed, he turned abruptly without a sign of recognition and bowled on down the Strand, his walk stiffening and his heels grating.

Quick joined her and said: "Were you looking at the rings?" and he laughed, taking her ringless hand and looking at it, work-stained, sinewy.

"No, not rings—Johnny! There he goes down the Strand as if Old Nick was on his tail. He saw me!" She put her arm in Quick's and they walked on, close together, but she felt as if death were in her heart. Quick said: "Did he stop and speak?"

"No, he thought I was a vampire, I think. He tore off. He probably—dreams—and I was it! I was in that ugly lamp and I looked blue to him!"

"No, you didn't."

"Yes, I did."

Quick laughed. "It's impossible. The man's colour-blind."

She laughed. "To me, yes."

"He's colour-blind, I tell you. I noticed that he kept asking me the colour of things, but in a canny way."

"Good heavens!" She was silent, reflecting. "I never knew."

"You didn't notice much about Mr Crow."

"No wonder he thought I was mad."

"You are."

"I can't believe I ever loved that man."

"You never did."

After a while, Teresa sighed bitterly. "It's dreadful to think that it will go on being repeated for ever, he—and me! What's there to stop it?"

THE END